STILLBRIGHT

Book Two of the Paladin Trilogy

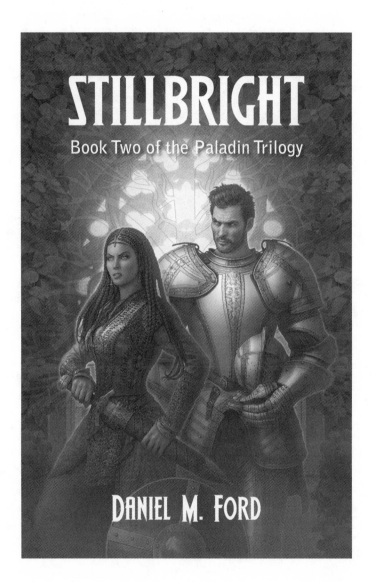

STILLBRIGHT

Book Two of the Paladin Trilogy

DANIEL M. FORD

sfwp.com

Library of Congress Cataloging-in-Publication Data

Names: Ford, Daniel M., 1978- author.
Title: Stillbright : book two of the paladin trilogy / Daniel M. Ford.
Description: Santa Fe : Santa Fe Writer's Project, 2017. | Series: The paladin trilogy ; 2
Identifiers: LCCN 2016033042| ISBN 9781939650580 (trade paperback : alk. paper) |
    ISBN 9781939650597 (pdf) | ISBN 9781939650603 (epub) | ISBN 9781939650610 (mobi)
Subjects: | BISAC: FICTION / Fantasy / Epic. | GSAFD: Fantasy fiction.
Classification: LCC PS3606.O728 St 2017 | DDC 813/.6--dc23
LC record available at https://lccn.loc.gov/2016033042

Published by SFWP
369 Montezuma Ave. #350
Santa Fe, NM 87501
(505) 428-9045
www.sfwp.com

Find the author at www.danielmford.com

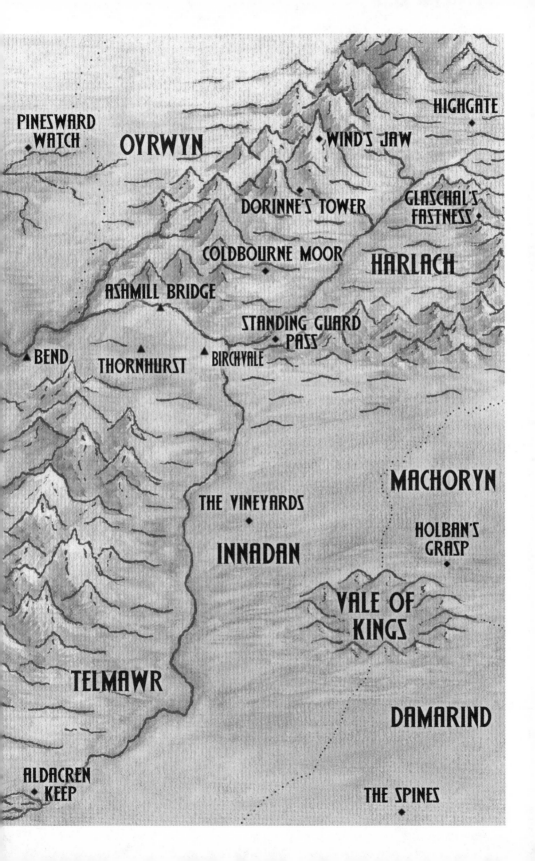

For my mother, for everything.

Table of Contents

Prologue 1

Chapter 1: Cost and Memory 7

Chapter 2: Sounds like Cursing 13

Chapter 3: The Boy 19

Chapter 4: A Distraction is Arranged 25

Chapter 5: A Rescue is Mounted 29

Chapter 6: The Distraction 57

Chapter 7: Tasks 67

Chapter 8: Names 75

Chapter 9: Mountains, Knives, and Ideas 89

Chapter 10: Into the Thasryach 97

Chapter 11: The Cave 109

Chapter 12: The Will 121

Chapter 13: Choice, Not Fate 131

Chapter 14: The First of Many Cooperations 141

Chapter 15: Homecoming 149

Chapter 16: A Task is Finished 165

Chapter 17: A Task is Begun 173

Chapter 18: A Vigil 199

Chapter 19: Labors 211

Chapter 20: Fortune's Priestess 219

Chapter 21: Finery 241

Chapter 22: Temple Politics 261

Chapter 23: An Old Trick 293

Chapter 24: Trial-at-Arms 301

Chapter 25: Who You Are, Not Who You Were 309

Chapter 26: The Grip of Despair 325

Chapter 27: Interlude 339

Chapter 28: The Will and the Dragon 341

Chapter 29: A Legend is Crafted 353

Chapter 30: The Minstrel and the Shadow 373

Chapter 31: Interlude 395

Chapter 32: Homecoming and Guests 399

Chapter 33: Battle is Joined 411

Chapter 34: Old Mountain Ice 427

Chapter 35: The Feel of Gold 453

Chapter 36: Shadows 459

Chapter 37: The Rest of the Message 479

Chapter 38: The Rite of Blooming Blood 505

Chapter 39: Stillbright 515

Chapter 40: The Sorcerers, the Islandman, and the Will 535

Chapter 41: Two Awakenings 543

His fair face cold and hard as winter dawn
and as beautiful in its wrath.

His mail mirror bright, all men fearing
the judging reflection.

His steed of purest silvered mane, a beast
light as cloud, swift as wind.

His arms bright bars of fire given shape in
his holy hands alone.

His the hand that drew the fury of the sun
and stilled the ocean's rage.

—The opening lines of the epic poem
Hammer of the Sun, attributed to
Derrinbad of Keersvast

Prologue

The sun shone on Londray Bay with the soft brightness that was particular to early autumn. It bathed the walls of the Dunes in warmth, and filled the towers of Baron Delondeur's keep with golden light.

The same light fell over the entire city of Londray, spreading from the massive, sand-colored castle walls at its northwest corner. Mixing the wide and regular streets of recent, planned construction with old cowpaths, Londray was one of the greatest cities in the Fourteen Baronies—one of the few that would even be considered a city by a Concordat southerner, much less anyone from the great city of Keersvast, stretching, as it did, across an entire island chain.

Still, it was an impressive place holding thousands of souls—all bathed in that sunlight that marked one of the last truly warm days of the year. Soon enough, the short autumn would give way to a winter that threatened to freeze the harbor for months. Today, the city could rest in its beauty, wealth, and warm breezes.

In the shadows that light cast all over the city, people went about their daily business. At the harbor, they hauled in nets to mend, swabbed decks, or sorted their catch. Foreign sailors, whether the huge, bearded Islandmen from the north or the lithe, fair-haired Keersvasters from the far southwest, rolled off of their ships and into the taverns, ale-tents, wine-shops, bathhouses, barbers, and brothels.

In the rich quarters of the city, knights, lords, and wealthy traders sipped their evening wine or settled in to the first course of dinner. They ate in front of expensive leaded windows from bright plates. Liveried servants stood ready to attend to every wine glass and utensil through every course of soup—chilled at great expense, against this last gasp of heat—fish, meat, fruit, cheese, and more.

At the city's margins, where the summer sun was broken into shadows by high-piled shacks that leaned into one another as they rose above the street, families jammed together over tables happily covered with what fish or bread they could afford.

At the gates leading out of the city, most along its eastern wall and others to the north and south, clusters of green-cloaked men gathered, awaiting the turn of the glass that officially ended their campaigning season. For a few months, the war was done. The war that had once been the Succession Strife—fourteen Barons alternately supporting a king, pulling him down, or fighting to put themselves on the throne—had now become a simple fact of life. No one under two-score years in Londray had been born in a city at peace. No kings were left to support or oppose; now the twelve Barons that remained fought for their own borders. Some, perhaps, harbored the ambition of a crown. Most claimed to simply be answering the grievances done to them or their people.

The signs of war were all over the city. Of course there were the gathered hundreds of men waiting to be released to their homes, hopeful of pitching into the harvest or the last months of fishing, or hopeful of heading to the drinking, dicing, and wenching with their pay. There were the armed and armored men who patrolled the walls of the Dunes still, green cloaks blazoned with a sand-colored tower; there were the ballistae that dotted the walls; there were the ram-prowed ships berthed in the harbor.

Yet there were quieter signs, as well. Men and women, lamed or missing legs, blind or one-armed, slumped against tavern walls with shallow wooden bowls in one hand and simple signs in the other. In the poorest parts of the city, the sign might be a crude charcoal drawing of a horse on a piece of hide, or a drawn bow, or a spear. Whether this signified the nature of their service or the source of their injury was never entirely clear.

These were the most numerous.

In tradesman's streets, the veterans slumped in the same way, holding the same bowls, but their signs were more likely to be lettered. Most contained only a word or two.

Aldacren.

Green Forks.

Thasryach Pass.

The Vineyards.

Giant's Winter.

One particularly elderly man, who managed a knobbed wooden crutch, a bowl, and a sign—by the expedient of having the latter looped over his head with a bit of string—had crossed out the last word upon it and written a new one. It had read Vale of the Kings. Now, it read Vale of the Graves.

Many walked past them without seeing them. Others, near their own age, who bore a scar or lacked a finger, tended to pause and drop links and bobs into the bowls, or to hand out stale half-loaves.

If such folk were seen on the streets of the richest parts of the city, it never took long for green-hatted, truncheon wielding guards to move them on.

In the Temple District, Fortune's white-surcoated guards in their conical helms were not shy about moving them on with the flat of their blades.

Guards at the Temple of Braech didn't always use the flat. If word spread that a ship of Braech's Dragonscales—the crazed holy berzerkers—had put into the harbor, most folk avoided the Temples altogether, and the beggars doubly so.

One man, his age hard to tell, stood up from his spot along such a tavern wall. Matted and overgrown brown hair fell into his dark eyes, which were ringed and clouded and stared into the distance while seeing nothing. He tossed aside a sign that read "The Crossing" and tipped the contents of his bowl into an older man's, seized up a crutch, and began walking, dragging a badly twisted left leg behind him.

Slowly, painfully, sweating profusely before long, the man made his way towards the docks as night slowly fell over Londray. He didn't turn aside to the calls of women walking in the streets in flimsy dresses, or to the ale and whiskey sellers in tents. When he passed by a stall where a man sat with beringed hands folded over an ample stomach straining against dirty robes, beneath a sign promising healing tinctures and mystic oils to soothe any pain or rheumatism, his hand moved instinctively to his belt for a weapon that wasn't there.

Not that it would've done him any good; the charlatan had leather-clad, heavily armed guards to either side of him. Still, the man spat in the direction of the alchemist's stall in a last small gesture of defiance.

He set his faraway eyes on an empty quay and kept walking. Each step was pain, but each step was closer to ending it.

When he reached the long stone quay he tossed away his crutch, heard it splash in the water, wished he could've turned to see the hateful thing sink. Instead, he hurried on.

At the first sufficiently far spot, where nothing was tied, he paused and gathered himself, leaning against a post for support. Ought to pray, he thought. Then aloud, he said, "Braech, Fortune, Urdaran…Cold, even the Elven Green, if any of ya hear me, then freeze you and yours for all you ever did for me."

Then he lifted his bad, twisted leg towards the small dark waves below, ready to plunge towards them.

He could've sworn that no one shared the quay with him. With the harbor not yet full, nothing had tied up on it; it was too far from the warehouses and known to be too shallow for the biggest ships. Yet, before he could fall, a hand seized his shirt and pulled him backwards. In his shock he fell upon his bad hip and bit off a yell, prepared to swing his fists wildly and fight for the life he'd been about to end.

Then he saw a woman appear out of the darkness of the air, the night's shadows simply peeling away from her like a dropped veil. In a surprisingly deep and raw voice, she said, "Water's still warm, but I take it you weren't out for a pleasure bath." One of her hands, rough and calloused, settled lightly on his head. "Why?"

It was a simple question. The simplest. And also the most complex. Yet he found an ease entering him, a warmth that began to spread from the woman's hand as soon as she had spoken.

"It hurts," he admitted, in a faraway voice. "I'm tired. And hungry."

"I've a friend who can help with the last one right now," the woman said. Despite the huskiness of her voice, there was a hint, nearly hidden, of a rich music behind it. But only a hint. "And the second takes but a few turns sleep."

"I don't sleep well," the man responded.

The quay was silent for a moment but for the play of the water against the stones. Her hand against his head still exuded warmth, and he felt himself dropping towards sleep, then abruptly yanked away from it.

"Can't let you pass out on the quay…ah, what is your name, anyway?" There was a pause as the woman sighed and he thought he heard a few muttered words. Something about someone else, a name he didn't catch, who was better at this.

"Tibult," the man replied, slowly, as if the word was slow in coming to him.

"Well, Tibult," the woman said, "I can help you with some of what troubles you. But I need privacy just now."

She raised her hand from his head and the warmth it had brought began to recede. Her fingers clasped his forearm with a grip as strong as any he'd ever felt and hauled him to his feet, seizing him with pain. He found himself leaning on the woman's shoulder and was surprised to note that she was taller than him, even if he could stand upright.

"Privacy was what I was after," Tibult muttered. The warmth and calm that had filled him dissipated, pressed out of him like juice from a grape. Pain and hunger and despair wrung it from him as they welled back up.

"I'm willin' to pay for it," the woman said, reaching for her belt. Her hand came back with silver dangling in it, three links. "Now I can give you this and you can watch the quay for a turn or two and then you can hare off and get drunk and fed. But if you're willing to earn a little more, tell me, Tibult—do you still know soldiers, where they'll be gathering tonight, and where to drop a word that'll get 'round?"

"Aye. What d'ya mean?"

"I mean, friend Tibult, for a rumor dropped in the right places, gold. And if all goes well, I have a friend who can do something about that hip."

CHAPTER 1

Cost and Memory

Allystaire, formerly Lord Coldbourne, War Leader of Barony Oyrwyn, favored knight of the Old Baron Gerard Oyrwyn, Castellan of Wind's Jaw Keep, currently the Arm of the Mother, Paladin and Prophet of Her Church, was intimately acquainted with pain. Pain was the price of the life he had lived before his Ordination. It seemed to him that pain was the cost of the life he lived now.

And at the moment, he was readying himself to pay a great deal of that cost. Bound to a rack in a lightless room in the bowels of the Dunes, at the mercy of Baron Lionel Delondeur's pet sorcerer, he was anticipating pain. On what scale, he wasn't entirely sure yet.

There'd been a beating on the way down to the lightless room in which he languished, after he'd been stripped of arms and armor. With his body held immobile by the sorcerer's power, and even the release of yelling or screaming denied to him, the Delondeur soldiers escorting them had taken a bit of their own back. His name had usually been foremost among the army that had killed their friends, or brothers, or, when he realized how young some of them looked, probably their fathers. He didn't begrudge them the odd thud of fist or boot. It was really just professional courtesy. Had better from your sisters, he might have said. Only I had to pay them in copper, he might have added, had he the use of his mouth. Though it didn't seem the knightly thing to say, it was customary to say something.

The guards had lost interest quickly when they saw they could earn no response, and none were eager to linger around Bhimanzir. That much was plain. So once he was secured, the chains pulled tight, off they'd gone, taking their torches with them. The features of the room barely impressed themselves upon Allystaire's vision as the door sealed the last of the light away. He knew he was bound to a rack of iron and wood by loops of chain and that his sorcerous bonds had dropped away once the chains had been looped taut. He'd seen an oddly shaped table for a moment. There'd been a rack of tools upon it. Sharp tools.

Submitting to fear earns me nothing, Allystaire told himself. *Think on how I got here. Down a lot of freezing stairs, yes. Some new construction? Near the keep's own dock, out over the water?* He felt entirely uncertain of any of these guesses. *Making guesses and developing a possible response is better than waiting for the cutting to start*, he told himself, but he'd just run out of guesses to make.

The sorcerer suddenly appeared, revealed in the darkness only by the light emanating from his hands. Allystaire strained to make out his captor's features, but could see only that he was bald, and that his skin appeared entirely smooth and unlined.

"No doubt you are steeling yourself to resist my blades and hooks, my whips and hot irons," the sorcerer said. "I have no need of such crude tools for such a simple task. No doubt you will end your life upon one of them." There was no more feeling, no more expression in the man's words, than in those of a bored child reciting a lesson for a tutor who wasn't listening.

"What I am interested in is inside you, yes. Yet I think the hook would not show it to me," the sorcerer went on. One of those fingers, warm with the promise of agony, reached out and pressed against Allystaire's bare chest.

The sorcerer uttered a single syllable that vanished before Allystaire's ears could reach out for it.

Then the fingertip ignited against Allystaire's chest and burned unbearably. He screamed, surprising himself, as the world collapsed around the brand of fire that pressed against him.

Unloosed, unfocused, his mind sought some way to comprehend what was happening. Memories flashed, battles and wounds he'd taken. Then suddenly an image flashed into clarity.

Michar, the Old Baron's chirurgeon. A stump of a dwarf, his hair gone grey, beard in three thick, short braids bound with caps of silver, gold, and a metal Allystaire couldn't name. The plain workingman's clothes and thin gloves, the apron with its pockets of gleaming instruments.

One of them, a thick rod with its handle wrapped in leather, that would heat over a good fire in the time it took to simply lay it in the coals. The dwarf had closed many a wound with it, sealed them with his potions soaking the tissues, keeping away the things a man feared more than a wound itself.

Allystaire remembered almost a score of years ago, the dwarf standing over him as three men held him down. Having cut away an arrow from the meat of young Allystaire's thigh, sniffing the barbed point and harumphing as he consigned it to the flames with a flick of his hand.

"Sorry, son," he'd said. "They've dipped the arrowheads in their own jakes. It's for the best. On three." Then, without counting at all, the dwarf plunged the heated rod into the young knight's wound. There was the smell of his own flesh burning before the world collapsed into the pain of it.

There, Allystaire told himself, snapping back into the now, into the sorcerer standing in front of him. He screamed still, but the scream turned into an improbable laugh.

"I have had that from a dwarf who meant to save my life," he spat, when the sorcerer lowered his hand, having taken half a step back in confusion.

"I suppose I must use all the Delvings," the sorcerer said, ignoring the Paladin's exclamation. "One at a time, of course."

That energy was directed at Allystaire again. He half expected his skin to start smoking. The light extending the half span from the sorcerer's finger seemed, by turns, smoky, greasy, and incandescent. That may have been his mind simply searching aimlessly to understand what was happening.

What Allystaire did understand, what he knew, was that this was a pain he'd felt before. It hurt certainly. Hurt enough so that he screamed till his throat was raw. But he'd felt it before, or something enough like it to call himself its master instead of being mastered by it.

Abruptly, it ceased. And the quality of the light bathing his skin changed, becoming thicker, less translucent, as did its form. Instead of a single ray boring—or seeming to—a hole into his chest, the sorcerer raised his hand above Allystaire's head and let it fall down upon him like slow drops of rain.

It was a different kind of agony, and it engulfed his whole body. But he didn't have to search long or think hard.

"The battle in front of some shit-hole keep in Harlach," he groaned. Inwardly he remembered trying to carry a wall defended by starving, exhausted men. Without anything else left, they'd boiled water and poured it over the walls. Some had splashed along his neck and inside his armor, scalded him. *Other men took it worse*, he reminded himself. *Not other men. Poorer men. They always did*, he added, a moment of clarity amidst the pain.

Still the sorcerer said nothing, did nothing, except guide droplets of power through Allystaire's body.

The paladin clamped his teeth shut, cutting off his cries of pain. He swallowed them, buried them behind a sudden loathing of his memories.

This drew a humorless laugh from the sorcerer. "Try as you might, you cannot resist the pain of the Delvings. None can. Give into it. Perhaps, if you are lucky, your mind will untether itself before I am done, and you will feel only the dimmest pain before I feed my divinations with your life. This is, however, unlikely. You will end begging to serve me. You will scream it before long."

"Scream? Aye, I will. Beg to serve you? Never that," Allystaire grated through clenched teeth. *Goddess help me, never that*, he silently prayed.

* * *

It may have been turns. It may have been moments. It may have been days. Allystaire wasn't sure. In the midst of the pains the sorcerer inflicted with new manifestations of his power, it was all Allystaire could do to search his memories and find something to tell him that he had survived the thing once and would do so again.

All too often the memories he sought reminded him that others hadn't survived.

When the sorcerer tried a kind of cutting energy that sliced at him, Allystaire laughed. *The lance at Aldacren keep. A dirk trying to find my ribs while I throttled the knight wielding it, both of our weapons lost. The captain's sword in the warehouse in Bend.*

When a faint web of lines, pulsing darkly red in the air flew at him and sank into his skin, surely he screamed. But he remembered being unhorsed by a lance for the first time, the feeling of helplessness, the way the shock and the pain hit his whole body all at once as he crashed to the ground.

I could barely crawl out of bed the next day. I was a mass of bruise. I was perhaps twelve summers old. And still they made me sit a horse and tilt against the quintain the next day.

Finally, lowering his hands, the sorcerer—his measured voice betraying his seething anger better than any yelling might have done—said, "Why do you keep recounting these pathetic anecdotes?"

It was only then that Allystaire realized he'd been speaking them all aloud, shouting them while he screamed.

He didn't answer. Instead he lifted his head and found the sorcerer 's eyes. It was easy enough to do now, as they had started to slowly pulse with thin lines of red like that which drifted from his fingertips.

"I realize that you will pride yourself on not answering even my most petty questions. This will prove foolish. In the main I do not need your answers."

Allystaire thought about summoning the strength to spit, discarded the idea, and simply met the gaze.

With an exasperated sigh, the sorcerer turned and vanished in a rush of red light, leaving Allystaire in complete darkness.

CHAPTER 2

Sounds like Cursing

A turn or two before she went walking on the quays, Idgen Marte found Torvul outside a metal-monger's shop along a street full of smiths of every description. The air was thick with smoke and the faint burnt scent of hot metal and it rang with hammers, though they slowly petered out as the afternoon wore on.

Inside, the alchemist conversed with a fellow dwarf in the harsh but flowing consonance of their shared language. The other dwarf was a bit taller than Torvul, and had a thick but carefully trimmed soot-black beard covering his face. When she came a few more steps into the shop, the conversation abruptly ceased as both turned to look at her, but Torvul smiled and said to the other dwarf, "She's a friend, Murnock."

As Idgen Marte walked to his side, the dwarf said to her, "You won't mind if we continue in our native tongue—it is a more satisfying language to barter in than what you people use, after all, and besides, I can't thoroughly defraud the good ironmonger here if I don't use Dwarfish."

"I speak the barony tongue too, wanderer," the other dwarf said, and his tone, Idgen Marte thought, was a bit cold for a man hoping to make a sale. "You'll defraud me in no tongue at all."

"The problem for you, Murnock, is that when I outwit a man in a bargain, which is to say when I make a bargain, he doesn't realize it till his deathbed."

"Cease your nattering and let's finish up. Past time for beer and bread."

"I couldn't agree more," Torvul said, his voice suddenly honeyed. "But I couldn't possibly pay more than three or four silver links per rod of your bar stock."

"Price is a gold link per, 'less it's a lot-price, in which case I can go as low as six silver."

"I only need two rods and I'd sooner walk out of here less my balls than two gold links for iron like this. Five silver links, not a bent copper-half more."

"I'll take no less than eight."

Torvul snorted and pushed away from the counter, holding his hands up in mock disgust. "Then I'll find another iron-monger." He turned and started to walk out of the shop. He was at the door when the other dwarf smashed a fist against his counter and cursed in their native tongue, then barked out, "Six!"

I think he cursed, Idgen Marte thought. *It all sounds like cursing.*

Torvul pivoted on his heel and smoothly walked back to the counter, already digging in the purse he'd produced from up a sleeve. "I want to pick my own bars," he said, before pulling free three linked chains of four bright circles of silver and laying them on the counter. Almost instantly, they were swept up by the other dwarf's hand.

The dwarf grumbled, but he took the money, then lifted up a hinged section of his counter. Idgen Marte quickly followed him through the door behind the counter and out into the larger part of the building where metal was stored in stacks; it was mostly iron, but she saw stacks of white lead, green copper, others she couldn't identify. Torvul gravitated instantly to a pyramidal stack of thick iron rods, and knelt down, tilting his head towards them and inhaling deeply through his nose. His eyes widened, briefly, but from where Murnock stood, he couldn't have seen.

Torvul made a show of sorting through them, sniffing around the entire pile, tapping one or two with his fingertip—but Idgen Marte noticed that he went right back to the bottom and carefully separated out the first two he'd sniffed. He picked them up, handed one to Idgen Marte, and the two made for the door. They were almost out when the shopkeeper burst out with another rockslide of Dwarfish. Idgen Marte turned to listen, watching their faces carefully.

Torvul looked pained, his jaw tightening and his eyes narrowing just a moment before he answered. Idgen Marte couldn't pick out where one word ended and another began, but she could've sworn she heard the word Thornhurst tucked into Torvul's response. Then the dwarf turned and left so quickly she was stuck standing in the doorway with an iron bar in one hand.

When they were ten paces from the storefront, Torvul shook off whatever had bothered him and let out a cackle. "Still got it. Could've taken him to three if I wanted to—but the poor benighted bastard has no nose for the metal at all, and half a wagonfull of hungry mouths 'round him."

"And you didn't because?"

Torvul shrugged, and pointed his free hand vaguely skyward. "Don't want to anger Her Ladyship. I figure I can bargain shrewd, I just can't rob a man blind anymore." He sniffed disdainfully, and said, "It's like deliberately leaving half a vein of ore in the tunnel. Goes against everything I was brought up to believe—there was actually a cult a few hundred years ago, preached that we ought to leave some of everything—ores, gems, where we found it, to appease the rock and the spirits inhabiting it."

"What happened to it?"

"Nothing good," Torvul said, darkly. "Now. Where is our man?"

Idgen Marte sighed, shifted the burden of the rod she was carrying, and pointed with a free hand towards the distant towers of the keep. "There."

Torvul whirled on her. "What? Why did you say nothing?"

"He was summoned. Not arrested. Invited."

"And he agreed to go?"

"Well, he was asked by a squad of soldiers—looked solid types, too." She glanced around, and said, "We shouldn't be talking about this on the street."

Torvul nodded and quickened his pace, and soon enough they arrived at the inn he'd taken rooms at and unburdened themselves of their cargo. Torvul stroked the edge of one of the rods, and said, "Got traces of other things in it. With some coal and the right fire, I'll make steel out of this that could string a harp."

"What're you planning to make?"

Torvul shrugged. "This n'that. You'll see. Now—Allystaire went to the Dunes?"

Idgen Marte sat down in one of the chairs the room provided, surprised that it came cushioned. "Aye—he told me to wait till morning. That if we hadn't heard, we ought to, well…go find him, I s'spose."

Torvul spat into the unlit fireplace. "He's a fool."

"If he had resisted, maybe that squad couldn't have taken us, but the city's full of hundreds more soldiers—campaign season is over."

"Haven't they farms to go back to? Mills? Fishing boats?"

"Some, surely. Not all."

"Well—what do we do?"

Idgen Marte shifted uncomfortably on the chair. "Wait till morning?"

Torvul shook his head. "I don't like it. We don't know what's going on there. Could be he's already dead, or in chains, tortured."

"And it could be he's having a bottle of brandy with the Baron and all is well."

"How much are you willing to bet on that?"

Idgen Marte let out a breath and looked down at the floor, lacing her fingers. She tapped her boot on the floorboard once, twice, then said, "I think if he was dead, we would know it. Yet I hate sitting and waiting."

"I could try and bluff us in."

She raised her head and glared at him briefly. "Are Baronial Seats accustomed to allowing dwarfish peddlers in?"

"Point taken," Torvul agreed, with an upraised index finger. "Nightfall?"

Idgen Marte stood up suddenly and wrapped a hand around the hilt of her sword. "I don't know. I don't know and I hate this…sitting, waiting, planning, wondering. I've never liked commanding, and this is why. I'd rather react than plan—"

"Idgen Marte," Torvul said, his voice smoothed and calming. "Her Ladyship didn't choose you for no reason. You've been followin' Allystaire's lead for months now, and I don't blame you. He's an easy man t'follow, and that's precisely why this Baron is probably scared of him. And you know if you want to get into the keep, there's no walls that can keep you out. Aye?"

Idgen Marte took a deep breath, her eyes still on her boots, and nodded. "Aye."

"Good. I don't think we wait till morning. Nightfall—you get inside, at least."

"What'll you do?"

"Doubtlessly something brilliant."

"Haven't the faintest idea, have you?"

"Ideas are but a very small part of brilliance," Torvul said, with a wave of his hand. "And no rescue should go on empty stomachs." He glared at the fireplace. "Or cold feet. That's a bit of a Dwarfish saying, really, though it's not rescue so much as 'moving gold from one vault to another under threat of robbery,' but it's got a similar sense."

Idgen Marte snorted. "Take your sayings and go get us food and fire."

Torvul nodded and headed for the door, then paused and turned. "Whatever's going on, Idgen Marte, we'll find him. We've got too much work left to do. She wouldn't let it end like this."

Idgen Marte smiled faintly, but said, "She's not the only god in the fight, I think."

Torvul smiled in return. "She's the only one who's got us on her side."

CHAPTER 3

The Boy

Allystaire wasn't sure how long he'd lain on the edge of unconsciousness in the total darkness of the room when he was suddenly startled to wakefulness by a quiet but steady voice.

"What were you speaking of while Bhimanzir tested you?"

The voice was soft, a young boy's voice, or a woman's, he really couldn't tell. The sudden intrusion of noise into his aching, pain-wracked senses brought him to full alertness, his tingling wrists training against their chains. "What? Who is there?"

"It annoyed him very much," the voice went on. Allystaire couldn't place the accent; it certainly wasn't Baronial, or Islandman. Keersvast, or Concordat, he thought, but he hadn't heard much of their tongues. "He was less angry than confused."

"Well I am glad I can at least do that, whoever you are."

There was a pause, long enough that Allystaire wondered if the owner of the voice had left, before it went on. "I am Bhimanzir's student."

A young sorcerer. Wonderful. "And does he know you are here?"

"I was to observe you while he was gone. Not to speak. I have only just learned the Seeing Dark and it is a test of my mastery, I think."

"Well, Bhimanzir's student," Allystaire said, "what did you think of your master being confused and annoyed?"

"It is better than how he usually is."

"Oh? How is that?"

"Angry. Demanding. You're a puzzle he means to unlock, and he prides himself on his cleverness."

"Do you find him clever?"

Another pause. "No. Powerful and clever are not the same."

Well. This is something. "No, no they are not. Do you want to know the answer to what I was saying?"

"If I do, and Bhimanzir asks me, he may force me to tell him."

"Then you will at least have known something he did not. That will make you the clever one."

There was another pause. "Very well."

"Whatever your master was doing," Allystaire said, "it hurt. Yet I have been hurt many times before. More than I can count."

"Yes," the boy's voice replied. "I can see your scars from here. They are quite ugly," he added, matter-of-factly.

"Well, ugly or not, I know pain. We are old friends, pain and me. Well, acquaintances—I do not mean to say I like them, the aches and bruises, the burning throb, the feeling of a blade on the wrong side of my skin. Yet I do know just about every kind of pain a man can know. Your master was not showing me anything new. I found it helped if I recalled when I had felt whatever he was doing before."

"The Delvings—at least in the way Bhimanzir was performing them—surely hurt more than any weapon of steel."

"Mayhap," Allystaire admitted hoarsely. "There is more to it, I suppose. That counsel I would keep for myself, for now."

"I see," the voice said, and Allystaire believed that the boy probably did. "He will not like to hear that." Another pause, then, "Yet I think I will enjoy telling him, if he asks."

"What is your name, student?"

"I cannot tell you that."

"Why not?"

"My master has not given me one yet."

"I see." *I really don't,* Allystaire thought. "In my experience, the name another man gives you is likely to stick whether you like it or not. Better, perhaps, to claim your own."

"It is the way of things. I must wait for the name I am given, even if it is given by a clumsy fool."

"You do not like your master, then?"

There was no answer, and once again, Allystaire was alone in the darkness.

* * *

If he dreamed, the agony he awoke to washed it away. The sorcerer was standing near him once more, illuminating a tiny circle of the room with the ugly red light that leaked from his fingers, that had once again formed a web of threads around Allystaire's body, from which tendrils dipped into his skin.

His breath was too quickly stolen from him for any kind of a scream, and his lungs began to burn before the web of energy grew quiet; it still hovered over him, but no longer flashed into his skin. The breath he drew was less a deep inhalation than a ragged, inward moan.

"No bravado for that, ah?" The sorcerer chuckled, while Allystaire simply sought to regain control of his breathing. "This must be getting wearying for you."

"I just lie here," Allystaire croaked. "You are the one expending all the effort."

"There is truth in that," the sorcerer admitted. "And I am no closer to discovering the source of your power. I find no evidence of thaumaturgy, sorcery, witchery, or possession. I run short of ideas to test."

At that, Allystaire laughed, though it was a dry, dusty chuckle. "You could simply have asked."

"And why would I expect that you would answer, or answer truthfully?"

"Well, you are right that I might not answer. Yet if I did, it would be the truth."

The sorcerer came closer, lifting his head to peer at Allystaire, who saw tiny lines and motes of red flickering where Bhimanzir's eyes must be, under his cowl.

"Well then. I have witnessed, or have reports I have no reason to doubt, attributing powers to you. Unnatural strength, mostly, though some speak of healing and others of being compelled to speak when they would have been silent. Where do these powers come from?"

Allystaire smiled very faintly. "A Goddess."

There was silence for a moment, then a small sound of indignation from the sorcerer. "And you expect me to believe that?"

"Your belief is irrelevant to me," Allystaire replied. "I have seen Her, been touched by Her, been called by Her. I know it as I know how to breathe or to sleep. I know that it is a part of me that no amount of pain can make me deny. So go on not believing. When I am given the chance to prove it to you, that will be enough for me."

"Whether gods, as you mean the word, exist, is something hotly debated among my order. There are those who insist that they do but are at best indifferent, at worst openly hostile to this world. There are others who suggest that they are merely the spirit or the residual energy of the most powerful practitioners of our or some other discipline. I find myself incredulous of the former and inspired by the latter."

"You talk too much."

"Suppose that a benevolent god did exist," the sorcerer went on, as though Allystaire hadn't spoken. "Why would any being of unimaginable power choose, as its agent, a disgraced minor warlord from this pathetic, fractured hinterland? You tried, briefly, to walk in the world of power. Believe me when I say that power—real power, the kind that moves the world—does not come clad in steel. It has no need of swords, or hammers."

The sorcerer stepped closer, raised a hand, and let go a shockwave of red power that smacked Allystaire in the face like a blow from a club. His head jerked back against the wooden frame he was bound to, and he gingerly pressed his tongue to his teeth, expecting to find them cracked and broken, and felt mild relief when he realized they were not.

"In short, Allystaire Coldbourne, real power has no need of you."

Bhimanzir let that statement sink in for a moment, then spoke again. "This conversation has, I believe, illuminated a possibility I had not considered. If a spirit is controlling you, but hiding that very fact within you…yes. But how to unlock it? Or how to turn it…" The sorcerer suddenly hurried out of the room.

In the darkness again, Allystaire let himself wonder, for a moment, what truth might be in the sorcerer's words. But the thought lasted only a moment, just long enough for the memory of the Goddess's voice, of Her hand upon his head, of the sound of Her tears at the farmhouse, and his doubt was replaced with a flash of anger and a deep pang of shame.

CHAPTER 4

A Distraction is Arranged

Idgen Marte waited on the quay impatiently. She wanted to wrap herself in darkness, disappear into the shadow. Standing there in plain darkness made her feel exposed. She had a feeling Tibult might not take it well if she disappeared on him. He was getting edgy as it was, grimacing and trying to find a comfortable position for his leg. More than once she started to scold him, only to stop herself short.

Patience, Idgen Marte, patience, she thought to herself. *You've never had a wound like that.* One hand strayed to her throat.

Finally, after an interminable wait, she heard the click of oars in muffled locks and a boat glided into view. Nothing fancy, a simple tar-smeared fisherman's rowboat, with Torvul a dim, round shape at the stern. He tossed a rope without a word and she caught it with a graceful shift of her wrist, pulled the boat alongside the quay, and tied it neatly on a cleat.

Torvul hauled himself up onto the quay with surprising speed, and even in the darkness she could feel his gaze slide questioningly towards Tibult.

"Thought Allystaire was the one more like t'collect hangers-on," he muttered.

"Tibult, meet my friend Torvul. Torvul, Tibult," she said, moving briskly past the dwarf's disapproval. "Man's hungry, dwarf," she added quietly.

"What's that got to do with me?"

"It's got to do with whatever food you're carrying," Idgen Marte said.

"What makes you think…"

Idgen Marte sighed and stepped closer to Torvul, lowering her head towards his. "Dwarf, take a closer look at the man and produce some biscuit or some dried meat, for the Goddess's sake."

Torvul stepped closer to Tibult, reaching for a large pouch on the side of his belt, drawing from it a cloth wrapped bundle that proved to be a thick wedge of cheese so white it was almost luminous in the dark.

"Some of the best your city has to offer," Torvul said, holding it out to the man. "Fresh goat's milk packed in honey," he said. "I've often thought that the finest part of living on the world above is the abundance of cheese. Go on."

"Why're ya doin' this? What'll ya want?" Tibult reached out and took the proffered cheese but held it cautiously.

"I told you. Nothing more than a word or two dropped in the right tavern. And gold in your palm for the trouble," Idgen Marte calmly replied.

"How'm I gonna make it to the right tavern," Tibult said, around a mouthful of expensive cheese. "My crutch is on the bottom o' the bay. I can barely walk."

"Might be I can do somethin' about that," Torvul said. "Nothin' permanent, mind. But I can ease the pain for a bit, make walkin' easier." The dwarf patted the pouches on his chest, fingering them as if he could divine the contents with the touch of a hand. He slipped one bottle out and held it towards the veteran.

"I've had enough o' freezin' potions and their peddlers," Tibult said with a snarl, one hand curling into a fist.

"You haven't had any like mine."

"That's what the last one said, after I saved up for months, hidin' links and starvin' myself—"

"The last one? You bought from a dwarfish alchemist? There is one in the city?"

"Dwarfish? No."

Torvul's voice went a little cold. "Then you bought from a false alchemist. This art has belonged to my people and mine only, and if there are a dozen with command of it left in the world I would count myself surprised. Now listen to me," Torvul said, stepping forward and pressing the potion bottle into the man's free hand. "This will ease your pain. It will make it easier to walk. It won't cure your wound and it won't make you forget that you've got it. Each spoonful will let you walk across this city with no more pain than most men your age. And it's yours to keep, no matter what you do or don't do for my associate. For this," the dwarf said, with a certain sober formality, "the product of my craft, I ask for nothing. I will accept nothing. It is freely given."

Torvul stepped back from Tibult, leaving the potion bottle snugly in the man's hand. The veteran stared at it for a moment, then tucked it away in his rags.

"Not like anyone in this city to give somethin' of real value away for free. Man's got to be short a leg or an eye to end a day w' a bowl full o' lead bobs and copper halves," Tibult muttered.

"Well there's not anyone else like us in this city, Tibult," Idgen Marte said, drawing a string of links from a purse with one finger. "Less the friend of ours we need to help."

"Eh? And where's he?"

Idgen Marte pointed across the water at the hulking shadow of the Dunes. "In there. And not like to come out again unless we go and fetch him."

"You're mad," Tibult said. "And just what am I to say, what words do I drop in anyone's ear, that's gonna make any difference in a madwoman and a dwarf stormin' the walls of the tightest keep in the baronies?"

Idgen Marte smiled. "It's not about helping us get in," she said. "It's about helping us make it clear of the wall. The city wall."

CHAPTER 5

A Rescue is Mounted

"**D**warfs were a sea-faring people once, you know," Torvul said, as he and Idgen Marte drifted along in their borrowed rowboat in Londray's harbor, the gloomy hulk of the outer sea-facing wall of the Dunes looming above them and casting shadows on the swells that lapped against the boat. "I think I feel it still in my blood as I make the oars sing."

"You're gonna feel it in your boots if you don't shut up, dwarf," Idgen Marte said. "And if the oars sing, we're done for, so keep rowing only when we stop drifting."

Torvul grumbled quietly and readjusted his grip on the oars. Idgen Marte crouched at the stern, bow in hand, sword shifted so that it rested against the small of her back, the hilt projecting out past her hip. The oarlocks were muffled with cloth, for all the good it did. She still thought they were far too loud.

"We didn't have to leave a gold link for the fisherman, you know," Torvul replied. "I'm sure it's worth no more than two silver." He gave the oars a quick and efficient pull, and the rowboat glided forward several more yards.

"Why did I even bring you along?"

"You can't row and carry the walls single-handedly at the same time, I suppose," Torvul murmured. "And besides, I have an idea or three."

That's more than I've got, Idgen Marte thought, but she shoved that thought down. *There's a problem. I'm reacting. I'm going to get him out. No thinking needed.*

"You sure our new friend will do what you asked?"

"Sure as I can be," Idgen Marte whispered back, with a shrug. "He won't throw himself off the next quay, I don't think."

"He does it, there's chaos. Maybe the city burns."

"It won't. Not where their anger'll go."

The wall was drifting closer. Torches were faintly visible along its top as guards went on their rounds, but either Idgen Marte's prayers for shadow were answered or the single rowboat simply wasn't visible from that height. "One more pull," she whispered, the dwarf obliged, and suddenly the boat was within the shadow of the walls. It struck the wall, stopped with a force that shivered its side, and, she was sure, was audible to the entire keep.

They'd sailed right into a portcullis set low along the harborside wall—a possible sally port, or a place for emergency supplies to enter in a time of siege, Idgen Marte reasoned.

"This, also, is why you brought me," Torvul replied. "Grab a hold and make the boat fast."

Idgen Marte leaned forward and found a cold iron bar, wrapped her free hand around it as Torvul rummaged among his many pouches. By the time he spoke again, she'd taken a spool of rope that was fastened to a cleat on the boat and tied a mooring hitch around the bar.

"Now," he said, "take this skin. It's uncorked. Do not squeeze it. I can't emphasize that point enough. Do not squeeze."

"Why?"

Torvul sighed, even as he carefully leaned forward to hand her the skin. "Always with questions. Just do it."

Idgen Marte took it, a small leathern bag that sat heavily in one hand, but wasn't terribly large. "Now," Torvul said, "this fleece. Pour some of the liquid onto it, then rub it across the bars, and work fast."

She reached out and accepted the thick piece of lambswool he handed her. "Why?"

"Because if it does what I expect it'll do to the gate, you don't want to see what it'll do to your hand, and the fleece will only absorb it for so long."

"Why aren't you doing this?"

"Well," Torvul said, still whispering, though his patience was clearly thin, "if you'd like to take the risk of flipping the boat as we clamber over each other in the dark, let's. But honestly, if you just want to clamber over each other in the dark, this is hardly the—"

"Finish that thought and die, dwarf," she whispered, before she went to work. As instructed, she made sure the fleece covered her entire right hand, holding the skin in her left; she carefully poured out a measure of the stuff, and instantly felt her hand begin to warm. She wrapped the fleece around a bar and rubbed, then a second, third, fourth.

The fleece began to smoke, and Torvul hissed, "Drop it. In the water. Now."

She did, and the ruined bit of wool hissed as it hit the water, and disintegrated on its surface.

"I've another. Now we need to work fast. This might make some noise coming free, and they'll send someone to investigate it."

Idgen Marte paused as she reached out for the second fleece, and suddenly voiced a thought. "Why are we bothering? It's not like the walls can stop me."

"Can you take me in with you? Or Allystaire out?"

"Ah." With that, she repeated the process, rubbing the strange, burning liquid all over the bars the boat rested against. From behind her, Torvul suddenly hissed in alarm.

"Stones! Cut the rope. Cut it now. Now!"

She saw the danger as soon as he said it, and time seemed to slow as she threw the fleece overboard and reached for a dagger. Her blade bit into the rope and began to saw through it, even as the portcullis gave a sigh and slid free, as if cut in half, everywhere she had rubbed the alchemist's strange liquid.

The rope gave. The resulting splash tugged on the boat, and was loud, but didn't drag them under, and Torvul gave the oars a quick tug to shove them into the channel of water flowing into the castle's bowels.

"Well," Torvul said, "that went well. We've got a quarter of a turn, mayhap a bit more. Hurry. Take that liquid with you. Mind that you get none of it on your skin."

"Noted. What'll you do?"

"I thought I might set a few likely places on fire."

"We aren't here to burn the keep to the ground."

"No, and I don't mean to. Just enough to give them something to think about." The dwarf struck something against the side of the boat, and quickly a tiny shuttered lantern flared to life in his hand. There was a ramp cut into the stonework and a small dock to tie up to, though with the amount of rope they'd lost, Idgen Marte simply hopped out, splashed along in the shallows with Torvul following, till they could tug the bow up onto the ramp itself.

"Goddess go with you, Idgen Marte," Torvul said, a bit solemnly. "If you find him, and you can't get back here, or I'm not here when you do, just go."

"We are all walking away tonight, Torvul."

"Oh, I don't mean t'die here. No. I'll get clear—but he has t'get out, and you know it. Promise you'll not wait for me."

"Shut up, dwarf," Idgen Marte said, filling her hand with a dagger and disappearing into the darkness surrounding them.

"Now," Torvul murmured to himself, "where would I be if I were Baron Delondeur's wine cellar?" He thought a moment, pointed the tiny ray of light his lantern provided, and walked off.

* * *

For once, the sorcerer came bearing a light source other than his own trails of red—an expensive and large wax candle protected by an even more expensive glass lamp atop a silver tray. The sudden intrusion of that small point of brightness after so many turns in the dark caused Allystaire to recoil briefly.

"I do hate polluting my work room with this unnecessary light, but I do not come alone," Bhimanzir said, and Allystaire could not help but note the hint of gloating in his voice. Behind him came a short, thin boy of perhaps ten or eleven years, Allystaire thought. The light from the candle was minimal, so details were hard to make out, but the boy's skin appeared dusky, lighter than Idgen Marte's, but darker than most barony folk. Whatever his hair might have looked like, it had been carefully shaved. His eyes were large dark pools above cheeks still round with youth.

And behind them came a guardsman, wearing Delondeur green, armored, with a sword hanging at his side, dragging a woman behind him. It wasn't hard to tell she was a prisoner, wearing a ragged homespun dress that was too big for her, chains on wrist and ankle, and her eyes downcast.

Dress probably fit her when they took her, Allystaire thought, and he felt his hands curl into stiff-fingered, aching fists.

"If I am right about what is going on in your head, well then, I think I have the key to unlocking it." He turned to the guard and gestured with the hand holding the candle towards the nearby table. "Put her there, if you would."

The woman mumbled something, but was in no position to resist as the guard roughly shoved her towards the scarred wooden table, then onto it. He had some fuss getting her on her back, but once there she simply lay there moaning softly.

Allystaire heard the chains bound around his wrists creaking, felt the metal digging into his skin.

"There will be no heroics from you, I think," the sorcerer said, and raised a hand. The chains binding Allystaire's limbs suddenly glowed, not with heat, but from the power Bhimanzir commanded. Suddenly their weight was tenfold what it had been, twenty. They drew tighter, and Allystaire felt his hands and shoulders and ankles going numb.

"Now, boy. Hold this." He moved the candle in the direction of his student without looking back at him, and the boy glided noiselessly to the sorcerer's side, reaching out and taking the silver and glass lamp by its curled handle.

The sorcerer moved to the table and laid a red-tipped hand upon the rack of instruments. His fingertips danced over them: shears; a long, flat blade with no point; a very long and thin knife; and a wicked, black-crusted hook with a wooden handle.

"All blood carries power. One of the gifts of my order is the ability to unlock it, you see," the sorcerer said, and his intentions, which Allystaire was already certain of, became perfectly clear. "Why, I believe you saw some of what Gethmasanar could do with even the thin, weak stuff of peasants."

The paladin felt the song of the Goddess's anger begin to flood his limbs, and yet the music was distant and hard to hear, and his arms were weaker than they should have been.

The chains did not budge.

The sorcerer took the shears and began cutting away the woman's filthy dress. She was an older woman, Allystaire saw. Not elderly, but a few years older than him, probably, and she could only struggle feebly, with her hands bound behind her. She was, he suddenly realized, of an age with many of the women who'd been taken from Thornhurst. He remembered Idgen Marte's words to him back in the village, on the day the Urdarite monks had come. Someone did see value in enslaving women of her age after all. The chill that had danced along his spine returned, only with a drumbeat of certainty in his thoughts.

They were sacrifices.

Allystaire strained against his ensorcelled chains, and he thought he felt them move, yet he was still bound. *Certainly they rattled*, he thought, grimly. *That's something.*

The student had turned to him, drawn, perhaps, by the noise, but his darkly shaded eyes flitted back to the sorcerer.

Impulsively, Allystaire spoke. "Boy. You, without a name. Is this the man you want to give you one, eh?"

The sorcerer turned to Allystaire then, his eyes narrowed red slits. "Why are you talking to my student?" Then his attention turned to the boy. "Did you speak to him? Were you instructed to do so? No!" the sorcerer roared, and the guard near the doorway quailed at the power in his voice. The woman on the table let out a long and loud sob, and Allystaire felt his ear pop.

The sorcerer backhanded the boy across the face, and while the student stumbled, he didn't drop the candle. He simply regarded his master silently.

"Answer me. Answer me or I will have you upon the table, regardless of what Gethmasanar tells me about your untapped power. Perhaps it is your blood that will unlock this upstart for me!" He leaped forward and seized the boy's tunic in one hand, dragging him close.

"You said yourself he was a clumsy fool. He is a coward as well, afraid to ply a blade to anything not bound for him. And you would have a name he bestowed?" *Not sure what good this is doing*, Allystaire thought, for while the boy's face turned to him, he still did not speak.

The sorcerer turned, eyes wide open and raging red, leaped towards Allystaire. "I will be reading signs in your vitals next. The haruspicy warned of a mother, and so I took mothers and I read the signs in them, and it showed me death. Death! As if something as insignificant as you could threaten me. I will have three upon my table tonight and I will wade in your innards till this farce is clear to me!"

As the sorcerer was raging at him, the student, still holding the candle, raised his free hand, and Allystaire felt some new note in the music that played, slow and dim, in his body.

The glow upon Allystaire's chains winked out of existence. They were no longer a heavy weight. They were linen, or silk, laying lightly against his skin.

The boy nodded, Allystaire thought, at him.

The sorcerer whirled upon his student, a wordless roar of frustration emanating from his lips.

The wooden frame Allystaire had been bound to exploded into splinters as he suddenly ripped his hands free of it, links of chain scattering across the floor. He leaped to his feet, his body flooded with rage, and he took but one step forward before his left hand closed around the sorcerer's neck. He meant to crush his throat, to tear his head from his shoulders if need be. It felt possible.

But when his fingers found the sorcerer's flesh, something rushed into them, some throb of knowledge suddenly in his hand. Rather than squeeze, Allystaire poured the anger, the crying out for justice, the molten power his body thrummed with, into the sorcerer's body.

And healed him.

The red glow in Bhimanzir's eyes and his fingertips guttered and died, and the sorcerer collapsed with a strangled cry.

Allystaire leaped past him and barreled straight into the guard, delivering a powerful over-handed right fist directly into the man's mailed chest.

The guard had his sword half out of his scabbard when Allystaire hit him, and he staggered backward against the door, breathing raggedly. His hauberk was broken where Allystaire's blow had landed, and blood trickled through where the torn rings of his mail had pushed into the meat of his chest.

"Painful," Allystaire said, as he crouched over the guard and snatched his sword away by simply ripping the scabbard from the belt. "Yet not fatal." He drew the sword, tossed the scabbard away, and said, "I will remedy that if I must."

Allystaire stepped to the table where the intended victim still sobbed quietly. He helped her sit up, quickly tugged the leather thongs binding her wrists free with finger and thumb, and then turned back to the guard.

He reached down and hauled the wounded man to his feet with his free hand; it felt like picking up a blanket. Pointedly, he lifted the man clear in the air before setting him back on his feet.

"Was the woman kept nearby?"

The guard nodded, clutching at his wound with one hand.

"Boy, can you manage the woman?"

There was a pause as the student considered, his head tilted to one side. "Yes."

"Good. Bring your former master's tools as well."

"Why?"

Allystaire wasn't listening to the boy's questions. He bent down, lifted Bhimanzir from the floor with his left hand, tightened his right around the hilt of the unfamiliar sword, and leveled it at the guard.

"Take—"

A strangled cry from the limp sorcerer gave him pause. With his sickly red light gone out, the candle seemed to blaze brighter than it had, and Allystaire peered closely at the old wisp of a man clutched in his hand. Before his very eyes, age overtook Bhimanzir's features. The sorcerer's skin creased and folded; his eyes clouded over and sank into their sockets. His cleanly shaven head sprouted hair that began brown but faded rapidly to silver and then to white as it grew, and all of this in the span of a breath.

He heard the nameless apprentice stepping closer behind him, could practically feel the boy's attention focusing on his master.

Bhimanzir raised a hand slowly, feebly, reaching for the boy. The skin turned papery and thin, as if the very bones were rising up against it. The sorcerer croaked some words Allystaire could not make out, then fell forward to the stones of the torture chamber and lay still.

Allystaire put a hand to his neck and probed with the Goddess's Gift for any spark of life. There was nothing but a dark and impenetrable blackness, something harder and meaner than mere death or injury.

"What was he saying," Allystaire asked.

"He was trying to utter a curse, but his power had utterly left him. How did you do that?"

"I am not quite sure," Allystaire replied. "I am sure that now is not the time to discuss it."

The boy walked forward and squatted down, putting his hand in front of the sorcerer's mouth, satisfying his own curiosity it seemed. The boy stepped back, then extended the toe of his boot to touch the sorcerer's limp head. Hair, skin, and bone crumbled away like ash, and the rest of his body followed, till there was nothing left but a pile of dust.

The boy stood and tucked the case of knives and hooks under one arm.

"He was a fool," the boy said. "I am glad he is dead," he added, simply, as he stood waiting, looking expectantly at Allystaire.

Meanwhile the guard had started to edge away. Allystaire cleared his throat meaningfully and the guard halted.

"Take us to where the women are kept," he said to the soldier. The guard looked from the sword that had never wavered to the sorcerer's limp and desiccated form, swallowed hard, and waved one hand.

It was not a long walk; the stone corridor outside was well lit. The torches lining the walls made each step brighter than the one before.

They rounded a curve, the guard in front, when a voice suddenly called out.

"Back for another one so soon? Well, we're empty. He usually takes a little longer. Be a mess for the mornin' change t'clean up."

Another guard, green-tabarded, mailed, sat on a stool in front of an iron-banded oaken door. Keys dangled from his belt, next to a heavy flanged mace.

The tone of his voice struck Allystaire, the casual discussion of the prisoners they guarded, of their fate. The disregard. It ignited the fury of the Goddess to a pitch beyond his endurance, and before he realized what he was doing, he had shouldered the first guard aside, lunged forward, and driven the point of the borrowed sword straight through the key-holder's chest, cutting him off in mid sentence. Allystaire didn't stop; he kept pushing the blade forward, stepping close till his bare skin brushed against the guard's mail and surcoat, till the hilt was buried in the dead man's body and his blood had poured in a torrent over Allystaire's arm and chest.

When the paladin stepped back, the sword he'd stripped from the guard was buried a foot deep in the stone of the dungeon wall. The guard's body slumped forward against it obscenely, the stool clattering away from under nerveless limbs.

Allystaire ripped the man's belt away with his suddenly weaponless hand, and threw it over his shoulder, drawing the heavy mace free and brandishing it at the guard who was backing away.

"You knew," Allystaire said, his voice cold and menacing. "You knew what you were guarding these people for. What end you brought them to. You knew," he repeated, spitting the last word out like a curse.

The guard backed away another step, a small well of blood seeping up between his fingers where he clasped his wounded chest. Allystaire stood before him, naked, half of his torso covered in fresh blood, his white knuckled grip so hard the haft of the mace he held cracked.

It was too much. The guard's nerve broke; he turned and ran.

He got two steps before the thrown mace took him in the back of the head. His skull crumpled like a curled leaf under a heavy boot, and he fell to the ground.

Allystaire spent only a moment contemplating the two corpses. "Take these," he said, tossing the boy the belt with the ring of keys still dangling from it. The boy was small, with thin, gangly limbs, dark eyes deep-set on his dusky face, with his head shaved so close there was no trace of hair upon it.

He caught the belt and simply wrapped it twice around himself, tying off the ends where Allystaire broke them.

Meanwhile, Allystaire picked up the mace and broke down the door. It took two blows. The first bent the door inward. The second ripped it clean off its hinges. Inside was a dimly lit stone room, much like the one where he'd been held.

"I do not think there are any more slaves," the boy called from behind Allystaire, and the paladin whirled on him, glowering.

"They are not slaves, boy. No one is a slave, not in my sight. Not in the sight of the Mother."

The peasant woman cleared her throat. Her eyes were red but her sobs had ceased, though she maintained a wary distance from Allystaire. "It's true though, m'lord. I was the only one bein' kept there."

Allystaire nodded, but strode into the room anyway. On the back wall, heavy iron rivet-loops had been driven into the stone, each holding a ring for chains to be threaded through. Allystaire set down the mace, took a ring in each hand, and, with a twitch of his song-filled arms, ripped them free; he moved first one way down the wall, then the other. There were a dozen rings when he started, and a dozen holes in the dungeon room when he was done.

"This work was new," he murmured, as he strode out, and reclaimed the dead guardsman's mace. "At least that much is true." He took a deep breath, fearing, if only briefly, the wavering of the Goddess's song, and the power it brought. But still Her presence filled his mind and powered his limbs.

"Do you know where my armor was taken? My arms?"

"No, but the guards you killed are wearing some. Is yours so different?"

"Different enough. Even so, your point is not entirely without reason." His ears alert for any sound of clattering footsteps, the jingle of mail or weapons, but hearing none, Allystaire paused to strip the dead guard of his tabard, and to throw it on over his otherwise naked body. *Cold of a lot of good it'll do to stop a sword, or an arrow.*

"What time is it?"

"Almost three turns past the new day," the boy answered, without pausing to think.

"Where does the Baron sleep?"

"I don't know." The boy tilted his head to one side, wrinkled his brow, and asked in a tone as if he addressed a simpleton, "Why would you think I would?"

"Never mind," Allystaire said. He thought about stripping the hauberk from one of the dead guards, but just as he knelt on the stone, he heard the sound he dreaded—the stamp of boots. Stone swallowed the noise, and the corridor ahead of him branched in three directions, so he could not locate precisely where it came from.

"Boy, is there anything you can do to help me in a fight?"

"Give me time to think on it."

"We may not have any," Allystaire replied, and as soon as he did, the shouts down a corridor became clear. *I know orders being yelled when I hear them. How would they know so fast?*

He heard some member of the detachment, a sergeant or bannerman, he was sure, yelling ahead of them. "Intruders in the keep! Fire! Ware the guards. Stand to, every man!"

Fire? Intruders? Allystaire had little time to puzzle over this before ten guards, spears at the ready, poured into the far end of the corridor.

He raised his mace and said, "Boy, good woman, stay behind me." Cautiously, holding the weapon in two hands, Allystaire began to move forward.

Two guards, he saw, cocked their arms and readied to throw, bracketing him with their aim from either side. *Solid plan, that*, he noted, then he charged, barreling to his right as he did. The spear thrown to that side took him in the left shoulder as he pushed himself against the wall, while the other clattered harmlessly to the stone.

More spears were raised, and he was still ten paces away and unarmored. He took a deep breath, expecting the pain, expecting the spear. Then, unexpectedly, he felt something, a presence, and he allowed himself a smile.

A long-limbed shadow materialized amidst the guards and began weaving between them, a crescent of darkness extended from one of its hands, cutting their legs out from under them, tearing throats open.

Allystaire paused for just a moment, switched the mace to his left hand, and pulled the spear free from his shoulder. The pain registered in his mind more than his body.

He reversed the spear in his right hand, took a step, and threw. It whistled in the air and made a horrifying crunching sound as it pierced one of the guards through the side of his body, punching through mail, flesh, and bone. He dropped, blood pouring from his side and his mouth, as Allystaire tossed the mace back into his right hand, and pressed his left awkwardly against his own wound. In a moment, it closed, and he let it be. *There will be pain, and a scar. As it should be*, he thought, followed closely by, *It was freezing stupid to walk in here like I did.*

There was little work left for him to do among the guards. When the Shadow had killed two and cut the legs from two more before the others could even react, it had taken the fight out of them. Allystaire's spear-throw had broken a pair of them, who turned and ran, but three now pressed upon the form that had ambushed them. She was still a figure of weaving shadow, hard to see, harder to catch, but one of the three remaining men—the sergeant Allystaire had heard bellowing—was smart.

"Backs to the wall," he ordered, "spears set for a charge."

Idgen Marte—he knew it was her as soon as he'd felt her moments before she'd appeared—vanished from sight. Unable to come at them any way but from the front, her advantage was diminished. Allystaire, the strength of the Goddess's Gift still flowing in his veins—longer than it ever had before—recognized the man giving orders as Chaddin, the sergeant of the detachment that had imprisoned him.

"Chaddin," Allystaire barked out, hoarsely. "Throw down your spears. You can better serve your barony if you listen to me. If you do not, all you can do is die."

The sergeant's gaze swiveled towards Allystaire, though the point of his spear never wavered. "I see it three against two. Even if one is some kind of demon."

Shaking his head, Allystaire took a step forward, though he kept his mace-hand below his hip. He took another step; one spear point shifted in his direction. "I do not seek your death," the paladin said, addressing the guard. "Yet if you stand in my way I will have no choice." He took another step forward, and reached down to one of the limp, cold bodies on the floor, its throat a ruined gash. He reached up, fumbling at the steel pot helm, with nose and cheek guards that sat loosely atop the dead guard's head. He left his borrowed mace sitting on the floor when he stood.

Pointedly staring at the three sweating, spear-brandishing guards, he pressed the helmet between his two hands and crumpled it into ball, then turned his hands and let it fall to the stone floor with a heavy thump.

The two guardsmen got the message. Their spears clattered from hands that suddenly shot up in surrender, even as Chaddin fumed. "I'll see both of you hung," the sergeant spat, before suddenly lunging at Allystaire with his spear.

The man was well trained; the spear was level, held properly with hands spread for power and control. He pushed off his back foot and led with strong, straight steps. The point was aimed straight at the center of Allystaire's mass, and would certainly have driven through his unarmored flesh.

The paladin did not move. He thought, simply and pointedly, *Try not to kill him.*

No training, no form, was a match for the Shadow of a Goddess. Idgen Marte barreled into Chaddin from the side while her sword described an arc in the air so fast it appeared as a blur, driving his spearpoint into the stones at his feet. The shaft splintered and buckled and the weapon was torn from his hands, and he collapsed in a heap. She was upon him instantly, sword laid against his neck.

"I don't think he wants me t'kill you," she said, her face grim, "but I'm not too keen on doing just what he wants right now. So go ahead and move for your sword."

"We have no time for this," Allystaire said, even as he bent to one of the moaning hamstrung men Idgen Marte had toppled. He laid his left hand against the man's pale cheek, and poured some of the Goddess's power into him. Not much, just enough to keep him from bleeding to death on the stones. He did the same to a second. Then he confronted Chaddin.

"Sergeant, I have escaped your Baron's torture, killed his sorcerer, and together with this…" He looked to Idgen Marte, then back to Chaddin, and said, "Demon, was it? With this demon, we have routed your men. Remember these two things: I did not come here meaning to fight, and I could have let those two men die. Instead, they will live because the Goddess I serve gave me leave to save them. I think loyalty matters to you, sergeant, but it is time to decide if you are loyal to your Baron, or to your people. Because you can no longer serve both."

Allystaire paused to let that sink in, then said, "Where are my arms? Where is the Baron? In that order."

"Compel him," Idgen Marte spat, through gritted teeth.

"If I must," Allystaire growled back. "What will it be, sergeant? Do you tell me what I need to know of your own will or do I tear it from you?"

He could read the back and forth of duty and uncertainty, of fear and courage, in the soldier's face. *I could bring him to my side*, Allystaire thought, *if I had time*. He knelt, reached out for Chaddin's neck. The man flinched, started to back away, but Idgen Marte's sword-edge came to rest on his throat again. He stilled.

Allystaire seized Chaddin's chin and throat, pushed against the soldier's mind with a sense he still didn't quite understand, and asked, "Where are my arms and armor?"

"The Baron meant them for a trophy. Probably the great hall."

"Where does he sleep?"

"Northwest Tower."

"Allystaire, we haven't the time for this."

"Fine," he said, adjusting his grip on the now wide-eyed and pale-cheeked man's jaw. "My last question. What did you know about the prisoners?"

"What prisoners?"

"Her," Allystaire said, gesturing with a jerk of his chin towards the woman he'd freed. "And there were others. Slaves, taken on your own barony's land with your Baron's knowledge and consent. Some, like she was meant to, met their death at the hands of a sorcerer, feeding his divinations with their blood."

"I just returned from campaign," Chaddin whispered, all the color now gone out of his face. "I was at the far reaches of the barony, working against Innadan—"

"I do not need your report, sergeant." Allystaire stood up, wobbling slightly, the first hint that the incredible strength thrumming in his muscles was waning. "I need you to understand the truth. You heard his words yourself. Rabble, he called you. To men like him, for all his soldier's affectations, you are just another resource, a tool, a possession."

Finally on his feet, Allystaire started to turn away, then whirled back suddenly and dropped a glancing blow from his clubbed first against Chaddin's temple. He sank to the floor, his eyes rolling up in his head, unconscious. "If he is perfectly healthy when they find him, they will kill him. Better this way," he explained to Idgen Marte, who was already darting ahead to the end of the corridor and scanning the ways ahead.

Allystaire turned back to the boy and the rescued woman, whose brown eyes were wide with fear as she clutched the shreds of her dress. "The two of you," he said, "follow us and nothing here will harm you, if we can prevent it."

"Why?" The question came from the boy. "You have repaid me for dispelling my master's sorcery by defeating him. Why would you do more?"

"Follow and I will do my best to answer. In the meantime, many angry men with spears are going to show if we do not move, and they will kill you." Allystaire looked around at the carnage before them, sighing faintly at the waste of it, and pointed to one of the spears that lay nearby. "Pick that up. Do not try to stab anyone with it. Just point it menacingly if I tell you to."

The boy shrugged, and did as Allystaire suggested, hefting the weapon uncertainly, with both hands, holding it across his body like a quarterstaff.

Idgen Marte waved them on. "We don't have time for all this. We've got to find Torvul and clear out."

"To the Great Hall. I am not leaving without my arms."

"There's not a shortage of them, you know," she hissed.

"Good armor is expensive, and that plate was custom made to my needs by the Master Armorer at Wind's Jaw. Besides, we may run into the Baron on the way."

Idgen Marte shook her head resignedly. "Never rescuing you again."

"Agreed," Allystaire replied. "Now where will Torvul be?"

"Follow the shouts of 'fire,' I suspect," she replied. "Now, let's go. There's a stairway down that hall." She pointed to a passage and trotted off. Allystaire waved the boy and the woman to go ahead of him and followed.

As they moved along, Allystaire grew impatient at the slower pace enforced on them by the woman and the boy. Down a passage, up a stairway, another passage, without encountering guards. *We're near the ground floor. All keeps are much the same from the inside,* he thought.

"This is still a terrible idea," Idgen Marte said.

"The Great Hall has no tactical value, confers no advantage. They will not expect it. We collect my arms and then we find Torvul."

They had just crested another narrow staircase when they heard the sound of tramping feet and the calls of "Fire! Fire in the cellar!"

Allystaire turned towards the nearest door, took three steps, and threw his shoulder into it. The Goddess's strength had not left him, and the door flew open, bursting its lock. "Inside. Now!" He stood in the doorway till the woman skirted past him, and the boy, the butt of his spear dragging on the ground. Then he and Idgen Marte darted inside.

It was a closet, the size of a small peasant's cottage. It held stacks of linens, piles of wood, coal scuttles, buckets and brushes, the kind of things that kept a keep running. He hefted his mace and slid to one side of the door. Idgen Marte bracketed the other, while the student brandished his spear and the farmwife crouched behind a stack of chairs.

Suddenly a voice sounded from outside the door. "I think you're clear now. The sight of half the Baron's precious wine cellar going up in flames ought to keep them occupied for a bit. Come on out and let's quit this place."

Allystaire nudged the door open, and Torvul smirked from where he leaned on his cudgel.

"How did you find us?"

Torvul tapped the side of his head with one long finger. "I used Her Lady-ship's Gifts, and my not inconsiderable store of wit and wisdom. Come on now. They'll get that fire dealt with soon enough. Once they're organized and start patrolling every floor…"

"The wine cellars of the Dunes are legendary," Allystaire noted, a touch of wistfulness in his voice. "Did you really?"

Torvul sniffed. "Only the barrels of the inferior stuff. And, well, perhaps a few tuns of the better won't pass muster. Let's say I merely helped it on its natural course."

"Meaning?"

Torvul tapped one of his many pockets. "I turned it to vinegar."

Idgen Marte stepped out of the room and smacked both of them on the back of the head, so fast they grunted simultaneously. "If you two are done, we've a castle to escape, and a Baron to kill."

"After my—"

"Yes, after we collect your toys," she spat, before stalking off to the end of the corridor, ripping her sword from its sheath and swirling the tip in the air in front of her.

Torvul grunted and retreated a few paces. "And in case you're wondering, the fire won't spread out of the cellar, but they'll have a job of getting it under control."

Allystaire motioned for the youth and the woman to emerge. "Stay behind me, in front of the dwarf. He is a friend."

"And they are?" Torvul asked, gesturing towards them with his cudgel.

"Fellow escapees," Allystaire muttered, as the small column began to move. *Take the next left, girl, then straight down the corridor. Stairway on the right leads up into the Hall. Bound to be guards. Put them down if you can.* Allystaire heard Torvul's thoughts before the rumble of his voice.

"I see. And given that you're escaping, I take it the baron didn't ask you over for brandy and a pipe?"

Allystaire snorted. "He turned me over to a sorcerer. Name of Bhimanzir."

Torvul coughed discreetly, and his scuffling boot-steps stopped for a moment." And what's become of said sorcerer?"

"I healed him," Allystaire said, as they walked. "Dragged the magic right out of him, and he aged, oh, three or four scores of years right in front of me."

"Five-score at least," the boy corrected. "Possibly twice that much."

The dwarf whistled low. "They aren't gonna like that, boy," he said, while turning his eyes at the nameless youth behind him.

"I said they would learn fear. Now is the time they start," Allystaire said, trying to edge between the dwarf and the former apprentice. Torvul noticed, he was sure, but said nothing.

Guards! He heard Idgen Marte's voice in his head and rushed to her. There were two guards at their post, and Allystaire arrived just in time to see Idgen Marte knocking them both senseless with the hilt of her sword.

The doors of the Hall were barred from the inside. Torches burning in sconces to either side of the wooden double doors. Idgen Marte stepped under the torches, where the shadows were thickest, and vanished. The bar scraped against wood and iron as she lifted it, and the doors swung open. Inside, all was darkness.

They hustled inside, Torvul messing with the cylindrical, shuttered lamp hanging from his belt. Soon the lamp was glowing steadily, a brighter, more direct light than that of plain fire. He adjusted some knobs and light pooled in a wide circle around them as they advanced. The columns with their trophies rose up around them like great stone trees.

"Lot of risk for some steel," Torvul offered.

"How can I be a knight in shining armor if I am naked?"

Torvul harumphed at that, moving his lamp to and fro, fiddling some more with the knobs on it so that it focused into a tight, narrow beam. "Damn if this thing ever worked half so well before." *They'll probably have found the boat by now. We need another way out.*

I have some thoughts on that score, Allystaire thought. *I think we will leave by the front gate.*

Goddess save us from you doing the thinking, Idgen Marte thought.

There are more ways out of the keep if we need them. Tunnels my Master used. He could Step, as well, but I am afraid he did not teach me. The voice sounding in all three of their heads was unfamiliar, careful, and unusually accented.

All three swiveled as Torvul's lantern-beam focused on the former sorcerer's apprentice. The boy blinked his eyes against the sudden brightness, and readjusted his grip on the spear. "I'm sorry. Was that rude? I thought if I could hear you, then…"

Allystaire, Torvul, and Idgen Marte stared, first at the boy, then at each other.

"Later." Idgen Marte spoke first, cutting off all debate with a single chop of the edge of her hand.

Allystaire's narrowed eyes lingered on the unblinking and wide-eyed gaze of the boy before returning to the search.

Torvul's beam swept the room, suddenly stopped. "Over here." The light canted for a moment as the dwarf set his lantern down, and then some clattering as he began gathering up pieces. "Here."

He handed Allystaire his belt, with the hammer still snug in its ring. Securing the belt back around his waist made the paladin feel a little less naked. He stuffed the mace through his belt on the other side. Resignedly he added the thick leather strap that held his heavy sword; through the thin fabric of the tabard he wore, it began to chafe his skin as soon as he settled it.

"No time to get the armor on," Allystaire said, but Torvul's hands were already flying among the straps and buckles, long and skilled fingers moving certainly and nimbly despite the faint light. Soon enough he had it tied in convenient bundles, took two for himself, and handed one to Idgen Marte. The dwarf handed Allystaire his shield, the light of his lantern reflecting brightly off the battered blue face and golden sunburst.

They found the stairway that led straight down to the keep's main gate, but below them they heard a clatter, raised voices, armor rattling, steel hissing against leather. Idgen Marte halted and the rest of them came to a stop behind her.

"We should make for the boat," she said.

"Long walk," Torvul offered. "And they've surely found it by now."

"Will five fit on this boat?" Allystaire asked.

Idgen Marte fixed him with a hard stare that Allystaire returned. She looked away, shaking her head, eyes narrowed in frustration.

"We go onward," Allystaire said. "The front gate."

Torvul spat between his boots with pinpoint precision. "Men are already raised. How many between us and safety?"

"Her strength has not left me yet. We can fight free if we must."

They halted as the tumult of raised voices became more distinct. A shout briefly rose above the din.

"You speak of mutiny! Treason!"

Similar calls rang out, but the rattling of metal quickly swallowed them.

At the bottom of the stairs, two groups of men in armor and Delondeur green shoved and yelled at one another. In the very midst of it stood a familiar figure, Chaddin, his blond hair standing out among the crowd of more anonymous men in helmets and coifs.

"You knew what the sorcerer was doing here," the sergeant bellowed. To Allystaire, Chaddin seemed young for his rank without his helm, like a child stripped of a vital part of a costume. "Your entire detachment knew, Sir Leoben." The sergeant was taller than the knight he stood face to face with. Despite the disadvantage of the steps, he gave the knight a hard shove that sent him reeling backwards, clattering onto the stairs in his green-enameled and silver-chaised mail.

Sir Leoben was quickly hauled up by his men, his face darkening with rage. "First you talk treason. Now you dare lay hands on your—"

Chaddin drew his sword in a flash, the point leveling just in front of Leoben's face. The knight froze. "Say it. Say 'upon your better' or 'upon your lord.' See how much that matters to me right now, Leoben."

There's hope for this one yet, Allystaire thought, smiling inwardly, even as swords were drawn all around. The men—common soldiers in tabards—who gathered in a knot around Chaddin appeared calm compared to those on the steps above them, who were jittery and shifting from foot to foot, unable to stay still.

"Your political debate is thrilling, gentlemen," Torvul hollered, advancing down the stairs. "But alas, it impedes my exit, and so it must end. This is your warning." They had gone unnoticed by the opposing bands of Delondeur men, but there was no clear way past them now.

Allystaire was already drawing his hammer free; the weight returned to his arm like a comfortable old shirt sliding over his shoulders.

Both groups turned to them. Chaddin was suddenly seized with indecision, the point of his sword wavering.

Cover your eyes, all of you, and get the woman's, too. Torvul's hand dove into a pouch and produced a small, cloth wrapped bundle. He began to stroke the back of the bundle with the ball of his thumb, chanting a few low, rumbling words of Dwarfish.

Allystaire caught a glimpse of a painfully intense brightness and saw Torvul's arm cocked to throw before closing his eyes. Even with his arm covering his eyes, there was an intense red flash and the sudden screaming of men and a clatter of mail and weapons as they fell about, toppling each other down the stairs.

"Now! The effect will wear off soon!" Torvul scampered down the stairs, moving as fast as Allystaire'd ever seen. Torvul crouched among the downed men, searching for something for a few seconds, before finally shaking his head and moving on.

Allystaire waved the woman and the sorcerer's apprentice down the stairs before him, then bounded down two at a time, his bare feet slapping hard against the stone.

They passed the heap of blinded, yelling soldiers and guardsman without a backward glance, and had reached the wide and ancient oak gates of the keep's outer wall when a voice of command suddenly rolled over them.

"Where do you think you're going, Coldbourne?"

Allystaire whirled, giving his hammer a tentative swing, and saw Baron Delondeur, clearly just roused from sleep but carrying a naked sword, with a pair of knights at his side. The Baron wore a green silk nightshirt with his sigil, the sand-colored tower, patterned all over it. He looked faintly ridiculous with his swordbelt cinched around him, Allystaire thought, but his voice was hard, his eyes were clear, and his thick-wristed arm held his sword with casual ease.

"I am forced to refuse your hospitality, Lionel," Allystaire said, "but I do not wish to destroy your home in the process."

"You up-jumped mountain simpleton," Delondeur spat, "you've destroyed nothing. You won't make it out of the city."

"I think you are about to have greater problems than what to do about me, Lionel," Allystaire replied. As if it were a cue, Idgen Marte took a couple of steps forward, ready to launch herself towards the Baron, but Allystaire stopped her with a sudden thought.

No. Not like this. It cannot look like an assassin in the night. It has to look clean.

He's right, Torvul added. *If he's killed by a blurry shadow, we're no better than murderers as far as the regular folk will see.*

"What problems are those?"

"As I see it, there are two," Allystaire replied. "The first is that too many of your men, your good, loyal, seasoned men, now know what you were doing here. One of them is damned unhappy about it, too. The second—how will the sorcerers react when they know that one of their own died in your keep, under your care?"

"You can't kill a sorcerer!" Lionel's voice was steady, but his mouth tightened, his lips twitched nervously.

"I already have," Allystaire said, lifting his chin. "Your sorcerer, your diviner of secrets, the weapon that would win you a throne, lies dead upon the floor of your dungeon. If you doubt me, send a man to find his decrepit corpse. I am afraid we cannot wait."

The Baron's eyes widened, and after a swallow, he pressed on. "Even on your best day you'd never have been able to kill a sorcerer. You're lying."

Allystaire laughed hollowly. "You know that I cannot, Lionel. And when his brethren come and ask what happened, you tell them the truth as I tell it to you now. Tell them it was me, the Arm of the Mother. I was unarmed, naked, and bound, before I took his magic. Tell them his bones turned into powder at a touch when the Mother was done with him." Allystaire paused, felt his rage swelling in his throat. "Then tell them where to find me. I will await their coming, and I will be neither alone nor unarmed."

"There are too many guards between you and the gates of my city, Cold-bourne," the Baron replied, though his face had paled noticeably and the sword in his hand shook, but the uncertainty passed in a moment, replaced with his casual military swagger. "Even if you make the wall of the Dunes, you'll get no further."

"Why, Lionel," Allystaire said, "one would almost think you were afraid to face me yourself, with that kind of talk."

"Don't try to goad me, Coldbourne. You know me better than that."

"No," Allystaire replied. "I knew you." Whatever he'd been about to add was interrupted by the clatter of footsteps as the conflicting parties of guards raced towards the gate, with Chaddin's hardened bunch in the lead.

"M'lord! Guard yourself from mutineers," came a shout from Leoben. The knight was suddenly silenced as one of Chaddin's soldiers—a broad and thick-waisted man taller than the Baron—turned and drove a mailed fist into his face. This set off a general scuffle between guardsmen and knights, mostly conducted with fists and elbows, hilts and blade flats. No blood was drawn, though surely it would have been had Delondeur not whirled on them and bellowed, almost wordlessly. A lifetime of shouting orders in the field gave his voice the unmistakable note of command, and the men stopped and snapped to attention.

"What is the meaning of this? Why do my own men fight? Why has one of my own knights had his nose bloodied by a man-at-arms?"

"There are accusations, my lord, that must be answered," Chaddin said, his voice and fair features barely concealing his anger.

"I must answer nothing," the Baron shot back, imperiously. "Especially not accusations leveled by the soldiers in my service."

Allystaire's eyes flitted from Chaddin to the Baron and back, and something suddenly fell into place, and before he knew it, he was speaking aloud.

"He is your natural son," he said, lifting his hammer to point to Chaddin. "He is, Lionel, do not deny it. He has the Delondeur features."

Chaddin's jaw tensed, and he defiantly kept his eyes locked on the Baron. Conspicuously he did not look at Allystaire, but he didn't have to. As soon as the words were spoken aloud, the entire crowd in the entrance of the courtyard realized the truth of the paladin's words; in many ways Chaddin was a young mirror image of the Baron. Before the Baron could deflect or defend himself, Allystaire pressed on.

"How long have you kept him under your thumb, kept him thinking that someday you will acknowledge the truth he wears on his face, in his eyes, his hair?" Then, a knot of anger growing in his stomach, he added, "His accusations will not do because he is what, a sign of your own inadequacies? Your own lack of will? Because you deny his parentage, his word is worth less than the words of that coward?" The paladin pointed to the knight, Sir Leoben, who was probing carefully along his split lip with his fingertips.

Leoben suddenly flushed and began to draw his sword. "I will not be called coward, sir. I demand—"

"If you finish that demand, you will die like the guard of Lionel's slave pen did," Allystaire said, "pinned against the wall like a tanning hide. Silence yourself now or be silenced forever. Choose." The paladin fixed Leoben with his clear blue gaze. He was still blood-spattered, much of it drying to a dark brown upon his skin, and he hefted his hammer speculatively. In his mind, Allystaire was already lining up the throw.

Leoben matched Allystaire's stare for a moment, but his brown eyes wavered and then lowered. He swallowed once, then slipped his sword back into its sheath.

Allystaire pointed to the woman huddling behind Torvul. "What of her? A woman of your own barony, taken by reavers, sold into slavery, and bought with Baron's gold," he shouted. "Thrown upon a table to be butchered by the sorcerer the Baron hired. This is the man you are taking orders from—no better than the commonest reaver!"

"Still your mad ravings," the Baron roared, turning to Allystaire and lifting his sword.

"If you deny it, then attack me, and prove your innocence upon my person," Allystaire said. He spread his arms wide. "Neither of us are armored, and I have just spent the day being tortured by your pet sorcerer. That ought to even us for your advanced age."

That, it appeared, was enough, for the Baron roared and leaped to attack. Allystaire swung the haft of his warhammer so that the base of its shaft thunked into his left palm and he used it like a staff to ward off the blows Lionel leveled at him.

Age had taken little from the Baron as a swordsman, his swings as strong and fast as many a younger man's. Allystaire was never the swordsman Lionel had been, but he didn't intend the fight to last long. A vestige of the Goddess's strength lingered. *It will be enough.*

He pushed the Baron, with enough force to send the old man staggering to one knee. Allystaire lowered his hands to the bottom third of his hammer, keeping them a few inches apart, ready to swing in a wide arc.

Lionel noted the change and began circling, shuffling his feet, shifting his weight. Both the Delondeur men and Allystaire's own party instinctively gathered in semi-circles to either side of the combatants.

His sword held in his right hand, Lionel lunged. He was a tall man, with long arms and legs, and his lunge was fast, impressive, and hard to defend for a man not wearing armor.

Allystaire didn't try to meet it with his hammer. Instead, he simply turned his body and let the blade score across his ribs as he stepped forward. The pain was a sizzling line across his flesh, but he had drawn close enough to the Baron to do precisely what he wanted.

When his left hand closed on the Baron's shirt, the paladin lifted him off the ground, turned, and ran a few steps, till the older man's body slammed into the outer wall. Allystaire slammed him once, then twice more, till the sword fell from his fingers. Then he dropped his hammer to the stones, and wrapped the fingers of his right hand around the Baron's wrist, as it dove for the dirk belted opposite his empty scabbard.

He squeezed, just a bit, and felt bones creak, saw Lionel's eyes water. For a moment, Allystaire felt a pang of guilt. The Baron's age had made this fight a charade when compared to Allystaire's strength.

Then he remembered the sight of the bloodstained table in the dungeon, the stink of fear in the slaver's warehouse in Bend, the misery that he'd followed like a determined dog for all these months. He remembered the indignation of a little girl he'd found huddled and freezing in the cold well of her father's inn when she learned, for the first time, that her lands were ruled by a Baron who simply did not care for the weakest of his people. Who simply did not care for her, her parents, or any of the folk of her village.

His hand tightened till a bone in the Baron's wrist popped under his fingers. He stopped himself from turning the man's arm into a limp tube of bone fragments, shredded muscle, and agony.

"Tell all of us, Lionel. Raise your voice so your men can hear. You know slavers operate in your barony, and you profited from it, yes?"

Through pain-gritted teeth the man grated, "Yes."

"You even bought some of the captives, yes?"

"Yes!"

"And some of them came here, to the Dunes. And you never saw them again, because Bhimanzir was murdering them by ripping their vitals out with hooks and barbed knives. You may not have known that, but you knew when you gave him a woman that she was going to die. Did you not?"

The Baron clenched his teeth and strained his jaw, trying to twist out of the paladin's grip to no avail. The two knights who had walked at his side suddenly leapt forward, swords in hands, but Idgen Marte darted between them. There was a heavy smack of metal against flesh and bone, and they dropped their swords from nerveless fingers as she retreated back into the shadows.

"Say it, Lionel. You were putting your own people on a sorcerer's table for slaughter in order to help your aims. To found your kingdom. I will tire of asking, Baron," Allystaire said, increasing the pressure around his wrist, "then I will tire of letting you live." He worked hard to keep the easy confidence in his voice, for he felt blood beginning to stick the tabard he wore to his skin, felt the strength slowly draining from his limbs, which began to ache from the effort of holding the Baron against the wall. This needed to end soon.

"I knew. They were sacrifices for their barony, for their lords. They couldn't be soldiers, but they could do this. Bhimanzir promised victory; his kind have never been defeated. He needed flesh, mothers, he told me. They were my people! Bound to serve me, and they did!"

Allystaire let the Baron drop in a heap, disgust rising in equal measure as anger. "My people, Baron, does not mean the same thing as my sword, or my boots, or even my horse. It does not mean that they serve you. It should mean that you. Serve. Them." He turned to the soldiers behind him; they looked angry, in the main. Most of the anger, it seemed, was aimed at the man slumped on the ground, holding his fractured wrist. Hands tightened around swords, but did not draw them. Jaws quivered with tension, eyes flared. None seemed willing to challenge the paladin.

"You heard it from his own mouth, Chaddin. You are a sensible man. Take charge of him. We are leaving. We will kill any man we see in green between here and the gate. Aye?"

The blond sergeant stepped forward, his sword level, not pointed at Allystaire, but not pointed at Lionel either—thought it wavered in the direction of the Baron. He swallowed once, and said, "I will send word to the gates between here and there. You will not be harmed."

"How will word go ahead of us? No. I need more than word."

Chaddin strode forward and squatted at the nearly unconscious Baron's side, then seized his hand. Lionel tried, weakly, to pull away. The sergeant, his son, held fast and quickly pried something free. He came to Allystaire, holding out his hand. In it sat a heavy golden ring set with stones that glittered darkly green in the guttering torchlight.

Allystaire took it, glanced at it briefly, and held it to Torvul. His arm shook, very slightly, as he extended it. Hope no one noticed that.

"This will come back, Chaddin. You have my word on it. I will leave it with the guard at the outer wall." As Allystaire and company turned for the last set of stairs that would lead to the castle exit, he heard Chaddin begin to speak to the men. Knight's voices raised and quickly shouted down. He slid his left hand under his tabard, wincing as it felt blood and the slash across his stomach. He reached for the compassion, the love of the Goddess, to heal himself. He almost fainted with the effort of it. It felt like trying to draw the foundation stone of a tower out of the earth with his bare hands. It shifted, but only just. Blood crusted and dried under his hand. There would be a scar.

CHAPTER 6

The Distraction

No sooner had they made their way outside than Idgen Marte gave Torvul a nod. The dwarf produced a potion, threw it high in the air. Before it hit the zenith of its arc, it burst into a long, streaming green flare.

"Is that to tell every damned guard in the city where we are?" Allystaire asked incredulously.

"They'll already know that. No—it's somethin' she cooked up," he said, pointing a thick finger at Idgen Marte. "I suggest we go to ground for a bit t'see if it works."

* * *

Tibult had been lurking around the edges of the massive crowd of soldiers at the small north and east gate. An impromptu tent city had sprung up, as it always did, and even with just a few turns till dawn, ale-sellers and wine-carts and tents selling food, companionship, and trinkets were too full of customers to consider closing.

The men gathered here would likely be heading up towards the Ash river, to fisheries and mills and ferries, though a few might be making for the far northern reaches of the coast. At the main eastern gate, better than a mile to the south, men massed in anticipation of heading out into Delondeur's central plain and the lee of the Thasryach mountains.

This gate's camp was the third he'd managed to visit in the turns since they'd sent him on his way with more gold in his purse than he had ever counted on seeing. With a few drops of the dwarf's potion in him, he'd almost been able to walk without a limp, though he sensed he'd pay for it tomorrow.

It had been easy to fall into the rhythms of soldier's speech again, even if he'd not been one for nearly ten years now. And it hadn't been hard to spread the rumors, especially since he'd been willing to stand his rounds.

A soldier about to go home for the winter would listen to anything from a man standing a round.

"Look at how early the season ended," he was saying even now to a group of men whose green cloaks showed the Delondeur tower backed by shovels and broadaxes—sappers and pioneers. "It's a feint. I'm tellin' ya," Tibult said, finding himself moving into the role as he took a sip of his own too-new, too-sour ale. "The city is t'be sealed. Leave home is bein' revoked, and the season is goin' right up t'winter, if not into it. When the signal comes, any man still in the city is goin' back out on campaign."

"Where'd ya hear that?" One of the pioneers, a burly and bearded man with fists so large his ale-cup nearly disappeared in one, leaned forward over the brazier they shared.

"I heard it from my old mate, a quartermaster with Thryft's lot," Tibult said. "He got his manifests and they had him drawin' supplies through winter."

"What's this signal then?" The burly pioneer spat into the brazier, turning his cup around and around in one hand.

"Froze if I know," Tibult started to say, but then there was a general commotion and men scrambling out of their seats and tents.

At the far northwestern corner of the city, a bright green flare blazed across the sky. Every man in the camp froze in place to watch it.

Tibult gulped down the last of his ale and bellowed, "There it is! They'll be closing the gates against us now! Any man still in the city at dawn is in for a winter campaign!"

There were few words more hated by barony soldiers, armsmen, and knights than "winter campaign," Tibult well knew. The freeze could start mere weeks after summer and last for six months. Men could die at their post, horses at their picket. He'd frozen through more than one truly horrid barony winter himself.

So he was not at all surprised when the hundreds of homesick men took only moments to stitch the rumors he'd spread together into a cloak of fear that settled over all their shoulders, all at once.

As one, as if a knight himself had barked the orders, the men turned towards the distant gate, seizing up weapons and ropes, and charged like they were taking an enemy's fortress.

Tibult grabbed the flagon of ale he'd provided and shuffled off into the night, keeping the wall hard to his left and making for the main gate.

"Smart woman, that one," he muttered. "Attack at outlying positions first t'draw men away from the center and then go in force at it."

* * *

"What in the Cold is going on?" Allystaire paused, drawing Torvul, the boy, and the woman into the alley between shuttered shops. There was shouting, the clash of men, the indistinct yell of crowds.

Idgen Marte appeared behind him, bundles of cloth in her hands. "What's going on is the distraction that'll allow us t'make the gate. Take this." She held out one hand and Allystaire took from it a Delondeur soldier's cloak.

"What did you do," he asked, even as he threw the thing over his bare shoulders, glad of something else to wear besides a blood-stained tabard.

"Spread rumors. You know how soldiers are."

"What rumor?"

Idgen Marte passed out similar cloaks to the rest of the party, though she didn't bother with one herself. "Just something that'll keep the gate guards occupied."

"Idgen Marte—"

She began to wave the rest of them after her, but stopped. Turning back to face him, exasperated, she said, "That the Baron means to start a winter campaign. That any man still in the city come dawn—"

"Oh Goddess," Allystaire breathed. "What have you done? They will riot. They will burn the city."

"Well," Torvul drawled, "they're not playin' at bowls just now. But I don't see too much aflame."

"I needed something to get us out. I needed something we could hide in. I had no idea you'd find a way to get safe passage, and that's even if it would've worked!"

Allystaire scowled and punched his balled up fist into his free hand. "Men will die."

"Men die every day," Idgen Marte shot back. "How many did you kill today? We needed a way out."

"Those are not the same. We do not make those kinds of compromises," Allystaire spat.

"You don't," Idgen Marte said. "I don't have a choice."

"Enough!" Torvul's gruff voice cut through the chatter while the woman and the sorcerer's apprentice looked on, one fearful, the other simply unnervingly observant. "We are getting out. Now. We can argue over it later," he said, then pointed a finger at Allystaire, "and you'll lose. Now go."

They filed out of the alley. A hundred yards ahead, a dark mass of men was visible in the light of torches and impromptu campfires, pressing forward into the massive gatehouse that led through Londray's outer curtain wall. Some campfires had been kicked over and the embers spread about, but Allystaire, for once, appreciated Lionel Delondeur's rigidly enforced edict about the distance between his city's outer walls and the houses within them, for no nearby building had gone up.

Green-cloaked men were in a frenzy to get over the wall. Many had simply gone through the gate by main force, but when that had proved too much of a bottleneck—or perhaps had too much resistance, for the sounds of struggle were audible—some had begun lowering ladders from the inside, and others swarmed up to the top.

From what Allystaire could see, the fighting was mostly fist-to-fist. With Idgen Marte a presence in his mind just a few steps in front of him, he drew his borrowed cloak more tightly around himself, extended his hand and clamped it around the woman's, and plunged into the crowd.

* * *

Tibult made decent speed from one camp to another, but even had he two good legs, he'd never have moved at the speed of rumor. Soldiers were the worst gossips he knew.

By the time he'd left the first camp, men had been pushing towards the wall in a standard-issue angry mob, waving fists and torches but no steel that he could see. But when he'd found the newly forming mob at the main gate—the stronger, better defended gate—he saw frantic green-cloaked soldiers prying cobbles from the road, knives drawn from belts, making cudgels out of tent poles. He felt a cold pit in his stomach. There'd be blood this night, and it'd be upon his hands.

Wouldn't be the first time, he thought, followed quickly with, *It would be the first time they were my own brothers of battle.*

It surprised Tibult to know that a thought, any thought, could still sicken him. "Freeze it all." He hobbled over to a torn-down tent, picked up a broken length of tent pole by the flat end, and, using it as a cane, started pressing backwards through the crowd. *Let that woman keep her friends and her gifts and promises,* he thought. *It can't have been worth it.*

* * *

Not long after they plunged into the crowd Allystaire had its measure. The men surging for the city gates weren't facing much resistance, it seemed, but such a mixture of anger and fright was upon them that they believed they were. City guard uniforms, with their distinctive green caps, made men targets.

He saw men wounded, bleeding, falling. He didn't see any dying but he was certain there were deaths. Such was the pace that Idgen Marte set for them, clearing the way with her Goddess-given speed and the flat of her blade. It was a mad press of bodies, and his muscles screamed, aching with the aftermath of the Goddess's Gift.

Even so, he pulled the woman and the boy in front of him, and Torvul instinctively moved in front of them. The dwarf was not shy about employing his cudgel, and many a rioter who ventured too close for his liking was soundly thumped on the back of the knee, or sent sprawling with a casual twist between his ankles. Where one man went down, others were sure to follow. Slowly, Allystaire realized,

Torvul was making his own contribution to the clearing of their path. Of a mind to help, Allystaire clenched a fist, but all the strength had fled his arms, and his hand shook.

Faith, he told himself, as he realized that he was simply in their hands.

* * *

Where is that damn cripple? Idgen Marte winced the instant she had this thought. *Tibult. His name was Tibult.* She moved through the crowd with an ease afforded the Shadow of the Goddess. Men might bump into her, and many were diverted from her path with the flat of her blade, but none saw her clearly enough to make trouble, and when they did see Torvul's cudgel or Allystaire's clenched fists behind her, they made way.

He probably couldn't punch wet paper just now, she thought, glancing at Allystaire and reading in a moment, from the set of his jaw and the slight hitch in his gait, how quickly he was reaching the point of exhaustion. Still, he pressed on, his green Delondeur cloak and stolen tabard conspiring with the darkness to more or less hiding the fact that he was mostly nude and smeared with a startling quantity of blood.

Suddenly she caught a glimpse of a man pushing raggedly against the tide of men that surged towards the gate. A man pushing himself along using a broken stick for a cane.

She started through the crowd towards him, flinging a quick thought back to Allystaire and Torvul as she went. *There he is! Try to wait!*

She ignored Torvul and Allystaire's complaints as she began slipping through the crowd. She was soon at Tibult's side, startling him for the second time by seeming to appear out of thin air.

"No time to explain. My friend who can help you is in the crowd. Come!" She could feel Allystaire and Torvul moving away from her, being pushed by the half-mad crowd. She grabbed Tibult's free hand and began the arduous task of fighting through the mob.

* * *

Allystaire was buffeted, almost taken off his feet, as soon as Idgen Marte stopped clearing the way for them. The Goddess's strength had fled, and it was slowly being replaced with a fatigue he couldn't stop. *We need out of this city, Torvul, and fast.*

Idgen Marte has got a project, the dwarf thought, stepping forward only when forced by the press of men, and occasionally whipping about with his cudgel.

They had to move, though, and Allystaire knew that even in top shape he wouldn't have been able to stop it. The crowd was too many, too mad. Bodies pressed on all sides. Pace by pace, they were being shoved ahead, away from Idgen Marte, who was making her way—much more slowly—towards them.

The gap between them widened. Drowsy-eyed, wine-addled, and crazed green-clad men kept appearing out of nowhere, swelling the crowd around and behind them. The gates must have been opened—there was suddenly loud cheering ahead, a roar that spread through the mob, and the pace of the crowd increased. They were swept along, forced to keep up for fear of being trampled.

Allystaire! Her mental voice sounded strained, though not quite frantic. *I can get out fine, but the man who helped us. He needs you!*

Torvul groaned and began pushing through the crowd, wielding his cudgel like an oar. Allystaire, still trying to shield the boy and the sorcerer's captive with his arms, while trying at the same time not to lean on them too much, looked for Idgen Marte. He saw her pulling a tall, broad, limping man along behind her, the two of them shoved side to side by the knots of men running for the gate.

Why? Allystaire had barely thought this before Idgen Marte's answer shocked him into action.

He's a veteran. Lamed. Was going to throw himself into the Bay!

"Take them to the gate, Torvul," Allystaire bellowed. "We will come behind!"

Gathering whatever strength he had left, Allystaire plunged into the crowd, swinging his elbows aggressively, knocking men aside.

Had he his normal strength, much less the Goddess's Gift, he'd have knocked them off their feet. As it was, they barely made way for him.

Idgen Marte drew closer, guiding the man towards Allystaire. Allystaire offered his left arm, stretching it as far as he could. He heard Idgen Marte yelling at the man to grab Allystaire's hand. The veteran didn't hear or didn't comprehend. Allystaire stretched, throwing himself across an escaping soldier. His fingers brushed across the veteran's neck. He reached for the Goddess's Healing.

Allystaire had only the briefest moment to assess the man, his wounds, his life, what he could draw on to heal him. There were memories of battle, of stabbing downwards from a horse, of feeling a mount founder on the stones and the terror of it going out from under him. A plunge into water so cold it felt like the shock alone would kill him.

Then there was pain, a huge red cloud that overwhelmed everything, then slowly receded—but not entirely. It was constant. Not overwhelming, but never less than a strong distraction, something that could be dulled, but never mastered.

Allystaire knew pain, but not like that, pain that could never, ever be ignored. He knew the shock and terror of losing a mount. He drew on the shared experience, poured the Goddess's empathy into Tibult, felt it seize and begin to reshape the man's mangled leg and hip. The healing was always a shock to the recipient, and he felt the other man stiffen and cry out as the Gift of the Goddess began to wipe the injury of years away.

And then a surge of the crowd, a gaggle of latecomers running for the gate, green cloaks billowing behind them, smacked into Allystaire. He felt his feet momentarily leave the ground, and he was left with little choice; he could go along with them, try to make the gate, or he could be trampled.

He tried to fix on the man's face in the moments he was pulled away, the fires that burned nearby brightening the night enough to make out some details—the shock in the big, broad face, the hope that might've been flashing in his sunken eyes.

And then Allystaire was gone.

* * *

Idgen Marte saw Allystaire get torn away from her and Tibult, and knew there was only one decision she could make. She thought to drag Tibult with her, but she needed speed now, and they all needed out of the city.

Some of the Goddess's words to her on the day she'd been Called echoed in her head. *Without you, my Shadow, he will fail. Without you at his side, he will fall. There are dangers he will never see,* the Goddess had said of Allystaire. *It is my hope that those dangers will never see you.*

She turned to Tibult, shouted. "Thornhurst! Find us there whenever you can, bring as many of your fellows with you as you wish!" She reached into her purse and pulled free a string of silver links, pressed it into his hand. "Thornhurst!" she shouted once more, then vanished. As always when Idgen Marte employed the Goddess's Gift, the world slowed around her. Light and dark came together in her vision, picking out the pockets of shadow as far as she could see; all color and most other shapes melted away unless she concentrated. While acting as the Shadow, all she could easily see were the shapes of the shadows themselves. There were many, with the firelight, the stars, the shouting, running masses of men, the looming walls. Her sense of precisely where Allystaire stood was unerring, like a beacon to the rest of her. With a single step, a single impulse, she was beside him, wrapping her arm beneath his shoulder.

Then the world moved again. Men shouted and pressed around her. Allystaire was a heavy weight at her side. Her blade was in her hand in a flash—a little bit of her speed, a little of the Goddess's. Her Gifts were amazing and powerful, Idgen Marte knew, but she took some pride in just how much of the speed of her draw was her own, and not the product of divine gift.

Bared steel gave men something to avoid, and the progress had carried them within sight of the inner gate, leading through the barbican. The greenhats and soldiers who'd had the guard of this gate had long since given up trying to hold back the tide of men, as all the gates and ports stood wide open, men streaming out of them.

She knew Allystaire seethed at her side. She also knew he hadn't the strength to argue. She half dragged him into what was now less a mob and more a rough but genial queue and flowed with it towards the plains and the night beyond.

* * *

Londray emptied itself of most fighting men as night rolled into day. They streamed out onto the plains carrying whatever they could, weapons, food, tools, wine, pay, plunder.

Most importantly, they carried tales of how close they'd all come to a forced winter campaign. Tales of how the Baron Delondeur had proven willing to sacrifice their harvest, the work needed to make their boats ready for winter, for his own glory.

What good did a larger barony do anyone if there was less food for more mouths?

So when rumors trickled out over the coming days that the Baron himself had been imprisoned in his tower, and that his own bastard son had taken charge of the capital for the winter, there was no immediate influx of loyal soldiers and knights ready to return Lionel Delondeur to his seat.

* * *

Torvul had been waiting for them outside the gate, his lantern bright in his hands, the woman and the sorcerer's boy standing safely beside him. Outside the walls, the crowd could and did disperse in all directions.

"I took my wagon, your mounts and our baggage out to a hostelry and inn a couple of miles up the road while the two of you were playin' at usurpation and civil unrest," he offered wryly, as they approached out of the crowd.

"What makes you sure that the place won't be burned down or looted?" Idgen Marte asked. Allystaire disentangled himself from her arm and stood apart. His knees wobbled once, but he slowly pulled himself upright.

"Faith," Torvul said, "in my ability to read people. Not to mention how I'd hate t'be the looter who tried to pry open my wagon or steal his horse," he added, gesturing towards Allystaire with the lantern. "Lose a hand either way. Mayhap a deal more."

He walked closer to Allystaire then, extending the lantern. "Going to make it a couple of miles, boy?"

Allystaire took a deep breath. Deep, aching pain was settling into his muscles. Such was the price of the Gift of Strength, he knew.

"I want nothing more than to lie down and sleep," Allystaire admitted, wearily. "Yet the work is not about what we want, is it? I will carry on. I have no choice." Another deep breath, trying to draw strength from the very air back into his muscles. "Lead on."

CHAPTER 7

Tasks

They were, Allystaire believed, the longest two miles he'd ever walked. They felt every step of twenty, with painful fatigue dragging him towards the ground at every step. Halfway there, Torvul offered up a flask of something. Uncharacteristically, he took it without asking, had a swig, and felt a brief flush of energy flow into his limbs.

That rush faded quickly, though. So quickly that Torvul grumbled incomprehensibly in his native language and had a sniff at the flask himself.

Allystaire ignored the dwarf's gimlet eye. He had no attention for anything but the setting forward of one foot after another, the brute forcing of it. The pain was shoved aside along with every other thing that might otherwise have preyed upon his mind: the crippled veteran he hadn't finished healing, the riots, where they were going, how to get there, how to guard the woman, the boy. What the boy meant, who he was. Allystaire had suspicions.

Or he'd had them, before life had become one step. Then another step. And another.

Idgen Marte, who'd ranged ahead as they walked, reported knots of green-cloaked men here and there, fleeing the city in all directions, some halting as the energy of the mob began to desert them.

She began to ask him a question, something about cutting branches for a litter. He waved her off with a curt gesture, and grunted out a single word. "Ardent."

"Your horse?"

"Get me to him. Sleep in the saddle."

She nodded and disappeared again, only to return in moments and confer with Torvul, their words reaching his ears only distantly.

"Men with bows guarding a cluster of buildings ahead."

"That'll be our innkeep. And his sons, I expect," Torvul said.

"How d'ya know?"

"What did I say about faith in my ability to read people? And, ah, to read the insignia on the matching tabards they'd all hung on the wall. Baron's Own Bows, or so it said. Seems to be the first stage of the family business. Followed by the inn, of course."

Sure enough, they crested a rise and in the earliest of pre-dawn light, they could all make out a pair of figures holding bows, arrows nocked, patrolling casually along the edge of a fenced enclosure. Within the fence sat a number of buildings, one three-story central frame that was the largest on the plot save the stables, with a scattering of sheds and outbuildings. Torches burned at regular intervals, giving the walking archers light to shoot by.

"Ware the 'stead," Torvul called out in his booming voice. "I left links on deposit with the master of the house."

One of the bowmen seized a torch and came forward, swinging open a gate. "Come along. We can see if food is to be found," he called as he approached. "Thanks for the advance warning of trouble in the night. We've got beds."

"We're unable to stay, goodman," Torvul said. "Unfortunately. Of course, the silver I left with your father is yours to keep."

The dwarf's voice droned on, with Allystaire losing the thread of what he said. Then Idgen Marte was at his side, propping him up. Without her arm around his back he surely would have fallen to the ground.

"Ardent," he mumbled, then fell to a knee.

He heard footsteps rushing, Torvul growling out requests. His mind swam right to the edge of unconsciousness. For how long, he didn't know.

Then Idgen Marte was gripping him under the arm and helping him to his feet and he heard the stamp of a horse's hooves and someone cursing. The hooves pounded closer, pulled up, and he felt Ardent's huge muscled shoulder suddenly there, beneath one outstretched hand. Where he found the strength to haul himself up, he didn't know, but he was sitting in the saddle, finally able to let go. till he remembered the Delondeur signet ring, heavy gold and emeralds, they'd carried with them out of the city.

"Torvul," he said. "The ring. Give it to them. They will know what to do."

Then Allystaire slumped forward across the neck of his enormous grey destrier and finally, blessedly, slept.

* * *

He snapped awake in the saddle, aching more than usual. The sun was well overhead and they moved at a slow pace along a well-kept baronial road. Heading east, he judged.

"How long," he asked, his voice emerging as a croak from a painfully dry throat.

"Only a few turns," Idgen Marte said. She sat her brown courser next to Ardent, the two horses moving calmly along the road. Without a word she held out a bulging skin, which Allystaire took and drank deeply from.

The water took the edge off his throat. "The boy? The woman?"

"Sleeping in the dwarf's wagon," she said. The wagon rumbled along ahead of them, powered by Torvul's placid and tireless team. "Her name is Bethe, by the way."

"And the wounded man back in Londray? What of him?"

"Tibult," she said. "His name is Tibult. And I had to leave him."

"How much had the Healing done?"

"I couldn't tell," she admitted.

"What will become of him, if he is found to have spread the rumors?"

"Folk like him are invisible. Everyone has made a practice of not noticing them. Believe me."

"That is not the point," Allystaire said, his voice on edge. "We do not use people for our own ends and then leave them behind."

"I had no choice," Idgen Marte said. She gave her horse a nudge with one heel and it trotted a few feet ahead.

"You cannot put others at risk for our purposes."

"I will do what I must," Idgen Marte calmly replied, without turning her horse.

"Men died because of your plan. Men who were not our enemies, who would otherwise be heading to their homes for the winter," Allystaire yelled. "They, their families, that is who we are called to defend!"

"I know very well who I am called to defend," Idgen Marte said, reining in her horse and turning in the saddle. She raised a hand and pointed a finger at Allystaire. "You."

"I can defend myself!"

"No!" Idgen Marte spat. "You can't. You pick a direction, usually one bristling with people that want you dead, and you go straight at it, blind to everything beside you. It almost got you killed this time. What happens, then, when it does kill you? What happens to the Goddess, Her Temple, Mol?"

Allystaire couldn't find words, but he glared daggers at her as she spoke, one hand opening and closing around his reins. "It would go on," he said, finally.

"No, it wouldn't," Idgen Marte insisted. "You're the one they'll make songs about, Allystaire," she added, more quietly, turning her horse and trotting it back to his side. "You're the Arm. The Knight. The Paladin. You'll walk in Her sunlight and then be illuminated forever in memory. I am the Shadow. If that means I have to live in yours, well, I made my peace with that the day She Ordained me. It is my task—one of my tasks—to see that you live to do the things you must. If that means I must do things you can't, or won't, then I must."

"It is our task to help men like Tibult, and his kin."

"And I did, as best I could," she said. "Don't presume to tell me what my tasks are," she added. "Because I'm going to do them, whether you approve of them or understand them. One of them is to keep you alive, no matter how stupidly and stubbornly you try to get yourself killed. Nothing you say is going to deter me from that, any more than what I might say would stop you." She nudged her horse again and pulled up alongside Torvul's wagon.

This time, Allystaire let her go without comment.

* * *

After another turn or two of riding in relative silence, Allystaire trotted Ardent alongside Torvul's wagon. As if he could anticipate the question, the dwarf spoke before Allystaire had even formed the words.

"Yes, I gave it back, but I can't understand why. In a day I could've made a copy that would pass for the genuine article, according to the uneducated fools you folk called gemmarers."

"We have not the day to spend. And what is wrong with our gemmarers?"

"Do you know what one of them told me a few years ago when I asked him where his diamonds came from? From the belly of a great snake, he said. He said they lived in a valley far to the west, past Keersvast, on a land at the other side of the sea. He said the floor of this valley was the source of all diamonds in the world. That the snake-tenders, this was the word he used, snake-tenders, would lure the beasts to the edge with food, and then pluck the stones from their bellies while they slept." The dwarf spat. "Primeval ignorance."

Torvul turned to look back at the distant speck of the city walls as if he could take in its many lights, its shadows, the stink of the sea that lofted over it. He took a last deep breath, closed his eyes, murmured a few deep and rumbling words.

The boy had quietly climbed out onto the buckboard next to the dwarf. He'd remained silent for the entire flight from the keep, through the riot and beyond the walls. Now he swung his head towards Torvul. "What tongue was that?"

"Eh? Dwarfish."

The boy cleared his throat. "What did you say?"

The dwarf shrugged. "Not sure how long it'll be till I smell that much weight in one place again. I was…acknowledging it."

"Weight?" The boy's head tilted to one side, quizzically.

"Gold. Silver. Even copper or bronze. Steel. Metals. The valuable and useful kind."

"Ah."

Idgen Marte walked ahead, leading her brown courser while the village woman rode upon it. Allystaire sat slumped and quiet in Ardent's saddle.

The day had dawned cold and seemed to be growing colder. Everyone occasionally, furtively glanced over their shoulders. There was no pursuit, and after they had moved east along the road for more than half the day, towards the looming shadows of the mountains that cut Barony Delondeur in half, the tension eased. Finally, with night coming on, Allystaire looked back once more and hoarsely said, "Looks as though Chaddin was as good as his word. I suspect we are safe."

"Well," Torvul said, "as safe as we can be in a barony where everyone with any power likely wants us dead."

"There is more than one kind of power," Allystaire replied.

"Aye, and they've got all of them. Magic, gold, religion, swords. That about covers it, I'd say."

Allystaire merely grunted in reply. Torvul tried a different tack. "Speaking of magic and power—now you know I'm not one to get between a man and his holy rage, least of all when that man is you, Ally, but…" The dwarf let the 'but' hang in the air for a moment. "When you were healing that sorcerer, couldn't you have left him alive? Tamed, he might have been turned to our benefit. Learn from him. Maybe he could've been a hostage—"

"He needed killing."

"Just think ahead next time. It's all I ask."

Allystaire stayed his horse and turned to face the dwarf. "I will think ahead on how to kill any of them that come within my sight. I will think on how to mitigate the kind of horror they can wreak. If you want one alive, you capture him, then hold him till I can kill him."

"And that'd be the holy rage," the dwarf murmured. "He would've been more useful alive…"

Allystaire was about to respond, and Idgen Marte groaned in exasperation, but the boy spoke again. "What is it you wish to know, Master Alchemist? I have been Bhimanzir's ward and apprentice for most of my life."

"Master Alchemist, eh? I like this one." Torvul turned from Allystaire to the boy next to him. "What's your name, boy?"

"I haven't been given one."

"Haven't been given one, eh? Take one that you like."

"It is not done. I must be given one."

"Well, I'll give you one. Let's see now—"

The boy cut him off with a curt shake of his head. "No." He lifted a hand and pointed to Allystaire, a huge shape in the darkness; his and Ardent's forms blended into a massive shadow. "Him."

Idgen Marte halted her courser and spoke up. "Before we settle the big questions—strategy against sorcerers, the boy's name, what we're even going to do with him—can we at least decide where the Cold we're going?"

"Thornhurst," Torvul answered, even as Allystaire grunted, "Bend."

Idgen Marte sighed in frustration. "Which is it?"

"Bend," Allystaire insisted. "I think the Choiron was headed there."

Torvul drew his wagon team to a halt and shook his head. "Mayhap he is, but I can't see it's our problem now. And we've got to get the boy and the good woman to safety."

"I will not leave the people of Bend to the mercy of Symod," Allystaire replied. "If that fool Windspar broke his Oath and the Choiron himself went to enforce Braech's vengeance—"

"He'll wipe Bend from memory," Idgen Marte said flatly, "and I can't say I'd miss it."

"Never been to Bend," Torvul replied. "Not eager to go."

"It was the most miserable patch of the world I have ever seen," Allystaire replied, "and that is precisely why we must defend it."

"We have to defend them, too," Idgen Marte said, gesturing to the woman asleep on her courser's back, and the boy seated next to Torvul.

"We managed with Mol the first time around," Allystaire replied.

"She managed us, more like."

Are we forgetting that we cannot return to Thornhurst without the Will? Allystaire tried to direct his thoughts at Idgen Marte.

Are you so sure that we would be?

"Do you mean me? What is The Will?" The boy, once again, had been hearing their thoughts, and responded aloud. "I am sorry if I am rude again, but it did sound as if you meant…"

They paused for a moment, stared through the darkening air at each other, and the boy. In the distance an owl's cry signaled nightfall.

Allystaire cleared his throat. "Any idea why you can hear our thoughts, lad?"

"I assumed it was some magic the three of you call upon, and my nature and training made it available to me."

"Speaking of training, there's a lot of questions I want to put you, when we've the time," Torvul put in. Then, with pursed lips and a delicate sigh, the dwarf went on. "Look, boy. It's not magic, not in the way you mean. It's, ah…"

"It's a Goddess," Idgen Marte said.

"I have been taught that even if deities exist, they are not as powerful as we believe, nor does their existence matter very much," the boy began, seeming likely to go on, before Torvul cut him off with a wave of his hand.

"You've been taught quite a lot of shit, I don't doubt. Among it, I suppose, would be the notion that a big dumb man with a hammer poses no threat to a sorcerer. Well, he's still here and your master's dead. So it might be best to think on just how much of what your master taught you was wrong."

The boy furrowed his brow and bit his bottom lip, his back stiffening a bit.

"It is a lot to take in, I know," Allystaire said, nudging his horse closer. "We have much to discuss. I cannot make you believe in something, but if you trust me, and Idgen Marte, and Torvul, well, all three of us have seen Her, spoken to Her, been touched by Her. She is real as the sun we've ridden under today—and that is setting on us as we speak. So rather than sit in the middle of the road and speak of dogma and heterodoxy and heresies and whatever the Cold else people do when they argue about religion, let us look for a likely spot to camp and sleep a few turns. Aye?"

"Every once in a great while you manage to say something sensible," Idgen Marte replied. She turned her horse and rode off down the track, pointing to a gentle, lightly wooded rise. "There." She continued a dozen more paces or so down the road before cutting into the grass. "We can all use the extra rest and be up all the earlier on the morrow."

CHAPTER 8

Names

Allystaire collapsed almost the instant he'd finished unsaddling and brushing Ardent and laid some blankets down on the cold, stiff grass. Torvul busied himself inside his wagon, but soon came out, holding a small stack of stone disks in thickly gloved hands. He moved carefully to the bottom of Allystaire's pile of blankets and slipped one of the disks underneath it. Torvul straightened up and repeated the process by each pile of blankets.

Idgen Marte cocked her head to the side as she watched him; finally he looked up and said, "Alchemy. Lots of complicated magical hoodoo your primitive culture hasn't prepared you to understand."

The boy picked his head up from beneath his blankets and peered at Torvul. "It isn't complicated at all. Those are made of dwarfish memory stone, which will assume characteristics of the atmosphere it is placed in. The secrets of making them were lost with the end of the Stonesingers, but…"

Idgen Marte began to laugh as Torvul coughed loudly. "Well, it isn't nearly as simple as you're making it sound. Get some rest as you can."

The boy shrugged and laid back down, and Idgen Marte followed Torvul to his wagon, leaning against it as the dwarf climbed towards the door, before he turned and sat on the step. She let her neck loll back against the wood, sighed heavily.

"We got out. Take a breath."

"It isn't that." She lifted her head. "He was already free when we got in. And had found the boy, who looks likely t'be one of us—"

"I'm not entirely convinced," Torvul replied, then, pitching his voice low. "And I'm not even sure we can trust him. Or that we should take him to the Temple with us. A little sorcery is still dangerous."

"He can hear the thoughts we share—"

Torvul shook his head, eyes drifting closed a moment before snapping back open. "Not enough to be sure."

"What would be?"

Torvul thought a moment. "Her Ladyship could clarify the matter right quick, I'm thinkin'."

"Faith, Torvul. She's given us a lot to support it, but there've been times—and I'm guessing there'll be more—when we'll need to find it in ourselves. Each other. We can't always be waiting for Her to arrive. That isn't why She's chosen us."

"There's truth in that," Torvul replied. "And mayhap I'm too old to trust easy."

Idgen Marte snorted and pointed towards the snoring heap that was Allystaire. "He's got that bit covered. Believe me." She shook her head. "I think he's got just about all of it covered."

"Well," Torvul said, "if he hadn't trusted me, I might have hung."

"If he hadn't trusted me, he'd be dead. More than once. And now he argues with me over it."

"You said it yourself. No hero of the stories or the songs is without his boon companions and shield bearers and such, eh?" The dwarf yawned and stood. "Give me a turn, then I'll be up and you can sleep." He pulled open the door of his wagon, and Idgen Marte shook her head.

"Take as long as you need," she said, looking back over the camp, the three sleeping forms in it, the one notably larger, and louder, than the other two. "I'll watch."

* * *

Allystaire's dreams were touched, albeit briefly, by trails of red in darkness, by the memories of a dozen kinds of pain. Each time it seemed likely to descend into nightmare, the dream dissipated into warmth and light, a bright golden disk that dispelled the darkness and the red within it.

When he sat up, it was brighter, though the day would be overcast. He was as sore as he had ever been. His shoulders and torso screamed with the effort of simply levering himself off the ground.

"Morning," Idgen Marte said. He turned his head and saw her leaning against a wagon wheel.

"Is it? How long have I slept?" It hurt to simply open his jaw, and his words were quiet and slurred. *Cold, I even think my tongue hurts.*

"Only a little over four turns."

He nodded, which he quickly found a mistake. The muscles of his neck wrenched and tightened in protest.

"Cold, but you wake up uglier and more painfully than most men die."

He laughed, but that caused him to wince and press a hand to the new wound on his stomach. It was healed, but the skin was raw and the muscles not entirely mended. "Listen a moment," he slurred. "I need to apologize. I should never have gone by myself. It was vain. Arrogant."

"Also foolish," Idgen Marte replied. "Stubborn. Naive. Short-sighted…" She lifted a fist and began counting points with her fingers.

Allystaire rolled his eyes, and was slightly astonished to find that it didn't hurt. Much. "Still," he said, slowly, "I knew what would happen. If it went bad, and it did, I knew you would come."

"You were already free when I found you."

"Not the point. The point is you found me. I owe you my life more times than I can count—"

"Well, it's not quite more times than you've got fingers."

"Enough with that. I cannot laugh for fear of bursting a rib." He took a slow breath. "I should not rely upon you so casually."

"Allystaire," she said, pushing herself to her feet and then wiping her hands against her trousers, "shut up. You're meant to rely on me. She told me as much." She walked to him, extended her hand, and helped him to his feet.

"Always behind me?"

"Always," she replied, with a slight nod. "Even when you're an idiot. Cold, especially then."

They stood, awkwardly, for a few moments, not much space between them, after Idgen Marte pulled her hands from his, till the creaky opening of Torvul's wagon provoked them into turning quickly apart.

The dwarf emerged from the boxy interior of his wagon, already dressed in his traveling gear, a fresh array of full pouches clipped onto the many rings of his hooded jerkin. His eyes darted to Idgen Marte and Allystaire, then rolled skyward. With a shake of his head, he muttered loud enough for them to hear. "Will you two just get it over with?"

"You haven't ever learned when to shut your mouth, have you dwarf?" Idgen Marte scowled while Torvul grinned.

"No," he said, "and I never expect I…"

He was soon left speechless as Idgen Marte seized Allystaire's head with one hand on either cheek and pulled close to him, kissing him hard on the mouth. Allystaire's eyes widened and he let out a wheezing moan of pain. Then she stepped away, Allystaire winced, and Torvul's jaw hung slightly open.

"Like kissing my brother," Idgen Marte said, before wiping her mouth with her sleeve. "Now put that thought out of your head."

Torvul slowly turned towards Allystaire, who placed a hand to his neck and rolled his head around on his shoulders. "Like kissing my sister," he agreed, "only it hurt more. Now. Where have my gambeson and armor gotten to?" He plucked at the bloodstained and torn tabard he still wore.

The dwarf grumbled in his own language, ducked back into his wagon, and returned with armfuls of steel. Allystaire walked to the side of the wagon and accepted them piece by piece, carefully untangling straps and buckles.

"Might not be best to wear it today. You might need some time to recover," the dwarf said, as he handed over the last pieces.

"I have slept, twice now. I will eat. And I would feel better wearing it than not." He gathered up the pieces and wandered several paces away from their little camp. He pulled the tabard off his back—first having to rip it free from where blood had dried it to the skin of his stomach—and knelt.

Idgen Marte had woken the boy and Bethe, and both sat up, now watching Allystaire walk off. When he removed his tabard and revealed the scarred geography of his back, Bethe turned away, but the boy simply tilted his head to the side, curious.

"He has been hurt a great deal," the boy said. "Injured. Stabbed, burned, arrow-shot, and such."

"Aye, as has anyone his age who has been at his trade for so long," Idgen Marte replied.

"He said as much when my master was trying to divine the nature of his power."

"The dead sorcerer isn't your master anymore," she said. "But what do you mean?"

"Well, he did not say so, exactly. Every time my—Bhimanzir—used his sorcery to reach into him, which invariably causes great pain, he would just talk about the pain. About how he'd felt it before." The boy paused, then walked towards Idgen Marte to accept a hard biscuit she'd taken from a sack and held out to him. "It was very odd."

"He's very odd," she said, handing a biscuit to Bethe. "But that sounds like him." She tossed a biscuit towards Torvul. Scowling, he made no effort to catch it and didn't watch as it hit the ground.

"Does pain bother him so very little?"

"Of course it bothers me," Allystaire said while pulling his gambeson over his head. "As it bothers any man. I have just grown used to it."

Idgen Marte whispered to the boy, "It bothers him less than any man I've known. It's uncanny and bizarre and if I were you, I'd learn better than him how not to get hurt."

"I see," the boy replied. He lifted the biscuit to his nose, sniffed, and said, "I think the first step to not getting hurt is not trying to eat this."

"Got to eat something, and these are mostly what we've got," Idgen Marte replied.

The boy sniffed at it again, set his teeth to its edge, then wrinkled his mouth in distaste and held it at arm's length.

"C'mere," Torvul said, poking his head out of his wagon door. "I can fix you up better than that." The scent of bacon wafted out of the open door.

"How can you have a fire in there?" Idgen Marte said, even as the boy and Bethe began drifting over. "It's not safe."

"Nonsense," Torvul said, pointing to the chimney in the rear of the wagon. "Every dwarfish wagon has its stove. Stones, I can make a fire in here that'd melt your sword."

"Show me," Idgen Marte said, moving towards the wagon.

"Tch," Torvul replied, shaking his head and letting the door shut behind him. "Nobody in here save me. 'Sides, you're all too tall. Except maybe the boy." The dwarf tilted his head and addressed the boy now. "How about Ur-brinchithaschurtingmal. One of my uncles was named that."

The boy frowned, crossing his arms over his chest defiantly.

Allystaire hauled on another piece of his armor. "If we are going to use family names, well…" He sized the boy up, chewing on his bottom lip. "Gideon. It was my grandfather's name."

"I like that better," the boy said. "Who was your grandfather?"

"First of our line to be lord of Coldbourne Moor. Dead before I was born, but, by all accounts, as stiff and frightening a son of a bitch as ever walked this world. It is quite likely he began his life as a peat digger on the land he came to rule. Earned his title with his sword, during the early part of the Succession Strife. Back when all this nonsense began."

"Do you mean that the people here have been fighting this petty war since your grandfather's days?"

"I would not call it petty," Allystaire said with a faint frown, cinching a vambrace tight around his left arm with his right hand. "Not to people whose lives it has ruined. Not to its dead or its living victims."

"My master always called it petty," the boy went on. "He said that Keersvast alone could conquer the baronies if it wished, to say nothing of the Concordat."

"Keersvast could buy the men for a season," Allystaire said. "Yet it could never hold on very long. Besides, an invasion that threatened all of the baronies, or at least a handful of the most important, that would put new grudges in the back of the mind, and bring old alliances to the fore. As to the Concordat—" Allystaire began to shrug, but his words were suddenly cut off.

"They could conquer the baronies," Idgen Marte put in quietly. "And hold it. Or burn it all, if they chose. Trust me."

"Enough of all this *hatschinlzaft*," Torvul suddenly put in, frowning. When everyone stared at him he went on with a shrug. "Dwarfish term. Means, ah…" He struggled for a moment, waving a hand in the air, "Means 'fourth flagon of the evening talk.' Things you only talk about when you're drunk or getting drunk. It's certainly not proper before breakfast talk, which should be limited to 'what is for breakfast,' and 'when is breakfast.' "

"You have just made that up," Allystaire said.

"Old Dwarfish is an ancient, nuanced language that is not easily rendered in your barbarous northern twaddle," the dwarf said with a sniff. "And if you live in hope of bacon you'll not insult it again."

Allystaire rolled his eyes, but he kept his mouth closed. At least till the boy offered him the biscuit he'd rejected. With a shrug that clanked pauldrons against cuirass, Allystaire reached out and took it, bit off a hunk with his back teeth, and crunched contentedly.

"Gideon," the boy said. "And your grandfather was a laborer who became a lord?"

"Well," Allystaire said, around a mouthful of dry biscuit, "a laborer who became a soldier, then a bannerman, officer, knight, and finally lord, as the family lore would tell. There was a portrait of him among the family gemmary. If you can tell anything about a man by his profile in carnelian, he was hard. The worst my father would say was that he was forceful. Nothing more."

The boy listened, then nodded faintly. "I think I will try Gideon. If you find a name that suits me better, please tell me."

"Pick a name that pleases you, lad," Idgen Marte said, as she dribbled grease from a rasher onto a broken biscuit, perhaps in the hopes that it would soften the hard, twice baked bread. "Not one of their dusty old grandfathers or great uncles or bastard sons," she added, gesturing towards Torvul and Allystaire, before fitting bacon and biscuit into her mouth.

The dwarf was oddly unresponsive, simply chewing and not saying a word. Allystaire quickly swallowed.

"I have no children. So far as I know," he said.

"So far as you know, eh? Not the answer a paladin ought to be giving," Idgen Marte said.

"I have been a paladin for but a few months. I was a soldier on campaign for the best part of twenty-one years," he shrugged.

"There's a story there," Idgen Marte said, suddenly inclining her head forward, eyes narrowing.

Allystaire's eyes flitted briefly, but meaningfully, towards the boy. "Another time, perhaps."

"I spent the last few months watching my former master tear the entrails and the wombs out of screaming women to help him tell the future," the boy said, suddenly, aware that he was being talked around. "I am not delicate. You do not need to avoid saying things around me for fear it will offend me."

The boy's voice took on a shade of heat for the first time in their hearing. Allystaire straightened up, startled, eyes widening. "I apologize, Gideon. I expect you have grown up as fast as any of us. Faster, mayhap."

"I have," the boy insisted, and Idgen Marte and Torvul offered muted apologies. Breakfast passed in silence from then on, though at one point Idgen Marte eyed Allystaire and looked about ready to question him again. He silenced her with a quick shake of his head.

When the food was gone, the braziers, blankets, and stone disks packed away, the fire out, the animals saddled, and the wagon pronounced fit for travel after much fussing by Torvul, Allystaire climbed into Ardent's saddle and gave the horse a gentle nudge with his leg and began to trot back to the road. Behind him, the wagon slowly rumbled forward, its great thick wheels rolling over the lightly frosted grass.

When the small column reached the hard packed dirt of the road, Allystaire turned one way and the wagon turned another. The paladin wheeled his destrier around and saw Torvul's head appear from over the top of his wagon.

"Where're you headed? Road to Thornhurst is this way."

"I am not going to Thornhurst," Allystaire yelled. "I mean to make straight for Bend. Besides, Thornhurst means going straight over the Thasryach, and it could be impassable any day now."

"Straight for Bend means we go right past barony watchtowers and some of Delondeur's most loyal lords. What's in Bend that's worth that?"

"My enemy," Allystaire replied.

"You don't know that," Torvul said. "And even if you do—"

Allystaire trotted his horse a few yards closer to the wagon and shook his head. "I know. I am sure of it. That idiot of a would-be baron likely broke his Oath, and Symod went to enforce Braech's will."

"What has any of that to do with you," Torvul said, and then tried to go on before Allystaire could reply. "He brought it on himself. Let him suffer—"

"He is not the only one who will suffer," Allystaire shouted, leaning forward in the saddle. "There is a town full of folk who will pay a steep price for Symod's rage and Windspar's pride, who will suffer for a feud they have no part in."

The dwarf took a deep breath. "Allystaire, you can't save everyone. We can save two souls who're with us now. Right here."

"Whether a definable soul actually exists is quite a point of contention among," Gideon began, but quickly silenced himself when Allystaire's hard-eyed gaze flicked towards him.

"Please," Allystaire said, biting the word off, "not right now." The boy nodded and Allystaire turned back to Torvul. "Listen to me, Torvul. I know who, and where, one of my enemies is. There may be an angry baron at our backs now, or a city in flames, more sorcerers on the way and looking for vengeance, but the Goddess Herself said to us that She and Braech were destined to oppose one another, and right now, Symod is imposing Braech's vengeance, with flame and fear, in the place where the Goddess first spoke to me. Windspar may be a fool, but his town is full of people the war drove there out of necessity."

"It isn't the smart approach—"

"And there, you are wrong. I have spent the better part of my life leading men into battle, and I won a good deal more than I lost, which is not something most of the war-leaders of the baronies can say. At the moment, we have but few advantages, mainly that we can move quickly, and that our enemies do not really know where we are. If we make for Thornhurst and sit and wait for them to come to us, we are done for—especially if Symod makes common cause with Lionel or a sorcerer or both."

"You might know battles, but I know the roads," Torvul said. "And you aren't sneaking past Delondeur liegemen between here and Bend. They don't much care what goes on past that oxbow in the river, as you well know. But they treat their side of it like a border. We'll be cuttin' through the mountains one way or another, Ally, no matter how much you bluster."

Allystaire's frown deepened. "You may be right about that much. These western plains are some of the best patrolled lands in the baronies."

"Snow we can dig through, or into if we're desperate," Torvul said. "You can't kill an entire garrison if we're spotted. Besides," the dwarf added, spreading his hands imploringly, "who could possibly be a better guide across the mountains than a dwarf, eh?"

"I do not relish the idea of passing the winter holed up in a snow cave," Allystaire said.

"Only because you're the biggest and we'd have to eat you first," Torvul teased. When Allystaire's frown cracked into a chuckle, the dwarf seized his chance. "You say it enough, Ally, so I'll say it to you. Faith. I know I'm right. Both roads are dangerous, but I know that one ends with us dead or in a dungeon. I know it in my bones. And if you get me to a high enough place, I can prove it."

"Fine," Allystaire said, throwing up his hands. "I relent, Torvul, so far as this. I will take you to as high a place as necessary. If we end up crossing the mountains, we end up crossing the mountains."

Torvul nodded, satisfied with his victory.

Allystaire rode around the side of the wagon, where Bethe sat, with Gideon between her and the dwarf. "Bethe, I know that a long ride to Thornhurst is not what you might wish. We can bring you home, your old home or a new one, if you will trust in us just a while longer. I can promise you this: while any one of the three of us live, no harm will come to you. Aye?"

The woman, the vacant and distant expression melting off her face, shook her head, vaguely at first. Finally, she cleared her throat, opened her mouth, and haltingly, as if searching for the words, said, "I've no home t'go back t'. I'll go where ya will, just don't leave me behind."

"We won't," Idgen Marte said, "not till we're somewhere safe. With other folk who'll welcome you home. Now," she said, "if you two are done measuring tackle, can we get the Cold on with it?"

* * *

The rest of the day was spent in the silence of hard travel. The breath of horses and ponies steamed, and Allystaire and Idgen Marte were careful to walk their mounts at regular intervals. Night descended more quickly than anyone expected, and soon enough they were pulling the wagon behind a copse of trees. Mountains loomed over their camp, and more days of travel lay ahead of them.

Torvul began setting out the campsite, producing warming braziers, blankets, and the like from inside his wagon while Allystaire stood beneath a tree that was slowly shedding red leaves and stared into the gloaming.

"You'd think you were trying to look back to Londray itself," Idgen Marte said, as she stepped up behind him.

"Who says I am not? I want to know what happened when we left," Allystaire's eyes continued to search the distance. "How will the sorcerers react? What will Chaddin do? Did we start a war within the barony itself? What kind of support would Lionel have?"

"He'd have a lot of support, and you know it," Idgen Marte replied. "And what happened to the bluster of this morning? The confidence?"

"Nothing," Allystaire said. "We are doing the right thing and the best thing we can do. I still want to know what might be chasing us. You can never know enough about the ground you are on, or the enemies you might face on it."

"Well, we know damn little about what might be up in the Thasryach."

Allystaire turned and was about to speak when Torvul nudged open the door of his wagon with a boot, and walked out wearing thick leather smith's gloves, and bearing a heavy iron pot. He walked a few paces away from his wagon and set the pot down on an iron ring he'd set on the grass, then lifted its lid. Steam billowed out, carrying wonderful savory scents with it.

"Threw this together and put it on the grate while we rode," Torvul said. "Bacon, cabbage, leeks, and a bit of that, and some of the other. Plain, not fit for a lord's table," he said, smirking in Allystaire's direction, "but good enough for honest traveling folks, I'm sure."

"Sounds better than anything my camp cooks used to make," Allystaire replied, his vigilance and curiosity forgotten as everyone gathered around the pot. Torvul produced a handful of spoons with thick wooden handles, and they sat or knelt and ate in companionable silence for a while. Wineskins were passed around. Bethe still didn't speak. Gideon seemed wary of the food at first, but after an exploratory taste, ate as much as anyone else.

"Gideon," Allystaire said, after pausing from the furious work he'd been doing with the spoon, "did any of your training include defending yourself? Weapons, bows, that kind of thing?"

The boy shook his head, his mouth still stuffed with food. When he swallowed and after he wiped his mouth with a strip of cloth pulled from his belt, he answered. "No. Some sorcerers might carry a dagger or a staff but usually as a prop. Bhimanzir said we were above the weapons of small minded men."

"I see," Allystaire said. "Well, Bhimanzir's silly rules will not do you much good if we meet bandits on the road."

"Or worse than bandits," Idgen Marte and Torvul echoed each other, and both received a sharp look from Allystaire.

"I do not think I need to learn how to swing a hammer," Gideon said uncertainly.

"Of course not," Allystaire replied. "Yet it would do you good to know how to use a knife, or a staff, or a crossbow, in a pinch."

With just a hint of sullen reticence, Gideon fitfully dug his spoon back into the pot, which seemed hardly as diminished as it should have.

"I am not going to try and make you a man-at-arms, lad," Allystaire said. "There are just a few things a man ought to know, and how not to get himself killed in a quick fight is one of them."

Some of the tension seemed to drain out of the boy, and he relaxed as he leaned forward to take another mouthful of cabbage.

When everyone finally sat in silence and made no more movement towards either the pot or the wineskins, Torvul stood up. "Well. Plenty left for another meal, eh?" He slipped the lid back on the pot and returned to his wagon. Bethe and Gideon began preparing their blankets, and Torvul reappeared with his stone disks to warm the bedrolls.

When only Torvul, Idgen Marte, and Allystaire remained, with the chill of night descending, the dwarf produced a jar of ikthaumanavit and they each took a swig before anyone spoke.

"If we are going to go across those mountains, someone has to say it," Idgen Marte finally said. "Legends of the Thasryach do not invite travelers."

"Aye," Torvul said. "Chimera." The word hung in the air a moment, as if none of them wanted to acknowledge or dismiss it.

"Legends are not something to fear," Allystaire said. "If there is trouble up there, it will come in the shape of men. Deserters, a warband gone for reavers, bandits gone to ground for the winter. I put no stock in legends."

"You're a legend, in the flesh. We all are," Idgen Marte reminded him. "If a paladin walks the world still, what else does?"

Allystaire didn't answer. Instead he lifted his head, craning his neck towards the unseen mass of mountain to the east. "Nothing that paladins cannot kill, if they have to." I hope.

"That's the spirit," Torvul said. "I'm sure when the hobs come at us on the back of their tame bears, with their twelve foot long blood-red lances, you can just tell them, 'Now now, a paladin's here' in your best frightening voice, and they'll all just drown in their own terror."

Idgen Marte snorted in quiet laughter, but said, "You mixed up a few legends there all at once, dwarf."

"You do not believe that will happen any more than I do," Allystaire said.

"A month ago I'd've not believed it. Since then I've spoken to Her Ladyship. My perceptions are realigning to a world proving itself radically different than what I thought it was. If bear-mounted hob lancers are out there, I'm not likely to be surprised."

They were silent a moment, till Allystaire finally spoke. "A hob could not hold a twelve foot long lance."

The other two didn't speak, they just turned to stare at him in silence. When the weight of their gaze finally dawned on him, he turned to them. "Well. Hobs are small, in the stories, aye? Twelve feet would be too long. They would over balance and spear the ground before they would find a target."

"And what of the bear mounts? Have you comments on the practicality of that?" Torvul's voice only barely contained his laughter.

Allystaire crossed his arms over his chest and sniffed. "Getting the bit between the teeth would be a chore. Still, a tame bear ridden into battle..." He looked to the dwarf. "Do you think you might have a potion that could—"

"Allystaire." Idgen Marte interrupted him. "Stop it."

"I know, I know. When it reared up on its hind legs it would toss the rider. Entirely impracticable." He paused. "Unless you caught a cub and trained it for years."

Torvul and Idgen Marte finally let out their bursts of muted laughter.

"We should sleep," Allystaire said, grinning as they laughed. "Well. The two of you should. I will take the first watch."

Torvul muttered goodnight and slipped quietly into his wagon. They heard faint sounds of wood creaking as he moved about inside.

"Why do you always take the first?" Idgen Marte asked.

"Old campaigner's trick," Allystaire said. "If you can manage it, take a watch that starts the night, or one that ends it. Get uninterrupted sleep that way."

"Or uninterrupted making of bastard children you don't know about," Idgen Marte teased.

"No hammock in the trees?" Allystaire asked, as he pushed off from where he leaned on the dwarf's wagon and stretched his neck.

"Too cold for that rot. No need for such now anyway, eh? I'll know if anything happens. The Goddess's Gifts are useful that way."

CHAPTER 9

Mountains, Knives, and Ideas

The next day passed much the same as the previous, plodding along the dirt track that served as a road with the shadow of the mountains growing ever longer. The ground grew harder under them as the cold settled into it, and as it sloped gently but inexorably upwards, their pace slowed. They camped in the evening on a relatively flat space by the bend of the trail, before it turned to head into the Thasryach Pass itself, ending the day at a considerably higher and chillier point than where they started.

Regardless, once camp had been made, Allystaire produced a pair of sheathed knives from one of his saddlebags. Both had glittering gems, one blue, one green, set in the hilts. He handed one to Gideon, who held it at arm's length as though he expected it to bite him.

"First rule," Allystaire said as he stepped away, "is never look confused, even if you are."

"So the first rule is deception?"

"Not as such, though a little skulduggery in a knife fight might go a long way," Allystaire said, reaching out and adjusting the boy's fingers so that his hand was wrapped around the knife, the hilt squarely in his palm. Gideon re-settled his fingers uncertainly.

"Now, we are going to keep the sheaths on for now so that nobody gets cut, but in future, you are going to have to learn what it feels like to swing the blade. Spread your feet."

The boy looked at him blankly.

Allystaire leaned forward, placed a hand on the lad's shoulder, and nudged his feet apart with the toe of his boot. "Spread your feet. You do this because you do not want to be knocked over easily."

"You would knock me over no matter what I did," Gideon pointed out.

"No reason to make it easier for me." Once the boy's feet were spread out to his liking, Allystaire regarded Gideon with a careful eye. "Hold on to the knife tight enough that no one can take it from you." He waited a moment, as Gideon's fingers moved on the hilt, before he darted forward and lashed out, one hand grabbing the boy's wrist, the other prying the knife from his hands. The boy frowned at him, and Allystaire offered him the knife again, flipping it around and extending it towards the boy hilt first.

Gideon took the knife, and set his lips in a thin, tight line, wrapped his hand firmly around the hilt, and extended his arm uncertainly.

Allystaire crouched slightly, leading with his left foot, keeping his own knife obscured with his left arm. "If it comes down to knives, you have to be willing to accept that you will get cut." *Cold, that's true of almost any fight,* he thought.

Even as this occurred to him, Idgen Marte snorted from where she watched, lounging upon the cold-stiffened grass. "Don't listen to him, lad. Only dullards get cut."

The boy mimicked Allystaire's stance, and even started to mirror the much larger man's movements, slowly shuffling side to side.

"The important thing to remember," Allystaire said, "is that if he can cut you, you can cut him." *Unless he's got a bow. Or a crossbow. Or is wearing good plate. Or is ahorse. Or knows how to hold a shield. Stop pretending. You'll get the boy killed.*

Allystaire suddenly lunged forward, bringing the edge of his sheathed weapon across Gideon's upper arm, while seizing his knife hand around the wrist.

"Why are you not trying to cut me?" Allystaire shook his head and stepped back. "Again. Do something with the knife this time. Whatever comes naturally."

Once more, Allystaire lunged forward, only to suddenly duck as Gideon's sheathed knife flew haphazardly through the air, tumbling end over end and sailing over his head.

"What in the Cold was that?"

Torvul and Idgen Marte, meanwhile, were doing a poor job of stifling their laughter.

"You said do whatever came naturally. So I did."

With a sigh, Allystaire retrieved the knife and handed it back over. "Gideon. This is a knife you stab with. A knife you cut with. Not a knife you throw. Those are mostly useless, unless you want to spend several years doing naught but learning how. Even so, they have to be specially made. What is more, never throw the only weapon you have except at desperate need."

"I've seen you throw your hammer," Idgen Marte quipped, smirking.

Allystaire turned to her, his face tight with anger. He raised his right fist, and said, "You have also seen me beat a man to death with this. So my rule about not throwing the only weapon you have stands."

Idgen Marte studied Allystaire closely for a moment, staring hard into his face as much as the light would allow. The laughter melted from her dusky features, and she nodded. Allystaire turned back to Gideon.

"Now," Allystaire said, "Your best bet with that short of a blade is to let your man get himself stuck on it. Again."

Once again, the sheathed blade held forward in his hand, thumb pressing just at the very base, Allystaire lunged. Gideon stood his ground, knife held tentatively before him. The boy did nothing.

The big man sighed, then gently prised the knife from the boy's hands. Gideon lowered his eyes to the ground and said, "I have failed. I will accept punishment."

"Punishment?" Allystaire tilted his head, brow furrowed.

"Yes. Bhimanzir believed that punishment hardened the mind and the body against future failures."

"You might have noticed that Bhimanzir is dead."

"Yes." The boy lifted his head, eyes narrowed. "Meaning?"

"Meaning we do not do things his way. Not now, not ever. No man ever won a fight the first time he held a blade. We just have to figure out what it is we can teach you. Torvul, surely, can teach you the rudiments of the cross-bow."

"The bows you have in these lands being barely worthy of dwarfish hands, rudiments is all I could possibly teach," the alchemist put in.

"And Idgen Marte, no doubt, could teach you something. About skulking or backstabbing, perhaps."

"We call that 'fighting smart,' not that he'd understand it," she said, briefly hooking her thumb at Allystaire.

Gideon nodded seriously, almost solemnly. "If this is what you ask of me as my new masters, I will do it."

There was a jumble of voices, as Torvul, Allystaire, and Idgen Marte all rushed to protest. Allystaire waved them silent with an upraised hand, and said, "Nobody here is your master, Gideon. You have no master any longer. That is in the past."

"Yet it is only natural for men to sort themselves into masters and servants. So said the Eldest."

"Eldest?" Torvul hopped to his feet, more sprightly than usual.

"The first sorcerer," the boy said. "Also the name given to the head of any given coven of sorcerers. Some accounts among the scriveners of the Concordat conflate the first Eldest with their own Georthg the Wise, yet that seems entirely unlikely given certain known facts about Georthg's life, distant though they are from our own days."

"You and me are gonna have a lot of nice long chats, boy. Starting tomorrow." The dwarf looked to Allystaire and said, "Provided it fits with your 'knightly training,' that is."

You couldn't make this boy a knight if you had a decade and a yard full of the best men you taught to help. The thought came unbidden to Allystaire's mind, and perhaps bitterly, but not, he knew instinctively, entirely without truth.

"Knighthood is a foolish and stultifying tradition," the boy suddenly said, "and I have no wish to take part in it."

As Idgen Marte and Torvul laughed again, Allystaire forced a grimace into a flat, calm expression. "I have no wish to make you a knight, but I do want to keep you alive between here and Thornhurst, and if you should happen to pick up the odd skill that helps me do that, so much the better. To that end, you," he said, pointing a thick finger at Gideon, "will rise with me, a turn before everyone else, starting tomorrow."

The boy's back suddenly straightened and his nostrils flared. "You contradict yourself. Just now you told me you were not my master, and now you speak to me as though you are. Which is true? I owe you, but I will not be misled."

Allystaire blinked in surprised, but slowly nodded. "You are right, lad. Let me amend my statement—should you wish to learn things, the staff, the crossbow, the knife—I will be awake a turn before everyone else, and I will teach what I can to you. Not an order. A request."

Gideon nodded, mollified, if only slightly. He turned and went to seek his pile of blankets, close to the fire, next to Bethe's. Torvul busied himself retrieving the stone disks he had set in the fire, using his thick gloves to slide them under each pile of blankets. Then he trundled himself towards his wagon, with a brief backwards glance at Allystaire and Idgen Marte and some grumbling in his own language.

Allystaire stared into the gathering darkness, while Idgen Marte turned her face towards the moon, a curved silver blade in the far sky.

"Boy's right. About knighthood. Still, I expected you to cuff him."

"Two years ago, had a lad of twelve spoken to me that way in the yard at Wind's Jaw, I would have done worse than cuff him," Allystaire said, grimly.

"Twelve?"

"In Oyrwyn we start them young. Twelve would be old enough to put on his first armor and take his first real blows. He would have had a sword in his hand at five, six summers, depending on his father."

"And you had the training of them?"

Allystaire turned to face her, his lips pressed thinly together. "There was no one better at it. Not in Oyrwyn, not anywhere. Understand that I do not say this with pride, not in the way I might have done once."

"So what would you have done to a lad of twelve, for the back-talk?"

"The first time? Mayhap I would just cuff him. If it kept up, there would be a good deal of running. In armor, carrying rocks, holding a shield above his head, that kind of thing. If it kept up after that? Into the yard with me, gambesons, and blunted swords."

"Cold," she swore, and let the word hang in the air. "You're a hard man, Allystaire."

"I was," he admitted. "Perhaps I still am. I come from a hard business, a hard country. And a line of hard men, so far as I know."

"Coldbourne," Idgen Marte murmured. "Did your grandfather choose the name, or was it given him?"

"Came with the fief and the Hall. Still, I often wondered if the Old Baron's father gifted him that estate on purpose. As the Succession Strife rolled on, there was no shortage of empty Seats."

"Why do you lot keep fighting over a throne none of you could hold?"

"Lionel's generation, and mine, we were born to it. A man is told 'this is what we do and this is who we fight' by his father, his Baron, by every piece of the structure he helps prop up, he comes to believe it." He paused and turned back to her. "That is no excuse. I know that now. I have no idea how to stop them, even if I had the army to do it with."

"Give them a k—"

"Do not finish that thought," he snapped.

"I didn't mean you. Cold, but you'd be a horrid king. Worse than the Rhidalish."

"Oyrwyn fought for the Rhidalish kings, you know. For or against, does not seem to matter much today," he admitted. "The Vale of Kings is naught but a ruin now, and what bits of valuable land surrounded it have been snapped up by Innadan, or Machoryn, or Damarind. Every once in a while a pretender shows up, but why one man over another, anyway, even if one could prove his patrimony? Strength is so often an accident of birth; Her words. So is kingship."

"So is knighthood—which is precisely why it is foolish."

Allystaire was silent a moment, his eyes searching the darkness that was now nearly total in the wood around them.

"That is true. And yet, mayhap it is just how we go about it. The idea of knighthood, Idgen Marte, that is not so foolish. It could mean something, if only we went about it the right way."

"What in the Cold do you mean, the idea? A rich man gets to stay rich so long as he's willing to put on five or six stone of steel and clobber other rich men?"

"Well, that is one kind of knighthood. What about knights in stories? What did they do?"

"Mostly kill things. Monsters and brigands and other knights."

"Aye, but it is not the what that matters. It is the why. I have heard a few songs in my day. Reddyn the Redoubtable, Reddyn of the Red-Hand. Cold, if half the stories have an ounce of truth it would be more like Reddyn-the-Red-to-the-Elbow. But why? Like other knights and heroes in stories, he did it so that other men, women, children—some that he knew, many that he did not—could sleep well by their fires and never worry about the darkness surrounding them. He did it without asking them for their links, or the fruit of their labors, or their daughters. If knights did that, could be made to do that? Then the idea would not be half so foolish."

Idgen Marte absorbed his words in silence. Finally, she spoke, smiling wryly. Though it was too dark to read her face, Allystaire could hear it in her voice now, he knew it so well.

"If knights could be made like you, then yes. The idea would have merit, as you say. But, Ally, they can't. The path you walk is a narrow one. Most men would founder."

"I might."

"You won't. And even if you did, I'll be there behind you to set you right." She clouted him companionably on the shoulder, then turned away. "Enough with foolish talk. Wake me in two turns."

CHAPTER 10

Into the Thasryach

A few short turns later, Allystaire was awake, dressed in his riding leathers, with his iron-banded gloves and thick bracers around his forearms, standing silently just a few yards outside the camp, a straight length of wood in his hand that didn't quite reach his shoulder. Bark still clung to it, but it was straight, strong, and dry—everything he had hoped for.

He stood, waiting, his back to the camp, for longer than he'd hoped he would. Eventually, he heard quiet footfalls on the grass, a few of the first-fallen leaves crackling under Gideon's careful steps.

"How're you awake? The sky barely suggests dawn. Bhimanzir knew tricks that would allow him to do without sleep for days, yet always with a price to pay."

"No tricks, just a long habit. I sleep when I can and wake when I must. Now." Allystaire turned to face the boy, who was rubbing sleep from his eyes, and held the staff out for Gideon to take. "Did you come to talk of sleep or did you come to learn?"

"To learn," Gideon said, then recoiled as Allystaire lightly tossed the not-quite-ready staff at him, but corrected himself in time to fling his hands out and catch it, one end dragging on the ground.

"Good. The first lesson, and our first exercise, just like the knife: hold on to that staff so that I cannot take it out of your hands." With only a moment's wait, Allystaire stepped forward and reached out, wrapping his left hand around the staff and giving it a rough tug, then another. Gideon held on briefly, but the second pull ripped it from his hands, the rough bark tearing at the skin of his palms.

"Again." Allystaire held the staff out to the boy, who took a deep breath and accepted it.

This went on for roughly half a turn, with Gideon struggling more and more, till eventually he fell to the ground and curled his legs around the staff, locking his feet at the ankle. With both hands, Allystaire grasped the staff and lifted it from the ground, bringing the boy with it. He raised the staff till he was looking Gideon eye to eye, and then nodded approvingly.

The boy uncoiled himself from the staff and dropped his feet to the ground, roughly. His thin arms were trembling, and when Allystaire relinquished his grip, the staff nearly clattered to the ground.

"Is this what training a knight is like?" the boy asked, panting softly.

"No," Allystaire replied. *This is much easier*, he thought, but did not say. "Besides, why would you want to know anything about training for such foolishness? Now. Carry that staff all day. At times I may ask you to do something with it, hold it above your head, say, or carry something with it. Will you do that?"

"I will try."

"Good enough."

"What would you be doing, if I might ask, if you were training me to be a knight?"

Goddess help me, I would be sending you away, to your mother, to the priests or the scriveners, where you belong, Allystaire thought, his mind instantly and unflinchingly sizing up the boy's spare frame, thin arms, and narrow shoulders. What he said, though, was, "Putting a chain shirt on you and making you run the yard."

"Seems it would be hard to run in a chain shirt."

"That is rather the point, lad."

They headed back to the small camp. Idgen Marte was slowly waking up and Torvul was sitting atop his wagon with his crossbow in his lap. He had fallen back asleep once Allystaire had woken up; his snores drifted on the morning air. Bethe, as was her habit, was huddled deeply into her blankets, unmoving.

After a moment of silence, Gideon said, "I don't want to be a knight. I do want to learn utility. I don't want you to regret bringing me with you."

"Listen, lad, that you want to learn is a good thing. Even if you did not, it is not as though we would leave you behind. Besides, you already saved my life once. What would I be if I abandoned you after that?"

That seemed to mollify the boy, and he nodded. He lifted one hand from his staff and studied the raw red lines that a half turn of scratching against bark had raised. "Can you teach me to do anything about this?"

"I can tell you two things," Allystaire said. "The first is that Idgen Marte probably has some sort of salve. The second is that you should talk to Torvul about cutting the bark away and smoothing the wood. He will have the tools."

"Could you not heal it?"

"I could, but I will not," Allystaire replied. "And I have reasons beyond mere cruelty," he added. Allystaire pulled off one of his gloves and held his hand out towards the boy. "Look at my hand. Tell me what you see."

The boy leaned forward, studying Allystaire's hand, turning it over to look at the back, and then again at the palm, gnawing his lower lip. "I see that you have broken two fingers and two of the knuckles on the back of the hand, and that they probably hurt in damp weather, that your life line is odd—long, but odd—that your nails are cracked and dirty…" The boy glanced at Allystaire's increasingly impatient face, and added, "And also that your hands are very calloused, which is what you wanted me to see."

"Yes. If I heal your scrapes, you will never grow them, and your hands will always be scraped. Proves my point, lad. Some hurts are good for a man, aye?" The boy nodded, let go his hand, and Allystaire quickly asked, "What was that bit about a life line?"

Gideon shrugged. "Parlor tricks sorcerers sometimes perform to impress their patrons. Reading the future in the hand. Mostly nonsense."

Allystaire shrugged it off and motioned the boy to Idgen Marte, who was groggily strapping on her sword belt. Gideon went to her, gingerly wrapping his hand around the staff and swinging it in front of him like a walking stick.

Allystaire rapped on the side of Torvul's wagon. The light sounds of snoring stopped, and were replaced with rumbling Dwarfish oaths.

"We leave in half a turn. I mean to make some distance today. No time for loafing."

"Loafing! Boy, in a quarter turn of sleep my mind does more work than yours has in a score of years," Torvul answered, through a yawn. "Never call it loafing."

"As you say, Torvul," Allystaire replied. "Nevertheless, it is biscuit and cold meat and breakfast in the saddle today."

As the dwarf rattled more stone-chewing words he clambered—rather nimbly, Allystaire noted—from the top of his wagon, to the board, and finally back inside, slamming the door behind him.

* * *

Two turns later, the sun was up and bright, but brought very little warmth as they climbed. Their winding track through the foothills had begun to cut back and forth across the mountain it ascended, and their going was slow, till it finally halted when Idgen Marte, walking a few paces ahead, called back for Allystaire.

Sweat streaming down his face despite the chill in the air, he swung from his horse, landing on his heels with a heavy, clanking thump, and trudged up to meet her. She was crouched to the inside of the track, near a pile of fallen rock and broken branches. She looked up, saw him coming, stood, and pointed with one finger—at a corpse.

Allystaire frowned and moved closer. The body was fairly fresh, not rotted yet, wearing the remnants of a mail vest and the scraps of a tabard. Allystaire knelt, reaching out with one gloved hand to rip free a strip of the cloth.

"Faded, but this was red once, I think. Innadan red," he said, as he held it to the light.

"Aye. When's the last time any Innadan man got this far into Delondeur?"

"The last time they were allied, I suspect," Allystaire replied. "Still, they made a good go of it, two years ago. Probably a deserter."

"Look at his neck," Idgen Marte said. She pulled her sheathed sword free from her belt and used the tip of the scabbard to push away some of the detritus obscuring him. His throat had been torn out, and dark brown stains covered his light beard and the neck of his mail and clothing.

"Torn out by a beast? Bear, wolf?"

"Body's still here. Bear or wolf wouldn't have wasted it."

Allystaire stood, wincing at the click of a knee, and said, "Unless they were scared off. This man was probably not surviving up here alone."

"Deserter's Brotherhood," Idgen Marte said, though without force or conviction.

"Could be," Allystaire replied, and was about to go on before he stopped himself short, frowned. "If so, they would have taken the body. Buried it. And the vest, his clothing…Cold, even his sword is still sheathed."

Idgen Marte looked at him, an odd light in her eyes. "Man dies with his throat slashed, his sword still in its sheath, and the beast or man that did for him does nothin' with the body?" Allystaire started to shake his head, but she spat once, and muttered, almost growled one word as she shifted her eyes back to the body.

"Chimera."

Allystaire spat, reflexively, over his left shoulder, moved by superstitious need. He collected himself, shook his head. "Plenty of reasons before we go reaching into legend to frighten ourselves. And," he added, lowering his voice, "the boy, and Bethe."

"Only one reason the stories put here in the Thasryach. Legends stay with us for reasons, Allystaire," she said, her words clipped short by thinly pressed lips.

"Then remember what you are, and act like it, not like a frightened child," Allystaire said, his eyes widening as his voice rose. "We have chosen our road, and that is over the pass. We will fear nothing we might meet upon it. Will you take the lead, or shall I?"

"I'll do it. Goddess only knows what you'd blunder us into." Her anger at his words was evident in the set of her jaw and clenched teeth. But, Allystaire noted, she stood straighter again, looked him in the eye.

Shaking his head, he headed back to where Ardent waited for him. The destrier's ears were moving, his eyes slightly wide, nostrils flaring. He didn't shy or protest when Allystaire took the reins and swung back into the saddle. He felt the stallion's restiveness in the bunching of huge muscles, and patted the long grey neck softly. "We have many turns of light left. Let us not waste them," he called.

The little column moved on in mostly uncomfortable silence for the time being. Behind him, Allystaire could hear Torvul speaking quietly with Gideon on the seat of his wagon, prying and needling information out of the boy about the sorcerers and their history. Most of the conversation was too quiet and too circumspect for him to follow, but he sensed the dwarf was learning quite a bit.

As morning gave way to afternoon, despite the brightness of the sun, the day seemed to grow colder. They were gaining height as they moved up the switchbacks, but Allystaire didn't think the elevation was enough to explain the cold.

Then something, a thought, a notion, a warning, perhaps just irrational, animal fear, tickled the back of his neck. He raised a hand to call a halt. Even though he did not speak, and she was dozens of paces ahead of him, Idgen Marte drew an arrow from the quiver at her hip and fitted it to her bowstring. He lowered his hand and began easing his hammer out of its loop, then looked behind him, towards the dwarf's wagon.

"Torvul," he said quietly, "is there room for Gideon and Bethe in your wagon?"

The dwarf puffed out his chest as if to complain, but when his eyes met Allystaire's, his demeanor changed. "Aye." He reached back and twisted the doorknob, swinging the door open. "Get in there, boy. And you too, lady," he said, waving to Bethe, who had slid off of Idgen Marte's horse, slowly, and begun taking tentative steps towards the wagon.

She paused, though, hesitating, looking around at the mostly barren trees, squinting.

Gently, trying to sound urgent, but not angry, Allystaire spoke. "Please get in the wagon."

She stopped, cold, turning suddenly widened eyes on him. "It…I don't… is it dark in there?"

Allystaire shot a glance at Torvul, who was stepping down off the step and extending a hand. "I'll set up a lamp for ya. Now please, go on in."

Gideon stuck his head out of the door, holding one of the dwarf's small metal lamps, fiddling with its pump and dials. "There is a stove," he pointed out, "and chairs. Dwarf-sized, but big enough for us. It is quite warm inside."

The woman hesitated, then nodded slightly and began to walk forward.

Allystaire started to release a breath he didn't realize he'd been holding, when suddenly, something hard and strong and vaguely man shaped swooped down onto him, knocking him clean out of the saddle. He landed on the ground with a clatter, his hammer knocked clear from his grasp. Bethe froze in place.

He didn't bother searching for his weapon. Instead, Allystaire pushed himself to his feet, his leather-and-iron clad hands curling into familiar fists. The thing that had attacked him was giving him no chance to recover, though, and was already pouncing. It was man-shaped, but with, he could see, one feathered arm. *No*, he thought, even as it leapt upon him, *a wing*. And a man's face, twisted into a muzzle, bristling with teeth that had no place in a man's jaw.

Chimera. The one thought, certain and overpowering, sounded in his brain like a bell even as the thing began beating its wing upon him. Its other arm was clawed, like a rodent's, and it sought his face. Allystaire caught the claw descending upon him with his left and began punching with his right, seeking out any vulnerable spot, but in the beast's wild thrashing his blows seemed to glance away.

The strength of the arm he had caught was wild and daunting, and it ripped free of his grasp, then descended again, clawing three hot lines of pain across his cheek. Then the thing hopped, skittered, fluttered away, crying out in some half mad sound that was neither the cry of bird, nor the anguish of man, nor the growl of a beast, and leapt towards the stock-still Bethe.

No. Allystaire thought, though the creature was faster, faster than him, and its clawed arm was reaching for her even as he dove towards it.

As his extended hand caught the feathers of its useless, flapping wing and tore a hank of them free, Idgen Marte had suddenly rippled into sight at his side, her curved sword swinging in a quick upward arc towards the chimera's face—even as a crossbow bolt from Torvul, who stood propped on the step of his wagon, bow in hand, pierced its side.

Still, it shrieked and turned in a rage upon the swordswoman.

That it got a claw briefly sunk into Idgen Marte's shoulder was a testament to its speed, a fact Allystaire had undue time to reflect on as he tried to grab the beast and missed, feeling like he was running through water to try and reach it. His senses sharpened in the way they always seemed to do when blood was first spilled. He could hear Torvul cursing as he drew back the string of his bow, could hear Bethe's rapid, frightened breathing, saw Idgen Marte twist out of the chimera's grasp and draw back her blade for a two handed swing.

He also saw that as fast as she was, even with the Goddess's Gifts aiding her, her swing left her too exposed. What's more, a sudden shift in the beast's stance told him it saw that too. With a control and agility unnatural as the muzzle growing out of its otherwise human face, it flung itself forward, jaws opening, claws extended, at Idgen Marte's midsection.

Allystaire dove at it, managing to seize one of its feet, a five-toed, padded cat's paw in mottled brown and grey fur, in one of his hands, and bore it towards the ground, just enough for its claws to slash Idgen Marte across the stomach, even as its jaws snapped shut on air.

He immediately threw his weight forward, trapping the thing's legs under his body and seizing hold of it with both hands, curling them into fists. Feathers tore free from his grip as the thing flapped its wing; its other arm could not break his grip, though he felt it loosening.

He didn't have to hold it for long, thankfully. Idgen Marte wasted no time; she sidestepped, brought her blade up, and then swept down into its neck, the blow sending a burbling spray of blood into the air. Allystaire ducked his head to avoid the spray, smelling the warm animal stink of the beast, not unlike a horse, or a dog, or a falcon, or some mix of all three. There was another blow, and another, till the chimera's head finally rolled free, and still the body beneath Allystaire twitched and quivered for a few more seconds till, finally, it lay still.

He pulled himself to his feet and went immediately to Idgen Marte's side, pulling off his left glove. She tried waving him away but he planted himself implacably in front of her. "You have wounds, and Goddess only knows what disease that thing might carry. Show."

"Not yet," she grated, through clenched teeth, pointing at Bethe, who trembled on the grass with her hands clutched over her head. Allystaire turned towards her, but Torvul waved him away. He shifted his crossbow to one hand, and with the other seized a potion from pouch and flicked the cork out of it with a thumb. He knelt next to the woman, speaking in hushed tones and holding the bottle out. With just a few seconds of coaxing, she took the potion and drank, and suddenly stood. The dwarf took her by the hand and led her up into his wagon, where Gideon shut the door behind them.

As Torvul handled one problem, Idgen Marte bent and began trying to clean her sword on the grass, but Allystaire grasped her, gently, by the shoulder. The slashes on her shoulder were not deep, but they had broken through heavy leather and into the muscle. His fingers moved over blood-slick skin, and he poured forth a measure of the Goddess's healing warmth into her body; he felt the scratches on her shoulder knit seamlessly and he lifted his hand.

"Your other wound," he said, looking down. Her hand was pressed over her stomach, occasional droplets of red trickling through her clenched fingers. He pried her hand away, pressed his against her wound again, and repeated the process. This wound was deeper, required more concentration. He stood stock still and barely heard her gasp when his fingertips pressed into her torn skin. She tried not to lean forward against him as the pain of the healing—and it did hurt, he knew—moved through her.

When he finished the healing his eyes drifted closed, and they opened with a start, staring straight into Idgen Marte's wide, dark eyes. She stepped away from him, slowly and deliberately, then she slammed her sword home in its sheath and turned to pick up her bow.

Allystaire returned to the chimera's corpse on the ground, toeing it over onto its back with his boot. The monster was a hideous amalgam of parts that did not fit. One leg was furred and bent like a cat's, with a paw to match, while the other was taloned like a bird. There was the wing, and the rodent-like claw, and the wolf's muzzle set into a man's face, atop a man's torso, covered with faded scraps of clothing.

Torvul stumped over to meet Allystaire and the two studied the monster in silence while Idgen Marte, bow in hand, joined them, and Allystaire bent to retrieve his hammer.

"Well," Torvul said, before pausing to chew his bottom lip briefly. "Chimera." He lifted his eyes to the other two. "Good tidings, though. They take a bit of killin', but they do die."

"We should not have come this way," Idgen Marte sneered, and Allystaire forced himself to meet her gaze, and was opening his mouth to retort, when the air was suddenly cut by a great wolf-like howl that sounded somehow too pained to be natural.

And then the piercing screech of a hunting bird.

And then a roaring bark.

"And that would be the bad tidings," Torvul managed to say, before the three exploded into motion. Torvul ran for his wagon and hopped into his seat, while Allystaire and Idgen Marte leapt into their saddles.

"You ride with the wagon. I ride ahead with the lance," Allystaire shouted. The horse's eyes were wide and the great grey beast tugged at the reins, but seemed to calm once a familiar weight was on his back. Allystaire quickly lifted his helmet from the pommel of his saddle and sat it on his head with one hand. The other lifted his shield free of the saddle cleat it hung on, letting it fall on his arm till the straps hit the bend of his elbow.

Now as armored as he was going to get, he lifted free his lance. Then he glanced upwards at the afternoon sun, forming in his mind and his heart a quick prayer. *Mother, please, your guidance. If there must be death here, let it be mine. Do not let them suffer for my stupidity.*

"No one's dying here, least of all you," Torvul shouted, and Allystaire was suddenly aware that both the dwarf and Idgen Marte had overheard his prayer. He had little time for considering the matter, as another chimera came loping down the track at them, its body some hideous mix of canine and man. Though it ran with all four limbs upon the ground, its back legs were those of a man, weather-burned and strong, even as it loped forward in its twisted, bent-backed run.

With no time left for thought, Allystaire's body—and more to the point, his mount—knew precisely what to do. His knees squeezed the horse's flanks, and the destrier gathered himself and flung his great bulk forward, hooves churning up dust. Allystaire lowered his lance and leaned forward in the saddle.

The chimera leapt, but the lance was too long, the paladin's arm too sure. Sharp steel took it in the collar and plunged straight out its back. The beast died with a pitiful yelp, its body writhing at the end of the lance, the force and the shock of its weight nearly tearing the weapon from Allystaire's hand.

He managed to hold on, his arm and shoulder straining, barely managing to keep the weapon aloft, as another chimera lumbered out of the forest at them. A bear's head, and massive shoulders, moving unsteadily atop a man's trunk and twisted, grey-furred, bent legs. It staggered towards him, whuffling at the air in seeming confusion, and then letting out a half-roar, half-moan, charged towards them, raising dangerously-clawed paws as it came.

Behind him, Allystaire could hear the singing twang of Idgen Marte's bowstring as she loosed arrows towards the top of the trees. He spared a glance from the bear-shouldered monster while struggling to lift his lance with a dead chimera on the end of it.

The sky was alive with feathered things. Allystaire saw one man-sized, winged creature fall when a second arrow pierced it near the neck. Another he briefly saw crouched in a tree. Like the first chimera, it had only one wing, a fact that became evident when it leapt free and spiraled, screeching piteously, to its death as a crumpled heap several yards away.

This is wrong, some part of his mind, the detached observant part that was not focused on keeping his lance aloft despite the weight and the pain it was rooting into his shoulder. *These creatures are as pathetic as they are monstrous.*

And yet this thought did not stop the chimera charging him from being a threat. With a roar of pain, Allystaire was able to keep his lance aloft just enough to plunge the tip into the creature's twisted, bent-kneed leg.

There was no hope of saving the lance now. It tore free of Allystaire's hand at the muted shock of impact, and it was like letting go of the weight of the world. His arm and shoulder were a flaming agony, but pain was an old acquaintance. The oldest friend he still had, and he let it wash over and through him, even as his hand closed around the haft of his hammer and drew it free. The twisted chimera was not dead, but it was down, buried beneath the weight of the first he'd speared and with several span of lance pinning it to the ground. There were no more apparent threats ahead, so he spared another look back.

Between Idgen Marte's bow and Torvul sparing his reins to take the occasional shot with his crossbow, the air was mostly clear. He saw one flying beast that had drifted away, circling off above the trees.

Reaching inwardly towards the dwarf and the warrior, rather than shout, he thought, *Time to put speed on. This cannot be all of them. We can find a defendable place before nightfall and make it down the pass tomorrow if we do not linger.*

We should turn back, came Idgen Marte's thought.

No, Allystaire thought back, and he would have shouted if he knew how. *We lose too much time if—*

We must go forward, came a voice that all three of them recognized as Gideon's, who had once again overheard them. *Please. I can feel something ahead. A kind of power. We should go to it.*

Why? The single word echoed in all of their minds as Allystaire, Torvul, and Idgen Marte responded together.

It is something that animates these monsters. I can stop it. There was a pause. *I think.*

CHAPTER 11

The Cave

There was no more discussion. They plunged upwards along the ascending trail. The wagon rattled alarmingly, and despite Torvul's sputtered assurances of the sturdiness of dwarfish construction, they could read the worry on his deeply lined features. They ran the animals for a long time, too long, and finally with no sign of further chimera attacks, horses and ponies slowed to a walk. It grew colder, and the sun sank lower. Ardent's breath roared in his chest and Allystaire slipped out of the saddle, but he kept hammer and shield ready.

Idgen Marte hitched her brown courser to the back of the wagon along with their pack horse, and trotted forward to meet Allystaire as they took a brief pause. Torvul's ponies drooped in their harness, and the alchemist clambered out of his seat. He fetched a bucket from a rope on the side of the wagon and emptied a waterskin into it, then tugged a potion out of a pouch and upended it into the water, then went to offer it to his team, letting each pony drink in turn.

"Boy best know his business," Idgen Marte murmured, as they watched the dwarf. Soon enough Torvul came towards Allystaire, and held out the bucket.

"Give that great beast of yours a sip or two of this. Not too much, now." Allystaire took the bucket, setting down his shield. He brought it to the horse's muzzle, and Ardent dipped his nose in and began slurping. Allystaire took it away quickly, though the horse stretched his neck out for more, giving his head a vigorous shake and stamping his front hooves. Ardent's eyes went a bit wider, and despite the lather on his shoulders and flanks, the destrier looked ready to run.

"What did you put into this?" Allystaire handed the bucket off to Idgen Marte.

Torvul frowned, the expression creasing his broad, hairless face from forehead to chin. "Somethin' to keep their heads up. It won't do the animals any good over too long a time. Enough of it and they'll run till they keel over dead. Still, for tonight, and mayhap a bit in the morning, so long's we give them a rest after, ought to be fine."

"Do you have more of it if we need it?"

"We won't. I don't think…" Torvul looked back at his wagon, where Gideon's head had emerged from inside. "Boy's a bit uncanny, but I think he means what he says."

Their rest came to a quick end after all the animals were treated with Torvul's potion, and they set off again, Gideon now riding next to Torvul, leaning forward, his eyes closed and his hands resting on his knees, concentrating intensely.

And so they rode, the horses and ponies showing renewed vigor, eating up ground till they were off the switchback trails and onto a straighter, albeit rockier track. The wind bit at them a bit more, and the pass narrowed in places, though never so far as to threaten the safe passage of the wagon. Rock walls and mountains loomed up on either side of them, and Allystaire gripped his hammer tightly, straining to hear any sign of further monsters. Soon enough, Idgen Marte rode up to replace him at the point, but he stayed up front rather than fall back, riding side by side with her. Neither spoke, for their state of watchfulness did not allow it.

Once, Allystaire heard an echo of the half-human, half-raptor shriek of a winged chimera, and he and Idgen Marte both started towards the noise, hands filling with weapons. The cry receded, but not their vigilance, till the moment when Gideon suddenly stood up on the wagon's board and pointed to the left. "There!"

Torvul hauled back on the reins to stop his ponies, and followed the boy's extended finger. Several yards away, over rough rock and scrub, a pile of stones didn't quite obscure the opening of a cave. It was positioned on a slight slope above the main pass, with no real tree cover to shield it.

"The opening is large enough for man and horse," Allystaire said, "if we can move some of the rock. Go." He slid off Ardent's saddle and began leading the horse up the slope, loose rocks sliding around the destrier's hooves and onto the track. Allystaire stopped just short of the cave, planted his feet, and began digging at the rock pile with his gloved hands.

No sooner had he begun than Torvul's wagon halted along the track and the dwarf leveled his crossbow with one hand while swinging the door open with the other. He chanced a glance back into his little cabin, and cursed.

"Ah dammit, the woman's asleep. I didn't…" The dwarf looked to Allystaire, shaking his head. "Didn't count on this when I gave her that little tincture."

Idgen Marte rode up behind the wagon, her bow at her side. "Allystaire! There's more coming. Half a score, mayhap a dozen. Slow, scared I think—but they're coming."

"Cold," Allystaire spat, even as he shoveled away another rock. The way was clear enough for most of them—but not for him. More importantly, not the horses.

Gideon, meanwhile, leapt down out of Torvul's wagon, holding in both hands a long piece of the bar stock the dwarf had purchased back in Londray. "I cannot carry her," he said, as he ran to join Allystaire at the cave mouth. "But I can do this. The right tool makes almost anyone as strong as a knight." With that, he plunged one end of the bar amid the rocks, rooted it around, and then began tugging on it, throwing all his weight into it. The pile broke free and rushed down around Allystaire's ankles, almost tripping him as he began running for the wagon. Torvul set down his bow, hopped up the steps, and ducked inside. The dwarf came out carrying the woman and handed her over to Allystaire.

Meanwhile, Idgen Marte had hopped atop the wagon and drawn her bow, tilting the arrowhead high up to give it distance, then loosed. The shaft was quickly out of sight, but Allystaire thought the wind carried to his ears a distant, canid yelp of pain.

Bethe was barely conscious in his arms; whatever Torvul had given her had dulled her senses considerably. When Allystaire ducked into the mouth of the cave, and the late afternoon sun was suddenly dimmed, she sat upright in his arms and tried to scramble away, her face frozen in a rictus of fear.

Wincing, Allystaire gripped her tighter and laid her down against the rough rock wall just a few feet in. She tried to break his grip and could not. Her mouth closed in a thin, tight line and she began breathing hard and sharp, her eyes wide open and her clawed hands scrabbling at his arms.

"Bethe," Allystaire said sharply, his voice echoing loudly in the cavern. "Bethe, listen to me. I know it is dark. I know why that frightens you, but there is no sorcerer coming with a hooked knife for you here. It is dark, but you will see light again, I promise. Have Faith in the Mother. Have Faith in my right arm, and Torvul's magic, and Idgen Marte's blade, and you will see such brightness that you never need fear the dark again." The woman's hands relaxed and she ceased buffeting him, and that would have to do. He stood, ducking beneath the cave's roof instinctively, though it was several feet above his head. Torvul appeared with his lantern in one hand, crossbow in the other, and Gideon in tow.

Torvul quickly sparked his lamp to life—how Allystaire never quite saw—and unshuttered it, throwing bright white light through the cave. It was enormous and full of points reaching gracefully up from the ground or somehow threateningly down from the ceiling like liquid stone, poised forever on the point of a drop. The light fell across a dark red smudge that drew his eye. He had little time to study it, but he knew instinctively that it had been shaped. Whether by hand or by instrument he could not guess, but it was some kind of painting on the stone wall, of a form walking upright, like a man, but with an unmistakably bear-like head and huge claws at the end of its outstretched arms.

"Allystaire!" He heard Idgen Marte's call and pulled himself away from the painting and towards the cave mouth, stooping to pick up hammer and shield as he emerged into the light. Idgen Marte had gathered up all the animals, cutting Torvul's ponies and Allystaire's packhorse free from their lines and harness, and was leading them towards the opening. Distantly, down the track, Allystaire saw monstrous forms loping towards them, hooting, roaring, calling, and barking.

The animals shied from the opening of the cave, protesting loudly, and Idgen Marte hauled hard on the tangle of reins and straps to no avail. Whirling on one foot, Allystaire barked out, "Ardent!"

The grey turned his head, yanking his reins from Idgen Marte's grasp, and ran to his master. "Go inside," Allystaire said. "Watch the entrance. Kill anything that comes in that is not one of us. Now."

The huge destrier whinnied and reared slightly, stamping his front hooves on the ground. And then disappeared inside the opening of the cave, taking the other animals with him.

"That's not canny," Idgen Marte said, as she came back out.

"Agreed, though I stopped questioning it some time ago," Allystaire replied. He and Idgen Marte moved a few paces away from the mouth of the cave, stretching their arms.

"How many shafts do you have left," he asked, rolling his shoulders beneath his armor, lifting his shield and hammer in turn to test his arms, the right still tingling.

"Half a dozen. No chance to retrieve any."

"Fine," Allystaire said. "Stay behind me, a dozen paces or more, till they are spent. Gideon thinks he can end this. We need to give him time."

"Is the boy a sorcerer or not?"

"I expect we will learn that soon enough."

The pack of chimera—more than ten but less than a score—were drawing closer now. Numbers were hard to determine, for they moved so quickly, so oddly, and close enough to distort one another. They seemed hesitant, but Idgen Marte nocked an arrow and raised her bow, and Allystaire lifted his shield and spread his feet, swinging his hammer in small arcs to keep his wrist loose.

One broke from the pack and charged. Idgen Marte loosed, and Allystaire set his feet and squatted behind his shield.

* * *

Inside the cave, Torvul had left the large lantern with Bethe, who had calmed but refused to leave the mouth of the cave and its view of the daylight. He produced an even smaller one from a pouch, little more than just a tiny dot of light in the immense darkness of the cave, and followed Gideon. The boy walked unerringly forward, picking his way through the formations of rock spikes without the slightest hesitation.

"What is in this cave that's so important, boy?"

The boy stopped, tilted his head to one side, but did not look back at the dwarf. "Power. Whatever is animating those monsters. Whatever has made them into beasts." He paused. "I think."

"Made them? So what were they before?"

"Men," Gideon answered as he adjusted his grip on his staff and set off again.

"They were what? What has the power to twist man n' beast into those… things?"

Gideon stopped, turned back, and said, "A god."

"Well, I'd hate to be put out like this for anything less," Torvul huffed, as he hurried to scramble over the rocks and catch the boy, who had already turned and moved ahead into the twisting, dark passages.

* * *

Idgen Marte put an arrow into the shoulder of the furred and scaled horror that crashed against Allystaire's shield, but if that slowed it down, Allystaire couldn't tell. The impact drove his weight onto his back foot, and chances were he was only saved from being overborne by having the high ground. There was no time to reflect on the odds. Claws and teeth scraped against his shield. The attacker was focusing on the blue-and-gold-painted oak, it seemed, rather than the man behind it. Allystaire had time to cock his arm and bring his hammer down in a savage and skull-shattering arc directly on top of the creature's head. It was as deadly a swing as he had ever managed; with the advantage of height, the economy of his arm's movement, and the way he was able to shift his weight, he felt confident it would have staved in the finest steel greathelm.

The creature staggered back a pace or two, roaring, and held its head at an odd angle as it tried to charge the paladin again. It tripped, and fell, and Allystaire leapt upon it, battering its skull with his hammer once, twice more. Finally he heard a loud and resounding crack and the beast, some mix of bear and fowl, twitched and spasmed on the ground in its final moments.

He shuffled back up the slope, keeping his shield facing the group of chimera that seemed cautious, hesitant to approach. From several yards away it was hard to tell just what parts each beast was made of; they were a writing mass of fur, feathers, claws, teeth, and the occasional and incongruous human.

"Up the slope. Slowly. One step at a time. If they rush us before we make the doorway—"

Don't give them ideas. They might know our speech. Idgen Marte's thought cracked like a whip in his mind, and he cursed inwardly.

They were within half a dozen long paces of the cave mouth when two of the stirring horde finally drove themselves against them. With sharp, curved raptor's beaks set in gaunt human cheeks, beneath huge yellow bird's eyes and winged arms, these two seemed more coherent, more whole than many of the others. They both attacked Allystaire, from either side, screeching madly, awfully, and driving themselves into the air in short hops, their wings not quite taking them aloft, but serving to lengthen their jumps dangerously. Too late, Allystaire realized that their attack was not just in unison, but in concert, as they hurled themselves at his shield arm and his hammer arm. The one to his right, that had lifted a leg and bent one taloned foot, claws flexing as it reached for the haft of his hammer, suddenly screeched and fell tumbling backwards in a storm of loose gravel as Idgen Marte's arrows feathered it twice.

The other, though, managed to plant both its claws on the rim of his shield and immediately threw its weight, wings beating the air, backwards. Allystaire felt his feet begin to slide on the loose rock beneath them, and even as Idgen Marte loosed an arrow—and missed—decided to let go of his shield. He slid his arm free of the straps and danced away, and the winged chimera tumbled to the ground, cawing in triumph, as its taloned feet flung the shield down the slope.

Grimly, Allystaire shifted both hands onto the haft of his hammer, stepped towards the shrieking beast, and swiped the head of the maul savagely across its face, smashing its beak, and scattering pieces of it amidst a fountain of blood.

He and Idgen Marte scrambled back to the mouth of the cave as the rest of the chimera began a charge upwards at them. Allystaire reared back and flung his hammer into the midst of them; it thunked into something but amidst the roiling mass of monster he couldn't see what he hit or how hard. Idgen Marte's final arrows joined it, and then she tossed her bow aside and both of them drew their swords, Allystaire's a wide and ugly hand-and-a-half, Idgen Marte's a singly edged and graceful curve.

* * *

Inside the caves, Torvul's breath puffed in his barrel chest as he scrambled, banged his shins on rocks, dislodged streams of pebbles with his boots, and occasionally crunched down on something brittle he preferred not to think about.

Finally his breath caught as he pulled up behind the boy in a massive round chamber. He knew enough of caves and tunnels to know that they'd been moving steadily down into the earth, and rock rose above them in a dome so perfectly formed that Torvul could not help but think, briefly, of the grace and art of the cities of his own people, lost beneath the same earth as they stood under now.

This dome, however, was natural. Torvul's eyes, at least, couldn't find the mark of a tool on the stone, and if any eyes would've noticed, he was sure they'd be his. Gideon's footsteps had stopped, and Torvul had to tear his attention away from the cavern around him to see why.

The dome arched over an underground pool, not really large enough to be a lake, but large enough that his lantern's light did not reach its far shore. What light his lamp did throw, though, was cast upon a small island, only a few paces wide, smack in its middle. On it stood a circle of tall, smooth shapes. Too regular and straight to be the natural stone, he thought.

"It is on the island," the boy was saying, his breath rapidly filling his thin chest.

"A god is on the island, boy?" Torvul lifted his lantern higher and peered into the darkness. The tall shapes…obelisks? Pillars? He couldn't put a word on them. They ringed the island at regular intervals, and something—dark irregular shapes—sat atop each.

"What is left of it," Gideon answered. He glanced up at the dome, then the island, and finally at the dwarf. "Follow me with the lantern. I may need your help."

Torvul's gaze was drawn upward again. He just thought he could make out, on the ceiling, more shapes of red daubed on the wall. Winged and feathered things, standing on straight, human legs. His attention was quickly torn away by the splash of water as Gideon began wading into the pool.

"Wait, you don't know what might be in that water," Torvul found himself calling out, before snorting and wading in after him. "Travelin' with Allystaire is startin' t'wear off on me," he muttered, as he plunged first one boot, then the other, down into the water, lifting his lantern high above his head.

Several paces ahead, Gideon had adopted a graceful swimming stroke. Torvul was only halfway across the water when the boy, skinny and dripping wet, clambered onto the island to confront the last vestige of a god.

* * *

Outside, the scene was chaos.

Idgen Marte dashed and darted among the beasts, using their own shadows to move from one to another, her arms whipping her curved sword from one chimera's leg to another's back to under another's arm. Her blows were not enough to fell any single monster alone, especially with thick fur, the occasional patch of leathery, near-armored flesh, and the bulging of unnatural muscle there to absorb her attacks. But the multiple cuts added up, and soon her blade was flinging droplets of chimera blood with every swing.

Allystaire, by contrast, had no grace in his swordsmanship. His blade was large and ugly and swung in wide, dangerous arcs. The sword's length kept the worst of the monster's claws from him and near constant movement kept any of them from trying the same trick that had divested him of his shield.

It was not, given the way his arms and shoulders protested, a long term strategy.

He whipped his sword to his left, felt it bite into the body of a furred and scaled horror that had been opening a wide-jawed, razor-toothed mouth and lunging for him. His edge had taken the monster under the arm and stuck. It twitched and bled, still trying to raise a bear's claw for him, when Allystaire leaned back just far enough to raise his boot and kick it away, hard. His sword came free with the heavy crack of ribs breaking.

With half their numbers dead or writhing upon the ground, the pack of chimera broke away, and Allystaire and Idgen Marte backed up to the very entrance of the caverns. Inside, they could hear Bethe's praying, her voice running from a shout to a mumble and back again, invoking Fortune, Braech, Urdaran, the Green, the Cold, and gods and powers whose names Allystaire did not know.

Heaving for breath, and only just avoiding falling to a knee, Allystaire locked eyes with Idgen Marte, who had streams of sweat running down her face.

"Your Gift," she said, pausing for a deep breath. "Why is it not—"

"I do not know," he said, turning his eyes to the roiling, wounded pack of monsters that cawed and roared at them. One, another that went on all fours—though one arm and one leg were those of a man, burned a dark brown by the sun, and the rest of his body was that of a wolf—suddenly broke back towards them, leaving Allystaire no time to finish his thought. He stepped forward, holding his sword straight out, the pommel braced against his armored hip, and the point steady in the air like a pike set to receive a charge.

The impact of the thing impaling itself and dying upon his sword staggered Allystaire, and he fell backwards, sword tumbling from his hands, the bleeding, spasming body of a dying chimera locked upon its end. The wind was knocked out of him by the force of the fall, and he had a dim sense of Idgen Marte standing above him, holding ground in a fight instead of leaping about, and with what seemed to him a painfully deliberate slowness, he pushed himself back to his feet, just in time to catch the birdlike chimera, a beast that seemed unfazed despite carrying two of Idgen Marte's arrows in its flesh. The raptor-like creature was able to dart its head in and sneak its razored beak past the cheek guards of Allystaire's helmet, and rip a strip of flesh from his face—below the eye, which Allystaire realized had been its target. He seized its neck with one hand and drew the other back, curled into a fist, and began raining blows upon its face.

* * *

When Torvul climbed out of the water surrounding the island he almost cried out in shock, as he saw Gideon kneeling in the midst of the pedestals, before some rough stone block that answered too well to the description of altar.

But what truly gave the dwarf pause was the boy's thin arms reaching out to some object on it and changing, one sprouting feathers, the other fur.

And then the boy shook his head, and Torvul felt, more than heard, the word *No* emanate not from Gideon's lips, but from his mind. It was the sound of a massive gate rolling closed in front of a keep. It was the sound of an executioner's axe striking clean and thudding into the block.

Gideon's arms were his own again.

Torvul dared not approach closer because he did not wish to spoil the boy's concentration. And, in truth, after feeling that resounding wave of power thud through him he was, perhaps, a little afraid. With two fingers he loosened the mouth of a pouch and began easing a potion bottle out of it.

He spared a quick glance at the pillars. Long straight tree trunks, crudely smoothed. And at the top of each one, twice his height, rested a skull. He saw bear, raptor, wolf, fox, and others too shadowed to make out.

Then the dwarf suddenly felt a tug as if at his own mind, and then it was as if something huge was smothering him, something that promised him hot blood in his mouth and fresh meat for his fire. The thing that touched his mind sang a dark and bloody song of strength and power, of animal bloodlust, of safety, and the dwarf felt his body being shaped by this force, reshaped for the necessity and the glory of the hunt. His lantern fell to the ground from fingers suddenly grown large and clumsy.

But it was too much, and though on some level he knew that this spirit, this presence, was trying to help him, he felt very suddenly and clearly that his mind would disintegrate beneath its presence.

And then there was another *No,* shouted into the air like the crack of a whip. It echoed in the chamber. Torvul found his thoughts realigning along with his body, and he flexed his fingers and breathed deeply, reassuring himself, as he bent to pick up the lantern.

By then Gideon had lifted something off the altar, some kind of crude stone idol. He wrapped his hands tightly around it and closed his eyes. Torvul saw a ripple of flesh along the boy's arm, as if the spirit was reaching out to change him as well, but Gideon shook his head and the movement along his arm stilled.

"I know," the boy said, speaking directly to the idol. "But you must understand." The boy shook his head, intensely. "We do not need this gift. We cannot use it."

The boy held the idol at arm's length, opening his eyes as he continued. "Your time is passed. We no longer need the caves. We are beyond this. We need not become animals to take prey. Your gifts are too much. They drive us mad. We no longer understand them, as you no longer understand us. It is time to let go."

The dwarf felt some kind of answer. It was not articulated, and he could not have explained it, except that it felt like a kind of mourning, a shade of regret. Perhaps in some way an apology. There was a sense of loss. Torvul had the impression of the end of a failed hunt, of partners in the chase parting for good.

Then there was a soft crack and the idol in the boy's hands shattered, turned to dust, and released a shockwave of power that the alchemist could feel getting ready to expand and fill the cavern.

Except Gideon raised a hand, and just as quickly as the power had fled, he gathered it into himself. It was like watching a tremendous wave being pulled into a small drain, and not of its own movement. It did not flow. It was drawn.

He turned then, to Torvul, his eyes wide and calm as always. "It is done. We should go now."

"What, what just happened? What did you do?"

"I expect that the others will ask the same questions. If it is all the same to you I'd prefer to explain once."

Torvul frowned and set his mouth into a grim line. "Why don't you explain t'me on the way? I might be able t'help the rest understand." He tried to let his hand rest casually on his belt, his fingers a quick twitch away from the potion he'd eased out of its pouch earlier. With his other hand, he gathered up his lantern, none the worse for wear from spilling to the ground. *Of course it isn't,* came his smug craftsman's thought. *I made it.* He lifted it high, and turned back to the boy. "You lead the way, talk as we go. My old legs are tired."

The boy nodded, bent and picked up his staff, and began walking towards the edge of the island, swinging it like a walking stick.

When Gideon turned his back, Torvul slipped the single bottle free from its pouch and palmed it. *Lady, grant that I don't have to use this,* he thought, with a genuine ache behind the words. Then, with a deep breath, he thought, *Grant me the wisdom to know what I just saw and what it means for You.*

Gideon had stopped, halfway across the pool. "Are you coming? I can see in the dark but you might want to follow me."

"Right. Coming." Torvul set off with one last look at the impossibly perfect dome of rock, and the just as impossible hand-daubed paintings that covered it like some temple's ceiling. Which, he had only just now realized, it had once been.

CHAPTER 12

The Will

Outside the cavern, as Gideon subdued the vestige of a god within, Allystaire and Idgen Marte found themselves driven to their knees by the sudden, ear-shatteringly loud screams of the handful of chimera they still faced.

The one Allystaire had come to grips with had tried to peck at his eyes again, and so he'd responded by doing his best to shatter its beak with his steel-clad fist, and had put a good crack in it when the thing suddenly seemed to forget that it was even fighting him, turned to the sky, and shrieked. It made a last desperate attempt to break free of the paladin's grip. When that failed, it simply fell limp, as if struck, still screaming. The intensity of the noise broke through Allystaire and Idgen Marte's weariness and concentration on the fight, and they backed away, lifting hands to cover their ears.

When the inhuman noise stopped, there were no twisted, half-made chimera arrayed on the ground around them. No wounded monsters.

There were men. Most of them clad in the scraps what Allystaire instantly recognized as livery: Innadan, Harlach, Delondeur, Oyrwyn, even far-flung Damarind. Each bore the wounds that had been done to them in the battle.

"Oh Goddess, oh Goddess," Allystaire breathed, one brief moment of shock before he acted. He stripped off his left glove and dropped it to the dirt, and scrambled to the side of the chimera—*No, the man*—he had impaled upon his sword. The man still twitched, blood leaking feebly from around the length of steel planted in his body. Allystaire threw himself down the slope, landing on his knees, stones falling loose around him, and placed his left hand upon the man's side and his right on the upper third of his sword. He felt the faintest fluttering of life within the body, and tried to reach for it with the Goddess's Gift. He found it, he held it, and began to pour life back into the man.

But Allystaire knew he had to draw out the sword, and it was deep. *All at once,* he thought. *All at once, and hold against the tide as it comes.* He gritted his teeth and with one strong pull, freed his sword.

He felt that spark of life extinguish itself, and the man gave a gurgling cry; blood and gore gushed from the wound as Allystaire pulled the weapon free. He pressed his senses, the Goddess's Gift, further into the man's body, seeking the trail of the spark. But it was fruitless. He continued to press, looking for any sign of life, any movement of the blood, a twitch of the muscles, the beat of the heart, things he had not known he could sense or feel or see with this Gift, and he tried to will them into working.

And then an impenetrable blank wall dropped over his extended senses. *You cannot—you will not attempt to—reach into Death's demesne.* The Goddess's words to him, when She had Ordained him and granted him this very Gift, rolled across his mind.

With a grimly clenched jaw, Allystaire stood and looked for the next wounded man. Even those who had been only lightly hurt seemed no threat, as most had collapsed or swooned. Only one stood, halfway up the slope, staring at his outstretched hands as if seeing them for the first time.

Allystaire moved among the broken and bleeding bodies scattered across the slope. Most were beyond his help, but the one he had just been struggling with still breathed. His face was battered so that his own mother might not recognize him, and one arm was badly twisted.

The paladin knelt and poured from the Goddess's endless compassion, knitted the bone and closed the wounds of the man that had been a chimera that he had just now been trying very hard to kill. And with that compassion flowing through him, Allystaire felt a grief begin to grip him. *I know now why your other Gift did not come to my arm, Mother,* he thought. *These men meant no evil. They were wild, like a sick dog. They knew nothing of what they did.*

When he stood up, the man now whole and healed, he saw Idgen Marte moving among the scattered and broken bodies, placing the back of her hand over mouths, or her fingertips to a neck. "This one lives," she called out. Nodding, if for no other reason than to clear his head, Allystaire hastened to her and knelt by the man, pressing his bare palm against the man's neck. He wore, Allystaire saw, the tatters of Delondeur's green and white. He needed but a bit of the Mother's grace to close a few of Idgen Marte's shallower cuts.

And then this process repeated itself, Idgen Marte moving ahead of him and finding three more men who would live, and Allystaire growing wearier by the moment.

The man who kept examining himself finally turned to Allystaire and Idgen Marte, his dazed eyes focusing for the first time since he'd shed his beak and feathers. "Who are you? Where...what..." Then his gaze, harried and fearful, settled on Allystaire. "Lord...Lord Coldbourne?" His hand went to his chest, to the faded grey remnants of Oywryn livery. "How?"

"Settle down, man," Allystaire said wearily, still seated on the ground nearest the man he'd last healed. "I have no more idea of what happened here than you. And I truly do not care if you are a deserter or how you came here." To the empty cave mouth, he called out, "Bethe. You can come out now. Danger has passed."

The three of them sat in silence for a moment. Bethe did not appear. Idgen Marte opened her mouth, closed it, then slapped her thigh and spoke. "We had to defend ourselves."

Allystaire stood up, his movements slow and measured. The former Oyrwyn man had knelt on the slope, watching him with fearful awe.

"I know," he replied woodenly. "I find no sin in this, for us or for them."

"Then why does it feel like murder?"

"If there was evil here, it was in whatever made them monsters."

"There was no evil in that either." Gideon's voice suddenly rang out, young, but clear and confident. They all turned towards him as he emerged from the cave, Torvul leading Bethe. "Only misunderstanding. Perhaps a touch of..." The boy paused, searching for a word. "Of senility."

"Senility?" Idgen Marte pulled a rag free from her belt and began to clean her blade. "Best explain quickly, before that one swoons like he's wont to do," she said, with a thumb hooked in Allystaire's direction.

Allystaire simply snorted and went to collect his sword, the greater part of the blade coated in blood. He sought something to clean it with, but stopped as he saw the men who'd survived focus on Gideon. The Oyrwyn deserter raised a trembling hand at the boy.

"It's…I can feel it in you. You've brought it out."

"Peace," Gideon said, raising one hand, the palm out. "The god of the cave can no longer reach out to you. I took its power, yes, and that is what you feel. But none of its essence. It has…" The boy paused. "Departed. Not died, precisely." Then, regretful, lips pursed. "At least I hope not."

"The god of the cave? Is that it was called?" The man lowered his hands, but fear was written plainly on his ragged features.

The boy is standing there speaking of killing a god and taking its power, Allystaire thought, and a fear greater than any he'd felt during the fight with the chimera gripped his stomach like a clenched fist of ice. *What have I done?* He glanced at Idgen Marte and knew from her widened eyes that she was thinking the same.

The response to Allystaire's question made him want to weep, or laugh, or both. The unmistakably bright, pure voice of the Goddess sounded in his head, saying, *Precisely what you needed to do, my knight.*

Suddenly made weak-legged by the wave of joy and relief that rippled through him, Allystaire let out a half-laugh and quickly dug the point of his sword into the rocky ground and leaned his weight on the hilt, staring through teary eyes at his feet. In another distant corner of his mind was the dim memory of a master-at-arms yelling at him to never lean on a sword, that this was how points snapped and blades bent. He found that he did not care.

When he laughed, all eyes turned briefly towards him, he was sure. He could feel the tension, Torvul and Idgen Marte probably wondering if he had snapped, but he didn't even bother to explain. He just waved a hand and said, "Go on, Gideon. Explain. Take your time." He lifted his head then, smiling faintly, still leaning on his sword. He glanced at Idgen Marte and could feel the curiosity roiling in her.

I rather enjoy knowing something she does not, for once, Allystaire thought, a bit smugly, as he turned towards Gideon, who had taken another step from the cave mouth and lifted his hands as if about to begin a discourse to a hall full of students.

"Long ago, more years than men count, I think, even in the Concordat, long before the first Eldest breathed…" He paused, shook his head, and with pursed lips, continued in a stronger voice. "Before people built with stone, before people had the idea of building, this cave was a refuge. A home. And a god found the men and women who lived here, and it gave them gifts. Wings, and fangs, and claws. The gift of hunting, of prowess equal to the bird of prey, the wolf, the bear. And those people thrived, and made this cave a temple."

The boy turned to the dwarf, a few steps behind him, who was listening, but, Allystaire could tell, thinking of something else, his left fist curled tightly around something in its palm. "You saw that, yes, Torvul?" the boy asked.

The dwarf nodded, and his eyes focused briefly on the boy. "Yes. As you said on our way back…" The dwarf cleared his throat, and gestured to Gideon. "Go on then, boy, it's your tale t'tell, not mine."

Gideon quickly resumed. "This god, the god of the caves, he spoke to men when they were not much more than the animals they hunted, or that hunted them. And surely he made them strong. But something, I do not know what, something severed this god from the world. Some great catastrophe, perhaps. When I touched what was left of its mind, I knew that it had no knowledge of walls, of iron and steel, of wheels. The things we make to master the world were all foreign to it. It had spent uncountable years alone in the place that had been its temple. Tell me," the boy said, suddenly looking at the Oyrwyn survivor, around whom some of the other newly conscious men had begun to gather, "when did you find this place?"

"It were summer," the man replied, nervously glancing at Allystaire. "Early summer, s'sthe last time I remember. I hope it was this summer," he added, faintly ill.

"It does not matter, I suppose," Gideon replied. "What matters is that someone did find it. Several of you, I would think."

"Aye," the man replied. "It were…the Brotherhood. We found the cave and spent some time exploring it and then, then I only remember…" He put a hand to his head and suddenly went to one knee upon the ground.

Frowning faintly, Gideon said, "It meant you no harm. I hope you can see that. There was simply too much distance between the men it had known and the men it found. It tried to help, yet no longer knew how to teach you, how to tell you what it was doing or how to control its gifts—"

"Don't you call it a gift, boy," the man snarled, springing back to his feet. He took a threatening step towards Gideon, fists clenched in anger. "I've lost months to this thing you call a god."

Allystaire and Idgen Marte both snapped into motion, stepping between the man and Gideon with several yards still between them. "And you would have lost a good deal more if not for him," Allystaire said, quietly. The man responded as though Allystaire had shouted, knuckled at his forehead, was half-way to a knee before the paladin caught his elbow and stood him up. "We can deal with all that later. For the next turn, at least, I do not care a whit how or why or when you deserted an Oyrwyn host, aye?"

The man nodded. Allystaire let him go and turned back to Gideon, waving a hand for him to continue.

The boy nodded and cleared his throat. "I...I spoke to it. I think I was speaking to it in my head since we came up into this pass. If it is possible for a god to be lonely, it was. It did not understand why its gifts no longer worked, or why its temple was empty. Even to a god, millennia can be a long time," Gideon said, sadness creeping into his voice, his eyes having dropped to the stones at his feet. "And even a god may dream of firelight and the sound of drums." He looked up then, at the Oyrwyn man. "If it helps, when I made it understand what it had done, what its gifts had wrought, it grieved, like a father might grieve when a son he loves will not listen to him."

The man opened his mouth as if to speak, but looked sidelong at Allystaire and clamped his lips tightly together.

"Gideon," Allystaire said, moving away from the man and towards the boy, "when you said you took its power, what did you mean?"

"It dissipated itself," the boy replied. "I gathered in what it tried to expel."

"How? Is this something the sorcerers taught to you?"

The boy shook his head. "No. Not at all. In fact..." He smiled, faintly, an almost predatory gleam in his eye. "In fact they would be distressed to learn that I could."

"What do you mean?"

"Bhimanzir was often frustrated with me. I was taken into their training because the Eldest said he sensed great power in me. Great will, he said. This is what they call their ability," the boy said. "Will." He shrugged. "Yet I always struggled to learn all but the most basic of lessons. I think it was because what Gethmasanar sensed in me was not their kind of power, not their ability to tap into the magic."

Torvul's eyes widened and his head snapped up when Gideon said 'will'. So did Idgen Marte's.

Allystaire only smiled and said, "No, lad. No, it was not." He grasped Gideon's shoulder. "You did well today, Gideon. Exceptionally well. And I suspect that tonight, when we make camp, there is a conversation you will need to have."

"Who with? About what?" The boy's brow furrowed.

"You will see," Allystaire said, then he turned to the men Gideon had saved. "You men, surely you are confused. Frightened, even. Perhaps hungry. Come with us, make a camp. Rest a full night in your own skins, your own minds. Then we can think on what to do in the morning."

"What about them?" The Oyrwyn man pointed at the bodies strewn about the slope. "Surely we can put them t'rest, too."

Allystaire scrutinized the man, trying to find his face or his voice in his memory. Try as he might, though, there was simply no possibility of having known every man under Oyrwyn arms. "What is your name?"

"Keegan, m'lord," the man replied.

"Keegan, we cannot carry the bodies out, and the soil is thin and hard this high in the mountains. Yet there are enough stones that might do for a cairn." *It'll be knocked over in the first good wind, and carrion will be at them soon after, but it's the best we can do,* Allystaire thought, and was inwardly shamed.

"That'll do, m'lord," Keegan said.

He could feel the accusing stares of Idgen Marte and Torvul on his back as he laid down his sword and bent to pick up the first stone. He said nothing.

By the time he was standing with an armful of rocks, both had laid down their weapons and joined him.

* * *

Camp was a subdued affair. They had not been able to get down to the other side of the pass, but everyone involved seemed to want some distance from the caves, so they had traveled right to the very edge of darkness before settling in. Torvul had built up the fire and somehow had come up with fresh bread for everyone, and another huge pot of stew.

"How, dwarf, do you do this?" Allystaire asked him, as Torvul carried his iron pot down the steps of the wagon and laid it on a metal stand he'd set over their fire. "Riding hard all day, a pitched melee, uncovering ancient secrets, and you produce fresh bread and," Allystaire sniffed the steam coming off the pot, and ventured a guess, "beef and bean? How?"

"And barley," Torvul grumbled. Lacking, for once, a witticism, he simply shrugged and added, "I simply see no reason to neglect supper."

The four men who'd come with them out of the pass kept mostly to themselves, and Allystaire left them to it. All were eager for the food though as they began digging into it with the spoons that appeared from Torvul's wagon. Allystaire noted Keegan picking at it, and once spitting to the side.

"Something wrong with it?" Torvul asked, rather sharply.

"No," the man protested, working his tongue around his lips for a moment. "I just, I find myself with no taste for beef. I mean no insult."

The meal resumed and the pot was quickly diminished, the bread mere crumbs around the built-up fire. Allystaire stood, feeling the ache of the day in his legs and shoulders, and gestured to Gideon. The boy stood, and Allystaire placed one hand on his shoulder and led him out of the camp, a few yards away towards where the horses were tethered.

"Gideon, you told me when we met that you were not convinced that gods and goddesses existed. Has your mind changed?"

"I think that they are not as powerful as most would believe," the boy replied, "but yes. Clearly evidence has amassed to force me to modify my position."

Allystaire searched the dark ahead of them and caught a faint but promising shimmer, and began steering the boy towards it. "Prepare to modify it further, lad," he said.

Only a few yards ahead, and they found the Goddess awaiting them in a clearing carpeted in pine needles, beneath a stand of towering evergreens. Allystaire knelt. Gideon, his jaw agape, remained standing till Allystaire tugged at his leg, and the boy sank awkwardly to both knees.

She laughed, then, and Allystaire and Gideon could not help but join Her. Suddenly She was standing directly before them, one hand atop each of their heads.

"My Knight," She said, and Allystaire's heart leaped against his chest at the sound of Her voice. The pain in his knees and back was quickly forgotten. "I knew again that I had chosen well when you grieved for the men you killed today."

Before he could even begin to formulate a response, Her hand had reached down and cupped his chin, tilting his face towards Her. She smiled. Thought was beyond him. Response was impossible. "I grieve for them with you, and I will do what I can for them. Yet you proved again the wisdom of my choice; you kill when you must and you save whom you can. This, My Arm, is precisely why I Called you. Most knights of this world do the opposite."

Allystaire felt himself lifted to his feet, and for the second time, felt the kiss of the Goddess he served fall upon his lips. It was overpowering. His senses could not perceive anything beyond the scope of it. If Her hand and Her lips were flesh, he was unsure. They felt, somehow, to be both more and less substantial. Her kiss lasted but a moment, but the impact lay smoldering on his skin with a tangible weight, like a punch. *Better than a punch,* his mind supplied, dumbly.

He knew, instinctively, when She let go and stepped away, that it was time to remove himself—all of their Ordinations, starting with his own, had been private, between only the chosen one and the Goddess. He could feel, as he walked away, the presence of Her mind, and the beginnings of Her reaching out towards Gideon, as the boy stood, and was wrapped in an embrace that Allystaire thought was, somehow, touchingly maternal.

"Oh, my Will, my boy," She murmured against the crown of the boy's head as She hugged him to Her. "I feared they would not find you, would not know you as I do." This was the last Allystaire heard as he drifted, slightly dazed from Her overwhelming presence, back to the camp.

CHAPTER 13

Choice, Not Fate

He found, once he'd reached the camp, that everyone but Idgen Marte and Torvul had fallen into their blankets, and the warrior and the alchemist were waiting for him in a tiny pool of light cast by one of the dwarf's lanterns. Torvul leaned against his wagon with a long-stemmed, round-bowled pipe stuck into the corner of his mouth, a faintly sweet smoke drifting from it, while she paced back and forth.

"Where's the boy?" the dwarf murmured, around the mouthpiece of his pipe.

"In the safest place imaginable," Allystaire replied, his eyes still slightly dazed, his voice distant. "They will be along."

"How did you know?" Idgen Marte asked, her restless curiosity written plainly on her face, even in the dimness of the lantern light.

"I did not," Allystaire replied. "That he could hear us sharing our thoughts, well, I suspected, but thought it could be some sorcerer's trick."

"It still could," Torvul pointed out. They both turned to him, glaring, and he frowned around his pipe. "I don't mean that way. If he could do it before he, ah, met with Her Ladyship, then, maybe it is something sorcerers can do. Need to be mindful of it, is all."

"The boy is not a sorcerer," Allystaire replied. "Nor could he have been. We know that now."

"How does it all fit together, Allystaire?" Idgen Marte asked. "Is She leading us along? Did She know you'd wind up in that dungeon somehow? That boy comes from half the world away, and he had to be—"

"Faith," Allystaire said. "I do not know how it all fits together. I cannot know. What I can do is carry on as the Arm of the Mother."

"Is it all to chance? Are we pushed along like game pieces?"

"Idgen Marte," Allystaire said, "were you pushed along when I hired you? No. You saw the chance to earn some weight. Were you pushed when you chose to stay? No. You stayed for the story. Your own words, not mine."

"I hope Her Ladyship doesn't mind questions," Torvul said, before taking in a mouthful of smoke and then blowing light, wobbling rings into the night sky. "Respectful questions."

"I know what you would ask me, Mourmitnourthrukacshtorvul." The Goddess, Gideon trailing in Her wake, glided into the outskirts of their camp.

As one, the three servants arrayed before Her—the Arm, the Shadow, and the Wit—knelt. She stood in front of the dwarf, who looked cautiously up at Her.

"My Lady," the dwarf began, removing his pipe and tucking it behind his back with one hand, "that we found Gideon, fated to be your servant, it seems an enormous chance. All of it seems an enormous chance. Are we fated to do these things? Are we—"

"No, my Wit," the Goddess said, frowning faintly. She motioned with Her hands, and they all stood, Gideon coming around to stand before Her, next to Allystaire. "I chose you, all of you, because I saw in your souls what this world most needed. Despite surviving great hurts, of spirit and body both, all of you share a compassion that the world, for all it has done to you, could not drive away. I may guide you, empower you, but the paths you walk and the choices you make will always remain your own."

"Then how'd you know, My Lady, that he'd hare off into the keep and fall afoul of a sorcerer, that the boy'd be there?" Torvul asked, without lifting his eyes.

"I did not know. I cannot know what it is any of you may do. I may only guess," the Goddess said, smiling gently, if a smile with such power could be said to be gentle. "And I excel at guessing what even you will do, Mourmit-nourthrukacshtorvul." She touched the dwarf's cheek lightly with one long-fingered, glowing hand. "Son of the earth, I will not abandon you so long as you do not abandon me. It is not given to me to control you, nor would I wish to if I could."

She stepped back till her features and her smile encompassed them all, and Allystaire felt his mind and senses being overwhelmed once more. "I know from the paths you decide to walk, that I chose well, in each of you. None of you are fated to be what you are. You are, and will always be, the results of your actions and decisions. It is that which has led you to My service, not fate.

"If you err, or you chose other than I might wish—so long as you do so in earnest service —I will keep my faith with you all. In deepest darkness, the narrowest of paths, the bitterest of ends—you will always have My love, and My Gifts, to sustain you."

With that, She slowly glided past them and into the camp, where lay the sleeping Bethe, Keegan, and the other rescued Brotherhood men. She bent over Bethe and laid Her hand atop the woman's head for a moment, then She straightened and looked over the sleeping men.

In Allystaire's head, Her voice chimed softly. *These men could be an aid to you, My Knight, if you can lead them back to the world. It will not be easy.*

Then, to all of them, She spoke once again before fading into the night.

"You must go, and the five of you together finish what you began in the place where I woke and began Calling to you. It must be a beacon in the days to come."

* * *

The next morning, Allystaire was up early, as usual, and stood a few yards away from the camp, staff in hand. As he heard the rustle of footsteps approaching, he looked up and saw that it was not Gideon, but Keegan. The man, looking a bit better for sleep, seemed taken aback to find Allystaire in his path. He made to tug his forelock and paused with his hand still upraised. He wore the blanket Torvul had given him wrapped around his shoulders like a cloak. Meager though it may have been, it was sturdier than the rags he wore, rags that Allystaire could, if he looked closely, see were once the leathers and livery of an Oyrwyn archer or scout.

"I am no one's lord any longer, Keegan," Allystaire told him, quietly. "There is no need for any of that."

The man nodded, but still didn't meet Allystaire's eyes. "Might I ask y'some questions, m'…ah …"

"Allystaire. And yes."

He lifted his eyes, grey, distant, and met Allystaire's for a moment before looking back to the dirt, to his tattered boots. "I'm tryin' t'figure out how long I've been out here. What year d'ya make it?"

"Two score and one since the death of Iridan Rhidalish." Allystaire replied. "Just short of three since the death of the Old Baron Oyrwyn."

Keegan's eyes closed and his head dipped towards his chest. "I walked off into the mountains on your first foray with the Young Baron into Delondeur. That'd be…"

"Two years last spring." Allystaire let that hang in the crisp morning air a while, as Keegan alternated shaking his head and staring at his hands.

"I cannot do anything to give you those years back, Keegan," Allystaire said, finally. "I can take you to a place where you can find whole trousers, a better pair of boots, and regular food, so long as you are willing to work for it."

"Ya don't care that I'm a deserter, m'l…Allystaire?"

Shaking his head, Allystaire replied, "No." At the look of wide-eyed disbelief on Keegan's face, Allystaire shook his head insistently. "I know. There was a time when admitting that to me would mean the lash, mayhap the rope. I know." Allystaire considered his next words, and said, "I might like to know why, but I have no right to hang you for it, whatever the cause."

Keegan sucked in a deep breath, tilted his eyes towards the sky. They were, Allystaire thought, roughly similar in age, though the leaner man had a thick red-tinged beard and thinning hair. There was a ropy, wiry strength to him despite the slenderness of his build.

"I just walked off one day. Had enough."

"Not the easiest thing to manage."

"It is when you're a scout and know your woodcraft," Keegan said, with a hint of pride in his voice.

"Fair enough," Allystaire replied. "How long did it take you to, ah, have your fill?"

"Every bit of ten years." He paused and looked at Allystaire, and went on. "Won more than we lost in that time, thanks t'you, or so most of us believed."

"How old were you when you took the Baron's link?"

"Not goin' t'ask if I were pressed?"

"I never wanted pressed men in my armies, Keegan," Allystaire said. "I will understand if I have earned your scorn. I may even deserve it. But if you were pressed, it is none of my doing."

The man nodded then, as if confirming something. "Aye, that's true. I was just twenty summers when I took the link. Were a huntsman in the service of Durnrock Hall. Knew how t'shoot, had me own bow, and I heard there was better pay for woodsmen, archers and the like, than for your spearman, and less risk. Thought I'd see somethin', all that rot. Well," the man went on, before Allystaire could reply, "what I saw were a lot o' marchin. Got outside a lot o' bad food. Killed my share o'men, took a nick here and a knock there. Never anythin' real bad. Weren't anythin' particular about the day I walked off. Just…" Here he gestured with his empty hands to the air before him. "Enough. Enough blood, enough stupidity. I had a full quiver and a pack of good bread and everyone knew there were Deserter's Brotherhood in these mountains. Figured I could wait out the campaign, then nip back o'er into Oyrwyn durin' the winter."

"Is the Brotherhood a real thing? Deserters, all over the baronies, forming bands, defending themselves?" Robbing merchants and raiding the odd village, Allystaire thought, but did not say.

"It's real enough," Keegan replied, with a tired shrug. "Not what ya'd call very formal. Just, we'd find each other. Some would decide to live the outlaw style. Most, though? Cold, we were too tired of fightin' for that. I met all kinds of men up in these mountains. Innadan men, Delondeur, Harlach, even Machoryn and Damarind now and then. We learned pretty fast that none of us had any reason t'kill each other so long as 'tweren't a knight or a lord or a warband captain shoutin' orders at us. Shared fire, shared bits of rabbit, shared a cave—" Then the tired shrug became a shudder and a slightly choked gasp.

"How many of you were there out here?"

Keegan shrugged. "More than a score, less than two. I dunno how many got turned by that god o'the caves. We tried to keep our camps small, not attract any o'the wrong attention."

Over Keegan's shoulder, Allystaire saw Gideon, rubbing sleep from his eyes with one hand, the other curled around his staff. "Listen, Keegan. There is time yet for you to sleep before we are off. I have some business with the lad here. Take some more rest, and if you decide to follow us, you can have a home again. For as long or as short a time as you want."

"That go for all of us, or just me because I was an Oyrwyn man?"

"I am not an Oyrwyn Lord any longer, Keegan. Any man who goes where we are headed, and does so in peace, will be welcomed."

Keegan sniffed. "Not all o'the men who've, ah, walked away from the war did so 'cause they were sick o'the blood or the marchin' or the rotten food."

Allystaire fixed Keegan with what he planned to be a mild stare, his eyes narrowed, and waited to see how he reacted.

Keegan met him stare for stare, and said, "If y'don't mind me sayin', seein' as how yer no lord anymore, y'hadn't the best reputation for welcomin' strays back."

"I know what my reputation was. There are men I would not welcome back. But the men who made your choice, to leave because they had no stomach for it? Them, I will take."

"And the cowards? What o'them?"

Allystaire pressed his lips together in a faint line. "I am less apt to call a man a coward these days."

"I see. And what o'the men who fled the noose or the lash, eh? Men who'd maybe taken a liberty too far with a farmgirl or drawn steel o'er the dice cups. What o'them?"

"I will not give harbor to murderers or rapists," Allystaire replied. "Not them."

From behind Keegan, Gideon stepped forward, his mouth pursed. "Does the Goddess not ask us to be merciful?"

Allystaire's eyes, briefly fired with anger, flitted to Gideon. "She does," he said, drawing the words out, "yet some men are beyond any forgiveness I can extend."

"Do not equivocate with me. My teachers may have been vile men, but they taught me logic," Gideon replied, lifting his chin defiantly. "I did not say forgiveness. I said mercy. They are not the same. You can extend mercy without forgiveness, and you can forgive a man's sins against you even as you kill him."

Allystaire felt his teeth grinding and his anger rising in his throat, liable to expel itself in a shout, but he choked it back down as a realization broke through, namely, that the boy was right. "Go on."

"What if these men who you say are beyond mercy—if they came to you and confessed their crimes and they genuinely expressed their sorrow—would you grant it to them then?"

"Boy, that's a pretty enough idea," Keegan put in. "But any man who knows that can just sing o'his sorrows and how he's a changed man now, well, there's many a magistrate or priest at the Assizes has heard that song and gotten out his hangin' rope regardless."

Allystaire was quiet a moment as he thought on Gideon's words. "They would have to be willing to accept any sentence we might impose."

Keegan turned to Allystaire then. "Are y'serious? If they know they can avoid a rope dance or a headsman they'll be linin' up t'tell ya their best lies."

"No man can lie to me," Allystaire replied. "The boy's plan has merit." Then to Gideon. "I will think on it. For now," he hefted the wooden staff in his hand, "let us have at it."

"No man can lie t'ya? What does that—"

"It means precisely what it sounds like it means, Keegan," Allystaire said. "I am no longer an Oyrwyn Lord, true, but I have become something much different. Go get that rest, or food, if Torvul is awake yet. I have got to give our young rhetorician a good thumping."

The puzzlement on his face clearly showed that Keegan had more questions, but Allystaire and Gideon drew away before he could ask them, and so he drifted back into the camp to stir the fire.

Several yards off, Allystaire and Gideon faced each other, staves in hand. "Part of me does want to give you a thumping," the paladin was saying to the boy. "I am unused to having boys your age speak to me like that."

Flexing his hands around his staff and shifting his feet as he looked for a comfortable and practical stance, Gideon suddenly took a frightened step back.

"I said part of me, Gideon. You were right to speak up. I am finding it hard to break old habits."

The boy nodded and took a half step closer. "Nothing is as difficult as change, whether in a man, a home, a village, or an entire country."

Allystaire took a step forward at just over half the speed he might actually attack, bringing his staff up in a fairly slow overhand, letting the boy see enough of it to get his own staff up to intercept it. "More rhetoric?"

Gideon intercepted Allystaire's staff, but frowned as he pushed it away with his own. "Yes, but there is truth in it. You have already been an agent of more change than most men who've ever lived," he said, trying a tentative swing, which Allystaire easily caught.

"It does not feel like so very much. Yet."

"No? You are the first true paladin to walk this world—this part of the world, at least—in at least three centuries, and that is a very low estimate; it is probably five. You have shaken the foundations of the most powerful of the warring baronies. You are the prophet and visible leader of a new faith."

Allystaire cut Gideon's lecture short by rapping him on the wrist with a quick, if light touch of his staff. "You cannot talk a man to death. Defend yourself."

"Actually I could," Gideon said matter-of-factly, even as he adjusted his hands on his staff and thrust it towards Allystaire's stomach like a spear.

Though he easily knocked it aside, Allystaire nodded and said, "Good. Most weapons can be used in more than one way. Never forget that." Then the words the boy had spoken sunk in, and Allystaire called a halt by stepping back and planting one end of his staff on the ground. "You could do what?"

"Talk a man to death. It might not sound like talking, exactly, but—"

"Explain, Gideon." One moment passed before he added, "Please."

"The power I absorbed from the god of the caves, I can redirect it."

"To what?"

The boy shrugged. "Whatever I choose, I suppose."

"And this is the Gift of the Goddess?"

"It is hard to say. I seem to have been born able to do this, yet, She showed me how to express it."

Allystaire was silently thoughtful for a moment. "Is this what you did when you released the ensorcelled chains Bhimanzir had laid upon me?"

"Yes, though I did not really understand it, nor did I actually absorb the power he'd expended. I merely dispelled it. I had time to think on it as we traveled, but She made it all clearer."

"And the things you can do are limitless?"

The boy frowned. "Your question does not make sense. Do you mean 'are there no limits on the type of things I can do' or do you mean 'is there no limit on how much I can do?'

Allystaire laughed mirthlessly. "You will teach me to be precise eventually, lad. I mean both, I suppose."

"Well, as to the former, I remain unsure. The Goddess told me that there are always limits. There are limits even on what She might do, and rules She must follow. As to the latter? The power of the cave god will run out in time, and with use. As will any further power I draw in."

"Gideon," Allystaire said, "pretend that I do not understand the slightest thing about magic or thaumaturgy or sorcery—Torvul tells me I certainly do not—and explain what you mean in the smallest words you can use."

The boy sighed. "In the presence of magic, of power, of will, as the sorcerers would call it, I can, it seems, dispel, absorb, and then redirect the power that is expended."

"So you swallowed the power of the god of the caves?"

"Yes."

"And you could do this to other gods? To sorcerers?"

"Well," Gideon said, "yes. If conditions favored it. It's unlikely that most sorcerers would be inept or imprudent enough to allow me to do that uncontested. And I imagine that most other gods are rather more reluctant to let go of their power than the god of the caves was. I also believe that proximity matters."

The clearing was silent but for a few hardy birds greeting the day as Allystaire considered the implications of the boy's words. Finally he said, "And you could use this power to kill?"

"Yes." There was something in the slightly cold, nonchalant way that Gideon said that single word that chilled Allystaire, and he took a few steps to close the distance between them, laying his free hand on the boy's shoulder, bending down to look him in the eye.

"I need you to promise me something, Gideon," he said, solemnly. "You reminded me just a short while ago that we should always be looking to expand our capacity for mercy. Promise me that you will not kill anyone with this Gift unless it is absolutely necessary."

Gideon frowned uneasily. "You and Idgen Marte and Torvul already abide by this rule. Or at least, I think that you make the attempt. What exactly are you asking?"

"Then kill only if it means your life, or the life of others, if you do not."

"How will I know if that is the case?"

"You will," Allystaire replied. "Please, I ask you again. Promise me that you will think of mercy first. Always."

The boy thought on this for a moment, and then nodded. "I promise," he said.

Allystaire nodded and straightened up, felt the cool morning air relieve his suddenly sweat-damp brow. "Thank you, Gideon." He looked with some consternation at the growing light in the sky, and said, "I think we will not get much more done this morning. Perhaps tonight. If not, tomorrow is another day."

"How many more days travel?"

Allystaire grunted noncommittally as he started ambling back towards the camp. "Depends on where we go."

"The Goddess told me we must be in Thornhurst as soon as we can manage. There is something there that is unfinished."

"The altar," Allystaire replied. His hand tightened around the length of wood he carried. "The Altar in the Temple of the Mother. It needs you and Torvul there to be complete."

"Why does this thought anger you?" Gideon gestured with his staff to the fist Allystaire had made.

"It is not that. It is the thought that Bend—another town, a town where, in many ways, all of this began—is laid open to the scourge of Braech's anger. I had thought to go there and confront the Choiron."

"Oh." Gideon went to Allystaire's side and looked up at him. "I think with Torvul's help I could show you Bend, if you wished. Bend as it is now."

"Show it to me? How?"

With a grin that imitated Torvul too closely for Allystaire's taste, Gideon said, "Magic."

CHAPTER 14

The First of Many Cooperations

Back in the camp, Gideon had knocked on the door of Torvul's wagon almost immediately. There were no signs of breakfast yet, though most of those sleeping around the fire stirred, if fitfully, and Idgen Marte soon appeared from whatever nearby tree she had perched in. They heard grumbling in a mix of tongues as Torvul answered Gideon's knock, though when the boy spoke to him in an excited rush, the dwarf ushered him in.

Soon enough, the pair of them emerged from the wagon. The boy carried a basket of long, thin pieces of bread that smelled sweet and proved light and delicate on the tongue.

"Where did you get the sugar for this," Idgen Marte asked, even as she stuffed half of a sweet stick into her mouth and reached for another.

"From his saddlebags," the dwarf said, pointing a finger at Allystaire. "Great big cone of the stuff, raw and pure."

"I do not recall being asked if you could go through my bags," Allystaire began, sternly, though at least half in jest, for he was already grasping two more of the breakfast confections in one huge hand.

"I took charge of food. That means any and all food or ingredients I found among our baggage," Torvul replied, testily. "Not that this is likely to be a problem, but make sure they all get eaten. They stiffen up something terrible if they are left over. Give us plenty of energy for the day's travel, too," he added, "after our little demonstration, that is."

"Demonstration?" Idgen Marte this time, taking more care with her second pastry.

"Yes. The boy here, quick study that he is, outlined for me how we might do a bit of scrying. Not like your Braech priestess's bowl of seawater, mind, or some charlatan's ball of glass. It might not be exactly what you're hoping," he said to Allystaire, "but it should do the job."

"What will it be then?"

"No divulgin' of secrets," Torvul said. "I can only promise when it will be," he added, snatching two of the last pastry sticks from the basket. "And that will be after breakfast." The dwarf ate slowly, with relish, and occasional swigs from a jug of ale that he somehow kept cellar-chilled in his wagon.

When that was done, Torvul and Gideon cleared up the breakfast detritus, the dwarf refusing offers of help, for Gideon seemed to be the only person Torvul routinely trusted with entrance to his wheeled home. With that finally done, they appeared again, Torvul holding a leather tube with hard leather caps tied at the top and bottom.

"Come with us," Torvul said to Allystaire, and the three of them wandered away from the camp. Torvul took the lead, setting a quick pace that belied his usual deliberate gait. Eventually he led them to a slight outcropping at the edge of the pass, not exactly a peak, but it commanded a reasonable view of the north and west. Torvul turned to Allystaire, and held up his tube, uncapping both ends.

"Gideon's notion is that he can pour some of his own power into mine, and since you're so keen t' see Bend, I had an idea how t'make it happen. D'you know what this is?" He held the tube out to Allystaire, who took it gingerly.

"Thought it was a map case, though clearly not."

"It's a glass," Torvul said. "In terms you can understand, it extends the range of your vision."

"All the way to Bend? It is a hard few days ride from here."

"No, no, no. It doesn't go near that far. Don't be daft." Torvul cleared his throat. "Though what we were thinkin' is if we apply a little of one of my concoctions to your eye and a little to the glass, and Gideon feeds a trickle of," the dwarf paused to search for a word and settled on, "of whatever he has, well, then maybe you'll get a distant glimpse."

"If the Goddess told him that we must head for Thornhurst, his word is good enough," Allystaire replied, nodding towards Gideon.

"Yes, but it'll be gnawin' at ya the whole way, and you'll be chompin' at the bit to head up t'Bend as soon as we're settled. This'll put your mind at ease—and it's a good test for me and the boy. Now." Torvul reached into one of his ever-present pouches, drew out a potion bottle and handed it to Allystaire. "Dab some of this into your right eye, then look into the glass, eh?"

Allystaire nodded. He poured a few drops from the thin-necked glass into his hand and let them gather at his fingertip before rubbing it carefully into his right eye. There was a kind of hum of power, a light trill of new sensation that ran through his head and down his spine, and he gazed into the glass, as Torvul indicated.

Allystaire was unprepared for just how far he was able to see. Not so far as Bend, but down into the gently rolling hills and fertile valleys of Barony Delondeur. He could see the odd village, the patchwork cloak of fields, all shades of brown, spread out before him.

"Torvul, this is a wonder," Allystaire said, in a hoarse whisper.

"Not yet it isn't," the dwarf murmured. "Close your eyes again. When I tell ya t'open them next, I want you to think very, very hard about the town of Bend. I take it that is where all this paladin business really started. Concentrate."

Allystaire did as he was told and felt something catch at the front of the glass he held—Torvul's surprisingly dexterous fingers applying some potion to the end of the glass, he thought. Then he heard the dwarf turn towards Gideon, who'd been silent this whole time, and say, "Go on."

Instantly Allystaire heard the strum of notes, the warmth that meant the Mother's power—it was a tangible presence, albeit one less overwhelming than Her own. He felt it flow into and envelop him.

"Now!" came the instruction from Torvul.

Allystaire's eye flicked open even as he struggled to remember the town of Bend. Muddy streets, the outlying warren of tents and shanties clustered around the flimsy palisade wall. The surprisingly large town within it. Bricktown, the thriving twenty-year old center of the place. The absurd toy keep that squatted within it. The warehouse on the Street of Sashes. The wall against which he had beat to death the slaver captain. The throb in his hand. The Assize, the awful storm, the widow he had bought a new life for on a boat to Londray.

Suddenly his sight flew over the landscape; his stomach flipped as though he were falling, and the expanses of Barony Delondeur rolled past him and suddenly his vision was filled with the squalid town where he'd first met Idgen Marte, rescued the folk of Thornhurst, and been Called by a Goddess.

Or, rather, his vision was filled with what was left of it. Bend had burned, and was, in places, still burning. Lazy, thin plumes of smoke drifted up, not the kind that signaled a blazing fire, but rather the smoldering ruins of one. Here and there, figures moved, but Allystaire's vision moved too quickly to make them out.

He tried to pull back, but realized that he was no longer controlling his vision. Some huge Presence, some indomitable willpower, knew that he was looking upon it and drew his gaze like a fisherman drew his netted catch.

Allystaire tried to exert some kind of control, tried to focus, and suddenly found his head swimming and his knees going weak. His vision rushed out onto the bend of the Ash from which the town had taken its name, and began following it on its course towards Londray Bay and the great sea beyond, a stream of blue blurring past his vision. His hand trembled on the glass. There were ships sailing upon it—long, sleek Islandmen ships, full of mail and hide-clad oarsmen and a handful of bare-chested men who wore only gauntlets upon their hands. He had no time to study them, for his vision was drawn to a tall, dark-bearded figure in robes the color of the sea. Standing at the bow of one of the ships, the man raised his hands in supplication to the waves, calling the wind that filled their sails.

That bearded figure, the Choiron Symod, suddenly turned sharply, sensing a presence. Then Allystaire thought he heard a voice call his name, a voice as deep and enormous as the ocean itself. That was all it said, *Allystaire,* yet even the sound of his own name, spoken by that voice, shook him to his core.

He knew, lurking somewhere past the river and the sea that drew it, something huge and immensely powerful knew him, and hated him.

"Cut it off, boy, cut it off!" He heard these words distantly, as though the speakers were miles away. He heard a cracking sound, felt something in his hand give way, and then his legs started to wobble.

Suddenly he jolted back to awareness. Torvul's hand was clamped onto the back of his shirt, dragging him from the outcropping they'd been standing on.

"Stones, but you're heavy," Torvul grunted. The dwarf had a grip like iron.

Torvul let go and Allystaire surged to his feet. He looked down to the tube in his right hand; it was crushed. Only the stiff leather case had kept the glass from cutting into his skin. He held it out to Torvul with a sigh.

"Not your fault," the dwarf was saying to Gideon, whose shoulders were slumped a bit. The dwarf laid one hand on the boy's arm and held the other out for his glass, Allystaire placed it in his palm and the alchemist stuck it in his belt. "We should've tested it in a smaller way."

The dwarf turned to Allystaire then. "What did you see? And what started, ah, tugging on you?"

"I saw Bend. Destroyed. In flames. The Choiron's work, no doubt. As for what tried to grasp hold of my mind? I think it was the Sea Dragon himself. Through his priest." Allystaire remembered, for a frightful moment, the power that grip had exerted, the fear it had stoked in him.

There was silence for a long moment before Torvul said, "Her Ladyship told us She feared that She and Braech were bound to be at odds."

Gideon, quiet and slumped, finally spoke. "How are we to contend with a god? Not a senile one like the god of the caves, but one in the fullness of His time?"

"Gideon," Allystaire said, "you just performed a miracle none of your previous masters would be capable of. Think on that, and worry not about the miracles to come."

The boy looked at Allystaire when he spoke, and smiled faintly. "I will."

"And it worked," he added. "No matter what else came of it, it worked. I saw Bend." He stopped then, suppressing a rising tide of anger, and went on. "Refine it later. No plan works perfectly the first time, eh? Come. I mean to make as long a ride as we can of today."

That seemed to brighten the boy's mood and he hurried off to the camp. Torvul and Allystaire lingered.

"How'd you know how to handle the boy like that? You've said you were never a father…"

Allystaire chuckled softly. "No. Yet I did spend a good long time turning boys into knights. There is a time to praise, a time to correct, and a time to punish. This was clearly the first."

"I s'spose so."

"Sorry about the glass."

Torvul shrugged lightly, without meeting Allystaire's eyes, and was silent a moment. "Allystaire, back in the caves, when he spoke to…whatever it had been. Stones Above!" The dwarf cursed, shook his head, and stared at his boots. "He frightened me—more than I've ever been."

Allystaire turned his head to watch the dwarf, but remained silent.

"I, on the way back out o'the cave, after seeing him just take in all that power, I started thinking about what I might have to do. Him being a sorcerer…"

"He is not," Allystaire pointed out.

"Didn't know that then, did I? All I knew at the moment was that a sorcerer's apprentice had just talked an ancient god into letting go of its hold on the world, and then sucked in all its energy for himself. It was a terrifying thought. And I, I started wonderin' if we were going to have to…"

Allystaire frowned, the expression deepening the lines on his face. "Torvul—another time, my life before all this, I would have thought the same. I will not fault you for it."

The dwarf was silent a moment before saying, "Thanks. D'ya think, is there some ritual for…cleansing ourselves? Asking forgiveness?"

Allystaire shrugged. "Not unless you want me to devise one. All in all I would just as soon you spoke of it to the Goddess Herself."

Torvul grunted. "Nothing like going straight to the top." A pause. "So that's it then? No lecture? Nothin'?"

"You did not hurt him. And you would not have done so except at greatest need. Remember, Torvul: faith. Faith in the Mother, yes, but also in ourselves, and in each other."

"So speakin' to the Goddess, d'you just…think in Her direction, as it were, or speak aloud? Does She answer back?"

"Betimes," Allystaire replied. "Certainly not as often as I might hope, but I suspect that is the point. If She always answered—"

"Then we would just be pawns," Torvul finished for him. "Let's get on the road already. Dwarfs belong under mountains, not atop 'em."

"Torvul, if I may ask, if dwarfs, as you say, belong under mountains, why are your folk above ground?"

Torvul sighed. "Not today."

CHAPTER 15

Homecoming

The descent from the Thasryach pass was far less eventful than the climb, and by midday they were entering the foothills Allystaire had looked across that morning. Idgen Marte set as fast a pace as she could, and Torvul coaxed speed from his ponies and his sturdy wagon's wheels.

To Allystaire's initial surprise, Keegan and the other Brotherhood men were able to keep pace even on foot. Though they were reluctant to respond to his attempts to draw them out, he'd learned that two of the remaining band were from Barony Delondeur, one was from Barony Innadan, and a handful wouldn't say even that much. All had deserted their respective armies within the past three years. Yet nothing else. Not even their names.

He wasn't overly troubled by it, but he did catch them peering at him sidelong and murmuring amongst themselves. He knew guarded fear when he saw it.

So when they paused—briefly, at Allystaire's insistence—to eat a midday meal, he was finally more direct.

Strolling over to where they gathered, several yards away from where he'd tethered Ardent, he announced his presence broadly and amiably. "Gentlemen," he said, and the only one who looked directly at him was Keegan, "might I ask what you find disagreeable about our travels?"

One of them, a Delondeur man, Allystaire thought, glanced briefly to Keegan and then back. "We're sorry, m'lord," he said, avoiding eye contact. "We, ah, we just…"

"They're frightened of you," Keegan said bluntly.

"Why?"

One of the silent men spoke all in a rush. "We heard all about how Lord Allystaire Coldbourne treated his own. That shirkers and malingerers were lashed, that breakin' rules was a hanging offense in your camp, and the noose for any prisoners ya couldn't feed."

Allystaire blinked at the sudden torrent of words. "So you are afraid I am going to hang you? Am I fattening you up for it by feeding you? Walking you across country to my favorite hanging tree?"

The man spat defiantly. "Could be some kind o'plot, you bein' a canny one fer a lord."

"I am no lord," Allystaire replied calmly, "and if I wanted you dead I would have let you die back in the mountains." A pause. "It is true that in the past I would have hanged deserters. Yes. But that man no longer exists. There is no more Lord Allystaire Coldbourne."

"So you say."

"So I do," Allystaire said. "And in time, you will come to learn what that means, I hope. Everything I have told Keegan—the sanctuary I am willing to offer him—applies to you as well."

The half a dozen men looked at each other; the arguer's cheeks had flushed a bit. "Does that mean we have t'tell ya why we, ah, walked off?"

Allystaire shrugged. "Eventually, mayhap. Now, I only want to go home."

Something, some note of the Mother's music, faint but unmistakable, chimed within him when he said that. Home had always meant Coldbourne Hall, or perhaps his own pavilion on campaign, with its few but coveted comforts. Yet home now meant Thornhurst, and he had not thought on it, not decided on it. It simply was. And despite having no family, few friends, and a list of responsibilities and decisions waiting for him, he wanted to be back in that village, back in the Temple Field. He wanted the five servants of the Mother to be gathered together at its altar for the first time and to finish the work three had started in raising it. And he wanted these things with a surety and an insistence that made Thornhurst stand out in his mind like a beacon in a sea of fog.

And then, Allystaire found that if he concentrated, closed his eyes, pushed everything else away, he could hear a single strain of the Mother's music, and that he could have, without recourse to maps or roads, followed the feel of it straight back to Thornhurst and the Temple.

He opened his eyes, and smiled, and somehow this only made the three reticent men more wary of him. "Follow me there, men, and you will see miracles that will remove all doubt. At the least, follow us, be fed, shod, and clothed when we reach our journey's end, and then set out again to make of yourself what you will. There will be no shortage of work for you, if you wish it."

With that, Allystaire signaled that the brief rest was over by loosening the light hitch he'd thrown around a bare tree limb to hold Ardent in place, then began walking, keeping the reins lightly in one hand. Ardent, always eager to be off, knocked into him, as if to show his approval. Soon enough, the rest of the little caravan was trailing them.

* * *

"So what did you see?" Idgen Marte had waited till they'd made camp for the night and eaten, and everyone else was asleep except for them, and she could contain her curiosity no longer. "And how?"

They sat near each other, by the banked fire, and spoke in hushed tones.

"As to the latter," Allystaire said, picking at the remnants of his third bowl of Torvul's onion and mushroom stew, "magic. To the former, Bend in flames. The Choiron sailing away."

She was silent a moment, absorbing the information, and said, "Town full of slavers, cowards, and pirates. Not sure they didn't have something like that coming."

Allystaire felt a spot of anger flare within him. "Town full of slaves, then, and victims, and fishwives, and people sick of war. Do they deserve to be burnt out, and worse, by Braech-crazed Islandmen?"

Idgen Marte sighed. "No. Yet as long as men have built towns, other men have wanted to burn them. You can't stop every enormity men like Symod are determined to commit."

"I ought to have been able to stop this one."

Idgen Marte reached out. Allystaire expected a cuff, but instead, her hand settled on his shoulder. "I'll not have you brooding on this all through the winter. Think of our victories first, our failures later. If you insist on thinking of who we haven't helped, well, the results will never be in our favor. We did what She asked, and we'll return to Thornhurst and set about doing what She asks next."

Grinning, Allystaire said, "What if what She asks next is for us to live in Thornhurst and take up farming?"

"Don't jest about that," Idgen Marte warned. "There's things I won't do, even for Her."

Allystaire chuckled. In truth, he doubted that any of them could refuse a request the Goddess made, given the effect of Her presence. He thought of the music of Her voice, that rich silvery harp song, the undeniable strength in Her hands, the searing fire of Her lips. *I know I couldn't.* A shiver went down his spine.

"Let us just focus on getting home," Allystaire said, turning to watch her sidelong, gauging her reaction to the word.

"Aye," Idgen Marte replied. Then she made a quiet, thoughtful sound, lips pursed, chin wrinkling. "Never thought I'd call a northern barony farming village home."

"Nor I. After all, farming and peat-digging villages are very different places."

Idgen Marte gave him the light punch on the arm he'd expected before. "Come off it. Your home was some Lord's hall, not a laborer's cottage."

"True enough, but the villages were nearly on the doorstep. And I probably spent as much time at Wind's Jaw, or on campaign, as I did at Coldbourne Hall. Hard to think of a tent as home, though." His eyes were drawn, momentarily, to a log that hissed as steam escaped it. "What was home for you, anyway?"

"A city far t'the south and west."

"Keersvast?"

"Farther south," Idgen Marte replied. Then, quietly, "Cansebour."

"Cold," Allystaire said, "I have even heard of it. Can it be as large as they say?"

"You could drop Londray into one quarter of it and not notice the difference."

"Surely not," he protested.

"Your barony cities would be the smallest of towns back where I come from, Ally," she said softly.

"How in the Cold did you wind up out here then?"

"Chasing stories," she said, a bit too quickly perhaps.

"I would think the Concordat would have better stories than those we northern savages tell."

She snorted. "Most of our tales are about how if anyone—usually a woman or child—doesn't follow the rules, they end up dead, or worse. Our songs are much the same. At least yours have some passion in 'em, some blood."

"You speak often of songs and yet in all this time I have never heard you sing."

"You never will. Don't ask about it any further."

Allystaire threw up his hands in surrender. "I shall not, then." He levered himself slowly to his feet, stretched his back till it popped, and said, "Wake you in four turns. Days of road ahead."

She nodded, watched him begin to walk off, then went to climb one of the bare trees surrounding their camp.

* * *

There was a crowd waiting when, on the afternoon of a day that had begun with frost on the ground, a tired party arrived at the outskirts of Thornhurst. At the front of the crowd was a small, brown-haired girl with large dark eyes, wearing a robe the color of the summer sky, her feet bare despite the cold. In contrast to the crowd of adults and other children behind her, the girl stood silent and still, her eyes on the curve of the road ahead. She stood apart from them, with an air of dignity that was uncommon for her age.

When the column came into view there was a great hubbub of talk and jostling, but no one broke from the crowd. Even the eldest among them seemed to be looking to the girl for their cue.

They got it when, as Allystaire came into view leading the column, his great grey destrier stamping along behind him, she broke into an entirely childlike and undignified run.

By the time she reached him, he'd knelt to throw out his arms and gather

her into an embrace, and those watching thought, on balance, the scene resembled a beloved uncle or older brother returning from great peril.

Soon enough, though, Mol wriggled out of his arms and smoothed down the front of her robe and turned her gaze on the rest. She smiled at Idgen Marte, who returned the girl's gesture with a lopsided, scar-tugging grin and a nod. She took in the others and instantly sorted them into categories. To Bethe and the Brotherhood men, she immediately said, "There's warm wine and food waiting for everyone. I expected you'd want clothes so I had some of the folk gather up what they could spare. Should be enough to suit you."

Taken aback by her self-possession and tone of easy command, the rest of the party was silent as Allystaire, smiling, said, "Allow me to introduce the Voice of the Mother, Her first priestess—Mol, of Thornhurst."

The girl gave a tiny sort of curtsy—less a noble mannerism of deference than an acknowledgement of new introductions. Then her eyes instantly found Torvul and Gideon, sitting together on the bench of the dwarf's wagon. "Right," she said, "you two must be the Wit and the Will, aye? We've work to be doin' and things to discuss, so eat quick." She waved a hand towards the village, as if sweeping everyone towards it. "Go on, go on. The Inn is the only three-floor building in the village. Can't miss it."

Meanwhile, certain men and women of the crowd came forward to tend to the animals. Allystaire and Idgen Marte began exchanging greetings with familiar faces. Allystaire clasped forearms with Renard, who smiled through his beard, even as Henri and Norbert came forward—together, Allystaire noted—to tend to the animals.

Torvul climbed down off his wagon, but shooed away the villagers who came to take charge of it. "I'll see to the wagon myself, if you don't mind. I'll let you take the ponies once we get it inside the town, aye?" Then he walked over to Mol, and without any trace of his usual flippancy, knelt in front of her, though he did not bow his head. "Lady Mol," he said, rather formally, taking her hand, which disappeared into his. "I am—"

"Mourmitnourthrukacshtorvul," Mol said, smiling a bit smugly. "I know. She tol' me ta expect ya. And if he's no lord, then I'm no lady either," she said, pointing with her chin at Allystaire. She turned the same smile on Gideon, who followed Torvul hesitantly, made uneasy by the crowd, it seemed. "And you must be Gideon. C'mon, both of you," she said, holding out her other hand towards Gideon, and pulling at Torvul's till he stood. "Let me show ya Her Temple." She glanced at Allystaire, and said, "Ya have visitors. Best go see t'them." Then she was leading Torvul and Gideon, both by the hand, towards their first glimpse of the Temple of the Goddess they served.

"Visitors?" Allystaire asked this question to no one in particular, yet it was answered by Renard.

"Well, something to that effect. Mayhap more like pilgrims," the gruff old soldier said. "In fact, we've had rather a lot of new arrivals."

"Where from? And any trouble?"

"A lot of places between here and Londray, I take it, and some from across the borders. And no, none I couldn't deal with."

"Which borders?"

"Oyrwyn, Innadan" Renard said. "And remember I already said there was no trouble. No sign of knights come looking for your head."

"What was it, man? Out with it?"

"Better y'see for yourself. Lots of folks been askin' after the two of ya— though usually they didn't know your names. It was all Arm this, Shadow that."

Allystaire grunted. "How's Leah?"

Renard smiled even wider through his beard, and it was all the answer Allystaire really needed, but Renard said, "In a family way. Mol tells her it'll be a girl." They'd reached the edge of the restored buildings on the outskirts of the village proper, and Allystaire could see, clustered here and there, groups of tents and makeshift three-walled shacks.

Renard followed his gaze. "Like I said, a lot of new folk come in. We haven't roofs for all of 'em yet, but we hope to by winter, or it'll be close quarters all around. Done that already when it rained." He pointed to a particular cluster of tents that stood well apart, and said, "Swords-at-hire that that wants to speak to you over there. We've invited them into the village proper but they haven't come. Said they needed your permission first."

Tossing a curious look back at Idgen Marte, who was following him as he expected, Allystaire set off for the tents Renard had indicated. They'd been pitched in neat, military rows, with stacks of weapons at regular intervals. A pole was planted in front of one tent, a grey and dark blue banner hanging limply from it. If the wind caught and unfurled it, Allystaire knew it would show a raven perched atop a round tower.

"That's a warband sigil," Idgen Marte. "I don't recognize it."

"Iron Ravens," Allystaire said. "Not very well known."

"Then how do you—"

Her words were cut off as the fourteen or fifteen black-clad swords-at-hire seated around a fire in the middle of that encampment caught sight of Allystaire as he moved towards them. First one, then two, then all the remainder at once stood up to face him. They offered neither salute nor obeisance nor recognition, just stood, watching him.

Allystaire approached one of them. They were roughly of a height, though Allystaire surely outweighed her by four stone at least. The woman was bald as a stone and tanned a deep brown, wearing a chain shirt and thick bracers similar to those Allystaire favored. Steel clanged dully as they clasped forearms, and exchanged a phrase: "Brother of Battle." And then Allystaire moved down the line of them, doing the same with each one, clasping arms and shaking, and saying, almost solemnly, "Brother of Battle." When that was finished, he returned to the very first woman he'd shook hands with.

"What in the Cold are you doing here?"

"What d'ya think," the woman said, her accent thick and nasal. "Come to serve with you."

"There is no weight or color in it, Ivar," Allystaire replied. "I do not expect the Iron Ravens to work for free."

One of the other men, stocky and with a fringe of dark hair, spoke up. "Ne'er really needed links t'shoulder spears if you were t'call, Lord Coldbourne." He flushed a little as he spoke, but there was a general murmur of consent from the men gathered around.

"I am not Lord Coldbourne anymore, Gern," Allystaire said, with a slight twist of regret shading his words.

Ivar smiled—a smile that was brown where it wasn't empty—and delicately stuck a finger inside one of her bracers and pulled forth a piece of parchment folded upon itself. "Luck is wi' us then, m'lord," she said, though the casual way she used the honorific made it seem more like a nickname. "We are commissioned t' serve ya already." She held out the parchment to Allystaire who took it carefully and spared a glance at his own name on the outer surface, written in a fanatically neat, tiny, rounded script that he knew as well as his own. He unfolded it with slightly nervous fingers and read.

Allystaire,

I cannot say that I approve of your leaving, or the method of it. The Baron could have been made to see reason, especially when he realizes he will have to campaign without the great and infallible Lord Coldbourne directing his armies. Yet Garth and Skoval told me the truth of their encounter with you, and I know that trying to talk you into returning would be trying to talk the Ash into flowing backwards.

I do not know if I believe what Garth told me you said. A paladin? The Mother? I know that Skoval believes, and that Garth is trying his best not to.

The day will come that the Baron will stir against you again, though Garth told me that the corpses of the other four knights, Casamir especially, were eloquent arguments for inaction. Still, I know you, and I know that you will make enemies. I would send all the strength of Coldbourne and Highgate to you if I could, and you know that if you asked, they would come. Yet I know just as well that you would ask no man to commit treason on your behalf. Garth told me what happened when he spoke of it in the village you are now calling home. So instead, I have sought out and commissioned your pet warband. I have paid them enough for a year, though I know they feel such a debt to you they would stay yours forever if you merely asked. Keep them with you. Even if you are a paladin, you are still a man.

I do not know how you would get a letter to me, but please try.

Love,

Audreyn

In the space left under his sister's signature, there were a few dense, closely written lines in even tinier letters that he had to strain to see.

The women of Barony Oyrwyn are forever indebted to you for killing Casamir. Should you come back you will find no shortage of would-be wives.

And beneath that, almost as an afterthought, was one more simple sentence that he knew instinctively was an apology for the previous line.

Garth has made sure that Dorinne's grave is kept the way you ordered.

Allystaire swallowed hard and carefully folded the letter back up. Then, with a deep breath, he turned to Ivar. "Welcome to Thornhurst then, Ravens. And welcome to the service of the Mother." The group cheered; several picked up shields and began banging their rims.

Allystaire raised his hands to quiet them.

"You may not find it profitable beyond the commission you already have. There will be rules." He paused and saw the knowing grins on the men's faces, and added, sternly, "More rules than in the past. We can speak of that tomorrow." He saw some of the grins fall, and pointed to the Inn that was visible above the cluster of cottages. "Tonight, you drink at my expense."

The good cheer returned, and with many a muttered "Brother of Battle" and clasp of forearms, the Iron Ravens—fourteen in all—tramped off.

"At your expense?" Idgen Marte was suddenly at Allystaire's right shoulder as he watched them go. "With what, exactly, are you going to pay for their beer?"

"Torvul has charge of all our expenses now, aye? I will refer Timmar to him."

Idgen Marte snorted. "I can't wait to see those two haggle."

"Be a duel worthy of song, I expect."

"What now?"

"Temple," Allystaire replied.

The route took them through the green and along the outlying cottages, past the first of the farms scattered in the valley and towards the High Road that paralleled the river Ash. And it took them past villagers eager to greet them. Allystaire and Idgen Marte clasped so many forearms, pressed so many palms, and accepted so many hugs and well wishes they were near exhausted from the walk. It, too, was a walk in memories. For Allystaire, of following a column of smoke for a day and finding the charred corpses of a massacre. For Idgen Marte, of watching the carnage as the Arm of the Mother ripped apart the shackles that knights had bound him with, and then of her own Ordination in the stand of trees to the west.

There were new faces in the crowd, as well—faces from Ashmill Bridge or Birchvale, from towns and villages and hamlets all over Barony Delondeur. Allystaire and Idgen Marte did not know them all, but most knew them, by reputation if not sight. They were farmers, laborers, city watchmen, whores, fishwives, tradesmen, children, and they had come to the place the Arm or the Shadow had promised them. They had come for safety, for shelter, for refuge, for curiosity, to make a new life or to forswear an old one. And now the Arm and the Shadow walked among them, growing ever more uneasy as the weight of responsibility began to settle heavily upon their shoulders.

The crowd seemed to understand their destination and so eventually parted to let them pass, and they had their first sight of the Temple of the Mother. What had been a waist-height wall of stone marking out the foundation when they left was now a temple; true to Mol's plan, there were windows spaced all around the building. From its hill it commanded a good view of much of the valley that Thornhurst and its farms nestled in.

"Goddess, is that glass in the windows?" Idgen Marte leaned forward, her mouth gaping slightly. "Where in the deepest Cold did they find that much glass? How did they afford it?"

"How did they build a dome?" Allystaire said. They shared a puzzled glance and then made for the doors, carved oak, bound in brass, with a sunburst painted in the middle of it.

Inside it was still simple: a floor of cunningly nestled planks had been affixed, and rough but sturdy benches stood in three rows up to the altar, itself still rough, seemingly unformed stone, joined together through the joint prayer of Allystaire, Mol, and Idgen Marte. Mol was standing to one side as Torvul examined it carefully. Gideon stood next to Mol, watching everything with his seemingly detached air. Allystaire realized that though the boy seemed indifferent, he was probably taking in more details of what was happening around him than everyone else together would.

Mol smiled as they entered. "D'ya like the windows?"

"Aye," Allystaire replied, cautiously. "We do wonder how—"

"A master glazier," she said pronouncing the word with utmost care, "came in not long after ya left. Said you'd healed him after he was knifed in a tavern brawl and spoke to him of Thornhurst. He came here with his tools and all. Name of Grigori. Said he had t'repay it somehow, pay the Goddess. I told him he didn't need to, but he insisted. He left when he was done, but I prayed wi' him at the altar and he's come to the Goddess. Said he'd be back after the winter."

"How many people have come, Mol?" Idgen Marte walked up to the altar and almost unconsciously dragged her fingers across the stone. Allystaire followed her and placed a hand upon it as well. He found it warm, and looking up, he saw panes of glass were set directly above it, allowing the sun to fall upon it as much as possible.

"To stay? More'n three score, maybe four. More have come and gone," the girl replied. "And there'll be more in a few days—folk fleein' Bend."

"How do you know," Torvul started to ask, but Mol simply swung her large, dark, knowing eyes to him and his question resolved into an "Ah."

Mol turned back to the rest of them and said, "Tomorrow, at sunrise, at noon, and sunset—we must gather here. The rest of the folk may come at noon. And then at night we keep a vigil. She will come and speak to each of us in turn."

Allystaire felt the strum of power in the girl's words, the binding of something true and important as she spoke, and he knew that the rest of them felt it as well—and that the sound was radiating not only among them but between them—as if each of them was a note. Idgen Marte's was so high-pitched it nearly escaped his senses, and were it sung or played he was not sure he could have heard it. Mol was something simple and pure and, he knew, harmonizing with every note around it. Gideon, an intense, blaring blast of some great winding horn, a sound that would carry across mountains. Torvul rolled like thunder, if thunder could carry the promise of home and safety in its thrum. He strained to hear his own but then the moment passed.

He looked to Idgen Marte and saw, he was sure, tears gleaming at the corners of her eyes, quickly blinked away. She moved to his side and whispered, for him only to hear, as the rest were still distracted by the moment that had just passed.

"Like a silver trumpet signaling a charge. Terrible and beautiful all at once."

* * *

Late that night, when even the Ravens had retired to their tents, Allystaire and Idgen Marte sat in front of the banked hearth inside the rebuilt tavern of Thornhurst, drinking beer that was slightly less sour than when they had left.

"With no need to stand a watch we hardly know what to do with ourselves," Idgen Marte said, idly, to break the silence as they stared into the faintly glowing coals.

"We could still stand a watch if you miss it that badly," Allystaire offered.

She snorted, had a sip of beer, and then did precisely what he expected. "The Iron Ravens, Ally? I have to know." Her tone wasn't demanding or imperious; it was almost imploring him. She leaned forward in her seat, bending slightly towards him.

He gave his head a small and uncertain shake. "If I tell you, Idgen Marte—if I tell you this, you can never speak of it. Not to Torvul. Not to anyone."

"That's not fair."

He lifted his head and met her gaze with a chilling solemnity. "Neither is what happened to them. Promise me."

She thought on it a moment, swirling the beer in her mug, and nodded. "I promise."

He drained the rest of his mug, set it down, and let his eyes unfocus among the flickering embers. "They were Oyrwyn soldiers. Some of them Coldbourne, some of them Highgate, Horned Towers. Four score I left to hold a tower that commanded a pass into Harlach. This was near a decade hence. And held it, they did. Harlach had fooled me, and had three hundred men behind me I did not know of. They besieged the tower. I had left them enough supplies to last two weeks—in my arrogance I thought I could pin Harlach's largest host, grind it down, and be back in that time, or near enough. They stood up to a siege of near four times their number, and they did it for more than a month longer than they had supplies for."

"How? What did they eat? Rat? Horse? Leather? Grass?"

"All of those, save horse. They had none. Oyrwyn armies are mostly foot."

"Well, Cold, Ally, everybody that's gone for a soldier has eaten his share of grass or rat."

"They ran out of all of those old tricks well before I was able to relieve them."

"Then, what?" Idgen Marte swallowed as she asked the question.

Allystaire turned to face her, his cheeks pale, his voice low and dark. "What does a raven eat?"

She gasped, sitting up straight and pressing a hand to her mouth. "Oh, oh, Mother, no, Allystaire. No. And they are here? They did, they did that and you forgave them?"

"It was my fault," Allystaire said, his voice quiet, but fierce, his body raising half out of his seat. "I left them there. I told them to hold to the last, I said it in jest as I rode away with the rest of the army and the food they should have been eating. Well, hold they did, to the last soldier and beyond.

"When we finally relieved them, they would open the gate only to me, and me alone. I found them shaking as they stood at their posts. They were sure I would hang them for their crime."

"You should've."

Allystaire made as if to lunge towards her, one hand curling into a fist. "How dare you? They were good , honest soldiers, young and strong and brave, and the gnawing, screaming, horrible demons of hunger drove them to something we have no right to judge. Not then and not now."

Idgen Marte sat back and away from him, considering his words, face twisted in reflexive disgust.

"I could not take them back. They knew that. So I gave them their release, and I wrote them a charter. There were just over two dozen of them left. As a warband, they had no past, no crime. Only their name, their skill, and their word. It was all I could do for them. I asked only that they take no contract to serve against Oyrwyn."

There was utter silence in the room save for the occasional crackle of the fire till Allystaire went on. "I could not hang them for my own mistake, Idgen Marte. Surely you see that. And if you do not, it is because you did not see them then, the shame and the guilt and the loathing they had for themselves, and each other." He lowered his head into his hands, rubbing at his temples with his thumbs.

Idgen Marte stood up from her chair then and turned as if to leave, thought better of it, and put a hand on Allystaire's shoulder. "I'm sorry, Ally," she finally said in a whisper-thin voice. "You're right. Even then you knew that mercy was no weakness."

"Speak to no one of this," Allystaire replied. "If word were to spread I would have to send them away."

"Do we want a warband here?"

"I want this one, yes. till I met you and Torvul, there were only three people I would have trusted more than I do Ivar."

"What are you going to give them to do?"

Allystaire drained his beer and stood up, setting the mug atop the mantel. "I will think on that tomorrow. Start building some defenses, mayhap. Watch towers, or a palisade wall."

Idgen Marte tilted her head back a bit, and he had the sense of being watched thoughtfully. "Think we'll need them?"

Allystaire took a long breath as he bent to pick up the hammer he'd laid by the side of his chair. He slid it into his belt as he exhaled. "Better to prepare for what could happen rather than what you think or wish might happen, aye?"

"I suppose." She picked up her sword belt from a peg on the wall. "Where in the Cold do we sleep?"

"They gave the house we had shared to a newly come family. Mol told me there were beds upstairs free, though."

"You're planning to sleep down here with your back up against one of the walls, aren't you?"

"I am," Allystaire said, though he'd meant to tell a harmless lie, like That is how I sleep best. The words simply didn't pass through his throat, and Idgen Marte laughed.

"Cold, take a bed. Have a decent night's sleep for once in your life. The Goddess didn't tell me to live like some kind of self-mortifying monk."

"No, She did not. It was my father who taught never to trust comfort too much. A man gets too used to soft beds and rich food, he starts imagining such is his due."

"Or," Idgen Marte countered, "he takes what comfort and joy he can get while it's there to be had."

He shook his head. "That ends in getting soft. I heard it too often as a child to stop believing it now."

"A skilled poet could exhaust himself coming up with ways to describe you and never, ever use 'soft,' Allystaire," she said. "And every time you talk about your father, about the Old Baron, about your life in Oyrwyn, it's like seeing another piece of a map get revealed, another note in a song being written down. I've a notion to dig around for bottles of wine and get you drunk, hear the rest of it. Hear what was in that letter, maybe. I saw your face when you read it. At the end you looked like you'd been punched in the gut."

"We have to be in the temple in the morning. The Goddess has nothing against honest drink, so far as I can tell, but I doubt she would take kindly to Her ordained coming to her presence with wine-ghosts battering the inside of their skulls."

She sighed. "I s'pose. There's stories I've yet to get out of you, though."

"Aye, and I have told one more than I meant to already. To bed with you," he replied, as he began eyeing the wall for a likely spot.

"And you as well and not up against a wall," she chided, seizing his arm with one strong hand. "If we're meant to keep a vigil you're sleeping on a bed tonight. No arguing. A little comfort won't kill you."

He opened his mouth to protest, but her questions and Audreyn's letter set his mind moving along familiar paths outside the massive castle in the mountains where the Barons he had served all his life, all of his first life, resided. And on a path leading from the postern gate, to a small tower that guarded a southerly approach—the route from the lands that had once been his charge. How, on a small battlement underhanging the crenellations and reachable only by a rope ladder, a patch of grass was carefully tended, planted with heather, mountain vetch, and loosestrife. A single rough, unmarked headstone stood amidst the flowers. When that image filled his head, his throat was tightly seized with a grief he had rarely allowed himself, and all the soldierly protest went out of him.

Forcing that grief back down, he let Idgen Marte lead him up the stairs and they sank into separate beds in one of the larger rooms.

Sleep took him quickly, but not before he found himself thinking of a petite, fine-boned woman of twenty or so summers, her hair an auburn, wind-tossed mass.

CHAPTER 16

A Task is Finished

The next morning came on too fast. It seemed his eyes had only just closed when they snapped open. Mol stood beside his bed, dressed in her sky-blue robe, her hair loose, her unblinking eyes watching him carefully. Slowly, he realized he could only see her because she held a thick white candle steadily in a holder in one hand.

"Gideon and Torvul are already on their way," she said, her voice filling the otherwise silent room. "Were fearful you two'd spent all night in yer jars," she added. "C'mon now."

Years of early rising had accustomed him. Allystaire went from sleep to wakefulness in one willed moment. He was standing and pulling on his trousers and belt while Idgen Marte was still sitting groggily on the far side of her bed.

Nodding, as if in approval of his quick response, Mol walked around the other bed and came to Idgen Marte's side. She placed one hand on the woman's knee and murmured words he could not hear, and the warrior stood up with a nod.

Soon enough they were all three walking briskly towards the Temple, Mol with her candle in the lead, Idgen Marte and Allystaire drinking mugs of tea and sharing a loaf and a thick wheel of cheese that had been waiting in the Inn. Timmar and his wife had been moving about already, after the myriad early morning tasks their establishment required.

Gideon and Torvul waited outside the doors, the dwarf examining the carving, tracing his fingers over it. The boy, only slightly taller than Mol, shivered slightly. Somewhere, someone had found boot, breeches, shirt, and vest for him, but not a cloak, and though the vest was wool, the boy was clearly cold.

Allystaire placed his hand on the boy's shoulder and gave it a gentle squeeze. "We will find you a cloak or a coat today, lad. It is the kind of morning where autumn is looking towards winter and thinking of inviting him in. Only going to get colder."

He nodded, though quickly all eyes were pulled towards Mol, who had stopped in front of the thick doors and pinched out her candle. "We do important work today, "she said, and Allystaire wondered at the way her voice seemed to switch from the uncultured tongue of an eleven year old village girl to the sonorous and wise tones of someone much older and much more educated. "This morning, when dawn breaks through the Temple windows, we will finish raising the altar. Afterwards the folk can come, with their petitions and questions. At noon, we celebrate. At sundown, a service. We'll all know what to do."

Slightly dumbfounded, Allystaire felt himself nodding at the statement. Of course he would speak, at the sundown service. He had no idea why or what he would say, but it seemed entirely reasonable that he would. From the corner of one eye, he noted Torvul nodding along as well.

"Tonight, the vigil. Four of us will remain outside the Temple, with one inside for two turns at a time, in the order that the Mother called us."

"If I might pose a logistical question, what of our provisions for the day?" Torvul asked, his thick, rumbling voice made delicate by his careful choice of words.

"She will provide. Her people, our people," Mol replied, "will bring us food." The girl smiled, broadly, joy radiating from her features. "Today is a happy day. Try not to look so glum. You 'specially." She turned to Gideon, a finger aimed at his ribs. Though the boy didn't flinch away from the touch, Allystaire saw him harden himself when Mol extended her hand, saw his lips press into a line and his shoulders and arms tighten. And though his stoic face broke into a forced-seeming smile, Mol stopped short. Instead, she took and gently squeezed his hand for a moment.

Then she looked up to the windows, and all their gazes were drawn with hers, as the first light of the sun began to filter into the Temple.

Without thinking about it, without speaking, they closed around the altar, hands reaching for it. It was a rough, three-legged thing of stone, no higher than Allystaire's knees, no wider across than his forearm.

Allystaire's thoughts were drawn to the Goddess, to the tests he had passed, from following the pyre of Thornhurst's villagers out of his own high country, to tracking the reavers and bringing them to account in blood. He thought of his honesty at the Assize, his decision to speak truth and be damned for it, giving the reaver widow a small fortune and seeing her away from Windspar's reprisals. He thought of the times, few though they were, that he had been in the Goddess's presence, his own Ordination, Idgen Marte's, the raising of the altar, Torvul's Ordination, Gideon's. He thought of the music that accompanied Her, the burning thrill of Her touch, the power of Her kiss.

He heard and felt the music of the day before, but not simply a harmony of notes, some kind of dazzling, powerful music he hadn't words for. Allystaire found himself moving to the side, found Mol slipping underneath his arm to stand beside him, saw and heard the others moving as well—but none ever lifting their hand from the altar.

There was a sound, a great crack, the altar suddenly sprang upwards beneath his hand; he felt it smoothing out and widening, the rough surface taking on the slick patina, not of marble, but of stone lovingly crafted, smoothed and sanded over countless turns. It reached well above his waist when it stopped rising, and it had expanded. No longer a block of stone, but a ring, an oval, supported by five smooth columns as thick as his arm. Mol stood at the center with her back to the door of the Temple, he to her left, and Idgen Marte on her right. He looked up and saw he was opposite Gideon, and Torvul was opposite Idgen Marte.

The music climaxed in his mind, a note shaped and sustained by the things that they were and had been and would be: five people, broken and scarred in their own ways, inside and out, granted powers from the boundless well of compassion, love, and strength of a being he could not hope to comprehend. The Voice, the Arm, the Will, the Wit, and the Shadow; arrayed like this, he knew that it made sense. To a congregation, the Voice would be front and center and the Arm at her right, the Shadow at her left hand. The Will was behind him, the Wit behind the Shadow.

Allystaire felt symbols appear on the smooth stone that now was a ring of red and gold, the colors of the sun. His fingers traced the outline of a carving. He stepped back and peered closely: a hammer. A fairly simple sledge, roughly like the one he carried, but not unlike a craftsman's tool for the shaping of metal or joining of wood, he thought. When he looked up, he saw that the others were examining similar carvings spread around.

Allystaire was about to open his mouth to speak when he heard Mol speak. "No use for all tha' quiet," she said. "Tell me what all o'ya see."

"An eye. Wide and open," Torvul rumbled.

"Cloud, I think." Idgen Marte's voice was slightly detached.

Gideon paused, his brow furrowed. "An open palm. Yet if I turn my head, a sunburst. And if I turn my head again…" He turned to Mol. "A flame."

Mol smiled, and to Allystaire it was not the simple joyous expression of the girl he thought he'd known. Altogether too knowing, he thought. "That is as I expected," she finally said, after wetting her lips. "They are symbols of what we are—and we will be different things to different folk. Even to ourselves."

"A hammer," Allystaire said, even as he bent his neck to left and right, trying to see a different shape, a different sign. He glanced at the others, and shrugged. "Still a hammer."

"You told me once you weren't a subtle man," Idgen Marte jabbed, grinning. Then, with a softer smile, "But you also told me that a hammer can create as well as destroy. That it is a tool in a way a sword can never be. I think She knows that, Allystaire. As much as any of us can claim to have created all of this, you can."

Allystaire felt Mol's hand slip into his. "The Shadow is right. Another man looking at this altar may see a clenched fist, or a gauntlet. Or at the Pillar of the Wit, mayhap a mountain, or a stream. The sign will mean what the supplicant needs it to mean."

Allystaire furrowed his brow. "Where did you learn a word like supplicant, Mol?"

The girl smiled knowingly. "She has been teaching me. And many of the visitors have had books with them." Then her smile dissolved into the slightly gap-toothed one he had come to know, she tugged her hand free and went to Idgen Marte, her bare feet all but soundless on the wooden floor. Mol took the warrior's hand and then leaned against her hip, while Idgen Marte's arm curled around her shoulder. They held the pose for a moment before Mol broke away and her face turned serious again, her childish grin transforming into an ageless-seeming wisdom.

She didn't say anything else. She simply knelt in front of her Pillar of the Voice and closed her eyes. Allystaire found himself doing the same. Around him, he could hear the rustling of clothing and the click of boots against wood as the others knelt. The planks were hard on his knees, but kneeling brought the hammer to his eye level, and he let his gaze unfocus as he stared in contemplation. He wondered what had brought the hammer to his hand in the first place, thought back more than a score of years to his teachers, his earliest times on campaign.

Ladislas. Lord Harding. He first suggested the warhammer to me—but he meant a spiked hammer with a small head. Never felt right. He was no longer staring at the altar, or even seeing it. Instead he was looking, as if from a great height, upon all the battlefields of his past, all at once, and seeing all the blood that had been spilled in the wars both great and small that had consumed the baronies for a generation or more, back to the death of the last Rhidalish King, whose name he couldn't even recall.

My family was made by that war, and undone by those that followed. How many other families undone by this?

No longer did he see a battlefield. Despite his tightly shut eyes, Allystaire believed that he saw his hands, and that they were the color of blood.

For the first time since he'd left his home with equally vague senses of dread and guilt hounding his heels, he thought about the cost of everything he had done before the Goddess had found him.

I had my rules, Allystaire told himself. *I hung the rapists and the murderers.* But the feebleness of his defense came to him in a flash. *Yet villages still burned in my wake, and I made as many widows and orphans as any other man alive. I did what I was brought up to do, and what I taught hundreds of other men to do—kill. That I tried to make it cleaner, somehow, or that I spoke of knightly ideals to the youth in my charge does not console a single widow.*

Why me, Mother? Why? Allystaire had not allowed himself to ask that question since his Ordination. There'd be no time, no peace and quiet to reflect in, always too much to do. But now he could not avoid it.

You know why, Allystaire, came Her voice, ringing clear and unmistakable in his mind, shaking his entire body with its majesty. *I told you why. Cut adrift from the life that had been made for you, you risked everything you had, everything you were, to save the girl whose very cries had awakened me from my long slumber, and then you risked your life to save her kith and kin. All of the knights of this world make widows and orphans, my Allystaire—you realized at long last that you cared what became of them.*

Allystaire remembered, then, the fishwife he had carted off to the docks. The anger that had been coursing through him after the way Braech's power had pressed down upon him at the Assize, turning into a fury that he'd wanted to unleash on the panders he saw working the quays.

I was with you even before then, Allystaire, the Goddess went on. *I spoke to you through my Voice, I guided and prodded you. There were so many times you could have failed, turned away, or given up, and yet, with no hope of reward save the goodness of the deed itself, you persevered. That, to use your own word, was* knightly.

Allystaire nodded, and felt her presence begin to recede and the physical surroundings of the Temple coalesced around him once more. His knees ached and his hands were white knuckled and shaking from the force with which he pressed them into one another.

He pulled himself up with one hand on the edge of the altar, knees creaking in protest. Around him, the others began to do the same, though all but Torvul hopped much more nimbly to their feet than he had.

Allystaire stole glances at their faces. Mol's was as unreadable as it had been before. Idgen Marte looked determined, somehow. *She always does,* he thought. Only Gideon, pale and rubbing at his eyes with his fingertips, seemed to show the same kind of disquiet.

With a couple of steps, he was at the boy's side, laying a hand on his thin shoulder. Allystaire said nothing, but Gideon spoke quietly.

"I wondered what I might have become had I not helped you," he murmured. "And that is what I saw. Some of it. And some of what I might do, even now, in Her service. It frightened me," he admitted. "Her own Gift frightens me."

"As it should," Allystaire said, quietly. "The only man fit to wield power is the one who is frightened by its consequences."

After considering this a moment, the boy said, "Then how will we know when to employ our Gifts?"

"When it benefits someone else."

"That is too simple," the boy complained. "What if it is a matter of saving two lives at the expense of one? That benefits others, yes, but it also condemns another."

"That's faulty logic," Torvul put in, having drifted over. "You'd not be the one doing the condemning."

"You will know when it is time to act," Mol said, her eyes still focused on her pillar. "You will know when it is time to employ the Goddess's Gifts. And if you fear that you won't, look at the people She has provided to teach you." The girl swept her hand over Allystaire, Torvul, and Idgen Marte.

Allystaire squeezed Gideon's shoulder then looked up towards the windows letting in the light of the risen sun. He frowned. "How long—"

"Two turns or so," Mol said. "Probably best to spend some time thinking about what we'll do when the folk come for noon service." She looked to Allystaire then, lifting her eyebrows.

"I need time to think about what She showed me," Allystaire replied. "I need to understand what it meant and how to…" He stopped and shook his head. "No. I know what it meant." He looked from his companions to the altar, and said, "We have to put an end to the war."

CHAPTER 17

A Task is Begun

That declaration was met with a profound and extended silence that was finally broken by Torvul. "There are five of us, and more than twice that many Barons and their hosts, unless you people have misplaced one. Or more. And we're to put an end to all their fighting? How d'ya propose we do that, exactly?"

Allystaire shrugged. "I do not know. I cannot know how, not yet. But think, Torvul—think of what the lives of these people have become. They look old and die young, but probably outlive their sons. If their farms or homes are not destroyed in any given season of campaign, they are more than likely to face starvation in the form of taxes to pay for the next season. It has become the dominant fact of life in the baronies. A whole generation has grown up never knowing peace. It must end."

"That's a noble goal," Idgen Marte said. "But—"

"What were we brought together for, if not noble ends?" Allystaire asked, more fiercely than he meant to. "What greater service could we render our people than to give them peace? Make no mistake," he went on, seizing the moment, as the rest seemed a bit stunned by his sudden intensity, "this is not something we can do in a day, or even a year. It may be our undoing. Yet how can we not try? How could I not try, and call myself a paladin?"

Torvul groaned, and Idgen Marte sighed—yet Mol was beaming her smile at him, and Gideon was as thoughtful as always.

"Tell me it is impossible," Allystaire said. "Fine. So is the altar we stand at, raised out of a pile of small stones into this." He ended with a flourish at the red and gold, five-pillared oval before them.

"We start where we can," he said, turning towards the doors, and the large, round window above them. "Here. From this day, these wars, the Succession Strife, are over for the people of Thornhurst, and any that seek honest refuge here. If anyone carries the war to us, I will hurl it back at them till they lose their taste for it."

"It's just a farming village, Ally," Idgen Marte started.

"And Londray was just a fishing village once, and Wind's Jaw was just a wooden bailey. There is a warband outside, a Cold-damned good one, who will do anything I ask. With them, forty men who know how to work a shovel, and you," he added, pointing to Torvul, "in a month, I can erect defenses that will turn any hireling band away. In three, I can give a small army pause. A year? I could find a way to break all Delondeur's gathered strength."

"You know you won't get a year, boy," Torvul rumbled, though his hand was thoughtfully stroking his chin. "Never. Word is out. Ya've seen t'that."

"We do not need to make it a year. We need only repel an attacker once. And then when word spreads that there is a haven, and that those who are done with war will be protected?"

"They will flock," Mol said. "To Thornhurst, and to the Mother."

"They're going to be flockin' outside the doors soon," Idgen Marte replied. "You said they'd come with petitions, questions?"

"Aye," Mol said. "I have done the best I can in that regard, and the folk generally abide my authority. Yet there are some matters that need Allystaire's attention. Or Torvul and Gideon's."

"What kind of matters?"

Mol raised her hands, palms up. "Folk accused of theft, a stolen beehive, a dispute over land—"

"A beehive? Can a man steal a beehive?" Allystaire's eyes narrowed in dismayed confusion.

"And they want him judgin' them," Torvul chuckled. "Course you can, if you know what you're after. With proper plannin' a man, or more likely a dwarf, can steal just about anything." Then, he suddenly turned to the altar and gave a polite cough. "Theoretically, I mean, of course."

"Fine. Where do I see to this?"

"Renard is arranging it even now," Mol said. "Out front of the Temple." Allystaire nodded and started off, boot heels loud against the wood.

"What about us?" Gideon asked. "We are not, I assume, set to judge cases of theft or robbery?"

"No," Mol said. "I have felt, and so have some of the wiser farm folk, that the weather has been…wrong."

Allystaire stopped dead and turned around. "Wrong how?"

"It should have rained more than it has in late summer and into fall. We've still some crops in the ground for late fall harvest and all our winter roots need—"

"What can any of us do about rain?" Allystaire replied. "It could simply be a dry year."

Mol frowned. "It has rained to the north and the south of us, and to the east and the west. Clouds have simply passed us by," the girl said. "It has not been natural."

"Braech," Idgen Marte snapped. "You know his priests could do such a thing."

"Are folk likely to go hungry because of this?" Allystaire asked Mol.

"This year, no," Mol said. "Visitors have brought stores and much is laid by. Yet if this keeps up…"

"No one is goin' hungry, this year or another," Torvul said, his face slightly flushed, his words a little sharper than Allystaire had expected. "And that salt god can go hang," he added. He clapped a hand against Gideon's shoulder. "Come on boy, we've work to do."

As he passed Allystaire, the boy swept up in his wake, Torvul muttered, "What can we do about rain? What can't we do, that's the only question that matters." His voice kept on rumbling but the words were lost under the thumping of his boots, swung in the longest strides his stature would allow, as he dragged Gideon out of the Temple.

Allystaire followed after them, his steps more measured. He heard Idgen Marte and Mol talking quietly behind him, tried not to listen or overhear, and was soon out of earshot, out of the Temple. *Not sure how I feel being a judge or holding an assize,* he thought, but just as quickly, he silently rebuked himself. *What was the Goddess's Gift of Truth given to you for then?* he asked himself and then, with a solid nod and an impassive face, approached Renard and a small crowd at the edge of the Temple steps.

A sturdy chair had been set out, for him, he supposed, and Renard was trying, and mostly succeeding, to keep the crowd—about a dozen or so—paired off in some way that appeared to matter. Probably the claimant and the accused, Allystaire thought. With a quiet but deep breath, he set his shoulders and stepped up behind the chair.

"You may take this away or set it aside, Renard," he said, patting the thick, smoothly polished wooden back with one hand. "If the folk who have come to see me must stand, then so will I." He lifted the chair and set it a few feet away, then spread his feet and laced his hands behind his back. "Who will be first?"

Renard pointed first at one man, then at another, and said, "You," to both of them, and they came forward, clutching their caps.

To Allystaire both looked older than he, but, he realized, were probably his age or younger. They weren't tall, and neither of them could match him for breadth, but their bodies had a wiry strength to them all the same. One was as bald as a stone, and the other had raggedly trimmed brown hair that he kept pushing out of his eyes.

Both of them started to talk at once, and all Allystaire could hear was babble about land rights and families and planting. He raised a hand even as his eyes narrowed in a mix of anger and confusion. "Stop."

They mumbled "Sorry, m'lord," and took half a step back when Allystaire sighed.

"First and foremost, I am not anyone's lord. Call me Allystaire. If you must have a title for me, Arm will do. Now. I am going to ask one of you to speak, and while he does, the other will remain silent. Then I will do the same to the second. Then I will offer a decision. Will you abide it, no matter what it is?"

One of them swallowed, but both nodded, with the bald one muttering, "So long as it's fair."

Allystaire cleared his throat and fixed his eyes, unblinking, on the muttering one. "What is your name?"

He cleared his throat. "Hugues, m…ah, Allystaire."

"Well, Hugues, will you abide by the," Allystaire paused with the word judgment on the tip of his tongue and carefully replaced it with "decision that I think is fair? If you will only abide by your own sense of fairness, coming to me was a waste of time, aye?"

The man bobbed his head and shrugged all at once, a gesture Allystaire found disconcerting, and not a little annoying. He worked hard to keep his face impassive.

"Good. Now, Hugues. The other man is going to speak to me and tell me his side of the story. Aye?"

Hugues made that same odd nod-shrug, his lips clamped tight over crooked teeth.

Allystaire turned to the other. "And your name, goodman?"

"Denys, Arm," the man said, and Allystaire uttered a small, pleased "hrm" at the use of his real title.

"Denys. What is the problem?"

"Well, since we resettled our farms, he's been tryin' t'claim one o'm'fallow fields fer his own," the man began, still tugging stray locks of hair from his face. "I was plannin' t' put cabbages fer the winter harvest in it, and he's been after fencin' i'off—"

Allystaire lifted a hand. "How long had this field been yours?"

"Well, always was," Denys said, slowly.

"How long is always?"

"I've lived in Thornhurst o'er five winters now," the man said.

Allystaire nodded, and turned to Hugues. "And you? Why do you think you have a claim to this field?"

"I been here longer," Hugues said, his voice scratchy and low. "And tha' field were ne'r part o'the land he bought."

"How do you know that?"

"'Cause I knew the man what sold it t'him. And I knew how much he sold to the rod and span. This field has lain fallow now all the years he's been here, he's ne'er worked it, but now he thinks he can spread out a bit, right? But if he's ne'er worked it, ne'er made impro'ments t'it, then e's—"

"And what were you planning to do with the field?"

"I was gonna put in cabbage as a winter crop now the field's ready t'be planted," he said, defiantly.

Allystaire's head swam, for a moment, with a vision of him shaking both men by the collars and giving them a good toss, but he willed the vision away. *Unworthy of me,* he thought. *Or at least unworthy of my role here.*

"So the question as I see it is who gets to plant the cabbages?"

"Aye," they replied.

"And what do you plan to do with the cabbages?"

"Well, go t'feed the village, aye, after we take our own share, and for a fair price" Denys said.

"I'd do the same," Hugues said. "Though usually ya get bet'r prices at market fair days and not local."

Allystaire tried to keep his face neutral; a smile and a scowl were competing for space and so, he hoped, neither one revealed itself completely. "Fine. Work the field together. Divide it in half if you must, lengthways or side by side, I care not. You will each have a third of the crop to do with as you please. The remaining third, by weight," Allystaire said, emphasizing that point with an extended finger, "will be donated to the common stores."

"What are common stores?" Denys asked. Hugues kept quiet but looked likely to ask the same question, given the puzzlement on his broad, sunbrowned face.

"Food that will be kept here at the Temple of the Mother, available to all in need of it."

The men frowned and seemed likely to protest, glancing warily at each other and then back at Allystaire, who cut them off. "You agreed to accept my decision, and there it is. Protest, or short the common supply, and the field and all its output for the next year becomes part of the common supply. And if it sounds as though I mean to punish the both of you, I do. This is the sort of squabble that should have been solved amicably, between the two of you, as neighbors," he said, irritation threatening to rise into anger as he spoke. "We are done. Make such arrangements as you can for the working of the field. I will come by and check the planting myself when it is time."

The two men stood there for a moment, equally confused, equally disappointed, which, Allystaire reflected, probably meant he had made the right decision. Finally, they walked off. To Renard, he said, "Remind me that we have got to build something to store these cabbages. And anything else the folk decide to donate."

The old soldier nodded, and scratched his bearded cheek. "Will do," he rumbled, and Allystaire considered that as good as it being written down. "Next," Renard called out then, pointing to another pair of men. "Stolen beehive, Arm," he said to Allystaire, indicating the pair.

"Fine," Allystaire replied. "I have not the patience to listen to a lot of talking and blame. Which one of you is accused of thieving?" Both men stared at him, one tall, the other shorter and broader.

Finally the tall one said, "He's accusin' me but I never—"

Allystaire walked over to him and carefully but implacably placed a hand on the man's arm. "Did you steal the other fellow's beehive? Do not attempt to lie to me."

"I…I did," the man admitted, his eyes widening in shock as the words squeaked out of his mouth.

"And why did you do this?"

"I wanted t'try mixin' honey into some o'the malt mash I had in my cellar."

Allystaire sagged a bit, letting go of the man's arm. "You make spirits, then? Strong drink?"

The tall man nodded sheepishly, his eyes downcast, his face scrunched up. "Please m'lord, I'll beg ya not t'imprison me, or 'ang me, I've a daughter, and my wife was killed by the reavers."

"Cold, man!" Allystaire exclaimed, startled. "I am not about to hang or imprison a man for simple petty theft. Give him the beehive back. And a small barrel of your best malt spirits." He turned to the other man. "Does that suffice?"

The other farmer seemed taken aback at the speed with which his claim had been judged. "I s'spose it would, Arm," he said.

"Good. Then go. Do it. And for the Mother's sake, be kind to each other. If you want honey, ask him for it. Trade for it." Allystaire turned away from them, trying not to roll his eyes.

"Next," he called out, even as Renard was waving another pair of village folk forward.

* * *

"That was more about farm implements and lands and fences than I ever wanted to know," Allystaire told Idgen Marte. The swordswoman had been, along with Mol, meeting with a group of a dozen or so of the village's women. As the sun climbed higher in the sky and noon approached, though, all the meetings and business the five Ordained had been about had ceased, with the villagers gathering in anticipation at the edge of the Temple field.

Gideon and Torvul came walking in unison down the road in animated conversation, if conversation could be said to include Torvul speaking and gesturing as he walked, and Gideon mostly nodding.

When they joined Mol, Allystaire, and Idgen Marte at the foot of the steps, Gideon was clearly deep in thought, but Torvul was grinning. In spite of himself, Allystaire felt the contagious pull of it.

"That look on your face can only mean you know something the rest of us do not, Torvul," Allystaire said.

Torvul snorted playfully. "If that were true, I'd look this way all the damned time. Yet, there's truth in your words—me and the bright boy here have put our heads together and have just about got this rain problem clubbed into submission. Only question remaining is whether we bring clouds here, or wait for some clouds to show up and give 'em a thorough shaking so the rain falls out." Pause. "Metaphorically speakin', of course. No actual shaking."

"Drawing clouds here would have widespread effects on the rest of the region's weather," Mol said. "The weather is like a loosely knitted muffler. You can't just tug on one end without unraveling some of it."

"Seems like the Sea Dragon's priests have already done that," Idgen Marte pointed out. "Keeping weather at bay could be just as dangerous as pullin' it towards you, aye?"

Mol frowned. "Doing wrong in order to combat the wrong done to us is not the Path the Mother would see us walk, Shadow," she said, her voice growing unmistakably grim as she spoke. "I would not see us create a drought on the Innadan border because we need the rain."

Idgen Marte's face stiffened at Mol's rebuke, but she nodded. Mol, impulsively it seemed, reached up and clasped the woman's hand.

"Heavy storm clouds should pass near enough within the next few days, or a week," Mol said. "We need not worry over it now. Come," she said, pointing to the Temple.

With Mol at their head, Allystaire and Idgen Marte to either side, and Torvul and Gideon behind them, the five Ordained ascended the short row of steps to the Mother's Temple and the newly erected altar within.

In a reverent silence, they each moved to their pillars, and felt the stone-walled space begin to grow brighter as the sun moved towards its zenith. Allystaire put his hand on the hammer carved into the Pillar of the Arm.

The stone quickly grew warmer, but not uncomfortably so. He felt, rather than saw, the other four place their hands on the altar, and the light inside the Temple grew.

The same sound as the night before began to fill his ears, the harmony of five notes—or was it one note shaped out of five sounds? He could not tell. And truly, it did not matter, for it was the Music and the Light of the Goddess, and the entire Temple began to fill with both, with a brightness so intense he shut his eyes against it.

The music rose and blended till Allystaire could not pick individual strains from it; he thought he heard the clear ringing of a trumpet such as Idgen Marte had described, but it slipped away from him, and then he simply heard the Goddess's own voice.

"Open your eyes, My servants, and look upon each other."

Allystaire opened his eyes slowly. The light was not painful, now, but lent a clarity to the world, burned away all that was fleeting. They were no longer standing in a Temple, but in a well of pure, streaming brightness. He looked to his right. Mol did not appear any longer to be a child of ten or so summers; she was tall, slim, clad in a simply cut blue robe, with a hood that deeply shadowed her face, leaving only her mouth visible. From her belt hung a sickle, and in her cupped right hand, a ball of green light.

His eyes flitted to Idgen Marte—and almost past her. When he could force them to focus upon her, she was still indistinct, but what he saw was much like the tall, long-limbed warrior he knew —only more so. Her skin was even darker and flawless, without the scars that trailed from lip to collar. The curved sword in her hand blazed with light—but only along its razor-sharp edge, so faint that most would miss it. She was nearly impossible to see unless she turned to face him fully. When she turned away, she winked out of his sight—yet he could still feel her there, at his side, like a limb or a weapon no one else could see that he held.

Torvul still had the proportions of his race, but he had grown in stature, and would have stood equal to Allystaire in height. His eyes were deep, wide pools of solid, liquid blue—and they were set in a face that had the texture of stone, and the mottled grey and brown of granite. He raised his hands, spreading them before his eyes in wonder, and Allystaire saw a familiar grin spread across the dwarf's mountainous face.

Gideon was a being of pure, gleaming fire. Almost featureless, still slim, and vaguely human-shaped, but as Allystaire watched, he changed, becoming more like the boy he knew, the fire shifting colors from blue, to white, to green, to deep orange.

Only then did Allystaire look at himself, and the reflection of light that came back to his eyes would have blinded him had he seen it with his mortal eyes. He was clad in armor straight out of a story. It was light against his skin, lighter than any steel could be. It was as bright as newly polished silver, and it clung to him from toe to chin, leaving only his face bare.

No, not only his face. Also his left palm, which pulsed with a deep golden glow in time with the pounding of his heart. His right arm, he now saw, gleamed even brighter than the rest of him—gone from silver to white flame, and at the merest thought, his hand held a hammer made of fire—fire of the sun. Though he could feel the heat radiating from it, it did not burn him.

The five Ordained Servants of the Mother stared at each other in wonder, speechless, till they heard their Goddess's voice.

"What you have been, who you have been, you must leave behind—take only the parts of your lives that strengthen you for the trials ahead. The Arm, the Shadow, the Voice, the Wit, and the Will—what you see now in each other is who, and what, you must become. More than a woman, more than a man, more than a mere alchemist, or sorcerer, knight, warrior, or priestess."

"Return now to the world of men, with my undying love. I will speak with each of you this night."

Suddenly, the bright, unearthly world was gone, replaced with the world of stone and shadows —but a powerful glow still filled the Temple, streaming through its windows to the crowd beyond.

Allystaire blinked, the afterimage of the vision the Goddess had given them slowly fading against the back of his eyelids. By the time he had recovered enough, Torvul's voice had begun to fill the Temple.

Allystaire knew nothing of the dwarf's native tongue, though he'd heard the dwarf sing in it many times. Still, he thought he recognized something in the words, though the tone of it harkened back to the day when the dwarf had saved Allystaire's life by cleansing the poison from his body.

The dwarf's voice was as low-pitched and potent as ever, and yet something—or someone, judging by the way Mol and Gideon were both staring intently at the dwarf—was amplifying the sound, for it filled the Temple and spilled to the field beyond.

Allystaire had nothing to offer the song and yet he felt it vibrating in his chest, as the unknown words rolled, lyrical and thunderous, from the dwarf's barrel chest. Torvul's eyes were closed and his hands upon the altar. Allystaire touched his own pillar and felt the oval of stone humming beneath his hand.

Torvul's voice did not flag or quail, and it began to seem to Allystaire as if the stone beneath his hand was not humming so much as it was drawing the sound into itself through him—that the entire Temple was absorbing the deep rumblings of the dwarf's voice.

Finally, Torvul broke off with a gasp, and the sound sank into the stones.

"It is done," Mol said, giving the silence that followed in the song's wake only a moment. "With the completion of the altar, and Torvul's song, we have completed the consecration of this Temple."

A warm glow still surrounded them, suffusing the air and spilling into the field. Mol gestured towards the doors. "It is time to go amongst our people and celebrate."

"Not yet," Allystaire said. He swallowed hard. "I have something I must say to them." With the set shoulders and hardened walk of a man striding into battle, Allystaire walked to the doors and threw them open. The people of the village cheered. He raised his hands for quiet, and began to speak, reaching for the voice that had served him well in courtyards and on battlefields—a voice that rolled out over the assembled crowd and gathered all of them in.

"People of Thornhurst, people of the Mother, people who are unsure whether they are either one. Many of you have come to know who I am—the Arm of the Mother. You know my name, even if many of you still refuse to use it when I ask," he said, his admittedly weak jest met with a smattering of muted chuckling.

"What most of you may not know," he said, sliding his hands behind his back, "is who I was for most of my life, before the Goddess came to me. The name, and title I was born to, was Lord Coldbourne, of Coldbourne Moor and Coldbourne Hall." He paused, and added, "We are not so good with names up north in Oyrwyn, I suppose." That got a rather livelier bit of laughter—none more so, Allystaire saw, than from the Ravens, who were a leather-and-metal clad knot in the back of the crowd.

"The name might mean something to you. It might mean nothing. What it meant for me, all my life, was war. In that, we are not so different. Yet the role I was given to play, bred for, prepared for, was very different than yours. I was a leader of men, a captain, a maker of knights. Over the last score of years I rode in, and eventually led, hosts to every barony that borders Oyrwyn, and some that do not. Whatever village, town, hamlet, or city you call home—in that life, I probably raided, burned, or besieged it."

He paused waiting for the reaction. There was only silence, wide eyes, slightly open mouths. He began to pace.

"To say I did those things is false, really. In the main, I ordered them done. I knew that there was always a terrible cost to men on every side of any battle. I knew that their families, widows, children, parents paid a price as well. I consoled myself that I was better than the men I fought against, because I had rules. I tried to take care of my own, I thought. I tried to minimize the harm they did, as if it were possible for one man to oversee the actions of hundreds, of thousands.

"And I tell you, I was skilled at it. I won more battles than I lost. I thought my men loved me. I gained honors, riches, acclaim. I never thought, not really, about the cost of what I did. I measured my success in battles won, lands taken, in the count of the enemy dead. I rarely questioned any of this—fighting, you see, is what Coldbournes did. My grandfather won the name and the Lordship for himself and his sons back in the beginning of the war that has plagued us now for more than two score years, and he did it with a sword, and a brutality that remains legendary among Oyrwyn's knights and nobles.

"I walked away from that life, and that privilege. Yet I cannot say to you that I did it out of outrage, or sympathy, or to begin to atone for all the sins of my class, or even my own life. I did it out of anger, and arrogance, and only days ahead of being exiled. I walked away and into this village, where I found a girl whose father had saved her life by hiding her, probably just moments before he was murdered. In those moments, I would say he did more good for the world than I had done in all of my six-and-thirty summers.

"Why am I telling you all this? Why am I admitting to you that I may very well be the man who orphaned you, or widowed you, or destroyed your home? How can that man be standing before you, telling you he is a paladin, expecting you to take his word and stand at his back?

"I am telling you all of this, my people, because I must beg your forgiveness. When I call you my people, I do not mean what I once might have meant—that you must call me lord and knuckle your forehead and hop to my command. I mean that I am your servant now, not your master. I will never," Allystaire paused, raising a fist with one finger extended, "expect any man to call me his master or his lord again. I rode into this village out of curiosity, and what I found, and what I did, beginning that day, was the start of something new. We are still at the start of that new thing. I do not know what to call it or where it will lead. Yet I will make a promise to all of you. The wars that have plagued your life, these squabbles between Barons who seek a crown none of them truly want—while there is breath in my body, those wars are over for you. That is how I will pay the cost of my sins. That is what the Goddess, who we call the Mother, has given me to do.

"I will not rest till you know peace. This is not to say you will not know hardship or labor. Yet no one must take up arms unless it is their choice and in defense of this place we will build together. And if Baron Delondeur, or Baron Oyrwyn, or any of their liege lords or knights would seek to bring that war to our doorstep, they will have to carry it through me, and through Idgen Marte, and Torvul and Gideon, and any who choose to stand with us. None of them could beat me at their game when I was just a man, just one of them, playing by the same rules. None of them will do so now that the Goddess has shown me how much more there is worth defending than the lines on a map."

Allystaire let the final echo of his words roll over himself and the crowd. "I ask, today, for your forgiveness. Stand with me, and I will spend all the life that is left to me, and employ all the Goddess's Gifts, to this one end: to peace."

He was met with dead silence till Mol came to his side and squeezed his hand. She tugged on his arm till he looked down at her. Then she pointed at the steps beneath their feet. He knelt.

She placed her hands on his temples and leaned forward to dryly kiss his forehead. "That you of all people believe you need the Mother's forgiveness is a sign that She chose well," Mol said, her voice somber, resonant—not at all the voice of the simple village girl he'd saved. "Her forgiveness is yours, Arm, so long as you do Her work."

"It is not Her forgiveness I seek," Allystaire said. "Or not only. It is their forgiveness I need ask for."

"Well," Mol said, turning the crowd. "Do you forgive this man the sins of his life?"

The crowd remained silent and still. He scanned them, seeing mouths hanging agape, others tight-lipped. A few began muttering to themselves, or their neighbors.

One young woman—Leah's age—stood up and stared hard at Mol and Allystaire. Her eyes were shining with anger, Allystaire thought, and her mouth quivered till she finally blurted, "My Raff was killed when he went for a soldier, killed 'gainst Oyrwyn men. Your men," she said, raising an accusatory finger at Allystaire. "We had just married. Now I'm s'sposed t'forgive him that?"

Allystaire offered her no reply. He glanced up at Mol who tilted her head to the side, her lips flattening a little. "Odette," she called out. "You would be dead, or worse, if not for what Allystaire did for you in Bend. Mind that."

"Oh I mind it well. I mind he walked in and killed a buncha men 'cause it's what he does, s'all he's done, is kill. And I'm sposed t'thank 'im for it? And b'lieve that this Mother, this Goddess you prattle on about, is all mercy and love and forgiveness, and she chose a blaggard like 'im to be her man? A killer, just like them reavers!"

"Yes, Allystaire has killed, and he will again. In your defense. Or mine. Or your mother and father's. The Mother is not so simple as to believe that bad men who are also strong will simply stop thieving, raping, and murdering because we ask them."

Mol's shout was so loud, so shocking, that Allystaire recoiled; it was a physical thing, a force like a punch in the chest. The crowd fell into a shocked silence as her words echoed over the Temple Field. Birds exploded out of a tree in the middle distance, tearing madly for the sky. Odette paled and took half a step back. The crowd parted around her.

"My father had strength, of a kind," Mol went on, much more quietly. "And he was a good man. But when bad men, rabid dogs of men, proved they were stronger, it was all he could do to save me from their depredations by hiding me. Yet he could not stop them from killing him, or anyone else. Compassion is not armor. Mercy is not a shield. Fatherly love is not a ward against evil." As she spoke, Allystaire saw, in the shadows of the hooded robe she wore, the tracks of tears leaking from the corner of each eye.

"I wish, oh how I do, that it were otherwise, that bonds of love were proof against steel and flame. Yet they are not. We forgive what we can, endure what we must, but the Mother is no eye-blinding god, asking us to ignore the world and bear any hurt done to us in hushed and holy silence. There are hurts which cannot be borne, and more importantly, should not have to be. Forgiveness may be extended without mercy. Between us, and those who would do us unbearable harm, She has placed a good man to bring Her justice into a world that has forgotten it. She has made him strong. If you do not understand why, I cannot explain it." Mol was weeping openly now, the tracks of her tears leaking down the side of her face. But she was smiling, if sadly.

"Even as I wish I could return your Raff to you, or ease your pain, I wish you could find forgiveness in your heart. Is it so hardened by grief that you cannot?"

The girl offered no reply, standing in a silence of grief and rage balanced in equal measure.

"Neither the Mother nor Her Ordained will compel or coerce the worship or forgiveness of anyone. So was the first law of our church spoken by its first paladin and prophet," the girl went on. "I would not order you to forgive any-one. Go if you wish. Stay if you wish. We go on now."

She turned back to Allystaire and placed her hands upon his head. "I can-not speak for all those who gather here, but I am the Voice of the Mother, and in Her name, I absolve you of the sins of your life. You, who were born Al-lystaire Coldbourne, are born again today in the boundlessness of Her Love and the warmth of Her Sun." Even as she spoke, Allystaire felt those silver-strung harp notes of the Goddess's music play along his nerves, felt some gathering of energy building in Mol's palms and then flowing into him. It was like drinking the finest vintage, tasting it, feeling it with his entire body.

"Rise now, Allystaire, Arm of the Mother. Rise, paladin, and enter fully, at last, into your new life in Her service."

Allystaire stood. His knee clicked in protest, as usual, and his back remind-ed him of too many long days in the saddle, too many nights of poor sleep, too many years of wearing armor. Yet he barely felt them. Something fell away from him as he stood up. Something that weighed upon him like steel upon the shoulders was lifted away.

He took a deep breath of air flavored with the chill of autumn frost; it felt like his first breath.

Meanwhile, Mol turned back to the crowd. Odette had stormed away in angry silence, and one or two in the crowd had followed her, though whether in sympathy or to calm her down, Allystaire couldn't tell.

"Anyone who comes forward to me, whether in public or in private, in any place, at any time of the day or night, and confesses to me a sincere wish to be forgiven for any part of their past, will have that forgiveness. If this is to be a new way of life, a new place, then we must have new lives to live in it."

"How do y'mean sincere, exactly," Torvul asked, from the doorway of the Temple, his silhouette outlined in the glow emanating from within. "Ain't the easiest to judge."

Mol faced him, mirroring his own casual, knowing smile. "Do you doubt that the Mother has given me the capacity to judge the truth of your contrition, Mourmitnorthrukacshtorvul?"

"Far be it from me to doubt Her Ladyship or you in any capacity," Torvul said.

As they'd spoken, some of the men and women of the crowd had begun to come forward. First among them was the farmer Henri, who approached Allystaire to shake his hand, and then went to Mol.

"You said in public or in private, right, ah…"

"My name is still Mol, Henri," the girl said, with no trace of mockery. "Or y'could just call me girl, or you, or dammit get outta my field you little wretch like you used t'," she added, her rough accent returning for a moment.

Henri laughed, though nervously. On a somewhat balky leg, he knelt before of the girl, and cleared his throat. "I got somethin' that needs sayin'. When we first came back t'Thornhurst, and the lad o'er there, well, Cold, you all know 'im. The first night he was among us, me and two o'thers who I'll not name, they'll do as their own mind says. Well, we wanted t'murder the boy. Hang him. Were ready t'fight Allystaire o'er it if need be." He swallowed hard, almost grimacing in pain as he forced the words out. "I wanted t'do murder. I was ready t'kill a lad o'er harm he di'nt do, not really. That's the worst thin' I can e'er remember doin', and that night, Allystaire told me t'ask fer Her fergivness, and I've tried, but I can't. I don't have the words fer it."

Mol nodded, then placed her hands on his head and leaned over him. She murmured words that Allystaire could only hear as a quiet rush of sound, but he felt, distantly, a gathering and discharge of energy like what he'd felt moments ago when Mol had absolved him.

When Henri stood, his face held the relief of a suddenly vanished pain. He threw his strong, wiry arms around Mol's shoulders and hugged her. The solemn little priestess whose imposing shout had frightened them just moments before surprised them all now by laughing and wrapping her arms around Henri in return. The man stepped back, wiped a rough hand against the corner of an eye, and said, "Thanks. To all o'you."

He melted back into the crowd, even as a line of village folk was forming in front of Mol. Allystaire looked to his fellow Ordained, and saw Idgen Marte and Torvul both eyeing that line, and smiled inwardly.

"Well, confessing is all well and good, and I encourage everyone to do so if they have a mind," Allystaire suddenly said aloud, pitching his voice to the carry to the back of the throng. "Yet this day is a celebration, too. And I cannot be the only one here who is thirsty!"

That got a great cheer, and jugs, bottles, and skins were suddenly produced in greater profusion than Allystaire had counted on.

"Talkin' sense again," Torvul rumbled at Allystaire, as he strolled to his side and grinned up at the paladin. "Gettin' to be a habit. Hardly know you anymore."

Allystaire snorted lightly. "Cold, in a lot of ways we hardly know each other at all."

"Nonsense," Torvul protested. "Just learned quite a lot about you."

"And yet I still know almost nothing of you, or Idgen Marte."

"Well, could be that's the point. New place. New life."

Allystaire nodded in the direction of the line forming in front of Mol. "Going to go confess, then?"

The dwarf's eyes narrowed and he rubbed a hand across his bald pate. "I don't think so," he replied, after a long pause. Then, he added, "Not today."

"I remember you asking me about it only a little while ago. When we found the god of the cave. Why the reluctance?"

"I've my fair share o'sins and dark deeds. I'm not with a caravan, and I'm guessin' you folk know enough of dwarfs to know that means nothin' good. I've lied and swindled, never really thought of it like thievin', but that's," he shrugged as he searched for a word, finally settled on "just fake weight, trying t'make scales balance when they shouldn't. Still, that amounts to pretty small beer. I don't think that's what the girl and Her Ladyship have in mind."

"You have lost me, Torvul."

"Well, boy, what I mean is—the worst things I've done, the things got me out here on my own? Not ready to repent o' them. Not sorry I did them. Not gonna try and lie to the girl and Her Ladyship and say I am."

Allystaire was silent a moment, letting his eyes wander the crowd. People had started breaking into baskets and jars, spreading out blankets on the ground, and passing skins and flagons among themselves. "No act of Faith will be compelled," he said, choosing his words, and his somber intonation, carefully. "Whatever it was, Torvul—if the Goddess called you, she knows of it, and she has either forgiven you, or seen past it. I will trust Her judgment, and I will not press you. I will say only this: not very long ago, I would have said the idea of asking forgiveness for the life I have led was absurd. Now it feels as though someone else did those things, someone I knew, once, and have grown distant from."

He smiled at the dwarf. "It is a good feeling."

Torvul snorted and gave his head a quick shake. "A couple drinks'd be a better feeling."

"I think we can just manage that," Allystaire replied, and the two began their way down the steps and out towards the crowd. "Yet none of your unnameable dwarfish spirits. We have a vigil tonight, after all."

"*Ikthaumanavit* is a boon to the soldier on watch till dawn, or the knight at vigil, as it were," Torvul said, suddenly spreading one arm, as if pointing to the horizon of possibilities, his voice smooth and soothing. "It warms the extremities and sharpens the mind. It—"

"Will put two old men to sleep when they try to stay up all through the night, which is a foolish goal even for the young," put in another voice, and the both of them turned, confused, to find Gideon smirking at them. "And no spirit that strong sharpens the mind. It makes you feel that it does, and only briefly."

Torvul gave a loud harumph. "As if you know anything about drinkin', boy. What say we teach him?"

"Not today," Allystaire said. "Soon, perhaps."

"I do not wish to imbibe fermented or distilled beverages of any kind," Gideon protested stiffly.

"Never let Idgen Marte hear you say that. Or Mol, for that matter," Allystaire warned.

"Stones above," Torvul said, "enough nattering. There's celebrating to be done. And I've got to get t'know the folk here." The dwarf cleared his throat, and called out, "Who among you thinks he knows how to work metal or stone and has a jar to put in my hand?"

There was a smattering of laughs at the dwarf's words, but Giraud—the tall, gentle stonemason who Allystaire knew had directed most of the building of the Temple—stepped out of the crowd, a bulging wineskin in his hand.

"I'm a stonecutter," the man had barely begun to say, in his soft and patient voice, when Torvul had sidled up and assaulted him with talk of stone and tools.

"You don't cut stone, my friend, not if you know what you're about," the dwarf said. "Better to find the shape within it, eh?" Allystaire could read the confusion, but also the curiosity, on Giraud's face as the dwarf steered him away.

Allystaire laughed and placed a hand on Gideon's shoulder, steering him into the crowd, and accepting a wineskin that was offered him. "How do you want to celebrate, lad?" He tilted his head back then and took a long drink of wine, squeezing the sides of the bag. Then he offered it to the boy.

"I said I don't—"

Allystaire frowned, and Gideon fell silent. "And you would insult the folk here if you do not accept some of their hospitality," he murmured. "Trust me. You need not get sodden." *Not yet*, he thought, trying hard not to laugh at the prospect. He handed the skin over and watched as Gideon squeezed a thin, brief trickle into his mouth.

"So, as I asked, how do you want to celebrate?"

"How do folk here celebrate?"

"I have not the faintest idea," Allystaire replied. "If I had to guess? There will be singing, dances, perhaps some wrestling."

"Wrestling?"

"Aye, it is a common enough pastime at festivals and feast days in this part of the world." Allystaire took the wineskin back and squeezed another long stream of the stuff into his mouth. "Nothing serious, just wrestle your man to a fall."

"Hmph. What point to it?"

"A man who finds himself in a fight, or, for that matter, behind a cart stuck in the mud, is happy to know something about leverage and force."

"I suppose you'll be wrestling then?"

"No," Allystaire said quickly.

"Why not? You'd be good at it, surely."

Allystaire drew the boy away from the crowd, passing him the skin. "Think of this as a quick lesson in leadership. Let us say that I am good at wrestling, at boxing—at leverage and force, and that I know how to apply the strength I have spent a lifetime building. How well do you think most of the folk around here are going to fare against me?"

"A lifetime of farm labor can be just as rigorous as a lifetime of fighting," Gideon said, thoughtfully. He lifted a finger and tapped the tip of his chin once or twice. "I suppose, though, it's unlikely any of the men here have the kind of experience you do. So you would probably win."

"Aye, I probably would. Let us say that I do so quite handily. How do the people feel about it?"

Gideon thought for only a moment. "You seem a bully."

Allystaire smiled. "Indeed. Let us say, then, that in order to forestall resentment, I let their best wrestler throw me in the final match. What then?"

"Unless you're a fine mummer, they will probably know. And some will suspect no matter how well you act."

"Good," Allystaire said, smiling again for just a moment. "Now, what if I were to simply lose early, against the first man I was pitted against?"

"You'd look weak."

"Exactly. So, the lesson: if you want folk to follow you, you should share in their hardships and miseries; if they go hungry, you go hungry. If they are in danger, you are in danger. If they are wet, cold, marching or riding on no sleep—you must be those things as well. However, you cannot always share in their celebrations. If you get wine-sodden with them, sing bawdy songs with them, wrestle with them—you have too much to lose that way."

"You must be at a little remove," Gideon said, grasping the concept. "I see."

"Aye. It does not mean you must think yourself better than them, and you certainly cannot say you are, or make them believe that you think you are, but you have to be able to maintain a distance. Not a large one, mayhap, but a distance nonetheless." *Makes it easier to ask them to die for you, too,* Allystaire thought.

"I suppose that makes it more possible to give unpleasant orders," Gideon said.

"Aye, lad, it does that, too." Allystaire took another pull at the wineskin to hide his surprise at the way Gideon had echoed his thought. Then he handed it back to Gideon and surveyed the crowd. Folk were still lining up for Mol's blessing, but the line had diminished. Some instruments had been produced: a drum, a flute, a set of pipes, and joyful music began to skirl and thrum outward. Hands clapped, feet stamped.

"It is fitting, though," Gideon said. "While they sing, and dance, while they labor and work, while they marry and raise children—this, this is what we will do, yes?" The boy lifted his eyes up to Allystaire. "Watch over them. So that those things—the working and the singing and all of it—may go on."

Allystaire smiled and felt a flush of pride—something he'd not felt in a long time. "Aye, Gideon. Out there, somewhere," he said, flinging a hand vaguely in the air, "is war and darkness and sorcery. Here, today, is music and light, feasting and song."

"I like music," Gideon said. "I always wanted to learn to play something. My master discouraged it."

Allystaire clapped the boy on the shoulder. He felt, suddenly, an impulse to embrace him, to wrap his arm around the thin shoulders and pull the boy against his side in avuncular affection. It surprised him, and he resisted it, settling instead for another clap and a gentle shove of the boy towards the crowd.

"Go, Gideon. Join the music. Find a girl to dance with, if you like."

The boy nodded and started tentatively off. He didn't get far before a gaggle of children, younger than him in the main, enveloped him. They were all shouted questions, Gideon's careful, thoughtful answers being quickly overwhelmed.

"And what about you? Going t'find a girl t'dance with?" Idgen Marte's voice came from just a pace or so behind Allystaire's ear, and he laughed.

"I knew you were there, you know."

"Didn't." Idgen Marte protested, poking his shoulder with one finger. "Decent little speech, though. Good lesson for the boy to learn, even if you did just tell him to do the opposite of what you taught him."

"Let him be a boy for a day. It may be the only such day he has. We do not all need to stand a watch all at once."

"True. What'll you do, then?"

"Drink a little wine. Eat something."

"And watch."

"Aye, that too," Allystaire admitted. Meanwhile, Gideon and the children who'd surrounded him had made their way to the flutist and the piper. The village children began a mad, foot-stomping dance. Only tentatively did Gideon try to imitate them, till two girls—both about his age—each seized one of his hands and began jumping with him in time, practically forcing him to keep up.

They laughed, then, the Arm and the Shadow, and turned towards each other smiling, if only for a moment.

"This can't last forever, Ally. We'll be in for a hard winter, I think. Bandits, the Baron, refugees—who knows what'll come with the snows?"

"Let winter do its worst," he replied. "I will be waiting for it."

"We will be waiting for it," she corrected.

"Still behind me, no matter where that path leads?"

"Always, no matter where. To the bitterest end, or the cruelest Cold," she replied, her voice suddenly solemn and formal despite its rasp.

He tilted his head, pursed his lips. "I think I have heard that before…"

"Damn," she cursed. "Was hopin' you'd not notice. It's from the cycles of Parthalian, part of the oath of his companions." Idgen Marte turned away and coughed into her fist. "Awful, though, isn't it?"

Allystaire shrugged. "I would not know. I always liked hearing a story or a song, but I was never too well educated on the subject of music itself."

"You mean to tell me the lords here don't bother learning music?"

Allystaire shrugged. "We gesture at it. I recall a few lessons. In Oyrwyn, though, we have enemies on all sides. The tundra, and all its attendant horrors, to the north, Harlach to our east, Delondeur to the south. They do not leave much time for music."

"Attendant horrors?"

"Elves. Gravekmir, Islandmen who have gotten mixed up with them."

"You've had elves in your borders, down off the tundra?"

Allystaire shook his head. "Not in my lifetime, no. Before the last Rhidalish king died, they still made raids. And they are still there, or so we are told; it is not as though we signed any treaties. But the giants? We had occasion to see them."

"No wonder most northern song and poetry is dross. Everything is either a dirge or a call to arms."

"Well, what are we supposed to sing about if not war and death? Mud? Snow? Mountains?"

"It's not only what you sing about. It's how you sing it," Idgen Marte said. Allystaire pointed to the reeling dance on the Temple Field, to the mass of stamping feet, and the drummer, piper, and flutist at the edge of the whirling crowd, directing it all with a skirling melody and the increasingly fast strikes of wood on skin-drum. He said, "Which one is that, a dirge or a war-march?"

Idgen Marte scowled at him and furrowed her brow. "It's just one instance," she finally, grudgingly admitted, her teeth practically clenched around the words. "It proves nothing."

"As you will," Allystaire replied. "Why not go over there and show them how to turn it into a dirge, then?"

Idgen Marte darkened, the mirth of the past few moments melting completely out of her features. "I don't sing, or play any instruments."

"You seem to have a great deal to say about it," Allystaire said, "for someone who does not engage in it herself."

She was silent for longer than Allystaire expected, bristling as her chin clenched. Finally, she wet her lips, spoke low and carefully, "I did, once. I still know all the songs, the cycles, the great stories. I can't sing, anymore—not properly. I won't sing any other way." Almost unconsciously, her hand strayed to her neck, and Allystaire saw her calloused fingertips briefly stroke the scars that trailed down from the left corner of her mouth.

She narrowed her eyes and put an edge to her voice. "If you tell anyone I said any of this, I'll have your head."

He raised his hands, palms out. "I will spread no secrets, Idgen Marte. You know me well enough to know that."

She snorted, and some of her casual insouciance seemed to take over her features once more. "It's the form of the thing. Threat has to be made." She looked towards the Temple steps, where the last few petitioners were waiting for Mol's attention. "Speaking of form, seems like we have a ritual, now."

Allystaire sighed. "I suppose. I want—I wanted—to avoid all that. Forms, rituals, observances. That is where it all goes wrong."

She nodded her assent. "Even so, can any church survive without a ritual, if there's more than a dozen folk involved? There have t'be rules, Allystaire. There have to be forms, or it'll never hold together."

"And what happens when the form overtakes the meaning?"

"You think Mol will let that happen?"

"I think all of us will only be a part of this for so long," he replied. "I want this to go on after us."

"Cold, man—we're having our first ever feast day and you're thinking of a legacy."

"Someone must," he answered, "so that our first feast day is not also our last."

She was quiet a moment, then said, "You're a hard man. I don't mean in the bad way, the wrong way, just—you never stop. You never pause, never rest."

He shrugged. "I am who my father and the Old Baron made me. They did not much believe in rest."

"How much of what they taught you d'ya believe in anymore?"

He considered a moment, crossing his arms over his chest. "Keep your weapons sharp. Scour any dirt off your armor the moment you see it. Plan as though your enemy is smarter than you and knows more. Sleep light. There is never a perfect course of action. Drink brandy when you can, wine when you cannot, and beer only at need. Only a fool claims to be fearless. In war, men will die, and nothing you can do will prevent that. Round towers are better to defend than square. It is better to force your enemy to react to you than to attempt to react to him."

Idgen Marte cut him off with a sharp wave of her hand. "Oh, for Cold's sake, stop. They just shaped you into some kind of blunt instrument, didn't they? War and nothing else."

"I learned politics, geography, history, hunting, riding—"

"Yet not music, philosophy, art, theology…"

"There are chapels to Fortune and Braech within Wind's Jaw. There were priests. I dimly recall some lessons."

"How dimly?"

"Well, the priest of Braech had fists of stone; I remember that. And the priestess of Fortune was shapely. And friendly," he added, smiling at the memory. "That obscured any lasting theological insight she was trying to impart."

Idgen Marte snorted. "They usually are. Have you noticed, for all their talk about how their goddess spreads wealth among men, an awful lot of it seems to stick to their fingers?"

"It was not her fingers I recall anything sticking to," Allystaire admitted, then broke off in a curse as Idgen Marte's fist landed solidly against his arm.

"Enough," Allystaire said. "How would it look if two of the Goddess's own servants fell to blows?"

"You'd never land one," Idgen Marte sniffed.

Allystaire waved a hand absentmindedly and looked back out at the revelers. "We have an awful lot of work to do, and we have no way of knowing how long we will be left alone to do it. We will have to make a start of it tomorrow."

"Fine. What d'ya need me to do?"

"I would like to see a weapon count."

"And?"

"Not just what arms are available. What can be made? What is lost in the rafters and hidden in the root cellars. Is there seasoned wood that can do for a bow, or arrows?"

"Why me?"

"You are more likely to get the answers than I am. Imagine what happens if the Arm of the Mother knocks on the door and says, 'Evening goodman. I was wondering if you have a rusty sword around the place, or a spear out back holding up some vines.' "

"Someone'll panic. Someone'll lie, but it isn't as though they can lie to you for long."

"I do not wish to employ the Mother's Gift against someone who has no need to fear the truth," Allystaire replied. "Yet they will fear. And if I do not hesitate to use that Gift for simple questions now, I may not hesitate in future. And where does that end?"

Idgen Marte's eyes widened. "The inquisition to end all inquisitions. How far ahead have you thought about these kinds of things?"

"Not far enough. So, tomorrow, a weapon count, and an idea of what materials we have. I will speak to the Ravens and we will begin to talk about constructing defenses. I will need to make arrangements for those common stores I spoke of."

"You'll have t'eat before you stand watch all night. Come on. Enough of planning and worrying and watching." She stopped and peered at his face, squinting. "You're never going to stop doing any of that, are you?"

Allystaire shook his head. "No."

"Fine," she murmured. "I'll bring food."

CHAPTER 18

A Vigil

Just like any other night on watch, Allystaire told himself, as he stood at the door of the Temple. Still, he could feel and hear the presence and the music of the Goddess inside, as She spoke with Mol, and though it was muted and distant, it remained distinct. There was no sound as full of joy, no brush of sensation across readied nerves, that compared or even approached it.

Makes it hard to concentrate, he thought, briefly sparing the time for a look at Gideon, to his left, who carried his staff and shivered beneath his too large cloak. Clearing his throat, Allystaire said, "Move around some. Stamp your feet, move your hands, roll your shoulders. It will help you warm up."

"I know that," the boy said, almost sullenly. Quickly, though, his voice regained its typical calm poise. "I am more concerned with going sleepless. How do you do it without stimulants?"

"Stimulants?"

"Tea? There are certain herbal extracts that can be ingested—"

Allystaire snorted. "No need for any of that. You decide you must do a thing. Then you do it."

"That is too simplistic," Gideon protested.

"Not in this case, my young philosopher. Nothing stands between us and maintaining our vigil but our own weak flesh. It is precisely as simple as deciding that the wants of the flesh do not outweigh the task."

"It still seems simplistic," the boy noted. "Yet it seems to apply in this case. The mind is the master of the body."

"Aye. And it applies in almost every case, really. That was the most important lesson I was ever taught, and still the way I measure people. Someone says they will do a thing, they do it, or they do not." Allystaire paused, then said, "Vigils are most often maintained in silence. However," he added, "if you have questions, important questions that you must ask, I will answer. I doubt Torvul can stop himself from answering, so if you find yourself falling asleep, walk around the Temple to his post and speak with him. It will warm you, wake you, and satisfy your curiosity."

The boy nodded, and they once more fell into a companionable sort of silence. Allystaire rolled his shoulders, trying to relieve the pressure of his armor against his neck, but the relief was temporary. *Always is,* he noted. *Don't know why I bother.*

Allystaire made a slight "hmph" as he thought that over. Gideon turned to look at him but soon looked away. *The point is to do something to alleviate it. The relief may be temporary, but for a moment, pain was diminished. That is worthwhile.*

He almost snorted at himself. *Beginning to sound like the boy. All rhetoric and logic, and I am only arguing with myself.*

You're arguing with the man you know you really are.

"Were," Allystaire said aloud, surprising himself and Gideon both. The boy turned to him, eyes narrowing. "It is nothing, lad," he murmured. "Just talking to myself."

"Do you do that often? It is sometimes a sign of—"

"Yes, and it is not madness. Just a habit. When I speak something aloud, even if no one else is around, I seem to understand it better."

"This suggests that you are confused or unclear."

"Cold, boy, I am usually both of those."

Gideon paused. Allystaire could feel him composing a thought, or a question. "Yet the essence of leadership is decisiveness."

"A man may be confused, may not know the way forward, may not know the ground he walks, or even know the lay of his own mind—that does not mean he cannot make decisions based on what he does know."

"I suppose, yet it will probably be a poor decision."

"A poor decision made sooner based on poor understanding is often better than waiting for totally clear weather, perfect maps, and a bagful of the enemy's dispatches—because if you hesitate, the day is lost."

"How can you act without hesitation if your own thinking is muddled?"

"You do it because you must, lad," Allystaire said. "Think back to our battle in the Thasryach. I could have stopped and demanded a thorough explanation of why you needed to get into that cave, and what you were going to do. I would have liked one, to be honest. What would have happened if I had stopped and insisted on it?"

The boy nodded. "We would probably have been overwhelmed."

"It is a rule of leading people, Gideon. You may be confused, or afraid, or overwhelmed, or all three—those who depend on you must never see it. Or, as the Old Baron once put it to me, you absolutely cannot be pissing your pants when your men are expecting orders."

"No pants-pissing. I see." Gideon's voice was even but Allystaire couldn't help the suspicion that the boy was laughing inside.

They passed a while in silence. Allystaire fell into a place within himself he had come to know well. His mind emptied except for the impressions of his senses, his body loose and seemingly still, but occasionally shifting—his shoulders shrugging, his feet flexing within his boots, hands tightening into fists. His perceptions moved into the night around him, its sounds and smells, the feel of it. It was autumn, and no mistaking it—the air was chill enough to feel it moving in the throat and the nose. Bird songs had changed, and the faint smell of rotting leaves rode in the air.

In this way, Allystaire knew, he had passed many night's watch—feeling the world around him, immediately attentive to changes with it, while also relaxed, allowing the active part of his mind to take some mild rest.

It was because of this state that Allystaire was already turning to the doors of the Temple as they opened from within, and Mol emerged. Light spilled from within along with her, from guttering rushlights set along the walls, but also from a brighter and deeper source, that did not waver or bend. Mol's face was hidden beneath her hood, but her small shoulders were straight, and her head turned towards Allystaire.

Without words, he understood. They quietly shuffled past each other, and Allystaire heard the banded wooden doors creak closed behind him.

His eyes searched for the steady source of light, and could find none. Inwardly, his heart sank, for while he felt the Goddess's presence closely, he knew that She was not precisely present; nor was She absent, really. With a fortifying breath, he walked forward, his armor clanking, till he came to the altar.

The Hammer that seemed to him to be permanently graven at the top of the Pillar of the Arm glowed faintly, and he knelt before it. His thoughts traveled to his knighthood vigil, in the chapel of Braech in Wind's Jaw, and he felt his lip curling as disgust welled within him.

Knighthood, he thought, and he could feel contempt in the word as it rolled across his mind.

Soon, though, the disdain was mingling with regret, a sadness over something lost. What had I expected, he wondered. And then his mind reeled back to his vigil then, the crude dragon, shaped of stone and roughly polished semiprecious stones that he had bowed before. Though never a religious youth, that vigil had been the culmination of every dream he'd had. Staying up all night in the chapel had not been difficult; the windows had been opened and it was late autumn in northern Oyrwyn. Thankfully, only a light snow had been falling, but no fires were lit save one candle.

Yet he had made it the night, as he had known he would. The ten years spent getting to that vigil had been harder. He had seen battle, for two seasons, as a squire to Baron Oyrwyn himself, an honor even his father had acknowledged with pride.

Even so, coming out of the chapel that morning, being received by the Old Baron himself, by his father, by Ufferth of Highgate, by Joeglan of the Horned Towers, accepted as an equal by men who were known and respected across all the baronies—it had been the single finest day of his life.

Or so he had thought. *What had I thought? What was knighthood to me then? It had meant a dream, a dream of leading men and winning glory. And winning the hearts of women,* he thought. "Or at least their eyes. At seventeen, their eyes were enough," he murmured aloud.

It had been all he had dreamed, all he had been, all he had wanted, as long as he could remember, from the moment his father had brought him to Wind's Jaw to learn what knighthood meant.

And then he was, in his mind, six or perhaps seven summers, riding with his father and a small train of knights and men-at-arms. He had been expected, even then, to sit his own horse. He hadn't ridden on the front of his father's saddle since he could walk.

And then walking his pony into Wind's Jaw—the largest and most terrifying structure he had ever seen, past the huge forward towers that thrust ahead of it on a spur of the mountainside, through and between which the high winds screamed and skirled, granting the place its name in a time lost to any memory. As they approached the gate and entered to the call of a trumpet and a mail-clad warrior yelling, announcing the arrival of Lord Coldbourne, his father—a towering presence behind him, his face and pate shaven to bare, gleaming skin, the blue-grey eyes and sharp nose, smelling of horse and leather and steel—murmuring to him.

"You are the son of Anthelme Coldbourne and the grandson of Gideon Coldbourne," he had said, his voice a rough, grating thing, shouted hoarse over the battlefield so often it had nearly given out. "The Coldbourne name means you will be harder than any other boy here. Stronger than any boy here. And if you aren't that, and much more besides, they'll break you for an upstart. And you'll deserve it. I'll have no shame attach to the name my father won."

A group of men who seemed to the young Allystaire much like his father had come to meet them in the courtyard, after others had taken their horses. At the head of them, dressed in grey silk trimmed with ermine, had been the Old Baron, Gerard Oyrwyn. He was not, Allystaire knew now, a particularly large man, but in the moment he had seemed huge, for he commanded the men around him by his very presence, his booming voice. He had a well-trimmed beard and his hair was held back by a simple silver circlet of office; both had once been brown but were by then half grey.

He was shorter than Anthelme, shorter than Allystaire would be when he began to approach manhood, but the way he carried himself, his back as straight as a blade, his dark grey eyes focused intently on whoever or whatever was before them, made him seem, somehow, the largest man the young Allystaire had ever seen.

After exchanging loud, expansive warrior's greetings with his father, the Baron had looked down at the son, those eyes focusing sharply upon him. Allystaire distinctly remembered that the man—his liege lord, he knew, without understanding all that implied—had not spoken down to him as so many adults had, but instead, had spoken to him in the same direct way he had to the warriors and knights that surrounded him.

"What is your name, lad?"

"Allystaire Coldbourne, my lord," he had replied, meeting that steady grey gaze with his own curious eyes.

"Looking a man straight in the eye, any man, is a good habit, Allystaire. Keep it," he had said. "Now, why have you come to my home?"

Allystaire cleared his throat, and carefully recited the words he'd been taught the past week. "To become a knight in the service of my Lord Baron of Oyrwyn. To defend with my life his rights, lands, and people; to strike with all my skill against his enemies. To prove my courage and temper my soul in his service, and the service of his descendants, till the end of my life."

Allystaire noted the Baron's eyes flit towards the towering presence of his father, and he nodded an almost imperceptible, but approving, nod. He looked back to the boy.

"I accept your service, Allystaire Coldbourne, on my behalf and for my descendants, till the end of your life. For faithful service, I will give faithful reward: food at my table, space under my roof and by my hearth. My treasure and my spoils I will share fairly in measure of your service, and the lands, titles, and possessions of your father's shall be yours in time. Break faith with me, or my heirs, and you will face exile and death."

The boy knew what to do next. He knelt, his right knee touching the rocky dirt of the courtyard, and lowered his head—but he did the last slowly, bearing in mind the Baron's advice about looking a man in the eye.

He felt the Baron's hand, strong, and with the hard ridges of rings on two of the fingers, settle atop his head. "Rise, Allystaire Coldbourne, and begin your life in my service."

The boy hopped quickly to his feet, full of energy, brimming with excitement, unsure of what to do next.

The Baron was still watching him, and said, "You'll begin your training immediately, boy."

"What am I to learn, my lord? The sword? The lance?"

There was a smattering of laughter from the gathered warriors, but they were silenced by a quick look from the Baron, who said, "There is nothing wrong with being eager, lad. Yet what you're to learn first, and every evening from now on, is not steel or horseflesh, but vellum and ink. No man is fit to be a knight in my service who cannot read, write, and think."

Allystaire had felt his cheeks flush at the laughter, but gathered himself to say, "I am already lettered, my lord."

"Good," the Baron boomed. "That's more than I can say for half of this lot. Still, there'll be much reading for you to do. Now, off you go—tell the Castellan you're to meet the tutors."

Allystaire knew enough to realize he was dismissed, so he hurried on through the gates of the keep, into the beginning of the life he had dreamed of since he knew what it meant to dream.

Suddenly Allystaire was back in the Temple, his knees aching as he knelt in front of the altar. He shifted his weight, lifting his left knee with a click so that he rested only on the right. It had taken more than ten years from that day for him to come to his vigil and his knighthood, years of sweat and blood and pain, with his father's words, and the Baron's, always driving him on.

He had been harder than the other boys, and stronger. Anthelme Coldbourne had made sure of that. The Old Baron had been as good as his word on that day, nearly thirty years ago: riches, spoils, honors.

And so had the Young Baron been: exile, for broken faith.

"Does breaking that oath bother you, My Knight?"

The Goddess's voice startled him out of his reverie, and he was suddenly intensely aware of Her presence, behind him, of the muted song, the steady, warm light.

"It…I do not know, my Lady," Allystaire replied. "I did not break it while the Old Baron lived, only with his son. I could never have broken faith with Gerard Oyrwyn. I do not truly know if I would judge him a good man, as I see such things now. It is likely that I would not, yet I loved him like a grandfather. It is not in my heart to renounce that now."

He felt Her hand settle on his shoulder, felt the tangible weight of it even through the steel he wore.

"Love, honestly borne, can never be a sin, My Arm," She said. "Why do you not turn and face me?"

He felt his cheeks grow hot. "It feels presumptuous, my Lady."

She laughed. "The Baron's advice to look men in the eye may apply to such as me as well, Allystaire. If Braech Himself were to confront you, would you not look Him in the eye?"

"I would," Allystaire admitted, his cheeks still flushed, though a tiny trill of anger at the mention of the Sea Dragon rolled through him.

"Then why do you not offer me the same courtesy?" He felt Her hand lifting him to his feet, and he turned around, meeting Her face to face.

She was, as always, beauty and power barely contained in a feminine figure. A soft, golden radiance, warm and inviting, filled the space around Her, emanating from Her skin, clear and smooth, without line or blemish.

She did not appear young, nor old, not as his mind could measure such things and make sense of them. She simply was.

"Much of what that man taught you has merit, Allystaire," She said, Her eyes—golden, without pupils or irises—searched his face, and, he suspected, his thoughts. "There is no good or ill in knowledge itself, or in the skill of your hands, and much of both comes from Gerard Oyrwyn." Her hands then closed upon his, and he shivered from the power of Her touch. His eyes closed, but he forced them open again, half-lidded.

"Do you know why you have the second part of this vigil, Allystaire?"

"It is the order that you came to us, Called us," he replied, his voice wavering slightly, for She still clasped his hands.

"Yes, though there is more to it. We are not in the deepest and darkest part of the night; that is for My Shadow. Yet we stand where the memory of the sun is as faint as the hope of its return. The only light is what we might make ourselves, what we bring with us. You must be that light, Allystaire—you and Mol and Mourmitnourthrukacshtorvul—steady, and still, and bright enough in the darkness so that all who see it may remember the sun, and know that the dawn is coming."

Allystaire tried to think on Her words, to understand them as they came and take them into his mind and his heart, but the touch of Her hands was so overwhelming that it seemed he might miss things he should understand. Then, in a flash, something came to him, and before he knew it, he was speaking.

"If the order we were Called, and the order of the Vigil we stand, is…then Gideon…"

She smiled, though it was something of a sad smile. "Is like unto the dawn," She said. "And it may be your greatest task to see that he is not a false dawn, my Knight."

"There is so much he needs to know," Allystaire said, a sudden trace of desperation creeping into his voice and his features, eyes narrowing. "He could be a great man, and a good one. I think he wants to be. Yet there is so much no one has ever taught him."

She smiled at him, fully, with nothing held back and no hint of sadness weighing upon her features, and for a moment, all thought fled. "My Knight, there is much he knows that you do not. Be mindful that you learn as well as teach."

He nodded, took a deep and slightly strangled breath.

"What is wrong, my Allystaire?"

He cleared his throat and closed his eyes, dipping his head slightly so as to avoid the full force of Her eyes. "Your touch is overwhelming, Mother," he replied.

One of Her hands left his, but suddenly cupped his chin and lifted his head to meet Her eyes once more. "Why do you call me that?"

He straightened up, took quick breath. "It seemed appropriate."

She thought on this a moment, and Her eyes moved from his face. It was both the lifting of a weight off of him, and a cause for despair. Quickly, the twin golden eyes rested once more on him. "I suppose it might. Yet I would ask you to remember that I am not your Mother."

Allystaire's mouth went dry, and he felt that if Her hands had not been holding him up, his knees may have buckled. "I…do you have a name, My Lady?"

"I have had many names, in many places," She replied. "Some of them even I have forgotten. Is it important?"

"I…it may be to the people, your people—to have a name to give you."

"Then let them give one to me, if they wish," She said, smiling again. "If I were to name myself, I would be limited, captured, defined by the name I chose." She laughed, and his heart thrilled at the sound, pounding against his chest. "Gideon will understand what I mean. A name given to me would be a symbol, and thus only a part of what I am. A name given by me would be the true thing. That would be a dangerous thing to loose upon the world, a tool in the hands of our enemies, and they have tools enough as it is."

"My Lady, forgive me if I speak out of turn—you have spoken to me, more than once now, of enemies, and of a darkness to come. Who do you mean? The Church of the Sea Dragon? The sorcerers? The Baron?"

"All of them and more," She replied. "I do not wish to be at odds with my brother Braech—but what He has become, I will not abide." She sighed, and Allystaire felt a sudden surge of desire.

"The longest night of the winter, my Arm—that is the time you must prepare against."

"Is there any more that you can say?"

"Only what I have told my Voice. She knows my mind as closely as any mortal can."

Allystaire nodded, gathered his breath and his wits, and said, "My Lady, I am hesitant to make boasts to you, to offer vainglorious promises of impossible victory. Yet if the Churches and the Barons and all the sorcerers of the world arrayed themselves against your people, I would stand between them, even if I had to do it alone."

"You are never alone, My Arm. I am always with you. And My Shadow, My Wit, My Will—do you think they follow you only because I came to you before I came to them? They see what I saw. I Ordained you my paladin not to make you a better or a greater man, Allystaire. I chose you because my Gifts could draw forth the greatness—and the goodness—that was already within you."

Then suddenly, She leaned forward and kissed him, Her mouth against his, Her hands clutching his, supporting him, for surely he would have fallen to the ground had She not. It was not a chaste kiss, and the heat and the power of it was so overwhelming that he could not have recalled his name if he were asked. He was not Allystaire, not a knight, not a paladin—he was a man being consumed by desire, by love, by something beyond him or any words he could put to it.

And then She stepped back, and he fell heavily to a knee before Her, gasping for breath.

"I have given you every Gift I can, save one, Allystaire," She whispered, Her voice thick. *With desire?* The question floated dumbly across his mind. "The longest night," She said, her voice growing faint, Her form fading from his adoring eyes. "Be a lamp in its darkness, My Knight."

And then, She was gone, and Allystaire's heart sank, if only for a moment. Once Her presence had receded, he could think again. He realized his heart was still thudding against his chest, and he closed his eyes and held his breath for a moment, till its pace slowed, then levered himself back to his feet.

"Well," he said aloud, with a slight chuckle rattling in his dry throat, "that was considerably better than a vigil in the Sea Dragon's chapel." He rolled his shoulders, stretched his legs, loosened his hammer in his belt, and began to pace, finding himself full of nervous energy. His steps echoed around the stone, his armor clanking and settling around him.

The doors creaked open. He felt, as much as saw, Idgen Marte step inside.

"Has it been two turns already? Surely not."

"Aye, it has," Idgen Marte said.

As they passed each other, they clasped hands and forearms for a moment, and Allystaire thought he felt the light that hovered around the altar take on a different quality, dimming and flickering.

As he reached the doors, he looked back, but instead of Idgen Marte, he saw her indistinct, shadowed shape. He turned away and closed the door behind him, savoring a gulp of cool air. *Warm in there,* he thought, then corrected himself, with a blush he hoped the darkness hid. *Only got that warm when She…* He cut that line of thought off, as he felt a bead of sweat drip down his forehead.

Gideon, he found, was doing a creditable job of staying awake, but his eyes were sliding closed, his head nodding. He gently prodded his shoulder with two fingers. "Take a walk, lad," he murmured. "It will do you good."

The boy frowned, and shook his limbs as if to clear the encroaching slumber from them. Then he shook his head, and said, "No." He looked up at Allystaire, adding, "If you can stay here, and awake, and alert, so shall I. I want to do the vigil properly, and that means guarding this door, with you. I will not have it cheapened by my own weakness. My mind will master my flesh."

Inwardly, Allystaire repressed the urge to slap Gideon on the back, or embrace him. Instead, he merely nodded and took up his post on the opposite side of the doors. "Seeing things done properly is a good habit, Gideon. Keep it."

CHAPTER 19

Labors

By mid-morning the day after the vigil, Allystaire stood in a rough line of about a dozen people, half villagers, half Ravens, and all of them digging.

Most of the villagers had shovels, but the Iron Ravens had a supply of good Oyrwyn mattocks among their equipment, and Allystaire had been given the use of one. His body had hummed with energy for turns after the sun had risen that morning, after the vigil—but a few minutes of swinging the mattock had dulled his senses and begun to set a good ache into his shoulders. His armor lay in a heap several yards away and, as he worked in his sweat-stained gambeson, quickly growing too warm, he knew his energy was fading.

The mattock, a part of him noted, was rather sharper than it needed to be in order to effectively cut into the earth, a point that was driven home when he nearly swung it into his calf.

The line of laborers was situated at the western end of the village, just before the road led into the closer farmhouses, and the earth they were digging up was the very first step in a plan that Allystaire had roughly hashed out that morning with Captain Ivar, and a brief consultation from Torvul. The dwarf had grunted a few comments before declaring himself too tired to do any useful thinking and retiring to his wagon.

The warband and the villagers seemed to be at some kind of unofficial competition to see who could throw the most earth the fastest, and the pile of dirt was growing quickly. *Still need to sit down and talk with the warband,* Allystaire thought, as he rested his mattock a moment. *And with Keegan and his lot. And Renard.* His throat began to grow dry and the thought of all the talking he had in front of him.

A cleared throat from Gern saved him from another near mutilation of his leg with the razor sharp adze edge of the mattock. "Couple o'visitors, m'lord," he mumbled, and the men all seemed grateful for the opportunity to take a break.

"Ah, posing manfully at the idiot end of a shovel or some other tool of ignorance. A noble posture I know all too well. It bespeaks a day of grueling but honest labor. All things I strive to avoid," Torvul said, as he and Gideon approached from the village. Both were carrying an odd assortment of equipment. The boy had long coils of thin rope wrapped around him, a small round-headed mallet in one hand, and a few wooden stakes in the other. The dwarf carried a large wicker basket.

"What exactly are you two after doing, besides taunting me with how well-rested you look?" Allystaire asked.

"Call it a proof of concept," the dwarf said. "The girl tells us we'll have the right kind of clouds in a few days, and I mean to be sure we can put the necessary tinctures and concoctions in 'em when they arrive." He walked a few paces beyond the piles of dirt, and scanned the line of workers. "You know, we could hire a dwarf mason who knows the proper way to build walls."

"We have not the weight nor the stone," Allystaire replied. "Earthworks and a wooden palisade will have to do."

"Walls don't do much good for the people in outlying farms," Gideon said suddenly. Allystaire suppressed a wince, and he saw that the villagers and the Ravens alike were turning sour faces at the boy.

"You have a point, Gideon, and you have identified a problem in our defense," Allystaire said, carefully. "By dinner, I want you to have three proposals for me on how to solve it."

The boy bit his bottom lip. "I have two already—"

"Dinner, Gideon," Allystaire said. "One fantastical scheme at a time."

The men milled around. Allystaire gave a discreet nod to Gern, and the gap-toothed man slapped a hand against his thigh. "Right. That's a break n' we'll all be well after it again in a quarter turn. Piss or sleep or go behind a tree t'tug your c—"

Allystaire cleared his throat and Gern stopped. "Sorry m'lord. Old habits n'that."

While they spoke, Torvul was unlimbering his basket, removing what looked like inflated paper bladders, and then a host of smaller, finer tools.

"With the stakes and the rope, boy, if y'please," Torvul said, and Gideon hurried over to his side, awkwardly unlimbering the ropes coiled around his thin shoulders with hammer and stakes still in his hands. Allystaire meandered over. He saw, when he got closer, that they were not inflated bladders, but rather incredibly fine, thin paper stretched over an internal frame.

"What in the Cold are those?"

"Risers," the dwarf said. "I'll fill 'em with the right vapors, coax those vapors to a controlled combustion, and the whole business'sll float straight up. Old dwarfish toy. Plenty of real application for it, though."

"Such as?"

The dwarf looked up at him from underneath hairless brows. "Well, pretty lights in the sky, mostly. I s'pose they can be used fer signals in an army n'such."

"See, that's a solution right there," Gideon said brightly.

"No, boy, it isn't, because I've not got an endless supply, and I'm not handin' over the necessary reagents to make 'em fly to anyone without a solid score of years training in the alchemical arts. Dangerous otherwise," the dwarf said, as he began producing vials, and a glass ball about the size of his fist with a waxed cork seal stuck into an opening at the top.

Torvul pulled the cork free, and Allystaire peered into the glass sphere as the dwarf quickly unstoppered two vials and poured them into the glass. He jammed the waxed cork back in, carefully levering his thumb against it to apply the pressure to push it in as far as he could without damaging the glass sphere.

Immediately the two liquids he'd poured in began to foam, then bubble, then suddenly it appeared as though the dwarf was holding a glass ball full of a steaming vapor, rather than liquids. He grinned, lifted his eyes up towards the bright, clear sky, and said, "Thank you, Your Ladyship." He produced a thin glass stem and prepared, it seemed, to slip it through a hole his finger covered on the cork.

"The stakes and ropes any moment now, boy. This'sll hold for a while, but not all day," he said.

Gideon had been just as entranced as Allystaire in watching the alchemical process Torvul produced. The boy suddenly scrambled for a stake and hammer. He held the hammer far down at the bottom of the handle and began to raise his hand above his head, holding the stake with his hand flat against the ground. Allystaire cleared his throat and Gideon stopped, turning back to him.

"Hang on a moment, Gideon," he said, then walked to the boy's side and knelt next to him. "Two suggestions for you: first, hold the bottom of a hammer if you want power, closer to the top if you want precision. I think you probably want the latter, aye?"

Gideon nodded, and adjusted his grip up the mallet's handle, resettling his long, thin fingers around it carefully.

"Second," Allystaire said, "bring your hand up closer to the top of the stake. Trust me."

The boy knitted his brows. "Why?"

"If you miss your strike and hit your hand when it is close to the top of your target, it may hurt a bit. If you miss and hit your hand while it is hard to the ground, or a piece of wood or stone…"

The boy's lips parted slightly and his brows lifted in understanding. "You'll crush it. I see."

Then, deftly, and carefully, with a few quick strikes, the boy had driven one stake far enough into the ground to satisfy Torvul and Allystaire both, the dwarf nodded to one of the coils of rope.

Adroitly, and without any assistance necessary, Gideon looped a quick, self-tightening hitch around the stake, and played out the rope till it reached Torvul. The dwarf, with thin glass stem and vapor-filled sphere in his hands, cleared his throat and looked to Allystaire.

"Would you mind?"

Allystaire chuckled, and reached for the rope, which was thin, pliant, and smooth. "I am no sailor, Torvul. You will want to check the knots." He saw then that each of the risers had a thin metal ring protruding from an open bottom, as the dwarf had laid them delicately on their sides. Allystaire threaded the end through the ring, then made a loop in the rope and pulled the end taut.

The dwarf snorted. "It'll do for now. Don't you know any proper knots?"

"One," Allystaire said, as he tugged with two fingers at the muddle he'd made of the rope.

"Well, then use it!"

"I do not think you want a noose."

Torvul snorted, but the way his eyes turned sideways to Allystaire he seemed uncertain whether to take it as a joke or not.

Then, as Gideon hammered a second stake into the ground and again made the rope fast to it, Torvul plunged his thin stem of glass through a paper seal around the hole in the center of a cork, plugging the end of the stem with one finger. Next, he lifted it clear, placing the thumb of the hand holding the sphere over the cork, and quickly slipped the end of the stem—now filled with the blue, smoky vapor—into the bottom end of one of the risers, and removed his finger.

The thin paper creaked around its framework, shifted, and suddenly lifted perhaps a foot off the ground. Torvul cackled delightedly. "Well, it's a start."

"If you knew you could get them off the ground, why the test?"

"I've got to know I can get them off the ground when they're heavier than normal, and I've added some weight to the framework by fastening a few scraps of wood and iron in place. Hold the rope so that it doesn't fly off on me yet, eh?"

Allystaire grabbed a handful of rope, as the dwarf carefully piped another stemfull of vapor into the riser. Allystaire felt it tug. Torvul said, "Two more ought to do it."

"Why must they be heavier?" Allystaire asked.

"When I put 'em up for the girl's clouds in a few days, I'll need to have a mixture in 'em," the dwarf said. "Something to make sure the clouds are drawn to us instead of pushed away, and a little something to tickle their thighs open, as it were."

"I see," Allystaire said, though he wasn't entirely sure that he did. Still, as Torvul piped more vapor into the riser, it suddenly tugged free of his grip and shot straight up, playing out the rope till it was nearly taut.

"Are we going to need more rope," Allystaire asked, his voice smooth and flat. "To get them up into the clouds?"

Torvul fixed Allystaire with a flat, blank stare. "You can't be serious. The clouds are thousands of spans above us, we've…"

The tiniest curl of a grin tugged at the left corner of Allystaire's mouth, and Torvul harumphed. "Even you couldn't be that daft. Anyway—we'll keep 'em tied up till the clouds arrive, then cut loose and wish them well."

"Will it work?"

The alchemist narrowed his eyes threateningly. "Of course it'll work."

"How do we know that the clouds will even get here?"

"Mol says she knows when the Dragon's priests are fiddling with the weather. She can feel it." He extended one finger towards Gideon. "And our young man here says he can stop whatever they try to do once she lets him know."

"Are you ready for that?" Allystaire turned his attention to the boy, who was making the second rope fast.

"It doesn't matter if I am or not," the boy replied. "It needs to be done."

"Well," Allystaire said, carefully, drawing the syllable out a bit. "It does not necessarily need to be done now. I have felt the weight of Braech's will, through the Choiron Symod. It is a powerful and oppressive thing."

"There's no way to prepare for it or test it," the boy replied. "Either I will be ready or I won't. If I'm not, testing my Will against his—assuming for the moment that he is directing this effort, which we don't know—will help me learn what I must strive against."

"I cannot argue with the logic," Allystaire replied, though he thought, if only briefly, that there was something else to be done. "When the time comes, do not risk yourself. If it is too much…"

The boy frowned and stared hard at Allystaire. "Would you give Idgen Marte the same advice? Or Torvul? Would you not risk yourself?"

Allystaire sighed and rubbed his brow with finger and thumb, lowering his eyes. "No, Gideon. I would not, and you are right." *Goddess, but I wish he were not,* he thought.

"If you'll risk yourself, you must be willing to let the rest of us do the same," the boy said, more quietly.

Meanwhile, Torvul had gotten the second riser off the ground and both now floated, lightly buffeted by the wind, at the end of their ropes. Some of the resting work crew gawked and pointed at the flying paper spheres.

"Very true, Gideon." Then an idea came to him, and he found himself trying not to grin. "Indeed, all of us, as the Mother's Ordained, must be willing to share our tasks and trials with each other."

Torvul, admiring his devices, suddenly glared at Allystaire. "I don't like the sound—"

Allystaire cleared his throat, and, cutting the dwarf off, yelled, "Gern! Two more shovels, if you would, and let us get back to it."

The villagers and mercenaries shoved themselves back to their feet and gathered up tools. Torvul began packing up his instruments, murmuring in Dwarfish as he did. Two more shovels were produced from a stack of tools. Allystaire took them by the shafts and held them out, handle first, to both the dwarf and the boy. Gideon took his without a word. Torvul glared at Allystaire for a moment, then set his basket and case of tools down and snatched it away.

Smiling brightly at Torvul in return, Allystaire took up his own mattock and set back to work.

Gideon, meanwhile, had extended the shovel as far as his arms would reach and ineffectually dug the head at the turf, barely cracking it. Taking care not to sigh, and keeping exasperation from his voice, Allystaire moved to his side.

"Once again, lad, let me give some advice. You are going to want to let the tool do the work—"

CHAPTER 20

Fortune's Priestess

The morning was chill, frost having turned the grass brittle beneath the stomping feet of the ten young men scurrying back and forth across the field. Each of them carried in his hands a large rock, except for those who carried a pile of smaller rocks.

At their head, wearing riding trousers and a vest that left his arms bare, was Allystaire, one large rock perched on each shoulder. His strides were long, his breathing even, and his arms and chest coated with a light sheen of sweat. He reached one end of the field, and turned around, returning the way he had come.

This forced several of the men to scatter out of the way, and one to drop his rock. There was muttering and cursing as it came near to smashing into feet and tripping unobservant runners. Allystaire left it behind, reached the other end of the field, where a pile of coats lay, having been tossed aside at the start of the morning's exercise.

He dug his fingers into the rocks he carried and flung them forward. They tumbled across the frost-tinged grass, and he turned back to the crowd. Instinctively, his eyes sought out Gideon. Though the youngest and smallest of the crowd by far, the boy was in the middle of the pack, the fourth to arrive after Allystaire and carefully set his rock down.

"All right," Allystaire called, his voice echoing across the autumn morning. "To Ivar at the Eastern Gate. Run."

They formed a fairly ragged line and moved off at a trot. Allystaire blew out a long breath and dug his fingertips into his bare shoulders, wincing at the ache. *Not young enough for this anymore,* he thought. *Who the Cold else is going to do it?* He had no answer for that.

He sighed, bent to gather up his belt, hammer, and cloak, and started back towards the Temple. In the Temple Field, two solid, square campaign tents had been erected, and Torvul's wagon was parked close by. The small round windows of the boxy home-on-wheels showed a light inside.

Allystaire tugged open the flap to his tent and ducked inside. The camp tables, chair, stool, and cot that furnished it had been given to him by the Ravens, like the tent itself. Much of it was a little too well made for a small, itinerant warband, even a successful one, and he suspected Audreyn's hand in it. One table held the jumble of steel and leather that was his armor, both the plate and the hodgepodge of leather and steel that was lighter and less obtrusive, and his sword, with his shield leaning against one of the legs. The other held a small stack of parchment, quills, ink, sand, and a quill knife. The tent itself was spacious enough that he didn't have to duck his head, and small conferences could be held with all five of the Ordained, at need.

He threw off his cloak and vest, found a shirt amidst a pile of clothing in a basket at the foot of his cot, and pulled it on gratefully, the warmth of exercise having fled his limbs in the walk. From outside the tent came a gruff Dwarfish murmur.

"You decent in there? Haven't snuck a girl in or anything?"

"No one in here but me, and I am clothed, Torvul," Allystaire wearily replied.

A long-fingered hand pulled the flap back and Torvul strolled in. "It wouldn't hurt you to sneak a girl in once or twice. Unless you're saving yourself for marriage, chivalry being what it is…"

Allystaire sighed heavily, and the dwarf trailed off, peering closely at the paladin's face. "Touched a nerve, eh?"

"Leave it, Torvul. Let us discuss business."

"You're pining over someone. Not Idgen Marte—"

"I said leave it," Allystaire insisted. Thoughts competed for space in his head. Auburn hair, highland winds, wildflowers. The Goddess, Her overwhelming presence, Her burning lips.

"Well, what's that about then," Torvul said, instantly honing in on a sudden flush in Allystaire's cheeks.

"Not Idgen Marte, who is like a sister to me, and all that implies."

"Well, you've hardly slept since we got back, much less had time for courting, so I can't imagine…" Torvul's eyes suddenly went wide and he glared at Allystaire. "Surely not…I mean, you're not pining over…Her."

Allystaire cut him off with a sharp chop of one hand in the air. "Stop. I cannot explain. I have not the words."

Torvul chuckled under his breath. "Well, I guess I can't fault your ambition." He ambled over to the stool and sat down, tapped a finger thoughtfully on his chin. "Did you ever marry? I'm assuming you didn't leave a wife behind. Doesn't seem like you."

"No."

The dwarf harrumphed. "Married to war, to glory in battle, n'that?"

"In short, and so you will let it alone—the only woman I would have married I was forbidden to. By the Old Baron, by my father and hers. I followed their commands. When they suggested other candidates, I ignored them."

"Aren't your father and the Old Baron dead many years?"

"So is she," Allystaire replied, clipped and cold. "Now I assume you did not come to see me to gossip?"

Torvul grimaced. "I'm sorry, Allystaire. For bringing it up. I'll let that alone from now on, till some night we're both good and drunk. Fair?"

Allystaire nodded. "Fair. Now, what have you come about?"

The dwarf pulled a heavy, full-looking pouch free from his belt, and upended it on the table. What emerged was Allystaire's gauntlet, the left-handed one, that Torvul had borrowed. "Finally finished what I set out to do with this. Nothing that'll sink a tunnel through bedrock or shunt lava— that's what dwarves mean when we say miracle in Dwarfish, by the way—but I think you'll find it useful."

"What did you do?" Allystaire began pulling it onto his hand and immediately felt the difference. The palm had been cut away and the rest adjusted so that it fixed firmly around the tips of his fingers. He tested the fit, flexing his hand.

"Thought it might be of use to be able to heal in the midst of a fracas without pausing to strip that off," the dwarf said. "Figure the exposed skin is probably worth the trade, no?"

Allystaire nodded, continuing to flex his hand, curl it into a fist. "Aye, it should be." He nodded a thanks and said, "Well done, Torvul. Fits better than ever."

"That's dwarfish craftsmanship you feel," Torvul replied. "I'm no great smith, not among my folk, but I know my way around a common forge— they're nothing like the old Great Forges in the Homes, mind you, or so I hear, anyway. Still, I did what I could." He paused, then added, "Made the girl a sickle, too."

Allystaire frowned, stripped off the gauntlet, then set it down on the table with the rest of his armor. "Is that truly necessary?"

"You saw the same vision I did. She carried one there. She'll carry one here."

Allystaire put his palms down on the table and leaned over it, dropping his head and closing his eyes. "I do not like arming an eleven year old child, Torvul."

"Be willing to bet you armed enough eleven year old boys in your old life. Don't see why it's different except that she's a girl, and we both know she's a great deal more than a child anyway. But it's not just about arming her. It's about becoming more than we are. It's a little bit like playin' a part, I suppose, though we're not trying to deceive anyone. She showed us what we could be, Allystaire—what we need to become. If we don't take our own steps towards that, what are we doin'?"

Allystaire stood up, wincing at the audible snaps his back made. "You are right. I never said you were not. I just said that I do not like it."

"Likin' it isn't the point, and you know it. That being said," Torvul added, and pointed at Allystaire's armor, "I need to borrow that. The plate. The best that you've got."

"Why? More adjustments?"

The dwarf shrugged, his eyes shifting evasively. "Something like that. I'd rather not say just yet, till I know if I can do it."

Allystaire sighed. "In for a copper half, in for a gold chain, I suppose. Do as you must. Please do not damage it; I have no idea how I would replace it. The armorer at Wind's Jaw worked weeks at it, made it to my fit."

"That plain suit was your best?"

"Best in the way that mattered. I had fancier plate. My arms engraved on it, stones set in places. I think it would not have stopped a sling-stone, and I would not have bothered to bring it with me if I had left with a wagon train."

"Your priorities never cease t'disappoint me," Torvul replied, before nodding to the armor. "I'll send someone around to gather it up later. I've got a few points of the formulae to work out."

"Just do not—"

"Damage it? Anything I did to human ironmongery could only improve it." The dwarf headed for the flap, but even as he opened it, Mol was standing outside reaching for it. Her hood was down, and the morning light behind her made the sky blue of her robe nearly white.

Torvul held the flap open for her. "M'lady," he playfully murmured. The girl laughed, and in the moment was young again. When she turned to Allystaire, her face was once more a nearly ageless anomaly.

It is like the face of the Mother joining with the face of the girl I pulled from the cold well, Allystaire thought.

"We're going to have visitors today," she announced. "Coming on the westerly track. The first will arrive soon. We'll need to greet them."

"Do you know any more than that?"

The girl paused for a moment. "Dress well."

* * *

Allystaire had chosen to interpret Mol's words as dress in such armor as you have not loaned to Torvul to experiment on, so less than half a turn later, he was wearing iron bracers, his iron-studded leather gloves, and thick leathers. His sword rode on his back and his shield was slung off of Ardent's pommel, with the hammer tucked securely against his right hip.

The destrier was happy for the exercise and tossed his head against the reins, stamping his feet and resisting Allystaire's gentle suggestions to relax. The horse wanted to run, so Allystaire let the reins go slack for only a moment. The huge grey gathered himself and practically leapt forward, thundering over the track that led through the village green.

Allystaire felt his own heart leap as the destrier did, wishing, if only for a moment, to give the big grey his head and let him run as far and fast as he would. All too quickly, though, he saw a cluster of other mounts on the road beyond the green, and had to rein him in, a decision that Ardent fought for a few moments. Mostly, Allystaire thought, for the look of the thing.

Mol sat atop a pony and Idgen Marte on her courser. He saw the warrior staring into the distance, her eyes narrowed.

"What are we waiting for, exactly?"

"She tells me we'll know it when we see it," Idgen Marte murmured from one corner of her mouth.

"I do not want to color your reactions with prior knowledge," Mol replied, calmly. "Shan't be long, anyway."

Ardent gave up on running and was soon nipping at the frost-rimmed grass. Mol's word was true, and in a few moments the early morning sun showed them a glint of metal that resolved itself into a party of three riders and a small crowd of men on foot.

Two of the riders carried banners or standards of some kind, and when Allystaire saw them, his stomach tightened. One of the standards was simply a wheel, left loose and spinning, mounted atop a pole. The other was a long rectangle of gold-edged white cloth, its length taut against the pole. It showed a female figure, nude, but the glinting he'd seen was from the precious stones sewn into the fabric at her fingers and throat and hair.

"Gemmary on a flag," Idgen Marte said. "Oh, Freeze me…"

"It would not do for the Goddess Fortune to go without Her Adornment, even on a standard," Allystaire said. "From what I remember of my lessons, this must be a ranking priest."

Mol was silent, watching the party approach with unreadable poise.

Besides the three riders, there were three pack mules and six armed men on foot. The riders to either flank held the standards. The woman carrying the banner wore a cloak lined with fox fur over a dress of a deep red hue. Her saddle was a leather Allystaire couldn't identify on sight, and all her mount's tack was tooled with silver.

Meanwhile, the man carrying the wheel practically wore rags by comparison. Young and hardy, if thin, his clothing was carefully dirtied and rumpled, though hardly threadbare. Allystaire felt something in himself snarling at the intimation of poverty and hardship. *His face has not got the look of a man going hungry,* he thought. *And there's many a peasant this country over wearing worse things into the fields today.*

What really drew the eye, though, what demanded attention, was the Priestess riding between them. Where the standard-bearer's saddle was set with silver, hers bore gold. She, too, wore fox-fur, only it was a rich and rare silver, and her dress, in slashes of white and gold, was richer silk. Her feet were slippered, rather than booted, and she rode side-saddle on a white palfrey that Allystaire estimated some men would pay as much for as they would for Ardent.

Her face was covered by a golden mask with translucent topaz inset over her eyes. The mask was exquisitely detailed, showing the aristocratic, indifferent face of the Goddess Fortune, and was bound carefully with ribbons of silk.

"I have come as a representative of She who bestows, withholds, and spreads the wealth of the world among men. I seek the man Alysander." Her voice was muffled by the mask, but resonant nonetheless, with the unmistakably rich and smooth tone of the educated. Her intonation was theatrical, and even behind the mask Allystaire could feel her eyes sizing him up. A hand, elegantly gloved in soft white lambskin, pointed a beringed finger at Allystaire. "You are he. I can sense a power within you."

Allystaire snorted. "I am the man you seek, though my name is Allystaire. Tell me plainly what has brought you here."

"My Mistress Fortune wishes to satisfy Her curiosity about the rise of a new power in this world. As Her servants, it is our duty to understand the currents and eddies of power, and at the moment, power is swirling around your name. Even if the passing of that name from mouth to ear has rather garbled it. I apologize for having it incorrectly." Her voice was honey, and her imperiously pointing hand lay demurely against her saddle.

Allystaire merely shrugged, which had the unintended but not unwelcome effect of rattling the scabbarded sword hung across his back. He eyed the retinue, and the cynical, detached part of him that evaluated such things went to work. *They look indifferent. Casual. Yet hard-eyed. They know their business. Weapons are well maintained, hilts are worn. None of them are trying for style.* Though they wore light brown cloaks with hints of gilt running through them, and rounded, spiked helmets that looked as likely to stop a hammer blow as wet wool would, the cloaks were all kept carefully away from sword and dagger hilts.

Two of them had wandered, nonchalantly, to the sides of the road, watching intently while trying not to appear as though they were watching intently.

"We have no intent to ambush you, gentlemen," Allystaire suddenly said to them. "Yet I commend your watchfulness." His eyes flitted back to the masked face of the priestess. "I am not offended that you had misheard my name. I do admit to curiosity about where you heard it—and about your own name."

The two guardsmen Allystaire had addressed turned to him, but slowly. *I do not like this at all,* he thought, then was suddenly startled by Mol's voice in his head.

This may be turned to our gain. Be nice.

"I am Cerisia, Archioness of the Goddess Fortune's Church in Baronies Delondeur, Telmawr, and Innadan."

"Well met then, Archioness," Allystaire said, scrambling in his mind for protocol he'd long since forgotten on greeting Fortune's clergy. *Her title sounds important. Why didn't I pay more attention to lessons?* "I am Allystaire, Arm of the Mother, Her Servant and Prophet, Revelator and Paladin. Welcome to Thornhurst."

She nodded graciously, the standard and wheel bearers bowed in their saddles, then all three began to edge their horses forward.

Ardent laid his ears back and bared his teeth, lowered his neck and tugged at the reins. Allystaire kept his own face free from similar signs of aggression, even if he felt them. He did not scold Ardent, though he subtly tightened his fist around the reins in case he needed to pull the horse in. He did not, however, give any ground.

"I am still unclear on your purpose, exactly," Allystaire said.

"To confer with you as the leader of this new faith, of course," Cerisia said, the bright warmth of her voice doing little to defuse the situation. "There is certainly no reason that Fortune and the Mother cannot come to a good footing with one another through their mortal representatives." There was an almost imperceptible hitch, the tiniest pause, before the priestess said "Mother." With what Allystaire could only assume was an imperturbable smile beneath her mask, she said, "Are you going to introduce me to your servants?"

"I have no servants," Allystaire replied, rather more sharply than he intended. "However," he extended his free hand towards Mol, "This is Mol, the Voice of the Mother, Her first Servant, Priestess, and Seer."

The girl's poise very nearly matched that of the Archioness. Though Mol had only a homespun robe and shaggy spotted pony, she held her own against Cerisia's golden mask and fine, snow-white palfrey. The older woman—though how old, Allystaire had no idea—had the accoutrements, the training, and the years of experience. But Mol had spoken, often and directly, to the Goddess Herself, and that had to count for something.

Indeed, it must have, for it was Cerisia who spoke first. "Well met, Mol, Voice of the Mother. I look forward to speaking with you as one godly woman to another." She turned then, distinctly back to Allystaire, and indicated Idgen Marte with one hand. "And she is?"

That was too damn clever by half, Allystaire suddenly thought, even as he found himself clearing his throat and answering. "Idgen Marte, Shadow of the Mother."

"My, my. Such titles we give ourselves," the Archioness tittered. "Arm, Shadow, Voice. And, of course, Paladin? That is a bold title for anyone to claim, even if it is on lips from here to Londray, and beyond."

"I have not claimed it. It was given to me, as the others were given to those who bear them," Allystaire replied. "Now, as to your business…"

"Certainly we shall not bar entry to those of other faiths," Mol suddenly put in, turning to Allystaire, then back to Cerisia. "I suppose that protocol would have me ask you to produce your charter or warrant, but I think we can let that go, as breakfast-time approaches, and no doubt you are dry and hungry from the road."

Allystaire cleared his throat and spoke up again. "I mean no offense, Archioness, but I will not have armed men I do not know or trust remain armed in a village that is under my protection. I will have their arms, to return upon your exit."

Cerisia turned to the guard standing nearest her horse, who gave a tiny shake of his head. There was no mark of rank to set the man apart, but his face was older, more heavily lined. *Captain,* Allystaire thought. There were heavy bags under his eyes, and Allystaire marked his face.

"This is dangerous country, and we approach the season of deserters and banditry, do we not?" Cerisia's voice was entirely reasonable, her head tilted to the side, though some of the effect was doubtless lost by the mask hiding her features. "You have my word that they will remain peaceful unless provoked and would aid in the defense of your village and people at need. They will also remain sober."

Mol spoke up. "We mean to cast no aspersions on you or your retinue, Archioness. We could accept your promise of good conduct."

"You will also accept the brunt of any consequences deriving from their actions," Allystaire put in, and then thought, to Mol, *On this, I will not budge. I mislike the look of these men; they are not lazy merchant's sons playing at being guards.*

"They will be good. I do promise," the priestess said, and Allystaire didn't like at all the tone of faint mockery in her words.

"Very well. One of us will go ahead to see that a proper reception is prepared," Mol said. "I am afraid that space is cramped and we may have no roof for you."

"We brought our pavilions in case of need," Cerisia replied, "though we may ask for fuel to keep them warm. It is growing chill."

Allystaire turned his horse, happy to leave the priestess behind, less happy to have her men where he couldn't see them. Idgen Marte had already turned her courser and, he could see, was about to give it her heel. *Find Torvul, Renard, and Ivar. I do not give a frozen damn if there is hot drink or bread for them, but there will be armed men about. And get Gideon out of sight.*

If they don't see him, they can't ask you about him? Devious of you. Her voice echoed with approval in his mind. *The boy isn't going to stay hidden, though.*

Try.

Allystaire set a slow pace for the rest of them, putting out of his mind the inane small talk ensuing between Mol and Cerisia, though a part of him was briefly amazed, and not for the first time, at how frighteningly fast the girl had grown up. Still, most of his thoughts were circling around the six dangerous armed men he was leading straight into Thornhurst.

* * *

Allystaire burst into his tent to find Torvul, Gideon, Ivar, and Renard all waiting for him. The sounds of men at work drifted in, as Cerisia's guards and servants were erecting their pavilions.

"Mislike them being this close to Her Temple," Torvul said, through sourly twisted lips.

"No other space for them. Besides, this way we can keep an eye on them."

"Why'd we even let 'em in?" Torvul lifted a hand to gesture angrily and ineffectually at the air. "No good can come of this."

"Mol thinks it might," Allystaire replied. "We can argue later." His eyes flicked to Gideon, and he said, "I thought Idgen Marte told you to get out of sight."

"She did," he said. "I came here."

Allystaire sighed. "We will manage." Renard and Ivar lingered a few paces away, and he waved them closer. "The priestess brought guards, six of them, and two servants, or demi-priests or something. I mislike the look of the guards. Not the fat fools one usually finds in temples." He focused on Ivar, catching the woman's weary, indifferent-seeming brown eyes, which Allystaire well knew to be a ruse. "I want the guards watched, all of them. If one of them wanders off, I want to know where he goes, what he does. I want to know what they talk about, who loses what at dice, how much they drink, what they eat. From where do they hail, why do they think they are here. Everything. Did I miss anything?"

Ivar grinned rather gruesomely. "Be wantin' to know when one takes a shit, m'lord?"

"If it seems relevant," Allystaire replied. "Do not worry about letting them see you. Or at least one of you. I do not want them to think they have a free hand."

"Got it. How many men d'ya want me t'put on it?"

Allystaire clenched a fist and shut his eyes, doing quick calculations. "Can you spare three?"

"I can. It'll slow down the earthworks and cuttin' timber."

"I will find a few more men from the village. Good farmer stock here; we all know how to dig," Renard put in.

"We do not have enough men no matter how many hands we round up," Allystaire said. "Yet we must look at the threat within, now, as well as that without." He looked to Renard then. "Any word from Keegan and his band? I lost track of them since we returned."

"Camping out in the wooded hills to the north and east," Renard said. "Asked for some supplies, clothes, a few simple tools we could spare—hand axes and simple knives, no real weapons. Said he'd come in and talk to you when he felt ready."

"If you know where he is and can get a man out there, I would love to speak to him," Allystaire replied. Then, he suddenly rapped his fist against the table. "Belay that. Tell Idgen Marte where he is. She can get there faster, and with no one the wiser."

Renard nodded and stood up straight, barely, Allystaire noted, refraining from clicking his heels. "Aye."

Allystaire nodded. "Off you go, then." He paused for a moment, and added, "Thank you."

Both Ivar and Renard strode out into the bright autumn sun, tent flaps swinging in their wake.

"Mol is going to be talking with the priestess. There may be a tour of the Temple. I still do not know why they are here," Allystaire said, turning to Torvul. "I want you to do as much of the talking in my place as possible."

"Hardly a bad decision, but not how you often think," Torvul noted. "Why?"

"She knew to ask me questions. Not Idgen Marte, and not Mol. She knew," Allystaire said, "or strongly suspected. I do not like what that implies."

"What does it imply?" Gideon's face turned between the pair of them.

"That she knows that I cannot or will not lie to her. Where she would have heard that, or from whom, I do not know, and the things we do not know about a potential enemy are the most dangerous."

"Why must she be a potential enemy? Why must two faiths be at odds?"

Allystaire sighed. "Gideon, do not mistake me. I do not want to be her enemy, or her Goddess's. Yet there were moments, signs, in my short meeting with her that tell me I probably will be. I dislike the fact, but I have learned to listen to my instincts."

"If you treat everyone like an enemy, everyone will become an enemy," Gideon stubbornly insisted, frowning.

"If they came in peace, they will leave unharmed and with my good wishes. Yet I ask you to think on whether it is seemly for a priestess to wear a mask made of more gold than all of the people of this village will see in all their lifetimes put together. When I come back—and it may be some turns, so I will have Idgen Marte try to bring you food, or anything else you might like—I want you to tell me whether you think that wealth has come to her clean, or if blood stuck to it somewhere in its provenance."

Gideon nodded, the distant look on his face telling Allystaire that he was already thinking on the issue. He settled into one of the camp chairs and rested his elbows on his thighs, hands steepling in front of his face. Allystaire nodded at Torvul and then at the tent flap, and the two of them exited into the daylight.

The priestess's guards set up a camp that Allystaire found entirely too professional for his taste, with clear lines of sight, and their own shelters circled around her much larger tent. They'd even erected a picket line for their mounts, and two of them were brushing down the animals, two unpacked the saddles and baggage, and the remaining two stood watchfully to the side.

"That stretches the definition of tent, I'd say," Torvul said, jerking his chin towards the rather ostentatious pavilion that had already been pulled into place and staked down. It alternated panels of white and gold, and stitched upon it were the symbols of Fortune—the Ever-Turning Wheel, and the Goddess in various poses, from reclining amidst a fold of cloth to judging two men, each standing in one upraised palm.

"Needs everyone to know that she is here, and that gold and silver drip from her fingers," Allystaire said.

"What've you got against Fortune, anyway?"

"If She is meant to spread the wealth of the world among men, why does most of it stay with the ruthless and murderous?"

"Maybe they pray to her the most," Torvul suggested. "Your northern faiths don't make a lot of sense t'me and I've had fourscore years t'get used t'them."

Allystaire merely grunted. Mol appeared to be leading Cerisia up the steps of the Temple, and he and Torvul quickened their step in order to join them.

"My, this is impressive," Cerisia was saying to the girl as Mol pulled open the heavy doors on smoothly oiled hinges. "To have built a temple so quickly, and with so much glass. Certainly Fortune has been smiling upon your village."

"Fortune has had nothing to do with it," Allystaire was saying, and rather sharply, before he even realized the words were leaving his lips.

He felt as much as saw Mol turn to him, her eyes wide and half-warning, half-imploring him to be quiet.

"Well," the priestess said, "I don't mean to stir up any theological debates. Not unless we've scribes present to record our words for posterity. We can deal with that later."

"Before we enter," Mol said, "I should note that no man or woman comes into this Temple masked or shadowed, obscured or disguised," sliding, as she spoke, to stand in the very doorway of the Temple, managing to promote a kind of presence that seemed to block the entry as well as Allystaire could have. "The Mother will see your face as you approach Her altar. And so will I."

"This is part of my formal regalia, and as I am here as an official emissary of my Church."

"I am afraid on this point I will not budge," Mol said, her voice clamping down like iron. "If you wish to enter this Temple, which is under my care and guidance as the Voice of the Mother, you will do us all this courtesy. Otherwise this Temple is closed to you." Torvul smoothly stepped around her to stand, almost nonchalantly, next to Mol.

Allystaire resisted the urge to mount the next step or two so that he stood right behind the Archioness, looming behind her and sandwiching her between potential foes; instead he remained a respectful few paces behind.

Cerisia delicately pushed back her foxfur hood with her lambskin gloved hands. The mass of dark hair upon her head was intricately pinned up with a Baron's ransom of gem-studded pins and combs. Deftly, she untied strong silk bands that held her mask in place, cradling it in her hands. She nodded, almost imperceptibly, to Mol and Torvul, then turned to face Allystaire.

She was, he realized, roughly of an age with him, though she wore her years considerably better. If there were lines of age or care around her eyes or mouth he would've had to look close and long to find them, and he wouldn't have minded. She was handsome, he briefly thought, rather than beautiful, but something about her drew the eye, and full red lips curving in a faint smile saw him rethinking the label he'd assigned. Her eyes were a pale green, almost a match for the translucent topaz that were fitted into her mask. Her smile and her eyes lingered just a shade too long on him, and he felt his cheeks tightening in sudden and inexplicable anger at her brief scrutiny.

"There," she said, turning back to Mol. "I have acceded to your request. May we proceed now?"

The girl nodded rather solemnly, then guided, for the first time, a priestess of another faith into the Mother's Temple. Torvul stumped along beside her, and Allystaire slowly brought up the rear.

"How was so much accomplished so quickly? If I understand properly, this building was raised in a matter of months, and the glass—"

"Was donated by a glazier," Mol replied. "And many hands took to the building of this place. We had a steady stream of visitors through late summer and early autumn, and all took the opportunity to work."

"Donated? Why, even the Temple of Fortune in Londray acquired its glass at considerable cost. Surely something was exchanged."

"Aye," Allystaire spoke up. "The man was knifed in some foolish tavern brawl he was no part of, up in Birchvale. I was there and I cured him of a wound that might have meant his life."

"How?" The Archioness turned to him and fixed him with the look that suggested that his answer to her question could possibly be the most riveting thing she would hear today, her eyes wide, but not too wide, leaning almost imperceptibly forward.

"A Gift from the Mother," Allystaire replied.

Her lips parted lightly, her eyes widened. Allystaire knew he was meant to read surprise and curiosity. "I shall have to see it."

Before he could reply she turned and approached the oval of the altar, gasping faintly. "Such fine stonework." She came closer to it, brushing past Torvul and Mol, reaching out as if to touch it, though stopping short.

"Surely this must be dwarfish craftsmanship," she said.

The dwarf chuckled. "No. Even my kin could not work stone as cunningly as She who built this."

"She?"

"Yes," Mol replied in Torvul's stead. "The altar was raised by the Mother acting through Her mortal agents, of which we are three."

Cerisia smiled, fetchingly, but her tone grated. "It is important for these founding myths to be established early, yes?"

Allystaire felt a surge of anger, but Mol's large brown eyes swung instantly to him, and he heard her voice. *Keep still, Arm. She is trying to provoke us. Do not give her this.*

"If you will," Mol said out loud, solicitous deference briefly coloring her words and face. "The stages of the altar's raising were witnessed by many of the folk of Thornhurst."

"Of course," the priestess replied, taking a moment to swipe an imaginary blot off her mask with the edge of her fox-fur.

"You might inspect it for the seams where stones were polished to look as one, or for the tell-tale marks of tools," Torvul replied, "if you were inclined. But you won't find them."

Allystaire felt himself counting and recounting the men and resources he had on hand, picking at the problems festering in his mind, at the puzzle of these servants of Fortune. He didn't notice Cerisia speaking to him till she repeated a question.

He shook away the occupying thoughts and turned his eyes on her. "My deepest apologies, Archioness," he said, reaching for his best manners. "I am afraid I was preoccupied. Please do pardon my rude inattention."

She smiled, winningly. She seemed to do everything winningly, so far as Allystaire could tell. "You do have manners after all. Tell me, Allystaire, Arm of the Mother, how you learned them? Your accent is not…" She waved a patronizing glove at the small stone-and-glass temple, "local."

Allystaire cleared his throat, buying time to think of a true answer. "I learned my manners from my father, Archioness." He tried to smile. "Surely that was not the question that I missed?"

"No," she said, her smile's brightness dimming. "If there are five of you—I see five pillars on this altar, after all—where are the other two?"

"Working, no doubt," Allystaire replied. "There is much to do and few enough hands." Before she could open her mouth to ask further questions, he seized the initiative. "I am sure that Mol, as the Mother's Voice, could do more to answer your questions than I could."

Her smile fully bloomed again, bright and welcoming as a roaring fire on a winter night. She almost spoke, but whatever the words were, she tamped them down and turned back to Mol.

The dwarf's voice rolled and rumbled in Allystaire's thoughts. *Make your excuses and get out, before she comes up with more questions.*

"If you will all pardon me," Allystaire said, "there is work being done that I must oversee." He turned for the door, till Cerisia's voice brought him up short.

"Please do say that you will dine with me this evening." She paused. "All of you, of course. I do look forward to meeting all five of the Mother's servants."

Mol replied for him. "Some of us may, yes, though all of us have duties that will require our attention. These days, our evening meals tend to be taken standing up."

Allystaire ducked out through the Temple door and shut it behind him. Idgen Marte was lurking by the steps.

"How d'ya feel," she murmured.

"Outmaneuvered. My left flank is crumbling and I have no reserves."

"We may have some reserves. I'm off to make contact with Keegan. What do you want me to tell him?"

Allystaire took a deep breath. "The truth. We could use his help."

"What do I have t' bargain with?"

"Your womanly wiles?" Allystaire's suggestion was immediately followed up with a hiss of pain, as Idgen Marte's hand, too fast to follow as usual, thudded into his shoulder. "Remind him, if you could, of what obligations he may already have to us."

"No matter how it may soothe the conscience, a man can't spend fulfilled obligations, and Deserter's Brotherhood aren't known for acting kindly to people needing help," she pointed out.

"Well, I am not known for acting kindly towards deserters. In his case, I have. My mind could yet change," Allystaire said.

"I think hard weight is more likely to get us somewhere."

"Oh? What of the saving of their lives? What of the food and supplies and tools they have already been given? We have treated them as guests, and asked nothing in return, left them to their own, as they wished—"

She raised a hand. "Fine. Point taken. Don't blame me if they tell us all to go freeze and go for banditry before winter sets in."

"I will not have bandits base themselves under our nose. I will fit them for ropes if they take so much as a bent copper half at knifepoint."

"I'll leave that part out," she said, and turned to leave, then paused. "And Allystaire, that priestess is here for you. In more ways than one."

He snorted, lip curling in disdain. "Then she will leave disappointed."

Idgen Marte nodded, satisfied, and soon slipped out of his sight.

* * *

Allystaire passed the next few turns by walking from one end of the village to the other, inspecting the progress, or the lack of progress, being made on the village's defenses. He offered rather futile words of encouragement and briefly took up a shovel before restlessness drove him back towards the Temple and his tent. He found Idgen Marte and Torvul waiting within, along with Gideon, who was reclining on Allystaire's cot, reading.

"Well?" Allystaire asked.

"Archioness Cerisia has retired to her pavilion for a midday respite," Torvul said, mockingly pompous, drawing himself up with the air of a herald or a declaiming bard. "Apparently being so close to the soil is cause for exhaustion."

"Good. Gives us time to react. Where is Mol?"

"Praying," the dwarf answered him. "Asking Her Ladyship for guidance."

"We should probably all do so, if we can find the time," Idgen Marte offered.

"Aye, we should. Remind me this evening." Allystaire paused. "Before sunset. Now—did you find Keegan?"

"Aye. And he's eager to speak with you. None too eager to come near the village in daylight, though. Said he'll come to you tonight. There was something about making a call like a nightjar to let you know it was him, and how, since nightjars are flown south by now there'd be no mistaking it, but…"

Allystaire snorted. "As if I would know a nightjar from a barn owl."

"I thought as much. Even so, listen for some screeching."

"I will." He took a deep breath, looked around, as if seeking a task, his hands opening and closing once. "What do we do about this?"

"Little we can do," Torvul said. "This was bound t'happen. You've already made contact with Braech's Temple, and Urdaran's. Was only a matter of time till Fortune came calling. It's a sign they're taking us seriously."

"Or see us as a threat that needs stamping out," Allystaire countered.

"We are a threat." Gideon didn't take his eyes off his book as he spoke. "We are preaching a faith that threatens most everything Fortune, Urdaran, and Braech stand for. However," he suddenly sat up, sticking a finger in his book to mark his place, "we have a chance at making common cause with Fortune's clergy."

"How do you figure that?" Torvul asked. "I don't see our esteemed guests making common cause with anyone that can't pay them well."

"Perhaps," Gideon said. "As I have not met or spoken to them I can't really guess at her specific intentions."

"I can guess at some of her intentions," Idgen Marte suggested, smiling wryly at Allystaire.

He felt his cheeks grow warm. "You are not going to see them, Gideon, not if I can help it."

"Why? I am one of the Ordained. I have a duty to represent Her."

"I know, Gideon." Allystaire closed his eyes in frustration. "You do have a duty. Yet I have a duty as well, laid upon me by the Goddess Herself, to protect you. You are safer if they do not know you. Not yet."

"It is better if they don't see you unless they have to," Idgen Marte said. "It's simple strategy. You don't show an enemy everything you have."

"Who's to say they are enemies?" Gideon carefully set his book down on the cot as he stood up. "Have they made any threats, or come in force?"

"You said yourself that we threaten their faith," Allystaire pointed out.

"Aye. Yet Fortune's dogma speaks of the distribution of goods and wealth, the shifting balances of power. Perhaps diplomacy could convince them that this is such a shift, simply on a massive scale."

"How does diplomacy do that, boy?" Torvul found a stool and sat on it. "It's a bit naive to think they'll treat with us like equals."

"No more than it is paranoid to automatically treat them as enemies. Nor is it honest to call them our guests and spy upon them and plot against them."

"The Goddess didn't ordain a Shadow for no reason, Gideon," Idgen Marte reminded him gently. "Sometimes what we do must be done out of sight."

"There is a difference between Shadow and darkness. The former requires light; the latter often begins with lies."

"Gideon!" Allystaire didn't raise his voice so much as pitch it to demand attention. "We are not lying to them. We are not lulling them so that we may fall upon them in the night. If the Archioness wants to know what I think of her and her kind she will merely ask me. There is not much I can do to prevent it. We are in the weaker position; we may hope for the best, but we must prepare for the worst."

"So we must think the worst of everyone we meet?" Gideon's cheeks flushed at the scolding, but he bore up well, kept his eyes locked on Allystaire's.

"It is not that simple," Allystaire said. "Surely you can see that."

"It is complex, but we do ourselves no favors by making it moreso with our own actions," Gideon said. "Ask them what they want. Tell them whether they may have it."

"Gideon," Torvul began, "what you say is not without ore among the silt. We can't treat everyone like an enemy, but there's an old Dwarfish saying—now bear in mind I have to amend it a little and your tongue does a poor job of handling complexities. In short, though, it says that when you sink a new shaft, hope to find ore, but be prepared to find clay. D'ya understand?"

"Hope for a good outcome, but prepare for a poor one," Gideon said.

"Aye," the dwarf replied. "We can hope that she's here to be our ally, but we have to be ready if she's not."

Allystaire crossed his arms and spared a glance for Idgen Marte, whose frown nearly matched his.

"Any sense of optimism is misplaced, I think," he said sourly. "I have known priests and priestesses of Fortune, and gold sticks to their fingers the way ice sticks to the top of a mountain. Her arrival portends nothing good for us. Interpret it how you will, any of you." He waved a hand at them all. "But the defense of this place and its people is my charge. I will go about it as I think best. Each of you will always be free to speak your mind to me and offer whatever counsel you have. I will listen to it, and consider it—but I will, in the end, make these decisions. Her people will be watched. We will remain on our guard."

He went to the edge of his tent and reached for the flap. "We will offer them no offense, and strike no first blow. We all have work. Go to it."

Idgen Marte and Torvul both nodded sharply, and Allystaire could read her approval in the set of her shoulders, her stride. Torvul he found harder to read, but the alchemist patted Allystaire's arm as he passed.

With the tent now empty but for him and Gideon, Allystaire said, "Continue thinking on the problems I have set you, lad. We will talk about all of them and more. And I want to make sure you understand—you may always speak your mind to me, on any subject, no matter how much you think I will disagree."

Gideon sat back down upon the cot and picked up the book he'd been reading, but he didn't open it. "Will I always know your mind? With no dissembling?"

Allystaire nodded. "Always."

The boy thought a moment, then nodded and opened his book. Allystaire watched him for a moment, then exited into the noonday autumn light.

CHAPTER 21

Finery

Allystaire's shoulders bore a deep, comforting ache from turns of work with shovel and mattock, but his mind buzzed relentlessly at the obstacles that he could not move as easily as he could a pile of earth. Having taken time to wash, he retreated back to his tent to find Gideon napping on his cot. In place of his armor lay fresh, new clothes: a long-sleeved blue shirt with the sunburst that was displayed upon his shield and pennant embroidered over the left breast, as well as a pair of breeches of finer and cleaner cut than any he currently owned. He fingered the material. *Good linen,* he thought. *Expensive. Would feel better in armor.*

Sighing, he pulled off his work-soiled clothing and carefully pulled on the new garments. He stopped, contemplated his belt and the hammer hanging from it, then tugged it around his waist and cinched it tight. Then, he contemplated what pieces of armor Torvul hadn't absconded with, and picked up his iron-banded gloves, slipping them behind his belt.

"Does that send the right message?" Gideon hadn't sat up from the cot, but apparently knew what Allystaire was doing.

Allystaire looked down at the hammer in its ring. It was a plain thing, a rough steel sledge bound to a thick hardwood handle, the bottom third of which was bound with iron bands. "I am so used to its weight that I feel wrong without it. Besides, it is as much a badge of office as I intend to carry."

Allystaire rolled his shoulders inside the linen shirt, feeling it settle lightly against his skin. *Would still rather wear armor.* "I will bring you back some food. Do not light a lamp."

"Don't need to," the boy said, a bit smugly, and Allystaire left him with a chuckle.

It wasn't a long walk to the inn, where the dinner was being held, but Allystaire had hopes of making it alone. They were dashed when he saw the Archioness exit her pavilion just as he passed.

Her white and blue silk had been traded for a simpler but just as richly made dress of dark green, and she carried a matching fur-lined wrap around her elbows, for the dress left her arms bare, and the square neckline was scooped rather low. Her hair was no longer bound up, but fell in a long, dark wave to the small of her back, though it still glittered with gemmary.

Allystaire found himself pointedly not looking too closely at her, though some instinctive remnant of his prior life forced him to stand and wait, then to stiffly offer his arm towards her as she approached, smiling thinly, with a twist of her newly reddened lips. *Might not melt iron,* some part of his brain noted as it appraised her, *but she'd get it nicely red.*

"And once again you show gentility," Cerisia murmured, as her arm slipped through his and her bosom brushed against him so faintly and so expertly he couldn't help but admire her. "You are not the roughly-worked blunt instrument you wish us to think, Sir Allystaire."

"I have no claim to the title you give me, Archioness," Allystaire replied stiffly. He found matching his stride to hers a challenge, and took a false step, causing them both to stop and teeter slightly.

"How long has it been since you walked arm in arm with a woman?" Her tone was gently chiding, but the intrusion of the question bothered him.

Nevertheless, he felt compelled to answer. "It has been the better part of ten years."

"Well," she said, setting off again, and managing a slightly longer stride, allowing him a bit more comfort, "that is a long time. And unusual for a knight. You are a knight, no matter how you may deny it."

"I have denied nothing," Allystaire said. He cleared his throat and an uncomfortable silence reigned, broken only by their staggered steps on the path. "Why do you ask? What I am now is what concerns you, yes?"

"Indeed, yet there is value in knowing your past, part of which I can guess. Your accent is northern, and your speech and manner are educated. Forgive me if I insult your home, but there are not so very many well educated folk farther north than where we now stand, and all of them are Oyrwyn nobility."

She leaned close to his ear—close enough that he had to try very hard not to shiver as he felt her breath fall warmly on his neck—and she murmured, "You are doing a poor job of hiding, Lord Coldbourne."

Her words broke the spell of her contact, and Allystaire mystified her with a peal of loud laughter. "Hiding? You think I am hiding?"

He stepped away from her, pulled his arm free, and held her eyes, reading confusion in their cast. She was caught off guard and doing a poor job of hiding it. *Lovely. I wonder how much weight she spent on the topaz for her mask to match her eyes,* he couldn't help but note.

"Archioness, if you have come here thinking you will expose some great secret, you have come in vain. The Young Baron in Wind's Jaw knows where to find me if he wishes, though of the six knights he sent to find me this summer, only two rode back to him alive. Lionel Delondeur made me a guest of his seat at the Dunes not a month ago, and I am sure he could follow the trail back here if he wished. So if you thought that my past, and my name, and my presence here was some secret you could peddle, some weapon of influence?" He shook his head, his lips twisting with a bit of scorn. "If anyone wants to know who I am, or where I am, tell them. Draw them a map and lend them a horse. Make sure they understand that they will find the Arm of the Mother waiting for them. Not Lord Coldbourne."

She leaned back as he harangued her, raising the fingertips of one hand to her neck and taking a deep breath. A calculated move, he realized, just as much as drawing out his declaration had been. Her eyelashes flickered, then suddenly she met his eyes again.

"Of course a man like you wouldn't hide," she replied, sliding her arms around his again, and pressing rather more firmly against him. "You are a master of yourself and much of what surrounds you, no matter what titles you carry or renounce. I will remember that."

Why do I feel like I've just been outflanked? Allystaire cleared his throat and they resumed their walk to the inn, passing it in silence.

When he saw the lamp-lit oilskin windows of the inn, he felt a little like a lost soldier finally stumbling back into camp.

Once he was through the doors, pausing to allow Cerisia to enter first, he caught sight of Torvul and Mol. The dwarf's freshly shaved scalp gleamed in the lamplight, and he wore, to Allystaire's surprise, something like Mol's sky-blue robe, though of a slightly darker color and more generous cut. The sleeves, in particular, were very short and did not impede his hands. Allystaire was comforted to see a few nondescript potion-pouches hooked to the alchemist's belt, however.

A long table had been set out in the common room, with four mismatched chairs set out to either side. His stomach rumbled at the smell of bread rising from a cloth-covered bowl, and he went around the table to stand next to Torvul. The dwarf gave a subtle tick with his eyes, indicating Allystaire's seat, to the far left. As far as possible from Cerisia, he noted.

Mol came from the kitchen, bearing a pitcher in one hand and a platter of mugs in the other, and set both down expertly. The Archioness, to whom Allystaire's eyes were continually drawn, despite himself, arched a brow.

"The Voice of the Mother herself serving at table? I would think you had weightier, more exalted duties."

Mol turned her smiling face to the woman, and for a moment the girl Allystaire had come to know so many months ago was looking up at them all. "Nothin's more exalted than beer. Had t'be sure we were gettin' the best." Her smile beamed a brief moment more, and then she sat delicately, her back straight, and the cool, poised face of the priestess replaced her girlish grin.

Cerisia swallowed, allowing her hands to clasp briefly. Then one of her servants, the imitation beggar who had carried the Wheel on its staff, pulled out a chair for her. She sat gracefully, briefly managing to arch her back so that Allystaire had a quick, tempting glimpse of the plunge of her neckline.

"I hope it will not offend anyone if we provide wine," Cerisia said mildly, even as her servants, who'd apparently preceded her, began to unpack a wicker basket they'd set upon a bench pushed against the wall, producing two corked jars.

I thought they clinked promisingly, Allystaire thought, certain there was more. He caught Cerisia watching him as he looked at the bottles for identifying marks. They bore Innadan crests, a greathelm wreathed in green vines, carefully painted. *Expensive. And she expects me to react—how much about me does she know?*

"I do hope it will meet with your approval," the Archioness said nominally to Mol, though her eyes flicked to Allystaire as she spoke.

"Never touch the stuff," Mol said, brightly. "But I am sure Allystaire and Mourmitnourthrukacshtorvul will appreciate it."

Cerisia betrayed herself, perhaps, by sneaking a glance down to where Allystaire sat. The woman, it seemed, didn't know how to deal with a child priestess who deftly matched even her mild opening gambits.

She was even less prepared for Idgen Marte to suddenly materialize at the head of the table. Allystaire had to hide a smirk by biting the inside of his cheek. Idgen Marte lifted her swordbelt clear over one shoulder and slung it carefully over the back of her chair, grabbing the beer pitcher and a cup, then filling it before she sat. Much like Allystaire and Torvul, she wore new clothes: a leather jerkin over a loose shirt, and tightly fitted trousers, all of it a blue so dark it was nearly black. No symbols or sunbursts gleamed upon it anywhere that he could see. There wasn't even a glint of metal on the straps fastening the jerkin closed; they were as dark as the rest of it.

That was not necessary. Mol's voice echoed in Allystaire's head, all three of their heads, he was sure.

Idgen Marte's response was quick. *Doesn't hurt to keep her off balance.*

By the time all four of the ordained had seated themselves, Cerisia rallied and indicated for her female companion to open one of the bottles of wine, which she did with practiced efficiency. Wine was poured into three cups, one of which was placed before the Archioness, while the lesser priestess took one each to Allystaire and Torvul.

Allystaire took the cup in one hand. It was a delicate thing of hammered silver that Fortune's party had provided, plate apparently being among their baggage. The Archioness raised her own cup. Gems glittered around its stem, though he could not identify them in the lamplight.

"To the meeting of differing faiths in peace," she said, her voice as smooth and sweet as honey.

Mol raised her mug of beer and echoed her solemnly. "To peace." The other three murmured the same and all drank.

The gods are good, Allystaire inwardly swore, as soon as the wine swirled around his tongue. It was a better vintage than he'd had in years. One of Innadan's best reds, strong and rich in the mouth and nothing about it sour. His pleasure must've shown on his face, even as the lamps began to lose ground to the night encroaching outside, because Cerisia spoke to him.

"I must say that your neighbors to the east do know how to grow grapes, don't they?"

Allystaire carefully set his cup down, but not before taking a deep nose of the wine's breath, which had a pleasant hint of smoke. "That they do. Despite nearly two score years of war an unspoken accord has protected the main part of their vineyards."

"Foolish way t'go t'war," Torvul piped up, after having tossed back his entire cup in one go. "Why leave an enemy a way to pay his soldiery?"

Idgen Marte snorted. "You wouldn't say that if you'd had Oyrwyn or Harlach wine. It's all sickly sweet."

"Those are the only grapes that will grow in our climate," Allystaire replied.

"The colder north does produce hardier, if somewhat rougher specimens," Cerisia said, moving smoothly on before Allystaire could puzzle out whether she meant grape vines. "Of course, any of the baronies are quite cold enough for me. I hail from the Archipelago."

"Never been to Keersvast," Allystaire said. "Sounds entirely too warm and wet and salty for my taste." Before he could even realize what he'd just said, Idgen Marte and Mol's voices both sounded in his head, variations on the theme of closing his mouth, with Idgen Marte adding, *Unless you are trying to bed her.*

He covered his sudden embarrassed distraction by having another sip of the wine, letting its dry and strong flavors fill his mouth.

Cerisia gave him a moment's quarter and, setting her wine down, laced her fingers under her chin to turn her attention to Torvul. "Mourmitnourthrukacshtorvul," she said. "What brings one of your people into this new faith? And where is the rest of your caravan?"

Torvul cleared his throat and met her gaze evenly. "I've no caravan. Not for years now."

She sat straighter in her chair, lips pursed faintly. "How does one of your folk lose their caravan? Surely you weren't cast out. From what I know, that is a criminal punishment."

"I was," Torvul replied bluntly. "Yet what you know of my kind, and our caravans, probably couldn't fill this cup, Archioness—which, by the by, is sadly empty," he added, lifting it and gesturing at the wine-bearer. "We're a close-mouthed folk, by and large, and what passes for crime among us might be quite different than among you and yours." The servant moved around the table, smoothly pouring a fresh measure into Torvul's cup.

The dwarf sipped and smiled broadly. "That's better. Now as to your first question, Archioness—I'm among this faith because this one here saved me from hanging," Torvul said, grinning all the while, and then pointing with the rim of his cup to Allystaire.

Cerisia laughed lightly and looked to Allystaire. "There's a story to be told there, I'm sure. Stories sprout around you like mushrooms after a rain—of thieves bested, folk rescued, vile knights whose bodies are shattered by the force of your lance blow."

"Don't forget the gravekling whose head he stove in weaponless," Torvul rumbled. "Crushed it like you or I might a raw egg. That does make me hunger; is supper on its way?"

That threw her once again, and so as Mol and Idgen Marte began trying to put a solid dent in their pitcher of beer, Cerisia recovered with a sip of wine before speaking to Torvul again. "Torvul— may I call you familiar in this way?" The alchemist nodded, and she went on. "I would be remiss if I did not ask. Just what gods do your people venerate? I have heard so little on the topic and all of it very confused and confusing—Braech? Fortune? Urdaran? I have heard it said you worship stone, but of course that is all nonsense."

"Not stone, but ores. Metal. And to a lesser extent, gems."

"Surely you do not worship gold?" Cerisia's question echoed the thoughts rolling in Allystaire's own head.

"Well, I don't. Anymore." Torvul paused to let that sink in as he had a slightly more moderate sip of his wine. Then he pressed on.

"And worship is probably the wrong word. Different ores embody different ideals that dwarfs strive to attain. Silver, for example. Soft and beautiful. A good silversmith can turn out work to rival any goldsmith, if only because he's likely to get more practice. Silver, though, is more practical than gold, y'see? You can work it into things that are of some use, rather than things you just wish to stare at and polish once or twice a day. Makes good medicine, for example. Many dwarfs who venerate the spirits of silver—they want to do useful things in a beautiful way. Help their caravan and make it look better at the same time. Silver has a very feminine principle, I suppose, and I mean that as the highest compliment to the ladies at the table," he added, running roughshod over the follow up questions Cerisia was clearly yearning to ask, and lifting his cup, so that everyone was obliged to follow suit.

Allystaire was inwardly thankful for the excuse Torvul gave him to take another mouthful of wine, as well as the respite from Cerisia's attention. Even with the way the priestess had thrown his thinking off, a part of him still pondered Torvul's words. *That was more lore about dwarfs than I think I have ever heard from him.*

A brief silence reigned till Mol stood up, gave a fractional nod of her head to excuse herself, and disappeared into the kitchen. "Be back with supper," was all she offered by way of explanation.

"Wherever did you find this girl?" Cerisia murmured, mingling admiration and disbelief. "One moment she is a child and the next she is an ancient sibyl."

"Well," Allystaire began, letting one fingertip rest lightly on the base of his cup, "since you asked, I found her right here." He gestured with his chin towards the newly erected wooden bar, with a rack of barrels behind it and a shelf full of smaller spirit casks bracketed to the wall above them. "In the cold well, with the village a smoking charnel house."

He couldn't help but feel like a point had been scored when the Archioness's back straightened and her eyes—which he was grateful he could only make out the shape and not the color of—blinked in confusion. "I'm not sure I understand."

"The village folk had been set upon by reavers—some taken, but many, especially those who resisted, slaughtered and burned upon the green. Mol's father hid her in the cold well. I heard her cries as I rode into the village, following the smoke." Allystaire shrugged, lifted his wine cup, and drank. When he set the cup down, Cerisia was still looking at him, puzzled.

"Then how is the village peopled once more? How do buildings stand? Who came back?"

"As many of the folk as were alive when Allystaire found them," Mol said as she emerged from the kitchen, bearing a tray that looked too big for her, yet she managed it to the table and set it down without help. It bore two huge pies, the slits in their brown crusts releasing a wonderfully scented steam, a stack of simple wooden bowls, and a large spoon. "Beef and onion in ale gravy," Mol said, pointing to one pie, "and hen and leek with prune," she added, pointing to the other. "Mind the steam."

The girl picked up the spoon and held it out to the Archioness, who took it uncertainly, then decided to hand it off to the male servant at her left hand. Mol frowned, not bothering to hide the expression, and sat.

"Are you so accustomed to being served that you cannot put food in your own bowl?" Mol waited till the servant was done putting delicate portions in Cerisia's bowl, then took the spoon and ladled herself a sizable serving, holding the spoon out to Idgen Marte afterwards.

"Part of the duty of my students is to attend me," Cerisia noted, just barely keeping a defensive tone out of her words. "And to learn service and etiquette that way. I did so myself when I was younger. However, your words do make a point. Few of us should ever be so exalted so as not to serve. I did bring a few delicacies with me for the meal. Do you mind?"

Mol shook her head, not speaking an answer aloud, for her mouth was full of steaming, savory pie. Allystaire's was as well, having dished more of it up onto his bowl than anyone else at the table, though Torvul was a close second. He ignored the steaming heat with the aplomb of a man who'd often had cold food, and too little of it, but he did watch as Cerisia stood and went to her basket.

Cold take me, it has been a long time, Allystaire thought, then lowered his face and tried to bury his thoughts in beef pie, blindly reaching into the bread basket and seizing a loaf to sop the ale and onion gravy. *Beef's good, he told himself. Maybe not as good as...*

His thoughts were interrupted as fingertips landed lightly on his shoulder. He glanced up and got an eyeful of the pale, smooth expanse of Cerisia's neck as she placed a tiny bowl in front of him.

"Fish roe," she explained. "A luxury from my home." Two other similar bowls had been placed upon the table. Allystaire reached for the one nearest him, though he paused and his shoulders tensed as soft, manicured fingertips just lightly brushed across the skin of his neck as Cerisia retreated to her own seat.

The bowl was cool, light, and smooth to the touch. He held it closer to a lamp that descended from a crossbeam and saw the light shimmer across its surface. A miniature spoon was thrust into a mass of tiny black dots. "Is this made of—"

"Nacre, yes," she answered, anticipating his question. "Purists believe that anything else can spoil the flavor. Please do try some. It is only rarely transported this far inland."

"Well," Allystaire said with a gentle shrug as he carefully set the bowl down, trying without much success to grasp the spoon between forefinger and thumb without looking like an oaf, "we do not see much in the way of saltwater fish in my home. But," he added, finally getting a grip and coaxing some of the stuff into the shallow spot on the spoon, "an old campaigner never turns down food."

Idgen Marte had already eagerly put a spoonful into her mouth. Eyes closed, she savored it, tongue moving behind her cheeks. Allystaire plunged the spoonful into his mouth. The explosion of salt on his tongue and the half-liquid half-solid texture were welcome. *Bit too delicate for a proper food,* though, he thought, even as he chewed and swallowed.

He inclined his head, gratefully, as he swallowed the last, jellied scraps. Cerisia smiled warmly and he felt her eyes linger on him as he turned his attention back to his meal.

"From what I remember of Keersvast," Idgen Marte said as she pushed the half-empty bowl of roe towards Mol, who eyed it uncertainly, "that much good quality roe could pay a small fisherman's license and catch tax for a year."

"Perhaps with enough left over for a bribe or two as well," Cerisia said, chuckling.

The room suddenly chilled for Allystaire, as though a window were thrown open and the warmth sucked away. "That much?" An angry note thrummed through him as he spoke, deadening his voice. Questions abounded in his head. *Was the right fish difficult to catch? How much profit could the man who caught it make? Why would a fisherman need to bribe anyone?*

The effect was noticeable. Cerisia turned to him, stiffened. Mol's voice sounded in his head, a resounding, *Do not!*

"Have I given offense, Lord Allystaire?" The Archioness's voice was careful, teetering on a display of wounded affection.

Allystaire swallowed a mouthful of pie and tried to choke down his anger with it. "Not at all, Cerisia," he murmured, though how much conviction he managed to put in the words he did not know. "Simply raised questions."

"Questions we may explore another time," Mol smoothly put in as her spoon clattered into an empty bowl, which she pondered a moment, before reaching for the serving spoon.

Allystaire sopped his bowl clean with fresh bread, filled it again and emptied it the same, as the Archioness traded investigative gambits disguised as inanities with Idgen Marte, Mol, and Torvul. His mind still seethed, if more as a faint, glowing ember than a truly roaring furnace. *The extravagance,* he thought aimlessly. *Does she think to buy us with luxuries? Has she any conception of what we are, what we do, whom we serve? Clearly she knows some, but how much?*

Finally, with the large pie plates more emptied than Allystaire might have expected, they all sat back, sated. Cups were refilled. Torvul produced a long sliver of polished bone and began to pick his teeth with it.

Mol leaned forward in her chair, hands steepling beneath her chin.

"We have shared meat, salt, and beer at table together now, Archioness. You are our guest, and entitled to all rights and protections of hospitality. I believe I am entitled to ask a question now."

Cerisia nodded gravely, a loose tendril of hair spilling forward onto her neck. "Of course, child."

Mol frowned at being called child, but let it pass, sitting straight up. "To what purpose have you come to the Mother's people and Her Temple? What ends do you pursue by assailing the mysteries of Her Ordained with your subtle questions?"

Cerisia smiled. "It is quite simple. The Arch-Council of Fortune's Temple believes there is a very strong possibility that this Mother of whom you speak is, in point of fact, a newly discovered," she paused, searching for a word, "facet of the Goddess Fortune Herself."

The explosion of angry noise nearly drove Cerisia out of her seat in fright, as Allystaire leapt to his feet, one balled fist pounding the table so hard that wine cups spilled and an empty nacre bowl flew off the table and shattered. He roared in a nearly wordless rage, uncertain and uncaring of precisely what he said.

He was not the only one, either. Torvul leapt to his feet, as had Idgen Marte. The clatter of chairs falling and voices mingling in anger made any words indiscernible, though Cerisia tried to answer in her defense. Her male servant suddenly stepped in front of her chair and drew a knife from his belt.

Allystaire's hammer was halfway into his hands before he knew it, but Idgen Marte was, as she always had been, faster. Her arm was a blur and her blade moving in the air in the time it took for him to think of drawing steel.

"Silence."

The single word that left Mol's lips was not spoken at a volume or a pitch that should have cut through the noise, yet it did, carrying enormous power with it. Allystaire felt his own voice strangled into nothingness. He could breathe, yes, but he could make no sound. He saw, from the startled expressions on the faces of Fortune's servants, that it had done the same to them. Idgen Marte frowned, but did not lower her blade.

Mol remained seated, the only one to do so, and somehow a common peasant's chair became a seat of office, occupied not by an eleven year-old child, but by a priestess of sober and powerful mien, her eyes practically flashing with radiant anger.

"Put up your weapons and be seated."

Allystaire was back in his seat, hammer on his belt, without thinking about it.

Cerisia's two acolytes, for whom no chairs were provided, suddenly folded their legs under them upon the ground.

Voice of the Mother, Allystaire thought in wonderment as silence spread throughout the room.

"So like the Sea Dragon, the Mistress of Wealth would seek to make the Mother subordinate. To control Her, and we Her Servants—"

"It is not about…" Cerisia spoke up, voiced meek and strained.

"I did not give you leave to speak," Mol suddenly snapped, leaning forward in her chair. "When I am finished you may respond."

Cerisia straightened in her own chair, skin drawing tight across her cheeks as her jaw quivered in what Allystaire estimated was her first display of genuine anger. She rallied herself somehow.

"I will not be ordered about by a child—"

"You are being ordered by the Voice of the Mother in the very place where the Mother woke in this world, where She spoke to me, the place where She and I are strongest. In this I will be obeyed. Test me at your peril."

The two priestesses locked eyes for but a moment. Anger and power radiated from Mol in waves that Allystaire could feel pressing against his senses. The two acolytes looked to one another. Allystaire saw the fake beggar's hand move uncertainly towards his belt and tightened his fist reflexively. He thought to reach for his hammer, but his fingers brushed his iron-studded gloves. He pulled them free of his belt and laid them carefully on the table. He made sure the studs thudded dully and loudly against the wood.

The man looked up, going half into a crouch, saw the gloves, lamplight flickering off the studs. Then he saw Allystaire's huge, scarred knuckles clenched on the table behind them, and his eyes finally climbed to the paladin's face.

Allystaire reached for a glove and tugged it onto his right hand, flexing his fingers into a fist, then out and back again, leather creaking.

The acolyte sat back down and folded his hands together in his lap.

Meanwhile, Mol spoke. "Do you act out of simple fear of what the Mother's rise might mean? Or is this a part of some longer game, some stratagem?"

"Everything is part of a longer game," Cerisia said, her voice slightly weary. "And to suggest that a tiny temple in a hinterland village where something is worshipped by three score peasants could be a threat to Fortune's church is absurd. What I come offering is your only chance of survival."

"Explain," Mol said, drawing her hands into her lap.

"This is how Temple politics work," Cerisia began. "New cults spring up more often than you would think. Take this fad for worshipping the Elvish Green, as if any of the fools going to its rented Temples even understood what the concept even means. It will die off. In a year or two the dilettantes who run those Temples will lose interest, or their parents will cease to pay for it, and it will melt away."

Mol snorted. "No one is funding us in the first place, so it can hardly vanish."

"That's part of your problem," Cerisia replied. "Yet I digress. New gods, new goddesses—they arrive and they disappear. If they survive at all, it is because we absorb them. Fortune, Urdaran, and Braech are the godheads of this world. Their worship has gone unbroken, undaunted, as long as there are records. Other spirits might claim divinity, or have it claimed on their behalf, yet in the end they are shown to be aspects or servants of one of the true three."

Mol smiled. "Urdaran tells his flock to turn a blind eye, literally, to the suffering around them, to focus on a peace in the next world. The Mother demands that we work to alleviate suffering as we find it. Braech is merely strength calling to strength, all bluster and noise and lust. The Mother tells us that strength is often an accident of birth, that mercy and charity are no kind of sin. Fortune concerns Herself with the wealth of the world. How much do you believe the Mother cares for gold or gemmary? Can they be eaten? Planted? Used to comfort the weak or the dying or the oppressed?"

As the rest of the room sat in rapt stillness, Cerisia raised a hand. "Fortune does not seek wealth for wealth's sake, nor is the gain of it the end of those who serve Her. If it were, we would not count being miserly a sin—and we do. Wealth, treasure, power, riches, these things are as rivers, meant to flow towards all who mean to work along their banks. Perhaps," she allowed, lowering her hand and adopting a reasonable tone, "it is that they have been damned up or diverted too long from too many. Perhaps this is why a new aspect of Fortune has arisen, demanding that they be freed up again."

For the briefest moment, Allystaire felt he saw a kind of sense in the Archioness's words. She was a reasonable woman, and Fortune was no evil, grasping goddess. Certainly it was possible, he found himself thinking.

Then Mol's laughter rang out, and reminded him of the times he had heard the Goddess Herself laugh, had seen Her, touched and been touched, been kissed by Her, and something bright and clean and sharp thrummed through him, and he joined the Voice in laughter, as did Idgen Marte and Torvul, and the room filled with it for a moment.

"You think this is about wealth? You think the Mother can be bought off with bright metal and glittering rocks?" A sneer played over Mol's face for a moment, then was replaced with a kind of warm, yet poised distance. "You poor woman. You have listened to nothing I have said. The Mother has not come to us to see us gain in riches, but to see us gain in love, in mercy, in charity, and kindness."

"Then why do so many of you carry weapons? Why do violence on Her behalf?"

Mol tsked. "You think to trip us with childish sophistry? There are those who will not accept love, and those who cannot earn mercy, but the truest answer is this—when our arms are raised to give battle, it will be truly in the defense of those who are weak, needful, desperate, suffering. It is not something we do for the Mother; it is something we do for Her people. Love is not a shield unto itself. Can anyone be said to love if they sit passively by and spout congeries of naive platitudes when what they love is threatened?"

"Then why did your paladin respond violently to my statement? What threat do we pose?"

"What a silly question. You threatened our very existence. Yet that is not what drove the Arm or the Shadow to their weapons; your acolyte drew his knife first," Mol pointed out. "And, I would remind you, he is not my paladin. We all serve the Mother and Her people."

"And if he bares steel in the presence of the Voice again," Idgen Marte suddenly put in, her voice as smooth and deadly as a blade as she stared hard at the acolyte Mol had named, "I will have his hand. At least."

"Peace, Shadow," Mol said. "They will remain our guests, though his action could have forfeit that right. I will grant them their surety so long as they remain in peace. That, of course, presupposes they do not wish to simply break camp and leave immediately, given the futility of their mission?"

"Please give my words thought, all of you," Cerisia said, her eyes flickering to Allystaire's end of the table, then back to Mol. "I argued for this course of action, to extend this chance, rather than to simply declare you anathema, to call you heretics. I warn you," she said, her voice turning urgent and pleading, "that is what will happen if I return to Londray with this answer."

"Our faith cannot be brushed aside," Mol declared, frowning. "Our Goddess is no part of yours."

"Very well," Cerisia sighed, a touch melodramatically. "I do hope you will allow us to stay at least a day or two, in order to recover from our journey—and to speak Fortune's words to such folk as might see enough sense to listen?"

Allystaire felt a denial rising in his throat, but Mol cut him off with a simple light laugh. "Speak to them if you will. It is unlikely you will turn folk aside from the Goddess who rescued them from slavery and death."

Cerisia nodded and rose slowly. Her eyes lingered briefly on Allystaire, but turned away in hurt from the angry silence they encountered. Without a word, she swept out the door, and the four ordained were left in the semi-darkness, the silence broken only by the creak of the front door and the clatter of departing footsteps.

Allystaire stood and came to Mol's side. Placing a hand on the girl's shoulder, he found her trembling, or shivering as if she were cold. He knelt beside her chair, saw Torvul and Idgen Marte coming towards her in concert.

"Mol?"

The girl shook her head and rose on unsteady legs. Allystaire caught her and she fell against him in an exhausted embrace.

"Sorry," she murmured against his chest. "'T'were like workin' all day at haulin' wood with no beer and bread at the end of it. Goddess but m'tired." She pushed herself away and stood, keeping one hand against his shoulder.

"You were brilliant, Mol," Allystaire said, smiling, feeling a swelling of pride in his chest that he wasn't sure he had done anything to earn.

"Aye," Torvul added. "You were the Goddess's voice indeed tonight. Masterful."

"M'gonna be masterfully and brilliantly 'sleep," Mol muttered, her eyes drifting closed and her shoulders starting to slump. Allystaire was close enough, and knew the signs well enough to catch her and lift her small form gently, already asleep, as he stood.

"I know well what it feels like to have the Mother's Gifts overtax your body and mind," Allystaire whispered to Idgen Marte and Torvul. "She will need sleep." He jerked his head towards the staircase and started to carry Mol there. "We all will."

Torvul and Idgen Marte nodded, and the dwarf gestured to the meal's detritus that lay spread across the table. "Let's deal with this. Then I'm for bed. Well for a drink and a pipe, but bed at the end of all that."

Idgen Marte began to respond with her usual disdain for chores, but Allystaire couldn't make out her words, as he was already halfway up the stairs, looking at the unconscious girl in his arms. He was not sure why he spoke aloud, but his heart and his throat were swollen with the need to express what he felt, so he whispered, "I could not be prouder of you, Mol. I could not love you more if you were my own daughter." She could not have heard him, he thought—but then, as he carried her into her room, in the darkness he thought he saw her lips form a smile.

* * *

Allystaire brought a cloth-covered bowl back to his tent, the wood hot in his hands after Torvul had done something he wouldn't explain to warm the heaping pieces of savory pie it held. Navigating by moon and starlight now, he pushed open the flap and stopped immediately inside the pitch dark.

"Gideon?"

There was a scratching sort of hiss, then a tiny dot of flame came to life, found a lantern at about knee height, and the interior of the tent suddenly flooded with surprising brightness.

"What was that?" Allystaire blinked at the sudden light and crossed to where Gideon sat on his cot. He handed over the bowl and took the lantern in exchange. He found a hook along the ridgepole and set it in place.

"A firestick. Torvul's been making them and spreading them around. Says it is more efficient than flint and steel." The book he'd been reading was closed on the cot, and Gideon eagerly pulled away the cloth and began tucking into the pie.

"A damn sight more, I would say," Allystaire said. "As you eat, if you can find a moment to pause for breath, I believe I put two questions to you that still need answers. The first—how do we protect the outlying farms?"

"We don't have to protect the farms. We have to protect the people on them," Gideon said.

Allystaire smiled. "Good answer, though it evades the spirit of the question. How do we do it?"

"We can't. Not properly." The boy hastily swallowed another mouthful. "We haven't got the men to post out there. We can't ask the folk there to move here, to trade their livelihood and land for safety."

"Stop telling me what we cannot do. Tell me what we can do."

"Fine. We can train some of the folk who live there, give them bows and spears."

"We will. Ivar could teach a blind, three-legged dog the rudiments of the spear. Still, they are hardly soldiers. And it is our duty to protect them, not to let them serve as pickets."

Gideon chewed thoughtfully. "We could build signal fires for them to light at the sign of danger."

Allystaire shook his head. "Too much fuel, too much maintenance, too hard to predict; they would have to leave someone at each fire every minute of the day, ready to light it."

The boy suddenly sat up straighter, his food briefly forgotten. "I have it. The early warning bit, at least. Torvul can make small bottles full of something that will ignite on contact with the air. I'm sure he can. They throw the bottle upon the ground, it breaks, it releases a colored gout of flame or smoke into the air."

Allystaire straightened his back and crossed his arms. "That idea has merit. Provided Torvul can, and if I suggest that he cannot I am sure he will do it just to spite me. Yes. That will do." He looked to Gideon, said, "So those are your two best answers? Bows and bottles of flame?"

"Well," the boy said, jabbing at his food with his spoon, "Torvul likely could make bottles of real flame they could hurl at attackers."

"And no doubt someone would hurl one at a lad or a lass sneaking back home after a late night's…" he stumbled over the next word, settling on, "mischief."

"Then bows and signal bottles are all I have," Gideon said. "That and quick reaction. It does not…I don't know that it makes them much safer."

"It is a balancing act. We cannot make their world perfectly safe. Nor should we try, for it would reduce them to children. We will do what we can. Now my second question, and then off to bed with you. With both of us, in point of fact," Allystaire said, even as he helpfully reminded himself silently, *You've a conversation to have with Keegan before too long.*

"You asked whether someone could wear as much wealth as the priestess did and not be guilty of some ill-defined crime somewhere in the acquisition of it," Gideon said. "The answer is no, but only on the rhetorical technicality that you never specified anything. When you cast that wide a net, you're bound to catch something."

Allystaire furrowed his brow and lowered his head into his hands. "I may be too tired to follow this, lad, but I will try." He took a deep breath, ambled a few steps, sank heavily into a chair that creaked as it took his weight. "Do you not see how wearing that much gold in a miserable and war-torn country is a kind of sin in itself? How much suffering could she ease if she stopped and gave some of it away?"

"This assumes the people she would give it to would have the opportunity to trade it for what they lack, an assumption that is likely to be untrue. They can't eat the gold itself." The boy quickly ate another spoonful before continuing. "And how do you know she doesn't? I saw the clergy of Fortune once or twice in Londray, when my…when Bhimanzir allowed me out of the castle. They were quite liberal about tossing links to beggars."

"Were they tossing gold, silver, or copper?"

He thought a moment. "Probably copper."

"They could do more, Gideon. So much more. So could Braech, so could the nobility."

"Not doing more is as much a judgment of the frameworks that exist as of the individuals," Gideon said, prodding at the bowl with his spoon. "If they think they are doing good, or doing right, because it is how they've been taught."

"Some things are right or wrong no matter what a man or woman has been taught," Allystaire growled.

"Yes, but wearing the regalia of her priesthood, which was probably either handed down to her or made specifically for that purpose, is not a sin in itself," Gideon said almost plaintively. "I think you are too quick to anger. She could be our ally."

"She told us plainly that she came here as an envoy to seek to fold the Mother's church into hers, to claim that the Mother is merely some newly risen aspect of Fortune."

Gideon's spoon paused halfway to his mouth. "That's absurd," he said, letting the utensil fall down and clatter against the bowl.

"Aye," Allystaire agreed. "Yet apparently it is politics. I knew her visit meant us nothing good. When she returns and tells them we have refused, it is likely the three great temples will turn against us in unison, declare us a heresy."

"Meaning what, exactly?"

"A host of things, none of them good." *As if bandits, the Baron, sorcerers, and refugees from Bend incoming weren't enough,* Allystaire reminded himself. "I think this is enough talk for the night. I need to find what sleep I can, as do you. Good night, Gideon. Rest well."

The boy stood. He hesitated a moment before saying, "Rest well," and then he slipped out the back of the tent.

Allystaire tugged off his boots and his new linen shirt, setting the latter carefully on the table, and then slipped the hammer from his belt and rested it, haft pointing up, by the side of his cot, which he fell heavily into. Details of the day began to fill his mind. *What does a nightjar sound like? How long till Bend's refugees get here—are they coming here? We should be scouting. Mistrust Cerisia's guards.* As soon as he thought of the Archioness, though, his mind filled, nearly instantly, with the way her figure tugged at her dress, how her hair looked unbound and spilling down her back, and the way her eyes had smoldered when he had raised his voice.

Embarrassed, flushed in the dark, he pushed the thought away and quickly found sleep.

CHAPTER 22

Temple Politics

Prodded by the damnable call of some bird or other, Allystaire woke up quickly. The hammer came easy to his hand as he stood, blinking against the light.
Left the lamp lit, you old fool, he thought, then lifted it off the hook and walked to
the edge of the tent, hammer dangling from one hand, lamp in the other.

He pushed the flap back with the head of the hammer and peered into the
darkness, stymied by how he'd ruined his own night vision. He let out a sigh,
and finally, softly, called out into the night.

"Keegan?"

A tall, lean shape suddenly materialized off the ground and, as it moved
into the small pool of light, resolved itself into the former Oyrwyn scout. Allystaire stepped aside and Keegan walked into the tent.

He still wore his tattered scout's leathers, but they'd been sewn and patched
with care. His red-tinged brown beard was trimmed and his hair bound in a
loose queue that lay upon his neck, and he carried an unstrung bowstave almost
as tall as himself.

"Where did you find that?" Allystaire said, pointing with his chin at the
bow while he set the lantern back upon its hook.

"I found a supply o'well-seasoned wood just ready for the carving, carefully wrapped and hidden, buried under a tree. Was there a bowyer in this

village?" Keegan studied the furniture in the tent, and Allystaire gestured to a chair as he sat back down on his cot, groaning inwardly at the temptations of sleep that it offered.

"Not that I know. Could have just been a farmer who knew his way around wood."

"Or a poacher making sure he'd not go short. I need some string and wax, but otherwise they're just about ready," Keegan said as he slowly eased himself onto the chair by Allystaire's paper-strewn table.

"Good," Allystaire said, then added, "Provided you mean to use it to defend yourself or to eat."

"I've nothin' else in mind m'lord, I swear it," Keegan said wearily.

"I believe you, but mistrust is in my nature. I apologize." There was a moment of heavy silence before he went on. "You could come live in the village, you know, you and the other men."

Even in the dim light of the lamp, which was, by now, surely low on oil, Allystaire could see Keegan's pained frown, and waited till the expression resolved into a heavy sigh.

"We've talked about it, m'lord, but...the world of men is...crowded now. Loud. We're only just learning to become men again ourselves." He stopped for a moment, toyed idly with his bowstave, looked down to his feet. "I think I'm doin' the best of us at that, at rememberin'. And I'm none too good at it."

Allystaire didn't linger in the silence this time. "What can we do about that?"

"Don't know."

Silence reigned heavy for a moment again, and Allystaire finally said, "You might want to start thinking about it a little more like a man instead of a child waiting to be told what to do."

"You've no right—"

"I have every right. Were it not for us, you would still be a mad beast, bound to the whim of a dying god. Maybe it is time to start thinking of what you can do in earnest thanks."

The silence was even heavier this time. Allystaire heard the wood in Keegan's hands creak as he wrapped his fists tightly around it, and he slowly began easing his hand towards his hammer.

"We're grateful. And ya deserve our thanks. I'm man enough still to admit that," Keegan said. "Some o'the others I'm not so sure of. One barely speaks; he grunts and howls."

Allystaire put his hand back into his lap and leaned forward. "Idgen Marte can help with that. She's a gift for easing the mind. It might be worth asking her."

Keegan nodded, breathed out heavily. "I will do, m'lord."

"You can stop calling me that, you know. I am no lord anymore."

"How in the Cold did that happen? I didn't think you lot could simply walk away like a common soldier," Keegan said, a bit of joviality inflecting his voice for the first time.

"I walked away ahead of writs of exile. Maybe just a step in front the headsman."

"The Old Baron would've never…well, if you don't mind me sayin', among the soldiers we all sort of thought the old man might name you his heir after Ghislain was killed."

Allystaire snorted. "I was in his favor, but not so that he would throw over his own issue for me." He sighed. "Took that death hard, though. But Gerard Oyrwyn was ever practical. I know he thought he could get a new wife with child before he would have to truly hand things over to Gilrayan."

"And t'were him what banished you?"

"I banished myself, really. I knew what lines I was crossing. Shamed him in front of his entire court, called him an idiot, a pretender, and a boy playing at war. Told him he would have to play at it without me. He called that treason, and I dared him to make good on it. While he sputtered, I took what I could carry and rode straight out of the barony."

"You probably did the right thing. He was an idiot. Proved it when'er he got his own command. I've got friends in the ground 'cause of him."

"Aye," Allystaire agreed. "The only thing that made me hold on for the two years I did was the promise the Old Baron asked of me. He knew his natural son was no fit ruler, no leader of men. Asked me to help him, teach him. And I tried. The gods know I tried." He stood suddenly, waving a hand in the air and making a scornful noise. "Bah. Noise and nonsense. We need to look at who we are now, where we are."

"Aye," Keegan agreed. "If we could have just a few supplies, bowstrings, as I said, maybe some store of roots or tubers."

"There will be common stores here in the village, free for any who need it. You need but come and take it."

"What d'ya want of me in exchange? I can't promise fer all o'us."

"What I want is a good man watching the woods. I can guard the roads, but it leaves us vulnerable in the north east."

"Watchin' for what exactly?"

"An attack. Brigands. Bandits. Men of any description, really, who do not seem to have a reason—"

Keegan frowned. "There are men out there now."

Allystaire felt hair rise on the back of his neck. "What?"

"A dozen or so. They're armed, it's true, but they seem t'just be campin'—"

"Keegan, how long have they been there?"

"First I noticed 'em was two days ago."

"There have been armed men close upon us for two days, and you have said nothing of it?"

Keegan lowered his head, sighed. "I told you, the world was crowded and rushed and loud. We don't...it's hard t'remember what matters to men. All I want to do is run and hide—or kill them, rend their flesh and crack their bones, if I can. D'ya understand? Can I make ya?"

"I suppose you cannot," Allystaire admitted. "From now on, if you can, I want to know it when armed men in groups of more than three pass nearby. Can you watch this group, without risking yourself unduly?"

"Yer askin' an Oyrwyn scout if he can watch a band o'thugs without bein' noticed?" A new note crept into Keegan's voice then: pride.

Allystaire smiled, was startled as the expression suddenly became a wide yawn. "It is late, Keegan, and I must sleep. You can stay within the village tonight, or—"

"I've no need for much sleep," the man replied. "I'll bring ya a report tomorrow."

"Good." Allystaire extended a hand, felt Keegan clasp his forearm, and they shook. "Be well, Keegan. The world of men—or at least the village of Thornhurst—is here when you are ready to return. So is the Mother."

"I've maybe had enough of gods," Keegan answered. "But I'll think on it."

The tall and lean man slipped out of the tent. Allystaire placed the lamp back on its hook, blew the light out, and collapsed gratefully onto his cot.

* * *

He didn't know how long it was till he woke again, unexpectedly, but it was pitch dark in his tent when he heard the footsteps outside and the tug at the flap. Allystaire came awake all at once then, reaching for the hammer where it lay beside the cot and pulling it up next to him.

He sat up, saw the tentflap twitch aside and a hooded figure enter, with a shuttered lantern swaying at its side.

"Lord Allystaire?" Cerisia's voice was instantly recognizable: warm, hon-eyed, soft.

Freeze. Allystaire swung his legs out of his cot and stood up. "What are you doing here, Archioness?"

"I found sleep a challenge, and I saw lights in your tent, heard voices. I couldn't decide if I should see if all was well." She lifted the lantern that hung in her hand, asked, "May I?" Before he could answer she pulled back the shutters, bathing the tent in soft light again.

Allystaire blinked at the sudden relative brightness, but his eyes instantly fixed—as he knew they were meant to—on Cerisia herself. She wore a loose, fur-lined robe over a too-thin silk nightgown that was only just the decent side of opaque. She pulled down her hood, loosing her hair in a dark cascade down her back and shoulders, drawing his eye again towards the pale expanse of neck and the swell of her breasts beneath the silk.

She took a step further into the tent, lifted her lantern, and then her breath caught as, he realized, her eyes took in his bare chest, and the network of white, puckered scars upon it.

"Fortune, but, your chest, it's…"

"I have been a fighting man for more than a score of years now, Archioness. If this surprises you, it is because you have not known many men who were."

"My father was an Archipelago sword-at-hire who made weight enough to send me to the Temple on Keersvast's central island, Lord Coldbourne—I know more of fighting men than you think, and I understand that to bear so many wounds and to still be counted among the quick is unusual, at the least." She took a couple of small steps deeper into the tent, fully unshielding her lantern and setting it down on the table.

Nowhere to retreat, Allystaire thought. *Got to stand firm.* He cleared his throat and turned his head, casting his eyes about the dimly lit space for a shirt. None came to hand. He turned back to the priestess, and said with a small shrug, "The Baron employed a fine surgeon. A dwarf. Saved my life more than once, I should think."

"What was the noise earlier?" She switched subjects quite suddenly, in an attempt to catch him off guard, he suspected.

"Just someone come seeking counsel with me."

"Why do you not meet my gaze, Allystaire?" Another two steps, a third, and she was arm's length from him. An expensive floral scent reached his nose as she approached.

He lifted his eyes to meet her challenge, pressing his lips into a thin line and smoothing the skin of his cheeks with the tension of his tightly shut jaw. "I will make it a point to do so from now on, Archioness."

"Please, do call me Cerisia. Why does my presence discomfit you so?"

"I know not how much you know of me, yet I am sure it is more than I know of you. I am, forgive me, not entirely certain of your motives, or whether what you told us this evening is the entire truth. I do not know the lengths you would go to in order to see the Mother subsumed or destroyed."

"I am as true a servant to my Goddess as you believe yourself to be to yours."

"I do not doubt that. I just have no clear idea what it means."

"I spoke no lies at our dinner tonight, if that is what you mean. I did argue to be allowed this opportunity to prevent you all from simply being called anathema, and hunted as heretics." With a slightly theatrical gesture, she held out her hand. "The rumors say that you can draw the truth from anyone who speaks to you. Take my hand and ask. Prove it to yourself if you must."

Allystaire took her wrist between his fingers carefully. He could not help but notice the warmth of her skin, its softness, the alluring perfume that grew stronger—not unpleasantly so—with every moment.

He caught her eyes with his, noted how they widened slightly, how her lips parted. "Have you spoken the truth to us since you arrived in this village?"

Without hesitation, she said, "I have."

"You argued that you should be permitted to travel here in an attempt to convince us to subordinate ourselves to your Church?"

"I did."

"Why?"

"To avoid the bloodshed and the horror of rooting out a heresy," Cerisia replied. "I have no love for that kind of thing. No desire to see it done."

"And would you risk yourself, your status, or your wealth, to see it avoided?"

"I have already risked my position by coming here." She bristled at the question as she answered it.

"That was a truth, but also an evasion," he noted. "How much more are you prepared to do in order to curtail bloodshed?" Anger began to rise in Allystaire, and he felt his free hand curling into a fist, though he was careful to keep the touch of his other hand around her wrist light.

"If I cannot convince you to see reason—"

"It is not reason," Allystaire half-shouted, dropping her hand. "It is madness. It is an absurdity. You have felt, however lightly, the touch of the Mother's Gift to me. Is it anything like what Fortune grants to you? I have seen Her, spoken with Her, ki…" Allystaire broke off before finishing the thought. He felt his cheeks flush, and no doubt Cerisia saw it as well, for her lips curled boldly.

"Kissed Her? Come now, Allystaire—when was the last time you kissed a woman of flesh and blood?"

And then she was pressed against him, the silk of her nightgown cool against his bare skin, the promise of flesh behind it warm and soft. Her hand snaked around his neck and drew his mouth to her painted lips.

They were warm, soft, inviting. The scent that she wore filled his mouth as well as his nose as their lips met, opened. His heart pounded in his chest like a marching drum, and he felt hers, a pipe, distant and fast, answer through their chests. The kiss ended, whether too soon or too late, Allystaire could not have said.

"Why am I drawn to you, Allystaire of Thornhurst?" Cerisia murmured, slipping both arms around his neck. "You are not the kind of man who attracts me."

Instinctively, Allystaire had placed one hand against her back. The other, he now rested on her arm as he asked, "And do I? Or would seducing me be politically expedient?"

"Both," she replied huskily. "I would not find myself enjoying the prospect half so much were it only the latter. Or even mostly," she added. She pressed her body more firmly to his, slid fingertips into his hair. "You are, to be frank, older and rather more worn than most of the lovers I take. The stories I followed paint you a knight out of a story, where they are always young, fair-faced, clear of eye. That is the man I expected to find. That, or a charlatan; the first, easily seduced, and the second, easy to expose."

She gently but insistently tugged his head down closer to hers, meeting him eye to eye as she rose onto her tiptoes. "And yet here you are: broken nosed, with eyes that fear where your next step leads. Yet you are going to take it anyway, once you have decided where to set it down. And woe to those who would stand in your way. You are forceful in a way I find," she wriggled slowly against him, pressing her hips to his, her breasts rubbing against his chest through the thin silk, "exhilarating."

She moved to kiss him again, and he allowed her to take the lead. It was a longer and slower kiss than the first. Allystaire felt her nudge him towards the cot only a few steps behind him.

Her touch, her body, her kiss and scent—they were nearly overwhelming. Yet not so much as the Mother's kiss, the memory of which, only a week hence, could make him weak in the knees in a stray moment.

He moved his hands to her wrists and gently but firmly removed them from around his neck, and stepped away from the circle of her arms. "No, Cerisia," he whispered hoarsely. "No."

She stepped back, confused, anger sending ripples along her jaw, though it was quickly hidden, her lips curling in a predator's smile. "Are you going to prove a challenge?"

Allystaire thought of the ageless beauty of the Goddess, the radiance that followed Her, the overwhelming power of Her kiss. "More than you realize."

She stepped forward, leaving him no space to move, and laid a hand upon his chest, soft fingertips moving warmly against his skin. "This need not be about whom we serve," she murmured, before leaning forward to try to kiss the base of his neck.

Allystaire let out an impatient groan and put his hands upon her shoulders, and carefully but inexorably pushed her away. "Cerisia, you do not understand who or what I am. Everything is about whom I serve."

"Have you saddled yourself with some foolish vow to be celibate, so as not to drain your strength or weaken your resolve?" Less able to conceal her hurt at being rebuffed this time, Cerisia began to curl her lips in scorn.

"Nothing so foolish or petty," Allystaire shook his head, grimacing. "You show how little you understand. What would it look like to the people of this village if I am known to bed with the Priestess of Fortune who came here bearing a message that threatened their very lives?"

"How would they know?"

Allystaire couldn't help but laugh. "The gossip in a village this size? Some of them are probably already whispering the possibility. I will not prove them right."

She smiled again. "If you're going to be accused of a thing, you might as well…"

She has a point. The thought was dismissed as soon as it occurred to him. "Till I know that I will not face an army raised by your church, this will not happen." Allystaire shook his head. "It cannot."

"You are an odd man, Allystaire," Cerisia said, biting lightly at her bottom lip. "I do not know what to make of you. But," her chewed-upon lip assumed the curve of a smile once more, "I note that there was a condition in your declaration."

"There was," Allystaire admitted.

She chuckled faintly and drew her robe closed, which action granted Allystaire the gift of slightly easier breathing. "Then you do—"

"Archioness, at the risk of being crude, had we encountered one another in my old life, we would not be having this conversation," Allystaire admitted.

She responded with her own light, throaty laughter. Then her face grew serious, perhaps even tinged with regret in the set of her mouth and eyes. "I do not know what, if anything, I can do to prevent bloodshed."

"And that," Allystaire said, "is the problem. No one does know, because no one cares to know. Fear of the cost of doing the right thing is enough for most to abide in ignorance."

Her jaw set as she briefly clenched her teeth. "I will do what I can."

"You will do what you must, I think."

She walked to the tent flap, paused, and turned back to him. "Your words are uncharitable, Allystaire. I am not as callous nor as cowardly as you would have it."

"I am not averse to being proven wrong. Goodnight, Cerisia."

Allystaire sat heavily on his cot as she collected her lantern and then exited, casting a backward glance. She opened her mouth to speak, but closed it again, and then was gone. The scent she wore stirred in the tent as the flap closed.

"Goddess, I do not ask for petty things in prayer to you," Allystaire murmured, as he pulled the blankets over his slightly sweaty chest. "But tonight, I humbly beg that I am allowed to sleep the next several turns in peace." He drifted quickly off, despite a voice that berated him for letting the Archioness walk away.

* * *

Allystaire's next semi-conscious thought was, *If that is Cerisia trying to wake me up, I am going to lie here and sleep while she has her way.*

But then, as he realized that the voice hissing his name was considerably rougher, and that the presence in his tent didn't smell nearly so fair as the priestess had, he sat up, blinking his eyes into wide awareness. The quality of the darkness in the tent had changed; dawn had not broken, but it approached. *Well, a turn or three at any rate,* he thought, as he finally focused on the interloper.

It was Ivar. She reeked of horse and sweat-soaked leather, and her voice, as it called Allystaire's name, was somewhat plaintive.

"What is it, Ivar?" Allystaire asked, cracking a yawn.

"One of m'boys is gone missin'," the warband captain replied. "Told me he was off followin' one o the priestess's guardsmen out o'the village. Regardless o'what he found, he was t'report in within three turns. Been four and a half."

"Is it possible he has gotten lost?"

"It's Evert, m'lord—knows how t'reckon better'n any man I know and has as good an eye for country t'boot. Never known the man to get lost any more than I've known rain t'be dry or shit t'smell like wine."

Allystaire paused a moment, steeled himself with a deep breath, and then swung his legs out of his cot. He sat up on the edge of the bed, feeling weights and worries settle on his shoulders. "Does that mean no?"

"He's no more like t'get lost than the freezin' stars are," Ivar said with a note of finality that had Allystaire reaching for his boots and tugging them onto sore feet.

"Where are the rest of the guards?" Allystaire stood and began dressing, pulling on the heavy iron bracers over his arming coat and the studded gloves over his hands. He slung his shield on his back, pulled his belt tight around a thick leather vest, and slid his hammer into place.

"Two watchin' the pavilion. Three sleepin'."

"Yet one left camp and you did not think to tell me?"

"I wanted a full report. He coulda been leavin' to piss or to have a bit of a knee-knocker with a lass…"

Allystaire frowned. "You used your judgment, and I have never known a reason to fault it. Did your man say which way he was headed?"

"North and east," Ivar said. "Into the woods."

"Freeze," Allystaire spat. "I learned just this night that there are men out there. Armed men, brigands. What, Ivar, do you think are the chances that this is a coincidence?"

Ivar held open the tent flap for Allystaire and then followed him out into the pre-dawn chill. "Lower than the chances of a Delondeur man bein' pox-free, I expect."

"Where do you find these lovely turns of phrase, Ivar?"

The captain grinned, leaving Allystaire glad of the darkness that hid her ruined teeth. "Bit o'natural talent, bit o'hard work." The grin faded. "What's our play?"

"We get Idgen Marte and Torvul up. And Renard." Allystaire paused, taking in a big lungful of cold-tinged air. "And any of the Ravens who are fresh."

"We gettin' the village up? They aren't ready t'hold a spear when it matters, but just havin' folk up and about, havin' men carryin' spears around might give bandits a second thought."

"No. Not in strength, at any rate. As you said, most are not ready. And I do not want panic getting in our way."

They quickly covered the few paces to the other tent. Allystaire rapped his fist lightly against the front pole and shook the tent slightly. *Wake up,*

Idgen Marte, he thought, closing his eyes and concentrating on her presence. He could feel her, knew she was sleeping, just a few feet away, knew that she stirred. *Wake up. We may have enemies among us.*

She came awake instantly and he heard movement inside her tent. Quickly, she appeared, wearing the same new, nearly black leathers she'd worn earlier that evening. She slipped a twisted leather band around her head to hold her unbound hair back from her face, and buckled her sword belt on as she joined them. "Where?"

"I will explain once Torvul joins us," Allystaire replied, already walking to the large boxy shape of the wagon. He lifted his fist to pound on the side, then lowered it, closed his eyes, and reached out. *Torvul?*

He felt the dwarf sleeping within, and Gideon, but tried to share his thoughts with only the former. *Wake. We may have enemies among us.*

Allystaire knew he'd failed to wake only the dwarf when Gideon's voice was the first to answer him. *Enemies?*

He sighed, lowered his head. *Both of you, get out here.*

Through the thick walls of the wagon, they could hear the deep, sonorous Dwarfish cursing.

"Where's Renard?" Allystaire asked Idgen Marte.

Idgen Marte replied through a yawn. "Leah has trouble some nights, dreams of the slavers. I can Calm her, but she found that sharing a roof with Mol means the dreams do not trouble her at all."

"And it means that Renard is in the same room as Mol," Allystaire replied, nodding in satisfaction. "Damn. I should have thought of that earlier. We should be watching her while Fortune's priests are here."

"The Goddess thought of it for you," Idgen Marte said. "And I don't think Cerisia is foolish enough, after she was shown up tonight, to challenge Mol. Nor do I think she'd harm a child."

Before Allystaire could argue with any part of Idgen Marte's reply, Torvul and Gideon came clattering out of the wagon. The dwarf wore his hooked jerkin with its many pouches. He had his crossbow in one hand, and a quiver of bolts on his belt, balanced by his metal-shod cudgel. Gideon carried only his staff and wore the plain homespun wool he'd been given upon their arrival.

"Boy, you best have a damn good reason for waking a dwarf up before he's good and ready," Torvul rumbled, rubbing at his eyes with the back of his hand.

"I spoke with Keegan tonight. He told me there is a group of armed men, a dozen or more, camped in the woods nearby. Been there for two days."

"Why'd he say nothing sooner?" Torvul stopped rubbing and spat into the grass, then reached into a pouch and pulled forth a dull metal flask. He unscrewed the cap with the thumb of the hand that held it, had a slug, and offered it to the rest.

Idgen Marte reached for the flask while Allystaire said, "He had his reasons. Now more to the point. Ivar tells me one of her men, her best tracker, followed one of the priestess's guards in that same direction and has not reported back."

"I don't like that for a coincidence," Torvul growled. Gideon frowned but said nothing. Idgen Marte handed Allystaire the flask and he had a sip. It burned, but he felt a jolt of energy ripple through him as the spicy liquid hit his stomach. He offered the flask back to Torvul, but the dwarf said, "We all ought t'have a nip. Give us focus, for a couple turns, anyway. Don't want to overdo it." With a nod, Allystaire handed it to Ivar, who tilted her head calmly back and had a long swallow.

"We need to prepare for this without causing a panic," Allystaire replied. "Ivar, show Idgen Marte where your man went, then get the rest of the Ravens ready for a fight. I am going to go speak to Renard. I would like Gideon to come with me. Torvul, if you need time to get anything ready, take it, but watch the Archioness's camp—if anyone comes or goes, I want to know of it."

Allystaire turned his head to face them all in turn as he spoke. They all nodded, and as he turned to leave, they dispersed in his wake. Gideon followed, taking a few quick steps in order to catch up to him.

"Why not simply go directly to Cerisia and compel the truth of her?" Gideon asked his question suddenly as he took rapid steps to keep pace with Allystaire's much longer stride.

Allystaire instantly thought of Cerisia's words just a few turns earlier. *She can't have been lying then, could she?* He cleared his throat, and said, "I have reason to believe she would not know of this. And if I go straight amongst her and her guards, well, then things are almost certain to end in bloodshed. I will avoid that if I can."

"And if they have killed Ivar's man?"

"Then they will have made their choice," Allystaire replied.

They covered the distance to the Inn quickly, with the sun rising at their backs. Between the slight added warmth of the sunlight and whatever had been in Torvul's potion, Allystaire felt energy building his limbs, the anticipation of a fight stirring him. A small part of him, he knew, was even looking forward to the possibility. It was as though some forge deep inside him was being stoked, readied for purposeful, meaningful work.

Inside the Inn and up the stairs to the room where he'd carried Mol the night before, Allystaire found the door opening as soon as he raised his gloved fist to knock. The girl stood there in her robe, yawning into her fist.

She looked up at him with, he thought, a mingling of joy and sadness in her eyes. "I can't sleep past the sunrise anymore," she said as another yawn set her jaw moving. "Too much o'the world starts t'speak t'me." She studied his face for a moment and said, "Looks like they want t'make a fight of it, doesn't it?"

"I am afraid it does. I need Renard."

The girl nodded and pushed the door half closed. There was the murmur of hushed voices, and then the door swung open again, with Renard leaning on it in a nightshirt.

"Armed men camping outside the village," Allystaire said. "There may be a fight in the offing. I thought that if any of the local men were ready for it, you would know. If they are—even one or two, I want them armed and turned out as soon as you can manage it."

As Allystaire spoke, he watched the exhaustion of sleep melt out of Renard, saw his back straighten, his eyes focus, and his expression harden. His feet shuffled as though he meant to click his boot heels, and he said, "Half a turn or less. Where do we rally?"

"The Temple. Yet do not do it openly." Allystaire turned to leave, then quickly spun back. "You are a sergeant born, Renard, and surely as much a gift of the Mother as anything else."

With that, he and Gideon clattered down the stairs and back out into the morning. By the time they reached the Temple field, Idgen Marte awaited them by Torvul's wagon, breathing heavily.

"They've got Ivar's man," she told them. "There's more than a dozen of them but their camp was broken up, made it hard t'count. For all that they looked like brigands they felt like soldiers," she added. "He'd been done up pretty badly. Broken leg. No chance of sneaking in and carrying him off."

Allystaire felt that furnace inside him begin to pump and roar as if a bellows were working it. He pulled his gloves tighter to his hands and said, "Any sign of the temple guardsman among them?"

"I never made their faces," Idgen Marte replied. "What next?"

"We take the initiative. Allystaire stretched his neck till he heard a click, and then balled his hands into fists and looked towards Cerisia's pavilion. "Gideon, go tell Torvul to cover us. Stay with him." He paused. "Please."

With that, he set off with determined strides, shield bouncing against his back. He knew, without looking, without asking, that Idgen Marte was just a few paces behind, matching his stride, watching his back.

Allystaire made straight for the huge white and gold silk pavilion. One of the guards emerged from his own tent, armored, sword belt around his waist, helmet clutched in his hands. The guardsman, one of the younger men, headed straight to intercept, holding out his leather-over-steel helm in both hands to block Allystaire's path.

"You cannot see the Archioness armed, nor can you enter without—"

As the man began to give him this command, Allystaire reached out and snatched the helmet from his surprised hands, feeling the weight and the solidity of it and registering the shock on the man's face. Gripping it by the chainmail havelock that descended from the back, he gave it a short swing right into the man's face, noting with satisfaction the crunch of the guard's nose and the spray of blood that resulted.

The guard went to one knee, moaning in pain, his eyes closed, and Allystaire threw the helmet down beside him. "Give me an order of where I may or may not go armed again, and I will break your jaw as well as your nose," he growled.

He set off again, feeling Idgen Marte's unease in the way her stride quickened to catch up with him, and her hand went to his arm.

He shook it off, and bellowed as he neared the tent, "Cerisia! You and your men will answer to me. Come forward before I come in for you."

Think, man, think! Allystaire heard Idgen Marte's voice inside his head and turned to see her face livid, teeth clenched. "You've just told them all we're onto them," she murmured, hand falling to her sword.

If there is fighting to be done I would rather it start now, and not wait till they have numbers.

Even now, though, the other guardsman, four in all, had closed in around them. Two of them appeared from within the pavilion inside an antechamber in the front, Allystaire reasoned, and the other two from within the tents surrounding it. The first pair were armored and had their swords half drawn, while the remaining pair wore only the clothes they'd slept in, but stopped to grab spears from their neat piles of weaponry.

Allystaire's hand fell to his hammer and Idgen Marte's sword was gleaming in the early sunlight faster than anyone could have followed.

Guardsman's swords cleared their sheaths. Allystaire swung his shield to his left arm, flexing his fist in the straps, and slid his hammer out of its ring.

"I should have barred you entry with your arms. Surrender them now and you may keep your lives," Allystaire said as he and Idgen Marte squared off with one guardsman each. He felt a tiny tickle, nearly an itch, grow between his shoulder blades. *There's a man with a spear standing behind me,* he thought, *and I'm not wearing armor.*

Allystaire heard Torvul's voice. *I've got him. The one on Idgen Marte will never hit her.*

Allystaire felt some of his tension ease. The furnace deep within him roared. He tightened his fist around the haft of his hammer. He felt his arm start to lift saw it all begin to unfold; he would simply lunge shield-forward to turn the blade, try to unbalance his man, and then come over the top with the hammer.

But then Cerisia's voice, strong and resonant, sounded out over the morning. "Fortune's servants, in Her name put up your swords. Stay this madness!"

The guardsmen lowered their weapons, but didn't drop or sheathe them. Cerisia's face, red from sleep but, Allystaire thought, still alluring, turned to him. "Allystaire—what is this? Why do you come to my tent with weapons drawn?"

Allystaire lowered his arm, but only halfway, keeping his elbow bent, ready to bring the hammer into play. "Tell me why there are a dozen or more armed men outside Thornhurst, coordinating with your guards."

Cerisia's eyes widened and her cheeks drew taut across the bones of her face. "I know nothing of this," she whispered hoarsely. "Nothing. I swear it upon Fortune's name." Her eyes focused on Allystaire's, and she held her slim arm out to him. "Compel me if you must."

The priestess didn't wait for Allystaire to respond, but turned to the nearest guardsman, the one Allystaire had identified as their captain, her voice cracking like a whip.

"Iolantes," she snapped. "What does he mean? Explain to me now!"

The man was clearly taken aback. With one eye on Allystaire, he lowered his sword till the point nearly touched the ground, and stammered as he searched for a response.

"But, Archioness, it was your own command."

Allystaire felt his arm rising, but whatever violence he'd been about to unleash was cut short as Cerisia's acolytes emerged from the pavilion behind her. Clad in white and gold, both were armed with small crossbows that fit neatly into one hand, loaded and cocked with bolts only a few inches long.

"No, Iolantes," the woman said. "You only thought it was Cerisia's command. One voice sounds much like another behind a mask in the dark. Still," the woman added, smiling, "you'll be rewarded for your service."

"What is the meaning of this treachery, Joscelyn?" Though a crossbow was pointed directly at her from only a span or so away, Cerisia was far more angry than she was frightened. She turned, placing her back to Allystaire and Idgen Marte. One of her hands, half hidden behind her hip, began forming some sort of sign, her fingers flexing and bending in ways he couldn't follow.

The male acolyte had his crossbow leveled at Allystaire, a fact which did not escape him. He caught the man's eyes, noted the hesitation in them, and smiled.

At the same time, Joscelyn laughed and answered Cerisia's question with the air of someone deigning to accept a task that was beneath them. "Your primacy in Fortune's service is over. She favors the quick to act, the decisive—not those who would mewl about peace and forbearance in the face of a threat to the church's very existence," Joscelyn said. She was younger than Cerisia, with finer, thinner features that should have been delicately beautiful, but now were twisted into a kind of lean, angry hunger.

"These fools will be presented as gifts to our allies at the Temple of Braech," Joscelyn went on, "while the peasants shall be suitably chastised. Most lives will be spared, provided they give up their heresy."

"You incomparable fool," Cerisia hissed, her face white with rage. "You have no idea what you would set in motion. You have no notion of what a Declaration of Anathemata means, or what it will lead to!"

How long am I letting this farce proceed? Idgen Marte's voice sounded, dry and angry, in Allystaire's head.

Joscelyn spat. "What do I care for the lives of a few peasants bowing down for a renegade lord?"

"You were a born a peasant, Joscelyn," Cerisia said.

"And look how I have risen." The woman raised her crossbow, smiled. "Look how much farther I have to climb."

Now, Allystaire thought.

There was a frenzy of sudden movement. Joscelyn was pulling the trigger on her crossbow, but even as she did, Idgen Marte had blurred right in front of her and brought the flat of her blade down hard across her wrist. There was a sharp crack as a bone in Joscelyn's arm snapped, and the bow discharged straight into the ground.

Meanwhile, the other acolyte tried to loose his bolt just a hair after Joscelyn. Some surge of power welled up from Cerisia's hidden, signing hand, and the string of his crossbow snapped. Allystaire stepped around Cerisia and, with a tight, controlled swing of his left arm, bashed his shield straight into the man, lowering his shoulder and stepping into the blow.

The acolyte was driven off his feet and back into the tent, crashing into a folding stand and sending the metal pitcher and basin atop it clattering. Though it must've hurt, he rolled to his feet, kicked the pitcher aside, and came up with his knife.

Well, he's got stones. I'll give him that, Allystaire thought, even as he raised his hammer and crouched behind his shield, yelling, "Think on it, lad. A knife versus my shield and hammer?"

"Drop them and make it a fair fight," he called, not entirely convincingly.

Allystaire sighed and stepped deeper into the pavilion, watching the acolyte's shifting feet. He feinted to Allystaire's right, attempting to get around the shield, but Allystaire simply bulled straight at him again. The knife scored into the heavy oak panels of the shield, barely. Allystaire was once more able, with brute force, to knock the man onto his back.

He landed heavily, and Allystaire gave him no time to recover. He stomped on the acolyte's wrist, pinning his knife to the ground, and began to let that heel take more of his weight, even as the acolyte yelled in pain.

Casually, Allystaire leaned over him and let the head of his hammer drop so that it rested, lightly, on his adversary's chest.

"Boy, to make this a fair fight, you would need a wall of spears and a siege tower. I have killed dozens, scores, mayhap even hundreds of foolish lads like you. I am not keen to add to that list." He leaned closer, scowling, and gently prodded with the head of his hammer to emphasize every word. "Do not doubt that I will if you force me to." He let that sink in, watching the man's face intently. He had an olive cast to his skin, though the underlying flesh now was paler with fear and pain. His brown eyes held Allystaire's blue for a moment, a moment longer, then closed in defeat.

Allystaire nodded. "Toss the knife away as best you can. Up and outside, and if you try to run, my dwarfish friend with the crossbow will stick you like a hunted doe." The acolyte followed him out, cradling his right arm.

Outside, Joscelyn was on the ground, holding her arm in pain and silently weeping. Cerisia's guards had gathered around her and Idgen Marte stood warily by, sword at her side.

The Archioness turned to Allystaire, flushing in, he supposed, shame that her acolytes had betrayed her without her knowledge.

"Is this more of your temple politics, Cerisia?" Allystaire prodded the acolyte till he stood next to Joscelyn, and kicked him in the back of the knee, not as hard as he might have, but hard enough that his legs folded and he fell hard to the ground next to her.

"Unfortunately, yes," Cerisia replied. "Such coup attempts are not unknown among Fortune's clergy." She watched her acolyte pick himself up and start to stand, and she snapped, "Kneel next to your companion in treachery, Gerther." He did as commanded, all the fight having gone out of him. Cerisia's anger and fear had subsided, pressed below the demeanor of self-assurance and power that she typically assumed, and she eyed Allystaire, frowning. "You need not resort to abusing him now that he has surrendered."

"He is lucky to be alive." Allystaire's fist tightened around the haft of his hammer. "As will any of your guardsmen be who do not disarm themselves, instantly, and till my curiosity is entirely satisfied."

Iolantes raised his sword, his grim mouth opening to speak, when Idgen Marte seemed to simply appear next to him, her sword held along his throat. "We'll start with you," she said, reaching for his weapon. Wisely, he let her pry it from his hands and drop to the grass with no resistance.

"Is this how a paladin negotiates? With a blade to the throat?" Iolantes's voice, even with the edge of Idgen Marte's curved sword held against his throat, was all calm.

She snorted before Allystaire could answer. "He's the paladin. I'll cut your throat in payment for the deception you've wrought and the danger you brought to this place. And I'll sleep well tonight after I do it." Idgen Marte swept her sword away from his throat and shoved him with her free hand, then leveled the blade at Cerisia. "Tell them to disarm, before I take literally your forfeiture of guest's right."

Cerisia's lips furled into a scowl, but she spoke in a commanding voice that filled the air. "Drop your weapons, all of you, and step away from them if you wish to live."

With Iolantes already disarmed and surrendered, the other three guardsmen surrendered their weapons and then stood, uncertainly, hands at their sides.

Finally settling his hammer back into its ring and slinging his shield over his shoulder, Allystaire took a deep breath. His heart still thumped in his chest and his muscles seemed to quiver with unspent energy. He stripped the glove off of his right hand, tucked it behind his belt, and unceremoniously seized the Archioness's arm.

He sought eye contact, wished for a moment he hadn't. It was a moment's chore to tear his concentration away from Cerisia's startlingly pale eyes and to look deep within himself to find the compulsion to lay upon her as he spoke.

"Did you know anything of armed men on our borders?"

"No," she replied simply. Her arm hung lightly in his hand, and he could feel that her pulse beat faster than her expression would've suggested.

"Did you suspect anything, any plot on the part of your acolytes and guardsmen in reference to the Church of the Mother or the people of Thornhurst?"

"No."

"Did you—"

She sighed, and closed her eyes in frustration. When she opened them again, they were fixed not on his face, but the ground. "Allystaire, the answer to the question will be no. I have been duped. I did not know the extent of Joscelyn's ambitions and I underestimated her resolve to see them realized. As I have said, I came here as an advocate of peace. Mine is not a vengeful or a jealous Goddess—at least not as I came to know her."

Without seeking to compel her answer, Allystaire asked, more from pity than anger, "How were you duped? How did you not know that a body of men larger than that of your own party was shadowing you?"

"Why should I know? I am from Keersvast. The first time I saw an inland wood I was past twenty summers."

Allystaire let her arm slip from his hand and turned for Iolantes. Unceremoniously, he grabbed the captain by the throat. Iolantes tried to pull away, but Allystaire's grip was firm, and Idgen Marte was suddenly beside him, her sword poking into his armpit.

"What was the plan? I want every detail."

"My man slips back into the village today. Depends on what went on at your meeting last night. Most like, they come on in the night, try and kill you, her, the dwarf first. If we could get even one of you as you slept, we figured that meant better odds to take the village."

"And you believed your orders came from the Archioness?"

"I did, though she left the details to me to plan," he replied. His voice grew a little hoarse, and Allystaire realized his hand had been slowly and steadily squeezing the man's throat, so he relaxed it incrementally.

"How many men are out there?"

"Fourteen."

"Swords-at-hire or temple guards?"

"Mostly the first."

"And you were willing to proceed with this plan simply because you were ordered? You thought what, exactly, of the people here?"

"Seemed a chance to profit. What is this village to me but more dirt and more peasants scratching at it?"

Allystaire gave Iolantes a hard shove, and, stumbling backwards, the man tripped over the acolytes, both of whom knelt in silence.

"Your mercenaries have one of my men. If he dies, this place will be something to you—it will be the spot of your grave—unmarked, unvisited, unmourned. You, you, and you," Allystaire said, stabbing a finger at the acolytes and at Iolantes as he started to get to his feet, "will be bound and held till I decide otherwise. And it may be a long frozen time before I do."

Silently, Allystaire pictured Torvul, imagined him kneeling atop his wagon, crossbow sighted carefully on the tableau of betrayal and recrimination. Indeed, if he concentrated, he could feel the distance the dwarf was away from him—and atop his wagon seemed a sharp guess. *Torvul, Renard should be rallying men. Get them. And rope. Then we have a day to make plans. Let us make the most of it.*

He felt a confirmation, a kind of mental nod, and Torvul drifted from his perception. Allystaire turned to the remaining guardsmen, who had retrieved their bloody-faced compatriot and were walking him, slowly, towards the pavilion.

"Do you mean to damage all of my guards?" Cerisia asked with a frown as she grasped the injuries of the man being helped to the pavilion.

"Are you sure they are your guards any longer?"

That hung awkwardly in the air for a moment, Cerisia tight-lipped in anger, and Allystaire took the time to try and center himself, to expel the energy and the fury that had built up in him.

He took a step closer to Cerisia, and pitched his voice low, turning his head and murmuring for her alone to hear. "We are going to need to talk about what happens to those who plotted against my people."

"Fortune's Temple has its own way of dealing with those who fail in their bids for power."

"I do not give a frozen damn for Fortune's Temple, its ways, or its justice. They plotted against the Mother's people. For that, they will face the Mother's justice."

"What would you do? Hang them? Take their heads?"

"If I decide that is what their crime warrants."

"Do you not see how that would only hasten a declaration against you? It would prove to my fellow Archions that you are anathema in need of suppression. They will come in numbers—"

"And do you not understand that enemies are going to come no matter what I do?" Allystaire's voice rose in volume till all heads turned towards them. "As I see it, Cerisia, letting them go is only delaying the inevitable. They will come marching back and I will have to kill them then." Even as he spoke, the realization of this truth settled heavily on Allystaire's mind, a nearly physical weight dropping to the pit of his stomach. *They will come, with flame and fear and steel and proclamations and the rule of their own precious law,* his detached and cynical side told him.

He shoved the thoughts away and stifled a sudden yawn. Further conversation was delayed by the arrival of Torvul and Renard, along with a pair of villagers carrying spears, with handaxes thrust through their belts that looked more likely to chop wood than flesh. The dwarf had several coils of rope and he set about binding the guards and the acolytes with a grim efficiency. The guards he shoved to the ground alongside the acolytes.

He turned to Allystaire, holding up a loose coil and, loud enough to be heard by everyone, asked, "You want to tie the noose, or shall I?"

Allystaire was briefly taken aback, till Torvul's voice sounded in his head. *Play along, boy. We scare 'em enough, maybe we don't have to hang 'em.*

"You have a better hand with the rope than I do," Allystaire said, forcing an affected nonchalance into his voice. "More likely to make the drop quick and clean."

Torvul nodded. "You're right. Better you do it, then," he said, and tossed the rope to Allystaire.

One of the guards, suddenly wide eyed, leapt to his feet and started a panicked run. One of the two village men with Renard raised his spear as if to throw, but a sharp command from the bearded soldier and the tip was lowered again.

Idgen Marte was in front of the man in a flash, one hand held out, the heel of her palm extended. He ran straight into it and flew, heels up. His head struck the cold turf with a heavy thud. As he lay gasping, Idgen Marte looked over at the rest of the prisoners and suddenly produced a knife, protruding from her fisted right hand.

"Anyone else thinks they can outrun me finds a knife at the end of their trip."

She hauled the stunned guardsman back to his feet and shoved him back towards the rest.

"If everyone is finished testing our resolve," Allystaire said, turning angry, but weary eyes on the bound acolytes before finding Renard. "I want every single one of these prisoners out of sight and under guard, and I want them held in separate places. Scatter them." He knelt and seized the guard captain by his arm, lifting him to his feet. "Once they are in place, I want their ankles bound and secured to their wrists."

None too gently, Allystaire walked Iolantes to his tent, and tossed him through the flap, sending him careening over a stool and falling onto his face. Allystaire followed him inside and was pulling his gloves on without realizing it. He was upon the other man before he could even roll over and stagger to his feet, one fist upraised, leather creaking, the iron rings along the fingers of the glove pressing into his flesh.

He is helpless, came the sudden thought. *And this is not knightly.*

With a wordless shout of barely checked anger, Allystaire pounded his fist into the ground by Iolantes's head, and leaned over him. He read the scars in the captain's face, the cold set of his eyes, the lips drawn in a fear that was well hidden.

"I ought to kill you," Allystaire growled. "By all rights of hospitality, and all common sense, I ought to string every single one of you up, and let your bodies hang for the crows."

"Yet you aren't," Iolantes replied, trying, and halfway succeeding, to force some confidence into his voice, "elsewise you'd be doing it already. Is it t'be ransom, then?"

Even as he'd punched the ground instead of the man, Allystaire knew a plan had formed in his mind. His strategies often seemed to come to him thus, seemingly instantly, but only after he'd set some part of his mind working at unpicking the knot.

"I have less use for gold than I do for the satisfaction of hanging you. And yet that satisfaction would avail me nothing, if Cerisia is correct, and she may well be." *You should kill him. One less sword when the time comes,* came another thought, unbidden, less knightly. "If I can have peace, I will," he said aloud, as much to his inner voice as to the captured guard captain. "And Thornhurst will have no peace if I kill the lot of you.

"Yet there is a way, one way, and only one, for you to buy your life, and the lives of your men, back. Listen. And listen well." He stood up, turning his back only briefly to Iolantes, righted the stool he'd knocked over by hurling the man into his tent. "I need to know all of it: sign, countersign, the duress sign, for your communications with your other detachment. They need to think everything is proceeding as planned."

* * *

Allystaire knelt in the stubbly field, his knee starting to ache, his lower leg going numb. The weight of hammer and shield, though comforting, did not make up for his relative lack of armor. Gideon squatted behind him, along with Torvul. Renard, the Ravens, and such of the village men as Renard judged ready—not even a half dozen—were spread out in three clusters where Henri's farm met the edge of the wood.

Somewhere in the distance, growing slowly nearer, he could feel Idgen Marte's presence, knew that she was calm and unhurt. *If it was all freezing over we would know it by now,* he silently told himself, not for the first time.

He wondered whether any of this was wise, whether a murderous ambush in the woods, a simple, brief cascade of blood and death, wouldn't have been better. *Easier, maybe. Not better,* he thought. *Not knightly. Certainly not worthy of us now.*

Behind him, he felt Gideon shift from one knee to the other. He resisted the urge to take a backwards look for fear of shaking the boy's confidence.

Then the first figures began to break from the treeline. The moon was slight, a slice of dim autumn orange in a clouded night sky, but thanks to a drop of Torvul's unguent rubbed around his eyes, he—and everyone else lying in wait for the incoming bandits—saw as though it were the bright, early part of the twilight turns.

The men sneaking from the woods came slowly, professionally, with a creeping vanguard of four men leading the way, bows in hand, arrows nocked but not drawn. *Always the worst part of an ambuscade,* Allystaire thought. *Waiting for enough men to come into the trap to make it worth springing.*

More men crept into the field, so that the initial four were well within the circle of ambushers hidden behind hay bales, a fence-line, or as in Allystaire's case, simply behind a fold of earth below the field. Nearly half a score now in his vision—and from the corner of one eye, a blurred, fast moving outline that the would-be reavers entirely failed to notice, a silhouette that he could see less of the more he looked for it: the Shadow of the Mother upon their flank.

Not all of them are out of the woods, he thought, having made a quick count. Yet they showed no sign of emerging, and given too long, those who'd already come forward would stumble into their positions.

Now! he thought, making the command into a mental shout.

I hope they remember to close their eyes, Torvul replied, even as there was a rustling movement, a hiss as a bottle was uncorked, and then the rustle and clink of leather and metal moving as the dwarf stood and threw.

You have a good throwing arm, Allystaire thought as he watched the bottle sail into the night, saw it describe a graceful arc of several dozen yards, and remembered almost too late the dwarf's injunction against watching. He shut his eyes and tucked his chin against his chest, heard the hissing rise in intensity, then felt, and even saw behind his eyelids, the brief but intense burst of light and smoke.

There were too many uncomfortable seconds of waiting, crouched, eyes closed, before Torvul's voice came rumbling over the night. "Now!"

Allystaire sprang to his feet. The better part of the enemy who'd crept out of the woods to ambush them now knelt or laid upon the ground, clutching at their eyes. Hefting his hammer and trotting a few steps into the field, his boots sinking into the soft, cold earth, he filled his lungs with chill night air and bellowed.

"MEN OF FORTUNE'S TEMPLE, YOU HAVE BEEN DECEIVED AND YOU ARE UNDONE." He paused, sucked in another huge breath, feeling every year of his age, every battlefield order and yell. "SURRENDER AND BE TREATED FAIRLY. RESIST AND BE DESTROYED."

A few men threw down their bows, still rubbing at their eyes, while others staggered uncertainly. The Ravens, the village men, Renard, and Idgen Marte had left their positions, weapons out, and loosely surrounded the enemies.

Even as three or four complied with his commands, a final four emerged from the treeline, one of them drawing his nocked arrow.

"Gather yourselves, lads," yelled the would-be archer, as he sighted down his arrow at Allystaire. "He's a hangin' bastard and would see us all dance the short drop!"

The string drew back to the man's cheek. Allystaire sighed. *There's always one,* he thought.

Then before the arrow could loose, a giant stepped out from behind Allystaire and into the night.

This was no Gravekmir, no giant of flesh and bone, of bloodlust and savagery. In fact, it doubled the height of the only giants Allystaire'd ever seen, reaching a score of spans into the sky. It was all of a color, a soft, radiant gold that shed light in a wide pool around it as it moved. A single step carried it towards the suddenly terrified archer, and a quick open-palmed swing later, the man flew several yards in the air, his bow tossed aside, bones rattling as he landed hard against a tree.

For good measure, the giant swung his other arm and knocked aside the rest of the men.

Then, turning monochrome golden eyes set in a plain, blandly featureless face over the rest of the men, the giant spoke.

"I am the Will of the Mother," it said, and for all that its tone was soft, the power and volume of the voice shook Allystaire's chest. "Lay down your arms, or face me in my wrath."

The last word the giant roared, shaking the very ground. When it spoke, its face and form suddenly erupted in livid flames, and men cowered. Somewhere, deep within Allystaire, the urge to bolt, to seek refuge, cried out, though he knew very well he had nothing to fear.

Allystaire risked a look back over his shoulder. Torvul stood with his crossbow, a bolt nocked, in the cover he himself had recently abandoned. Hidden and sheltered from bowshot by Torvul, Gideon knelt, eyes shut, hands fisted, intense concentration writing lines on his face and drawing droplets of sweat onto his forehead.

Most of the men had recovered by then. A few of Allystaire's own men stepped back, shaking, but one of Fortune's mercenaries let loose with a fearful howl, yelling, "Sorcery! Foul magic!" and drawing back his bow. In his haste, the first shot went well wide of the giant that Gideon was projecting into the middle of the field.

His second shot never left his bow, because as he drew the arrow free from his quiver, Idgen Marte's sword bit into the arm that held the string, only seconds before Ivar's spear was driven into his knee. He collapsed, his yells gone to incoherent, pained babble.

Following their commander's lead, the Iron Ravens raised their weapons, spears and polearms mainly, and advanced. Allystaire bellowed once more. "LAST CHANCE. TO BE ARMED IS TO DIE!"

He joined them in the advance, rushing in on a mercenary who threw aside his bow and drew an axe and a dirk from his belt, only to throw them to the ground. Amidst the moans of the two wounded men and the crackling flames of Gideon's giant, the mercenaries surrendered.

The Ravens began to gather up the discarded weapons. After some sharp-tongued prompting from Renard, the villagers joined in. At spear and sword point, the mercenaries even tossed away their sheathed daggers, watching as they were thrust through the belts of the men who began to herd them into the center of the field.

Few of them could tear their eyes away from the giant that stood amongst them, though Allystaire could see its edges flicker and its body begin to waver.

It looked down upon the defeated men beneath it, and spoke once more, the volume of its voice dying slowly away.

"Remember what you saw. Tell all who will listen that those who would do harm to the Mother's people must face me. Those who come to the Mother in peace are under my guard. Make it known."

Then it raised its hands, palms out, and began to dissipate, dissolving into streaks of light that flew upward into the night sky.

"Which one of these sorry cowards is in command?" Allystaire addressed his question to Idgen Marte, having slung his shield and stowed his hammer. The anticipation of the fight still hammered away at him, his limbs jostling with energy. Beneath the wave of it, though, he could feel the gaping trench of fatigue that was going to swallow him sooner or later.

Idgen Marte, her sword still out, began searching among the captives, even as the Ravens began to clasp a hotch-potch of manacles, ropes, and improvised cordage around wrists and ankles. Once or twice she encouraged one to move out of her way with the flat of her sword, finally tapping the point against the chest of a tall and sturdy looking bearded man who remained unbound. He wore a coat of mail over leather, and appeared a few years younger than Allystaire.

"This's the one who talked business with our man," Idgen Marte said. "I heard one call him Altigern," she added.

"Tell me, where is my man Evert?" Allystaire said, addressing Altigern. After a beat, he added, "I hope for the sake of you and your men he is still alive."

The man drew himself erect and lifted his head slightly. "It's no concern of mine what happens to those who consort with dark and unnatural powers."

Allystaire sighed, then began tugging the glove off his left hand. "I am not a patient man tonight, Altigern. Cowards and would-be assassins ruining my sleep do nothing for my mood."

The man spat near, if not quite on, Allystaire's boots. "As if killing a warlock in thrall to some child witch could be anything but a good night's work," he snarled.

Allystaire pinched the bridge of nose and tried to find some fresh store of patience within himself, but even as he tried, the other man gained momentum.

"What're you going to do with us? Hang us upside down beneath the new moon and flay us? Or simply spill our entrails for your witch-whore's magics?"

The anger, the frustration, the pent-up tension of waiting and worrying for the whole of the village suddenly welled up within Allystaire the instant the man said "witch-whore." Before he knew it, his right hand curled into a fist, his arm bent at the elbow, and his body torqued as he drew back his fist and then hurled it, with the short, compact movement of a beautiful punch. It traveled less than a foot before it exploded on Altigern's jaw.

The force, delivered through his iron-banded glove, dropped Altigern to the ground like a man struck dead. Allystaire felt the impact jar his hand, heard the man whimper in pain as he went to the ground.

Bending over the prone form of the mercenary, Allystaire reached down and grabbed him by the collar. Though Altigern swam on the very edges of consciousness, the sudden shaking, and Allystaire's angry voice, stirred him awake.

"This need not end in blood. My man. Where is he?"

Allystaire instinctively pushed out towards the man with the Mother's compulsion, and was astonished to find it drawing forth a response through broken teeth and bloodied lips.

"Dead," Altigern moaned. "No men t'guard 'im, no use for 'im."

"At your command?"

"Aye," the man confirmed, before slumping to the earth, finally giving into oblivion with a clatter of teeth falling from his mouth.

Allystaire's fists curled in rage. He gave thought to simply caving the man's skull in with his fists, or to drawing his sword and taking his head. Idgen Marte probably sensed the bloody thoughts, or at least read them in his body language, for she stepped between him, shoving him away from the unconscious mercenary.

"Go," she said. "Before you murder them all in a haze. Sleep. Renard and I'll see to their disposition."

"We need to recover Evert's body," Allystaire replied. "And—"

She cut him off with a curt shake of her head. "I said we'd handle it. Go. I don't want t'spend the rest of the night digging graves." *And take Gideon with you.*

He nodded, turned, plodded heavily back to the edge of the tilled earth and down the slight hillock to where Gideon and Torvul still waited. The alchemist's unguent was starting to wear off and darkness was impinging on his vision, but he could see Gideon resting heavily upon one knee, a light sheen of sweat on his face despite the night's chill.

Allystaire lowered a hand upon the boy's shoulder and squeezed gently. "You did well, lad. We took them all with no death." He paused, then added, "No more deaths."

"I was just tellin' the lad that more than one hardened man out there is likely walking around in wet trousers," Torvul added.

Gideon nodded and pushed himself to his feet. "I was…sloppy. The flames did not need to be flames in truth. Merely the seeming would have done," he said, half to Allystaire, half to himself. "It was a waste of energy."

"Remind me in the morning to ask what it is you mean," Allystaire said wearily. "If you explained it now, like as not I would not remember it. We are off, Torvul," he added, giving the dwarf a nod.

The two of them walked with increasing weariness. By the time they'd reached the Temple field, Allystaire's eyes had lost all of the brightness Torvul's potion had magicked into them, and the night was night once more.

"Why'd you hit that man, their captain," Gideon suddenly asked as they stopped between Torvul's wagon and Allystaire's tent.

"I snapped. Spent all that time waiting for a fight, some part of me needed one to happen, and the man said something that cut straight to that need."

"It didn't look good to his men."

"Gideon, in the morning, we may hang them all. They meant to murder as many folk in the village as they could, starting with us. They killed one of Ivar's men, who was trying to protect us."

The boy frowned. "We can't kill every would-be murderer."

"No, Gideon. Not all of them; only those that we find. Goodnight." With that, Allystaire turned, lifted the flap of his tent, and barely managed to tear off his outer garments and set his hammer down by his bed before the abyss of unconsciousness rushed up to claim him.

CHAPTER 23

An Old Trick

Morning was like a blade to the eyes, a hammered fist to the mind. Allystaire woke up with a start and swung his legs out of the cot, the walls of his tent already letting in bright sunlight.

"Overslept, you old fool," he said aloud, before forcing himself to stand. *Ivar is going to want blood,* he thought as he dressed and armed himself for the day. *And I may damn well give it to her.*

No sooner was he outside than Cerisia, maskless but in formal white-and-gold silk vestments, was sweeping upon him in a rush. Though her lips were painted, her eyes highlighted, and other cosmetics he couldn't name were applied to her face, there were taut lines along her cheeks from the tension in her jaw.

Fear. She never showed me fear before. She addressed him with a hand laid upon his arm.

"Allystaire," she said, her voice as tight as her skin, on the far edge of panicked. "What happened last night? I did as you asked and did not leave my tent. But I could feel the power that was unleashed. What did you do?"

He tried to force a cold distance into his face and voice. He found, to his surprise, that it wasn't difficult.

"I did nothing, Cerisia. What you felt? That was the Will of the Mother. Surely, as observant a plotter and a watcher of men as you did not fail to notice that there were five Pillars to Her altar, and yet you met only four of Her servants? Did you not find that curious?"

That bought him a moment of her stunned silence, and he turned, pulled his arm from her grasp, and began striding away. She crossed the distance with hurried steps and grabbed for him again.

"What will happen to those men? Surely you can't mean to kill them all."

"You mean surely I cannot plan to do to them what they would have done to this village?" Allystaire turned on her again. The furnace of anger that had built within him the day before no longer roared as it had, but its embers stirred. "No. I will not do that. There will be no murder done. Yet they will face the Mother's Justice."

"You would smear your people's hands with their blood then, and confirm all the worst fears of my temple, of Braech's—"

"I do not give a frozen damn for your temple or Braech's. And as for reddening their hands? No." He shook his head, took a step closer to her. "Only my own. I will make you this promise—if I sentence any of your would-be murderers to die I will knot the rope or hold the blade. They will die quickly, as mercifully as I can manage. And believe me, Cerisia, I know that work like a smith knows his forge."

He turned again, only to be brought up short once more as she called out.

"You cannot. I forbid it. They are Fortune's agents, under my—"

She was brought up short as he whirled around once more, lowering his face towards hers, his cheeks livid with rage. When he spoke, however, instead of the roar she probably expected, his voice was as quiet and deadly as a sword clearing a scabbard.

"You will forbid nothing in this place," Allystaire whispered. "You, whose word on the conduct of her people was proven dross, you have no power here, no word. I deny you and your goddess and all her servants any authority here. Speak again if you wish to chance hanging with those men."

Cerisia was silent for a moment, but she bore up under his threat and spoke. "You will not hang me. I was as deceived as you, and came here as an honest envoy. And you, Allystaire Coldbourne, will not hang anyone who has done no violence. Especially not, I think, a woman."

Damn her. Allystaire could make no reply, so instead he turned away, pushing his anger down and choking on it, counting on longer-legged strides to outpace the priestess till he reached the dwarf's wagon. He pounded a fist against the side, and before he could knock a third time, Torvul stuck his head out of the door.

"Make a mark on my home and it'll be the last thing you do, boy." The dwarf stepped out into the morning, wearing his thick blue robe and no boots, his gnarled, wide-set feet slapping heavily against the wood of his wagon steps. He turned and saw Cerisia following hesitantly, spat into the grass, and let out a short string of Dwarfish curses. "He might not be willing to hang you, but I'm not decided yet. I'll not trade any further words with you. Out of my sight before I get angry."

The priestess retreated, but with a slow, deliberate pace, maintaining her regal bearing.

Once she was out of earshot, Allystaire said, "I would not let you hang her."

Torvul shrugged. "I know that. She doesn't. You're the one who can't bend the truth to suit his purposes. Now, for business. Idgen Marte and Renard simply tied the lot of 'em together and let 'em sit out in the night, wonderin' what was to happen to 'em. I've an idea on how to proceed. Wait here."

The dwarf disappeared into his wagon, re-emerged shortly, and tossed Allystaire a small, hard, cloth-wrapped bundle that he neatly caught. He unwrapped it, found the hard, grainy surface familiar, and snorted.

"A whetstone? That old bit, then? Go sit there and sharpen my sword while they sweat? That lot has seen it before, Torvul. Cold, half of them have probably done it."

The dwarf snorted. "I'm insulted, Ally, that you'd think that such a prosaic bit of theater would be the best I could do. Well, of course, you are going to go sharpen your sword. But that's only the start of it. We're going to be feeding them breakfast, y'see, treating them decently—"

"I will not have you poisoning prisoners."

"I'm no common poisoner! Never touch the stuff. Professional pride as much as ethics. Just a little power of suggestion. They aren't going to be seeing a man in musty leathers sharpening a sword, that's all."

"What is it they will see, then?"

Torvul smiled toothily. "The Arm of the Mother readying the judgment of their very souls."

* * *

Growing up on the Spirit Islands well north of Keersvast instilled a healthy respect, if not precisely fear, in men like Altigern. They worshipped Braech because the Sea Dragon was Strength Against the Storm, proof that courage was always a man's best option, a reminder that the strength of the arm was a real and a powerful thing. Yet Braech's church and his rough, seafaring priests seemed to have no answer for the spirits of his island home, the spirits of the wind and the night.

And Braech surely had no answers for a giant of light and flame, and so Altigern spent the night of his captivity—after the dwarf had set his broken nose and given him something to take the edge off the pain of his shattered teeth—alternating between prayer to the Sea Dragon and a frantic, gnawing fear for his soul.

When he and the other men had been roused by the dwarf, he'd been too numb and too hungry to refuse the bowl of porridge offered. Besides, he'd thought the dwarf seemed kinder, perhaps, than the leader, this Allystaire they'd come to kill.

After eating, their hands were bound again. They remained guarded by men in black mail and grey cloaks, armed with spears and halberds, who aimed dark looks and muttered at the swords-at-hire and temple guardsmen who were Altigern's companions. This tension increased as, shortly after daybreak, the body of the man he'd ordered killed had been brought back.

And just when one of those warband soldiers, with cracked teeth and an ugly, fierce countenance, spat on the ground and looked like lowering her spear and coming for his blood, Allystaire came back to the field.

Only, Altigern thought, he was changed. Taller, broader, somehow more terrifying, wearing a glimmering suit of armor that threw back the sun in brilliance and clung to his muscles like a second skin. He unlimbered an enormous sword—Altigern doubted he himself could lift it—and began sharpening it with a huge block of stone in his other hand. His face shown with a kind of radiance that was hard to look at.

Sparks fell from the blade with every stroke, in red and orange and white and green, and Altigern swore he felt the sword itself reaching for him.

He meant, Altigern was sure, to murder them all, to take their heads, and quarter their bodies and bury them out of sight or hearing of moving water.

My soul will not know the way to the sea, he thought in growing horror. *I will be left locked in earth till Braech's tide washes all before it.*

Altigern summoned all his strength and looked to the uncovered face of his would-be executioner, forcing himself past the pain of it.

And instead of the grim joy he expected, he saw regret. Anger, to be sure, but an anger that he was being driven to this, a sadness, an unwillingness to do this task if there were any other way.

And then Altigern heard a voice tell him to beg for mercy, to ask this huge, gleaming figure, this angry goddess's judge, for a clemency he hadn't thought was possible.

It was only then that the Islandman realized the voice he heard was his own, and not the only one; all around him, his men were falling to their knees, watching in fascinated horror. Some, strong men, men he knew were hard and bloodied, wept. They wept for their souls and their lives, and some, only some, wept for the first dawn of self-knowing.

The fear Altigern felt for his soul somehow turned into revulsion. Somewhere deep down, he knew that if this shining knight before him took his head and butchered his remains, it was probably no worse than he had earned.

And then, amidst the babbling appeals for mercy, the knight, the man he had come to kill—no, to murder—sheathed his sword, stood, and raised his hands for silence.

Then he spoke a miracle of forgiveness.

* * *

Dwarf, I do not know what you did, Allystaire thought, hoping Torvul could hear him, *but I hope their minds are not permanently addled.*

He had done precisely as Torvul had suggested: strolled into the field as the prisoners finished their meager breakfast, unlimbered his sword, and sharpened it. *Tried that once before on a captured Harlach spy, ten years ago. Maybe more. He laughed at it,* Allystaire had thought, when he began.

These prisoners did not laugh. They stared, open-mouthed. Some began to weep, some cried out incoherently, while others fell to the ground. They spoke out in the quick, darting Keervasti tongue, or in the harsher and more grating dialect of the Islandmen.

They begged for mercy, for clemency, for forgiveness. When even the man he'd punched the night before, his cheek swollen and bruised black and purple, fell to the ground in supplication, Allystaire put away his sword and slipped the whetstone into his belt.

"Listen to me. I, as paladin and Arm of the Mother, protector of Her people in this village, suspend the sentence of death upon you." A ragged cheer went up, he raised his hands again, and the men fell silent. "I said suspend, not commute. The Voice of the Mother will come to speak to you of repentance, and any who wish will have that chance. Your arms, however, are forfeit, as are half the value of all other goods you brought with you. Agree to this and you may leave this place alive, but be warned: return to it as aught but a friend, and I will see you dead." He paused, surveyed the field, and said, "Be silent now, and think on what I have said."

With that, he turned and strode away. The Ravens, who'd drifted a few cautious paces backwards as their prisoners began shouting and falling to the ground, once more stepped forward, adjusting their hands on their weapons and shooting sidelong glances at Allystaire.

He found Torvul waiting for him just out of sight, behind the sloping walls of Henri's sod-roofed farmhouse. Allystaire opened his mouth, but the dwarf cut him off with a raised hand.

"I haven't hurt them. I gave them, ah, a truth serum, for lack of a better word, which your northern tongue almost always lacks, in point of fact." The alchemist recovered from his brief digression with a wave of his hand, went on. "It made them see you for what you are, for one. More to the point, it made them see their own deepest selves. I'm thinkin' most didn't like what they found, aye?"

Allystaire nodded slowly. "I suppose not. But how do I explain this mercy to Ivar and her men? Our ways are not their ways, at least not yet. Their brother of battle is dead, murdered by those men."

"You folk and your brothers of battle," Torvul said. "As if war and killing were the only noble thing a man can turn his hand to."

"We owe him something," Allystaire said. "He died at our command, defending our people. Her people. That is worth something. The Ravens will want blood."

"I think Iolantes will oblige them." Idgen Marte suddenly stepped around from the other side of the farmhouse. She hadn't slept, he could tell that much by the dishevelment of her clothes and general weariness in her brown eyes, heavily bagged and lidded. Still, her shoulders were set and her walk determined. "I've just come from the shed where we tossed him. He's demanding a Trial at Arms."

Allystaire frowned and let loose a deep sigh. "Against whom?"

Idgen Marte snorted. "Who d'ya think?"

"We don't have much t'gain by listening to him. You want him dead, string him up," Torvul said, as the three of them drifted away from the farmhouse and back towards the village.

"Too much to lose by refusing," Allystaire murmured.

"This is more of that brother of battle rot, hrm?" Torvul eyed Allystaire warily.

"Aye. And I would not call it rot where the men might hear you. If this Iolantes is demanding a Trial at Arms, then he must have it, for the form of the thing."

Torvul began to speak but Idgen Marte cut him off. "If we hang him, we're murderers. That's the tale carried back to Londray. If he demands a Trial at Arms, is given it, and dies?"

"Then we are beyond reproach. More than fair and proven right," Allystaire said, nodding in agreement. "He will have his chance."

CHAPTER 24

Trial-at-Arms

"**I** want a day to prepare, dictate my last testament, regain my strength, and pray with Joscelyn."

"You're fartin' higher than your ass," Torvul shot back at Iolantes.

What in Cold does that mean? Allystaire had little time to ponder it. "In truth, Captain, you are putting on a good show of indifference for a man who slept his last night in a cow byre," he said.

Iolantes was redolent of his quarters, which he'd only just been let out of. Despite blinking against the sudden brightness, the man stood with a straight back, and as soon as his eyes adjusted, met Allystaire's gaze evenly.

"You are not in a position to demand anything."

"A Trial at Arms will never be seen as even or fair if I'm to go to it half-starved and with no chance to see to my goods or my soul," Iolantes responded coldly, rubbing at his newly freed wrists.

"You will be fed and allowed reasonable chance to recuperate," Allystaire said. "I will not grant you audience with another prisoner. Cerisia, yes. Joscelyn no."

An odd light passed through Iolante's dark brown eyes, and for a brief moment, he broke the held gaze. "She will not see me. I am certain of that."

"Then your soul will be left as your Goddess finds it," Allystaire said.

The man's jaw clenched in sudden anger. "And will you fight me honestly? Man to man, steel to steel, no sorcery involved?"

"I am no sorcerer," Allystaire replied. "I have met one, and I killed him," he added slowly, studying the other man's expression as he spoke. A slight swallow, perhaps, a drawn cheek. No sign of real fear.

"A vain boast at best," Iolantes snorted. "Will you agree to like arms, then? Swords, mail, shields?"

"Why do you think you get to dictate terms to me when you are my prisoner?"

"Because you stand to lose by refusing me. You have everyone in this village looking to you, hanging on your words, watching your actions—you've no choice but to play the hero," Iolantes said. "And because I haven't yet met the man who's a better swordsman than I am."

"It might behoove you to note that I have not either," Allystaire replied. He could feel Torvul and Idgen Marte's restlessness a few paces behind him. "Well, better swordsmen, mayhap." He thought briefly of the reaver captain in his green brigantine coat, his fine, thin blade. Bits of flesh and bone smeared against the wall as he pounded the man's face away. A twinge in the knuckles of his right hand. "But none who are still alive."

"No doubt you can kill me," Iolantes said. "No doubt I can kill you, too. If I do, I salvage something of my mission here. If I don't, then I have a better death than I'll get back in Londray, or on the Archipelago. Either way, I force you to it. Play the hero, paladin. Or kill me like a coward and show everyone here what you really are."

"Enough," Idgen Marte spat. With sudden and savage grace she stepped between them and slapped Iolantes hard across the face once, twice, a third time, her hand leaving a bold white impression upon his flesh. He seemed too stunned to respond. "That, Captain, is my challenge to you. I've heard enough talk. You'll have a Trial at Arms with me, not him."

The white outline of her hand was suddenly livid on his face, and his hands started to clench into fists. "I'll not be spoken to by some outcast Concordat whore who thinks she's a duelist—"

"I will make sure every one of your men, and Joscelyn, and Cerisia, know that you refused my challenge, then. Who's the coward now, you worthless frozen shit?" Idgen Marte's voice was as quiet as the drop of a noose, her face as expressionless as the hangman's mask.

And she's never been more terrifying, Allystaire thought, even as Iolantes's jaw clenched in sudden anger.

"Fine. Will you accept my previous terms?"

"Aye. Noon on the morrow. Blades, mail, and shields." She patted her sword and turned away with one more comment thrown back over her shoulder. "I'll only need the one."

As she strolled quickly out of sight, Torvul chuckled broadly and held up Iolante's manacles. "All right. Tomorrow at noon. Back in your shed for now, Captain of Cows," the dwarf said. Iolantes eyed him angrily, and his eyes darted to the side, as if looking for room to run.

Allystaire's hand fell to his hammer at the same time Torvul's did to the metal-bound cudgel on his belt, but the dwarf spoke first.

"Do it and save us all the trouble, Iolantes. I've no objection to simply having a good go about your head and shoulders with this, right now. I doubt he'll stop me," he added, hooking a thumb at Allystaire behind him, who simply shrugged.

Iolantes raised his hands and accepted the manacles. "That she's a woman will not stay my hand," he said as the dwarf locked his wrists back together.

"She'd be insulted if it did," Torvul answered him, ushering him back into the cowshed. "Someone'll be along with meals, and you'll be freed but under guard till tomorrow."

"I will kill her," Iolantes insisted.

"No," Torvul said, giving him a gentle shove. "You'll die like the dog you are. Were I you, I'd leave her something in that last testament you're so concerned about. A little incentive to make it quick." The dwarf shut the door of the shed, latched it, and he and Allystaire walked off.

"Got to get a message to Ivar or Renard that he needs to be let out, but under guard," Allystaire said. "Any idea where they are? And have you any thoughts on how to carry messages man-to-man faster than me always asking you or Idgen Marte where they are?"

"How'd you do it in large armies? And if I were to bet, Renard'll be somewhere in the village proper, and Ivar'll be guarding the prisoners and hoping one of them tries to run or fight."

"Fast runners, fast horses, fast birds. And all that trumpet and drum and flag nonsense," Allystaire replied. "Not really practicable here. Not what I am asking."

"I know," Torvul replied. "And the answer is no, unless we get walls around the whole place. I can't." He paused, placed a fist against his mouth as he searched for the word. "I can't simply magic up one thing to another over a long distance when they aren't touching. I could do something, like I said, with walls and far more raw gems than we're ever going to have. And they'd have to be mined from the same shaft, the same vein, born into the world touching each other in the same rock, knowing their grain, for me to attempt something like that."

"No would have sufficed."

"Never use one word when you've time for several," Torvul proclaimed. His expression grew briefly wistful, brows knotting very lightly, a tiny half-frown dragging at his mouth. "Besides, you reminded me of the Homes. The Loresingers speak of a place where that very thing was done, where stone called to stone, they say."

They picked up the pace and walked in silence for a few moments before Torvul finally spoke again.

"You've no worries about Idgen Marte taking him on?"

"None."

"Why not?"

Allystaire let out a slight chuckle. "Have you any worries?"

"Not as such. Still, if she means to fight him fair, blade to blade, bringing none of her gifts into play, could he take her?"

"Idgen Marte was faster than anyone I have ever seen before the Goddess Ordained her. I would not like my chances against her, so I do not rate his. At the same time, any idiot with a sword in his hand can stick someone with it, and he is not entirely an idiot, nor is he green—but she will have thought of that and made her decision. She does not take risks without weighing them first."

Torvul grunted, nodding agreeably. "That's what makes her fit to you, I suppose. You can barge in head-first, as you do, and make a good, clear path of blood and rubble for her to follow so she can sort out the mess."

"That is not how I would say it, but it seems to have worked well so far."

"I'm off to find Renard, because he is more likely to be closer to something cold and wet and last night was thirsty work," the dwarf said as they found themselves back in the center of the village. "You ought to escort Mol to the prisoners so they can repent if they've the mind."

* * *

As it turned out, Mol had not waited for his escort. Anxious to make it there, Allystaire had taken Ardent from the stable attached to the Inn, barely taken the time to saddle him, and ridden the destrier out to Henri's farm. The horse's sense of his rider's urgency wedded the stallion's own desire to run after only walking for several days, and Allystaire arrived at the richly brown, unplanted field windblown and a bit hard for breath.

He need not have worried. With Ivar keeping order, the prisoners had lined up, and one, even as he swung off the saddle and felt his feet sink into the earth up to his ankle, knelt before the Voice of the Mother in her priestly robes. Her hands were settled on either side of his head, and she spoke quiet words that Allystaire could not hear, was not meant to hear.

He gave her a wide berth, watched as her hands slipped from the man's head. Wiping tears from the corners of his eyes, the man shuffled back off to his comrades, who stood in a loose knot. They made no eye contact with each other, or their guards, and spoke little.

Beaten men, Allystaire thought. *They will give us no further trouble.* The way they milled about spoke to him of men waiting to be told what to do next, and not expecting to like it. Or fight it.

Mol beckoned him over. When he neared, she lifted her hood and murmured to him.

"Some of these men may choose to stay with us. When the Wit made them look inside themselves, they might find the desire to be better men. If it is so, would you have them, Arm?"

Allystaire bit back the bitter reply that came to him. "All are welcome. None are compelled. We could find a use for anyone. Ivar and Renard could see to their induction into the militia, if any should stay. In the meantime, if you are done here, there has been a development. Iolantes has demanded a Trial-at-Arms."

Mol looked up at him. Her eyes were large and daring, knowing and wary. "You are bound by no law to give it to him."

"Not bound, no. Yet…"

She sighed. "When are you meeting him?"

"I am not. Idgen Marte is."

"Must there be blood for blood? Must there be revenge?"

"I do not think it is about revenge, though you have said yourself, what was it—strong men, who are also bad men, will not cease thieving, raping, and murdering because we ask them."

"Not quite my words, but yes. It is a different thing, though, to defend yourself, your kith and kin, against an attack, and another to coldly take a life in some spectacle."

"No one need watch, though I would prefer if the rest of Fortune's party saw it."

"Are you so confident of her victory?"

Allystaire nodded. "Aye."

"Pride is a dangerous thing."

"Not as dangerous as Idgen Marte. And if it starts to go ugly, I will not let her die."

"You would interrupt the ritual that you apparently value the form of?"

"I weigh Idgen Marte's life more than that of all of Fortune's servants currently guested with us," Allystaire replied. "Would you not?"

"I would rather not have this barbaric ritual at all."

"It is a good deal less barbaric than hanging or beheading the lot of them, which is what I thought I was going to do this morning. One man dying in the place of a dozen is an improvement, if you ask me."

Mol sighed sadly, frowning. "It is, yet it is not good enough."

"It will never be, Mol." Allystaire laid a gentle hand on the girl's shoulder. The gesture surprised him, as it took that physical touch to remind him of her age, and that she stood barely to his chest. *Come to think I'm speaking to a woman grown older and wiser than me when I talk to her now,* he thought.

"Unless we make it so," she insisted.

"So long as we do not sit idle. The Goddess did not call us to wait for the world to change around us," Allystaire replied. "Now we have a lot of arrangements to make." He cleared his throat and called out, "Ivar! I need two men for a guarding party."

In a moment, the black-mailed, spear-carrying warband captain pierced the air with a sharp whistle. "You and you," she called out sharply, pointing black-gloved fingers at two men. "Go wi' Lord Coldbourne and do as he asks. On the hop."

CHAPTER 25

Who You Are,
Not Who You Were

As the appointed time of the duel drew near, Allystaire found himself look-ing for Idgen Marte. He tried her tent, the Inn, and finally it came to him: The Temple.

He found her kneeling before the Shadow's Pillar, wearing the midnight blue leathers that she'd appeared in the night Cerisia had arrived, her scab-barded sword resting on the ground beside her, hanging from the belt she wore across one shoulder.

Allystaire waited a respectful distance away, though he was certain that she knew he was present. He could hear no words coming from her, though her lips occasionally moved, but he could feel the faintest hum of the Mother's song.

Idgen Marte straightened, hopped lightly to her feet, adjusted the hang of her sword, and took a deep breath.

"Asking for Her favor?"

"Not favor. Permission," Idgen Marte replied, "and perhaps a bit of knowing."

"Knowing what?"

She frowned faintly, the corner of her mouth tugging at the scars that ran down her neck. "I...your Gifts from Her, they come and go as you need them, aye? Mine, my speed, the shadows? They are always with me. I no longer know how to move anything less than that fast when it matters."

"Am I hearing you say you want to win this fight fairly?"

Idgen Marte scowled at him and fiddled with the hilt of her sword. "I want to meet him skill to skill. I've fought my share of duels. I know the speed of my wrists is his match, and more. I don't need the speed of my Gifts."

"You are not Idgen Marte the duelist, sword-at-hire, the adventurer any longer," Allystaire replied quietly. "You are the Shadow of the Mother. You have responsibilities to live past this day, however you must."

"Would you take that advice?"

"If the Mother's Gift of strength came to my arm, I would not ignore it. I would end the fight as quickly as I could."

"Allystaire, for the last half score of years, all I had, all that I was, I earned with this," Idgen Marte wrapped her hand around the hilt of the long, curved sword she always wore. "I don't mean to stand here and tell you my story, but when I left my home, I did it with nothing but this sword, a decent pair of boots, and some stolen clothes. The boots and clothes are long since gone. I've earned a fortune, drunk it away, earned it back, and lost it again more times than I care to count. I've lived and fought and collected stories in the Concordat, Keersvast, and Goddess help me, this frigid northern waste. Because of this, and what I could do with it," she said, lifting the scabbarded blade off the frog on her belt. "Because my wrists and my feet were faster than anyone else's. The sword-at-hire, the warband life, it's hard on a man, you know that. The weak die quick, the cowards never last, and most of 'em who do live have seen so much they've given in and become right bastards. Now just imagine it for me."

Idgen Marte paused for a deep breath, looked down at her sword, wrapped her hand around the hilt again. "I'm not asking for pity. I could've chosen another life, after the one I wanted was barred to me," she rasped. "I chose it. It meant something to me, something about myself that I can't put into words. You probably felt the same about your knighthood, about teaching, about leading men at war. Well, the Goddess may have made us something better, something more noble or pure, than a knight or a hired blade. Somethin' closer to a story. Yet there's a part of me that wants to know, am I still the woman who made her own way? Am I still my own master? Can you understand that?"

Allystaire thought a moment, taking the time to let "after the one I wanted was barred to me" sink into his thoughts and lay there till he knew he'd remember to ask about it another time. "I do, Idgen Marte. I do. I felt that way when we came upon that press gang back in the summer, and that Delondeur knight with the blue cockerel lowered his lance. For a moment, I was doing what I was bred to do, spurring Ardent into the charge and couching my lance and trying to find the spot where his shield would not be. For a moment I was my old self again, Lord Coldbourne, Castellan of Wind's Jaw, Marshal of Oyrwyn, almost always a winner in the lists. And then I remembered whose knight I was now, and Her strength filled my arm. Who we were only matters as it prepared us to be what we are now. Please do not forget that."

"As if I could. And yet if I lunge and run him through faster than anyone can follow, am I helping our cause, or hurting it?"

"Maybe just slow down enough for everyone to see it."

She snorted. "Why's he doing this, anyway? He knows the rest of his men are walking away."

"He is afraid of what he faces if he returns to his church in disgrace. And I think he is a little ashamed of how the acolyte duped him."

"As if he were the first man led astray by the promise of parted legs?"

"I do not think Joscelyn's were the legs he had in mind, and I believe that weighs on him as well."

"Well, he's a fool. A little ashamed is better than dead."

"Mayhap. Could be that a clean death here is what he is really after. Under the sun, with a sword in his hand, rather than knives in the dark, or a quick fall off a ship."

"You think Fortune's temple would murder him?"

"I do not doubt that Braech's priests would. And do you think most of Fortune's clergy are more like Cerisia or more like Joscelyn?"

"Not sure what the difference is."

"Joscelyn was willing to do murder to advance herself. Cerisia came here hopeful of avoiding bloodshed."

Idgen Marte stopped near the door, her silhouette outlined by the thin band of bright daylight it let in. "Are you so sure of that? Not at all distracted?"

Allystaire frowned thinly, choosing his words carefully. "I may have been, at points," he admitted. "Mildly. Yet not when I compelled the truth of her. She is genuine on this point, if not others."

"Let me hazard a guess. You valiantly resisted her advances in the name of chastity and piety."

Allystaire laughed, though faintly, as the memory of Cerisia's fingers, her lips, her scent drifted across his sense. "I would not say chastity and piety so much as politics."

Idgen Marte sighed, shaking her head in mock sadness. "You probably made the smart choice. After a fashion. Still—when it comes to Fortune's clerics, I never saw one didn't have gold sticking to their fingers. And she's no different."

"Enough gossip. You have a duel to fight."

Allystaire led Idgen Marte out of the Temple, acting as her second. On the long walk to the roped-off field at the other side of town, a crowd tried to follow without pressing too close upon them. When they reached the Temple field, Ivar and her Ravens had joined with Renard and his villagers to keep the crowd back, and the disarmed prisoners cowed. Cerisia paced nervously, wearing her white silks and her mask, while Joscelyn and Gerther, hands bound, hunched miserably nearby in dirtied rags.

Iolantes wore his mail and helm and a longsword and a heavy dirk on his belt, though he'd dispensed with Fortune's surcoat. His guards stayed a pace behind him as he approached Cerisia and knelt.

Fortune's Archioness, unreadable behind her mask, seemed to pay little attention to whatever Iolantes had to say. The man knelt before her, speaking quietly, no words carrying across the stillness to Allystaire's ears. He made no grand gestures, did not raise his eyes to her mask, simply staring at the ground as he spoke. Finally, after several moments of this, Cerisia raised her hand to his head and bent over him, speaking, Allystaire assumed, some kind of blessing.

After a few quick words, she turned away from the kneeling guard. There was a kind of finality in the gesture. He called softly after her, then stood, his back as straight as the blade on his hip, and awaited his opponent.

The day was cool and cloudless beneath a bright sun. Allystaire led Idgen Marte to the edge of the flat space that was serving as their field.

Cerisia had circled around and met them, as well as Iolantes and the guard serving as his second, in the middle of the field. Mol did the same, gliding from one side where she had stood with Torvul.

"Is your servant bound to this foolishness?" The young priestess addressed her older counterpart directly, with that curiously adult, unmistakably educated voice Mol had grown into.

"He is no longer my servant." Cerisia's voice was flat and muffled by her mask, but colder than Allystaire remembered. "His life is his own to throw away as he wills it, foolish or not. Do not look to me to dissuade him."

"Enough of this," Iolantes snapped. His skin was tight across his jaw, but otherwise he was the picture of professional, soldierly calm. Even his voice softened when he spoke again. "Let us set the terms."

"The terms are that you die when I kill you," Idgen Marte said, "and that afterwards your men go free, with what food and stores they can carry. Their weapons, armor, valuables, and mounts are forfeit."

Iolantes spat. "That is no fair bargain."

"It's the only one you're getting," Idgen Marte said cooly. "Take it and die clean. Refuse it and you're the first of many to hang today."

"Fine. And if I win?"

"Hadn't given it thought," the swordswoman answered.

"If I win, my men go free with all their gear and goods. All my men, any that were witched into staying must be set free."

"Believe what you like and make peace with this world. May the Mother grant you mercy in the next." Idgen Marte turned sharply away and barked, "Clear the field."

Allystaire tried to catch her eye as he, Mol, Cerisia, and the other guardsman all hurried away, but Idgen Marte's eyes locked on Iolantes as she turned to face him. The bright, deceptively gentle curve of her sword gleamed as it cleared her sheath with hardly a whisper. With her left hand, she lifted the scabbard free of the frog it rested upon on her belt and gave it a good toss, clearing it away from her legs.

Iolantes drew more slowly, his heavier blade coming free with a loud and angry skirl. He lifted his shield and, mail rattling, trotted straight towards her, picking up speed as he moved. Shield lifted in front of him, he raised his sword for a brute-force overhand swing straight down at her.

Rather than even attempt to parry, Idgen Marte stood still, so still that even as his blade reached the top of its arc and began to descend, she seemed not to move. Allystaire's breath caught in his throat.

The heavy longsword swung through empty air. With an economical grace, Idgen Marte had sidestepped, planting her left foot wide to one side and pivoting on it. Her right foot only whisked against the ground. As Iolantes's sword overswung, she lifted hers and lashed a sharply snapped kick at his hand. His arm shook and his hand loosened around the hilt, but he wasn't that easily disarmed.

Iolantes swung his shield in an arc in front of him, but Idgen Marte was already rolling away. She popped back to her feet several paces in front of him. Resettling his grip on his sword, he danced forward again, more warily this time, shield advancing, sword probing.

She declined to meet any of his attacks with her own blade. Tentative as they were, she simply skittered to either side of them. Finally, some frustration beginning to wear on him, he tried a vicious, wide swipe at navel height. She brought the edge of her sword down along his flat and knocked his sword harmlessly away. Holding his weapon pinned with one hand on her sword, her left hand darted inside his shield.

Whatever soft spot or gap in his chainmail she found, or technique with her hand Idgen Marte performed, was hidden from their view, but the effect was immediate. Iolantes's left arm dropped nervelessly to his side, shield starting to slip from his grasp.

She didn't wait to press him, but stepped forward even closer, and snapped her elbow straight into his face.

His helmet's noseguard smashed into the soft bone and cartilage it was meant to protect with a loud thud. His nose wasn't broken, but he was stunned in surprise, and she used the moment to dance around behind him, unpinning his sword.

He spun around to meet her, shield trailing on the ground and slowing him down, forced to advance with his right hand, his sword hand, forward.

"Don't worry," she taunted, "your arm will come back in a few moments. Provided you're still alive."

"Witch!" Iolantes shouted through gritted teeth. With a hard shake of his torso, he swung his dead arm loose of the straps and let his shield fall to the ground with a clank.

Idgen Marte smiled, but otherwise stood pat, her posture relaxed, sword at her side.

She is taunting him, Allystaire thought. Then, trying to direct the thought at Idgen Marte, hoping she would hear him: *Stop this! Be what you are, not what you were.*

She was distracted, for a moment, by Allystaire's thought, her eyes flitting towards him from yards away. Iolantes saw her brief distraction and lunged forward, leading with his right shoulder and swinging his sword in an upwards arc, its tip starting near the tops of his boots.

Idgen Marte stepped backwards to avoid it, casually, as before, barely shifting her grip on her own blade.

And then she tripped.

She recovered quickly, flinging herself backwards and rolling back to her feet in little more than a blink. But the effect was chilling, her easy confidence replaced, if only briefly, with uncertainty, and her sword flickering as she brought it up into a more secure guard position, both hands on the hilt, fingers moving uncertainly.

I have never, Allystaire thought, a slight shiver moving down his neck, *seen her put a wrong foot. Even in her cups.*

Iolantes took another wild swipe, and instead of tumbling away, Idgen Marte lifted her sword and turned the swing away with her flat.

Finally, Idgen Marte lashed out with her own attacks, darting her sword in three short, swift swings to his left, then right, then left again, clearly trying to exploit his weakened, shieldless arm.

Iolantes parried the first and second, swinging his sword almost blindly. The clash of steel on steel was made louder by the silence surrounding the combatants. The third swing, faster than the first two—but not with the unnatural speed Idgen Marte had since her Ordination—he danced away from, backpedaling with deft, if not graceful, feet.

Allystaire spared a moment to look at Iolantes's dangling left hand, saw the fingers flex, curl into a fist.

Idgen Marte saw it too. She stamped forward and launched a low, sweeping swing at his left side. His blade met hers, guided as much by instinct, by luck, as intent. Again the clash of steel, again her attack knocked harmlessly aside.

Iolantes, gritting his teeth with the effort, brought his left hand up and wrapped it around the bottom of his swordhilt. Smiling then, he lifted his arms, bringing his hands up to his right shoulder as if preparing for a swing.

She went on the offensive again, a cut starting low near his left knee that sliced towards his right shoulder. Trying to draw him one way and go the other, Allystaire recognized, even as she made her cut.

Iolantes knew it, too, and he swung his blade down faster and harder than his bad arm should've allowed, trapping her sword against the ground for a moment. In that moment, he lifted his boot, stomped down on the tang, and snapped Idgen Marte's sword off less than a span above the hilt, the bulk of the curved blade falling to the dying grass in a brief, mirror bright shower of steel.

Iolantes let out a loud but inarticulate cry of triumph, and while shock widened Idgen Marte's eyes, she wasted no time. She flung the broken end of her sword at Iolantes with her right hand, while seizing the dirk on his belt with her left. He deflected the improvised missile by batting it away, but as he swung, she sprang backwards and away from him. Luck may have been with him in the fight, but speed was hers.

Staggering backwards a few steps, she shifted the dirk into her right hand and crouched, making a smaller target of herself, and holding the dagger in a forward guard.

Allystaire realized he was holding his breath, and felt a kind of curious, anxious buzzing creep up the base of his spine. His hand fell to his hammer, contemplating the distance, weighing consequences.

The buzzing grew louder. Idgen Marte backpedaled, catching and turning away a few probing strikes from Iolantes's sword. Blood trickled down around his mouth where her kick to his noseguard had opened his skin, turning his smile into a bloody rictus.

Suddenly a voice rang out over the crowd, and the combatants froze. The faces of the crowd snapped towards the source of the noise.

Gideon stood an arm's length away from Joscelyn, who still knelt, hands bound behind her back. One of his hands was upraised, and Allystaire could feel some power flowing between the boy and the acolyte.

"Break it! Break it!" the boy was shouting. "Break it or I swear I will draw so much of your Goddess's power through you that none will ever feel her benison again!"

Iolantes looked over Idgen Marte's shoulder, distracted by the sudden interruption, though she kept her eyes locked upon him. *Take him now,* Allystaire thought, at her. *He is distracted!*

She gave no indication that she heard. Her mouth moved, forming words he could neither hear not make out.

"It might kill me," Gideon suddenly hissed through gritted teeth, "but it will kill you. And it could kill your Goddess. The world will not miss you. Will it miss Her?" He raised his other hand. It began to glow, then his flesh seemed to disappear behind the dazzling concentration of light at the end of his arm. Joscelyn's eyes rolled back in her head, her mouth clenched, and she collapsed.

Gideon's hand clenched into a fist, and then he released the coruscating ball of energy that he'd gathered. Tongues of heatless flame had begun to lick around his hand.

A cloud passed across the sun as the ball dissipated.

The tableau was broken. Iolantes charged, sword raised in both hands for a killing blow.

As the shadow from the moving cloud fell over her, Idgen Marte blurred from view. Iolantes stopped in his tracks, then suddenly stiffened as his own dirk was plunged into the back of his skull, slid just beneath his helmet. Behind him, Idgen Marte had reappeared, though instead of the tall, dusky-skinned warrior Allystaire had met, she was the Shadow of the Mother, a twisting, barely visible figure of light and dark blended into a shape of terrible reckoning.

The blade was placed with the precision of a dwarfish chirurgeon. Iolantes fell straight to the ground, bone and muscle gone slack.

Idgen Marte stepped back, leaving Iolantes's dagger buried in the back of his own limp head. As the cloud passed away from the sun, she was herself once more.

Allystaire started to her side, but then veered towards Joscelyn and Gideon. *I wanted you to stay out of sight.*

"I couldn't any longer," Gideon answered aloud. He knelt beside the prone but steadily breathing form of Cerisia's acolyte, put a hand to her neck, and then her head. "I felt her calling upon her Goddess, drawing power. She was modifying the probabilities of the fight. It is what they do."

"In words I can understand, Gideon," Allystaire said.

"She was lending unnatural luck to Iolantes," the boy said. "Did you not think his blind parries meeting Idgen Marte's strikes was unusual?"

"It is one of the ways we can direct the power of our Goddess." Cerisia spoke, having glided carefully and quietly across the field to them. "I should have felt it. That I did not speaks ill of me as Fortune's servant. I am sorry for allowing her to endanger your comrade."

I think she endangered herself, Allystaire thought. "It is what you did to this idiot's crossbow just two nights past, aye?"

"It was," Cerisia admitted, her voice not only muffled by the mask, but subdued on its own. Her unreadable, jewel-eyed gaze moved from Gideon, to Allystaire, and back. "Who are you and what did you do to her?"

The boy didn't answer immediately. He looked at Allystaire. "I began drawing the power she asked for through her, more than her mind or her will could sustain…"

"Not Joscelyn," Cerisia snapped. "Her. Fortune. My Goddess. What did you do to Her?"

Gideon shrugged. "Nothing of any consequence. She is far too vast for me to do Her any permanent hurt unless I took great risk…"

She lunged towards Gideon, a wordless cry rising in her throat, hands clenching, only to be barred by Allystaire's outthrust arm. "Take another step towards the boy, Cerisia, with your body or your mind or your Goddess's power, and I will treat it as the beginning of a war. There is still a chance to avoid any further bloodshed. Leave before the road is darkened and I will give you Joscelyn's life."

"It is not yours to give!"

"She forfeit it when she interfered in this Trial. I am trying to show mercy, though I am sure I will come to regret it." His eyes flicked sidelong to Gideon, who was not, as he'd expected, watching the two of them. Instead, the boy's head was lowered, his eyes closed, face tightened in an expression of deep concentration.

"You wouldn't—"

"Stop trying to imagine what I would not do and focus on the things I can do. I can take her head, and those of all your men. Begone from this place before dark."

"You will want to leave," Gideon said, "if you want to speak with your Goddess again. I have been," he waved a hand vaguely, fingers spread, "checking. She is gone from this place, from Thornhurst and its environs. Not forever, by any means. But for a while." The boy thought a moment, eyes turning skywards before settling back on the priestess.

Cerisia brought her hands together and muttered something Allystaire couldn't hear, but the words trailed off into a muffled shriek. Quickly, though, she composed herself, her back stiff, and took a deep breath.

"What are you?"

Gideon stared at her, unblinking, then turned to Allystaire, who shrugged.

"He is the Will of the Goddess. The Fifth Pillar." Allystaire let out a faint, resigned sigh. "Now begone, Cerisia. At sundown, our doors are closed to you and yours, unless you wish to stay and earn your bread." He nodded at Gideon, and the boy followed him as he left Cerisia silent in his wake and crossed to Idgen Marte, who knelt on the field, having gathered the broken pieces of her sword.

"Go on," she murmured, as he approached. "Tell me you were right about all of it."

"I was merely going to suggest that you might want to look over the gear we are confiscating from Fortune's guards, see about a suitable replacement."

"There won't be one," Idgen Marte said, looking at the smooth-worn hilt she held delicately in her hands.

"A sword is just a sword," Allystaire replied. "I have lost count of the weapons I have carried, broken, or lost. My hammer fits my hand well, but I could replace it if need drove."

"Their swords are northern garbage. Islandmen blade? Might as well try to cut a man with a rock. A dull, heavy rock," she spat. "Keersvast work would be mildly better. But this," she said, holding the remnant to her eyes, "this was Concordat work. Light, flexible, strong—"

"And you were a Concordat sword-at-hire. Now you are the Shadow of the Mother. Gather up the pieces and take them to Torvul if you must, but we have work to do."

She nodded. "Aye. Let me find a rag to gather them in," she said as she stood and walked off, the hilt with its half-span of broken steel curving from it still dangling from her hand.

* * *

"You can have a pair of bows, and such arrows as my men consent to give you," Allystaire said, addressing Fortune's gathered servants as he, Ivar, Renard, Torvul, and Idgen Marte inspected the gear they'd confiscated. "As well as any knife with less than half a span of blade. Everything else stays."

Idgen Marte diffidently picked among a pile of swords, shifting them about with a studied frown and one extended hand. She quickly stood and walked off in evident disgust.

The gathered mercenaries, minus the two that Mol had granted leave to stay, milled around uncertainly. Cerisia sat upon her palfrey as though it were a throne, wearing her furs and silks, but without her mask. Neither the Banner nor the Wheel were in evidence, both broken down and tucked away.

Joscelyn was slumped over the pommel of a saddle, tied into it. In the turns that had passed, her senses had not returned to her. As she'd been secured into the saddle, Allystaire had used the Goddess's Gift of healing upon her, but had found nothing to heal. Gerther, his hands bound, was secured to the same pommel Joscelyn slumped over by a long lead.

"M'lord," one of the guardsman—the one Allystaire had hit with his own helmet, judging by his swollen, mottled-purple nose—spoke up. "What of Iolantes's arms?"

"What of them?"

"Ought to go to his kin."

Allystaire made a show of thinking this over, with pursed lips and a finger tapping heavily against his chin. "Tell them to petition Fortune's clergy if they are in want of money—he was a loyal temple servant, aye?"

"What d'ya think they'll do for 'em?"

"Nothing," Allystaire replied, dropping his hands to his belt. "And when they get that nothing and learn they cannot eat Fortune's lying promise, nor live in it, nor sleep warm beneath it, tell them to come to Thornhurst and petition the Mother, and they will have what we can spare."

He spared a glance then for Cerisia, who refused to acknowledge him or meet his eyes, though on her pale cheeks he thought he spotted a shamed blush.

"Begone, then. And know that you have seen the Mother's mercy. Return here with weapons to hand, or plots and deceptions brewing as before, and none of you will leave here alive."

Allystaire watched as Cerisia kicked her mount rather too sharply into a trot, leaving the rest of the party hurrying to catch up. Ivar and Renard stood with him till Fortune's delegation was nothing but a dust cloud.

"Well," Allystaire said, "this does a good deal of solving the problem of arming the village, eh?"

Ivar spat at the ground and said, "Doesn't do anythin' for Evert."

Allystaire shook his head slightly, and spoke in as kindly a voice he could manage. "Nor would it have done anything if I had killed each and every one of them, Ivar. Evert was my brother of battle, too, and I will mourn his loss, but they paid for it, one man for one man."

"And when they come back—and they will—with more men?"

"Then we will kill them—in defense of our lives, our home. Not for cold vengeance. Surely we can all see the difference."

Ivar looked at the ground, spat again. "Lord Coldbourne I served woulda seen 'em all dead rather 'an wait only t'fight 'em again. Woulda called that nonsense."

"The Lord Coldbourne you served is dead, Ivar," Allystaire said. "There is only Allystaire, the Arm of the Mother. Get some rest while you think on it," he added, and though quiet, there was still a tiny snap of command in the voice.

Ivar only just avoided clicking her bootheels. "I'll get the men over t'take charge o' this lot, get it cleaned up and inspected." She walked off, boots thudding rather more heavily into the ground than they needed to, raising clouds of dust as she went.

Allystaire sighed, and wandered off towards his tent, though he looked sidelong at Idgen Marte and Torvul, who knelt upon the ground, the dwarf examining the broken pieces of her sword, humming quietly to himself.

Leaving them to it, he walked alone, burdened only by his thoughts and no need to converse, give orders, make demands, or interrogate. *My thoughts are plenty burden enough,* he told himself. *The Longest Night. Two months away, at best.* Then he snickered at himself and said aloud, "You are no horologist, old man." *Got to speak to Torvul about the armor. Mol and Gideon about the rain. And the refugees from Bend—ought they to be here by now?*

These thoughts knotted up his shoulders and the muscles of his neck by the time he arrived at his tent and slipped inside.

A curious scent lingered in the air inside: strong, floral, strange, not at all unpleasant.

"Cerisia," he said quietly, letting his eyes adjust to the dim light and searching the space.

On his writing table he saw a folded sheet of parchment with his name written in a looping and graceful hand.

He lifted it with two fingers, or started to, but something held it down. As it pulled free of the desk, two objects of like size and weight slid free and gleamed against the wooden slats of the table.

The topaz eyes from Cerisia's mask. He scooped them into his hand, felt them cool and smooth and heavy against the calloused skin of his palm, and held the letter up—closer to his eyes than he would've liked—to read.

Allystaire,

I did mean to avoid bloodshed, and it pains me to know that not only did I fail, but that the deaths are my own fault. Had I watched my own acolytes more closely, or kept a better eye on Iolantes, some kind of accord could have been struck between us. I know you would not accept my Temple's proposal, but surely any arrangement, any acknowledgment, would be better than what you will now face.

I still find you an exhilarating man, an enticing man. Yet you are also a frightening man, at turns as warm as the noonday sun, as protective and sheltering as a castle wall, as chilling as the north wind at the turn of the year.

The certainty I leave here with is that you will always do precisely what you say you will, and that makes you as terrifying as anyone now living.

I will tell my Church what I have seen, and what I believe, from the above: that you are what the stories say you are, what you claim to be—a Paladin.

I leave you these gems as a way of chastening myself, and a sign that I am not, I hope, as awful as you may think. I am Fortune's Priestess, and that is not a life I would willingly set aside for anything. Yet even I can be sympathetic to the life of the folk of Thornhurst, and those like them all over your baronies. Do as you think best with them.

I leave you also with a word of warning. Whatever it is you plan, whatever change it is you think you can effect in this world, I do not doubt your ability to bring it about. I question your ability to control those who will follow in your wake. Think on this.

Cerisia

Allystaire set the letter down and picked up the gemstones. They were cleverly faceted, cut so that one surface was wider than the other, and had been carefully removed from the settings. "Nowhere to spend them now," he murmured, and went rummaging among his baggage till he found the small, soft sack he was looking for. He took a few moments to work open the knot its strings were tied into, and carefully slid the pair of topazes inside, drawing it tight. Some impulse made him open it back up, however, and pull from it a single piece: the portrait of a woman worked in carnelian. The features were soft and indistinct, as they must be, but the profile was as familiar to Allystaire as his own.

"When you sent me the Ravens, Audreyn, did you know what you were sending them to? Will I have to ask them to fight a war, alone, against Braech and Fortune and Delondeur, all together?" He sighed, held the gem up to the light, then slid it back into the bag and tucked it away among his things. He took a deep breath, squared his shoulders, and opened the flap of his tent to the afternoon light. "Refugees. Weather. Armor. Palisade," he murmured, as he stepped out.

CHAPTER 26

The Grip of Despair

"**Y**ou'll have no rest till you satisfy yourself about the refugees from Bend. I know," Torvul said, as the five Ordained sat around a table in the Inn sharing a quick morning meal. "Ivar and Renard'll handle the men, and the digging. I've got more than enough work to do."

"About my armor," Allystaire began.

"Another few days," Torvul said. "Take some of the captured stuff if you simply must strap some inferior iron on."

"Everything is wrong without it," Allystaire said. "I hardly know how to swing my hammer."

"You'll remember how to swing that hammer for years after you've died," Torvul replied, pausing then for a long pull from a mug full of small beer.

Idgen Marte finished chewing a piece of ham and shrugged. "I could use the ride. I'll join you."

Allystaire looked up at her as she stood, searching for words, but she cut him off.

"I've my bow still, and knives. Don't even say it."

Allystaire pushed away his own mug and the scant crumbs of his thoroughly eaten breakfast. "Gideon? Care for a ride?"

"I'm not much of a rider," the boy offered hesitantly.

"Time to learn, then," Allystaire said, thinking on his words to the Goddess. *There is so much no one has ever taught him.* "Come on. My palfrey is still here. It is an easy ride."

Mol looked up at them as they all stood, then back at the table, saying nothing. At the glimpse of her dark, unreadable eyes, Allystaire felt a slight chill run down his back. He dismissed it, though, and led Idgen Marte and Gideon to the nearby stables.

Ardent seemed to know he was coming, sticking his huge, thickly-maned grey head out of his stall. The destrier stamped and shook his head impatiently as Allystaire neared him. Idgen Marte's brown courser was a bit more subdued. Ardent quieted down as Allystaire retrieved his tack, entered the stall, and began to saddle him.

The work was familiar to his hands, and his mind drifted, if only for a moment, till he noticed Gideon struggling to lift the palfrey's saddle. He secured Ardent and went to the boy's side. After watching him try to lift by tugging on the pommel, Allystaire reached out and laid a hand lightly on Gideon's wrist.

"Get your arms under it. It is easier to carry a weight, any weight, when it is atop your arms instead of under them, especially when you have not got much to grab hold of."

The boy nodded and slid his arms under the saddle. He still grunted with the effort, but he lifted it and brought it towards the palfrey. Allystaire gave him a hand settling it on the back and with the various straps and buckles, then lifted him by the belt to help him into the saddle.

"Can I not just ride double with one of you?" Gideon asked as he settled on, trying to fit his feet into stirrups that were just slightly out of his reach.

"No," Allystaire replied curtly. "Ardent will bear no one else, and Idgen Marte may have need of her mount's speed."

Without complaint, the boy nodded. With one hand on Ardent's bridle and another leading the palfrey, Allystaire walked both horses outside, keeping the lead to Gideon's mount in his hand as he pulled himself into the saddle.

As soon as he settled on and adjusted his seat, Ardent tensed, the muscles bunching underneath him; the destrier wanted to run. Allystaire held him in check, thinking of Gideon, and with his horse protesting beneath him, he set a mild pace as they headed west.

A few dozen yards out of the village and Allystaire was suddenly struck by memory of a season ago, leading three animals and trying to keep Mol atop the palfrey, tracking a crew of reavers he knew nothing of, wrestling with his natural impulses to leave it all well enough alone. The girl's stubborn insistence. All the times he could have left her, could have abandoned her quest for justice. *What did it have to do with me? With me as I was then, anyway? Allystaire Coldbourne made more orphans than whoever I am now will save,* he thought.

Not the point, he answered himself silently, as Idgen Marte rode ahead and the palfrey flowed into an ambling gait that let it keep pace with the much larger destrier. *The point is that now someone stands with the orphans, instead of making more.*

Suddenly he remembered the heat, the way it baked him, the way it seemed to torture the landscape as he rode out of Oyrwyn and down into Delondeur. *Seeking what, anyway? Sword-at-hire work? Getting up a warband? Finding the Ravens? And if the sun is of the Mother, why was it…*

"The weight of sin," he suddenly spoke aloud, causing Idgen Marte and Gideon both to turn towards him. "Mine," he added, quietly.

"Are you talking t'yourself," Idgen Marte called, over her shoulder.

"No," Allystaire shook his head. "No. I was merely remembering the first time I rode this way, with Mol. Were those weeks of summer particularly hot?"

"Not to me," Idgen Marte said, "but remember that I was born a good thousand leagues to the south or so. We've got it a bit warmer down there."

"In my memory, they are the hottest days I have ever lived and I have spent summers campaigning in Innadan dust. I think…I think the heat was the work of the Goddess."

"What do you mean?" That was Gideon, peering at him with narrowed eyes.

"I think She was testing me, even then. There were so many times I could have turned back. So many times the thought came to me, unbidden, that I could abandon the girl's kith and kin, if not the girl herself. Take her to a temple, find relatives, even a kindly nearby family, convince her that all was lost."

"You'd've had no luck with that," Idgen Marte said. "Remember, I was taking your links and drinking on your credit just to watch Mol in a room. She set to talking and next I knew I was skulking around a warehouse full of slaves and watching your back."

"That was probably the Goddess's hand at work," Gideon pointed out. "Mol was the first she called, after all, and we have all seen what Her Voice can do now that she understands what she is."

Allystaire shrugged beneath his borrowed mail. "Just memories, are all," he said. "First time I have ridden this way since. Enough tongue-wagging over it." He looked over his shoulder at Gideon. "Do you think you can manage a run? Keep your hands on the reins and use your legs to stay in the seat. I am afraid if I do not give Ardent some room, he will decide to take it, and I cannot hold him back if that happens."

Gideon nodded, but swallowed nervously, and tightened his hands on the reins till his knuckles whitened.

"Not like that; a horse understands how you feel about it. Show nerves, it will show nerves. Show fear, it will be afraid. Understand?"

The boy nodded again and relaxed his grip. *Mother, keep him safe,* Allystaire thought, even as he gave Ardent the slightest prod with his spur. Idgen Marte did the same with her courser, and the three of them were off.

* * *

"Tracks," Idgen Marte called out, while kneeling where grass met road. "A large number of them, walking off the road, probably to make a camp."

"We may have to do that ourselves," Allystaire said, leading his and Gideon's horses as he strode to her side. "We have gone farther and later than I expected."

"A night of short rations and cold sleep won't hurt us, and the mounts can graze," she replied, standing up and peering at the ground. "Something odd about how they were walking. Slow, dragging steps, like they were clubfooted. And no baggage, no sleds, no wains pulled along behind them."

"They may have left in a hurry and had no time…"

"How many columns of people fleeing a battle or a siege have you seen in your life? Cold, how many have you sent fleeing? There are always wagons or carts, and animals, dogs and horses and goats and chickens. None of that. Just a half dozen or so clubfooted peasants."

Gideon, who still sat atop his mount, ordered so by Allystaire to get more accustomed to the saddle, suddenly lifted a hand and pointed.

"They're back there," the boy said quietly. "Only...not. I feel something. Sorcery. Be ready."

Before he had even finished speaking, Allystaire's hammer was out, and Idgen Marte had an arrow to the string of her tightly curved horsebow. They dashed through the trees in the direction the boy had pointed, Allystaire pausing only to toss the leads he carried towards Gideon, who was surprised as they struck him.

Allystaire crashed through the trees. He knew precisely, without thinking or wondering, where to find Idgen Marte. She stood with her bow hanging limp in her hand, the arrow fallen from the string, her eyes wide in something closer to terror than he'd ever seen in them. She pointed, and his eyes followed her finger.

What he saw was a horrifying tableau of a half-dozen people frozen in positions of twisted, painful horror. Heads were twisted backwards upon necks, knees were bent and locked the wrong way, as were elbows.

All of their mouths were open in silent screams.

Mute and horrified, Allystaire slid his hammer back into its ring, and approached the nearest figure: a man a decade younger than him, wearing warm fisherman's clothing and a knit cap.

His fingers slid against a smooth, hard surface, like marble. Cold, as though it had absorbed the chill of the air. He placed his left hand against the stone-like cheek, closed his eyes, reached for the Goddess's Gift. As he pushed his senses into the man, he felt the faintest spark of life, a tiny, barely glowing coal amidst a bed of ash. He reached for it, puffed it back to a flare.

The cold smooth skin turned suddenly warm, and with a creak of grinding bone, the man's neck turned, painfully, awkwardly, and wide eyes now suddenly aware focused on him.

"Palllllladinnnn," the man groaned, even as Allystaire felt that lifespark drain utterly away, snuffed out like a candle. "You are nothing to us," the corpse then said, and was suddenly joined in a chorus as all of the frozen bodies started to life and began to speak.

"Your goddess is nothing."

"You saved none of them."

"You cannot hope to stand against us."

"Your ruin lies at the end of this year."

Allystaire, briefly taken aback, moved to the next closest one, a fairly young woman, who snarled and babbled as he drew closer. His hand flew to her pox-marked cheek, but he felt nothing, no life within her. He moved towards the next as he heard Idgen Marte's bowstring stretch and tighten.

"Where were you?"

"They needed you."

"As if it would have mattered."

"We will kill you in the end."

"To live among the weak is to become weak."

The groaning, the creak of their bones as their bodies twisted more and more viciously, the feel of their very lives, of some very slim hope they had draining away even as he moved among them trying to bring the Goddess's Gift to bear, to save them, began to eat at him.

Suddenly Allystaire thought the twisted dead things were right. *I could not save them,* he thought. *Who can I save? The more I try to protect, the fewer I can help. Who have I saved? Mol,* he answered himself.

"And yet so many more died," one of the corpses said, twisting its neck unnaturally to look him in the eye as he began to sink to a knee.

"So many more will die," another said.

"So many."

"And for what?"

"A deity from where?"

"A deity who means what?"

"A power that pushes you about like a stone on a gameboard."

"Like cards on a table."

Allystaire began to shake, to tremble, feeling his resolve cracking, feeling the need to call to the Goddess's Gift, to try and save them, waning. He heard Idgen Marte speaking behind him, but not her words.

The air was a weight upon his neck. *If I led the weak and the poor in an uprising, thousands would die, and for what?*

The cold burned his lungs. *It is not about revolt.*

The noise of the groaning blended into a sustained and unintelligible cacophony that threatened to burst his ears. *Then it is pointless. Nothing will change. Born into misery and toil, ending in futile death.*

His heart pounded, then faltered. *So many have already died so pointlessly at my urging.*

The world started to grey at the edges.

Then, suddenly, the noise stopped. But the weight of it was still on his mind and his heart, and he grasped at his throat, his fingers feeble and clumsy. The words echoed in his ears still.

The futility of his life threatened to crush him.

He heard Gideon speaking behind him, but again, could make out no words.

Then he felt Idgen Marte's hand upon his cheek, and her whispers floated through the echoes. "Sorcerous lies," she said. "They cannot hurt you."

Color returned to the world. His heart stuttered back into a steady beat. "The Mother offers safety and refuge, and you are Her bulwark," came another whisper. "Her shield and Her sword."

His lungs filled with cool autumn air, and the burden of despair that weighed on his mind dissipated like fog under the morning sun. "No darkness can stand against Her sun, before the hammer She can make of it."

Allystaire remembered himself, and despair gave way to anger. He stood, whirled to face Gideon, still shivering slightly. Idgen Marte stepped away from him, her hand dropping from his neck. "What was that?" he said.

"A trap," Gideon said. "Laid by a sorcerer. For you."

Allystaire looked back towards where the refugees had stood, and saw only bodies. Bent and tortured, their necks twisted and backs broken, but truly dead.

"How? What?"

"I'll need time to examine them and the area," the boy said "Take a moment."

Allystaire collapsed onto one knee, pressing a hand to his chest. Idgen Marte squatted next to him, laid her hand companionably on his shoulder. "I couldn't feel what you felt, but I knew it was hurting you," she said. "They were wind, empty sounds. You heard them, though, didn't you?"

Allystaire nodded. "They spoke of futility. Convincingly."

"You started to fade from my senses. As if you were disappearing."

He said nothing. Gideon knelt by one of the bodies and grabbed it by the wrist, closing his eyes. He placed a hand upon the ground, then suddenly started, standing upright, his eyes flying open.

"This took a great deal of power," he said. "Someone a good deal more powerful than Bhimanzir ever was. His master, Gethmasanar, may have been capable of this, but I doubt it."

"Who, then?" Allystaire asked.

"I don't know," the boy said, shaking his head. "Think of the planning this speaks of, to know these folk are fleeing Bend, and coming here."

"Or to have been told by the Choiron," Idgen Marte muttered darkly.

"I doubt that," Allystaire said. "Symod is capable of much, but not this. An attack with steel and flame, yes. Casual cruelty, yes. But this? No, I doubt he would condone this. Too complicated."

"Aye," Gideon said, "it certainly was that. The sorcerer took over their minds, their very bodies, then preserved them, feeding his spell with their own life force, banking it like a fire that has to last for days on limited fuel, so that it would last as long as possible as it drove them on towards Thornhurst. The second half of what was done to them would engage only if someone came along who sought to heal them, who reached into their bodies to begin repairing them. You," the boy added, pointing at Allystaire. "And then came the Grip of Despair."

"Is that—"

"A powerful enchantment laid upon the mind," Gideon replied. "With it, a sorcerer with enough will, enough knowledge, enough sheer power, can make a target simply lose any connection to the world, any will to live. It can strike a man dead without hurting him. That it nearly worked on you— your will and vitality are far stronger than most—well, I'd not like to confront him. Not if he knew I was there."

"Could you expend this much power? Not to achieve this goal, but at all?"

Gideon thought a moment, then nodded slowly. "Yes. But it would expend most of the power that remains in me from the God of the Cave."

Allystaire stood with Idgen Marte's help. "If they wanted him dead, why not a simple thunderbolt or a ball of fire?" she asked.

"The Grip of Despair is a statement," Gideon said. "If a sorcerer's power is so much greater than your desire to live, it demonstrates how insignificant you are."

"Well, I hope the bastard knows I am not dead," Allystaire said raggedly. "I will remind him of that fact, eloquently, with my hammer, when I find him." He looked down at the corpses, and said aloud, "We have not the tools nor the time to bury them."

"I can set them upon a pyre," Gideon said. "Of sorts." A pause. "Not a literal pyre, made of wood. I've no need of that."

"Fine. Do it. Then we start back."

"Are we sure of traveling in the dark?" Idgen Marte hesitated a moment before going on. "I'm not some child afraid of hobs waiting in the night, but it's dangerous for the horses."

"I am sure," Allystaire said. "All three horses can use the work, and he can see in the dark," Allystaire said, pointing to Gideon. "We will walk if we have to. I do not care if it means we are up all the night. I will not sleep till I am back in Thornhurst."

He knelt on the ground once more. Dimly he was aware of the bodies being lifted from the ground and moved, felt the tiny hum of power emerging from the boy behind him as he did it, then a flare of light as the bodies were consumed. His mind, though, was elsewhere.

Mother. Goddess. I do not know how to fight a power that can make me forget all that I have felt and known in my life as your servant. Please, if you have any answer, tell me.

He was met with silence. He thought back to his encounter with Bhimanzir, how he had drained the power from him with the Healing Gift. *I will never get that close to one of them again,* he told himself. *They will be prepared. If just one of them can come so close...*

Stop. The voice that he heard within his head was not his own, nor was it that of the Goddess. He looked up saw Idgen Marte standing over him.

"They're powerful, but they fear you. Why else would they set this trap?"

"What do we fight them with?" Allystaire pushed himself to his feet. From the corner of his eye, he saw the twisted, tortured forms of the folk who'd fled from Bend consumed in a soft but powerful light that Gideon seemed to conjure from the air. It could have been awful, yet somehow it was not. There was no reek of flesh, and with each flare of light, the sense of gloom, the powerful interior darkness that infected the area, was lessened. The corpses straightened and uncurled themselves, lost their grimaces of pain.

"Him," Idgen Marte whispered, pointing at the boy, who seemed absorbed, peaceful, even relaxed. Allystaire could feel the suffering ease out of the bodies as Gideon's light touched and consumed them.

"Will he be ready?" Allystaire's voice was barely audible.

"That's up to you, isn't it?"

The last body lifted into the air at Gideon's will, and was cleansed in the light he moved along it. He turned towards them. "They're with Her now," he said. "I cannot do that endlessly, but for a few poor folk like these…"

"I understand." Allystaire thought a moment. "They have gone to a rest, and it was the best you could offer."

"Let's head home," Idgen Marte said. "Can you take the lead, Gideon?"

The boy nodded. They followed him out of the small screen of trees and found the three mounts more or less where they'd been left. Idgen Marte's sleek brown courser and the palfrey had wandered, nosing at the scrubby, browning grass. Ardent had remained exactly where Allystaire had left him, and whickered as the paladin picked up his reins.

"That horse is uncanny," Idgen Marte said, as she gathered her own horse and gave its reins a gentle tug to start leading it on.

"Not the first time you have said that," Allystaire pointed out.

"Doesn't make me wrong." She paused. "You know, the stories the songs, they often mention the paladin's mount."

"Aye, and usually it is a dragon or a great wolf or a bear or some celestial creature in equine guise."

"Well are you sure that thing isn't a bear, maybe wearing a horse's skin?"

Gideon, without looking back at them, spoke up. "Are you two going to do this all the way back to Thornhurst? It's going to be a long night as it is."

Allystaire smiled despite himself. "You have been spending too much time with Torvul."

"There's much I can learn from him," Gideon smoothly replied.

"Aye, and when you get bored of mixing tinctures and old lies, and you're tired of standing in the cold and hauling rocks and learning to get hit with a stick," Idgen Marte put in, "come to me and I'll teach you something useful."

"Like?"

"How to lift a purse or spring a lock," she said. "How to woo a girl and stomach your drink. Cold, get just the right amount of wine in me and I might teach you the lute."

That declaration brought a moment of stunned silence. Allystaire and Gideon stopped in their tracks. Ardent bumped his nose into Allystaire's shoulder, surprised by the sudden halt.

"You play the lute?"

"It's not that uncommon," Idgen Marte responded, and the hint of evasion in her tone made Allystaire wish for more light to make out her features. "You've said you had music lessons as a page or a squire."

"Oh, they tried," Allystaire said. "The harp. But I had no hands for it. My fingers were too thick and clumsy to find the right string without two or three wrong strings coming along. Then they banned me from trying it at all after I broke one."

Idgen Marte spat to the side, started walking again, forcing the other two to keep pace. "On purpose?"

"Aye," Allystaire admitted.

"Breaking an instrument with intent is a sin."

"If it makes you feel any better, I broke it by hitting a young Casamir over the head when I saw him try to shove a charcoal boy into a live fire."

"Cold, he was a piece of shit, wasn't he?"

"Who's Casamir?" Gideon asked.

"A dead man," Allystaire said. "And well deserving of it." He paused, looking over at Idgen Marte, imagined he could see the faintest trace of the white scar that curled down her lip and around her throat.

"Going to have to hear the lute some day, Idgen Marte," he murmured.

"About it, maybe," she answered softly. "Me play it, though? No."

* * *

The walk was long and cold and dark, and the sun lit the eastern sky as they approached Thornhurst's outlying farms. The horses were drooping. Once, Allystaire placed his left hand upon their necks and did what he could to ease their weariness.

"The horses will need a good rub, then rest and fodder," Allystaire said. "Gideon, you stay with me so you can learn how it is done."

The boy, who'd found the determination to walk every step of the way back, and was now on the fading edges of consciousness, looked wearily back at Allystaire. "Can't we just feed them and then sleep?"

"The first rule of keeping an animal, any animal, as a partner in your work, be it a horse to ride, or a dog or a pard or a falcon in hunting, is that you see to the beast's needs before your own. It eats before you, sleeps before you, drinks before you. You never break that rule except at utmost need."

"No would have sufficed," Gideon tiredly muttered.

A brief flare of anger brought sharp words to Allystaire's lips, but he bit them back. *He's not a lord's son in need of breaking,* he reminded himself.

The three of them wearily trudged their last yards to the stables outside the Inn. Allystaire sent Gideon to fetch water while he and Idgen Marte unbuckled saddles.

"Boy saved your life tonight," Idgen Marte pointed out, as she fetched a pair of stiff brushes, tossed one to him, and began to comb her courser's coat. "Ought to make sure he knows that you realize it."

"I will. When the time is right."

"The praise comes dear and the list of tasks never ends, eh? He's not a squire."

"No, but that is no reason to abandon a sound method."

"I suppose." She continued brushing and Allystaire did the same, and for a moment there was only the sound of the thick brushes against the coats of their warhorses, pulling free tangles, cleaning out the mud and dirt of the road. "How long do you usually get to teach a boy to be a man?"

"Wrong question. You can never teach that. You can only teach the things you think a man ought to know, mayhap have some say in the kind of man he becomes on his own. Yet, to your real question—they would come to Wind's Jaw as young as seven or eight summers, and become knights at sixteen, seventeen? Most would start marching on campaign at fifteen."

"So eight years or so. With Gideon, how long do you think you'll have?"

"Can it be more than two months till Longest Night?" Allystaire sighed. "So, that long."

"It'll have to do."

"I suppose I can skip the finer points of the list and getting accustomed to armor."

"How does a boy get accustomed to that, anyway?"

"In my day, we had chainmail thrown on and had to climb the highest tower in Wind's Jaw if we wanted to eat that night."

"And what did your charges do?"

"The same, but carrying sword and shield as well."

"Cold. You must've made some hard knights. How'd your barony not conquer?"

"Well, we did, a bit. Lord Mornis, one of Harlach's primary liegemen, was swallowed up entire by the Old Baron, and I carved a good third of Harlach away in my time. We took pieces of Delondeur or Varshyne or Telmawr, but rarely held them. And if our knights were hard, well, Delondeur knights were just as hard, as were Harlachan. Never enough of us." He paused. "Enough of them," he added, with a snort.

"Hard to forget who you were," Idgen Marte muttered.

"Could be that it is easier for me because I was already walking away from it," Allystaire offered after a diplomatic pause.

"I've learned that lesson. No need to dance around it. I tried to be my old self. She decided to let me. It was no accident that my sword got broken, after I spent all that time blathering over what it meant t'me."

"Torvul can make something out of it. Something new." He stopped in his brushing, having mostly gotten the tangles and mud out of Ardent's coat. "And that would be the point, aye? Take the parts of what we were to make something new."

"Leave the explanations to the bards and the minstrels," Idgen Marte said.

"Have I not been saying that, or near enough, since we met? On with the work of the day," Allystaire replied as the door of the stable swung open to admit both clear autumn daylight and a cold gust of wind.

Gideon entered with them, hauling a full bucket manfully with both hands around the handle. Allystaire took it from him, nodding his thanks, and emptied it into the trough. All three horses came forward to nose into it and began noisily drinking.

Allystaire handed Gideon the comb he'd taken. "Now," he said, "we have work to do. Your horse wants brushing, combing, and feeding. Hold it like this," he said, adjusting the boy's grip on the comb, and then pointed him towards the palfrey. "Careful with any knots."

"I could probably do this with magic," Gideon mumbled. "Carefully, but I could."

"You will not. A certain amount of working with the hands is good for everyone. And it is especially good for a man and his horse when you have the time," he added. "Now to it, and no more delays."

CHAPTER 27

Interlude

"**H**e escaped the Grip of Despair."

The words were as much felt as heard, for the voice that spoke them was mostly a hollow whisper. The speaker was a mere outline, a stick figure in a robe, with glowing trails of shimmering blue energy leaking openly from beneath the hood and the sleeves.

"We are aware." The voice that answered him, from a similarly thin robe, was something closer to two voices echoing each other.

"He killed one of the Knowing."

"He killed Bhimanzir, who was counted one of us by but the slimmest of margins." The reply echoed through the stone-walled chamber.

"It is easy to speak glibly of the dead, but we did not count him so slightly when he still lived," replied a third, much more human voice. "I say this not because he was my student, but because there was a time not long ago when he was well valued among us for his power, his potential, his gifts, and his willingness to act. It is the latter trait that we most miss."

"Be easy, Gethmasanar." Two trails of sickly green spread across the darkness as the echoing figure turned towards the younger, more hale sorcerer, whose own eyes and fingertips leaked a bilious yellow. "Bhimanzir's loss was unforeseen and regrettable. It will be paid. Let us not speak of moving in haste or of foolish concepts like revenge. We do not get revenge. We advance our aims, consolidate power. What other goal should power have?" The words rebounded off the stones, chasing each other in their dual tones.

"This man and his deity are a threat to us in precisely this way," the hollow voice answered.

"You also forget the boy," Gethmasanar pointed out. "How much of our knowledge does he carry with him? What power, what will, did we lose? He is a dagger held over our heart."

"You may feel free to plunge a dagger into our heart if you wish," the voice that was two voices answered. "It will have as much effect upon us as tossing a stone into the sea. The boy is nothing. He is a failure. Our order's history is littered with them."

"When is the last time our order faced something as dangerous as this man, his deity, and his movement?" The whispery voice rose to a ragged high, and Gethmasanar's spine stiffened, hands tensing beneath the sleeves of his robe.

"Deity? Dangerous? Are you beginning to believe this babble, Iriphet?"

"There is power there we do not see, power we cannot understand."

"He is a man with a hammer. He may as well be an ape with a rock bashing open grubs." The final sibilant hissed its way around the chamber.

"And yet, he escaped the Grip of Despair. How many men can have done that, in all the time the Knowing record its use?"

"We do not keep count of such things. What we do is not sport, nor clumsy battle losses tallied by an historian, nor trade goods upon a ledger."

"No, but there are those who do," Gethmasanar ventured, feeling like he had overturned a dice cup as he spoke. "Keep a count of such things. In song— and there is a song collected from these lands that speaks of it being thrown off by a paladin of legend, a Reddyn the Redoubtable…"

"We do not know that name."

"Because it is not known does not mean he did not exist," came the whisper.

"We do not acknowledge that name. The two of you go and do as you must, as you think fit. Speak not of this Allystaire again to us till he is dead or broken. Leave us."

The weird, pitchy yowl of the two voices was an end to the conversation. Iriphet stood and Gethmasanar went to his side, and they left, both feeling the piercing stare of bright and terrifying power across their backs.

CHAPTER 28

The Will and the Dragon

"Are you certain he is ready for this?" Allystaire stood with his thumbs hooked in his belt. Despite the deep chill hanging in the air, he wore no jacket or vest, and his arms and neck were thick with dust and sweat.

"For the past two weeks, you've had him up at dawn, hauling rocks, getting hit with sticks, hitting you with a stick, fetching water, riding, running, cutting timber, and Mother knows what else sort of fool's labor—and you're wondering if he's ready to do the kind of thing he was made to do?" Torvul looked up from the tools he was preparing—his risers, his glass stems, bottles of vapor. Torvul wore his deep blue robes, with the sleeves pushed up over his elbows as he tinkered.

"The work I have had him doing is for his own good, and ours."

"He's not a knight, Ally. Ya can't make him one."

"If I wanted him to be a knight I would be having you make him a set of armor." With only the slightest pause, he added, "Speaking of armor…"

"I've almost got it ready," Torvul held up a hand to forestall him. "We get this done with fast enough, and it'll be tonight. I think."

"You told me that two nights ago."

"Ah, well, there was a bit of a hang up. I had it right, ya see, precisely how I wanted. But, ah, well. Then a thought came into my head, unbidden, just sort of tunneled its way in as thoughts are wont to do, crashing about like trolls."

"What thought?"

"The thought of how much weight I could pull by selling what I'm working on," Torvul said hastily. "I know, I know. Her gifts are contingent on charity. It was unworthy of Her service. It came and was gone, and so were my results."

"Have you damaged—"

"Stones above, no, I've not damaged it. Anything I do to it will improve it. Now go tell Gideon we're ready."

"Aye." Allystaire turned on his heel and followed the dirt track deeper into the village, towards the Temple where the Will of the Mother waited in prayer for his task. Grey clouds, heavy with rain, circled Thornhurst. A half a day's ride in either direction, Allystaire was sure, would mean rain, but Braech's priests, according to Mol, kept it at bay. It was time for Gideon to pull it down.

At least that is a longer game, Allystaire thought. *Gives us time to breathe.* Though how much time they truly had, he wasn't sure. Not enough. Even so, the timber in the northeast hills was being cleared and slowly turned into a palisade wall around the village proper, and such of the village men as could work metal or stone were busy figuring out a pair of gates as designed by Torvul.

He swung open the doors of the Temple, letting the cold air in with him. Fires burned low in braziers set around the room, warming it, but the sweat of labor had dried on his skin and he found himself unrolling his sleeves and pulling them down.

Gideon stood by the altar, in front of the Pillar of the Will, one hand extended to it, pressed against the smooth red-gold stone. Though it had only been a few weeks of working with him, Allystaire thought he could already see a change in the boy. A straighter spine, a thicker chest, a more possessed manner.

Without turning to face him, Gideon said, "Is Torvul ready for me?"

"Aye. Are you ready for this?"

"Allystaire," Gideon said, turning from the altar and stepping away from it, "I've faced down two deities already. What great matter is a third?"

Allystaire frowned, carving deep lines around his mouth. "That kind of arrogance does not become us."

Gideon stopped and tilted his head. "I have heard you, and Idgen Marte, and Torvul, all speak that way. Not about gods, it is true, yet the point remains; why may you express confidence while I must not?"

"Confidence is good. A man needs to carry some with him, certainly. Braech, though, is not Fortune, and his clergy are not going to be unprepared. The Choiron himself may be involved, and he can wield his power like a blade or like a maul—if you let confidence become arrogance, and you do not take him as a genuine threat to your life, and the lives of everyone depending upon us, he will find a way to hurt you."

"How did you withstand him, then? Didn't he try to bring his will to bear on you?"

"The Mother was already behind and within me then. Truthfully, though, I am not sure. Most of what I remember of that moment was an anger I had never known before. It was cold and bright and hard, and it was like a goad driving me away from him. Through him, if need be."

"How can mercy and anger come from the same source?" Gideon wondered aloud, but was cut off when Allystaire gave him a gentle, almost playful shove on the shoulder.

"Enough words. Time for action."

Gideon brushed his hand away but went outside all the same. Allystaire gave him distance as they walked. The boy began chafing his arms against the cold, only to look back at Allystaire and drop his hands to his sides.

Don't be daft boy, put on a cloak or a coat if you're cold, Allystaire thought, but didn't say, as he felt the chill move up his own arms. *At least it is not quite a freeze yet. We'll have rain and not snow.*

They found Torvul with his inflated paper-and-wood contraptions, four of them, staked to the ground, leaving little slack in the ropes. Mol waited next to him, silent as the dwarf worked, and turned to face Gideon as he approached.

"The clouds are near, and Braech's priests hold them back unnatural-ly." Mol gestured with one hand towards the sky. "Do what you think you must—if they are too strong, or you need time to understand what it is they do, remember that this isn't a crisis. We'll not starve this winter if it doesn't rain now."

No, Allystaire thought grimly, *we will starve in the summer or the next winter.*

"I know," Gideon said. "Everyone stand back. And do not be concerned. Whatever happens. I will come back."

The boy went to a knee. He placed one hand on the grass next to his leg, and the other he rested on his bent knee. And then, to the shock of the three standing there, he disappeared.

* * *

His task was in the air, among the clouds. So, he reasoned, he needed to be in the air.

He needed to be air.

He realized almost instantly the flaw in the plan. As it was formless and without sense organs, air could see nothing. So as fast as the speed of thought, as fast as the idea formed, he was no longer simply formless, barely collected air, but rather air in the shape of himself.

No. He was himself, the Will of the Mother, in a familiar shape. The shape he knew the best, only it was a shape that was as light—no, lighter than the air—and as invisible. He floated, observed the clouds. Understanding that he needed wings to propel himself, he willed them, and they unfurled from his shoulders. Or, he thought, they felt as though they unfurled—since they had no discernible weight and no visible shape, unfurling was simply how he made the sensation intelligible.

Flight was a new sensation. It was interesting, but he could not linger. Drawn by the feel and even the smell of the rain that fattened the nearby clouds, he beat his wings and flew like a loosed arrow straight towards one.

Near the edges of the air above Thornhurst, he felt it. If he had to describe it, he would've called it a net, a great, finely woven net of air and water. The word, of course, was an imperfect reflection of the thing. *All words are,* he reasoned.

A net can be cut, he thought, and in the next moment, one of his hands had lengthened, flattened, and sharpened into a kind of blade. He reached for the net with his other hand and set the blade against its edge, and began to cut.

* * *

In the Great Temple of Braech in Keersvast, a huge blue marble edifice occupying its own island on the Keersvast Archipelago, the island chain on which the greatest city of the northern world was built, a circle of priests knew instantly that they were threatened.

The weather over the eastern border of Barony Delondeur, many hundreds of miles away, had required their specific attention this day, according to the Choiron Symod and his Marynth, both of whom had come to the City of Islands some weeks ago and taken council with the present members of the Choironate. Artifacts that resided in the Great Temple, and could not leave it, were needed to battle some threat to the Sea Dragon, or so the gossip would have it.

This was why, headed by the Marynth Oritius—a stout, bearded man of middle years and tremendous will, if very little political acumen—a circle of half a dozen priests in Braech's sea-blue robes stood around an incredibly finely wrought and detailed globe, with islands and continents worked in gold and silver and set into a massive blue crystal so minutely faceted it appeared round.

When they felt the presence begin to assault the construct of their will, they did not panic, and they did not scatter. Oritius's back stiffened as he stood up straighter. "Harden it," he commanded. "Harden yourselves."

* * *

For the briefest of moments, the Will of the Mother thought the moment would come easily. The blade of his hand parted a few strings of the net, and he could see how the whole would unravel.

Then the net became a chain, and his blade snagged inside of a link. He pulled it free.

He set both hands against the link and pulled. Slowly, agonizingly, it began to part, but he felt even as he was tearing it, the others were growing smaller, tighter, offering no purchase.

What he wanted was neither tool nor raw strength.

What he needed was fire.

* * *

It was a sudden and intense agony for the six blue-robed priests, till Oritius, sturdy and strong-willed Oritius, yelled another command. "Separate! Pull the clouds away but do not give this thing a target to focus upon!"

* * *

It was as though the lengths of chain suddenly became a flock of birds that exploded from his grip and disappeared. Even as he sensed that he was chasing after them, for they weren't flocks—rather quickly they coalesced into larger birds, and they gripped the clouds, the prize he had come for, in their talons and began to pull them, wrench them away from Thornhurst.

His weightless and invisible form stretched and expanded, his wings growing huge and ready to pound the air and throw him forward like a spear, but then a new thought overcame him, and just as quickly the wings became leathery, his neck stretched and thinned and his face became a snout rather than a beak, and feathers drew flat against his body and turned into scales.

With a contemptuous snort that turned the air in front of him to steam, the Will of the Mother, in the aspect of a great dragon of the air, dove for the nearest of the Sea Dragon's priests.

He would admit that the irony appealed to him.

His jaws closed around one of the fleeing birds before it even knew what hunted it.

* * *

Oritius fell to the ground like a man stunned by a hammer blow. With their leader down, the others instantly abandoned their task, drawing their wills back through the globe in the center of the room into themselves.

"Oh, Braech," one cried out, as they all stared at the artifact in dawning horror. "It follows!"

And then some enormous Will, something that dwarfed any of them on their own, was in the room with them. Its attention fixed upon the globe, and almost contemptuously, they heard a simple, resonant, "No."

* * *

Gideon's form slowly materialized on the ground in Thornhurst again. "Let them go, Torvul," he said hoarsely "And if someone would bring me water I would…" He coughed then, weakly, and sank forward onto the ground, hands and knees both beneath him.

The dwarf cut the ropes holding the risers, and the contraptions sped into the air and towards the clouds.

* * *

Symod paced the room that had held the artifact, the globe which the Sea Dragon's priests had used for hundreds of years to monitor the weather, to assist or impede vessels at sea, to guide their favored army or stymie the efforts of another.

Nothing was left of it but fragments of crystal and blobs of melted metal. There was a rap at the doorway behind him. Symod did not turn around.

"They say that Oritius's mind is gone," Evolyn ventured cautiously. She chose her steps carefully, stepping between hunks of the blue crystal. "He lives, but with no more sense than an infant."

"Better to send him to Braech than to let him live on as a mockery of what he was," Symod replied, his deep and rolling voice subdued in the wreckage of the room. "What of the others?"

"They will live, though the chirurgeons will have a long night of it, picking fragments of crystal and metal out of their skin. They do babble, though."

"What of?"

"A dragon in the clouds. A demon of the sun. An air spirit that cut and burned and pursued them."

"What is it, then? A dragon or a demon?"

Evolyn sighed. "They do not know, Symod." She bent down and picked up a bent and twisted blob of metal that had been one of the main islands of the Archipelago. "Will the destruction of the artifact fall back upon us?"

"Oritius was in charge. He has paid. We set the course, but did not steer the ship. If anything, it will drive the rest of the Choironate into our arms. They'll have no choice but to see Allystaire as a threat now."

Evolyn recalled her one face-to-face encounter with the paladin, frowned, and stole a glance at Symod. He projected calm and poise, yet there were new lines graven into the sides of his face, a pinched quality to his cheeks that belied the smooth surface, the aura of easy power. "Do you think this was him? The paladin?"

"Certainly not. He hasn't that kind of power, whatever he is."

"He seems more likely to confront you more personally."

"Why, Lady Lamaliere," Symod said, turning the full force of his sea-green eyes upon her. "That almost sounds like admiration."

A tiny note of panic sounded in Evolyn's head, but she suppressed it, and didn't waste time wondering if any of it showed in her features. It hadn't. "Not at all, Choiron. Merely that this does not seem like his work. And, if I may speak freely…"

"Your rank entitles you to that."

"It does not seem Braech's way to confront our enemies thus. To attempt to use our wills to, what, make a few score peasants starve to death?"

"We play a greater game. Surely you are aware of the stakes."

"Why not simply scatter them? Trod the place to dust. Salt the ground. Tear the stones of their would-be temple down and use them to build a shrine to the Sea Dragon."

"And it would be so simple? Perhaps I should simply give you command of some men and have you take charge of it." Symod took three slow steps towards her, a faint air of menace gathering around him, as bits of crystal shattered under his boots. "And yet I already did as much, at great expense and much risk. And after that, your assassin failed—at great cost to our Temple's treasury. Why should I throw two or three score more men, and all it would cost, after that one? That one who could not fail, and yet did."

"There are unforeseen powers among them, Choiron," Evolyn said, meeting him eye to eye and standing her ground. "There must be. Without the corrective immediately to hand he should have died."

"And yet he lives, and this new faith grows. Tales of the 'Arm' and 'the Shadow' have even reached the Archipelago. Here, in our city, where the Sea Dragon first roared, there are people who speak of them, speak of some inland cult of weaklings. Already the rabble of the baronies flock there. Do you know what happens if our own begin to do this? Have you any idea what it means? With greater numbers, greater power. Literally! Their goddess's strength will wax, and it will be us, and our allies in Fortune's Temple, that suffer."

"Fortune's delegation met with failure." In fact, Evolyn pondered the message she had just received, the first letter arriving on Keersvast explaining what had happened. Their losses, the catastrophic failure. She considered sharing more of it with Symod, but said nothing. *That is for calling my people rabble, Symod,* she thought.

"Of course they did. Led by that weak-minded strumpet, how could they not?" He smoothed his beard with one hand, and said, "In truth, though, Lady Evolyn, you speak with some measure of insight. It is time to return to the baronies and prod the one with the most to lose to move on Thornhurst."

"The Baron Delondeur?"

"The same."

"How can he move on Thornhurst when he cannot even control his own seat? Rumor has him imprisoned in the Dunes by his natural son. Half of Londray has declared for this bastard pretender, and riots in his name. By the time any delegation arrives there his men will long since have settled into winter quarters."

"Proper leverage, Marynth. Which is up to you to provide. You will depart the Archipelago within two days. You will take with you a small escort of priests and Islandmen warriors."

"What of the Dragonscales? If we are to confront the paladin, let us make an end of him with our largest and most dangerous weapon."

Symod tsked. "No need. And besides, it would be unwise, perhaps, to loose the berzerkers upon the lands of a Baron we wish to ally with."

Evolyn lowered her head to concede the point, and she heard Symod chuckle. "Besides, there is leverage to hand right here in Keersvast. You need only find it."

"What do you mean, Symod? Please, spare me the guesswork."

Symod swept through a cluster of once-priceless crystal as he walked to an opened window and leaned his hands against the stone sill. "It is a tradition for the Delondeur children to leave and engage in errantries, to write their names in blood and deeds. Whichever returns with the best roll of deeds attached to their name is named the heir."

"With all due respect, Choiron, you need not speak to me of the traditions of my own home barony," Evolyn said, barely keeping the sneer out of her voice. "I knew all of Baron Lionel Delondeur's children when I was younger."

"Then you will have no trouble locating the one who is said to be in Keersvast, leading a crew of swords-at-hire," Symod said, turning from the window to face her with a smirk. "Landen, I think."

Evolyn tried not to let her surprise show, but as Symod whirled on her she knew she had failed. "And what am I to do?"

Symod exhaled heavily. "Tell me, Marynth, what your plan ought to be."

She considered the question, her face impassive. "Encourage Landen to return and seek the Baron's rescue, submitting that as proof of fitness to rule as Lionel's heir."

"That is a first step, yes."

"Provide assistance in the rescue and in putting Lionel back on his seat."

"Then," Symod said, the corners of his mouth quirking upwards, sharp grey beard bristling. "Lionel must be driven to attack and destroy the paladin and his nascent heresy. The fact that Fortune's emissary failed becomes two pieces of luck. First, that Fortune's church is unable to fold this new faith into its own. Second, with their backing, you will carry a Declaration of Anathemata upon the Mother, Her so-called paladin, her other servants, clergy, and followers."

Evolyn stood straighter, curling her hands into loose fists to keep them from clutching at her belt. "Declaration of Anathemata?"

"A rare thing, yes, but politically useful. Urdaran's church will do nothing, of course. That is rather their trademark, after all. Yet two of the three Major Temples will suffice. With the Anathemata issued, and indebted as he will be for his rescue, Lionel Delondeur will have little choice but to marshal a force to stamp that village, and everyone residing in it, to dust."

"No matter what pressure is brought upon him, Lionel is unlikely to put men on the march in the depths of winter," Evolyn said, thinking of the barony winters she had known in her life, the daily grinding misery of them. The entire Lamaliere family and most of the servants tried never to leave the great hall of her father's keep, with its massive, never-cold hearths, once the sky turned and the wind grew its winter teeth. Men on watch upon the curtain wall froze in their steps if they went too far from a fire and were caught by a bad wind. The snow piled taller than her, taller than Symod, taller than one stacked upon the other in a bad year.

"He will," Symod said. "He will have no choice, for not only will you bring him his heir and the Declaration of Anathemata. You will be bringing him new allies to replace one he has lost."

"Are Braechsworn and Dragonscales going to do battle there or not, Symod?"

"They will not be required."

"Then who?"

"Do not burden yourself with an answer to that question." Symod cut her off sharply, in a tone Evolyn well knew she shouldn't challenge. "You have two days to find Landen Delondeur. Do not waste them."

"What if more of Lionel's children rush to his aid? We would be throwing a Temple's weight behind a question of succession. Wars have started over less."

"You needn't worry about Lionel's other children. I am given to understand that one has settled quite happily in the Concordat as a warband captain. And another will not be returning home under any circumstances." Symod looked down at the shattered crystal and melted gold around him. "Fetch someone to clean this up as you go," he murmured.

I know a dismissal when I hear it, Evolyn thought. She bowed very lightly, barely inclining her head and not lowering her eyes, and began stepping carefully among the wreckage of their priceless artifact on her way to her work.

When she passed near him, Symod leaned close to her, enough that she could feel the power emanating from his long, self-contained frame. "I suggest making sure of it, this time. I doubt he is likely to allow you to walk away yet again."

Evolyn took a moment to gather herself, trying to push away the image of a hammer resting upon her desk, of the horrible certainty in the eyes of the man holding it. "Braech, Sea Dragon, Father of Waves and Master of Accords," she murmured in a quick prayer, "grant me the strength to see him dead this time."

CHAPTER 29

A Legend is Crafted

Allystaire and Idgen Marte sat before a fire in the inn, a flagon of the best wine Timmar could come up with at Allystaire's elbow, listening to the sound of rain drumming on the roof. The place was fuller than usual at lunchtime, with few out in the rain to work. The village folk gave them space, engaged in their own conversations and stories and snatches of song, so that the two of them could more or less speak alone behind a buzz of noise.

"It is not an altogether unpleasant sound, is it," Allystaire mused.

"What, rain?" Idgen Marte toyed her mug and shrugged. "I suppose, though in parts of the Concordat there are rainstorms that will last for a month or more."

"A month? I would go mad."

She shrugged again. "It's what you know when you're born there. Not the part where I'm from, mind, but we could get a good week long soaking now and again. Hate how cooped up it makes me feel. No going out-of-doors. I'm not the domestic type," she said, twisting her lips in distaste before pouring a long swallow of wine down her throat. "Not one for staying put," she added, almost an afterthought.

"You are doing well enough with it here," Allystaire pointed out.

"D'ya recall that we thought we wouldn't? We hung about waiting for a sign, then left for the road and were glad to be quit of the place. Don't lie, you were just as happy to be moving again as I was. Should've taken Rede with us, though, kept an eye on him."

"I think we will see him again, for good or ill," Allystaire replied absently, picking up his cup and stroking its rim with a thumb. "Anyway, you are right—I was glad to be moving again. Then Thornhurst started to feel like home."

"That's a bit sentimental for a knight and warlord," Idgen Marte chided.

"Not how I meant it. I meant it has the same responsibilities, the same claims on my attention, the same preoccupying space. Home, as a lord of a place—at least, as one who takes it seriously—is a job of work as much as it is anything else." Allystaire started to raise his cup, and caught Idgen Marte's glare. "Not as much work as for the peat cutters or the farmers, I know. I would not claim otherwise. Still, home, when it was not a tent and a cot, meant a good deal of parchment moving across a desk and endless hearings and councils. Even being at home amongst an army was constant work, of a similar kind. Like being the headman of a large town, only one that is constantly on the move and cannot feed itself."

"And that," Idgen Marte said, "is why I prefer staying on the move by myself. If no one knows where you are, no one can pin any responsibilities on you."

Allystaire chuckled, finished his wine, then reached for the flagon. The clatter of the door swinging open and then shut, rain and wind howling in, and boots dragged against the scrapers cut through the background noise of the common room, followed by the stumping, powerful steps that could only be Torvul's.

The dwarf stopped at the entrance and cast his eyes about, settling on Allystaire and Idgen Marte. Then he waved, and called to them in a voice that cut across all the noise.

"C'mon, hero. I've got the process ready. I want ya t'see it."

Allystaire set down cup and flagon and stood, wincing just a bit. The advent of the rain the previous day had woken old aches in his left shoulder, and he felt them as he pushed against the table.

"Hear that," Torvul said, pointing a longer finger up at the roof, and, presumably, the rain driving against it. "That's dwarfish work, that is."

"So long as it stops at some point," Allystaire said. "We do not want to drown the, ah, cabbages." He paused. "Can cabbages drown?"

"Mother help us all if we ever need to turn your hands to farming. And nothin'll drown. My work is precise. The rain will tail off over the night. The ground is dry enough that it'll soak it all up, and we should be more or less back to normal. Now," the dwarf said, throwing open the door, "out into it. They gave me the use of a little house, on account of the fumes. Come now. It'll be a quick walk, but a sodden one."

* * *

Torvul checked and re-checked his table of instruments and the three glass vials of liquid, each stored in a separate rack. Around his bald head he'd tied a silk band that held dark lenses inside wooden frames, resting on his forehead. Allystaire had never seen them before, and couldn't imagine their purpose. Idgen Marte stood close, watching, fascinated. Allystaire, dubious and dour, leaned against the cottage's doorjamb with his arms crossed.

Laid out on the table about which the alchemist paced was Allystaire's armor: dark grey steel, pitted, scored, and dented. "I cannot see anything you have done to improve it, besides the gauntlet you showed me before. What exactly is the point to this, then? Armor is armor and there is no enchanting it, not with gifts such as yours." The dwarf turned and scowled at Allystaire, and the man lifted his hands, palms out. "Your own words, Torvul. Not mine."

Torvul scowled even deeper. "Don't quote my own words back at me, boy. And as for what good it'll do…" He sighed. "Showmanship. A little majesty won't hurt you any."

"I wouldn't go using 'majesty' in his direction, dwarf," Idgen Marte put in. "You know how twitchy he gets."

"I don't mean with crowns n'plenipotentiary powers. I mean the looks of the thing. What do your stories of paladins all have in common?"

"They are all probably untrue," Allystaire offered.

Torvul waved a hand dismissively. "Truth, untruth, all just shades when it comes to stories. Stories aren't facts, and they aren't meant to be. This," he went on, pointing at the armor and the instruments laid out—a boar's hair brush, several small hooks, a glass dropper—"gives you a certain quality that'll make people take notice. People who otherwise wouldn't. And," Torvul smiled faintly, "it'll put the fear of the Goddess into your enemies."

Then he turned back to the table and sniffed each jar, one after the other, and went on. "Back to my original question. Your stories have a certain style in common. Knights in shining armor. Bigger than life. Fair to look upon. You're big, I'll give you that, but I've seen bigger. Fair passed you by ten or twelve years ago, I'd say." He narrowed his eyes under craggy brows and added, "Fifteen, even."

"That leaves shining armor," Idgen Marte pointed out. She opened her mouth to go on, but Torvul beat her to it.

"Precisely," he said, snapping a finger. "And no—I can't enspell your armor. Not like a thaumaturge could. But I can give it style. " He smiled the devious, knowing smile they had come to know.

"What good is style? Style, I have often said, gets men killed."

"What he means is that he will make you a beacon." Mol suddenly sidled in, the door shutting almost noiselessly behind her. "Of hope," the girl added. Water dripped off the cloak she'd thrown on over her robe as she came to the hearth and set the wet outer garment carefully on the stones. She reached up to take one of Allystaire's huge, swollen-knuckled hands in both of hers. "When he is done, no one who sees you in this armor will have any doubt. Those with call to fear you will know their fear, see it thrown back upon them, and be weakened by it. And those whom we fight for—they'll be able to look at you and know their own strength."

The door opened again, and this time Gideon entered with a spray of rain before coming to the table and peering at the instruments and vials.

"Awake, finally," Torvul asked him.

The boy nodded, and reached for one of the vials, till Torvul grabbed him by the wrist. "Just because you're the aetherial shapeshifting troll' o' the' hill today, doesn't mean you get to touch my instruments or my tinctures. Got to do more than defy a god or three to do that."

"I wouldn't have harmed anything. Not sure I could muster the energy to change its composition even if I wanted to," the boy protested.

Allystaire walked forward and put a concerned hand on the boy's shoulder. "Gideon, did you overtax yourself? Expend all—"

"Not at all," the boy replied, shaking his head. "I'm just tired. Too tired to focus, except for a small thing."

"Good." He gave the boy's shoulder a squeeze. "You did well today, lad. Too much longer without rain, folk would have started to get suspicious, fearful. You rewarded their faith, and that is what we are here to do."

"Well if we're done speechifying, let's get t'work." The dwarf stopped, thought a moment, and said, "Well, I'll get t'work. The rest of y' just stay out of the way. Even you," he added, glancing at Gideon and shooing him with a playful swat.

Torvul selected the first vial. Its contents were colorless, but when he lifted its stopper, it released a metallic scent into the air. "To bind," he nearly chanted. "As the Goddess has bound us."

He began carefully pouring the liquid, in tiny droplets, starting at the top down: helm, pauldrons, cuirass, upper and lower cannons of the vambraces, the greaves, and last the gauntlets. But he did not merely pour; he picked up one of the hooks on the rack and began carefully scraping the liquid, which clung viscously to the surface of the armor, spreading it carefully into every crevice. When the hook he had picked did not reach, he selected another, smaller, and yet again another smaller. Then he set down the empty vial and took the second, full of what appeared to be cool liquid silver.

"To brighten." Now, Torvul was either into the role, or absorbed in his work, for there was no nearly chanting. He sang in his deep rumble. "So none in this world will miss his coming."

Again, he poured with a hand as steady as a mountain, and again he picked up a thin hook and began scraping, teasing the liquid he poured, till every bit of the armor was covered. Allystaire stifled a yawn. Idgen Marte shuffled her feet. Mol and Gideon fidgeted.

Finally, Torvul finished, set his tool and the empty vial down, interlaced his fingers, and cracked his knuckles. Then he took up the last vial and uncorked it. Its scent filled the room.

To Allystaire it was the smell of a cold late winter morning in the mountains of his home, when the sun was dauntingly bright and the entire world seemed fresh.

"To reflect." Torvul lifted the vial in both hands. He poured.

The room was suddenly filled with an intense, almost blinding light. Always prepared, Torvul tugged down the thick lenses he'd had stuck over his head, and continued. Allystaire had to shield his eyes in order to watch, as did Idgen Marte.

Mol and Gideon looked on, apparently untroubled.

Torvul took an age scraping and brushing. And when he was done, the room glittered with the radiance of the overhead lamps cast back by the armor upon the table.

Its surface gleamed like a mirror of pure silver, throwing back their reflections in dizzying multiples as they crowded around the table.

Allystaire leaned forward and brushed a finger against it. Torvul did not stop or scold him. He could feel the scarred and rough surface of his armor, as familiar as his own hand. Yet his fingerprint left no mark upon the bright, perfect surface. "Is it an illusion?" He turned to Torvul, lifted his hand from the armor.

"Yes and no," the dwarf said, shrugging.

"Is it a lie, then? A seeming, only? A glamour, with the truth of my old gear beneath it?"

"Hope is never a lie," Mol said, as she stood on her tip-toes to look down upon the table.

"The girl has the right of it," Torvul said. "'Course she does. Not known her t'be wrong yet. When I said yes and no, I wasn't just playin' games. The armor is what you were, it's a part of you, and it is ugly and hard. That's true. Yet you're a paladin now, the paladin, the Arm of the Mother, and that's what people will see in this armor—and that is true as well."

"We have all been Called," Allystaire said. "You and Idgen Marte and Mol and Gideon as surely as I."

"Not in the way that matters to folk. People will need this, Allystaire. People here, in Thornhurst, will need it, and you know it." Idgen Marte answered this time. "I'm the Shadow—I am meant not to be seen. Torvul is the Wit; his strength isn't in arms the same way ours is. No offense," she added to the dwarf.

"None taken. Most weapons are just a stick with a blade at one end and an idiot at the other, you ask me."

"Fine," Allystaire said. "Help me gather it up and I will go put it on."

"Wait," Gideon said, coming forward suddenly, his voice halting. He lifted a hand, the fingers and palm outlined in a faint whitish glow. "Could I?"

Torvul smiled broadly and crookedly. "Go ahead."

The boy had to pull a chair to the table and kneel on it in order to press his hand directly onto the center of the breastplate. "Close your eyes," he said, suddenly, and they did—but the sudden brightness that filled the room turned Allystaire's vision red behind his eyelids. When he blinked back into clarity, the Golden Sun of the Mother stood in brilliant relief against the silver of the cuirass.

Gideon stood up and admired his handiwork, then frowned. "Not quite," he said, and leaned back down, one finger outstretched. He traced a quick outline, then stood back, and gestured towards the cuirass. They crowded around the table to see the small outline of a hammer within the eight-pointed sun.

"Put it on," Torvul said. "I've improved the fit and shortened how long it'll take."

"I have not got my gambeson," Allystaire said.

Torvul smiled and pointed to the curtained-off bedroom. "I took the liberty."

Allystaire gathered up the armor with Gideon's help and marched off, waving the boy with him. "Best you learn how to help me in and out of it," he said. "I want you next to me till the point of battle."

Their voices trailed off as they pulled the curtain. There were some muted orders, a thud as some piece hit the floor, some rattling and creaking, and finally Allystaire emerged, helm under his head, glittering in mirror-bright silvered armor.

"I feel a little ridiculous," he murmured.

"Do I really need to remind you that you look as you did in the vision the night we built the altar?" Idgen Marte cocked her head to one side.

Mol closed in, leaned forward to touch the sun on his chest, the hammer within it, tracing the outline with her short child's finger. "This is what they might call you one day, Allystaire, a long time from now," she half-whispered. "Hammer of the Sun."

"Might?"

The girl looked up at him with a sad weight in her eyes. "Nothing is set, and all remains in flux. We may yet be conquered, our light snuffed out. It is not given to us to know how this ends. Not even to me."

Allystaire sighed and wrapped his arm around the girl's shoulder, hugging her, careful of the weight of the armor. "Nothing is being snuffed out. Not today, not ever." He let the girl go and looked to Torvul. "Have you got polish for it?"

"Don't need it," Torvul said. "It'll never smear, never stain, never be marred. Damaged, yes, broken, maybe. But give me iron stock and the right earths and I'll give you steel, and however patched, however mended, that armor will be forever this bright. All the soils and sins of the world will keep from it as if in fear."

Allystaire nodded, lifted the helm up to his eyes with both hands, and blinked at the distorted reflection of his own scarred and broken-nosed face in the crown. "We have work to do, to make sure that people remain for us to inspire, aye? Let us be on with it." He tucked the helm back under an arm.

The hearth spat, and a flame lifted from a log that suddenly split, flaring brightly in the rain-darkened room. When his armor caught the firelight and reflected it, Allystaire heard the smallest note of the Goddess's song, and despite himself, his heart swelled.

* * *

Hundreds of miles distant, like the firelight reflected in Allystaire's bright armor, the harbor in Londray was a mirror of dancing flames. And while the city burned, the handful of knights and men-at-arms that had, in the early days of autumn, imprisoned the Baron Delondeur and installed his natural son Chaddin as Baronial Regent, were hunted men.

Having tossed aside their badges—grey cloths wrapped around the upper arm—three such men alternately elbowed and skulked through the alleys and lanes of the capital city, moving always towards the wall and the gate.

"I hope the rumors are true," one murmured quietly, his breath puffing visibly into the air. He was younger, shorter than the other two, cradling a crossbow with a loaded bolt like an infant against his chest, errant blond hairs straying from underneath an iron-banded leather cap.

"We'll know when we get clear of the city and make for the rally point," another replied, his voice smoother and more educated. He wore a sword on one hip and walked with a long-handled axe in one hand, thick spikes at the head and opposite the single blade. He was the tallest, with a well-groomed brown beard and the clank of mail beneath his clothes.

"If I may ask, sir, why're we headin' to some village the other side o'the Thasryach," the third man asked. He was the oldest, a lined and scarred face with deep-set, wary eyes surrounded by creased and wrinkled flesh. He walked with an unstrung bow standing in for a walking stick, trying and failing to conceal its true purpose, and a shorter, cruder sword on his hip.

"Because that was Chaddin's plan," the second man replied. They stopped at the end of an alley and the youngest one went into a crouch and crept around, his loaded crossbow sweeping side to side. He stopped and waved the others forward. "You two were not present when that knight escaped the dungeons and exposed the Baron. He made quite an impression."

"True what they say of 'im, m'lord?" the younger one asked, turning hopeful eyes towards the knight. "A paladin?"

"He killed a sorcerer, and he showed the strength of many men," the knight answered him. He paused, resting for a moment against the wall of a building. "Chaddin…the Baron," he corrected himself, "he wanted this kept quiet, but the man, the paladin, he was Lord Allystaire Coldbourne."

"Out of Oyrwyn? Couldn't be," the bowman said, spitting to the side. "A paladin? I seen his handiwork these years."

"Lionel Delondeur called the man Coldbourne, and he would know," the knight said. "At any rate, enough. We can make the wall by dawn and be on our way."

"Be lucky to get to the mountains before deep snow," the bowman muttered.

They went on in silence, the sounds of violence or a scream occasionally intruding upon the night.

They turned a corner only to find their way blocked by a semicircle of figures shrouded in darkness. No weapons were evident, but the air of menace was palpable.

The beardless crossbowman snapped his weapon up and fired his bolt, even as the knight raised his axe and the bowman took his bowstave into his left hand and drew his sword.

The bolt thunked home in one of the shrouded figures, in the center of the chest. Its barbed head would do untold harm to a man's vitals. It was, against any target at this distance, a fatal blow.

The figure did not move or flinch or even cry out. The bolt seemed to hang loosely in folds of clothing.

The knight shifted his axe to a two-handed grip and advanced half a step before he suddenly stopped, bound in place by invisible chains. His companions found themselves similarly frozen.

From behind the ring of tall, silent, cloaked figures stepped a smaller one, hooded, with faint, sickly yellow trails of energy emanating from his eyes.

"Three more volunteers," he murmured. Though soft, his voice seemed to reach out and caress the three men who were caught, passing across their skin with an air of casual mastery. "You are bound now to great service for your Baron."

"We don't serve that slaving blackguard." Through gritted teeth, the knight managed to squeeze out a few words. "We're Lord Chaddin's men," he added, grimacing with the pain and the effort.

"In life, yes," the hooded figure replied, stepping close so that the knight could see the ruin of his face, the bilious yellow light leaking from his eyes and the corners of his mouth. "But that life has ended. In death you will serve Baron Delondeur more faithfully, more capably, and more fully than you ever could have done before." He raised one gloved hand and made a sharp gesture. The cloaked figures that had penned them in came forward.

As two of them closed in on him, the knight had only the time to catch quick impressions: a hand that seemed made of broken bits of metal tied together with ropes of sinew and patches of flesh, a face that was more bone than skin. And then darkness.

* * *

The crossing from Keersvast to Londray had been the most miserable time of Evolyn's life.

Not because it was late in the year to sail. Not because she shared an opendeck with Islandmen swords-at-hire. A true priest of the Sea Dragon did not fear death at sea, and if the weather had become dangerous, there was power she could bring to bear. And Islandmen were the most devout of Braech's worshippers; they treated priests of any rank with something akin to awe.

It was because she had not sailed on the boat with Landen Delondeur, missing the chance to renew a childhood acquaintance and perhaps curry favor with the future ruler of Barony Delondeur, not to mention coordinate strategy for the coming fight.

But even that was only a small part of what had bothered Evolyn. Namely, it had been the other passengers. She had felt something wrong when she stepped on board to find the captain of the vessel dislodged from his cabin. Her feelings were confirmed when she saw the mysterious mottled yellow and blue light that leaked under its doorway.

The lights did not go out during the entire crossing. They flickered, they dimmed, but they were ever-present. After three days she felt them like an ache in her eyes, thought she could scent them like rotting fish at the bottom of a barrel. She knew what they portended. When, steeling herself, she had gone to discuss the conduct of the coming battles with them, she had been laughingly dismissed. They had no need of gods, she was told; only men.

Which is why, now, with the battle for control of the Dunes quickly won by Landen and two ships worth of swords-at-hire—and the horrible craft of two sorcerers—Evolyn found herself kneeling at an altar of Braech in a small, hidden chapel in the Temple at Londray.

Have you any honest faith left, Symod? Would the Sea Dragon truly have us make an accord with such as them?

She stared hard at the sculpture of Braech. Small, crude, less adorned with gemmary than most of the others in this grand Temple, Evolyn had come to it precisely because it promised solitude. During her novitiate she had discovered it while penance-sweeping; the layer of dust over the statue, the chains that held it above the altar, and the altar itself had spoken of long disuse. Since then it had been her private place to pray, to reflect, to seek guidance.

She stared hard at the Sea Dragon, the dull greened bronze, and willed it to answer her.

"Father of Waves, Master of Accords, Dragon of the Sea, guide me," she mouthed, the words barely audible even to her. "This is not our way. Honest battle or cunning bargain, yes. There are loyal servants, holy berzerkers who would go to this battle simply for the asking, others who would do it for plunder or to make their name or their fortune. We would strive against this upstart, strength for strength. Or find the leverage to move him from his heresy." *Though Fortune's soft glove has already failed.* "But to make dark bargains that no one must know of, to pay in promises and whispers to things that were once men and are now, what?" She resisted the urge to spit when she though of them, of the reek of death that she caught when she was forced to talk to them, of the way their whispers had buzzed at her ears like a repulsive serpent's tongue.

"Tell me, Braech. Lead me, Sea Dragon."

Evolyn stared hard at the old and tarnished image of her God, hoping to hear some whisper, some echo.

Nothing came.

Evolyn stood up, smoothed out her robes, and made a decision. She had brought Landen and the swords-at-hire to the fight. She had aided the rescue of the Baron. But parts of Londray were in flames and fighting continued in the streets.

She would not go to battle in Thornhurst. Not like this, not hiding behind other powers. If Braech was not to lead, then Braech would not go.

"Surely the sorcerers will destroy them," she murmured. "They will not need me to help them, nor will I risk the lives of Braechsworn guardsmen or warriors. Braech will be represented, but the Sea Dragon leads, or the Sea Dragon does not fight."

* * *

As the last of fall's two months gave way to winter's early frosts, Allystaire sat in a tent grown increasingly uncomfortable. With braziers of glowing embers pulled close to the table he used as a desk, he staved off sleep with an old habit. One by one, he listed the forces, the assets, at his command, examining them for weakness, considering strength.

"The Ravens," he murmured in a barely audible voice. "Solid. They can hold a wall, or go over it in the dark. Yet I cannot ask of them what I might of men who serve the Mother, and not my sister's links."

He paused, spreading his hand out on the table. "Renard, his militia. Decent enough bowmen. Not real soldiers. They cannot be left alone in the heat of it. Keegan and his wildmen."

He sighed, lifted his hand and cradled his forehead. "Then me, Idgen Marte, Torvul." He paused, and then added, "Gideon."

He stared into the glowing coals in one of the braziers, and said aloud, having thought the words several times already, "It will not be enough."

The walls are nearly up, and gates. All the folk here will know what it means if they are taken.

The walls will not stand any engines, he thought. *Not likely Delondeur would bring one, if it is him I have to worry about. And bandits will not have them.*

If sorcerers come, he began to think, but he cut the thought off with a clenched fist rapped lightly against the table. "Let them come. Gideon and I will find a way."

If Delondeur brings a hundred men? Two hundred? A thousand?

"A hundred I can keep at bay. Even two or three, mayhap. He could not muster a thousand men as winter comes on. Not unless most were untrained rabble rousted off the streets of Londray."

Even so, whatever men Delondeur could bring were sure to have among them well-trained, well-equipped veterans. And when it comes to veterans, there are the Ravens, me, Idgen Marte, Renard, and Torvul. He paused. *Keegan, I suppose.*

"That is if it is Delondeur who comes," Allystaire spat. "What of Fortune? What of Braech? The sorcerers?"

He lowered his head to his hand again, then stood. He felt the cold more than he once did. His knees protested, as did his back and his aching shoulder. He felt every one of his collection of scars and hurts.

Without knowing exactly why, or even considering the impulse, Allystaire placed one hand against the edge of his table and knelt, wincing as first one knee, and then the other, touched the ground. Rugs and mats had been laid down where there was space, but even so, the cold leeched through the ground and into him.

And then bowing his head, the paladin reached out to his Goddess.

Mother. He stopped, cleared his throat, and started again, murmuring the words aloud. "Goddess, I have tried to do your will, use your Gifts as I thought you would wish. And my best judgments, and my plans have come to this, to sitting and waiting. I have made your people a target. I know nothing of what our enemies plan. The walls I have built, the stores and the trenches and the cunning plans, may all come to nothing."

As he spoke the words aloud, admitting to his worst fears, Allystaire began to feel the same kind of cold, gnawing despair he'd felt in the sorcerer 's trap on the road. "And this is a trap of my own making. Goddess, if you would but give me a sign, some indication of whether I have done well, or done ill…"

He waited, shutting his eyes, trying to turn inward, trying to stretch his hearing for some note of Her song.

He waited. For how long, he didn't know. Then, with a sigh, Allystaire levered himself back to his feet and wandered over to the other table his tent held, pulling back the cloth that covered his armor.

In the breastplate, he could see his reflection as well as in any mirror he'd ever owned. His oft-broken nose bent to the left side of his heavy, square face, more deeply lined than the last time he saw it. More flecks of grey in his hair and in the two-day's worth of beard upon his face. *Much more,* he silently admitted. Besides age and the odd new crease, there was nothing changed in it; it had been the face of Lord Allystaire Coldbourne, Castellan of Wind's Jaw Keep, Oyrwyn war-leader for the better part of a score of years. Now it was the face of whom?

"Allystaire, the Arm of the Mother," he murmured.

It was the same face, of the same man.

"So what would Lord Coldbourne do in this moment? With no army to speak of and unknown enemies with unknown plans on his position? Develop some freezing knowledge of my freezing enemies," Allystaire answered himself forcefully, thumping a knuckle down on the breastplate. He turned his eye towards the tent flap and the dark and cold of the night beyond, considered a moment, then grabbed a fur-lined mantle from the top of the small chest that held his clothing and strode into the night.

* * *

"You," Torvul said groggily, "had better have a good reason for wakin' an old dwarf in the middle of the stone-crushed night."

"I do," Allystaire said. He knelt on the floor of the inn, pushing an iron into the coals of the hearth and stirring them up, then laying on a fresh log from the nearby pile. He straightened up, and surveyed the weary faces at the table he'd dragged near the fire: Idgen Marte, Renard, Torvul, Gideon, and Ivar. Only the last of them didn't appear surprised. "What," Allystaire began, "have we been doing wrong?"

"Layin' up like a rat in a hole," Ivar said fiercely.

"Precisely. We surrendered the initiative to our enemies. Whoever they are."

"Allystaire, the Archioness herself told you they'd be coming back with a Declaration of Anathemata." Idgen Marte's voice was weary.

"Aye, but who is enforcing it? More Temple rabble? Will Delondeur come? Does Lionel Delondeur even live? Or did his natural son execute him? We do not know any of this."

"To tell the truth," Torvul said, "I've been waiting for some peddlers, minstrels, other folk who carry news t'come by. They haven't."

Idgen Marte sat up straighter, her eyes sharpening as she woke up completely. "The minstrels are the first to know to avoid a place. Word travels faster than you'd credit."

"Thornhurst is unlikely to have been on most of their routes," Gideon, quietly confident, said. "Birchvale and Ashmill Bridge are larger towns with more links to earn, but close enough that folk from here could travel there."

"For the better singers and players, aye," Idgen Marte allowed. "But for those still makin' a name or those can't handle the competition? Thornhurst'd be ripe."

"There'd be little traffic here, but some, surely," Torvul said. "And there's none. Pilgrims and folk moving here aplenty, but not anyone looking to make some weight. And they'd see it on the road, the patterns, the movement. If I were still out there, be Cold-damned sure I found my way here with the kinds of things farmer folk are usually wantin'."

"They know someone will target us. We know someone will target us. We have to do something to find out who." Allystaire's eyes flicked from Gideon to Torvul. "Have you two any thoughts on that score?"

Torvul pulled at his beer and sat back, rubbing his stubbly chin. "Might be we could do something."

Gideon looked as though he wanted to speak, but closed his mouth and merely nodded.

Allystaire frowned. *Ask him later. Privately.* "Good. And Idgen Marte?"

"I suppose I could roust Keegan and his lads and we could start scouting parties. Depends how far you want us to range how much good it'll do."

"Use your judgment," Allystaire replied. "Hardly your first time heading scouts." He looked to Ivar and Renard and said, "As for us—we need to redouble our efforts at getting the men ready. Any man who has taken up arms, that is all he does. Less what need drives to feed his family, from now till the longest night."

"What 'appens then?" Ivar leaned back in her chair, grimacing.

"I know only that the Goddess told me to be ready for it. And ready does not mean lying like a rat in a hole. Now all of you, back to your beds. I want to hear plans after breakfast tomorrow."

They stood to leave, but Allystaire waved Ivar aside. When the others cleared the door, he said to the woman, "Captain—if you already knew what I was doing wrong, what stopped you from speaking up? You know I have never been one to grow angry at anyone for speaking the truth."

Ivar sniffed, fixing Allystaire with an indifferent stare. "Not sure what 'tis ya do anymore, m'lord," she replied. "Lord Coldbourne I knew ne'er woulda let murderers go w'out stretched necks."

Allystaire frowned, hardening. "I was prepared to do that if it proved necessary."

"It oughta been necessary when m'man turned up dead," Ivar retorted hotly.

"There is more at stake than a warband, Ivar." Allystaire tried not to shout, and only barely succeeded. "More at stake than an army. I serve a different power now, one that seeks more out of this world than merely perpetuating itself."

"Tha's a lot o'words don't say anythin' 'bout lettin' a brother o'battle go unavenged, and no matter how ya pretty it up, that's what ya did."

"Vengeance and justice are not always the same."

"It ain't justice I'm freezin' after." Ivar was just short of shouting through her gap-toothed mouth, the words whistling over bare gums and around what brown and cracked teeth remained. "Ne'er was. A warband don't work if it ain't everythin' for yer brother. Was a time you knew that. Now I hear a lot o'mercy and Goddess and love and other horse-shit I can't see, spend, taste, drink, lay, or fight beside. Tha's why I didn't speak. S'why I don't speak now 'less you ask. Now I'm seekin' my bed and I'll be up when ya need me and we'll serve our accord. The Iron Ravens have ne'r broken one. Don't be shocked when it's up and we vote t'leave. All I can say." With that, the leather-clad woman turned and left without a backwards look.

"Is she going to be trouble?"

Allystaire should perhaps have been startled by Idgen Marte's voice so close behind him, but part of him wasn't. He realized, unconsciously, he'd known she was there. "No. They will do their duty, meet the terms of their accord with my sister, even if that means dying to the last."

"Think it'll come to that?"

"I do not mean it to."

"This isn't their fight."

Allystaire laughed. "No fight is a warband's fight. And every fight is. You know that as well as I do."

"Have you spoken to them of coming to the Mother? Have you even tried?"

"If warbands have a faith, it is in themselves. If they must have a god, they will take Fortune, perhaps Braech. You said as much yourself, once."

"Seems a long time ago." She paused, and then stepped out of the shadows to face him. "Listen, Keegan and his lot can scour the woods and the hills. I'm better off if I set out myself up to Ashmill Bridge. Speak to the singers and the traders and the wanderers. I'll learn about what's going on in the barony. We shouldn't have been this cut off—there'll be news out there if we turn our ears to hear it. I'm leaving at first light." Her voice was quiet, but firm, and her tone brooked no argument. "I'll be back in a week. You know there'll be nothing in that town can touch me. Aye?"

Allystaire nodded mutely and Idgen Marte walked hurriedly off. *Feels good to be doing, instead of waiting.* He followed her footsteps outside and found Gideon just outside the door in the weak grey light of pre-dawn.

The boy didn't meet his gaze. "When…during my strike against the Sea Dragon's priests who held the rain away…when I left this form?"

"I was there watching, Gideon, but you never spoke to me about what you did. Only that it worked."

"Well, when I left the form of my body—not left it, but changed it, I became a dragon of wind and air." He frowned. "That is not quite right. I became my thought. Became my imagination and my will, and what I did could best be described as having been done by a dragon made of wind and air." The boy suddenly lifted his head and stared at Allystaire. "Do you understand?"

"No. Yet go on, and see if I learn something by the end."

"It was wildly freeing. And I can do it again. In a short time I can scout the entire valley of the Ash for you."

Allystaire felt the possibilities opening before him, and his mind briefly reeled. *To know exactly where an enemy is, and how many of him there are, at any given moment.* He stemmed the tide of thought before it swept him along, cleared his throat, and said, "Gideon, if you can do as you say, it would be of immense value to us."

The boy nodded. "I know. It is just...I fear it, Allystaire. I fear that I will not want to come back to this flesh," he said, poking his thin chest with a finger turned inward, almost disdainfully. "Since then I have felt so confined, so slow and small."

Allystaire felt his heart sink even as his stomach rose up to meet it. "Truly?"

"I have lived a life of the mind—what could be more tempting than to live entirely as will?"

"What do you need to make you able to, ah, come back, as you put it, to your flesh?"

"I simply have to be able to master myself."

Allystaire shuffled next to the boy and put an arm around his thin shoulders. "Gideon—in my days as a war-leader, I would have given anything to have access to the ability you have just described. And had I found a man who could do it—I would have given him no choice. Whatever leverage I could apply to him, I would have. I will give you no orders. I will say only this." He paused for a quick breath. "Doing this could save lives. Could save the Mother's folk, Her Temple, everything we are trying to build. If sacrifices are to be made, it must be by those of us She has called." *That's a Cold-damned hard thing to lay on a boy of twelve,* Allystaire thought, recriminating himself.

"And as for mastering yourself—that is the hard bit. It always is. A man must look straight at the end he seeks, the same way he looks straight at anything. How he gets there, what he is capable of, what he is willing to do, all depend on that first act."

"Looking straight at it?"

"Yes."

"I will think on it. And I will have an answer by noontime. Fair?"

Allystaire nodded and stood, patting the boy on the shoulder. "Whatever you decide, Gideon."

As the boy walked off into the cold, Allystaire thought on the Goddess's words to him at the vigil, and silently prayed. *Goddess, Mother, Lady, please do not let him be a false dawn.* Then he remembered precisely what she had said, and amended the words of his prayer with downcast eyes.

Mother, I beg you. Do not let me fail him.

CHAPTER 30

The Minstrel and the Shadow

"Cold, but it's good to be among people again," Idgen Marte murmured, as she mingled with the flow of traffic on Ashmill Bridge's main thoroughfare. The Bridge from which the town took its name arched high in the distance, and the now derelict mill next to it.

She felt a twinge of guilt even as the words left her lips. The folk in Thornhurst were people, after all. *Good to be back in a city then,* she amended.

A thought flashed when she thought of the small town before her as a city. A vision of tall gleaming towers and paved boulevards wide enough for carriages to ride three abreast.

"A town, at any rate," she muttered, banishing thoughts of cities and concentrating on the dull buildings around her, most of them made of clay brick that seemed the color of rust. Like most barony towns it seemed to have no plan; streets started and stopped and bisected each other in mystifying ways, and if it were true to form, she'd bet the locals guarded knowledge of navigating them like sages on mountaintops in some stories she knew.

But any town with more than a few buildings jammed together and more than a couple of hundred souls seemed to speak to her, draw her in. Always had. So she simply drifted along with the crowd, another sword-at-hire at odds and ends since the end of campaigning season.

She kept one eye out for signs that tended to bunches of grapes, barrels, horns, foaming mugs, or beehives, with the occasional fanciful animal.

It was one of the latter that caught her eye: a green and gold dragon coiled protectively around a barrel, more skillfully painted than most she'd seen in this part of the world. The building was a bit larger, too, with stables behind, a noisy but not raucous crowd within, and a warm, inviting light filling the windows.

She pulled up short just outside the door as the first notes of music trickled into her ears. She knew instantly the melody, knew it was being played on a ten-course lute with a higher chanterelle than any barony-born minstrel played. No quill; the player was plucking the strings bare-fingered, and he knew his business well.

Long time past, she told herself silently. *Be who you are, not who you were.* With a determined hand she shoved the door open and made her way in. She couldn't help but spare a glance towards one of the fireplaces in the corner of the room, where the music came from.

She never got tired of being proved right. He was a Concordat man and trained in one of the better schools, probably the Tower. His skin was darker even than hers, that much was clear through the haze of smoke that hung in the taproom. She couldn't make out too much of the lute in his hands, but the shell gleamed in soft bands.

She couldn't keep a tiny grin from twisting the corner of her mouth. *Let fools ask for gold inlay and pearl pegs,* she thought to herself. *A musician cares about the wood.*

Quickly realizing that she was blocking the door, Idgen Marte stepped smartly up to the bar, a well-polished and well-attended slab of thick wood, its edge bound with hammered copper. As she was taller than most who stood or sat, and well-dressed, it wasn't long before one of the three keepers who manned its length slid in front of her.

A silver link already palmed, she spun it out to the tips of her fingers and then set it carefully down on the bar. "Red, Innadan."

He nodded and swept the link up, dropped it through a slot in the back wall into, doubtless, a strongbox. He returned quickly with her wine, a flagon and one well-made if plain clay cup, and set them down. "Anything else? Food?"

"Just a question," she said softly, even as she carefully poured from flagon to cup. "The lutist—is he house? Where'd he come from?"

"He's been in town a fair while," the barkeep said. He was younger than her, thin and dark-bearded. "Working his way 'round the better places. Most o'the owners'sve tried t'make him offers, though he says he don't mean t'stay. I think he's just anglin' fer the top bid."

"Good plan," she said, then turned around, cup in hand, to watch him play. She had a sip, found it too warm, too heavy for her tongue. *Allystaire'd love it,* she thought. *At least this means I can sip and not guzzle.*

He's better than this place deserves, she thought. *Better than this country deserves,* she amended, as she studied him. His hands glided across the strings, never giving an impression of effort or hurry. He had just the right aloof distance from the crowd, just the right combination of easy smile and concentration mingling on his features. The song she'd known had long since changed into something she suspected he was making up on the spot, and it had drawn nearly every eye and ear in the place. She felt it build, a run of impressive notes that called that high chanterelle into plenty of use, then resolve—as she knew it must for a drinking crowd in a small-town tavern—into a down-the-neck cascade and a final soft strum.

He straightened his back, easing his hand off the strings, and flashed a small, confident smile at the crowd. Offers to buy him drinks began singing out from the listeners, and links, mostly copper but some with the more friendly gleam of silver, began to arc into the small box open before his stool.

He sat casually flexing his hands for a moment before he adjusted his grip on the instrument. He stood and offered a brief, neat bow. Then he addressed the crowd in a resonant voice, and she shivered when she heard the rich accent of her homeland in his barony tongue.

"A brief respite, good people," he said. "To replenish my strength, revive my voice, and reinvigorate the hands, if you would be so kind as to extend your forbearance." He waited till the last coin made its way into his box, then snapped it closed. He reverently cased his lute, and carried it to the bar slung on one shoulder.

Idgen Marte cleared her throat as he approached, and pitched her voice to carry over the suddenly noisier room. More importantly, she spoke in the lyrical Concordat tongue.

"You're a long way from home."

He was a few seats down the bar, but a musician's ears hear most everything, as she was counting on, and she thought she'd hear their native tongue if it were spoken as a whisper on a battlefield.

He turned, smiled, rose from the stool he'd taken, and came to her side. She slid off her own stool and pushed it aside with her boot to make room. He wasn't quite her height, with skin like well-polished dark copper, a thin beard around his mouth, and hair cut so close it was practically shaved. The flickering lamp and torch light, not to mention the smoke, made his features harder to see, but Idgen Marte was reasonably sure she liked them.

"Home is the road," he replied in the same tongue.

She stopped herself just short of answering, *And its next bend will surely take me there,* forced a polite smile, and said, "Must get terrible drafty in the next few months."

She studied his reaction. It wasn't the answer he'd expected, she could tell by the set of his eyes, but he was a performer and had a tight rein on his expressions. "Well, that's what stops on the road are for, eh?"

She sipped her wine and nodded in agreement. When she set her cup back down, she said, "That was the best version of 'Flames on the High Tower' I've heard in a long time. Perhaps ever."

"You're too kind," he demurred. "I've played it better before, in truth." He extended a hand, even as the bartender was setting up some of the first of his free drinks. From what she could see, all of them were small beer, and well-watered at that. He was a professional. "Andus Carek."

She took his hand, feeling the familiar musician's callouses thick on the pads of his fingers. "Radys Glythe," she lied. *Why bother? The odds he'd know my name are so long they're beyond the counting.* "Where are you from, Andus Carek? I'm of Cansebour, myself." Speaking that truth felt almost physically painful. *But it's the place I can best describe,* she thought, a longing for those wide streets, gleaming towers, and clean canals seizing her heart and tugging it hard for a moment.

"The diamond of the south," he said admiringly. "I grew up in Fen Isil, less a diamond and more a festering boil. What brings you to the warlike and increasingly frozen north, so far from the greatest city in the world, Radys Glythe?"

"The former part. Just a sword-at-hire."

He looked pointedly down at her hip and said, "It's a curious sword-at-hire who doesn't carry a sword."

Idgen Marte nearly clamped her teeth to keep herself from spitting a curse and forced herself to keep smiling. "Just a term," she rebutted. *Got to tell that dwarfish braggart to hurry up when I get back.* "In fact, I'm not at-hire either. I've a job through the winter, little village a couple of day's ride south and west of here."

"Oh?"

She nodded. "Aye, a place called Thornhurst." She tried to read his expression again but the falling dark and his tight control made it a challenge. "In fact, I'm here looking for musicians."

He held up a hand, palm out. "Whatever it was, I didn't do it. Never met the girl, nor the boy. Never saw the jewels. And so forth." He grinned with his own joke, the delivery smooth and natural.

She laughed, then shook her head. "Nothing like that at all. Folk down there are aching for music. I volunteered to try and drive some in."

The man shrugged helplessly. "Wish I could help, if only to hear my native tongue all winter. Alas, I am contracted within Ashmill Bridge."

He lies, Idgen Marte thought, and for a moment wished she had Allystaire along. Though if he were he would've frozen it all up already. Scared him away or started a fight.

She responded by waving a hand, casually dismissing his protest. "Easily bought off. Plenty of links to make in Thornhurst. I've got their proxy. Tell me what you're making here, we'll beat it. I guarantee."

"Where would Thornhurst get the silver? Thought they were farmer folk in rough times."

She snorted. "All time is rough for farmers in this country."

He glanced around the bar and leaned closer to her. He had a clean, masculine scent and she decided that she did indeed like his features: fine, high cheekbones and rich hazel eyes. "Listen, a friendly word from one who's lately covered the barony. You'll not want to be in Thornhurst long."

"Eh? What've you heard?"

He shrugged. "Nothing certain. Just…too many whispers. Too many rumors. The fighting in Londray might spill out there, though, to be honest, that seems largely over now. Some rot about sorcerers and cultists. Too much stink attaching to the name. When you meet brethren on the road, you warn or are warned—nobody wants to be caught there."

"Wait, the fighting in Londray is over? What do you mean?"

"One of the Baron's children returned and made quick work of most of the grey-bands. Supposedly the pretender is still alive, but eh?" He drained his tea and set the cup down. "Unless he comes back to win and hold the seat, it won't be much of a song, so what do I care?"

"What is the rise or fall of a great man but for the song to be made of it?" She smiled at that and lifted her wine, drinking to the sentiment, still minding how much she actually imbibed. "There must be some price that'll get you down in Thornhurst. Even for a week." She leaned forward just enough to press her leg against the inside of his. *Lutist's hands,* she thought, surprising herself. *A singer's mouth. And lovely eyes.*

He smiled, and there was more warmth in it than performance, she thought, but a wistful tinge to those eyes of his. "Afraid not." He tilted his head, shifted his hips to press against her lightly. "I may not stay here all winter, but for the next week at least. And if you'd like to continue this talk, native tongues and all, I'm staying at the Sign of the Silver Fish, west of the bridge. And now," he said, smoothly pulling away from her, "I'm back to business. Got to talk to the publican, then more music. Maybe I'll play something from home for you." He grabbed a small drink out of his queue and tossed it back. He disappeared through a door behind the bar with a backwards glance and a sensual smile.

She drained her wine, trying to ignore the heat she felt moving up her cheeks. She refilled her cup, intending to toss that down as well. Caution and self control kept her to another sip. *Sign of the Silver Fish,* she thought. *May have to take a walk. That would count as developing intelligence of the wider picture in the barony, surely? He's recently crossed it, as he says. Probably got dust from it everywhere. It would be the work of a good scout to find all of it.* She let the thought die, watching the crowd. Mostly it seemed like local tradesmen, but the well-to-do sort who could drink better than swill and pay for top music.

No dirt under their nails, no more ache in their hands, she thought as she studied them, the fur-trimmed collars, the occasional flash of gold or gemmary on fingers or necks. *So long as they killed no one for it, not my place to judge,* she told herself.

There were a few swords in the room, worn by men dressed for traveling, and a smattering of less common weapons. She mentally inventoried her own: mainly the two long knives strapped underneath her coat, her bow and quiver with her mount at a cheap livery near the road.

Her attention was drawn to the minstrel as he made his way to his stool. He carefully set out his coin-box, then even more carefully uncased his lute and sat, making a great show of tuning and strumming it to his satisfaction. To Idgen Marte's ear, most of the adjustment was unnecessary, but it served to quiet the crowd and draw their attention.

Once he had it, he began, with the fast and familiar "Wastrel of Arabel," which soon had the crowd singing, or at least chanting, along. *Never my favorite. If they want to sing, let 'em learn how first,* she thought, keeping her own mouth clamped shut.

From the raucous, bawdy crowd favorite to a thumping adventure, he next played "Fenren's Final Ride," and Idgen Marte found herself admiring not only his speed, but also his precision. *Hard to be both,* she admitted. Again, she considered the Sign of the Silver Fish and just whether or not it might be worth walking.

Then he took a brief pause to wet his whistle from one of his free drinks, that she was more than half sure was water, before clearing his throat to introduce his next song. "A song many of you may not have heard, from my homeland far, far south of here, from its largest and greatest city."

Her back straightened. She quickly guessed what he meant to play, and the first chord proved her right. "The Streets of Cansebour."

Her mind was drawn instantly back to the wide clean streets, the gleaming white stone, the towers both graceful and imposing, the light of dawn flaring purple through the stained glass windows of one particular tower, of the music heard and played there.

Of blood splashed on the stones beneath it.

She tossed a link on the bar and stood up, made for the door. She heard the small hitch in the music, in his voice, could feel his eyes on her as she left.

Once out in the night she took a deep, gulping breath of stinging winter air, and pulled her coat tighter, felt it tug against the knives on her back. She began walking the narrow, dark streets of Ashmill Bridge with the song of her home taunting her ears all the way.

She wasn't sure how long it was that she walked, but a long stretch of night passed. She stared at the bridge and wondered if it was still worth finding the Sign of the Silver Fish, and giving Andus Carek the waking of his life. *But then I'd have to explain why I left,* she thought. *Not if I'm too busy to talk and he's too busy to listen.*

The streets were largely deserted, but she suddenly heard staccato footsteps on the street behind her. Instinctively, she rolled her shoulders inside her coat to loosen the fit and make it easier to shed in order to draw her knives. When a side-alley approached on her right, she ducked into it, loosening a blade.

The footsteps went right on past the alley, the product of a thin figure wrapped in a thinner cloak. Idgen Marte quietly counted ten and then returned to the wider street. The figure was distant, but not out of sight.

Some sense, some tickle along the back of her neck, told Idgen Marte to follow.

She let herself blend into the shadows, which were abundant. The Goddess's Gifts to her, primarily this—the blending, the movement through the meeting of light and dark—felt so natural, came so easy, she sometimes couldn't remember what life had been like without them. And yet she had resisted using them flippantly, despite herself. *Not that Allystaire couldn't use a good scare now and then,* she idly thought as she followed the figure that scurried through the streets.

After a few yards, though, Idgen Marte let the shadows drop away. *I could follow this one in broad daylight.* For all the nervous movement of the figure, looking over its shoulder, flattening against walls, she—Idgen Marte was certain it was a she—did a terrible job of keeping out of sight.

It was a simple matter then to simply stick close to the walls, duck into the occasional alley, and stay in blind spots.

The longer she followed, the poorer the town got. Ashmill Bridge was large enough to have its prosperous and its poor quarters, and looking around, Idgen Marte realized that she was in the worse half of the latter; the houses got smaller, meaner, closer together. The stench of the place tugged at her nose, but she pushed it aside and flattened herself against a wall, trying not to think of the wet now sloshing around her ankles, as the figure she followed stopped at a door and knocked carefully, speaking some hushed words. The door opened and the figure slipped inside, pulling it tightly closed behind her.

When she turned to pull the door, her face had been clearly visible, if distant. Something of it tugged at Idgen Marte's memory. Thin, young, blonde.

Well, I've come this far. Idgen Marte dashed across the open space of the lane and pushed herself against the stone wall of the house the woman had disappeared into. The windows were all tightly shuttered but still the faintest hint of light leaked out.

Nobody in this part of town wastes candles or lamp oil this late. Couldn't be more obvious if they tried.

Why do I care? Where have I seen that woman before? And do I wish to get in there? She felt herself melting into the shadows the starlight projected against the wall, started envisioning the shadow on the other side of it. She could move between the two—but would there be enough room inside the tiny hovel to contain her? Was it her business? *Happenin' in this part of town, women trying to hide? Sounds like my business.*

Then she heard the unmistakable tramp of booted men moving with swift purpose, and the jingle of armor and weapon. Without a second thought, she blurred away from the small house, to the shadowed top of a wall roughly ten yards distant, crouched invisibly upon it.

Men, perhaps a dozen of them in long cloaks and scarves around their faces, half of them bearing torches and the other half clubs—and all of them armed further, she was sure—swarmed around the house. The door was forced open amidst the sound of screams, and Idgen Marte's arms tensed as she heard the unmistakable dry thud of a club on flesh. *Greenhats,* she thought, *have to be. But why?*

Her hands went to her knives, and she started to pull them free. *My business now for sure,* she thought, but then one of the men started to speak, pronouncing his words with a casual assumption of mastery and power that caused her hands to go white-knuckled on her hilts. Even so, she paused to listen.

"You are in violation of several proclamations of the Baron Delondeur, all of which have been read publicly," he began, holding a torch aloft while half a dozen women were pulled from the building. "It is past the twelfth turn since noon and you are not in your homes. You are engaging in a secret meeting for seditious purpose. You engage in a heathen faith that has been proclaimed Anathemata by the Temples of Braech and Fortune, an Anathemata that is endorsed by the Baron."

By the time Anathemata was out of his mouth, Idgen Marte had pulled her knives free and began stalking across the street. She heard but barely registered one of the women cry out that they were only praying, while another sobbed. One, whom Idgen Marte believed was the one she'd followed, took a defiant step forward, lifting her eyes towards the man who threatened her.

"The Mother cannot be put down or tossed aside. Not with torch nor club, not with knife nor hangman's rope. What is it about poor unarmed women you fear so much?"

The man's hand slipped inside of his cloak and pulled free his short-sword. He laid the tip of it casually at the woman's throat. She swallowed, started to take half a step back, caught herself, angrily jutting her narrow chin.

"You're just a whore with airs on," the man said. "Why would I fear you? Tell me, foolish, dead woman, does your Mother have a sword?"

"No," Idgen Marte whispered into his ear, suddenly standing behind him. "She has a Shadow." His body stiffened as she slipped the point of her knife upwards into the unarmored juncture of his arm and chest. He gurgled bloody froth from his mouth and his eyes rolled into his head. She stepped back, let his body fall, and blurred into motion among the rest of the men, who were suddenly swinging torches and drawing swords, screaming alarm and yelling orders.

With the Goddess's cold anger flowing with her through the shadows cast by their torches, Idgen Marte made quick work of four of the remaining guards, slipping behind, beneath, and amongst them, the points of her knives sliding into groins or the edges across throats. With five of their number down, courage fled and the remainder chased after it. Idgen Marte picked one of them out and darted after him.

Before he was ten yards away, she was beside him, tossing him to the ground with an outstretched leg. Torch and club went bouncing away. She bent over him, placing a bloodied knife against his neck.

"Why? Why terrorize them?"

The man babbled in fear. She pressed the knife harder, drew a thin red line of blood. "Answer me!"

"I'm just taking orders. Please, I have a wife, and children. Please. Please." His voice came out in a hushed whine.

"What about their children, their husbands?"

"Orders come down from the Baron. From the Baron! He's coming here, that's the rumor, coming this way, soon, chasing down the grey-bands and heretics." He shut his eyes tightly, trying to gather himself with a shallow breath. "Please," he hissed out once more.

"Go. Tell the others that the Shadow of the Mother showed you mercy." Her voice was a ragged and angry rasp. "Tell the other soldiers, the other green-hats, whichever you are, that Her folk are not to be hunted." She swung away from him, pulling her knife away from his throat, but not without nicking his cheek first, ripping open a tiny line that would scar. "That," she said as he clambered to his feet and clapped a hand over his cut, "is so I'll know you if ever I see you again. Don't let me."

Without a word, he hared off down the street. She turned to the bodies, cleaned her knives on a dead man's cloak, and slid them back into place along her back.

The defiant girl walked up to her, admiration and anger warring on her young, fine-boned features. "Why'd ya let him away?"

Idgen Marte eyed her. The familiarity was nagging at her. "I know you," she said, gliding past the question. "What's your name?"

"Shary," the girl said. "An' yeah, we met—you saved me, me and another girl called Filoma. Saved us from—"

"From a pimp and his fat bruiser," Idgen Marte finished. "I looked for you in Thornhurst."

"I decided it was important t'stay," the girl said quickly. "Tell others what I saw. We started having meetings, praying together."

"That's brave of you, Shary, and brave of the rest of you, but there are five greenhat bodies cooling in front of one of your homes and seven more running away. That'll bring more of them. We don't want to be here when they arrive."

"What have we to fear? We have Faith, and the Mother sent Her Shadow," Shary began, wide-eyed. "Let them come. We'll be armed."

"Even if I could defeat a whole troop of them on my own, I'll not turn this town into a bloodbath in the Mother's name. Take what you will from their bodies if you've the stomach for it, but otherwise, you need to scatter to your homes or come with me. Which will it be?" Watching Shary and two of the other women patting the corpses down, Idgen Marte was hit with a sudden twinge of conscience. *Ought to leave some links for the families,* she thought, but then immediately countered the thought with another. *Anything left'll just get stolen by the other greenhats anyway.*

"What it's going to be," Idgen Marte said, once purses were stripped, knives tugged off of belts, and a couple of stout clubs liberated. "Going to ground or coming with me?"

"I don't want to leave," Shary protested. "I'm no coward. I don't want those bastards t'win."

Idgen Marte sighed. "Shary, this town's not big enough t'hide in forever. And those bastards will win if you try to fight. Even against me, if there's enough of them, one will get smart, or lucky. I can't stay here forever. If you come with me, I'll be able to throw them off and I'll defend you on the road."

"Some of us have family, little ones. Have we the time t'fetch them?"

"Go now, immediately. Meet me at the south road as soon as you can. Anyone who isn't there in a quarter turn isn't coming."

Idgen Marte turned and began running. She'd always been fleet of foot, and sure of every step she took. But with the Goddess's Gifts her speed was something more than natural. It would be a thing for song if anyone could see her move when she ran flat-out. *Be the kind of thing I'd write a song about if I had a mind to write songs,* she thought, before forcing her mind back to the moment. *I've a quarter turn to think on how to get a score of people out of town. How would Allystaire do it, anyway? Kill or terrify everyone who got in his way.* As she thought, she headed to the livery stable where her horse was quartered. There were no signs of greenhats or unusual activity, but that would change sooner rather than later.

The stable was locked up tight. She began to work on jimmying the bar when she snorted in disgust. There was light enough to make shadows on either side of the door, so she simply stepped into one on this side and flowed through to the other. She had her courser saddled and ready in moments. No use in slow stealth when her mount's hooves would sound loud on the streets no matter what she did with them, so she rode hard to her rendezvous.

Ashmill Bridge hadn't size or wealth enough to build proper walls and gates, but it did post guards at its entrances and take note of comings and goings. Thankfully she was the first to reach them, dropping from her her saddle a dozen paces from a three-walled guard shack.

There was no reaction from the ramshackle building as she closed in, one knife slid carefully inside her right sleeve. She edged up against one wooden wall, edging carefully around to its open side.

They were asleep. *Of course they are. They aren't paid enough t'stay up all night,* she thought, and briefly, she considered slitting their throats. *It's what I would've done a year ago. Now, though?* Instead, she dropped the knife from her sleeve into her hand, and rapped the pommel hard against the inside wall.

They startled awake, reaching for spears and coming clumsily to their feet, blinking in the dim light of the coal-filled braziers they dozed near.

"Gentlemen," she murmured, "I hate to disturb your rest, but a sizable group of my relations are going to be coming past your gate any moment. I don't want them counted, named, or, frankly, looked at too closely. What'll it cost me?"

Her honesty seemed to take them aback. One, older, with grey stubble all over his chin and cheeks, spat to the ground. "Gold link and a tumble for each of us," he snickered.

"You couldn't count the number of links you'd need to make that happen. How about a pair of silver links each and I forget the insult?"

The other one, large shoulders straining his jerkin, poorly-dyed green wool cap clinging to a mass of thick black hair, snorted. "What's t'say we don't just take what's in your purse, and anythin' else we want, hrm?"

"I tried to be polite about this," she sighed, before she kicked him hard in the knee, causing it to buckle. Then she shifted her weight onto her back foot and snapped the toe of her boot into the point of his chin. His mouth shut with a hard click and down he went, knocking over a brazier and sending hot coals skidding into the dirt. He was profoundly unconscious when he hit the ground.

The other greenhat had his knife only half free by the time her point was against the side of his neck. "You can still make a link out of this, provided you don't say another freezing word. Are we clear?"

He nodded very carefully, mindful of the knife held against his throat, and swallowed shallowly.

"Good." Knife still pricking his throat, she pulled free a thin circle of silver from her purse and pressed it into his palm. He took it. She lowered the knife. "When they ask you what happened, tell them it was the Shadow of the Mother—and that she could have slit your throats while you slept."

Before she turned to go, she gave the larger one a sharp kick in the guts as he appeared to be stirring. *Seemed like he could use another bruise in the morning.*

Outside of the shack she found a gathering of folk milling around her horse.

And distantly, in the town proper, there were torches, the clang of weapons, the shout of orders.

She sprinted back to her horse. "How many children have we?" she hissed. Most were wide-eyed, frightened, the few men and children rubbing their weary eyes, all huddled miserably in cloaks that did little for the cold.

"Three babes, three old enough to walk," Shary answered. For her part she carried a rolled and tied blanket slung over one shoulder, and many of the others carried similar bundles.

"Put the three who can walk on my horse's saddle, carry the other three, and run south. Just hold to a straight southern course, as fast you can, stay together, and I'll find you. Go. Now." Idgen Marte helped hoist three nervous, sleepy children onto her courser's saddle, and then retrieved her bow and quiver. She turned towards the guards, whose forward elements were rounding a curve out of the town proper and beginning to descend along the dirt track leading out of it.

They hadn't brought bows that she could see. *Small grace. Thanks, Mother, even if you'd naught to do with their piss-poor decisions.* Without bothering to pick a specific target, she nocked an arrow to drew, and let fly in a lazy arc that dropped into their torch-lit midst. *By all means, gents, continue to present me so very many targets.*

She turned to see Shary and the other townsfolk watching her wide-eyed. "I said now. Run! I'll catch you."

"We've no lamps or torches—"

"Don't fear the darkness," Idgen Marte cut her off. "There's light in its midst. I promise you. Go. The Mother will not abandon you. Neither will

I." She turned, and was already nocking another arrow, when she heard the sound of footsteps as the townsfolk broke into a run, of hooves as her horse began to trot.

She blurred into the dark shadows amongst trees to one side of the road, drew back her bowstring, and loosed another arrow, taking more careful aim. The men had scattered, showing that at least one man giving orders had some sense, but her arrow found its target—one of the torchbearers. It took him high in the arm, and he dropped his brand. Dry, the grass instantly sparked into flame, and two of them were distracted with stamping it out.

Idgen Marte spared a moment to count her arrows against the number of men, as they split into pairs and spread out even farther, covering their flanks and moving fast. *These are professionals. Not just greenhats.* A pair made their way cautiously towards her position. Her bowstring sang its badly pitched note once, twice, and both were down. She ran forward and snatched up the torch that fell from one's grasping hand, ran with her unnatural speed into the road, and heaved it at the watch post. It struck once side and bounced away. The little shack didn't catch fire, but the shower of sparks got the attention of her pursuers.

She paused, making sure they saw her. When half dozen of them produced loaded crossbows from under their cloaks, she wrapped herself in shadows and sprinted away with every ounce of speed, natural and supernatural, at her disposal.

They're not even after the faithful anymore, she thought to herself as she imagined crossbowmen firing at a high angle, hoping to drop their bolts down on her. *They're after me.*

A bolt landed in the dirt far behind her, but closer than it ought to have been, and she ducked into the bare trees that lined the road. She thought again of the number of arrows she had, the number of men pursuing her. *Be knife work before it's over, unless I can make them pay too dear for getting that close.*

She judged the approach of torches through the trees, fitted an arrow to the string. The face of the man whose cheek she'd marked swam for a moment in her vision, but she banished it and loosed, not waiting to see if she'd hit.

It looked a long, bloody night.

* * *

Shary led her ragged group down the cold dirt-packed track by starlight, some-times kneeling to feel at the ground to make sure they hadn't strayed off the track. Mostly it was straight and well-edged, but the fear nagged at her.

She kept silent, willed the rest to do the same, and clutched onto the wood-en club she'd taken off a dead greenhat with white knuckles, carrying it like a talisman, like simply holding a weapon would keep at bay the guards, the priests, the torturers she imagined hard on their heels.

Occasionally in the night, as they walked, they'd hear a ragged scream in the distance behind them. Always a man's scream, Shary told herself, confident she knew the difference, but her hand would get a little tighter on the club each time.

The first few times it happened folks would rush to clap their hands around the children's ears, and the children would start crying, only to be hushed, start to ask a question, only to have a hand clamped over their mouths.

Shary walked in circles around the group, a tight ball of nerves and energy in the pit of her stomach, occasionally pausing to touch Gend's arm or hand in passing. Gend, who'd been a thief and a drunk and become a laborer and a drunk, which was still an improvement. Gend who'd also met a paladin and had been one of the few who'd believed her story, just as she'd believed his. He may not have been much of a man, really, but didn't try to put her on the street and never hit her, never hurt her, never wanted to hurt anyone. What he did want, she knew, was to stop being a drunk. He just didn't know how.

Finally, when one of the sounds that split the silence open was less scream and more angry yell, he stopped her with a hand on her arm, careful but firm. "Gimme the club, lass," he murmured, and she tried to make out his face by the moon and star light, which wasn't bright. She could just about make out the shape of his eyes and the ragged beard on his cheeks, and not much else.

"Please," he finally said, as he pried it from her hand. He turned to watch the road behind him, such as he could in the dark, as there was another yell and suddenly a torch visible. He yelled, "Run!"

She froze, but soon other hands grabbed her and pulled her along. She glanced back and saw a struggle of bodies, heard the thud of weapons or fists landing against skin, heard and felt and smelled death in the air, and started stumbling forward faster, trying not to listen to the brawl behind her.

* * *

She was out of arrows, carrying her unstrung bow awkwardly in her left hand as some kind of ersatz club or shield, with one of her long knives in the right. The other knife was gone, bonestuck in a dead man's ribcage. A long trail of dead men, hamstrung men, men with throats slit or groins ripped open, lay behind her. She had a shallow cut along one side and a throbbing in her left shoulder, from the blow of a spiked mace, that made her wish Allystaire was at her side.

Not his kind of fight, she thought as she tried to get her bearings. *He'd just be in my way, or have bulled amongst them and gotten himself killed by now.* She'd moved so much, and so far, blurring from one group of men to the other, sprinting to attract pursuit, she wasn't sure where she was anymore in relation to the road or the people she'd sent hurrying along it. *Brilliant plan, that*, she thought, trying to ignore the pain that radiated from her shoulder.

The sounds of a fight grabbed her ear, cursing, muted strikes landing on flesh, a ragged yell. She made for it, resettling her hand around her knife.

Her fingers were wet and slippery and the knife's hilt was slick.

Two men were wrestling over a knife as a third lay on the ground, bleeding, a torch sputtering into the dry grass. She hadn't the time to stomp on the flames. She hadn't time to sort out which combatant was which, so she lowered her shoulder and plowed into them, biting down a howl of pain as she realized she'd led with the wounded shoulder. Both hit the ground, their surprised shouts cut short as the fall stole their wind.

One stayed down, while the other popped back to his feet, growling. There was a short blade in his hand, and for a moment, light gleamed against the armor under his cloak.

"You don't have to die tonight," she rasped, her voice made even harsher by her wounds, the night's exertion. A part of her cringed at how it sounded. "Put down the blade and walk away."

"And miss my chance at collectin' the links on your head?" He lunged at her, or tried, but she was gone, slipped behind him. She tried slipping the knife into his ribs but the point snagged on his mail, so quickly, savagely, she reversed her grip so that the knife pointed out of the bottom of her fist, and just slammed it with all the strength that remained to her where his neck and shoulder met.

The result was bloody and drawn out, but conclusive. She worked the knife back and forth, opening a huge gash, tearing the mail open.

The man died ugly, whimpering and clutching at the wound, forgetting the sword she'd told him to drop, kicking it about in the dirt as he thrashed.

She stamped out the sparks the torch had spread in the grass, picking up the brand after sheathing her knife. She held the guttering light over the bodies. One was a greenhat with the side of his head stove in, his identifying cap soaked in blood. The other was a thin man with a nasty wound on his side and bruising on his forehead and his bearded cheeks. She was about to move on when he took a ragged breath.

She dropped to a knee and let her bowstave fall out of her hand. "Easy, easy," she murmured. She drew her knife again, used it to cut ragged strips off one of the dead greenhat's cloaks, and began to staunch his wound with them.

"Stop, stop," he croaked. "I'm done. I know it. Another wound like this'sun in m'back. I did time as a soldier," he added, his voice rasping and growing fainter. "Nothin' t'be done."

She pressured the wound anyway, and he feebly slapped at her hands. "Not helping. Save t'others." He coughed, his breath rattled in his throat. "I got the bastards though, didn't I?"

"You did. What's your name?"

"Gend," he wheezed. "Tell Shary I died sober, eh? For her. For the Mother, I guess. Leave me here. Go." His were words barely audible now.

"The Mother doesn't want you dying for her, Gend," Idgen Marte whispered. "She'd rather you live for Her, for Shary. Come on. Stand up, I'll walk you back."

He didn't answer; his hands fell limply to his sides.

She slid her knife back home, collected her bowstave, and pushed painfully back to her feet. Pursuit seemed to have lost her or broken off. *Or I killed enough of them.*

She looked down at Gend's cooling corpse. "I can't carry you. And I can't stop to bury you. But they'll know what you did, and what you said. I promise you that." She turned to leave, then turned back and knelt painfully to the ground. She placed a hand over his forehead and gently closed his eyelids.

Then, searching for words she expected to be difficult and remote only to find them ready to hand, she whispered, "May the Mother find you in the next world, may Her hand guard you, Her tears wipe away your burdens, Her love free you of all your pains." She turned and started to limp away, muttering fiercely, "He died for you, Mother. He best not have died in vain."

Even as she said the words she felt, as much as heard, some tiny ringing note in the chill of the night.

* * *

She caught up with the rest of them not even a quarter of a turn later, dragging herself down the road at as fast a walk as she could make, ignoring the pain, forcing it into a part of her mind she could ignore. *Lucky Cold-damned shot anyway,* she told herself.

She heard the tired plod of her horse's steps, heard the quiet, fearful muttering of the folk, heard a calmer voice telling them to quiet down and keep walking. They were shadowy forms, indistinct in the darkness, except for one that kept moving from the back of the group to the front, every point in between, and back. *Shary,* she thought. *Mother, I hope she's as tough as she seems.*

She called out softly, "It's me. Idgen Marte. The Shadow. I think I've shaken the pursuit." *I think I murdered them all in the dark, actually, but I oughtn't tell you that.* The group stopped as soon as they heard her voice, but she could hear the sighs of relief, the quiet murmurs of thanks.

Idgen Marte called out again. "There's a lantern and oil in the saddlebags. I think you can risk it now."

As the others halted the horse, pulled exhausted children out of its saddle, and began rummaging in the bags, Shary came towards her with a determined stride.

"Gend? Did ya find him? He stayed back to hold the bastards off…"

Idgen Marte wiped her free hand on the back of her trousers, unsure how much good it would do. Then she touched Shary's arm. The girl's exposed skin was pebbled with the cold, and shook slightly. "I found him," Idgen Marte whispered carefully.

"Then where is…"

"They found him too, Shary. The soldiers. He wanted you to know that he died for you. For the Mother. And that he did it sober."

Even in the dark she could see the girl's features start to scrunch up, and then saw her fight back the grief, swallowing it, clawing herself free. Idgen Marte recognized that process when she saw it; she'd done it enough herself.

"And the men that killed him?"

"Both are dead," Idgen Marte softened her voice as she went on, but it was like a file against steel no matter what she did. "He'd fought them. Killed one, hurt the other, but he'd taken a wound himself, too big and too deep for me to staunch."

"You killed the other?"

"I did." She paused. "It's no small thing, an unarmored man with a truncheon taking on armored men with swords."

"Gend was a pretty small man," Shary replied in a voice that wavered between bitter and sorrowful.

"Maybe he was once. Not anymore."

"Don't make him into some kind of hero."

"I'm not," Idgen Marte said, casting an eye towards the people fumbling in her saddlebags in the dark behind them.

"He was a thief and a drunk, and I'm a fool for…" She stopped, bit her lips closed.

"If he was a thief, or a drunk, he came to the Mother in the end, and he's earned something for that."

"We should go back, bury him, or take him with us," Shary said, starting to brush past Idgen Marte, who tightened her hand on the girl's arm.

"No," she insisted. "Just because they've gone for now doesn't mean they'll stay gone. We've got to press on. If they come at us in numbers again, I don't know if I can stop them. We need to make Thornhurst as fast as we can. And I need you to lead these people there. I gave him a benediction when I left him…"

"A what?"

"A blessing. A prayer. The Mother will see to his soul, Shary. I promise you."

The lantern sparked to life. Shary turned, pulling her too-thin cloak over herself, and softly clapped her hands together. "Enough standing around," she said, her voice hushed but urgent. "We've got a long walk ahead of us."

Idgen Marte followed Shary towards the crowd, seizing her horse's bridle and leaning on the animal's weight a bit, to help her walk. She heard some hisses of indrawn breath when she came into the light. She saw her own hand on the bridle, saw the wet stains there on her fingers, her wrist, climbing up the sleeves of her jacket to her elbows.

She let go of the bridle and retreated to the shadows outside the lantern's light.

CHAPTER 31

Interlude

It was good to finally feel proper cold, even if it was a month later than it would've been at home. Nyndstir hadn't seen home, of course, in almost a decade, but he still compared most everything to it.

And right now hireling work in the baronies was freezing dismal, mostly because he hated being near the glowing-eyed bastards in robes.

Glowing eyes, glowing mouths, glowing Cold-damned skin. *Un-freezing-natural,* he thought, as he spent the greyest part of dawn trudging along with other swords-at-hire while one of their employers rode in a large, boxy wagon behind them.

He started to feel uneasy as soon as they came upon the bodies. Not because they were bodies. Nyndstir Obertsun had seen enough corpses, made enough, woken up next to them, spent time on ships with them. The form of a man that had once been quick and was now gone to the Cold had no effect upon him.

Nyndstir felt fear because he knew what was coming.

The wagon creaked to a halt and the hirelings spread out along the road. An odd lot: barony men, one other Islandman, a smattering of dark-skinned Concordat, fair-haired Keersvasters. Only about a dozen men. *Not counting what's in the wagon,* he thought. *If they're still men.*

The sound of the steps lowering, the soft footfalls as the sorcerer made his way to the front of his men, the sound of the contented sigh as he looked upon the bodies. "Three more for our cause," he said, almost brightly. "Strip them."

Two were greenhats, Barony Delondeur's guardsmen in cities and towns big enough to need them. Quickly the mercenaries pulled off their armor, their weapons, laying it all carefully aside. The third was a thin, wiry man, probably in his thirties but looking older, with a nasty wound in his side. One of the greenhats had his head bashed in, while the other looked like a spirit of the night air had grown claws and ripped the side of his neck and top of his shoulder open.

Nyndstir didn't assist in stripping the bodies. There was a hierarchy to these things. Men with his experience didn't pull the shit jobs. They stood around till there was something to kill.

He made himself watch as the sorcerer drew signs over the bodies, the sickly yellow runes hanging in the air. He'd seen this once already, and found it made his stomach uneasier than the worst sea voyage he'd ever had, but he'd be damned before he'd turn away from it.

The sign drawn over the thinner, unarmored man dissipated like smoke.

The sorcerer frowned, leaned over the body again, and drew his hand through the air. Nyndstir heard words on the wind, an obscene whisper he didn't want to listen to.

Then a tiny chime, like some silver bell on a dancer's scarf, and again, the sign vanished, carried away as if by a breeze.

Nyndstir worked awfully hard to keep a smirk off his face, but he found he liked seeing the sorcerer failing. He just knew better than to be seen liking it, so he stared hard at the dirt while he felt the tension around him thickening.

"What trickery is this?" The sorcerer 's whisper was barely audible, yet something about it raised the hair all down Nyndstir's neck.

The sorcerer, a slight figure who hadn't lifted a hand at real work that any of the men had seen since he'd been hired a few days hence, knelt on the ground. He extended one finger, a tiny beam of light projecting from it, and used it like a hook to rip the shirt and coat straight off the corpse. It came away like paper.

But where his finger touched the dead man's flesh, nothing happened.

He spread his fingers wide, and the glow around them intensified. He began muttering in a harsh and guttural language, and the world seemed to vibrate as the words spilled into it. Yellow light gathered in a cloud around the body as he spoke. He brought his hand down, smacking the flesh of the dead man's chest.

And once again, his power vanished like morning mist.

He stood up, squaring his shoulders. "You," he said, suddenly whirling on Nyndstir. The Islandman reflexively hefted his axe. He'd seen the sorcerer do terrible things, but he wasn't going to stand around with his hand on his stones while they were done to him. "Hack that body apart. Spread its pieces where you will as I attend to other business."

Nyndstir stood still for a moment, hands wrapped around his axe haft. "I'll take it off there," he said, jerking his head to the side of the road behind him, where a copse of pine stood in the near distance.

"No. I want it done here. I will not ask you twice."

The Islandman stood on edge for a moment. *I'll die someday. Maybe soon. But not out of sight o'water,* he thought to himself, and so he nodded, spat in his hands, and wrapped them around the haft of his weapon, the smooth, familiar hardwood worn into grooves where his fingers sat.

He looked down at the body, thankful, at least, that it spared him the sight of the other bodies, and what was happening to them even now. He heard it, the sick, impossible sounds as the sorcerer did his work, the ripping of flesh, the grinding of bone, the squeal of metal. He focused on the body before him. That wound in its side was gruesome; what swords did to unarmored flesh was never pretty. Nyndstir decided that this one must've killed the other two men, though he wasn't sure how. But the thought comforted him.

I don't know who you were, you poor bastard brother of battle, Nyndstir thought as he lifted his axe, *but you're better off than the frozen sods you took with you.* He raised his axe.

CHAPTER 32

Homecoming and Guests

Allystaire sat atop Ardent, his and the destrier's breath both blowing out in great clouds, even now at midday, the few turns ride along the northern track towards the High Road and the Oyrwyn border having left both of them sweating even in the sharp cold. Overloaded saddlebags rode on the horse's rump, along with an enormous bedroll, and a half dozen wineskins were tied to his saddle's pommel.

I hope the boy's scouting was right, he told himself, not for the first time. Then, aloud, he snorted. "Of course it was." And in truth, it wasn't long till the ragged party came into view: one horse, perhaps a score of people walking around it.

He gently nudged his heel into the grey's flank, and the massive horse started a deliberate walk up the road to meet them.

She's in rough shape, he thought, as Idgen Marte, leading her horse, which bore three exhausted children on its back, came into focus. Her left arm was hanging nearly limp, and sweat had plastered her hair to her scalp, but she walked purposefully. It took even him a moment to realize how she was leaning on the bridle of her horse. He dismounted and came forward to meet them, only to hear her voice in his head.

Don't you dare. Them first. I'm walking every step of the way back to Thornhurst on my own. I'll cut you if you try.

He pulled his heavy studded glove off his left hand, and saw her eye narrow as he did. "Are any of you hurt?" he asked as he came forward.

"Just exhausted and footsore, I think," answered a girl. At least, he labeled her girl but her age was hard to guess. She was thin, and her face looked young, while her eyes did not. Her thinness had the spark of urgent vitality about it, as if she used so much more energy than those around her that her body couldn't keep up with demand. Indeed, she walked straighter, spoke louder, and met his gaze more evenly than the rest of the crowd.

"Well, your journey nears its end. Thornhurst is only a few more turns. I brought bread, hot wine, cheese, and warm milk for the little ones." He lifted the wineskins—which were, indeed, quite warm to the touch—and passed them out, then opened his saddlebags and handed out wrapped bundles. "Blankets as well."

"How'd you keep it warm?" The girl who'd spoken earlier had seemed to instantly take charge of the food and drink, passing it where it was needed.

"What is your name, lass?"

"Shary. Don't call me lass. I'm older'n I look," she replied, her jaw jutting with lightly wounded pride.

"My apologies, Shary. In answer to your question, I did not keep it warm. If you want to know how it was done, ask the dwarf when we make Thornhurst." Allystaire paused a moment, then added, "I do not exactly recommend that you ask unless you have a spare quarter turn and a stomach for being told in advance how little of it you can understand."

"Eh?"

"Sorry. There's a dwarf who did it. Name of Torvul—if you ask him how he did it, he will answer. At length. With a great deal of insult thrown in. I was merely…" He stumbled while looking for the word, and Idgen Marte cut in.

"Stop tryin' t'make jests. You've no tongue for it. And we've not the time to waste standing around, either. Eat and walk."

Allystaire sidled up to Idgen Marte as they began to walk, dragging a reluctant Ardent behind him. He slipped his hand onto her shoulder, felt her tense and start to pull away, but it was too late; the Goddess's song filled his limbs and he pushed the energy into her, like a stream diverted into a dry dyke. He felt her body soaking up the energy, knitting itself, healing, with almost no direction from him.

Idgen Marte straightened up as if a weight had been taken off her back, let out a small sigh of relief, and shrugged his hand away. "Good enough," she muttered. "Save it for them if they'll need it."

"Your shoulder was badly mangled. There was hurt done to the bone, and it would only have gotten worse."

"I've had worse."

Allystaire hmphed and then was silent. "Eventful trip, then?"

"How'd you know t'look for us? How'd you know I was bringing folk with me?"

He was silent a moment. "Gideon."

"I would've guessed Mol."

"No. In fact, she says it is getting harder for her to hear…well, we will talk about that at home. About many other things as well. We have guests."

"Guests? Who?"

"I would rather show you than explain," Allystaire said. "Now mount up on Ardent for the rest of the way." He stopped, holding the huge grey still. Idgen Marte stared flatly at him for a moment, then turned and walked on.

"Every step of the way," she muttered.

* * *

"It is hardly Wind's Jaw keep, which has broken every army that got as far as its towers," Allystaire said as they approached the newly walled edge of the village of Thornhurst. "Yet it is something, at least," he said, to Idgen Marte and to the folk that followed them both. The Ashmill Bridge folk seemed palpably relieved to be within sight of a friendly town, and much invigorated by the food shared with them.

It wasn't a proper gate, of course, to Allystaire's thinking. What was needed was stone, and a lot of it, a barbican and flanking towers to give archers good angles, a curving path uphill to a real gate, barred by an aged and fired oak and iron portcullis.

What they had were lashed timbers and fittings of what iron Torvul could spare, but it swung open and closed and was barred shut with thick, iron-bound planks from the inside. When they passed through it and heard it close, Allystaire felt a tiny buzz of energy, perhaps heard a chime.

"When did you finish that," Idgen Marte asked, eyeing it professionally, mouth quirked to one side.

"Just this morning. Torvul says he is not quite done, that there is something more he must do at sunset. Which, come to think on it, cannot be long."

"How many can fit inside the walls?"

"All that need to," Allystaire replied.

There were new tents thrown up near the one Allystaire had been staying in since they returned to Thornhurst in the midst of fall, and a line of horses picketed together outside the stable to which Allystaire led Ardent and Idgen Marte's courser. The villagers he dispersed to the tender care of Mol, Timmar, and Renard, all of whom were waiting near the Temple, within close sight inside the nearly complete walls. The girl was already moving among them, touching a hand, speaking, guiding them to shelter and rest. The children, in particular, seemed to flock to her, though there was something more distant than usual about the little priestess.

Once Allystaire and Idgen Marte had some distance from the others, she asked him, "What's wrong with Mol? And what did Gideon do?"

"Mol says that as winter deepens and the days shorten, it is harder for her to hear the song of the Mother. She is not gone, our Gifts do not wane—at least I have not felt it to be so—but what Mol hears and feels is different from what I do. It frightens her, I think."

"I'm not thrilled knowin' She can weaken with the season myself," Idgen Marte said.

"I do not think She is weaker. I think that Mol…the girl has lived with the Mother whispering to Her, watching her, teaching her, every day for months now. If that is gone, or harder to hear, it is bound to be troubling."

"And what if the Mother's Gifts weaken in us on this Longest Night you prattle about? What then?"

"Then I will fight our enemies with my own strength, and you will sew my wounds, and Torvul will poison everyone. It will be quite nostalgic."

Despite herself, Idgen Marte laughed. Allystaire clapped her on her newly repaired shoulder, and said, "And now for the guests who arrived the night you set out."

"They look like armed men, anyway, if their horses are anything to judge by. Bit run off their feet, but good mounts."

Allystaire led her towards the new tents, rapped a knuckle sharply against the pole, and threw back the flap.

Inside, wrapped in a heavy grey cloak and looking older than when she'd last seen him, but with the unmistakable features Allystaire had pointed out months back in the Dunes, was Chaddin, formerly sergeant Chaddin, briefly reigning Baron of Delondeur, natural son of Lionel Delondeur.

His blond hair was longer and a bit ragged, and his cheeks bore a new scar, but it was him.

"What in the Cold are you doing here, you freezing moron?" Idgen Marte's shout surprised both Allystaire and Chaddin, and the two men sharing the tent with the latter both hopped to their feet.

The larger of the two, a young man with anger brightly firing in his eyes, got two steps towards her with a hand falling to his sword and a haughty, "You mind your tongue when you speak to your rightful Ba—" before Allystaire's fist took him in the stomach and blew the breath out of him. Allystaire stepped back and let him crumple to the ground, then he turned on a clearly astonished and suddenly ashen-faced Chaddin.

"I let you and your men in here under very specific terms," Allystaire said, as he stood over the wheezing man. "One of them, as I recall, was that if any of them bared steel without my express permission, I reserved the right to expel all of you. I also recall having issued explicit statements about calling anyone the rightful lord or true baron of anything inside these walls, which, as far as I am concerned, are no longer part of any barony. Discipline your men. Or I shall. Understood?"

Chaddin nodded mutely, swallowing hard. "Aye."

To the man on the ground, Allystaire bent down. "And you—next time I will not stop with taking your breath. Let this be a lesson. When I say a thing, I mean it. Understood?"

Still struggling to find a breath that he couldn't quite catch, the man nodded. Meanwhile, the other attendant—older and quieter than the first one—came over, grabbed him by the arm, and hauled him to his feet. "Let's get some air into you," he muttered. "Do you good."

After the two exited, Chaddin sighed heavily, eyeing Allystaire wearily. "Did you have to hit Rasby? He's a good man, just excitable."

"If he hadn't punched him, I'd've killed him," Idgen Marte replied flatly. "And I still haven't got an answer out of you. Why are you here?"

"Solace. Help. I haven't come seeking any obeisance or fealty. I just thought you could help us."

"What happened to your rebellion?"

"I don't quite know," he said with an inadequate shrug. "I was used to leading men, just not quite so many of them. Things turned quickly. Boatfuls of men loyal to the Baron—or at least to the Baron's weight—poured into the harbor, led by Landen Delondeur come back from Keersvast. There was another sorcerer with them, or so they say. All I know is I was woken in the night by my best knights telling me we had to flee the castle and that Lionel Delondeur had been broken free of his confinement."

"I told you once and I will tell you again," Allystaire said, "you should have hanged him from the highest tower the instant you had his seat."

"It isn't done," Chaddin replied, pressing his lips into a flat line. "You don't depose and execute a reigning baron without appropriate proceedings, especially with the inheritance an open question given Delondeur's practices. Braech's church had agreed to oversee the matter."

"If you had wanted to stay in the baronial seat, it is exactly what you should have done," Allystaire said. "Now that the Shadow has returned, we can convene and decide whether we will grant you refuge. You can stay at least through the morning. Now we have work to do."

"If you'd only listen to my offer, I could make your hopes for this place a reality," Chaddin said, surging to his feet, slight desperation in his voice.

Allystaire, though, was already on his way out of the tent and into the oncoming dusk.

Idgen Marte followed after him, but not without a dark look back at Chaddin.

Outside, she found Allystaire massaging his knuckles. She jabbed him in the ribs with a finger to get his attention. "You probably didn't need to hit the boy."

"You have not listened to his lot prattle on about rightful this and rebellion that. It was high time one of them got his wind knocked out."

"How many men did he bring?"

"Just over a score."

She sighed heavily. "We could use them."

"At what price?"

"What's the offer he spoke about?"

"I will answer in council—which we had better get to." He pointed towards the Temple, which Torvul had just exited. As they started walking, the wind brought to their ears the low and rolling wave of his voice, lifted up. Everything seemed to stand still around it; the wind quieted, the sounds of a village at dusk gave way to silence, the sinking sun fought for a few more moments of hard-won light.

They could make out no words, for as usual when he sang in his native tongue, it blurred together into one unbroken line of resonant sound. Allystaire felt it settling over him like a soft rain falling over a field, was reminded of Torvul's voice pulling him from the brink of a dark end some months ago.

They saw folk on their way from the day's labor, or back out the gate to their farms, pause to listen, could feel it sinking into each one of them, to the stones and the mud and the slumbering grass of the place around them.

Just as quickly as they were caught in this reverie, the song ceased, and the dwarf took a deep breath, and seated himself on the top step of the Temple. He was taking deep breaths and clutching a small silver flask.

"Voice gets harder t'find, the older I get," the dwarf said as they trotted up the steps towards him. "Twenty years ago, or thirty, I could've drawn that on a full quarter turn."

"You know dwarf, you could make good weight singing bass for a troupe of musical players," Idgen Marte said. "You'd be the envy of the circuit."

He looked up sharply at her and drew himself back to his feet. "It'll startle you to hear this, I'm sure, but among my people, singin' for links is simply not done. I'd never take gold for a song. Not any amount," he added, with conviction.

"What were you singing?" Allystaire asked, breaking the silence that ensued for a few moments after the dwarf's pronouncement.

"A declaration, an invitation—I was calling this my home and inviting my friends and my family to share it. Telling them that while they rest here, nothing that I have the means to stop will ever harm them. Inviting them to share the safety of its walls, the warmth of its hearth, and the bounty of its table."

"When was the last time you sang that?"

Torvul squinted up at Allystaire. "When did you get so clever as to ask that kind of question?"

"It is a simple question with a simple answer."

The dwarf grunted noncommittally and turned into the Temple. "Come along then. We've a lot to discuss."

They found Mol and Gideon waiting for them in front of the altar, and a few others sitting on benches nearby—Keegan, Ivar, and Renard foremost among them.

Allystaire turned a quick, worried eye on Gideon. The boy, usually so oddly, intently focused, was distracted, his gaze continually drawn towards the clerestories Mol had been so insistent upon building. Allystaire cleared his throat discreetly, and the boy's wide eyes flitted back to the gathering council. And, Allystaire noted, stayed there.

"We all know what we need to discuss," Allystaire said, his voice filling up the space and drawing all eyes to him. "We have an upstart baron in our midst, and he wishes to negotiate with us. With him, he brought over a score of fighting men, their weapons and supplies. We all know that our enemies are closing in on us. Keegan tells me that Delondeur scouts are sniffing not far away. Meanwhile, Gideon says that a party of men—two hundred or more—have made from Londray and appear to be headed here, skirting the mountains. Given the banners he has described, I think that Baron Lionel Delondeur travels with them."

"I have news as well," Idgen Marte said. "It's known among the folk who travel the roads—minstrels, players, and such—that Thornhurst is to be avoided. Even the promise of ready links couldn't change their minds. It may not seem like much, but trust me, it's bad. And there's worse," she added, turning and surveying their faces. "A proclamation of Anathemata has been issued by Braech and Fortune's temples, and endorsed by the Baron. All who worship the Mother are outlaws—and the hunting has begun. If it's so in Ashmill Bridge, likely enough it's so in Birchvale and Ennithstide and Londray, and soon enough it'll be so in Oyrwyn and Innadan and Telmawr. There were Baronial soldiers among the greenhats in Ashmill, and they were ready to hang folk who met in the Mother's name."

"The priestess was right, then," Torvul said. "Anathemata. Hobnail boots and truncheons and hangings. Burning at the stake."

"We knew it was coming," Allystaire replied. "What we did not know was that we would have Chaddin in our midst."

"I say we use him to work a deal," Ivar put in sourly. "Give the Baron what he wants, see if it'll buy us a winter's rest."

Allystaire turned towards the warband captain, eyes hard as frost. "Truly, Ivar? You would throw away a life, a score of lives, for a few more months of your own?"

Ivar returned Allystaire's gaze and the room was still for a moment. "I s'spose I might do it t'buy the lives of all the folk who live here since it's them I'm protectin'," she finally, slowly said.

"No one who comes seeking the Mother's refuge will be turned over to a man like Lionel Delondeur," Mol put in, her voice distant, her eyes focused on the middle distance. "That is final."

"And we're takin' our strategy from a child," Ivar muttered.

"No," Allystaire said, "I am taking direction from a priestess and prophet, and you are taking orders from me. If there is something you find troubling about the latter part of that arrangement, I believe the contract can be altered as soon as you are prepared to return your advance pay. On the former, I do not require your opinion."

Ivar went sullen, folding her hands into her lap.

"If we're done measurin' our manhoods," Torvul said, clearing his throat loudly, "then it's time to make a decision—we haven't offered the bastard baronling his asylum yet. What has he offered?"

Allystaire let out a long-held breath, his shoulders slumping a moment before he pulled them back upright. "He believes we can weather an attack—I suppose he must believe it. And that if the Baron is bloodied, support will evaporate. Says he has only second-rate troops and swords-at-hire who will vanish in the snows. Chaddin wants asylum now, and," here, he frowned before carefully going on, "aid. In the future, and when he becomes Baron, he will grant Thornhurst independence from Baronial rule, formally recognize the Mother's Temple in Londray, and establish a chapel at the Dunes."

"What aid is he asking for?" Idgen Marte leaned forward, her eyes narrow and lips pressed thinly together. Her tone suggested she knew the answer.

Allystaire he forced himself to meet Idgen Marte's piercing brown eyes. "Me leading the army that establishes him in the Seat."

"You can't," Mol said, her voice smaller and quieter than he remembered it being for a long time. "The Mother forbade that kind of glory for you."

"It would not be about glory, Mol," Allystaire said quietly, earnestly. "It would be about the Mother's people, about securing their future."

"It's hardly a well-shored up tunnel," Torvul said. "There's the rather sizable problem of the Baron. And his armies. And the Dunes."

"We've already proven that no castle wall can keep us out, you and I," Idgen Marte replied.

"So what are we to be, then? Assassins in the night?" Gideon finally spoke up.

"Isn't it better for one man to die clean than hundreds or thousands to die over him?" Idgen Marte fixed Gideon with a sharp look, which the boy met with calm poise.

"If you mean in a protracted battle or siege—if I had the energy, and I suspect I still do, I could simply pull the walls of the Dunes down," the boy replied softly. "Or put men on the other side of it. Or pluck him from his tower."

"Remember what you promised me, Gideon," Allystaire said.

"Then remember who you are," the boy replied, a little heat creeping into his voice. "Does the Mother truly take sides in these kinds of struggles? In politics?"

"I feel pretty certain suggestin' that Her Ladyship ain't on the Baron's side," Torvul mused. He turned to Allystaire. "You're certain you can win?"

"I am not certain we can hold Thornhurst just yet, but I think our chances might be a lot Cold-damned better with Chaddin and his men inside our walls. As for after—if the Baron is beaten once, at one of his own villages? Men will abandon him, and many will be easily persuaded to rise against him. Especially if we sing loud and long of the truth of his crimes. For all the wrong we have done to the common people of the baronies, we never put them in literal chains or subjected them to thralldom."

Mol looked as if she wanted to speak, but instead she slumped into her chair, shaking her head.

"That his crimes deserve punishment does not mean we fight a war to lift up his replacement," Gideon said, his voice rising angrily. "If we fight a battle to defend ourselves, so be it—we have that right. But we are not swords-at-hire!"

Look straight at it, Allystaire—that's what you've taught me to do. Doing the wrong thing for the right reasons is still wrong. It is not what She has called us to do."

Allystaire sighed, lowered his eyes to the floor, then lifted them up again. "The boy—the Will of the Mother—is right. We cannot do this. Dip our hands into those streams of politics and war even once, and we are forever tainted by them." He sagged. "Sometimes I feel as though the Goddess has set us at war against the world itself—against the slight and meaningless circumstances that lift one man over another, that give one family generations of wealth and power while others toil endlessly for their bread. I do not know how to unravel what we have made of this world, or how to make those circumstances any more just." He shook his head, straightened his back and shoulders.

"Like as not, who is rich and who poor will never be subject to what is just. Yet there is a difference between destroying a man for the evil he has done, and will continue to do, and destroying him because his children squabble over which of them should inherit his mantle. I will defend them, if they will stay. I will not fight their war for them."

Mol bounded to Allystaire's side, wrapping her arms around his waist and pressing her face against him. He clutched her shoulder.

"And if they take exception to that decision?" That was Renard, sitting up straighter. "They've got enough men to give us trouble."

"They haven't got enough men to give me trouble," Gideon said very quietly. "Nor the rest of us. And besides, it will be in their best interest to stay. Surely Chaddin is cunning enough to see that."

"So we'll be putting about three score men up against two hundred, if it breaks in our favor?" Ivar's face was sourly twisted once more.

"No, Ivar," Allystaire replied with a confident smile. "Against two hundred, we will put three score with the Arm of the Mother at their head, Her shadow beside him, and Her Will and Wit and Voice behind."

CHAPTER 33

Battle is Joined

"That is our decision, and it is final," Allystaire said, with the air of a man repeating himself, thick arms crossed over his broad chest. Torvul stood at his elbow, leaning a bit on his long bronze-shod walking stick-cudgel.

"But the man is in a weak position," Chaddin insisted, pacing the far corner of his tent. "He must destroy you before the next campaigning season and his support is waning."

"None of that changes any of what I said. The Mother is not going to be a part of your revolution."

"What about guarding the weak? What about punishing the wicked?"

"You've got it confused with choosin' among the strong," Torvul said.

"My father must be destroyed," Chaddin said with, Allystaire thought for the first time, real heat creeping into his voice. "Whatever he was, he's become a beast."

"That we agree upon," Allystaire said. "And we will give you and your men shelter from him. If our purposes work in tandem while you take that shelter and we can join our strength to defeat him, all to the good. But any alliance stops at the wall of Thornhurst."

"And those walls will do you no freezing good when my father gets here, unless there's three thick feet of stone I can't yet see."

"It has never been the walls as much as those who stand behind them," Allystaire replied, with an assurance he did not feel.

"There's more to 'em than you think or can see, boy," Torvul interjected.

Chaddin was silent a moment. "You honestly think you can defeat whatever my father brings? What if there is another sorcerer? Hired Islandmen? What then?"

"I have killed more hired Islandmen than I can remember," Allystaire said. "And you will recall what I did to your father's first sorcerer."

"We'll have what, three score? Against two hundred? Perhaps three? You're mad. Perhaps if we fled, went into the mountains—he can't kill what he can't find," Chaddin said, speaking in a sudden rush, curling one hand into a fist in front of him. "Staying behind the walls, we've given up all mobility, all initiative…"

"Remember who you are talking to," Allystaire grumbled. "I was teaching your father what mobility and initiative meant before you were holding a sword."

"Enough babble," Torvul suddenly rumbled, smacking the bottom of his cudgel against the hard ground. "Make a decision. You stay and you've got the Arm of the Mother beside you. Sixty against three hundred make long odds, but a damn sight better than twenty against the same."

"I am offering you something no other baron will grant you," Chaddin said, his voice almost pleadingly desperate now. "Independence for your village—no interference from the Temples, legitimacy for your Goddess…"

"Thornhurst will prosper or fail on its own faith, its own strength, its own people," Allystaire replied. "And my Goddess, our Goddess, requires no one's approval for Her legitimacy. I will not make her Church and Her name, small though they may be, a tool in a fight over an inheritance. That is my final word."

"You're a mad man," Chaddin said, shaking his head slowly. "You're giving up what you say you want for some notion of purity…"

He was cut off by the sound of a yell, which sent Torvul and Allystaire scrambling outside.

In the distance, beyond the southern wall, a column of bright red light plumed into the sky.

"Torvul…"

"That's one o' my signals. Red means more than a dozen, armed and close."

"My armor, now," Allystaire said. He didn't run for his tent; he walked with long confident strides.

"What's our play," the dwarf huffed, laboring to keep up.

"You, me, Idgen Marte, and whomever else is ready." Even as they walked, Allystaire was assessing the way the response was meant to unfold. *Idgen Marte, Renard, Ivar, and Gideon to my tent. Women and children to the Temple. Ravens preparing the mounts.*

He felt a calm and familiar assurance spread through his limbs, felt the rising energy that danger brought, tamped it down, banked it like a fire that needed to last long on too little fuel.

Then he and Torvul were in his tent and Allystaire was throwing off his tunic and pulling on the gambeson that lay on the table with his armor. The silvered, mirror-bright surface caught his eye for a moment, then Torvul was pulling pieces off the table and arranging straps.

"Just a warning," the dwarf said, as Allystaire was pulling the gambeson on. "If you ever call me your squire, I'll poison you."

No sooner was the quilted gambeson on him than Torvul was strapping pieces to his arms. The dwarf's nimble fingers made quick work of buckles, and soon Allystaire's arms and hands were plated with vambraces and gauntlets that left only the palm of his left hand bare.

By the time they were hurriedly fitting greaves over Allystaire's legs, Idgen Marte was throwing back the flap. Her own dark blue leathers were pulled over a thin coat of tightly ringed mail, and her hair was held back by a wide metal band, with a matching piece about her throat. She had her bow to hand, and two bristling quivers, one on her hip and one on her back.

"Ivar sent her three best bowman out as skirmishers. Renard is having trouble getting his men to the wall. Gideon has said he'll go to the Temple. He asked me to say not to worry, that he'll still be on the field." She reached out and tapped his cuirass, finger pinging against the golden sun the boy had magically inscribed there. "Didn't explain."

Allystaire choked down a spike of anger. "Orders are meant to be followed, yet they never are. Someone always thinks he knows better."

"Renard was trying to make sure none of his militia fell on their own spears or shot each other," Idgen Marte pointed out.

Allystaire grunted noncommittally. "Horses?"

"Saddled, being led here."

He nodded, and knelt down as Torvul threw the straps of his sword-harness over his back. Allystaire's gauntleted fingers fumbled with the strap, but Idgen Marte snatched it as he stood up, and cinched it tight.

The dwarf picked up his helm off the table, and Allystaire slid it into place without comment. It felt heavy and close, as it always did, with the cheek and nose guards digging into his flesh.

"Should have a visor," Torvul grumbled. "Be more proper knightly that way."

"Never favored it," Allystaire said. "Cannot see half of what you are fighting with one." He picked up his hammer, hefted it for a moment, then slid it home, picked up his shield, and headed out into the night.

Ivar was waiting, holding the leads of Ardent and Idgen Marte's courser. The huge grey destrier was pulling at the reins, bursting with energy, muscles bunching, fighting the warband captain every moment. The animal settled, though, as soon as Allystaire emerged.

Ivar's head turned, and, slightly shocked, she said, "What the Cold kind of armor is that?"

"The kind I wear now," Allystaire said, grabbing the grey's reins and pulling himself hard into the saddle. He felt his mount gathering itself beneath him, ready to run.

He knows battle is close, Allystaire thought. *He always did.* Another Raven came trotting up, held out Allystaire's lance, and he took it, adjusting his grip so that he held it far up the shaft.

"String along beside me on the way out," Allystaire said as he settled in the saddle, pitching his voice to carry as the Ravens gathered around their captain. "But do not obscure my path. If I start Ardent in a charge, he will not stop—do not be in his way. Remember that our own people are out there, the people we are here to defend—be mindful of that as you choose targets in the dark." He paused, gathered his breath, and said, "Forward."

He felt a tiny thrill as he said that, though whether it was the Goddess's approval or his own, he couldn't say.

This, he knew.

No pitfall negotiations. No preaching. No priestesses with one hand on his trousers and another on a knife. No frozen cabbages or stolen farm implements. His horse, his saddle, his lance and hammer and shield.

As he rode Ardent through the gate that Renard's men hastily pulled open, a cheer, ragged but honest, went up behind him, and he smiled coldly against the metal pressing into his cheeks. *It was for this that I was made, for this that you Ordained me, Goddess. Let me not fail you,* he thought, as he gave his mount its head, and, wearing painfully bright armor that carried light through the darkness like a lamp, went out to meet Her foes.

They were not cunning, or hadn't expected much of a response, for there was no proper ambush set. A handful were tossing lit torches at the buildings of a farmstead, while others assembled on the road. A score at least, though it was hard to tell as many of them were moving, shouting, torches in one hand and weapons in the other. There was enough light to see the green of their cloaks and tabards.

He heard a shriek, a woman's, pierce the night, rising above the noise around him.

A squadron was assembling on the road, heavy footmen, with long spiked hammers and bowmen on the flanks. Were they led and organized properly, were they veterans, they'd cut mounted men apart.

Bowmen first, he thought, directing the words at Idgen Marte. He felt a sort of nod of acceptance, and then she and her mount vanished from view.

Confusion, shouts of alarm among the men assembling to hold the road.

Panic as two of the four bowmen suddenly screamed as fletchings sprouted from their chests, driven deep through their boiled leather by the Shadow's short, powerful horse bow.

"Get people clear of the fires," Allystaire shouted, knowing his voice would carry. Even as he did, he felt the strength of the Goddess's Gift filling his arm, and he lifted up his lance point in the air, then swung it back to couch it against his side.

It was as light as a reed; it was nothing.

It was twelve feet of strong ash with a foot of sharp steel on its end, and with a forward thrust of his arm it plunged through the chest of one of the skirmishers who was too slow to figure out what to do with his long pole-hammer.

The force of the blow ripped the man's torso in half, sending an arm and shoulder careening into the darkness.

Allystaire felt the lance shiver and the cracks beginning to run up its length. Dimly, he registered the screams behind him as he tore through their ragged line. It took hard tugging with his knees to wheel Ardent for a second charge at them, and by the time he did they were already scattering. More arrows sailed into them from Idgen Marte's position in the darkness. They threw down their polearms and fell to their knees, holding out their hands. One had a splash of blood and gore along the side of his face.

His anger was so great, beating so powerfully at his mind, that he spurred Ardent, intending to ride them down.

There was a harsh, discordant note within him—the music that filled his limbs gone, for a moment, horribly awry. It was a sound of desolation and pain and darkness, and if he had to hear it again he would surely lose his mind.

He steered with a sharp knee pressed into the destrier's side, and Ardent veered away from them, onto the patchy, winter-killed grass.

The farmhouse was perhaps the smallest building on the plot, with a much larger cow byre, and another shed of a size with the house. Perhaps for that reason, the green-tabarded soldiers who'd moved into the area had gone to the larger buildings first.

Idiots, Allystaire thought, but even as the thought came to him, he saw a trio, bared blades in hand, kicking down the barred door, heard shouting inside.

He slid from Ardent's back, unslung his hammer, and ran across the ground, covering the yards at a speed no man in armor should make.

* * *

The first one through the door had gotten a bolt from her father's crossbow. The crossbow had been given to her father by the dwarf, who'd slipped her a handful of hard candies at the same time and told her not to worry, which meant she did, because when you were a child and told not to worry, you absolutely should.

Lise had watched her father practice with the crossbow, carefully, shooting at the broad base of a dead tree, every morning, as the dwarf had shown him.

So Lise worried when her dad had gone outside and flung down the bottle the dwarf had brought, the one of red glass, and gotten out the crossbow and the bolts and thrown the bar over the door. She'd become positively terrified when the banging on the door started, and her father had ordered her down to the tiny cellar he'd dug out beneath the kitchen, but had stopped at its entrance long enough to watch the door splinter and shiver and finally burst open, her father squeeze the handle of the bow, the short bolt flying true into the first man, who dropped with a scream.

Then she ducked down into the dugout, hearing another scream, which she thought with terror, sounded like her father's voice. Then quiet, and footsteps inside, with shouts and horses and muffled screams outside.

Booted feet scurried through the house. Things were tossed and overturned, crockery was shattered, and finally the door of the dug-out cellar hauled open, and a hand reached in, pulling her out by the front of her dress and tossing her raggedly on the floor.

Lise had been taken by the reavers along with her father, those many months ago, and she had learned well not to scream, not to speak, not to give any satisfaction, so she bit down on her cheeks and was silent.

There were two men, both wearing long and mud-stained green tabards; she could see that much by the light of the kitchen fire, both with swords, one of which looked dark and wet to her eyes. She tried to stand up, only to have her legs kicked out from under her.

"Your da shot our chosen man," one of the men snarled. "Right in the gut. Did for him. Now what do you think is good payback for that? What is due us for our grief?"

Lise swallowed hard, biting back the tears from the pain and searching for her breath and the words to answer. She heard a new set of footsteps creaking on the floorboards, and lifted her eyes hopefully, thinking that her father had crept upon them with the crossbow loaded again.

It was not her father, but Lise smiled all the same when she saw the gleam of the armor.

The men whirled around as the room brightened, but too slowly—the first turned straight into the paladin's glittering, mailed fist.

It met the side of the soldier's cheek and stove in his head with a loud, and, to Lise's ears, entirely satisfactory crunch. The man dropped to the floor of the kitchen bonelessly, and, she hoped, dead. From the way his head lay flat as the blade of a hoe on one side, she assumed he was.

The other tried to bring his sword to play, but the room was close and the paladin was already inside his guard. He caught the soldier's wrist in one hand, there was another crack, and the sword thunked to the ground. Then the same hand went around the man's throat and lifted him off the ground.

The soldier's boots had to be a foot clear of the floorboards, but the silver-armored man didn't struggle, and there was no hint of strain in his voice.

"What were you going to do to the girl?" The paladin's voice was low and calm and yet, even to Lise, some way more frightening than the leering soldier, or the snickering reavers had ever been.

"Kill her, maybe—"

"Enough." He gave the man a slight shake, with a rattle of armor. "Why?"

"Orders to leave none alive, and her da shot our chosen man—"

"Who was breaking down a man's door in order to murder him and his child." The paladin, still holding the soldier aloft, turned his head to Lise, and said in a softer voice, "Turn your head, Lise. You need not see any more death this night."

She turned her head—but not all that far, and peeked back out of the corner of her eye. She was hoping maybe he'd take out his huge sword and cut the man in twain; instead, there was simply a crunch as his hand made a fist around the soldier's throat.

Lise did turn away then. She heard two distinct thumps. One with the heaviness of a body slumping to the ground, the other smaller. She tried not to think too hard on why there were two sounds instead of one.

"Come on, girl." Then the paladin was at her side, picking her up, and carrying her out of her kitchen, wrapping one coldly metal-clad arm around her back. She expected to pass her father's body, and was keeping her eyes tightly shut.

Instead she suddenly found herself being shifted to other arms, more familiar arms. She opened her eyes to see her father—pale, ragged, with a wet hole on his shirt that her leg brushed against—shaking with relief as the Arm of the Mother handed his daughter to him.

"Get to the walls," the paladin told her father. "Take nothing but your bow and your daughter. The way is clear."

Lise's last thought as she saw the paladin walk away with flames and stars reflecting brilliantly, was to wonder why, despite what she'd seen him do back in the kitchen, there hadn't been a single spot of blood or dirt on his armor.

* * *

Thank you, Mother, was all the prayer Allystaire had time for as he turned away from the girl and her father, and let out a loud call. "To me! The night is not yet ours!"

Idgen Marte raced up, winking into his vision from the night itself, with Ardent following close upon her courser. Allystaire swung himself into the saddle.

"There's maybe two score of heavy foot coming down the road. Take more than a single man's charge to break them," she said. "Still a good quarter mile out but making good time. Look like they know their business. And this is just the tip of the spear."

Allystaire pulled his lance free from the boot forward of his stirrup, felt keenly the shivered and fractured timber of it as he settled his grip around it. "We shall see." He tried to focus, tried to think through the searingly cold anger that filled him, past the music that lifted his spirit and pounded his heart into a drumbeat, past the flooding of his limbs with strength. "Ravens," he cried out, and soon the warband had assembled. They'd made short and bloody work of the amateur skirmishers, and though fires began claiming buildings around them, a stream of folk was headed back to the walls. He spared a look back and saw a group of men moving from the gate to meet them.

When the Ravens, spears in hand, had amassed, he ordered sharply, "Stage on the road, fifty span ahead, loose line—leave room for twice as many men. Hurry!"

Ivar began translating the orders more colorfully, and Allystaire tuned her out, struggling to think clearly, to think of the land as it lay on a map.

"The farms are lost," Allystaire replied, "but we need to blunt their edge. Show them that no foot of this ground is given cheaply. Find a good shadow ten yards beyond the Ravens."

Idgen Marte nodded. "Where are you going to get the men to fill out the line?"

He swallowed hard, and said, "From Gideon."

She nodded, turned her horse and ran off. His next thought was to bow his head and send his thoughts outward, back towards the walls, seeking out the Will of the Mother.

Gideon's mind was not difficult to touch, and the force with which it met him was daunting.

Gideon, Allystaire thought. *I need you. Can you...*

It felt for a moment as if a massive presence sorted through his thoughts, then Allystaire felt Gideon's voice calmly saying, *I see. And yes, I can. Through the sun.*

You may have noticed that it is dark out, lad.

The sun on your armor. That is why I put it there. Go.

Allystaire felt the contact break. He thought he felt the Goddess's song grow a little dimmer as Gideon drew on his own power. He spurred Ardent and found the road, covered the place where the Ravens were setting up.

Up the curving west-bound road they could see the mass of men moving in the dark, the torches lighting their way.

"How exactly are we gonna hold off that many heavy foot with a dozen of us," Ivar was grumbling, as she shifted her grip on her spear and spat heavily into the dirt.

"There will be more of you momentarily," Allystaire answered him as he pulled up behind. He held his lance gingerly, then felt a buzzing enter the music that still filled him. Then a chime and a flash from the Sun on his chest, and suddenly for every living, breathing Iron Raven on the road, there were three more.

They would not pass a close inspection, or battle. Largely they mirrored the movements of the men they stood beside, wearing the same blackened mail, carrying the same spears and other arms.

In the dark, at a distance? *It should do,* Allystaire thought.

The line of soldiers murmured in shock and surprise, a few jabbing their spears at their insubstantial partners.

"Calm, and hold," Allystaire bellowed, a long-accustomed note of command in his voice. The Ravens snapped back to their rank, forty soldiers holding the road with spears bristling outwards.

The Delondeur foot came on, Allystaire searching their ranks as they closed. There, he thought suddenly, seeing the shape trotting alongside them—a mounted man, a knight or officer, leading them forward. In the darkness he couldn't make out any standards or badges. *Ask Torvul for something for the night vision next time.*

Once he thought them in reasonable shouting range, Allystaire called out, "You come seeking to kill and burn your own people at the behest of a slaver baron! A man so bent on power and plunder that he will tie his own people to the oars and row them to death so long as the ship sails him towards glory. Turn back or die."

Take the bait, he thought. *Take it.*

The column halted at a muffled shout and the mounted man rode forward. He was an indistinct shape in armor, carrying a lance. A hand reached up to push his visor to the crown of his helm, and he yelled back across the distance. "You have raised arms and hired warbands against the rightful Baron of this land. That you speak treason only confirms your intent."

"Might I know who I am addressing? I like to know a man's name before I kill him for defending his Baron of shit, his Baron of rapine and filth. A man is who he serves, and I will suffer no man like that to live."

"Sir Leoben, given command of these Salt Spears," the man shouted shrilly, and Allystaire's mind was drawn back to the Dunes and the knight Chaddin had threatened. "And it will be my honor to kill you," he added. "I have personal dishonor to avenge upon you, Coldbourne!"

"Come forward and die in the service of your Baron then," Allystaire felt Ardent tensing beneath him, hoped his lance would hold together. The Ravens stepped to the side in a neat, long-practiced maneuver, clearing space for him to bring the destrier through.

He spurred Ardent and felt the destrier's huge muscles bunch and flex beneath him as it leapt to the charge. Leoben's horse was of a similar size and breed as Ardent, and though moon and starlight, and the distant fires lit the field poorly, man and horse together were too large to miss.

The lance had the weight of air in his hand, and he aimed it true, striking the center of Leoben's shield. But the wood couldn't take another blow and it exploded in his hands, fragments pinging off his armor and scattering into the night, and too little of the force was transferred to do more than rock the knight in his saddle.

At the same time, he felt Leoben's lance strike the tip of his shield and slide over it. It took him square in the chest. He felt the sick sensation of air being pushed from his lungs, the sudden deep well of black sleep that rose up and threatened to claim him. He felt himself slumping.

Stupid, he cursed himself through gritted teeth as his legs lost their grip on the saddle and he fell over sideways, hitting the ground with a clatter of armor. At least his feet pulled clear of the stirrups, and Ardent rode clear. *Too freezing full of yourself,* he thought groggily as he struggled back to his feet. *Did not even look for his lance. Idiot.*

Allystaire swallowed a wave of nausea and pushed himself to his feet. His shield had tumbled from his hand but he still had his hammer. His right hand found it and brought it out, holding it easily, even as he wavered uncertainly in place, searching for Leoben.

"You are unhorsed and undone," came the knight's joyful shout. "Yield yourself as my prisoner, return to the Baron to face justice for your crimes, and perhaps some of the poor folk you've led astray can be granted mercy."

The only thing worse than an old fool is a young one, Allystaire thought as he whirled to the sound of the words. Leoben sat his horse a dozen yards away, the destrier's tail flicking angrily.

"I will not yield," Allystaire called out, biting off the wooziness that tried to infect the words. "Not to the likes of you. Meet me on foot or on your horse if you must, coward."

Leoben merely laughed and waved to his footmen, who, Allystaire suddenly and sickeningly realized, were much closer to them than his own, and every bit of two score men.

"Take him," the Delondeur knight yelled, and the infantry broke ranks and charged towards him.

Now or never, Shadow, Allystaire thought, and before he knew he was doing it, his left arm, shieldless, had reached up to seize his sword and pull it free. Despite its length and weight, with the Goddess's song still powering his limbs, it was like swinging a dinner knife. He charged towards the oncoming wave of spearmen, hammer and sword swinging, dimly aware that he was yelling as he ran, that all trace of grogginess and nausea had fled, that Idgen Marte had answered him and that a cry had gone up as arrows began to fall among them from behind.

Allystaire did not dwell upon the odds, only on the mass of men and the continual movement of his weapons. He led with the blade, swinging it in a long arc before him, and followed with the hammer when men drew inside his reach. He felt arms and legs part under the force of his sword. Ribcages and armor, helms and skulls gave way like eggshells to his hammer. He felt the nick and cut of their blades, too. No man came for long into the press and crush of a battle and went away unscathed.

Part of him noted that men in blackened mail under black leather had rushed beside him, their own broad-bladed spears defter and deadlier than those of the Delondeur foot.

Soon he found himself face to face with the blurred and shadowy outline he knew to be Idgen Marte. Without a word, spoken or otherwise, they turned their backs to one another and faced a ring of spears.

"Whatever devilry this is, honest Delondeur steel will bring you down," Leoben gloated from beyond the ring, rising up in his saddle and lifting his sword point to the air. He seemed to gather breath to yell an order, when the fletchings of a crossbow bolt suddenly sprouted from his eye, and he slid bonelessly from his saddle.

"It's hardly steel and it sure as Cold ain't honest," came a shout from a powerful and resonant voice that brought a smile to Allystaire's face. "And it's not got an asshair on my devilry," Torvul roared, his voice made all the more commanding because he was unseen.

That was followed by a sudden gout of flame springing up just behind the Ravens, who had backed off the ring that formed around the two Ordained.

The Delondeur infantry, wide eyed at the display, suddenly broke and ran.

Allystaire's very first thought was to whistle sharply, and Ardent came trotting to his side. He slid his hammer into its ring and grabbed the bridle, leaned heavily on the destrier, and shouted, "Gather any that live and such weapons, mounts and gear as we can use, then make for the walls!" He started to sheathe his sword, only to feel a telltale weariness start to seep into his limbs, and he had to steady himself and summon strength to do it.

The Ravens burst into action. Bodies lay strewn around the road, and Allystaire took solace in the fact that all that he could see wore green tabards.

Idgen Marte blurred away, and Torvul strolled up, the strange coiled stock of the *mchazchen* crossbow wound around his right arm, one of its sighting rings locked upward.

"Figured the longer this went the more likely y'were to need me," the dwarf groused.

Allystaire merely shook his head, pulled himself painfully into Ardent's saddle, a task monumentally more difficult than sheathing his sword had been. For a moment he teetered in the balance, afraid he was about to spill ass over appetite into the road, but, with a last surge, he swung his leg over and down and slumped on the saddle.

"Have we wounded?" He had meant to bellow the query like an order, but his voice came out in a rasping croak that only Torvul heard.

"Probably none more than you. Snap out of it and heal yourself before you pass out."

"Got to save it for them," Allystaire said, and twitched his destrier into motion only to have Torvul seize the bridle with one powerful arm.

"There won't be any of it for anyone if you don't attend to yourself first," Torvul hissed. "Not to mention that the men on the walls and the people inside them need to see you ride back in tall in the saddle and unhurt. Understand?"

He's right, Allystaire told himself, and with a weary shake of his head, he raised his left hand, slid it onto the back of his neck where there was space beneath his helmet, and reached for the Goddess's Gift of healing.

"Took it worse than you thought, didn't you?" Torvul said.

Allystaire could only nod in agreement; one spear had taken him hard in the hip. Others had nicked his thighs and side, points finding gaps in the armor, and one had found his elbow. None of the wounds in themselves were overly dangerous, but all together they might have put him off his feet, in time.

Her song flowed from his mind to his limbs and the wounds neatly sealed.

"Wounded to me as soon as we make the walls if they can walk," he yelled then, his voice regaining most, if not quite all, of its former commanding timbre. "Now if they cannot!"

None were brought forward, which he regarded as a good sign. All of them bearing prisoners or weapons, and with Idgen Marte having grabbed the reins of Leoben's destrier, they set off back for the walls of Thornhurst.

A good bit of the farmland outside was in flames, but they would die or be doused before reaching the walls, he was sure. Most, maybe all of the folk who'd lived on it had fled safely inside. "People matter more than land, more than buildings," Allystaire muttered as they rode.

As they neared the walls, Torvul produced his lantern, kindled in it a bright white beam, and centered it tightly on Allystaire.

The reflection was dazzling, lighting up a circle around him for ten spans or more as he rode in.

Renard threw the gate wide and a ragged cheer went up, and as Allystaire came closer, hushed words began running through the Thornhurst militia manning the walls in their hodgepodge of blue tunics, with their spears and axes and knives.

"Spotless," Allystaire heard one say. "Untouched," another. "Impossible."

But two words circled the crowd more than any other. When Allystaire heard them, he imagined he heard a tiny note of the Mother's music behind them.

"Still bright."

CHAPTER 34

Old Mountain Ice

Torvul stood outside Allystaire's tent, puffing thoughtfully at his pipe, beneath the cold canopy of stars.

The flap swished open, and Allystaire—having traded his armor for the dark blues, riding boots, and fur-lined cloak—sidled up to him.

"Thank you, Torvul," he murmured. "I think I might have gotten us killed had it not been for you."

"Not the first time, boy," the dwarf allowed from around the stem of his pipe. "Won't be the last."

"I did not think I would see you use that bow…"

"Nor did I," Torvul replied. "We came to an understanding, though, it and me. I needed it. She needed it."

Allystaire nodded. "I was foolish and overconfident."

"Aye, that you were. Of course, if your lance had held, it may've worked anyway."

"No wood that I know is going to take two blows like that when the Mother's Strength is upon me."

"If I had but a single stalactite of *mchazchen* I could make you a lance worthy of the songs the bards'd sing of it. Made to your arm, all smooth polished stone, too much force for any shield to stand." Torvul sighed, tamping his pipe's bowl with a thumb. "Like all my people, I'm reduced to the poorer earths, the baser metals and common gems."

"Have you any other thoughts?"

The dwarf shrugged. "The usual. Band it with iron or steel. I could make you one purely of steel, had I enough iron—but then you'd not be able to lift it except when the strength came on you, which has its own problems."

"Aye," Allystaire said. There was a silence. "We won the first day."

"We did. But only just. And it'll get worse before it gets better."

"You seem unusually glum, Torvul. Is it simply the coming siege?"

The dwarf made a noncommittal noise in response, pulled the pipe stem from his mouth, and spat on the grass. "No. It's what I just said, about poorer earths and my folk. It's likely enough that I'll die here in the next few days, but all over these baronies and beyond, my people are dying the same way, by one and two. And even those that aren't lost or exiled or forsaken are trying to make a home in a wagon. Home means stone and smoke, not wood and sky!" He spat again, and said, "Don't mind me. I'm old. The melancholia is bound to take hold now n'then."

He looked up, turned his pipe down, and knocked out the dottle by tapping it on the sole of an upturned boot. "Go get a turn or two of sleep. We'll keep the watch, me and Idgen Marte, and have you awake the instant anything shows itself."

Allystaire nodded, unable to stifle a yawn, and returned to his tent, disappearing inside the flap.

A few more minutes passed in silence before Idgen Marte emerged from the darkness behind the dwarf. "Still bright?" Her tone was as sarcastic as usual. "How'd you plant that?"

"Every good peddler knows how t'throw his voice."

"Why?"

"Rolls trippingly off the tongue, don't you think?"

"Really, why?"

"People need a symbol, knight of legend, a simple phrase they can shout and follow into battle," Torvul said. "They don't quite have that yet. If we survive this, they will."

Idgen Marte murmured something to herself, nodding faintly. "It'll do."

"It has to," Torvul said bleakly.

"It will," she affirmed, reaching out to squeeze his shoulder. "And Torvul? If I have t'fight the rest of this siege with just knives, I'm cutting off one of your ears."

He harumphed pointedly. "An artist cannot be rushed."

She snorted and walked off. "Good thing there're no artists here, eh?"

* * *

Certainly it wasn't much more than a turn till Idgen Marte was shaking him awake, a lamp throwing light around his tent.

"They're circling the walls, staying out of bowshot. Probably time to get you up."

Allystaire felt the weariness that followed the Mother's Gift still clinging to his limbs, but he pushed himself out of bed anyway as Idgen Marte hooked the lamp on the ridge pole. "How many?"

"Hard to tell without enough light. Gideon told me he could count them, but…"

Allystaire shook his head. "I do not want him on the walls. Or in the air."

"He can really? I mean, I saw him disappear that day."

"Aye," Allystaire replied. "And I do not want him doing it except at need."

"Why? It is a tremendous advantage."

Allystaire held up fingers as he counted off points. "First, we do not know how much or how long he can do it. Second, we do not know who or what can feel him do it. And third—he told me that each time he takes to the air it becomes harder to bring himself back to earth and take up his body again. Says nothing can match the sense of freedom. And a lot of other nonsense about pure thought and no limitations that I do not understand."

"If we're going to survive this, you'll have to be willing to let the boy expose himself to danger."

"Just help me with the armor," Allystaire grumbled.

A few minutes later the two of them were heading out of the tent, passing a small wineskin between them.

She led Allystaire to the western wall, and the two of them climbed the parapet, which was really a simple scaffold. Eyes followed Allystaire and his silvered armor as he walked. Torches reflected off of it, murmurs ran among the villagers, armed with spears and bows, who stood along the wall.

Too thin and too green a line to hold this wall, Allystaire thought, though he tried to keep his face calm, his manner casual.

The torches that spread out along the farmland outside the wall spoke to scores of men, but not the overwhelming host Allystaire had feared.

Awaiting him on the wall, Renard gave voice to the very thought. "Something troubles Delondeur that he can put only so many into the field against us." He leaned, unworried, upon his spear.

"That is assuming we see all of them. Yet it matches with what the Will told us," Allystaire offered. "Not as many as I had feared."

"Probably enough," Renard murmured, voice pitched for only Allystaire to hear.

"Maybe it is simply confidence, then. Lionel Delondeur has never lacked for that."

"Should've killed him when you had the chance, Allystaire," Renard said, not hiding the reproach in his voice. "Might be that his heir would've come after us anyway, but not with the backing the old man has."

"Mayhap I should have. Yet it felt like the wrong time, and the wrong way. People need to see what he is. Had I killed him in the Dunes, then I would be a murderer, disposing of the rightful Baron in favor of a bastard upstart."

"That's what folk'd think. Don't make it true," Renard grumbled.

"Oh, but it does," Torvul said as he made the top of the scaffold behind them. "And Allystaire's got the right of it. Now, who wants to go on out there and get this over with?" There was a bit of laughter, most of it forced.

"What do we do now?" one of the village men asked, fingering the string of his bow, and the quiver of arrows on his hip.

"The thing a soldier does most," Allystaire replied. "We wait. We wait for the sun to rise. We wait for Delondeur or his proxy to ride forward and make demands. We wait to laugh our answer in their poxy faces. Then we wait for them to attack, and while we do, we try to figure out where and how. Then we wait for it to be over and to see if we are still standing."

"What's t'stop 'em from simply settin' the whole o'the wall afire while we're doin' all this waitin'?" The villager couldn't keep his hands still. Allystaire fought the urge to reach out and grab the man's arm to quiet him.

"I am," Torvul replied. "You mind the skins hangin' every three span along the wall, and the barrels under the scaffold. No wall o'mine is going to burn, even if I did have to make it of wood rather'n stone."

The villager swallowed hard and turned his eyes back towards the dim clumps of men that moved beyond the wall, straining to see them.

Allystaire did a bit of straining into the darkness himself, then snorted. "Torvul. Have you any of that potion of yours for the eyes?"

"Be specific, boy. I've got more than one."

"The one for the dark."

"Eh. Save it," the dwarf said, as he swung his reclaimed crossbow up to rest upon the wall, and flipped up one of the sighting rings. Allystaire couldn't see the color of the crystal that filled it, but he suspected it was a dark red.

"Well, I've got the Baron's standard," the dwarf said, as he swept the bow slowly and evenly back and forth. "A lot of spearmen. Not too many bows. I don't see any engines, and we've done a number on the timber hereabouts. Heavy horse look few and far between."

"More trouble than they are worth in winter," Allystaire reasoned. "Not enough fodder, and the terrain turns bad for it in a hurry."

Torvul grunted noncommittally and lowered the bow. "I don't like it. Seems like too trivial a force, like we're not worth the bother. There's got to be more coming than this."

"Gideon said there were some coming from the north, but not nearly as many. Swords-at-hire, perhaps a couple of warbands worth, with wains behind."

"Don't like the sound o'that. Got to be somethin' we're missing."

"Patience will show us," Allystaire said.

Torvul turned around, and Allystaire had the sense of being glared at, then he heard the dwarf's voice in his thoughts.

You know Idgen Marte could simply sneak out there and slit the bastard's throat.

I do. And I will consider that at need.

This best not be about needin' to do it yourself, or any other prideful nonsense.

I may not need to be the one to do it—but the folk need to see it, if they can.

Torvul grumbled and turned back to the wall, and they waited. Waiting, like the fighting earlier that night, was something Allystaire well knew how to do. He let his mind drift, let it seek out the connections and examine his assumptions about what was happening and why, let it work over old sieges and stratagems.

His body barely felt the cold, or the weight of his armor, though weariness yawned under him like a chasm. In time, before he really knew it, the sky was filling with the day's paltry measure of light.

* * *

Dawn hadn't fully broken when a small party of mounted figures rode forward, perhaps half a dozen. Three banners were held on equally long poles: the Delondeur Tower, gem-encrusted Fortune, and an even more opulent dragon, picked out in dark-blue gems on sea-green silk. Each banner had a sash of white drawn across its middle, holding it in.

Torvul grunted. "I would've that our reception last eve would've let us skip all this parley-under-drawn-banners rot."

Allystaire shrugged, armor clanking as he moved. "It is the form of the thing, the show. Lionel always believed in forms. And showing off, even more."

Chaddin and two of his knights had joined Allystaire and Torvul on the scaffolding, and the blond-haired sergeant-turned-Baronial-pretender nodded. "Seems like you know my father well, Coldbourne."

"Stop calling me that, for the last time, Chaddin," Allystaire grumbled. "I left that name behind. I will not own to it again."

There was a rustling among the few militiamen within earshot, a whispering that Allystaire couldn't catch. Torvul grinned but said nothing. Allystaire turned his attention back to Chaddin.

"And I do know your father. I should. I have fought with him or against him—mostly against him—for near as long as you have lived."

He turned back to the waiting delegation and told Torvul, "We have no banner to answer them with. Can you tell them that the Arm and the Wit of the Mother come forth to treat with them?"

Torvul cleared his throat, pulled a small silver flask from one his many pouches, and took a careful sip, clearly savoring. He resettled the flask, drew in a deep breath, set his hands around his mouth, and bellowed in his deep and powerful voice. The sound that carried across the entire village behind, and to the host camping before them.

"We come forward to answer! Prepare to receive the Arm and the Wit of the Mother."

Torvul cleared his throat when he finished, and looked to Allystaire. "We takin' anyone else?"

"You needed a potion for that?" Chaddin's derisive interjection was delivered with pursed lips.

"No," Torvul said, his eyes narrowing. "I needed a drop of good dwarfish spirit. I also need you not to speak at me again unless spoken to."

Chaddin opened his mouth to protest when Torvul suddenly lifted his cudgel threateningly, placing the brass cap against the man's jaw. "Listen here, boy. You're here as a guest, and that against my judgment. We're going t'parley with your loving father now, and if I think for a moment that I can trade you for the lives of the people of this village, I won't hesitate."

Both of the knights flanking Chaddin looked to Allystaire, and he shook his head. "Have done, Torvul. Come on."

Carefully, Allystaire descended the steep wooden stairway that led to the scaffold, the wood creaking under his armored weight. He heard Torvul descending behind him. They waited in silence as two of the Ravens unbarred the gate and dragged it back, then walked out to meet the delegation.

Before they'd even come within a dozen spans, Allystaire recognized Delondeur on the back of a charger that, while not quite as big as Ardent, was certainly prettier, its coat a sleek black. The Baron wore brilliantly green-enameled armor inlaid with gold leaf picking out the Delondeur Tower, a theme repeated in the horse's tack and saddle. His bannerman Allystaire guessed to be the heir who'd come home to free Lionel, wearing armor made similarly to the father's, if not quite as richly.

Allystaire also recognized, with a certainty that sank to his stomach like a rock, the delegation from Fortune. Despite the extravagant, spotless white fur robe that she wore, Allystaire knew that the Archioness Cerisia had returned before he could even see the pale green eyes behind the empty sockets of her golden mask. Beside her sat a temple soldier in gold-painted mail and conical helm, carrying the same gem-encrusted banner he had seen on the road to Thornhurst weeks before.

The priest of Braech he did not recognize, though he had expected either Symod or Evolyn. The man was young, with a blond and patchy beard, wearing blue robes over bronzed scales that he seemed unaccustomed to. The banner-man beside him was an Islandman straight out of a coastal villager's nightmare: all fur and iron, wild-haired and bearded, with three throwing axes stuck in a bandolier across his chest.

The heart of Braech's leadership is not in this, Allystaire thought, hoping Torvul would hear him. *Or Symod himself would have come. They fear us.*

They fear Gideon, and they're smart t'do it, Torvul thought back.

They had time for only that much reflection, for as they approached, Delondeur rose up in his saddle and lifted the visor of his helm.

"Coldbourne!" he bellowed. "I have many grievances to express upon you. But first, I am persuaded by two-thirds of the Temples Major to give them time to persuade you to save some of those who've decided to follow you into oblivion."

"That is not my name any longer, you slaving coward," Allystaire spat back. "And at least one among your number knows that I will not be persuaded, for she knows what I am, and what is behind me."

"I do," Cerisia answered, nudging her palfrey forward a bit. Though her voice was muffled by the mask, Allystaire thought he heard an edge of desperation in it. "Which is why I would ask you to give yourself up—you and the other four among you who claim to have been Ordained by your Goddess. Do this, and the rest of your villagers will be offered clemency."

"So long as they will be godsworn to the Sea Dragon and to Fortune, of course," the priest of Braech put in.

"This does not include my bastard son or his followers," the Baron quickly and heatedly added. "They will all die traitor's deaths on the gibbets in Londray, and any crow-cages I feel like putting up along the road."

"Archioness, you cannot possibly believe that any clemency will be offered, no matter what oaths these people take. You also cannot possibly believe that I will abandon them," Allystaire answered, quietly and evenly.

"The Baron has sworn to it. The declarations are drawn up."

"The Baron is a liar!" Allystaire's shout, the heat and the volume of it, surprised even him.

"I will not stand for that abuse of my lordly father!" The Delondeur bannerman spoke up. Clumsily, the knight began trying to unstrap a gauntlet while holding the banner pole with one arm.

Allystaire rolled his eyes, but also set his shoulders and spread his feet, though before he could prepare a response, the Baron had reached over and grabbed his bannerman's hand with his own. "Stop it, Landen," the Baron growled.

"His abuse should not stand," the bannerman protested, voice muffled by the visor. "Let me prove his lies upon him, my lord."

"Landen," the Baron said flatly, "I need you to remember something. Whatever it is you think, the man you were about to challenge is still Allystaire. Coldbourne."

"What of it?"

"He'll kill you," the Baron replied. "You've some blood on your sword from your summer, but it's too little, too fresh, and too seawater-thin. His blood is old mountain ice. Oyrwyn ice. He'll kill you and yawn while he does it. Leave him to me."

Landen's hands wrapped back around the banner-pole.

"Allystaire, please listen," Cerisia said, urging her horse forward a few more steps. "You have a chance to save—"

"Spare your words. You had a chance to see and do what was right, and you have chosen to save yourself, and to soothe your conscience with a pair of bright gems that cannot feed, house, clothe, or arm the people you now come to crush. Absent yourself or silent yourself," Allystaire said. "But do it quickly."

He heard her sigh, saw her eyes close behind the mask, then open again, perhaps slightly wet at their corners. But she turned her horse and rode back next to her bannerman, and she did not speak or seek Allystaire's eyes again.

The priest of Braech straightened in the saddle, though he didn't gain much height by doing it. It was hard to guess with him mounted, but Allystaire thought himself likely a head taller than the priest, who said, "The Sea Dragon's Temple will not be as easily si—"

Allystaire swung narrowed eyes to the man. "I think the Sea Dragon has already been turned away from here once," Allystaire said. "And that neither the Choiron Symod nor the Marynth Evolyn could find it in themselves to face us." He turned from the priest, who paled beneath his boy's beard, back to the Baron. "Are we done?"

"Not till I've got you drawn and quartered and burning, Coldbourne, or Allystaire, or Arm of the Whore, or whatever you call yourself these days. Yet we are done treating." The Baron turned his horse and spurred it, followed closely by Landen and the Braech priest and bannerman. Cerisia lingered a moment. Perhaps, Allystaire thought, she was waiting for him to say something, anything else.

Instead, he stared at the retreating Baron's back, even as Torvul's voice sounded in his head. *I could shoot him from here. That'd be that.*

Not under drawn banners, Allystaire thought in reply.

Finally, Cerisia turned her horse and her banner followed. Allystaire and Torvul turned and walked for the gate.

"Never seen a man more determined to repel a comely woman's attempts to warm him up," Torvul muttered. "You didn't have your tackle cut off somewhere in your endless warring, did ya? Or does all that time in the saddle just deaden everythin'?"

Allystaire snorted. "I have no wish to be bound to that one. Too many games, too much at stake."

"Stones above. If I hadn't seen quite so much of your blood myself, I'd be inclined to think it was ice."

"I think that was the highest compliment Lionel has ever paid me. Frankly, I am a little touched."

"So long as it doesn't stop you from killin' him, you get the chance."

"There is very little in the world that could."

* * *

Allystaire and Torvul clambered quickly back up the scaffolding and watched the banners depart.

"How long d'ya think he'll make us wait," the dwarf muttered.

"Not long. Now that the form has been observed, Lionel will want to stamp on us, and fast."

"Not sure he brought enough men t'stamp."

"I think he brought as many as he could raise. None of Delondeur's major lords, save the Baron himself, are present. Had Ennithstide or Tideswater Watch or Salt Towers been here, their banners would have been present at the parley."

"You people need t'think a little harder on the names of your fiefdoms."

"Be that as it may, the fact that they are not brings us a little closer to understanding the constraints the Baron faces. He has the largest barony, half again as large as Oyrwyn and as big as Innadan once you consider the Telmawr fiefdoms Delondeur has swallowed up, and old barony Tarynth. He can field thousands of men. Why bring three hundred or so?"

"You're forgettin' that Idgen Marte sent them all running while you were a guest at the Dunes. They've gone to winter quarters now, and they're not coming back out." Torvul said.

"Yet some of them would have come, surely, if Delondeur commanded," Allystaire pointed out. "He has not. And that can only mean that he does not trust them. Surely word that he was deposed and imprisoned spread. How many rode to his rescue? How many turned out their knights and men-at-arms? He has to show them something. Some strength, or power. The longer we can hold, the more his position erodes."

"As if his lords and their knights don't know about the slavin'? Who's rowing their galleys, after all?"

"Mayhap," Allystaire said. "Yet they surely do not know of the folk being cut to pieces in the dungeons of the Dunes to feed the power of a sorcerer. And even if they do, they cannot be seen to know it. The longer we hold, the more they are forced by circumstance to distance themselves."

"How've you people let these wars go on so long, anyway? I'd've thought a war-loving son of a bitch like Delondeur would've been thrown off the parapet of his keep years ago."

"I cannot answer that. I was on the wrong side of it for too long. Some sickness, mayhap, some malaise that settled over us."

"Where'd you learn a word like malaise?" The dwarf turned to glare up at Allystaire with one eye, then sighed heavily. "I think it's just power. Those who have some and want more of it, and those who're afraid of it and do as they're told. I'll give ya two guesses who're the ones with the spears in their hands marchin' on enemy walls." The dwarf spat, shook his head, and reached into a pouch on his belt, pulling free a brass-bound tube with glass on either end much like the one that had shattered in Allystaire's hands back in the mountains. He held it up to his eye and moved it slowly across the camp on the farmland before them.

"Where did you get another one of those?"

"A prepared dwarf believes in redundancy. Looks like they'll be tryin' fire first."

He held the tube out to Allystaire, who peered through the smaller end in imitation of the dwarf. Indeed, a square of infantry was forming up. Heavily armored in scale, with green tabards, and carrying thick oak shields with the sandy Delondeur tower crossed behind by a white spear.

"Must be the salt spears Leoben talked about."

"Salt spears?"

"Name of the battalion. My guess, it is something Lionel threw together out of what guards and garrison soldiers he could find. Never heard of them before."

He watched as the infantry hefted their shields and began advancing. In the middle of the square, three braziers, flames flickering at the edges of the bowls, had been placed on a cart, and it was trundled forward as the square moved. The shields went up in front, to the flanks, and above, but there was a gaping hole in the center, open and vulnerable, where the fire was.

"You are sure that fire is not a problem?" Allystaire asked, as he lowered the glass and handed it back to Torvul.

Torvul grinned up at him. "Faith."

Allystaire glanced at the bulging skins, reached out, and took one in his hand. The skin itself was not well-tanned, for it stank, but it held tight against the liquid within. And that liquid felt heavier, denser somehow than water or wine would have. They hung at regular intervals, and the cauldrons and buckets below were, he knew, filled to the brim with some liquid that looked like water, but did not quite smell or feel like it.

"Where did you find the time to make so much of it?"

"I made the time."

"Even you cannot conjure time from the day, Wit of the Mother though you are," Allystaire said.

"No, but I can steal it back from the night." The dwarf tapped a pouch on his belt. "I've not slept much these weeks. Haven't needed to."

"Is that safe?"

Torvul glared up at him, one eyebrow cocked. "We're about to be set upon by men who outnumber us five to one at least, and you're wonderin' whether somethin' is safe? Tend your patch, boy. Let me tend mine."

Allystaire shrugged and drew in a deep breath. "Looks like they will try fire! Look to your weapons! Bowmen, nock arrows but do not draw!" Allystaire's command rolled powerfully over the scaffold. Half of the Ravens and half of Renard's militia began adjusting their armor, resetting grips on their weapons. The black-mailed warband soldiers did so much more casually than the villagers.

"Mind yer skins and the cauldrons below," Torvul yelled.

"Bowmen stay on the scaffold," Allystaire called out. "Spearmen and others will refill the skins as needed."

Allystaire eyed the bowmen—a dozen of them, mostly villagers. He smiled to see Norbert and Henri standing a few spans apart, both drawing arrows from the quivers on their hip. *Mother, let him live to finish the sentence I set him,* Allystaire prayed.

Then he turned his senses inward, projecting his thoughts to Idgen Marte. He had a brief image of her pacing the more thinly manned scaffold at the other gate, nearer the Temple, her own bow held lightly in her hands.

They are going to try the front door, he thought. *With fire. Torvul assures me. What do you see?*

Nothing, she fired back. *No swords-at-hire, no soldiers, no wains.*

How are your men?

The Ravens are a bored lot of murderers, to be sure. Keegan's bunch won't speak t'anyone. And Renard spends most of his time trying to keep the militiamen calm even though we've seen naught but our breath. Are you sure Gideon was right about what was coming this way?

Do you think Gideon was wrong? No doubt the picture has changed since the last time I let him go aloft. Where is the boy, at any rate? Allystaire felt a brief mix of shame and anger at himself for not keeping track of the boy this morning.

In the Temple with Mol. He said he'd know if we needed him, that he needed to make some calculations.

I will let you know if we need you. Be well.

He could feel her chuckle. *I'll know if you need me before you can arrange the thought.*

Allystaire's attention snapped back to the present. The square of heavy foot was still out of bowshot, but they could see it advancing slowly.

"Why does he send three-score if he has three hundreds," Allystaire murmured. "This is starting not to feel right. Like a feint."

"Let me know when it starts to feel like a punch," Torvul said. "I'd hate to miss it."

The last few moments of waiting were terrible. *They always are,* Allystaire thought. Even as the square of foot picked up speed, as shieldless men in the middle began lighting brands, they seemed to crawl.

Allystaire raised an arm and bellowed, "Draw!"

He heard the pathetically small noise of a dozen bowstrings drawn back.

He waited, waited till the last possible moment, and dropped his arm, a dazzling gleam of sunlight rippling off of it from pauldron to gauntlet, and yelled, "Loose!"

The arrows arced into the sky, not the thick torrent Allystaire would've liked, but instead an all-too-thin trickle.

The Salt Spears broke into a run, and the first torch, thrown far too early, was hurled out of the square, arced up, and hit the ground with a puff of sparks and smoke.

The Battle for Thornhurst was joined in earnest.

* * *

Though she could feel the turmoil at the other end of the enclosed village, Idgen Marte tried to close herself off from it, to focus only on the side of the wall Allystaire had asked her to take charge of. She had the slightly smaller portion of such forces as they had, with less wall to guard and, they reasoned, lesser threat given that the better part of the barony lay west of Thornhurst.

"Watching the back door is an important job," she reminded herself, as she paced along the thin line of scaffold that served as a battlement. Ivar and the remaining Ravens, longbows unstrung in their hands, lounged at intervals, with the bored competence that only professional soldiers knew how to demonstrate.

She spared a glance towards the Temple, wan winter sunlight palely resting on the stones of its oval dome and the thick, leaded windows dimly glinting as if in reply. She brushed her fingers through the arrows on her hip, shuffling them in their quiver.

There was a sudden snap in the trees beyond the gate; her head whipped around. She saw nothing.

Keegan climbed up the scaffold, shuffling towards her, occasionally looking north and craning his neck, lifting his nose in a movement reminiscent of a cat sniffing at an unfamiliar scent in the air. His band had kept to themselves since they'd come inside the walls, bringing the bows they'd found or been given, and an impressive cache of nuts, acorns, wild tubers, and smoked and salted game— far more than half a dozen men would've needed for the winter.

"Somethin's comin'," he half-growled. "Somethin' that don't smell nat'ral."

She slipped an arrow from the quiver and nocked it, but did not draw the string, eyeing the man uncertainly.

When he turned towards her, his eyes were wide and white. "You don't believe me." His voice was low in his throat. "But something…"

Her concentration was interrupted by Gideon's suddenly loud warning in her mind. *Sorcery!* the boy yelled, and she whirled back to the Temple to see him emerge from it, running faster than she'd thought him capable. She had but a moment to reflect, absently, that Allystaire's training must have done him some good after all, when there was suddenly a louder snapping, as of trees being felled.

She turned back to the treeline just in time to see a knot of trees explode, as an ordinary-looking covered wain rolled through them like a knife through hot bread. Some wedge of force was projected around the wagon; she could see the faintest outline of it, practically feel the air thrumming with it.

She drew her bowstring, yelling commands as her eyes searched for the driver.

There was none.

She loosed anyway. The arrow came no nearer to it than a yard away when it suddenly tumbled off its flight and skittered to the ground.

Gideon! She felt, not panic, but a kind of despairing anger rise within her. The wagon, and whatever was projected around it, was headed straight for the wall—and there was nothing, she knew, that her arrows or her knives could do about it.

Then she bared her teeth in anger, turned and blurred with unnatural speed to Gideon's side, wrapped an arm around the boy's thin chest, and appeared back on the scaffold, panting with the exertion of dragging another body through the shadows.

Gideon was not thrown by being suddenly moved so fast across the dozens of yards, or if he was, he didn't show it. He closed his eyes, flung out an arm, and Idgen Marte felt the power in the air buzzing towards him, draining into his extended hand.

The wedge that surrounded it seemed to disappear, and Gideon relaxed, looking suddenly sleepy.

But the wagon itself did not slow.

"*Gideon!*" she yelled, and the boy's tired eyes snapped open. He flung his hand out again and she felt force again project from his hand, saw a hazy line drawn in the air at the height of the wagon's axles.

The carriage of the wagon flew off the axles. The wheels spun crazily away in four directions, rapidly losing force and speed. The top crashed heavily into the wall with a thundering sound of splintering wood.

The wall buckled, and those on the scaffold reached out hands to steady themselves. Idgen Marte heard the creaking screech of stressed timber, but the wall held.

Those on the parapet, Idgen Marte included, nocked and drew, holding the points at the canvas covered wreck below them.

Suddenly the wagon's cover was torn open from the inside by a long, ugly blade, then another, then two more, and the defenders recoiled in horror as monstrosities poured forth began climbing straight up the wall.

* * *

Allystaire ducked beneath the wall as arrows sailed back and forth, staring in amazement as flames hit the wall, then guttered and died as they came in contact with Torvul's thick and viscous concoction.

For his part, the dwarf cackled madly each time one of the Delondeur soldiers darted forward with a flaming brand, or hurled it, yelling insults at them in Dwarfish. At least, Allystaire assumed they were insults. When opportunities arose, Torvul would pop over the wall and unloose a bolt. Allystaire had not yet seen him miss.

He heard a voice on the wall cry out after the impact of an arrow, saw a village man go down, and began rushing across the parapet to his side.

As he bent next to the man, pressing his left hand to his sweaty, stubbly neck and pouring health and warmth into him, he wasted no time in pulling the arrow free from the ribcage with his right. Allystaire winced in empathy as the man cried out in pain, but he could feel the quickening of his pulse and the healing of the muscles and bones that the Mother's Gift sped along, and knew he would live.

An arrow clattered off the back of his own armor, the impact more surprising than painful, though it would likely bruise.

"Back on the wall," Allystaire yelled, as he helped the village man to a knee. "Good man!"

He was turning back to his own position when he heard Idgen Marte and Gideon's voices both in his head.

Allystaire! To us! Your wall is a feint! The real fight is here, came Idgen Marte's silent voice.

Gideon's message was much simpler, but much more dreadful, a cold sickening lump forming in his stomach as he heard it, though he did not understand what it meant.

Battle-Wights.

Allystaire turned to Torvul, knew instantly that he had heard as well, saw the wide-open eyes, the fear written in those bluff, square features. "Go," the dwarf yelled. "We'll drive 'em off here. Take Chaddin and his knights with you," the dwarf yelled. "You'll want 'em!"

Allystaire nodded and ran down the parapet steps, bellowing as he went. "Chaddin! An attack at the other gate. Now is the time to earn your place." Then, gathering breath for a louder yell, he bellowed, "Ardent! To me!"

He heard an answering whinny and began running along the road, only realizing after his first few steps flew by that the Goddess's strength had come to his limbs.

While he easily outpaced the former guard-sergeant and his men, who were slow to respond to his call, he heard the hoofbeats of his destrier on the road behind him, knew without thinking when the horse had matched his pace—for though his song-strengthened limbs propelled him faster than usual, his speed was nothing on the stallion's. Barely slowing, he threw out a hand onto the pommel and vaulted himself into the saddle, kicking his feet into his stirrups by blind chance on the first try.

He lay flat against Ardent's powerful neck and drew his hammer. The village flew past, with the Temple coming nearer. He rounded the bend, the big grey's hoofbeats pounding loudly on the frozen mud of the track.

Before him, he saw what warranted Torvul's horror.

Things, monstrosities made of bones and metal grafted horribly together, swarmed the walls, attacking its defenders. They were man-shaped, vaguely, each seeming to have two legs, two arms, and a torso topped with a skull, but the limbs more often ended in ragged blades, bitted axes, or simple iron clubs than they did hands. The ragged bones were wired together with iron and steel, and each skull seemed to be encased in a strange metal that glowed darkly.

No time to gawp, you old fool, Allystaire told himself, even as he spurred the horse that had slowed to a walk and drew back his hammer. One had been tossed off the wall by a Raven using his spear—thrust inconsequentially through its gaping ribcage, with shriveled flesh and putrid sacs that were once organs clinging to it—as leverage to take it off its feet.

The spear was pulled from the black-mailed soldier's hand. The Raven clutched at his belt for the axe that hung there. Before he could pull it free, a blade punched through him at navel height and he screamed horridly, raggedly, till the Battle-Wight's other hand, mace-headed, whirled down upon his skull and crushed it with horrifying strength.

Allystaire grimly set his teeth and cocked his hammer. The Battle-Wight turned for him, the spear stuck awkwardly through it and impeding it not at all, and charged.

Allystaire bent to one side in the saddle and swung the head of his hammer for the center of the thing's mass. He hit it square, felt the impact reverberate up his arm. *Like hitting steel,* he thought, *not bone.* Still, the sheer force of it as he rode past was enough to break it into two pieces. The lower half crumbled, the spear clattered away, but as he looked back, he saw that the thing's bladed hands were pulling it slowly but inexorably along the ground after him.

He gritted his teeth and wheeled Ardent around, feeling through the horse's eager muscles that the destrier knew what he had in mind. Allystaire spurred, squeezed, and the horse raced forward, gathering speed and trampling straight across the half of an iron-and-steel wired corpse that remained.

Should grind the Cold-damned thing into dust, Allystaire thought, just before the impact. He thought he saw sparks fly, struck from Ardent's hooves against the wight. The impact jolted him in the saddle, sending a shockwave through his body.

He glanced over his shoulder once more and saw that an arm had been severed, but still the thing came on. Allystaire swung out of the saddle, swatted Ardent's rump to send the horse away, and ran towards the Battle-Wight that struggled on the ground, raising his hammer up and bringing it crashing down upon the skull, smashing it flat to the turf, splintering and shattering it.

Allystaire knew that only the Goddess's Gift of Strength let him smash it in one blow. The resistance he felt beneath the hammer was more than mere bone could have offered. More, even, than well-worked steel.

There was a ripple of power released into the air that he could sense, though he could not have explained how. It felt wrong. It felt like life and knowledge and craft all bent together into something not simply evil, something wholly unnatural, something that was not meant to be.

It reminded him, dimly, of the feeling of the Grip of Despair, and his heart lurched. Then it was gone.

Allystaire turned back to the wall, seizing his hammer in a two-handed grip.

A half-dozen more of the things clung like spiders to the wall, and the defenders were the worse for it. His hammer whirling in his hand, Allystaire ran into the fray.

As he sprinted, he looked for familiar figures. A shadow blurred along the wall, too fast to see distinct details. Where it appeared, the Battle-Wights fell, but not permanently. Legs were tugged out from under one; another was levered over the wall to crash against the wreckage of the wagon.

He saw Gideon standing calmly on the frozen grass in his blue robe, with one of the Wights closing fast. Allystaire pumped his legs faster, sent out a panicked thought to Idgen Marte, then saw Gideon's hands spread apart and a staff of light appear in them, about the size of the staff Allystaire had used to teach him. With better form than he'd ever displayed in his lessons, the boy stepped forward and thrust the staff out like a spear, his hands meeting together at the end. He stepped into it perfectly.

It took the Wight straight in the skull. Allystaire felt the air grow taut against his skin. The horror began to shake and then slowly disintegrate. A cloud of dirty yellow light appeared in its place, floating in the air like grease on water. The staff vanished from Gideon's hands and the boy thrust out a hand, palm out, pulling the energy into him.

Then, to Allystaire's horror, Gideon dropped in a boneless heap, his head hitting the ground with an audible thud.

His heart hammering with a terror it had never known, Allystaire rushed to the boy's side, extending his left hand and skidding to his knees at the side of the prostrate youth.

He felt the lad's heartbeat, strong and steady. There were no wounds, no disease, no poison crowding his veins. How he knew these things he could not have said, and there wasn't time to ponder.

Idgen Mar—

The thought was only halfway out before she leaped out of the air before him. She held a knife in each hand, though one of the blades was snapped off a few inches above the pommel. Blood flowed from a wound upon her cheek, and she favored one ankle.

Allystaire lifted Gideon in one arm and held him out to her. He didn't bother to use words, for thinking was simply faster.

He is unhurt. I saw him kill one of the things and drop after absorbing its energy. Then, without knowing precisely how, he shared with Idgen Marte his impression of what he'd seen; the sickly, bilious yellow outline that had hung in the air for the briefest of moments. *Take him to the Temple. To Mol.*

He felt her angry reply. *That color…the villagers. Allystaire! The same sorcerer!*

"Go," he said aloud, already running for the parapet. The Mother's Song sang in his limbs like it never had before. In his mind he beheld a picture of a family farm turned slaughterhouse, of bodies lying gutted and quartered upon their own table, of a family's blood splashed upon their own hearthstones.

He heard once again the weeping of the Goddess, felt it tearing at him like barbed hooks.

That sound propelled him up the stairs.

The first one he reached was struggling with a wounded Raven over the black-mailed mercenary's spear. Allystaire gave it a contemptuous backhanded swipe with his hammer and sent it careening over the edge. He paused, hurled his hammer straight down at the Battle-Wight as it struggled to rise.

The heavy iron-and-oak maul was a blur in the air. It crashed straight through the darkly gleaming top of the monster's head and crushed its spine.

Allystaire didn't think for a moment about the loss of his weapon. He did not need it; his mailed fists would do.

He found himself facing a third that had crested the wall, the one Idgen Marte had thrown over. He reached out and grasped its wrists, stepping to the very edge of the wall. With his unarmored left palm he felt the unnatural hardness of the thing's limbs.

The Arm of the Mother closed his hands into fists and squeezed, and the Battle-Wight's steel-and-bone arms were crushed through his fingers like a handful of sand.

Allystaire seized the thing by the neck. With his other hand, he punched through its chest, shattering bones and bits of iron and steel grafted to it.

He lifted the thing off its feet, felt it struggling against him, flailing its useless arms. One of its legs kicked his chest, thudding hard against his armor, but the steel took the brunt of the blow.

Gritting his teeth from the exertion, he bent the Battle-Wight, pressing the back of its covered head towards its heels till he tore it in half. The metal shrieked; the bone splintered. He tossed the lower half over the wall, and brought the other down, helmeted skull first, atop a pointed timber on the parapet, once, twice, a third time, again, then flung it high in the air over the wall, screaming as he did.

"Sorcerer! Coward!" he bellowed, his voice rising over the sounds of struggled and booming through the air.

"I AM ALLYSTAIRE, THE ARM OF THE MOTHER," he screamed, his voice going raw, the skin of his throat hurting with the effort of it. "AND I DO NOT FEAR YOU. COME AND FACE ME!"

Allystaire realized then that, canny fighters as they were, the Ravens, Renard, and Keegan's lot were doing their best to herd the remaining Battle-Wights towards him, luring them his way at risk of wounds or worse, or gathering with a mass of weapons and shoving one of the monsters, inch by inch, across the parapet towards him.

He waded into them, punching, elbowing, kicking, using his armor and the force of his anger, the Strength the Goddess had given him, to hurl them across the wall, snap pieces of them off, and send them flying.

All the while the sound of Her weeping. The blood on the hearthstones. The promise he had made.

I will tear apart the world of men to find the man who has done this thing in your sight, he had said. *To find the man who has made you weep.*

The Battle-Wights were not what he wanted. He wanted the sorcerer's throat in his hands, like Bhimanzir's, one moment to swing a mailed fist through the craven sorcerer's face, to snuff out the bilious light that burned within. That very man, the man he had sworn to Her he would find, was out there, somewhere, sending monstrosities to do battle in his place. The Battle-Wights, horrors though they were, were only a diversion.

But for now they would do.

Then they were gone too suddenly, torn apart, thrown over the side, ripped to pieces, and he was screaming with raw and inarticulate fury. The Strength had not left him, and he searched for another enemy, peered beyond the wall at the gathering gloom hoping to see a flash of yellow, thinking for a moment of leaping the wall and running in search of him when the Shadow appeared at his side.

"Allystaire," she said, her voice cutting through the veil of rage that fogged his features. "The wounded need you. We have won this moment."

He took several long, ragged breaths, prepared for the Goddess's strength to flee, gripping the wall.

Her song remained in his mind, his limbs.

"He is here, Idgen Marte. Here. And I will have him."

"You need to see t'Gideon," she said, shoving hard against one shoulder. "The attack is done for now."

"The danger is not passed," he rasped. "Her Gift has not left me."

"Then we'll keep an eye out, but there's men'll die if you don't get down there," she snapped. "Now."

He took a deep breath, trying to calm the fury that called within him like a hunter's horn. *Gideon.* "Aye," he agreed, then stumbled down off the parapet with a backwards glance over the wall.

"The boy has not awoken?" He asked her the question as he carefully descended. The Strength still suffused his limbs, and as he closed his hand on the rough wooden railing, it cracked.

"Wounded first. He's not dyin', just gone," Idgen Marte murmured. And indeed there were men who were closer to death than not. She paused to finger the crack that ran along the railing where he'd touched it, and added, "Mind you don't speed 'em on."

There was one dead Raven, and another whose arm hung by a thread. Ivar knelt next to him, pressing a dressing to the wound which slowly and weakly pumped blood. The gap-toothed, black-mailed Raven captain leveled steely eyes at Allystaire as he approached. The paladin ignored her, laid his palm as carefully as he could on the man's wound. The mercenary, a round-faced, broad-shouldered stump of a man named Donal, groaned weakly. His voice rose in volume and pitch as the wave of the Mother's Healing flooded into him.

First, the bleeding stopped, then the bone righted itself with an audible snap. Donal cried out still louder, a dry scream, then sagged against his captain as new flesh sealed the wound and all trace of it, save the rent in his mail and the pallor of his cheeks, vanished.

Allystaire rose without a word, though he felt Ivar's eyes boring into his back as he moved to Keegan's side, who squatted low near one of his own. The archer straightened up and shook his head as the paladin approached.

Allystaire knelt by the man anyway. His shoulder was completely smashed in, his arm in tatters, and there was a flat patch of his skull where it had been nearly crushed. Either wound alone would kill a man for certain. He felt only the faintest beat of life. He tried to feed it, gently, as he might blow on a spark in a lantern.

The man's life steadied, and held on, but that spark did not catch. Allystaire tried to pour the Goddess's Gift into the man, but found his flesh already dying around him. Not knowing how, he could feel the man's panic, could sense the spirit within him flailing blindly in fear.

Her words, heard so long ago, came to his mind then. *Comfort the dying,* she had said.

Allystaire thought, for a brief moment, of the men he had seen die on the battlefield, or after it. Thought of his own father, the hardest of a hard lot of men, dying with a leg lost, the way he'd been reduced from an invincible giant to a shriveled man gone old before his time, and he seized upon those moments, those memories, tried to imagine what it was like for those men who were facing a final battle they couldn't win, and the vast unknown that lay beyond.

Those memories made a bridge to the man Allystaire knew he couldn't heal, and he reached out to the dying spirit that quailed and raged in its fear and pain. And he remembered then that this man had spent time—months? years?—as a Chimera, a pitiful half-man, half-animal, mad with the rage of the senile God of the Caves.

Calm, Jeorg, he thought, not knowing how he knew the man's name. *You need not fear. The Mother waits for you.*

Jeorg, the man's weakening spirit answered. *That…that is my name. I am a man. I am a man and not a beast.* Allystaire had impressions of the man's life all in a flash: a peasant in Barony Innadan working the vineyards gone for a soldier. A soldier who broke, one day, and ran, with no more choice in it than breathing. A deserter, yes, but not a coward.

Yes, Allystaire reassured him. *You were a man, and you died a man, and if you look for Her in the next world, the Mother will ease the pain of your passing and soothe the suffering of your life.*

Jeorg. Died a man.

The thought was so faint Allystaire barely understood it, but he felt the fear melt away, the panic dissipate, replaced with the impression of warm sunlight on acres of vines, of a tidy cottage, of sand-rimmed Innadan lakes. Allystaire sensed a distant brightness hovering beyond the man, and then his spirit faded as well.

Allystaire stood, popping quickly to his feet. "I am sorry, Keegan. He was beyond the Mother's Gift of healing. I could only comfort him on his way."

Keegan nodded faintly and sighed. "He hadn't spoken since ya saved us. None of us knew him from before. He spent a long time as a beast—maybe the longest of any of us. Not sure he understood why he was fightin'."

"His name was Jeorg," Allystaire said. "And he was much the same as the rest of you, and I mean that as no insult. He remembered who he had been."

Keegan nodded, then tried to clasp Allystaire's forearm. The paladin shook his head. "I dare not, Keegan. And again I mean no insult. Her Strength fills my limbs. I might break your arm."

The rangy man grunted, scratching at the side of his head. "If ya say so. I'm happy t'be yer man in this fight, Allystaire, or Lord Coldbourne or Arm or Lord Stillbright or what'er yer name is now. I'd rather not die in it, though, all the same."

"I do not want anyone to die in this fight, Keegan," Allystaire replied, before turning to go. He stopped then and looked back. "Stillbright?"

The man shrugged. "Just somethin' goin' round last night after that first skirmish. I didn't pay it much mind."

Allystaire turned towards Renard and his militia, but the bearded man waved him off. "None bad enough hurt here. Go'and see t'yer boy. We're gonna need him before this is done."

He looked over the militiamen. As Renard had said, none of their wounds seemed all that threatening. The wounds of their flesh didn't, at any rate. Allystaire had long since come to know when fear threatened to overwhelm a man's good sense, and he saw it in the wide whites of their eyes, in the skittish movement of their feet and hands.

Luckily for him, Renard saw it too and turned, bellowing orders. "Right. Enough standing around for you lot. Back up on the wall and a weather eye for those things. The Arm's got better things t'do than stand around nursemaiding the Mother's own fighting men, eh? He's not the only one around here can kill some manky corpse, right? Let's prove it."

Despite himself, despite the battle and the rage, Allystaire grinned as he listened to Renard work. *The man is an artist,* he thought, as he set off for the Temple, feeling the Goddess's strength flooding his limbs with every step, turning over the battle and thinking on the army beyond his walls as he walked.

CHAPTER 35

The Feel of Gold

"Well," Nyndstir said, crouched in a copse of trees with the rough wooden walls of Thornhurst in the distance and a half dozen other swords-at-hire circled around him, "I wouldna want t'fight that bastard." The bastard in question was standing atop the wall in glittering armor, screaming, as he ripped apart one of the sorcerer's monstrosities by hand.

"What's this? Our bold, bearded Islandman boaster a craven?" That from one of the southerners with his curved sword and fancy words.

The Islandman turned, spat, and clouted the southerner so hard with a balled-up fist that he wouldn't have been surprised to see blood trickling out of the ear he'd struck. The man gave a cry and tumbled over.

Nyndstir spat again, on the man for good measure. "We may be brothers o'battle for the time being, southerner, but some words don't get said to Nyndstir Obertsun, and craven is one o'them. Now pick yourself up. We're t'report back."

With that Nyndstir stood, wincing at the way his knees and back shot with pain as he moved. He leaned a little more heavily on his axe than he'd have liked as he walked, with no great relish, back to their little camp.

It was a good hundred span north and forty span or so off the road behind a tangle of trees, and it was damned hard to see even for a man who knew it was there.

In fact, as Nyndstir and the three other scouts he was detailed with drew near, he almost felt as if something was trying to twist his attention away from it. For just a moment, he stopped, staring at the bare-limbed trees and finding his vision sliding away from them, till he gave his head a shake and locked on the small clearing, the circle of ragged shelters, and the small fire burning.

He did, for just a moment, wonder how the smoke from the campfires didn't clear the treeline and why he couldn't smell it till he was stepping within the circle of warmth. But he knew the answer lay with the remaining wagon and the men within it and that was not something Nyndstir liked to ponder overlong.

Both sorcerers had brought their own crews, and met up just a few miles north of their current position, so there was still some sorting out among the hired men of just who was in charge. The men paying the links didn't seem to care much; they issued orders to whomever was convenient.

Still, among those who made their living with weapon in hand, there was some sorting out to do. An order needed establishing. Nyndstir didn't much care for the yoke of responsibility, but when he looked around the camp at the score and a half of men who were pointedly ignoring the angry sounds coming from inside the wagon, he snorted and spat again. He was doing a lot of spitting these days. Even the men he'd pulled for his party, including the one he'd clouted, drifted away to their tents, their bottles, or just into the woods.

"Well, I'm not gonna stand here watchin' you lot holdin' yer cocks like boys ain't figured out what they're for yet," he growled, and marched up to the wagon, giving it a sharp rap with the back of his hand.

The sounds inside ceased, and the tongue he didn't speak and didn't like the sound of broke off with a whispered hiss.

"What?"

"Back from the job. The, ah, attack. Didn't go well." When delivering bad news, Nyndstir thought, understate.

The door flew open. The yellow-eyed one, Geth something, Nyndstir thought, glared at him from the dark interior.

"Do you think we don't know that, you great fool?"

Nyndstir shrugged heavily. "Ya told me t'watch and report, so that's what I'm doing."

"Well then," the man said, his voice faintly ghostly, focusing those awful pools of glowing yellow that filled his eye sockets on the Islandman. "What did you see?"

"I saw somebody in real pretty armor tearin' your, ah, troops, t'pieces and tossin' em over the wall like so much broken crockery. With his hands."

"We felt them destroyed. But no man can contend with a Battle Wight for strength."

"Well, I'm reportin' what I saw, and I'm not one t'lie t'the man with the weight. He climbed up on the wall screaming his damned head off, picked one of them, and ripped it apart like fresh bread. Did a number on the rest of 'em too."

"'Pretty' armor?"

Nyndstir shrugged again. "Bright silver. Could've seen it gleaming from twice as far away as we were, seemed like."

"And what was he saying?"

"Ah, I believe he was askin' for you to face him yourself. Had some comment on your willingness to do so."

The sorcerer opened his mouth as if to scream, and Nyndstir didn't like, at all, the way that sickly yellow glow started to emanate from the man's throat. But then it was cut off, as another voice—a voice that felt to Nyndstir's ears like getting scraped over barnacles had once felt to his back—came from inside the wagon.

"Gethmasanar," it said, thrumming slightly. "Do not lose yourself in petty anger. All is not lost." A string of links, gold and silver, flew with unerring accuracy from the darkness of the wagon and landed at Nyndstir's foot. "You have done good service, Nyndstir Obertsun. You will continue to do so. Wait for darkness. Organize some men. Move forward and retrieve the pieces of the Battle-Wights the man in the pretty armor threw over the wall. Can you do this?"

Nyndstir eyed the links, but didn't bend to pick them up. "I can."

With that, the wagon door was shut as the sorcerer withdrew, and Nyndstir found himself glad to miss the rest of the conversation.

Finally he bent and picked up the links, but for perhaps the first time in his life, he found that he didn't much like the feel of gold in his hands.

* * *

Inside the now darkened wagon, Gethmasanar seethed, the yellow energy that leaked from him growing darker, pulsing visibly.

The other presence in the enclosed interior spoke calmly, though the words were slightly distant, distorted.

"He has left us our raw materials, and we should never run short at the place of a battle anyway. That is the entire point of the procedure. Eventually we will have enough and we will overwhelm them. Now to the matter of Bhimanzir's lost apprentice."

Gethmasnar let out a quiet harumph. "On that point at least we may claim victory. I felt him come into contact with one and spring our trap. I am quite sure he is accounted for."

"Do not be sure till we have the body, and may study it."

"He is done for, I tell you. I felt his will flee his body."

Multiple points of blue light moved in the air as the other sorcerer stood. "Yes, but did you feel him die? Know you for certain that his flesh is quiet?"

"There was nothing of him left."

"On this point, Gethmasanar, we must leave no room for doubt."

"We'll sift the rubble after our Wights have done their work, then."

"That will not be sufficient. When their collapse nears, you shall have to move close enough to make sure of the boy yourself."

"Iriphet," Gethmasnar began haughtily, "surely we need not be so cautious over a barely trained boy."

"Silence." Iriphet's voice was barely loud enough to be heard, the echo of it fainter still, yet it hung in the air as Gethmasanar instantly obeyed. Trails of blue streaked across the small interior till the elder sorcerer stood directly before the younger, whose eyes lowered to the ground.

"It was at your insistence, Gethmasanar, that the boy was given to one of the Knowing. Though he was the least among us, Bhimanzir's power should have been sufficient to clear this land of its threats. Had he been here by himself, certainly he would have succeeded. Instead, we allowed you your fancy and planted with Bhimanzir the seed of his own destruction. You have come perilously close to loosing the Negation upon us by handing it to the very power

Bhimanzir was dispatched to counter. That has not gone unnoticed by me, nor by the Eldest."

Gethmasanar remained silent, eyes upon the floor, letting the power that danced unsubtly behind the words wash over and through him.

"Certainly, Bhimanzir shares some of the blame," Iriphet went on. "For not realizing and unlocking the boy's true potential. For his failure, he paid, but do you realize the enormity of what happened? Do you realize that a primate with a hammer killed one of the Knowing? Death does not come for such as us in this way, Gethmasanar. Never."

Iriphet turned away and Gethmasanar lifted his head, eyes narrowed. The other sorcerer's retreat granted him new leave to speak. "There are those who have fallen in battle."

"To infighting, yes," Iriphet allowed. "To a lucky Thaumaturgist, as those dabblers style themselves. To cursed Dwarfish Stonesingers, though we long ago won that war. And perhaps, under great duress, to a stray arrow or a freak chance of a greater battle. The man was a prisoner, bound to Bhimanzir's rack, the secrets of his power ours to know, according to his final message to us. And then he is dead. That, Gethmasanar, is unique to the history of the Knowing. And it will remain unique. Go and bend your hand to some useful work now. Likely by now the Baron will have gotten some of his men killed and wounded. Material and fuel. Send some of the men to gather it."

CHAPTER 36

Shadows

Allystaire strode into the Temple on legs he expected to go weak and wobble at any moment. That they did not, that the Goddess's song still sang in him was worrisome, though it had receded to the back of his thoughts.

Mol sat before the altar, cradling Gideon's slack neck in her lap. Allystaire rushed to her side and knelt. He reached up to remove his helmet, but thought better of it when he imagined it crumpling in his hands.

As carefully as he could, he extended his left hand, and gently lowered the palm onto Gideon's bare forehead.

He felt the perfect health of the boy, and nothing else.

Allystaire pulled his hand away, gingerly, and straightened up on his knee. Too much flowed and warred within him to notice the pain the joint would ordinarily spear him with.

"Mol? Have you any insight?"

The girl, her hood pulled back to reveal her features, didn't respond at first. Her face had lost none of the odd change that had come over it, the strange ageless quality, but some of the wisdom of her presence seemed diminished, her poise ruptured. She looked, in short, more like a girl of twelve or so years than she had since Allystaire had returned to Thornhurst.

Finally, she lifted her head and looked straight up at him, her brown eyes unblinking. "I think it was a trap, meant just for him. I…I don't know if it worked." She swallowed hard. "I can't hear him, Allystaire. And I don't know if he can hear me." She paused a moment, then added, "I can't hear Her, either. For the first time since the reavers."

"Her? The Mother?" Allystaire tried to keep his voice even. "Have you always?"

"Almost always. And when I didn't, I knew it was because there was something I needed to understand on my own. I always knew She was watching me. I could feel it. Now, the Longest Night. Gideon seemed to think it would be soon. Perhaps She is weak because of it?"

"Mol," Allystaire said, leaning forward, reaching for the girl before he remembered the strength that lingered in his hands and dropped them to his sides. "She is still watching. Her song lingers in my mind, and Her strength fills my limbs. That means Her people are in danger, yes—but it means She has not abandoned them. She never would."

Mol gently slid her legs from beneath Gideon's head, lowering him carefully to the stone floor. He didn't respond, just went on breathing slowly, almost imperceptibly. She stood and moved to Allystaire's side, putting her arms around his neck and leaning for a moment against him. He resisted the urge to return her embrace.

"Promise me it can't end like this," the girl murmured as she pulled away. Her eyes were large in her face, frightened, but dry, and their gaze was steady. "We have so much work left to do."

"So long as any strength remains in my arms, no monster, no sorcerer, no slaving Baron will have Her people uncontested," Allystaire replied. "I will tell you what I once told Her. If the whole world arrayed itself against us, and I was left to face them alone, I would." He stood, careful to step away from the girl and the prone boy. "Find him, Mol. Do what you must. Get Torvul if you can. We will need him if we are to see the dawn."

He watched her kneel beside Gideon again, and lay her hand upon his forehead. He wanted to kneel beside the girl, call the boy's name, heal him, pull his mind back from wherever it had gone. Allystaire's hands clenched at his sides, and for a moment he was afraid to move, afraid to touch anything, for the power in his hands had still not abated.

He is as close to a son as I am likely to have, Goddess, he silently prayed. *Please.* Allystaire could not finish the thought.

"We remain in danger, Mol. I have to see to the walls."

The girl nodded, but didn't respond. She knelt over Gideon, murmuring words Allystaire couldn't catch. He turned and was halfway to the door when her voice rang out.

"Allystaire—did the people bring their animals inside the walls? Cattle? Dogs?"

"Some, I think," Allystaire allowed. "Torvul put aside lumber for a cow pen to be built along the north side. Cold, he probably built it himself while he should have been sleeping. Why?" *Not sure why,* he thought, *but did not say. This cannot last long enough for us to be slaughtering cattle.*

As if she plucked the thought from his head, Mol said, "Torvul did it because I asked him to. Animals have a great value to Her people, and thus, to me."

"As you say, Mol," Allystaire said quietly. With a last look back at Gideon, he slipped out the door, stepping gingerly, trying not to rip it off its hinges as he went.

* * *

"I've been on shit jobs before," Nyndstir said to himself. "I've collected corpses and pieces of corpses, dug jakes, hauled garbage, butchered meat," he murmured as he crawled along. "Dug graves, repaired wagons, shod horses, built pyres, burned bodies on them, built cairns, hauled water, ale, wine, mead, cheese, meat, salt, bread, fruit, tents, lumber, stone, iron, peat, and coal," he went on, pausing to check the wall, to check his side for cover, and to think of more shit jobs. "Cleaned armor, sharpened weapons, repaired sails, portaged boats, and stood more guard duty'n half o'the soldiers in this barony put together." On one wonderfully memorable occasion, he'd volunteered on a hunch and found he was guarding the officer's brothel and that his silver spent there just fine despite having no badges tied around his arm. "What I wouldn't give to be crawlin' drunk and dazed outta that place again," he said.

He was enumerating these things to himself because no matter how dangerous, boring, or odorous any of those tasks had been, none of them had compared to crawling around in the dark looking for pieces of those things the sorcerers had unleashed upon the town.

It didn't help that there was at least one bastard up on the distant wall who could see him and his detail and had already put a bolt through one of the two southern lads he'd brought with him, if the southerner's distant, wheezing cries were any clue.

If they were after real bodies in order to give them a proper grave, Nyndstir would've had no qualms about standing up weaponless, waving a hand, and asking for a brief truce to gather them. He'd done it a dozen times before.

Nyndstir knew that he didn't deserve a truce for what he was doing.

Cold, he wasn't real sure he wanted one.

So they crawled, staying behind what cover they could, and picked up bones and bits of metal, but more often things that looked like bone and felt like metal.

He shivered every time his hand closed over something like that. Him, Nyndstir Obertsun. He hadn't shivered in the cold since he was six summers, or thereabouts, and he couldn't remember shivering in fear.

But there was a kind of wrongness about these things that he hated, hated from deep down, and he didn't want to be putting them in a sack and bringing them back to the sorcerers. No good would come of that.

Nyndstir gave a brief longing look at the wall that loomed in the dark in front of him. *Being honest with myself, I'd rather be the other side o'that,* he thought, and he found himself wondering how good his throwing arm might be with his sack of bones and bits, only to realize it was all he could to do to lift it.

Besides, you took their links. You take a man's weight, you do the task he sets you, he told himself.

Maybe it wasn't much of a code. It wasn't something the bards sang or told stories about. But going against it had never done him any good.

So Nyndstir crawled and ducked and hugged the earth as tight as he could, feeling the cold seeping into his bones like an old friend—there was no cold here like island cold, anyway—and he kept finding pieces of Battle-Wight and stuffing them into his sack.

Nyndstir found himself reaching for something—a hipbone that glittered like tarnished silver despite the dark. His fingers brushed it and it was numbingly cold. It stung.

Then something whizzed out of the darkness. He felt it brush past his knuckles, drawing a burning line across them, and impact the bone he held. Sparks flew. He tried to shut his eyes but his night vision was ruined, so he pulled his arm back tight to his body and curled behind the fold in the ground that offered cover.

"Cold and salt but that hurts," he bellowed, more in surprise than pain, really, though it did hurt, the flesh ripped open in a thin but deep cut.

Much to his surprise, a deep and powerful voice answered him from the darkness beyond. "Then don't be skulking around outside my wall!"

"Braech's scaled balls, man, I'm not bringing the fight to ya. I'm not even armed!" Nyndstir had to summon his wind and work to project his voice.

"I can see what you're doing," the voice replied. "And if you think being armed changes anythin', you're talkin' to the wrong one of us!"

"Well which one am I talkin' to?"

"You've got the pleasure of addressing the Wit of the Mother and the best crossbowman you're ever likely to meet. Pull your head but half a span to the left and I'll make sure that hand troubles you no longer," he added with a rumbling cackle.

Cold, how can the bastard see that well at this range? Nyndstir wondered to himself.

"I already did for your men. Well—one of 'em might be alive still, but not for long," the voice called out. "I was aimin' for his heart and got a lung and I'm sorry for that. The other one died fast and clean. I'd do the same for you."

"Both of them? Now I've got to carry three times as much of this back t'our camp," Nyndstir yelled. "If my man's hangin' on I don't suppose you could take him in and treat him, eh?"

"I'll check but I wouldn't count on it. And I can't just let ya walk away."

Nyndstir didn't answer. Instead, he hunkered down and began gathering himself, tensing muscles and stretching them without moving much, taking in quick lungfuls of air and pushing them back out.

In one fluid movement he rolled up onto his knees, heaving the sack of bones onto his back, and then levering himself upright onto his feet.

Then Nyndstir engaged in an act he typically found distasteful: he ran, a bagful of bone and Battle-Wight on his back providing cover. He hoped.

His hopes proved fruitful when he felt something punch him in the back with enough force to nearly knock him over. Thank Braech and Fortune it was nearly, because if he'd gone down he probably wasn't getting back up. Instead, he was able to keep his feet, zig and zag between bare trees, and finally gain the cover of the more thickly wooded road.

All the while he was anticipating another punch in the back or a burst of pain at the back of the skull.

He slumped behind a thick tree trunk, slinging the bag off his shoulder and heaving for breath. He felt sweat on his forehead and cheeks cooling in the winter air, and gave a snort of disgust. "Young man's foolishness, this," he muttered, then spat in disgust.

"What has a young man got that I haven't?" He stood back up, slung the heavy bag defiantly onto a shoulder. "Fewer scars, less know-how, and a smaller cock," he muttered, answering his own question. The hike the rest of the way back to camp was easy enough, though it tried to elude his eyes again. The big boxy wagon was still there, and in the darkness he thought he could see hints of color through its doors and shaded windows. Not of torchlight, but of unearthly blue and sickening yellow.

Still outside the camp, he reasoned. *Doubt the idiots on guard have seen me. Could just sod off into the woods, dump this lot into a stream, and tell them the bowshot was too strong and they had the range.*

Nyndstir looked into the woods, then back at the wagon, considered the bag on his back, and spat again. Then he squared his shoulders and took an angry, stomping step towards the wagon.

"Took their weight," he muttered as he shifted the burden he carried.

He neared the wagon, paused as he heard raised voices, two that he didn't like hearing and a third that he didn't recognize.

He suddenly realized there was a fully armored knight standing in front of the wagon. Cloaked in green and wearing a surcoat with the Delondeur Tower quartered with a symbol he didn't recognize, a ship sitting atop a spearpoint, the knight was only up to his shoulder, but that was typical; Nyndstir was used to being the tallest man in sight.

Nyndstir chuckled inwardly as he studied the knight's arms. *Inlanders and their pretty pictures,* he thought. *As if any of 'em know the first two things about seamanship anyway.*

A shout, followed by quieter murmuring, came from inside the wagon. The knight standing at the door started to reach for it and Nyndstir cleared his throat.

"I wouldn't. Ya don't walk in on such as them uninvited. Trust me."

The knight turned to him. "Mind how you address me, man. I am Landen Delondeur, Heir of the Baron and one of your employers."

Nyndstir dropped the bag at the knight's feet. It landed with a heavy metallic clank. Then he fixed the steel-clad youth with a hard stare, to see if he could get that visor up. Nyndstir wanted to see the knight's cheeks pinch, his skin flush, his eyes cut away from the force of an islandman glare.

The visor did come up, but Nyndstir was the one whose skin flushed. Instead of a young knight's affected mustache and pale cheeks, he was staring at the sharp cheeks and sea-sky grey eyes of a young woman.

Nyndstir Obertsun was ill-equipped for the series of recalculations he was forced to make in the moment. Landen Delondeur never stopped staring back at him, never moved.

So he inclined his head—not a true bow, but just enough to satisfy—without lowering his eyes.

"Beggin' your pardon, m'lo…m'lady" he rumbled. "I'm sure the sorcerers won't mind bein' interrupted. By all means."

The door of the wagon swung open, spilling blue and yellow sorcerous light across the camp. Another armored, green-cloaked fellow stomped out. Him, though, Nyndstir knew by sight. White-haired, but sizable, back straight despite the steel he wore, wearing a cloak and surcoat of fine green silk over his green and gold armor, and the sword he'd won fame with at his side.

Lionel Delondeur took in both of them with a moment's glance. A smile creased his features, split his beard, as he clapped Nyndstir companionably on the shoulder, saying roughly, "Good to know we've Islandmen with us, eh Landen? Toughest men around. Tougher than Harlachan mountaineers even."

"M'lord," Nyndstir said, bowing a little deeper this time. "Good t'serve," he added, thinking that if he were actually serving Lionel Delondeur—whose grip was not too diminished with age, the Islandman thought—he might have more of a stomach for all this.

"The horses, Landen," the Baron ordered lightly. "And round up their draft animals," Nyndstir heard him say, as he walked off. "We need to cart our wounded over to this camp."

Nyndstir felt a cold tightness in the muscles of his belly, looked at the sack of bones and metal at his feet, and found that his stomach for any of it had just about died.

* * *

The rest of the day had been quiet, to Allystaire's surprise. The Goddess's song receded but did not vanish. He saw to the wounded and the dead, silently thanking the Goddess for how few in number the latter were, then walked a circuit of the wall with Renard and Idgen Marte in silence.

As they walked, Allystaire was struck by how small the size of the ground they had chosen was. But then, Thornhurst was no true crossroads; just the space where the barony road rose towards its meeting the old High Road as it paralleled the Ash. The inner village held just over a score of buildings, closely built upon one another, where the road really began its upward sweep. There were no points within the boundary of the walls where he couldn't see the stone oval of the Temple.

Near the end of their circuit, he stopped, faced the Temple, and took a heavy breath. *Let me be equal to this, Goddess,* he prayed. *However it must end, let me meet it well. Let all of us.*

He felt a sharp rap of Idgen Marte's knuckled fist upon his armor, and turned to face her, finding her eyes hard and her face sharp. "Enough of that," she muttered.

Renard, leaning upon his spear, heaved a small sigh. "That's odd, you know. Unsettling. When any of you five start talking in your heads and answer aloud."

Allystaire turned a quizzical eye on the bearded veteran. "You know of this?"

"'Course I do. Mol told me. Cold, she showed me once. She can speak to any of us that way. I'd wager she can speak to anyone she likes in their mind."

"Can she hear them answer?"

"Aye," Renard answered, nodding faintly, his coif clinking lightly against his mail coat. "Said she'd only do it at need, that most of us weren't prepared for it, could hurt us. Only you lot could truly stand it, something about the touch of the Mother upon your minds."

"Renard," Allystaire said, drawing a step closer to him and raising a hand as if to clap him on the shoulder, only to see the canny old soldier back up.

Then, grinning, Renard said, "I'll take my chances with the Delondeur troops and the patchwork monsters, but I've no wish to see my shoulder crushed to rubble because you got maudlin, Arm."

Allystaire and Idgen Marte both laughed. Allystaire's mouth quickly drew back into a line and the mirth that briefly flared in his dark blue eyes vanished altogether. "Renard, if there is a way to get some of the folk out, to escape before this draws to its end, I want you to leave with Leah. A man with a child coming has obligations greater than any other."

"Don't you tell me what my obligations are," Renard said, with sudden heat creeping into his voice. "I'll be staying right here, child or no."

"Renard—"

"Don't," the man said, shaking his head sharply from side to side. "I decided to follow you those months ago—seems like more than months—regardless o'where it took me. I was puttin' silver in my purse, but a man can't live on silver, not and feel like a man. And when you called me out on what I was doin' in front o'that fat man's toybox, well, I felt shame like I never had. And I thought, well, I'm done taking that greasy silver. Decided I'd rather see where a man like you was goin'. A man with naught more than I had, arms, armor, will to use them, a better horse maybe, standing alone in front of a man with spears at his command, and a priest with a bully of a God behind him, and tellin' 'em no." Renard's gruff voice made the word somehow triumphant. He went on after a breath.

"Maybe they were petty lords, but they were men used to forcing their way, like the bastard slaver outside is, and you wouldn't let 'em have it." He didn't wait for Allystaire to nod before rolling on. "And now I know what you are, and what she is," he said, pointing at Idgen Marte, "and Torvul, and Gideon, and Mol, well, now I'm not going anywhere. Not because I think it's grand to be part of a story bein' born, though mayhap I'll look back and think it so some day. Lords and heroes alone don't win a battle, yeah?" He paused again, wetting his lips.

"Someone else has got to do the little work, the organizin', the shoutin', the cursin'. Other folk, folk not blessed with Her Gifts, have got t'be willing to look at the bastards who own everything and want more still, and tell them no the way you told the fat baron and the Choiron. Maybe all I got is this," he said, hefting his spear and butting the bottom of the shaft against the ground. "For the first time in all the years I been carryin' it, I can know for cert I'm usin' it on the better side o'the fight, for somethin' more than silver. For the first time, maybe the only time, I'm fighting for my own home, my wife, my child, all things I'd not have if not for the Goddess. You don't get to take that fight away from me, paladin or not."

The soldier's defiant outburst hung in the air a moment, till Idgen Marte stepped forward and took his arm in hers. "Brother of Battle," she said quietly, and he echoed her, a faint flush in his cheeks.

"Renard," Allystaire said softly, "I have known dozens of knights and lords whose deeds minstrels sing of, men in glittering armor on horses whose blood-lines make Ardent look like a nag, with every manner of axe and sword and mace and hammer made to their own hands by master smiths. And there are none of them I would rather have next to me than you."

"Fine," Renard said, rolling his shoulders beneath his mail and shifting his eyes from one to the other of them. "Can we stop all this rot and get back t'work now?"

Allystaire and Idgen Marte laughed and resumed their walk. When they reached the north-facing gate, Renard moved off to resume his post and talk to his militiamen. Idgen Marte started to head towards the scaffold, and then paused and looked back.

"Should you be posted here in case the Battle-Wights come back?"

"No guarantee they will come back to this gate. They could attack either gate, or both. We need to get the men some cudgels, staves, maces—anything heavy. I cannot be everywhere, and if we face more than eight or ten, or they attack in two places…" He trailed off, shrugging.

"I can borrow Torvul's head-knocker," Idgen Marte replied. "Gather up stones and…"

"…drop them from the top of the wall? Let the fall do the work for us," Allystaire said, nodding approvingly. "Can you get up a party for it?"

She nodded, glanced to the wall, and then back to him, resting a hand upon her hip. "We're going t'need Gideon," she muttered.

"I know," Allystaire said, nodding slowly and biting the inside of his cheek. "I cannot imagine that the Goddess would let him be taken now."

"I don't think She's got anything to do with it." She toed the ground and kicked at a frosted clot of dead grass. "I like to think She has a plan, or a goal— but She told us herself that none of it is fated, none of it is destined. Whatever happens, we have to make it happen. And pay the costs."

"Gideon cannot be the cost. Not now. Idgen Marte, She told me in the chapel, during the vigil—the order She Called us, it mattered. We are…" He grimaced, searching for the words. "I think we are the phases of light in its struggle with the darkness of night. Mol at the very fall of twilight. You, at the darkest time, when light exists only in shadows. And Gideon…"

"Is like unto the dawn," Idgen Marte said, echoing the Goddess's words. "I know."

"Well, if dawn is to come then it is up to us to pass through the night. The Longest Night."

"That'll be in the next day or two. If I'm any judge."

"Gideon thought so, apparently."

"Knowing him, he's likely right. Anyway, why haven't you northern barbarians a decent horologist or star-gazer about to know these things for certain? And your seasons, your damned longer winter and summer. You people don't know a proper spring here."

"I am sure the Rhidalish kings employed one or two such men, and I am equally sure they took a good look at the start of the Succession Strife forty years ago and scarpered off back to wherever they came from."

She waved a hand in the air dismissively. "Back to the watch with you. I'll be listening for any word," she added, tapping the side of her head.

Allystaire made quick work of the walk back to the other gate. Stretching his muscles gave some vent to the song that pulsed in them, but what he knew he wanted—what the song wanted, what his Gift wanted—was an enemy and room to swing.

Too soon he was back on the scaffold, and equally too soon the sun had all but vanished. Torvul was nowhere to be found, so Ivar had the wall, along with a thin scattering of Ravens. The mercenary captain kept her eyes staring off down the road, where a few burnt out farmstead buildings were visible as shadowed hulks from the glow of campfires as the Baron's men bivouacked among them.

"Ivar, what is it that you do not approve?"

"Not my place to approve," she said, with a shrug of her mailed shoulders. "I'm a hired spear only."

"Nonsense. We have too much history to—"

"History you've forgotten," Ivar said, lofting a gob of spit over the wall. "The Allystaire Coldbourne I followed never would've cornered himself at bad odds. Never would've chosen t'believe fool notions of goddesses and defendin' peasants," she added, heat rising in her voice.

"The man you followed is dead, Ivar," Allystaire said, his voice calm and even. "There is no more Allystaire Coldbourne."

"Oh, and don't I freezin' know it," the woman replied with a vicious laugh.

"You took my sister's weight and agreed to serve."

"I know Cold-damned well what we signed on to. We just didn't know who we were signin' with. We'll stay here and die for our silver 'cause that's what we're expected to do, aye? That's what we were always expected to do, even in the old days when you didn't take airs you weren't born to."

"I cannot make you believe and I will force no man to profess my faith. If what you have seen with your own eyes cannot convince you, nothing I say will. I know you are not a coward or a traitor, Ivar, so I will not warn you against it." He took a deep breath and went on. "If we are to die here, at least I know I am not doing it for silver."

"I don't want t'die here at all," Ivar said. "Not in Delondeur. In Oyrwyn, maybe. Innadan if I must. But here?" She spat again, shaking her head all the while. Then she grabbed her spear and walked off down the scaffold, turning her back to Allystaire.

Allystaire sighed and looked out over the walls towards the distant camp, but only for a moment, as he heard the tramp of Torvul's heavy boots behind him.

"They sent men t' collect the parts of those monsters y'destroyed," Torvul grumbled. He leaned, sagged really. His eyes closed. Then he pulled himself upright and took in a deep breath of air. "I got two o'them," he said, patting the crossbow that was slung across his barrel chest. "Third got away. Talkative sort. Things were different, seemed like he might not be a bad man."

"He is on the wrong side of the wall till he surrenders," Allystaire said. "How much did he get away with—and what can they do with it?"

"A right heavy bagful, and I'm not certain. Make more of their Wights, I s'spose."

"You know of these things?"

"Have read about, never seen," Torvul replied. "It's a practical thing, I guess, if awful."

"What do you mean?"

"What are two things no battlefield is ever going to run short of? Corpses and broken bits of metal," he said, answering his own question. "You make the one remember what it was to be a man and the other what it was to be a weapon and then you fuse 'em together into one awful whole."

"Any thoughts on how to fight them?"

"Funnel 'em your way?" Torvul stopped a moment, cocked his head to one side as if listening to some distant voice. "I...no. Not just now I don't. There was a time when my folk contended with sorcerers, or so the lore is sung. I've not the weapons or the knowledge. I'm sorry."

"Not just now? Meaning you did once, or you might?"

"I told you that's how the lore is sung. Ya remember anything I've told ya about my people, ya'd know some of what that means. My magic, such as it is, the craft of it—it is nothing to what my folk could once do. I would be among the meanest of apprentices to the truly gifted. They were artists to give sorcerers pause," the dwarf said wistfully, his eyes drifting off towards the distant camp.

"Artists?"

"If something is worth doing it ought to be done beautifully," Torvul said, then waved a dismissive, frustrated hand. "Enough, Allystaire. I haven't the time to try to explain. Unless I were very lucky and came upon him unawares, I don't think I have what's needed t'fight a sorcerer on my own."

"Then we need Gideon."

"Aye. I went to see the boy while you were walking the interior. I've got no potions that'll touch him, I fear. If Mol can't reach him…"

"He is not dead, and he is not gone. Not forever."

Torvul didn't answer. He lifted his crossbow and flipped up one of the crystals, sighting down it. "Looks quiet for now. Think it'll keep?"

"Not all night. No reason you cannot grab some rest."

"There's every reason. A moment spent asleep right now is a moment wasted."

"Fine," Allystaire said, dropping his voice. "We need to prepare a fallback position, and get all the folk inside the walls ready to move into it."

"The Temple," Torvul said. "It's the only building they'll all fit in. Not likely they can get a fire hot enough to burn the stone. Might be the sorcerers could."

"What can we do to shore it up?"

The dwarf sighed heavily. "Makeshift barricades, I suppose. I can do some work on the doors, bless them—"

"Bless them?"

"Are you going daft on me again? Didn't I just say that?"

"What good will blessing them do?"

"You've got your Gifts, boy, and I've got mine. I'll explain when I have to."

"Fine. Get up a working party. I have the wall."

"This'sll help with watching the night." The dwarf reached into a pouch and removed a familiar potion bottle, motioning to Allystaire to hold out his hand. "The other one," Torvul groaned, when Allystaire held out his right hand. The dwarf carefully squeezed a few drops onto Allystaire's bare palm, dipped a finger into them, and motioned again, indicating that Allystaire should bend down.

The drops were carefully massaged into the skin around Allystaire's eyes. When he opened them, the night was already growing lighter and clearer.

"Lady be with you," Torvul said, and then trudged off. His first two steps were taken wearily, slowly, but as he descended the ladder he seemed to gain strength and speed, and Allystaire heard his voice booming as he moved on, calling out names.

Allystaire narrowed his eyes as he looked in the direction of the Delondeur camp. He felt weariness creeping into his limbs, and a yawn cracking wide his jaw. He looked to the sky; it was heavily clouded, with little star or moonlight. For a moment he thought he saw a shadow passing across it, but it was just as quickly gone.

He lowered his head and closed his eyes, trying to push his thoughts into the world surrounding him. *Gideon?* The thought was aimed nowhere, everywhere.

There was no answer, not even a ghost of one, not even a sign that he'd been heard. *We're going to need you, Gideon. We cannot do this without you. It will take the five of us, together, to do the work the Mother set us.*

He tilted his head to the sky, slowly opening his eyes. It was brighter yet than it had been, but shadows teased at the corners of his vision.

He let his eyes slowly unfocus as he lowered them to the ground.

Then, much too close to the wall, he saw shadows, man-shaped shadows, flitting among the bare trees.

He stared a moment, and his vision focused and brightened even further. Wearing dark grey cloaks and carrying ropes with hooks tied to the end, a party of men, perhaps a dozen, moved with careful swiftness on the walls. They didn't make a sound that wasn't covered by the normal sounds of the night, the wind, horses picketed nearby.

His first instinct was to raise an alarm, and he was filling his lungs with a deep breath to do just that, when he suddenly went silent, tried to look calm, dragged his eyes away from the surreptitious forms.

Idgen Marte. Check your frontage. A dozen men are advancing on this gate with rope and hook, trying to go unseen.

And you saw them? He could feel the mockery even in her thoughts, and smiled at the sense of relieved mirth it brought him.

Torvul's potion helped.

Our frontage is clear. Renard has lanterns out, and men patrolling the walls in pairs with Torvul's flare bottles. I'm coming to you.

Ideas?

Allow me to show them what Shadows mean to the Mother.

* * *

Moments later, Idgen Marte was crouching at the farthest end of the scaffolding in a pool of darkness so impenetrable that even with Torvul's potion, Allystaire could only feel her there, not see her.

He'd sent off the half dozen men upon the wall as if for a regular change of watch, and started walking it alone, a shining beacon of a target. His shoulder blades had started itching before he'd made his first turn.

The whistle of a thrown rope, the slight metallic clink as a hook, expertly aimed, clinched into the wood not much more than an arm's length from him. The rapid, biting thud of boots with climbing studs ascending the wall. *These men,* he had the time to note, *are professionals.* Then the crown of a man's head, hooded in dark green over a thin helm, appeared. He felt Idgen Marte dash into action farther down the wall.

Allystaire darted for the man nearest him, grabbing him by the arm he'd just thrown over the timbers of the parapet. The knife he held—its blade blacked to keep from betraying its wielder—clattered away as Allystaire broke the wrist with a simple squeeze. Then he raised the man high and tossed him over the back railing of the scaffold. The man let out a shout of pain, cut off as he hit the ground with a thud.

Beneath the scaffold, Allystaire heard the men he'd ordered off the wall rush to their fallen enemy, and winced despite himself at the sound of fists and feet thudding into him.

The rest of the interlopers had made the wall by then. Blades were drawn, and the Arm of the Mother moved to meet them with hammer and fist, while at the other end of the scaffold, the Shadow worked towards him with knives and speed.

It did not take them long. By the time the first three lay dead, leaving eight still upon the scaffold, Allystaire simply backhanded the next he came to across the face. He felt the jaw shatter, saw and heard a meaningless babbling moan of pain and blood coming from the ruined mouth, when one in the middle suddenly threw down a short sword.

"Yield," he said. "We yield! Lay down your arms," he yelled to his men. "We are beaten!" Knives and swords and a hand axe or two thunked to the scaffold. One man still waved a knife vaguely in the air at a patch of shadow in front of him, till Idgen Marte appeared behind him, twisted the knife out of his grasp, kicked savagely at the back of each of his knees, and threw him down upon the narrow boards.

"Your captain told you to yield. I'd take that order," she said, bending down and resting the point of a knife against the nape of the man's neck.

Allystaire pushed his way along the scaffolding towards the leader. He seized him around the collar and lifted him easily off the ground.

The man struggled, to no benefit. He was taller than Allystaire, with broad shoulders and a lean build, a closely cut brown beard, and a finish to his gear that suggested family weight, if not title.

"Your rank, your company, and your mission," Allystaire said, looking up into the man's eyes.

"Captain. The Long Knives. And…havoc," he replied.

"What do you mean, havoc?" Allystaire asked, though he knew full well the answer.

The man swallowed. "I yielded. You may ask me no questions about our plans! It is not done!"

"It is now," Allystaire roared, lifting the man higher. "Now tell me—what is meant by havoc! You cannot resist my question. Do not try."

The man twisted feebly in Allystaire's grasp, kicked out at the paladin's knee, but without any way to leverage his weight properly, the blow simply glanced off the armor.

"Set fires," he finally said, his voice thin and strangled. "Slit throats. Kill animals. Note the layout, and then slip back over the wall."

There was a pause, till Allystaire suddenly lowered the man back to the scaffolding, but did not release him. "Whose throats?"

"Any," the man said, his voice very thin and harder to hear now.

"Did you have any specific targets?"

There was more struggle, the man twisting in Allystaire's grasp. Ravens and militiamen had started to filter back to the top of the scaffold, gathering the fallen weapons and taking rough hold of the surrendered warband.

Finally, the captain's resistance broke again under the assault of Allystaire's Gift, even as the paladin stood silent and unmoving.

"The girl-priestess," he finally said, choking on the words. "The boy, too."

Allystaire stepped back, releasing his hold of the captain, who instantly began massaging his neck.

"You come on a mission to murder children of less than thirteen years," Allystaire muttered quietly, icily. "And yet you would lecture me on the niceties of battle and the rules of treating prisoners."

"They're peasants. I'm a brother of battle, captain of a warband with friends and family who'd ransom me handsomely."

"Pick up your sword," Allystaire said, retreating a step and lowering his hammer to the planks of the scaffold, letting it sit upon its head with the handle straight upwards.

"What?"

"Pick. Up. Your. Sword." Allystaire's voice was probably quieter than it had been since the battle had been joined the night before, yet the silence around made it deafening. Though the men around him couldn't have seen his face, many took an unconscious half-step away.

"I yielded," the man protested, backing away. "You all heard it."

"Pick it up, or die unarmed. It makes no difference to me. Will it make a difference to you?"

The man hesitated a moment, then fell to his knees, extending his hands away from him.

"You all see this," he yelled. "Your paladin! Your holy knight of song, prepared to murder a man who has yielded."

Allystaire. Idgen Marte's voice was sharp and reproachful in his mind. *You cannot.*

I shouldn't. But I can.

No. He could feel Idgen Marte tensing, ready to leap between him and the captain if need be. He turned to her.

The captain saw Allystaire was distracted. The paladin heard only the flit of steel against leather and by the time he looked back to the captain of the Long Knives, the man had slim blades in each hand and was lunging him.

Allystaire felt one of the blades slip through his greaves and into his left knee. The other was foiled by his armor when the man tried to slice it up into his armpit.

The paladin reared back and brought the crown of his helm straight down onto the top of the man's skull.

There was a tremendous and unmistakable crack.

The captain of the Long Knives was dead, Allystaire was sure, before he hit the ground, though he twitched for a long while. He pulled the knives free, the one from his flesh and the other from his steel. He took a moment to heal himself, pressing his left palm to his neck, then raised one knife in his right hand, held it out towards the gathered remnants of the warband, and crushed it by closing his fist.

"If any of you would-be murderers opens your mouths without a question put to him, goes for a weapon, refuses a request, or attempts to hide information from me when I ask it, you will get the same. Who will tell me what they know, be it rumor, order, or speculation, about the rest of your Baron's plans?"

The top of the scaffold was suddenly abuzz with eager volunteers.

CHAPTER 37

The Rest of the Message

Bannerman Orin Milfair was not, if he really thought about it, entirely sure he'd made the right decision in agreeing to carry the paladin's message back to the baron's camp, but he'd been the highest ranking man left alive after Captain Tierne's head had been crushed, and it had been his duty.

As the paladin had told him in that bone-rattling chill of a voice, *Going over the wall and firing the town and slitting throats had been your duty, and you went to that eagerly enough. Returning to the Baron who holds your contract and speaking the truth of what happened should be far easier.*

Sneaking and skulking had been the stock in trade of the Long Knives as long as warbands'd had names. Creeping in darkness, scaling the walls to spread confusion and terror, kill guards as they slept, start fires, poison wells. Once or twice, memorably, their action alone had been enough to tip a battle one way, but more often they were simply another arrow in the quiver, as the Baron liked to put it.

Milfair felt naked, walking out upon the road with his weapons stripped from him, and the cold biting through his leathers and his heavy cloak. Any moment he expected an arrow in the back from one of the hard-eyed zealots who'd given him a good kicking after he'd been tossed off the scaffold during the fight, by something that flitted in behind him that he hadn't even seen.

"Unnatural," he muttered, though he recalled, earlier in the day, as the wounded in the Baron's camp had been carted up and trundled over to the other camp, the secret camp that only officers were supposed to know about, and tried not to think too hard about what was unnatural on his side of the wall. Orin hadn't been with the carts, but he'd talked to men who had, who spoke of how the wounded grew frantic and how many had tried to run when they saw their destination, and the screams the men pushing the carts had heard.

The carts had been empty when they came back.

While he was lost in this thought and what it meant he found himself challenged by the pickets. Milfair had to search his mind for the countersign, and by the time he gave it, a man in a green tabard with a freshly painted shield and a new-looking spear had come forward to glare at him. The spear point hovered towards him for a moment, then slid away once he responded. Even so, he held out his hands and spread his cloak wide to show the empty scabbards on his belt.

"I've got parole to bring the Baron a message, then I'm t'give myself back up," Orin told them.

"What're you, a knight now?" He didn't recognize the man who'd challenged him, but they shared the general camaraderie of soldiers on campaign, something they fell into as naturally as breathing. Milfair had found that few enough of the men on this expedition were truly veterans. It was easy to recognize those who were.

"Never that," Orin responded with a nervous chuckle. "Just point me to the watch officer and from there I can get to his Lordship."

The other soldier gave him directions and he followed them dumbly. Soon enough he was saluting and reporting to a dark shape huddled close to a brazier.

"Bannerman Milfair, sir, of the Long Knives," he stated. "Returning with a message from the enemy for his Lordship."

"Well let's hear it, Bannerman," the officer snapped.

"With respect, sir, it was laid upon me to speak my message to the Baron himself."

"The Baron is in conference in the other camp, and unreachable. We are not to send messages for him there," the officer replied. "He left specific instructions on that score."

Milfair sighed, "Have you any suggestions then, sir? I am to report back to my captors within two turns of the glass."

"Nonsense," the officer said, waving his hand. "They were fools to let you go. I'll find two other officers to witness and you can make your report to the three of us."

Once again Milfair felt that tiny prickle in his back, that thought that he was the fool. "As you will, sir," the Bannerman replied, still standing stiffly, trying not to eye the brazier, or the stand with the carafe upon it that, he was certain, he could smell wine in.

The officer waved a hand and they moved towards the center of the camp, where higher ranks, knights, lords, and officers were camped. There weren't too many of the former, but eventually the officer, who wore the Tower-and-Spear of the newly formed unit full of half-trained guards, merchants sons, and new volunteers, was able to round up a knight wearing yellow and purple with a crest of a horse rearing upon a wall, and another Salt Spear officer wearing expensive armor, but with no crest of his own.

The knight must've been a minor one, for Milfair, having fought all over the baronies for his entire adult life, didn't know the crest. *A sword-at-hire with a sir is still a sword-at-hire,* he thought, dismissively. The three officers found an empty tent, complete with seats, braziers, lit lamps, and wine for themselves while once again leaving Milfair standing to in the cold.

They'd also gathered a scribe, who fussed with his writing-case and produced from it parchment, ink, and pens, though he muttered constantly how it was too dark to do any proper writing.

Once all was finally ready, Milfair stepped smartly to the front of the camp table they'd set up. "I would like the account to show, m'lord, sirs, that I attempted to carry out the charge laid by my captor to deliver my message to the Baron himself."

The scribe began scratching at the parchment, tsking all the while under his breath. The knight, who had a greasy blond beard and hair, slapped the table lightly with the flat of his hand. "Out with it then, man. The night is cold and we've other duties."

"Very well, m'lord," Milfair began. "I was told by the pal—"

At this he was cut off by the original officer waving a hand. "Give the man no undue titles. His name is Coldbourne."

"Yessir. The first part is that I was told by Coldbourne that upon our retreat from Thornhurst he would be willing to release the other captured members of the Long Knives based on certain conditions."

"How is it that you failed so singularly in your charge?" The officer had a careful way of speaking, an educated polish to his words, that put Milfair off even as he tried to match it.

"They seemed to know we were coming, sir," Milfair replied. "Killed the first few men over the wall and then Captain Tierne ordered us to yield."

"If Tierne was alive to order a surrender, then why does he not stand before us?"

"He ordered it, sirs, but then the…then Coldbourne asked questions of him. The answers were, ah, not to his liking."

"Why did Tierne answer them?" The knight leaned forward, blinking weary, red-lined eyes. "Why was this Coldbourne even asking? That is bad form, to put questions to a man of rank who's yielded."

"I don't think Coldbourne is too concerned with those kinds of form, m'lord," Milfair said, then swallowed as he felt a droplet of sweat, despite the chill, run down the back of his neck. "And his questions—they must be answered."

"Torture, then? By a self-proclaimed paladin?" The knight sat back, waving a hand dismissively. "I ought to ride forward and call the upstart out."

"No, m'lord. No torture. He just asks. And then something bright and hard seizes your mind and the lies and evasions that spring up into it can't pass your throat. You choke on them, and then you tell him the truth. That's what Tierne did. And then he died."

"What? How?"

"The paladin killed him."

"A yielded foe?"

"Tierne slipped his knives into his hands. Then he sprang at Coldbourne with them, and got a crushed skull for his troubles." Milfair swallowed again, and said, "There's more to my message, sirs and m'lord."

"Go on, go on," the first officer waved, then poked a finger at the scribe. "Are you recording all of this?"

"Aye," the man answered, annoyance plain in his voice and features. "Even the nonsense about paladins and truth magic," he added with a weary sigh.

"You'd not call it nonsense if it'd been done to you, you cowardly scraper," Milfair spat at the man, who simply ignored him. Then he cleared his throat. "Ah, he also says he will turn the bodies and effects of the men who died over to us upon our retreat," he said delicately, "provided that it is proven to his satisfaction that benefits are paid to their surviving kin." He paused. "I think I have that right. Bit longwinded, Coldbourne."

"And that is all?"

"Not quite."

Milfair spun around, his hands clenching into fists, because he hadn't been the one to speak the words. The voice was a woman's, husky, angry, and a bit terrifying, but there was no one and nothing to be seen.

"The rest of the message is this," the voice went on, sounding as if it came from behind him, behind the gathered officers, who were also scrambling dumbly to their feet, knocking over the table. They nearly upset the scribe's writing case, but he deftly pulled it into his lap, even as he fell from his stool and tried to gain his feet.

"That if you wish to play a part of this out in shadow, with fear and flame, then know that we also will do this, and not with murderous warband men as our tools."

Then a woman's shape, tall and dark and little more than an opaque silhouette, was standing behind the first officer and plunging something into his shoulder. "We will do it with the power of the Mother," she said as she leaned forward. Though she seemed an insubstantial figure of shadow, the knife point that pressed through the officer's mail on the right side of his chest seemed very real, and very wet.

Before any of them could react with drawn weapons, the Shadow was a blur among them. The other two men cried out as the knives slashed at them, the form wielding them slipping in and out of sight, then a brazier was kicked over, and the lamps smashed and flames were licking the sides of the tent.

The scribe had run for it and Milfair heard him screaming outside, raising an alarm. He heard more hard wet sounds of knife meeting flesh.

Milfair knew when it was time to run, and so he did, putting the burning tent behind him and emerging into the dark of night. Regular torches lit the camp, as did the campfires, so he could see a clear path, but he made it no more than a few span before something tripped him, and then that same voice was at his ear.

"This message was supposed to be for the Baron himself. Make sure you tell him that if you've not got the courage to come back inside the walls of Thorn-hurst like you said you'd do. Tell him the Shadow of the Mother is longing to meet him again."

Then the voice was gone and Milfair was briefly alone in the chaos of the camp waking up to an attack in its midst.

Orin Milfair thought of that bright and hard thing that had seized his throat back in the village and made him speak truth when he'd wanted to lie, and of the blurring Shadow that had just wounded, maybe killed, three well-armed and trained men like they were children. They frightened him, and he was no parade-ground soldier.

But what frightened him most, somehow, was not returning to face the paladin. What frightened him most was giving that man, that bright hard thing within him, reason to notice him, reason to judge him and find him lacking.

So Bannerman Orin Milfair got to his feet, and started pumping them down the road. When he made it past the pickets, he could still hear the noise and alarm behind him, and he began worrying at the stitches of his patches of rank, three green circles, upon his sleeves.

* * *

"In my own camp!" Lionel Delondeur raged. "An assassin! That woman that follows him about, it had to be!"

The raging, the volume of it, was a problem for Nyndstir for two reasons. First was that it was keeping him from sleep, which very little had the power to do. Second was that it meant an assassin had come for the Baron and failed. *Shoulda made freezing sure,* he thought to himself, as he rolled out from under the wrapping of furs he'd pulled right near the edge of a campfire. Nyndstir sat up, feeling his age, and listened to the baron yell.

Delondeur had been in council with the sorcerers earlier that night and had taken the long route back to his own camp, and then returned at haste with a strong mounted guard all bearing lanterns.

Not very well hidden anymore, he thought to himself, eyeing the Baron's guards standing about in the leafless wood, lanterns forming shifting pools of light, as he stood, rewrapped his furs casually about himself, took up his axe, and went looking for something to drink.

He didn't wander too far, though, because he wanted to hear more of this. Why, he wasn't sure he knew; knowing the plans of men like the sorcerers and the Baron was a good way to find yourself included in them, or dead.

"We must hit them with everything. Everything, as soon as we can," the Baron was yelling from inside the wagon. There was some hushed discussion, as if the sorcerers were trying to calm or dissuade him.

Nyndstir was staring hard at the door of the wagon when it suddenly opened, and he turned back to his search for a drink. Finally among the jumble of packs he found a clay jar that sloshed promisingly, uncorked it, and had a sip.

The Baron stormed out, cloak billowing dramatically behind him, and immediately his lantern-bearers surrounded him.

"Why the lanterns, Baron?" Gethmasanar followed Delondeur out, the yellow trails leaking from him hanging sickly in the air behind him.

"She calls herself the shadow. Keep it bright enough around me to banish shadows and the witch can't find me," the Baron huffed.

"I see." The sorcerer paused. Nyndstir liked to imagine that he was holding in laughter, but didn't think he wanted to know what a sorcerer's laughter sounded like. "No doubt we can devise a more effective protection, given time."

"There isn't time," the Baron yelled. "I want this town erased, this religious nonsense stamped out, I want Coldbourne's head. And his witch's, for good measure."

"We want the man Allystaire," the sorcerer replied. "As well as the body of the boy, the dwarf, and the girl priestess. You may have the witch."

"I'll have what I Cold-damned want," Delondeur yelled. "You've been paid a lord's ransom, thrice over, to help me get it. Make it so."

"We will have new Battle-Wights ready in short order. If you launch an attack as soon as you can, in force, we can have more than a dozen of them moving in to support you. Mayhap as many as a score. If your men can force the wall we'll be able to overwhelm them in no time. Perhaps it is time you ask the religious forces with you to commit themselves."

Delondeur spat at the ground. "They're observers only, or so they say. That Choiron was cagey about sending any of his so-called Dragonscales. The priest his Marynth left with me is an idiot and a coward and hasn't more than half a dozen ceremonial guards. She kept the rest in Londray to, as she put it, stamp out the last sparks of rebellion. The Archioness says she can petition Fortune but that too many of her soldiers already spent their lives here. It's my men, yours, your creatures, and you. It's time you showed on the field yourself."

"We are waiting for certain favorable conditions. We will send the Wights. If they all prove insufficient, we will make more Wights, and eventually they will overwhelm the walls and the peasants upon them. It has never failed us before. It will not fail us now."

The Baron spat again, kicking at the ground. "Dead men draw no pay, at any rate. Fine. We'll launch our attack within the turn. Get your men into it as soon as you can. I'll leave you two riders to coordinate with our camp."

Freeze this, Nyndstir thought. *M'not stayin' here t'be turned into one of those things.* He hefted his axe and walked off a few paces, grabbing at the fur and armor belted around his waist as if he were heading into the woods looking for a likely tree.

Once he was outside of the wide pool of light cast by the lantern-bearers, he trotted off. He wasn't the best or quietest of scouts he'd ever known—that'd have to be an elfling he once rode with, down from the tundra in some kind of exile—but he'd picked up some woodcraft here and there, and in the darkness, and with no proper guard kept up, Nyndstir Obertsun disappeared into the bare trees, only pausing to reach into a pouch on his belt, pick up a big handful of silver and gold links, and toss them on the forest floor.

"Have your frozen weight back, bastards. Choke on it."

* * *

Renard, Ivar, and four militiamen led away the string of securely tied prisoners. Allystaire watched them move off into the village, trying not to clench his fists hard enough to rip his gauntlets apart.

"We've every right to put them in the ground," Idgen Marte said, her voice thick. "They came here meaning to murder Mol."

"And Mol will decide what to do with them when this is done. And we may need them to bargain with."

"You already decided what t'do with their captain."

"He made his choice when he stabbed me."

She grunted and glanced down at the array of weaponry, mostly short blades, that had been stripped from the Long Knives. "What'll we do with these?"

"Pass them to every man and woman who wants one. Those with children especially."

"Allystaire!" The shock in her voice told him she had understood his intention instantly.

"What would you have them do, Idgen Marte? If we fall, they will be tortured with exquisite care and forced to renounce the Goddess. And when they are messily killed in public, it will come as a mercy," he whispered harshly. "If nothing else, I would spare them that."

"Fine. Where's the dwarf?"

"Doing what he can to secure some defenses about the Temple. It is time to move them into it. Lionel has probed and played at strategies with us so far. If he wants to take the walls by main force, he can do it simply by attacking in more places than we can defend. And it is what he will do next."

"How do you know that?"

"Do you think this is the first time he has besieged me? He is impatient by nature. The weather and the politics will make him moreso, but this is his method. Two attempts with craft, a third with a bludgeon."

"Fine. I'll take the weapons over and then start going to houses and rounding folk up."

He nodded. "We will need all of Chaddin's men, and anyone Renard says can manage to fight from horseback, gathered centrally. I will need Ardent and as stout a lance as can be found."

"I'm not your freezing squire," Idgen Marte protested.

"I know, but you can move faster to give out those orders than I can, and while Torvul's potion lasts," he said, pointing at one eye, "I want to stay on the wall."

She nodded and turned away into the darkness, streaking off. He climbed back up the scaffolding. One Raven and a handful of militiamen remained on guard, and he strolled back and forth among them for a few minutes.

"Ya ought t'sleep, m'lord," one of the Ravens said carefully as he passed.

"There will be time for sleep when this is done," Allystaire answered, with a practiced, gruff ease that he did not feel. In truth, he was scared of sleep. He felt no fatigue, no weariness of battle; the Goddess's strength kept it at bay. But he remembered the toll he'd paid for employing her Gift in the past and did not like to think what would happen when the Song no longer filled his limbs.

He turned his eyes out to the fires of the distant camp, wishing for one of Torvul's looking-tubes, or another potion for his vision.

But even without them he could see men moving, a mass of shapes too far away to be distinct. Too many shapes for a change of guard or a simple patrol. Then larger shapes, mounted men, moved to the forefront, carrying with them a bubble of light, like torches or lanterns gathered for a procession or a fete. The sound of a drumbeat, faint but regular, reached his ears.

"I know you too well, Lionel," he muttered. "And I am going to end you."

"What's that, m'lord?" The solicitous Raven leaned towards him, trying to catch the murmured words.

Allystaire filled his lungs with air and bellowed. "STAND TO ARMS. Delondeur moves again, in strength! To the walls, all who can hold a spear or draw a bow!"

Did you hear that? This he directed towards Idgen Marte and Torvul. *Lionel is coming for us with everything. As I knew he would.*

I've only just got to Chaddin. Getting his men mounted and armed will take time, thought Idgen Marte.

That's not enough time to get folk to the Temple, Torvul's strained voice came back to him. *I've only just started.*

Leave that to me. Mol's voice sounded, clearer and more powerful than Allystaire had ever heard it.

Then her voice again, like a herald's through a speaking-trumpet. *Folk of the Mother! Of Thornhurst! All of you to the Temple, now, with your kin. Leave behind your possessions. Now! All who can bear arms, to the walls at the side of the Arm, the Shadow, and the Wit! Worry not for your beasts, for I will send them to safety. Now move, all of you, at once.*

Allystaire knew from the reactions along the wall that all of the men gathered there heard it too.

He unslung his shield and secured his left arm through its straps. His right hand found his hammer and slid it out, letting it come to rest head-down, haft up, on the floor of the walkway next to him. "They are going to need time, men," was all he said at first. Then he thought for a moment, rolled his right shoulder, and said, "Any spears, rocks, throwing axes—anything that can be hurled and that we can spare, bring to me."

* * *

Nyndstir had turned his course north, intending to make for the high road and the towns along it as it approached the Ash. Somewhere among them a merchant would need a guard or a tavern would want someone to calm the rowdies. Or, Cold, the greenhats in some larger town might need another man on the wall. He was never short of work in winter.

He didn't get a quarter mile before the thought came to him. *You did their freezing work and took more weight than you tossed back.*

Nyndstir stopped, set down his axe, and leaned on it a moment. "My left stone for a young man's wind," he muttered, breathing heavier than he expected to.

He turned and started walking back the way he'd come, swinging his legs in long, determined strides that ate up ground.

"What the Cold am I gonna do when I get there? Piss on the ashes?"

He walked on.

* * *

Allystaire held out his right hand and a nearby villager dropped a heavy stone into it. He cocked his arm, turned his hips into it, and sent it sailing into the night.

His vision still brightened by Torvul's tincture, he followed the arc it described before crashing into the shield of a Delondeur man in the formation as it moved up the road, saw him fall and cause another couple of men to stumble to the ground around him.

All alongside him, the villagers and Ravens peppered the advancing line with bowshot, most of them simply firing into the mass. Torvul alone seemed to carefully pick his targets, and every one of the dwarf's bolts that Allystaire followed seemed to find a mark.

It is not going to be enough, Allystaire thought.

The Delondeur forces had already paid in the past fighting, but so had the defenders, and it was never an equation that had favored Thornhurst. And even as they advanced, the Delondeur column began to spread out into longer lines with sizable gaps, their flanks spilling well off the path and into the rise of hills on either side.

"Do not waste arrows," Allystaire yelled. "Choose targets and aim, or hold!"

What I wouldn't give for some light horse to hit the end of their lines and turn them straight around, he silently cursed. Without the threat of mobile troops hitting their sides, they were free to string along in those loose lines and minimize what his archers could do, despite the height they held.

Behind those lines, Delondeur had drawn up his heavy horse, fifty or better. Half a dozen banners hung above them, unreadable in the darkness even to his brightened eyes.

With a frustrated sigh, he held out his hand again, feeling the heavy haft of a spear settle into it. *Throw with the legs, through the hips and trunk,* he thought, recalling long ago lessons from the previous Castellan at Wind's Jaw, Ufferth of Highgate, Garth's father. Even as the weapon flew straight and true, splitting a Delondeur shield and the man behind it through the thigh, he remembered a fellow page's complaints. The spear was the weapon of the levy, the peasant, not fit for a knight's hands.

Ufferth, who'd looked like a barrel on legs and from whom his son Garth had gotten his fair complexion and pale hair, had clouted the boy across the head with the butt of one. *And those peasants'd spit you like a capon for the cookfire, you frozen shit,* he'd yelled, disgusted. *A weapon is a weapon and no man is fit to be an Oyrwyn knight who disdains the one that comes to his hand at need.*

Allystaire gave his head a quick shake, snapping back to the moment. The Delondeur foot were making the final push across the last dozen yards. Rocks and other spears joined the thickening arrow fire. Nearly a score of Delondeur men dropped, but the rest rushed to the wall.

They'd been forced to build straight, rather than with the curves or breaks for overlapping killing fields that Allystaire would've preferred, so with the men right below them, it was a good deal harder to get his aim, especially with the solid thicket of shields.

The Delondeur foot swarmed to three points: the west gate, and yards away along the north and south. Allystaire would've bet his arms they were assembling ladders of wood and rope to be thrown over the wall.

Idgen Marte! Are Chaddin's horse assembled?

Aye, she replied. *And I'm nearly there.*

We cannot repel them at all three points. Cold, not even at two. And we will be flanked and overrun if we do not. Can you delay them at the southern point?

He looked to the southern part of the wall, saw hooks tossed over its top and pulled firmly in. *And quickly!*

Suddenly she was there in his sight, poised carefully atop the rough timbers of the palisade, bow in hand, leaning with a dancer's balance over the side and shooting down as men climbed towards her.

Hooks on ropes, with flexible ladders attached, were being thrown up at several points. One was no more than a step to his left, so he darted to it and ripped the hooks free, tossing them back over the wall contemptuously. The sound of armored men crashing back to the ground reached his ears.

But he could not be everywhere, and it was apparent that Delondeur was throwing his main strength against the gate and the scaffold along the wall above it, perhaps four score men.

Against which Allystaire had barely a dozen, and more than half of them barely blooded.

"They are going to make the wall," he yelled, years of practice carrying his voice above the din. "Bowmen fall back. Spearmen to me."

He saw the clutch of village archers hesitate a moment, and yelled again, "Fall back twenty yards and prepare to cover us!"

Delondeur men were clearing the wall in three places along his parapet, and the work was about to turn close. Ivar spitted one in the belly with her spear, quickly pulled it free, and then darted it down over the wall. A muted scream and then a louder muddled one as men fell back to the ground.

Allystaire bounded to another rope-and-hook ladder, saw a helm rising above the wall, swiped at it with his shield. He felt the shock of the blow up his arm as the metal rim of his shield stove in the side of the man's helm, and his skull with it.

Unluckily for Allystaire, the momentum of his blow carried his target sideways off his ladder instead of down it, and more men swarmed up in his place. He ducked away a few steps, retrieved his hammer, and came back swinging.

Where he went along the parapet, such as it was, foemen died, their skulls crushed, chests caved in, knocked back over the wall or to the ground below.

But he was one man, and the wall was too much for him to cover alone. He saw Ivar fighting desperately, spear a blur, another Raven overwhelmed and a Delondeur footman viciously thrusting a short, broad dagger through a rent in his black mail and into his ribs.

Allystaire fought his way there, swinging hammer and shield both in wide arcs and sending men tumbling, but the mercenary was dead by the time the paladin reached his side.

Torvul! He wondered if the dwarf could sense the panic in his mental voice.

Ready as we're going to get. I'm bringing up Keegan's lot to cover your retreat. Back wall does us no good either.

Allystaire sucked air deep into his lungs and shouted. "The wall is lost! Fall back!"

Something, some instinct, some sense of a battlefield bade Allystaire turn to his left and raise his shield. At nearly the very instant he did, he felt a hard thump as something bit into it and stuck. His eyes darted over the rim to see a Delondeur footman pulling another throwing axe from his belt.

He squatted, shortening his torso and thrusting hips out behind him, putting as much of himself behind his shield as he could, and bulled forward. The axeman released, but too late, and his weapon bounced away into the night. Allystaire was already cocking his arm as he ran forward, and at the moment of impact on his shield he straightened his legs and brought his hammer down.

He had misjudged the angle; instead of the skull, it crashed hard down on the man's left shoulder. The force of the blow sent bits of mail flying into the darkness and the man collapsed, screaming as blow crumpled the left side of his torso, driving the shoulder down into his chest.

Allystaire spared a quick glance for the wall around him. His section was clear, but wouldn't remain so for long. Ivar and the remaining Ravens were pulling back, keeping enemies at bay with veteran spear-work. He looked out over the wall. Delondeur's horsemen were closing. A thought struck him. He slid his hammer back onto his belt and ripped the throwing axe free from his shield.

It was well balanced, with a long head and a very faintly curved haft. He looked out over the line of mounted and armored men.

Near the standard of the tower, he told himself, and he picked out a likely suspect, cocked his arm, adjusted his aim, and threw.

* * *

Baron Lionel Delondeur watched with calm approval as the shapes of his men swarmed over Coldbourne's pathetic excuse for a wall. The strong bubble of lantern light he'd ordered kept around him didn't carry too far into the darkness, but each squad of foot carried a torch or two, and the night had brightened as some cloud cover moved away from the moon and stars, so he had a commanding view.

"Runner!" At his yell, a footman dressed in leathers and lightly armed appeared at his stirrup. "Go find Captain Verais. Give him my compliments for his attack. Tell him that once they have the wall he is to secure it and allow our horse to stage within the village before we advance."

"Yes, my—" Something flashed out of the night and beside the Baron's horse, which shied away several steps. The runner's words were cut off in mid sentence with a horrid wet gurgle. It took Lionel a moment to wrestle the charger back to his command amidst a sudden clamor.

The man he'd just issued orders to crumpled to the earth, a throwing axe embedded where his neck met his shoulder, blood pumping freely from the wound. The soldier twitched and struggled, more and more feebly, as blood poured from the rent in his neck. Finally, he went still. The knights and lords around him seemed impressed and fearful, chattering uselessly to each other.

"Impossible throw."

"At such a distance."

"Warlock."

"Madman's strength."

Delondeur silenced them with a yelled order. "Forward the horse! The foot will have that gate open or I will have every tenth man lashed!"

He gave his charger the spur, and the animal dashed forward, iron-shod hooves churning over the fresh corpse of the message runner like mud.

* * *

"Well," Nyndstir muttered to himself as he crested the hill, "at least I didn't miss everythin'."

Down at the bottom of the slope he could see a small group of Delondeur spearmen struggling to assemble their rope ladder.

"Get that ladder up! We're missing the fun, lads," one of them boomed, all fake cheer and stupidity, announcing their location and intent to anyone nearby. "C'mon, there's the knack," he added as the flustered men fumbling with it finally got a few of the wooden slats straight.

Can just hear the freezing stripe on his arm, Nyndstir thought disdainfully. He considered his position. He had elevation and surprise, but there were five of them, and likely more within earshot.

What I wouldn't give for a throwing axe or two, he thought. *Even the odds a bit.*

But then some other part of him rebelled at the thought. *Evening the odds wasn't always my way.*

Before he knew it he was striding down the hill, axe in hand.

He heard one of the idle men, huddled in his cloak and stamping his feet in his boots, say to another, "Can't wait to get in there and start burning something, eh?"

The other one snorted. "I'm thinkin' more about gettin' into somethin' warm," he replied, with the sneer of a man certain of his prospects of plunder. Nyndstir knew it well.

"Cold, did that bastard just go to his dungeons and hand out spears?" Nyndstir called out to them from a few paces away. As one, they jumped in shock and whirled to face him. *Freezing amateurs,* he inwardly cursed. *Didn't even post one man as a sentry.*

The one Nyndstir had picked out earlier as a chosen man turned to face him, hand on his short sword. "Do not be speaking of our Lord Baron Delondeur that way, Islandman. Not when your own Sea Dragon blesses him, and us, with victory this night."

Nyndstir didn't get the chance to answer, because one of the shirkers pointed a finger vaguely at him. "Steady—aren't you one of the hired men from the other camp? I've seen you about. Shouldn't you be joinin' in? There's work for all hands."

"I'm about to," Nyndstir replied, then brought his axe in a tight, controlled swing straight into the neck of the man who'd just spoken. It cut through mail and leather and bit deep into the flesh, blood spilling out in torrents as he pulled the blade free.

The others were too shocked by the sudden attack to respond immediately, so Nyndstir had time for a second cut at the chosen man. He swiped low, taking his legs out from under him and knocking the man to the ground with a scream as he fumbled for the shortsword he never had time to unsheath.

One of the shirkers came at him with his spear leveled, but it was too close for that kind of weapon to do much good. Nyndstir took one step to the side, then another towards the man, and brought the haft of his axe in a vicious uppercut into the bottom of the spearman's chin. His legs flew straight up as he was taken off his feet, and his head thudded resoundingly against the ground.

The two men fumbling with the ladder finally disentangled themselves from it. One went for his spear, which he'd leaned against the timber palisade, while the other drew a knife from his belt.

The other shirker was also coming with his knife, and he held it like a man that knew from knife fighting, in a crouched guard, with the blade forward and his body a small target, bouncing lightly from one foot to the other.

Nyndstir quickly backstepped a few feet and sent a whirling cut towards the man's head, which he easily ducked beneath, then did the same on the backswing of the spike that balanced the heavy blade.

Nyndstir grinned in the darkness, feinted another cut. The grin became a smile as the man took the moment to dart within the axe's arc, knife out. In the starlight, Nyndstir could read the greedy, triumphant smile on his opponent's face.

A quick step to one side, a reversal of the axe in his grip, and the would-be knife fighter's smile turned to a grimace as he charged his belly straight onto the first six inches of the axe's footlong spike.

Nyndstir pulled it quickly free and drew back a heavy boot, kicked the man in the wound, and sent him sprawling with a scream.

The fourth spearman took a look at his three dead or dying comrades and turned away, running into the night.

"He'll be back with other men," the last remaining soldier warned him, knife held out awkwardly as he backstepped, free hand searching behind him for the wall and the spear that rested there.

"Don't see how that stops me from killin' you," Nyndstir said with a shrug. He lunged towards the man, raising his axe in a feint. The green-tabarded soldier dropped his knife and ran, knocking his spear aside as he went.

Quickly, Nyndstir secured his axe to his back, strapping it in place with heavy leather thongs that were stiff from lack of use. He looked at the three men he'd felled: one dead, one dying, one twitching and trying to roll over to push back to his feet. He gave that third one a couple of solid boots to the ribs, and the man crumpled to the ground in a ball.

Then he picked up the tangled remnants of the rope ladder and found the bit he needed: the hook. That he tossed over the top of the wall, thanking Fortune when it set on the first try. Grasping it in both hands, he lifted one leg and placed it squarely against the rough-cut timbers, and then pulled himself up and did the same with the other leg.

The muscles in his shoulders protested, but he gave his head a sharp shake, and hauled himself up with quick steps, wrapping the rope around his forearms as he went.

"Been up as many walls as I have, ya never lose the knack," he muttered, congratulating himself as he crested the wall.

The congratulations turned to a curse as he realized there was nothing on the other side, and he tumbled over into a longer drop than he'd been ready for.

"Cold dammit, there's usually some freezing steps or a parapet or something." He pulled himself out of the dirt, giving each limb a careful shake to see that they were still in working order. Then he unlimbered his axe and ran off towards the sounds of fighting.

* * *

Allystaire pulled himself into Ardent's saddle, ripping a lance free from the ground where three had been planted for him, points driven into the dirt to hold them up. *In another life I would've run a squire off his feet for doing that,* he noted absently.

Around him, Chaddin's score of men were similarly mounting and pulling lances from stirrup boots. Not all of them were armed and armored to function as heavy lancers; some were unfamiliarly couching spears under their arms.

"Chaddin!" Allystaire bellowed, searching for him amidst the crowd of riders. Finally one of the better-armored figures rode up to him, pushing up a visor. Chaddin sat his horse a bit stiffly, and he kept shifting his grip on the lance.

"We do not want to come straight up against their foot," Allystaire told him, once he could see his face. "They are all spears, and would tear us to pieces. But I think your father means to bring up his horse, and we have to give them a bloody nose, keep them from racing beyond us. A loose line, charge only at my command, and remember, it is not a freezing tourney list. You are trying to kill them, and they you."

Beyond them, there was the sound of commotion and frightened shouting, as the folk of the village poured into the Temple. Torvul had worked a minor miracle, erecting barriers made of carts, barrels, crates, even his own wagon. At the moment, the dwarf, laden with a heavy crate and leather straps full of tools, was trying his best to empty the contents of his boxlike home into the Temple one trip at a time.

Renard, his clearly frightened militia, and the remaining eight Iron Ravens manned the makeshift barricade, spears and bows at the ready. Mol glided among the crowd, stopping to speak with children, or with the most obviously frightened. Idgen Marte moved along behind her, a heavy sack in one hand, from which she drew the confiscated weapons, pressing them into the hands of unarmed adults that passed by.

The sound of horns in the distance froze the scene for a moment. Allystaire listened to the pattern of the blasts, then said, "They are calling formations, trying to organize. Let us not do them any favors! Horse, forward with me!"

He nudged Ardent and the destrier responded, tugging at the reins he clutched in his shield hand as he and twenty of Chaddin's loyalists went off to meet the Baron's horse.

They hadn't far to go, and Allystaire had surmised correctly; the Baron was drawing all of his horse inside the walls, screening them with infantry as he drew them into lines. At a quick guess Allystaire thought he was drawing up two lines of twenty each, with his remainder in reserve, but it was taking a while. Against the force staging inside the western gate, the line of horse looked paltry indeed.

The line of spears in front of them was thin, but it was thicker than his own, and charging it brought the risk of getting cut to ribbons. *Idgen Marte. Torvul. What can we do to disperse their foot?*

Call in another army, Idgen Marte grumbled back.

Depends on how careful y'need to be about fire now, Torvul thought to him.

Not at all, Allystaire replied. *I will use any weapon I have now.*

Good. I'll send 'er up.

Among the enemy lines, orders were being shouted, but in the dark and in the confusion of any battle, on unfamiliar ground, it took untested men a long time to respond to their orders.

It did not take nearly so long for Idgen Marte to appear out of the darkness behind his horse. The animals to either side of him shied away, stamping at the ground and tugging at their reins. Ardent barely acknowledged it.

She held out a clinking bag in one hand. He set his lance in his stirrup boot and took it. "Hope your arm is still good. He says it won't burn for long, or very hot, but it ought to give them a good scare," she said as she handed it over.

He let the bag dangle from his hand and started to open it up. She had already disappeared. He considered for a moment the problem of how to pull the three bottles out of it individually without crushing them in his hand, then spat an oath, yelled, "Hold your line," to the horsemen around him, and spurred Ardent.

The destrier's muscles bunched and the huge grey leapt into motion. Before they'd traveled more than twenty yards, Allystaire was swinging the bag over his head in long circles. Another dozen yards and he released it, then pulled back on the reins. He couldn't follow it in flight, but he knew when it landed. A gout of flame erupted that would've filled the largest fireplaces in Wind's Jaw keep, hearths that were made to hold entire tree-trunks. The flame billowed into the sky and rolled out behind the front line of spearmen.

Panic erupted, frantic officers calling frantic orders. All sense of discipline among the Delondeur foot vanished when another, much smaller fire erupted on their far right flank, and then another close beside it. A dozen men turned and ran, then a score. Some of them, passing too close to the flames, suddenly found their cloaks and tabards catching on tendrils of it, and a few were too mad with fear to drop and smother themselves.

At the sight of their comrades running, and a smattering of them screaming as they burned, the trickle became a torrent, and the Salt Spears turned and ran. Allystaire heard their screams of panic, caught the words "Witchery! Sorcery!" among them.

Allystaire turned Ardent and trotted him back towards his thin line of horse, who cheered. He heard one man call out, "Cowards!" at the retreating foot, others simply celebrating with wordless cries of triumph.

"Quiet," he bellowed at them. "Burning a man to death is nothing to celebrate! They were unblooded boys, tradesman's sons. The Baron's knights and men-at-arms will not be driven off so easily. With me, at the trot," he finished, snapping command into the words with a lifetime of practice.

He picked up his lance and turned Ardent again, letting the horse take his head. In his stomach, he felt a brief flare of shame when he saw the fires burning ahead of him. *Oh, Goddess,* he thought in a quick prayer. *I am sorry I could not give them a clean death, or better still, a cleaner life. It could be that they are not truly your enemies, only men who are badly led. I am sorry.*

With that, his trotting line had come within sight of Delondeur's horse as they forced their way around the panicked foot. He saw more than one Delondeur knight laying about his horse with a weapon, mostly horseman's axes or flails they kept on loops around their wrists, driving away or simply felling their own panicked spearmen.

There, he thought then, steeling himself and finding the song flowing louder in his limbs, *are better targets.*

And there wouldn't be a better time, as only a trickle of them had managed to pull themselves free of the retreat and started to form a ragged line.

As he began to fill his lungs to give the order, a stray thought crossed his mind. *I really ought to teach Gideon the trumpet calls.* Then with a pang of sorrow and anger that turned his voice hoarse, he bellowed, "CHARGE!" with all the force he could muster.

Ardent pulled away from the rest of the line before they'd all run five yards, eager for the run, his energy seemingly boundless. Allystaire leveled his lance and picked a target among a knot of little more than half a dozen Delondeur men who'd only just begun to spread out. Two of them tried to turn their horses and run for the flanks rather than confront the charge. Most brought up their shields and tried to wrestle lances into their hands.

His chosen target, whose arms he could not read, got a heavy shield up to take the blow, but had only just got his horse moving and couldn't hope to match Ardent's speed, and the force the pair of them brought to bear.

Allystaire's lance shattered with an explosive sound, and he heard a sharp crack. The other man's shield or his arm, he hadn't time to care, but he turned his head to see the man thrown from the saddle as his horse reared back and only just managed to keep its feet.

Luck had been with them. Most of the men of his line were successful on this first pass, though he saw one unhorsed as a Delondeur knight from further back, with more time to prepare, had met a man with his own charge. Even as Allystaire was yelling for them to fall back and reform, he saw three of Chaddin's knights, emboldened by their success, go racing into the second ranks of Delondeur horsemen, who were quickly finding themselves and splitting into two columns to pass by the flame.

"Fall back, you fools," he yelled, his ragged voice still carrying, but to no avail. He saw them crash amongst the armored ranks. "Back! They will surround you!" But the trio had gone too far, discarded broken lances, and were now drawing swords or swinging flails. They were quickly overrun. He could hear the sounds of the combat, the yells, the sound of weapons beating on armor, the cries of men wounded or killed.

"BACK!" He whirled Ardent. Those men were lost the moment they kept charging, he told himself. They raced back to their original spot, the two lances that someone had planted in the ground serving as his target. He pulled one free and turned his mount with his knees, counting the other men as they arrived around him.

Sixteen. They'd hurt the Delondeur men, but lost a quarter of their own. "We cannot afford to overreach," he yelled. "One charge, one target, then pull back as fast as you can."

He struggled for just a moment to settle Ardent, who wanted back into the fight, when he heard Mol's voice from too close by for his comfort.

"Hold," she said, the word ringing out.

Instantly, Ardent settled, letting out a heavy breath. Around him Allystaire could see the mounts of the other men doing the same, instantly rooting themselves in place. *She was ordering the horses,* he thought, with some slight awe. *Not us.*

The girl walked to the front of the line. Allystaire swung out of his saddle and stepped in front of her. "Mol. Please, lass. Back to the Temple. You cannot be exposed out—"

"I have a part to play in this too, Arm," Mol intoned, turning to face him. He could see a tear glinting on her cheek, a glimpse of her true age behind the aura of the Voice. "Though I hesitate to do it."

She turned to face the darkness. Beyond, Allystaire could hear orders ringing out, knew that the Delondeur knights were fanning out into a line and starting forward. If he squinted, with the very faint dregs of Torvul's potion remaining to him, he could make out their shapes coming forward, the fires behind them having all but died out.

There was another sound, though, a deep rumbling. And then a long, mournful howl. *A wolf?* He turned to the girl with puzzlement. Then he heard the baying, and the rumbling grew louder. *Not wolves,* he thought. *Dogs. Dogs, and...*

His thought was cut off as the Delondeur line came rumbling into his vision, lances couched. He bent as if to snatch Mol up. Then the far left of the Delondeur line exploded, man and horse flung about and crushed under the weight of a stampede of ordinary cattle.

And then the dogs swarmed over what was left. Village and farmfolk gathered dogs around them everywhere, Allystaire knew, and for a moment felt keenly the absence of the favored hounds he'd left behind him in Oyrwyn. The dogs were of no particular breed or stock; they were large, small, and in between, and they darted at the horses and the knights utterly heedless of their own safety, dozens of them flying in from all directions in the darkness. Those with the size or the legs leapt at the knights in their saddles, breaking teeth on armor and dragging a few from their seats.

Others darted at the horses themselves, snapping at fragile lower legs or flitting beneath them to tear at their bellies.

The sound of their howling and baying filled the night, all too often punctuated with loud yelps as one was stamped on by a horse or fell to a Delondeur weapon.

Allystaire stood watching, transfixed and slightly horrified at the display. Chaddin and his knights did much the same.

"Now!" Mol yelled, snapping him back from the sight. He could hear no small grief in her voice. "Don't let it be for nothing!"

Allystaire leapt into the saddle, lagging behind, as the other horses leapt to the girl's command. He could feel Ardent's impatience, and he didn't bother to snatch up a lance, instead pulling his hammer free.

The village's dogs peeled away. He hadn't time to count but he suspected that less than half of them ran off to safety. He lashed out with his hammer mechanically, too stunned by what he'd just seen to pay enough attention to the fight. He took a hard blow off his shield, and another that skimmed off his helmet and pauldron, blooming pain in his shoulder. Allystaire snapped into focus and bashed out with his shield, sending a man from his saddle. Then he turned for another, hammer swinging in a tight arc and crushing the side of another knight's chest.

The shock of circumstance and the sudden close combat took the fight of the Delondeur men, and they broke in short order, retreating. Allystaire heard Chaddin's voice. "After them! On their heels," he yelled.

"NO," he yelled. "HOLD!"

Chaddin turned towards him in the saddle, his armor dented and wet, as was the sword clutched in his fist. "We have them on the run! Now is not the time to fall back."

"Hold," came Mol's voice, rising over the yelling and the din of the Delondeur retreat, though it hardly seemed loud enough.

Once again, every horse stopped in its tracks like it was rooted to the spot, and turned, placidly, to face the girl. Delondeur mounts whose riders had been killed or knocked clear did the same, trotting towards her as eager and pliant as if she'd trained them all their lives.

As one, the men—the dozen that were left—swung from the saddle. Mol walked, barefooted, towards Allystaire's side, and reached up for Ardent's bridle.

The huge grey lowered his neck towards her, pressing his nose against her shoulder more gently than Allystaire would've believed possible.

She murmured to the destrier. Ardent tried to lift his head away with a whinny, but she tugged his face back towards her and murmured again. "Ardent will lead the rest of your mounts to safety out the other gate. The enemy has abandoned its camp there," she announced suddenly. Then she reached up and deftly unclasped the warhorse's bridle, tugging the bit from his mouth and tossing it to the ground. "Free their mouths," she said. "They may need to graze."

Reins and bridles were tugged free by gauntleted hands as the horses all fell into place behind Allystaire's destrier.

The huge grey came to Allystaire's side and nudged against him, pausing for a moment. Allystaire patted the side of his neck carefully. The huge grey gave its mane a shake and pulled away from him.

"Avoid any men," the girl yelled after him. "Come back only if you hear me."

The herd of horses fell into place behind Ardent, then thundered out of Thornhurst and into the darkness.

Then she turned to Allystaire, and said hoarsely, "The Temple." She started walking, and the men, Allystaire included, followed her.

"It's not fair," he heard her saying, grief choking the words. "Not right to ask this of them. Not what She would've wanted."

Allystaire took a few steps to her side. "Mol, lass. You may have saved us all tonight."

The girl stopped and leaned against him. He carefully set his arm against her back, and she muttered, "Her Gift can't hurt me, you know."

Still mindful of it, he bent slightly and picked her up. "We do what we can, Mol. And then what we must. She would tell you the same, I am sure."

She gave him a quick embrace, arms wrapping around his neck, then leapt free to the ground. "That we needed it does not mean it was right to have asked it."

Behind them, horses, men, and cows cried out in pain and terror, lying broken and dead or dying along the path of the stampede. Allystaire paused and turned back to face them. "You go to the Temple, Mol. I must see to the men and beasts."

"Aye," she replied. "Bring all the wounded in first. Gather bodies to burn if you can."

"Aye." In his mind he was already reaching out to Torvul and Idgen Marte, and telling them to bring volunteers.

* * *

Nyndstir had been crouching by the cattlepen, taking the lay of the land and wondering where he could do some damage, when the stampede went off and the animals crushed the fence like parchment and went lowing off into the darkness. He'd given a wide berth, then crept closer to watch the carnage as they crashed into the exposed flank of the Baron's heavy horse.

When all the shouting was done and Delondeur's men retreated, he had half a mind to go out onto the battlefield and present himself to the man in the bright armor. Something about him tickled Nyndstir's memory, but he couldn't put his finger on what.

Don't want that man takin' me for an enemy, either, he thought as he watched him and a few others beginning to sweep the battlefield. Staying hidden along a fold of ground seemed the smarter choice.

He expected them to make knife work of it, quick and merciful ends for the wounded. He was all the more surprised when he saw the man in his armor kneel at the side of a man whose legs were crushed under his felled mount. He rolled the dead horse away like another man might a mid-size log for the fire, and then placed his hands upon the blessedly-unconscious knight.

Then the man suddenly woke with a long, harsh scream, swinging his arms wildly about him. Still the knight just knelt by his side.

When the knight stood up, the other man looked down at his legs. Then slowly, disbelievingly, he rolled over, pushed himself to his feet. With wobbling, impossible steps, he followed after the man who'd just healed him.

"Braech bugger me if I've ever seen the like," Nyndstir muttered, awestruck.

Then he watched the man move about the battlefield, one by one, waking the dying and the broken and setting them back on their feet.

As he was watching these miracles unfold before him, he heard a lowing and saw a line of cattle moving past him, headed back towards their pen, re-tracing the lines of their own stampede. Their numbers were reduced, but they were perfectly calm.

Nyndstir Obertsun was at a loss for the right oath.

CHAPTER 38

The Rite of Blooming Blood

"Landen," the Baron Delondeur bellowed, moving back and forth across the half-empty camp. "LANDEN!"

Men and horses milled around him, stunned by their reversal in the battle. Officers and knights tried to gather what was left of the Salt Spears to form them into units and take note of casualties. While the general panic had subsided, confusion reigned.

The Baron knew, inwardly, that he needed to assume control, show them confidence and flair, and allow the men to settle down.

But first he had to find his heir.

"M'lord. M'lord Baron," he heard, and whirled to find a young man in armor, unhelmed, with one arm loose and broken, limping towards him. His face was bathed in sweat and soot-stained. Lionel struggled to recall a name, but found none as the boy sank to a knee.

"Up, lad. No time for that kind of formality in the field. What is your name and what have you to say?"

"Sir Darrus Cartin, m'lord. I was given my spur this past fall as a member of Landen's company—and I am sorry to say, m'lord, but I saw her unhorsed. I tried to fight to her side, but…" The man tried to lift his clearly wounded arm, grimacing in pain. In the lanterns he'd once again ordered gathered round him, he could see how the boy's face paled when he moved it. "I didn't see her killed, m'lord," he added hastily. "But she took a wound."

"A wound valiantly earned in honest service is not something I'll forget. A lordship is yours when we conclude this business," Lionel bellowed, drawing the eyes of the men around him. "A hundred gold links, armor from my own smiths, and a horse from my own stables to the man who finds my heir in the coming day's fight."

He felt the immediate effect the words had as they moved through the camp, passed by whispers and shouts. His command asserted himself. Composure was contagious, as was optimism about the coming fight. Delondeur turned for his tent, lantern bearers pacing him, smiling to himself.

He stopped short of the flaps as he saw the unmistakable blue and yellow glow on the frozen ground.

Lionel Delondeur gathered himself with a deep breath and held out one hand to pause his lantern-bearers, then threw open the flap, and stepped boldly in.

Gethmasanar and Iriphet were both seated on the only camp chairs within the tent, leaving just his cot if he wished to sit. His bones ached, his shoulders protested the weight of armor, and his knees screamed in pain.

Command the moment, he thought as he drew himself up imperiously. "Why did you not support our attack?"

"We noted some heretofore unknown powers at work. We needed to evaluate them," answered Iriphet, his words hanging in the air, an eerie echo of themselves. "We will have a suitable number of Wights ready very soon. In the meantime, we had a further notion."

"Soon? We could've crushed them with a dozen of the blasted things tonight!"

"Tomorrow night would be more suitable. It is the midpoint of the winter season. This has symbolic as well as thaumaturgical significance," Gethmasanar put in. "The omens were not quite right for this night. We should have told you but we had not consulted the runes nor the charts. It is, of course, our mistake."

Lionel's stomach chilled, and despite his willpower, his years of practice, he felt himself shrinking down in the face of the trap they'd sprung. And it was, indeed, a trap.

"We will," Iriphet was already saying, "require the dead and the wounded. And as to this further notion…"

"What of it," Lionel answered, wearily shuffling to a table and leaning upon it. *Tired. So Cold-damned tired.*

"Imagine the ache in your limbs, gone. Imagine being suffused with a strength unlike any you'd ever known, even in your days as Lionel Giantsbane." Iriphet's voice was a wavering, grating thing. Sometimes it almost sounded as if it echoed in his own throat. "Imagine, most of all, matching Coldbourne strength for strength."

"He has your daughter as a prisoner. We have confirmed this. With the power we offer, you could challenge for her return."

Lionel didn't turn to face them. He splayed his fingers on the table before him, considered the gnarled and swollen knuckles of each hand, the bent fingers and scarred backs. "What must I do?"

"Give us the necessary time, and the tools." A pause. "A man, hale, or nearly so. A few of the wounded."

"The sooner we can begin the better. Outside our wagon we will have our implements prepared. Meet us there before dawn, which is coming in but a turn or two."

The sorcerers vanished into the shadows at the back of his tent. Lionel's first impulse was to call for his lanterns, but he checked himself. He stood, gathered his hands into fists, and straightened his back. He went to the tent flap and pushed it back.

"You," he said, gesturing to one of the lantern bearers. "Fetch Sir Darrus Cartin. Tell him I wish to take counsel with him on a walk before dawn. Quickly now."

* * *

"Landen Delondeur," Chaddin spat, jabbing a finger towards a figure in the back of the knot of Delondeur prisoners. "Coldbourne," the man yelled excitedly. "We have the Baron's likely heir!"

Allystaire looked up from the wounded man he was healing. Space was at a premium inside the Temple, which was jammed with the Mother's people and the Delondeur prisoners. Idgen Marte, Torvul, and a party of Renard's men moved in the distance still, finding wounded and bringing them back to be healed, along with a few Delondeur volunteers that Allystaire had already put back on their feet.

The place felt anything but holy, now. It was rank with fear, with metal and sweat-stained leather, and the faint but unmistakably coppery tang of blood. Families huddled together, the children's eyes huge and distant. Torvul moved among the families with the youngest in particular, dispensing cheer where he could. Allystaire saw him pressing something from one of his huge, creased palms into the hands of a child more than once.

It's going to take more than boiled sugars, Allystaire thought to himself. As he stood he saw Torvul turn and fix a glare on him, then go back to moving among the people and talking quietly to them in his low rumbling bass.

Allystaire pushed himself to his feet. He expected to tip over and lose consciousness before reaching his full height. He expected to soon feel the sudden accumulation of the exertions of his muscles all in one moment.

Still the song, though faint, rushed through him.

People made a path for him as he walked. The candles and lamps they held and huddled over gleamed brightly back at them when his armor caught their reflection. His perfect, unblemished armor. The armor that should be covered in the wear of battle and spattered with mud, and worse. Instead it shone like purest hammered silver.

Their eyes followed him whenever he moved, and he could feel them like a weight. He felt them as he walked to the prisoners, who were shoved against one section of wall.

Chaddin was dragging a prisoner forward. It took Allystaire a moment to realize that the struggling figure was, beneath a bulky and bloodied gambeson, a woman. There was a long stain along her left arm, held awkwardly against her body. Her eyes were downcast and the resistance she offered to Chaddin's pulling was token, at best.

"Take your hands off of her, Chaddin. She is no more threat."

"I tire of your orders, Allystaire," Chaddin shot back. "We need to find out what she knows."

Allystaire fixed Chaddin with a hard stare for a moment. "If I need to ask her any questions, I will," he finally said. "For now, take your hands off of her, and try to get some rest. This battle is not done."

Chaddin stepped away, but not without a last shove that sent Landen sprawling against the stone wall. Allystaire took a half step towards the pretender, half-snarling. "It is not worthy of the Goddess's Temple that a wounded, defeated enemy should be roughly used, especially by one who claims the rights of rank and rule."

"And once again I say I tire of your orders," Chaddin snapped back. "I'm not interested in your Goddess. My father was beaten, and had we pursued him we could have won. Instead we have retreated in here, and for what? To nurse the enemy wounded back to health? They should've been seen to on the field and left to rot."

His last comment sent a general murmur of assent through his remaining men, and, Allystaire thought, some quizzical looks among the village folk. Allystaire waited for the room to quiet down.

"You are a fool. First, he was not beaten. He will not be beaten till he is dead." Allystaire flicked his eyes towards Landen and said, "I am sorry to say that in front of you, but it is the truth." Then he looked back to Chaddin. "Second, had we pursued him, his numbers would have told the tale sooner rather than later. His foot would have organized and bought time for the horse to do the same, and we would all be dead. Third, and fourth, why do we not leave the enemy to die upon the field?"

Allystaire looked at the knot of beaten, wounded, yielded enemies, then at his people, the Goddess's people. "It is not enough that we fight Delonduer. It will not be enough if we win. We have to be better men. Yes, ruthlessness might serve us here and now. We could have made quick work of the wounded and evened the numbers a bit more. But then the story goes out, after the fight: the Goddess thirsts for the blood of those who oppose Her, and Her paladin orders their throats cut. And then we have lost."

Allystaire leaned close to Chaddin and added, "And the more corpses upon the field—the more of those monstrosities Delondeur's sorcerers can make." He made sure that the Delondeur prisoners heard him, waited for them to grasp the implications, and began to walk away.

"If you're determined to be better men, why did you turn sorcerous fire upon us? Why is the captain of the Long Knives dead after yielding? Why do two of my father's officers and one of his finest knights lie dead, assassinated by this Shadow of yours?"

Allystaire turned on Landen, who had found her voice and pulled herself erect against the wall. Her face was pale, showing clear lines of pain, but her voice was strong and clear.

"It was alchemical, in point of fact," Torvul casually answered as he picked his steps from halfway across the room. "Calling what I do sorcerous is an insult, girl."

"A death in flames is not something I wish to offer anyone," Allystaire said. "But I did not look for this fight. Everyone who has died here in the past few days has done so because of your father. That blood, along with so much more, is on his hands."

"And the yielded man?"

"Attacked me, but not before he admitted to me he meant to do murder, to slit the throats of children in the night. I will not suffer a man like that to live." Allystaire felt his anger rising. "I cannot suffer a man like that to live. If you believe for even a moment that I am what I say I am you will understand that. That so many of you draw breath, and walk, and move your limbs freely still ought to be all the proof you need that my Goddess is no delusion, that my Gifts are no lie."

Suddenly the door swung open, and Renard stuck his bearded head in. "Allystaire—we have found a wounded man we cannot move. You'll need t'come to him, and quick."

Allystaire darted to his feet and was a step from the door before he stopped and said, "Landen. Chaddin. Both of you come with me."

* * *

Gethmasanar moved with casual serenity around a folding table that had been erected outside his and Iriphet's wagon, occasionally lifting one of the sharp tools laid upon it and examining it with a critical eye. Iriphet stood silent and unmoving some distance away. Periodically, some of their fearful swords-at-hire approached, carrying the dead or nearly dead. They had ceased questioning the necessity of delivering such material, though their own numbers grew fewer as the night passed.

As if he plucked the thought from Gethmasnar's head, Iriphet said, "Men cannot be relied upon except in short bursts. You know this."

"Of course," Gethmasanar agreed as he thumbed the edge of a knife. "Like as not their bodies lie upon the field and will come to serve us anyway. What was it the Baron said? Dead men draw no pay."

Iriphet laughed, an odd and disturbing echoing noise. "Indeed." There was a moment of silence interrupted only by the rustling of wind against bare tree limbs and Gethmasanar setting a barbed hook down upon the table.

"Must you use such crude implements?"

"No. I simply prefer it," Gethmasanar answered. "I find there is less wastage when I use a knife."

"And you are certain you can perform the Rite of Blooming Blood? It is hardly commonplace."

"It is not so different from preparing Wights."

"As you say," Iriphet said. "Our employer approaches."

Baron Delondeur wandered into the clearing, preceded a bit by a much smaller circle of light than had followed him for most of the night. He held a lantern in one hand, as did his companion. They stopped just beyond the tree line, with the younger man eyeing the sorcerers warily.

"M'lord, what is—"

Lionel cut him off quickly. "You wish to serve your Baron, yes? And help me locate my daughter?"

"Of course, m'lord, but—"

Iriphet waved a hand contemptuously, and the young knight's mouth moved soundlessly as he was lifted from the ground by bands of luminous blue. Delondeur himself started slightly and retreated a step, but then calmed and watched as Sir Darrus Cartin floated gently through the air and settled out upon the sorcerer's folding table.

Gethmasanar came forward, and, with a beam of yellow light extending from one finger, began cutting the young man's armor. It curled like wood under the hasp, falling away in long strips.

Cartin struggled, such as he could. His eyes were wide, and soon the small clearing was rank with the stink of piss as his fear mastered him. Lionel watched at some remove.

Iriphet waved the Baron to his side, and Lionel hesitated only momentarily before obeying.

"There are parts of the Rite of Blooming Blood that you may find unpleasant, Lionel," Iriphet began, his voice sounding even more alien than usual. "You will have to banish such thoughts from your head."

Gethmasanar picked up a knife. Strips of metal and gambeson lay curled upon the ground like shorn hair. Despite the sorcery that was gagging him, Cartin's scream was audible as a kind of whine as Gethmasanar's hand plunged down and began to slice.

With his free hand, the sorcerer gestured, and a wide goblet made of some strange dark metal floated into the air next to him.

"You must steel yourself and do as instructed, Baron," Iriphet went on. "For it is only after this Rite that you will survive the construction of your new armor. Remember—in order to match the paladin's strength, you must do as we say."

Lionel eyed the goblet that floated above the knight as he was butchered. He tried not to think about the dark substance flowing into it. He especially did not focus on the thrashing, mewling form on the table, pinned fast by glowing blue bands of twisting light.

"Armor?" Delondeur asked the question absentmindedly, his voice faint and drawn.

"Yes. It is not entirely unlike creating a Battle-Wight, you see."

* * *

Allystaire didn't give Landen or Chaddin time to pause or consider his demand to follow him. He simply went, hot on Renard's heels, hoping they would follow a commanding voice without thinking on it.

When he heard the tramp of feet on the frozen ground behind him, he knew that they had.

It didn't take him long to understand the nature of Renard's urgent request, because the soldier's steps took him straight out to the battlefield they'd recently held, to the scorched and blackened spot where Torvul's potions had bloomed into fire.

Idgen Marte knelt at the edge of it, next to a form that screamed so faintly that Allystaire thought the man's lungs must have been damaged. A wordless, wet sound, it was a horror to the ear, but from more than fifteen feet away, no one could have heard it.

Allystaire slid to his knees at the man's side, offering his hand. How old he had been, or how he'd looked, was anyone's guess. The chainmail he'd been wearing had scalded against his skin, and all along the left side of his body and his face, it was as if the metal had been grafted to him.

The sense of pain that washed over Allystaire as he pushed his Gift into the man was so overwhelming that he nearly blacked out.

Goddess, please hear me. I know that you are distant. I know that I have asked much of you, Allystaire quickly prayed as he tried to pour healing into the burned man. *But this man is in pain because of me. I did this to him. I do not know if he is an evil man. I do not know if he is truly our enemy. Even if he were, I would not wish this upon him.*

Allystaire built the compassion, the love that the Mother's Gift offered to him, into a raging torrent, and tried to pour it forth into the Delondeur soldier. He found the resistance to it more than he could imagine.

Please, my Lady. I am sorry. No matter his crimes, no man can deserve to die this way. Do not let this be done in your name.

Unlike Jeorg the night before, the man he tried to heal now did not seem to remember his own name. There was only pain and loss and fear and Allystaire found himself muttering, "I am sorry, I am sorry," audibly, pushing and pushing and pushing against the enormous wall of pain that threatened to engulf him.

And then suddenly it broke and the man's scream grew louder and more intense for a moment, and then the healing began to wash over him in earnest. The links of metal that had melted into his skin were pushed free as his flesh knit, and the screaming subsided till the man lapsed into unconsciousness.

Two of Renard's volunteers delicately picked him up, and began carrying him back to the Temple. Allystaire stood and turned towards Chaddin and Landen. "Do you still doubt me?"

"I have seen sorcery before," Landen muttered darkly.

"Aye. Seen it kill and maim and plunder, no doubt. I know without thinking on it that the power the sorcerers wield—the sorcerers your father pays to do his bidding—can never heal."

"Why?" Chaddin's arms were crossed over his mailed chest. "It still makes no sense to give so much aid to the enemy's wounded."

"And is this man my enemy? Is he yours? What lured him here, Chaddin? What promises or lies? And I healed him because I am the man who nearly killed him, who made him suffer with fire." Allystaire turned to Landen then, and said, "I will do what I must to protect the people I serve. But I will also do what I can for anyone who suffers. Could you claim any of that to be true of your father?"

Allystaire didn't give the Baron's daughter a chance to answer. He followed the men bearing the newly healed Delondeur soldier, leaving Chaddin and Landen to exchange curious looks before rushing after him again.

* * *

Lionel Delondeur fell to one knee, simultaneously gasping for air and fighting to keep his gorge from rising. *Surely some of the men heard the screams, he thought. Surely they will come looking.*

Wild-eyed, he looked up at Iriphet, who stood calmly and immovably above him, goblet in hand. "We are only just begun, Baron. Do not think of it in the crude terms that are causing your mind to reject it. Think of it thus: Sir Darrus Cartin's life, the strength of his youth and manhood, are now given to you. They would have been anyway, over a lifetime of service. Now they are given to you to use in the coming days. Do you understand? In this, the man still serves you. You must have steel enough to accept that. Up."

There was no denying the snap of command in the sorcerer's odd voice. "Yes," the Baron spat, pushing himself to his feet. "His service, still," he added weakly. *His service ended with him a mewling, whimpering thing. Dressed out on a table like an animal taken on a hunt, with less dignity.* The suddenness of his own thought surprised him. He pushed it away, straightened, and reached for the goblet. "Let's get this over with," he said, trying to put a bit of his flair back into the words.

Next to him, Iriphet offered no reply except to hold out the goblet and its dark reeking contents.

CHAPTER 39

Stillbright

Allystaire picked his way through the huddled shapes of all the folk crammed into the Temple. Most of them had been driven to sleep by their fear, and he could hear the regular soft rush of their breath, feel the warmth of it filling the air.

He found Mol, seeming asleep, leaning against the Pillar of the Will, where Gideon's body also lay. The two were surrounded by a mismatched bunch of the village's surviving dogs. In particular, Mol curled up with her back against one grey-muzzled, shaggy coated herding dog. Her peaked ears swiveled as Allystaire approached, and she lifted her head, considering him.

"He is a friend," Mol muttered, and for a moment he wasn't sure if she was talking to him or the dog, but then the dog closed her eyes and lowered her head upon crossed forepaws.

The girl uncurled herself, put her bare feet under her, and stood up. She pushed her hood back and gazed up at him. Though most of the lights in the Temple had gone out, the sky itself was beginning to brighten, and through the ring of windows Allystaire could make out the tracks of tears on her face.

"Mol," Allystaire whispered. "Do not despair."

"How could I not? I cannot hear Her, Allystaire. Not at all. Gideon is lost to us. And the day that breaks now brings the Longest Night with it. There is nothing more we can do."

"Yes, Mol, there is. I am not defeated. Nor are Idgen Marte or Torvul. We may not know what it is that we must do, but we are not done, and I will not give in to despair even if I am dragged before the sorcerers in chains. If is true that this will be our last day, then let us honor Her with how we live it."

"Pretty speech," a nearby voice hissed. "Not gonna do us much good when we all die, is it?"

Allystaire turned to face Ivar, her face painted with dirt and blood, leaning heavily on the haft of her spear.

"What is it that you want, Ivar? To be released from your contract so you may try and flee? I never thought I would see the day."

"We'd make it fifty span out the door before those sorcerers would churn us up into pieces of those bone monsters. Freeze that for a game I want no part of. I'll stay here and die for my weight because that's who I am. What I want is for you to remember who you are, and give up on this holy knight nonsense and find your way out o'this."

"As much as you have seen these months, and still you doubt and deny me and call me a liar."

"Or a madman."

"Either way, Captain Ivar, I care not and will hear it no longer. I release you from your contract, along with any of your soldiers who choose to go. I believe my sister paid your commission for a year. For your service, our history, and your losses I will not ask for any of it to be returned. Begone."

Ivar's face was stunned, her eyes wide dark circles in the weak pre-dawn light. "Dismissin' us? How're we t'get out?"

"It will be turns yet before Delondeur will raise another attack, and I feel confident that the sorcerer's abominations will not move against us in daylight. You have time to get over the wall. Be gone."

Allystaire raised a gauntleted fist and pointed towards the door. Ivar looked at him in disbelief, following the direction his finger pointed. Her gap-toothed mouth moved silently several times. Finally she gathered up her spear and stalked off.

The herding dog Mol had reclined against lifted her head and let out a low, soft growl.

"Shhh," Mol said, and the animal went instantly quiet, but still looked intently at the mercenary's retreating back. "That may have been a foolish thing,

Allystaire," she muttered as Ivar began waking up other black-mailed forms and speaking quietly but animatedly to them.

"It is not their fight. It is an old bond of mine, and past time they were all broken. Let the rest of this be upon Her Ordained and our people."

"If you're done widening the odds against us," Idgen Marte's voice came from behind him, "Torvul'd like to speak with you outside." He could read the anger in the flat tone of her words, and said nothing as he turned to follow her after nodding to Mol. The girl sank back against her grey-muzzled companion, which curled protectively around her.

Once they were outside, Idgen Marte rounded on him. "That was a damn stupid thing. They're practically the only thing keeping the militia from breaking."

"And I did not want to spend the rest of the fight waiting for Ivar to sink her spear into my back. It was coming," Allystaire shot back. "I could feel it."

"Cold, if you're going to send anyone out, it ought to be the women and children."

"They'd not go," Torvul said. He knelt on the steps of the Temple, working by the light of his sturdy little lamp. A mortar and pestle, several clay jars, and a few crystal bottles lay scattered around him. "And even if they did, they'd never get far."

"Have we any cards left to play, Torvul?"

"Need you even ask?" The dwarf picked up a clay jar and sniffed at its powdered contents. "I think I can do a Forbidding."

"Meaning what?"

"I can keep the creatures from entering the Temple. Not so hard, really, simple matter of seizing upon the energy generated by the faith within and the sense of community and belonging it brings with it. Then I channel it into a song and—"

"Save the theory, dwarf," Idgen Marte said wearily. "What does it mean?"

"Precisely what I just said. I can seal this building. Cold, I think if I have the time I can funnel them right to ya. Means I'll have to test my craft against the sorcerer's will." He paused then, and heaved a deep sigh. "I'd feel better about it if the boy were able to help."

"If you can deny them entry, then as long as we can fight them off, the folk inside are safe."

"From the Wights, yes," Torvul pointed out. "I haven't got a way to bar men. Only things with the taint of sorcery. There is, ah, one problem."

"Go on."

"Once I do it, no one can go in or out. So those inside the Temple are stuck, and those outside..."

"Likewise. Fine. Prepare and do it. The three of us out here, everyone else in there."

"I rather thought that's what ya'd say," Torvul replied, and he went back to his jars and vials.

"In the meantime," Allystaire said, "let everyone else get as much rest as they can. You and I," he pointed to Idgen Marte, "make a sweep of the village. Look for any survivors, anything useful, food and drink. Aye?"

Idgen Marte nodded. "Yell if there's trouble," she said, tapping the side of her head.

The door opened behind them. Ivar and five more of the remaining eight Iron Ravens filed out, carrying little beside their weapons and armor.

The captain glared hard at Allystaire as she stalked off, a look he returned calmly and evenly. The others refused to meet his eyes as they slunk off into the morning.

"I'm not even goin' t'ask," Torvul muttered as the men moved at a trot down the road.

* * *

Baron Lionel Delondeur had never felt so strong. Not even in the halest day of his life, not even among the elves on the tundra and earning the name Giantsbane, had he been anything like the man he now was. He could simply feel the strength flowing through his arms and legs. All the pain of his age, all the wounds he had ever taken, vanished beneath a flood of power.

"Remember, Baron," Iriphet said as if hearing the thought, "this will only last for a day or two. What we will do now will take much of the available time."

"It doesn't take you so long to craft a Battle-Wight," the Baron countered.

"If that is what you wish us to make of you then it will take little time at all," Iriphet said, the barely concealed threat hanging in the air as his voice echoed itself. The sorcerer cocked his head to the side and waited. "I thought not. Now, strip yourself of your common steel. We shall need it."

Lionel nodded and began unbuckling his armor. His fingers moved among the straps with long-forgotten speed; no pain clogged the joints of his knuckles.

No sooner had bits of his plate begun falling to the frozen grass beneath him than it was lifted into the air and unraveled by tendrils of yellow and blue light.

He tried not to look at the pile of other material the sorcerers had gathered, as it, too, was lifted in the air and stripped. As he watched, bone and steel were melded together in the air, woven inch by inch. The result was the kind of hideous dark metal that ran through the bodies of the Wights and coated the skulls set atop their crudely-knitted forms.

The process was slow and the sounds of the bodies of his men being ripped asunder, the sounds of their clotted blood being heated and pressed against the bone-steel to quench it, might have sickened him, once.

As it was, he barely noted the cold and waited eagerly for the tools suited to his new power. "A sword as well, I think, if we have the time," he said with casual assurance.

"A sword indeed, Baron," Gethmasanar answered. "A sword fit to bring down a paladin."

* * *

"The sun's movement today is not natural," Mol said as she stood on the steps of the Temple and contemplated the quality of the light filtering through heavy clouds. "It ought not to be so far past noon. It will be dark all too quickly."

"Then it's best you get inside the Temple, lass," Torvul said. "For I'm about ready to work my Forbidding." The dwarf clutched a heavy jar that sloshed as he moved. Exotic and unnameable scents rose up from the wide neck as he moved past Allystaire and Idgen Marte.

"Make sure the people know they cannot come out till it is settled," Allystaire said.

"They've food enough for a few days now," Idgen Marte added wearily. In addition to her bow and her knives, Torvul's cudgel was thrust awkwardly through her belt. "Though I pray the Mother won't let it last so long."

Mol nodded and opened the doors, then looked back to Allystaire. "Is there anything you would say to them?"

"I have no words left. Only what I can do for them. If you must tell them something, say that if it is to be their last night, let them live it in love and affection with each other. Not to let fear make them forget Her."

"Ask them to pray. For us if they've a mind," Idgen Marte added.

Mol nodded and went inside, closing the doors behind her.

Torvul set down his jar and pulled an aspergillum from his belt, dipped it in, and began flicking droplets of the liquid all along the walls of the Temple and the ground beneath it.

"If one of you'd like to carry this for me it might go a bit faster," the dwarf said, eyeing the jar. Allystaire bent to pick it up.

They made a long, slow circuit around the walls, across the steps, the dwarf quiet, intent upon his work. Allystaire thought on the coming night, on the Goddess's words to him. If he closed his eyes, banished all other thoughts, he could almost fix in his mind the image of Her. But then the beauty, the overpowering radiance, would force his mind aside and the image would shatter, leaving behind a surge of desire, a powerful sense of loss.

As they walked he thought of Gideon lying insensate and mindless upon the floor of the Temple. He'd seen a man kicked in the head by a warhorse once who'd lived a few months in much the same way. Food could be forced down his throat, and water, but it was no life; the mind, everything that made the man up, was gone.

And are you gone, too, Gideon? Too soon, my boy, he thought wistfully. *So much I had left to teach you. So much to learn from you.*

He drove these thoughts away, but they kept coming back. The Goddess. The feel of Her kiss. The desire he probably imagined in Her voice when last She had spoken to him. Gideon, lost.

Suddenly, out loud, he said, "I should have killed Delondeur when I had the chance."

"Aye," Torvul agreed. "Like as not, you should've."

"Why did I not?"

"You said it couldn't be like that," the dwarf said, dipping the round head of his silver implement back into the bowl he'd filled with the thick, slightly opaque, and heavily-scented liquid. "Couldn't be assassins in the night. Had to be public, the world had to know why. All that sort of knightly rot."

"Knightly rot is rather the point."

"I might argue that the point is seein' to Her Ladyship's folk, and Her church."

"If I had killed him then, the entire barony would have risen to see us crushed. He would be a murdered hero, a martyr."

"Could be. Or maybe our man Chaddin could've seized the reins of power more fully and come to an understanding with us. Doesn't do us any good to wonder. We've a job tonight. Which, as Mol has kindly pointed out, is not as far off as it ought to be."

"Are the sorcerers so powerful, Torvul, that they can bend the rules of nature?"

"Depends how many there are," the dwarf said with a shrug. "Might be Braech and Fortune working with them as well. I doubt their clergies just packed up and went home with no share of spoils or credit. Those bastards are powerful, though, as I recall tellin' a hard-headed knight some months ago. They'll not make the mistake of getting within your reach twice, I don't think."

"What are we to do against them, then?"

"Idgen Marte might have a chance. I…" the dwarf lowered his tool and cocked his head to the side, as if listening to something. His eyes narrowed and his mouth drew into a thin line, crinkling his chin. "I don't think…I can hold them at bay, maybe. Hold them off. With my craft." He shook his head as if clearing it. "There were days when they feared my folk, ya know. But I haven't that craft in my hands. There's no one who does, and if there were, no songs left to answer them."

"Answer them?"

The dwarf shook his head and wetted his tool again. "Come on. Let's mark out the path we want the Wights to follow."

"Straight up to the stairs. Give me some height. Where will you be?"

"The roof, I suppose. Don't look at me like that," he responded to Allystaire's sudden glare, even though he hadn't turned around to see it. "I can do more work from up there, and if one of them gets t'me, they're through anyway. You know by now I'm no coward."

"Never thought you were. Well, maybe back in Grenthorpe I did."

"We haven't got time for a lot of reminiscing," Torvul grumbled. "Besides, I don't figure on dyin' tonight. But in case you're thick enough or slow enough to get your own self killed, I want you to know what you've given back t'me. Not my life from the noose, mind. Something more important than that." The old dwarf faced him, eyeing him from beneath cragged brows. "You made me belong t'something again. I can't make you understand what that means to a dwarf. Family, clan, caravan—that's who we are. Exiled from that, I was dead already, just takin' a long time t'notice. It's why my craft was failing me. You and Idgen Marte and Her Ladyship gave that back to me. A place. A family. I can never repay that," the dwarf said with uncharacteristic solemnity. Then, grinning, he added, "Well, if anyone can, it'll be me. I'm sure I'll manage to save your life again tonight somehow, eh? Come on." He stretched, and they went back to the work at hand.

* * *

The notes of Torvul's song hung in the air as the dwarf stood before the closed doors of the Temple. They could feel the power that resonated from his words, feel as it settled into the stones around them.

For a moment the droplets he'd blessed the building with glowed. Thousands of tiny pinpricks of bright white light flared with the power the dwarf gathered and released, and then sank into the stone. Torvul stepped back, stumbling and falling to one knee.

"Stones above but I need a good lie-in," the dwarf muttered.

Idgen Marte helped him to his feet, and the dwarf, with the crossbow slung over his back and a heavy bag of potions in one hand, began clambering nimbly up the side of the Temple.

Allystaire studied the stones of the wall for a moment. The lights Torvul had created pulsed faintly within it, shifting and moving and eluding his eye if he looked too closely.

He settled his hammer in its ring on his belt and flexed his hand within his shield. Next to him, Idgen Marte unlimbered Torvul's cudgel and gave it a few experimental swipes in the air.

"Still with me, Shadow?"

She grinned humorlessly. "You even have to ask?"

Allystaire smiled, though the expression was equally grim. "No. But it fills up the silence."

"That it does." She paused, tapped the cudgel against her open palm, and said, "The story doesn't end here, you know. It can't. It doesn't. I won't let it."

"It was never a story, Idgen Marte," Allystaire replied softly. "A dream of one, mayhap."

"No, but it will be," she answered with sudden forcefulness. "And in it, you'll have some foolish name or title that the children think is bold, and that old men secretly thrill to hear. You'll not be a broken nosed old warlord, nor a bachelor, and that armor you wear will be magic, not just look it."

"If you say so," he answered, laughing without much feeling in it. "I am not a bachelor by choice, you know."

"Out with it. We may be dead soon. I want one damned piece of your story finished before we are."

"Fine. The woman I wanted to marry? Her name was Dorinne. She was the natural daughter of Lord Joeglan Naswyn, of the Horned Towers. Her father acknowledged her but would not dower her, and my marrying her was out of the question, according to my own father. I went to the Old Baron to plead my case, but he refused to listen to me. Told me I was a young man looking to marry for the wrong reasons, my head turned by a comely shape. That I needed to think of the future of my line and so forth. It was the only time I ever had harsh words with Gerard Oyrwyn. Not long afterwards, he ordered me away on a campaign. While I was gone, my father died. He'd lost a leg a few years before, and was never strong after that. A flux had come to the barony and he succumbed to it. When word reached me, I rode for home, determined then I could marry whomever I wanted, dowry or no."

"And why didn't you?"

"The flux was particularly savage."

The words hung in the air for a moment before their import settled fully on Idgen Marte.

"Allystaire," she murmured. "I'm sorry. I had no idea it was...Cold. It's awful."

"It was fifteen years ago. A lot of time for it to heal."

"Then tell me it has. Tell me the sting has gone out of it."

Allystaire fell silent, looked off into the fast-falling darkness.

"I'm sorry, Ally. I didn't realize it would be that way."

"It is how things end most of the time," Allystaire shrugged. "Ugly, painfully."

"Well let's make it ugly and painful for them, eh?" She pointed with her cudgel at the path leading towards the Temple. No shapes crowded upon it yet, but as the unnatural darkness settled around them, they both seemed to know, somehow, that Wights lurked just beyond their sight.

* * *

Nyndstir hated skulking. Hated it. But he'd proven to be damn good at it, and now found himself huddled against the wooden wall he'd climbed over, gnawing on a loaf of stale bread and swigging from a jar of beer he'd pilfered from an abandoned house. He'd hidden from the paladin as he'd moved through the village, unsure of getting the time to explain himself.

Nyndstir was no coward, but he wasn't an idiot, either.

He suddenly lowered the bread as he heard a faint wet scream float over the village from the west.

When it died, another followed it. And another.

And with each one, it got noticeably darker.

"Braech," Nyndstir muttered haltingly, his tongue unused to prayer. "I don't think ya bless this, priest in their camp or no. I think ya bless those who're brave with no more than steel in their hands."

Another scream. Night fell, all at once, in a manner so clearly unnatural that Nyndstir felt his hair standing on end.

"Bless me tonight, Braech, if ya would. I set a bad course. Every man is bound to do that now'n then. Bless me and help me set it right."

With that, he downed the last of the beer, dropped the jug, hefted his axe, and skulked off into the night.

* * *

The quick, awful screams and the falling dark raced each other across Thorn-hurst to the steps of the Mother's Temple. From behind the stone walls, Al-lystaire heard the sudden cries of dismay.

He set his feet and unlimbered his hammer.

Battle-Wights swarmed down the road, dozens of them. Not as large or as fierce as the Wights that had assaulted the town the first time. They seemed more carelessly made, loosely stitched together. Well behind them, what re-mained of Delondeur's men marched on. The crowd of them seemed improba-bly small, but Allystaire didn't have time to think on that at the moment.

The entire world, the darkness that crowded in on the Temple, the scores of people crammed into it, fearful and crying, all of it melted away from Al-lystaire's mind.

There was only his hammer, only his arms, and the Wights that pressed upon him. Bone flew away in chunks whenever he struck. Limbs were shat-tered, exposed spines severed with a blow.

Funneled towards him by Torvul's Forbidding, they came in twos and threes, loping awkwardly to their destruction. Some tried pushing themselves against the line Torvul had drawn around the Temple, and one or two were crushed against empty air by the press of their own fellows.

He had his feet planted on the stones of the Temple he had helped to raise, the Temple that had started with a pile of rocks in a field. The song of the Moth-er flowed still in his limbs, though fainter than it had. No matter, though. What strength it still granted him would be enough.

In the place he stood now, with the Shadow of the Mother at his right hand, they could come as long and in as many numbers as they wished. They could come and be crushed upon his hammer. He could feel cracks in the stout oak haft lengthening towards the head.

When it broke, and it would, he would have his fists.

Allystaire felt as though the proud boast he had given to the Mother was closer to true now than when he'd made it. Let the whole world come. Let the Choiron Symod bring the Sea Dragon's devoted berserkers, and the Marynth Evolyn bring all the assassins she dared to hire. Let Fortune bring

Her hired blades. When they came within the range of his hammer, they would die.

He realized, only then, that he was speaking aloud, bellowing his rage at the mindless Wights that crowded in on him. A small one, barely cobbled together out of mail rings pulled and spliced into wire and hastily wrapped around bones scuttled at him, swinging broken blades from the ends of its arms. He smashed its skull contemptuously. He saw the others pull back, and he laughed raggedly.

"Even your abominations fear us, sorcerer," he yelled, and he heard the cold wind carry his voice, sending it ringing over the ruined village. "Even the dead will not face the Mother's wrath! Do they learn their cowardice from you?"

Many of the Wights continued to press upon Torvul's barrier. He saw one, suddenly bathed in a chilling blue light, begin to push a bladed hand purposefully through it. The lights embedded in the stone began winking and dying.

I can't hold it, Allystaire. Torvul's mental voice sounded thin and worn in his mind. *I've got…we have to drive them off.*

Suddenly the Wights that had scuttled away were bathed in an intense, pure white light. Allystaire had but a second to wonder before he heard Torvul's voice from the roof bellowing above even his, and he spared a glance back to see the dwarf holding up his lantern in one hand, the wide beam it threw unnaturally bright.

"The Arm still strikes for the Mother," the dwarf yelled, his voice thunderingly loud. "He stands still and bright!" he roared. "A lamp in the darkness! No mark upon him! Why does he stand alone?" The dwarf jumped nimbly from the roof, landed hard on his feet on the steps, and charged to Allystaire's side, yelling again. "Still. Bright!"

From inside the Temple, Allystaire heard the words echoed, rising into a chant that stirred him from his place upon the steps. The doors of the Temple burst open, and the folk who'd sheltered there poured out of it, weapons in hand. Giraud the mason, rock-hammer swinging, led the way. At his side, Henri and Norbert brandished unstrung bows like staves. Behind them came Renard, all his militiamen. In one voice, they roared the name the dwarf had put to him, and with them behind him and more on their heels, Allystaire charged into the pool of light cast by Torvul's lantern.

The dwarf ran beside him, matching him step for step. In Torvul's other hand, he held his crossbow, but had turned it around on his arm. Allystaire glimpsed the odd, smooth blue stone crossbow shift and change in Torvul's hand, saw the curled end straighten into a spike. With another bellowed cry, this time in his own tongue, Torvul rushed forward and drove it through the head of a Wight that stood inert, and then crumbled into powder and broken metal.

Allystaire swung his hammer almost blindly, felt the cracks threaten to take it, dropped it to the ground and swung with his fists, his elbows, his knees. Without even thinking it, without checking to look, he knew that just beyond the lantern light gave Idgen Marte raced ahead of them, her borrowed cudgel a deadly blur in her hands.

He sought out the Wight that had brought down Torvul's barrier. The glow that had suffused it was gone, but he smashed it to pieces nonetheless.

Before them, the Wights were overwhelmed, destroyed bit by bit, levered to the ground and crushed under boots, cudgels, and heavy rocks. Beyond them in the blue-black dark they could hear what was left of the Baron's spearmen and horse pounding away in full retreat, officers cursing and urging the men, whether to stay or to fly faster, Allystaire couldn't have said. He took a few steps down the path after them till he heard Idgen Marte's voice in his head.

No, she hissed. *This is still not done!*

He drew to a stop, fists clenched, and yelled after them. "Come for me again, Lionel! Bring your sorcerers and put an end to your shame!"

He turned then, looking around for his hammer, saw Giraud smashing at what was left of one of the Wights, legless, as it tried to crawl away. The two dozen or so men that had charged out in the stonemason's wake stood in the circle of Torvul's lamp-light. He walked to join them, and the white light made a dazzling radiance against his untouched, unmarked, unbloodied armor.

The men, among them Chaddin and one of his knights, stared at him in open-mouthed wonder, till again, someone spoke the words the Wit had made a battle cry, then another voice joined in, and another, till the remaining defenders of Thornhurst chanted it as one word. A word that he knew, now, replaced the surname he had left behind.

"Still-BRIGHT, Still-BRIGHT, Still-BRIGHT." Torvul's voice, deep and resonant, chanted the loudest of them all.

He raised his hands, and they quieted instantly. "We are not done, men," he said, his voice practically a ragged croak. "We are not yet clear. till dawn," he said. "till dawn we must carry the light ourselves. We must hold for the return of Her sun."

And with the men behind him and flushed with their temporary victory Allystaire Stillbright, the Arm of the Mother, made his way back towards Her Temple.

We may yet win, he thought, sharing the notion with Torvul and Idgen Marte.

And then he heard a powerful voice behind him yell into the unnatural darkness.

"Allystaire! You've called for me to face you. Now come and reap the fruit of your boasting!"

Allystaire, Idgen Marte, Torvul, and the village folk turned as one. Torvul lifted his lantern.

It was a feigned retreat, Allystaire thought, suddenly sickened. *Meanwhile, he circled back.*

In the light thrown by the dwarf's lantern, Baron Lionel Delondeur stood in a suit of armor that seemed to drink in the light. Dark grey, dull, yet somehow sickeningly reflective. Where the light hit it, the surface suggested a dark red-brown was mixed in among the grey.

It was made of the same stuff as the Battle-Wights, Allystaire could see. The Baron wore no helm. His eyes were wide and bulging in a face that seemed to have lost a decade or more, and his white hair seemed blond once again. Planted in the turf next to him was an enormous sword, as long as he was tall, made of the same stuff as his armor, as wide across as Allystaire's hands laid next to one another.

Armor and a sword made of men, Allystaire thought. *Made of the very bodies of men.*

"Pausing now, I see," the Baron boomed, striding forward and lifting his enormous sword casually in one hand, cutting at the air. "Afraid to face me now that I'm on equal footing, eh?"

Behind him stood a ring of spearmen, fewer than the two score there ought to have been. But enough, given how exposed Allystaire's remaining men were.

"What have you done, Lionel? What have you become?"

"What I needed to become," he bellowed. "What you drove me to. You with your demon's bargain, the strength of ten or more. You with your Gifts and your talk of a Goddess and the presumption to lecture me on how to rule my own people. You did this."

"My people does not mean the same as my furniture, or my sword, or even my horse, Lionel. It never did. But you are beyond understanding that now."

Allystaire drew his own sword and held it out with both hands, pointed it at the Baron as he addressed the spearmen behind him. "Do you see it? Do you see that he is wearing your comrades, your brothers of battle? You are nothing to him. You are things."

"ENOUGH." Delondeur charged forward, swinging his sword in a wild, two-handed arc that Allystaire easily shifted away from. The blade drove a long furrow into the ground; the grass that it touched sizzled. "Those men served me in life, and now they serve me in death."

Allystaire circled warily, his sword held out, watching Delondeur's blade carefully. "How many of them died too soon, Lionel? How many were killed to bring on this unnatural night? How many died to give you that sword to fight me with?"

"It is their honor to die for me. It is their duty to die for me." Another wild overhand cut.

This time, Allystaire met it with his own blade. The shock that traveled up his arms when the swords met took him aback, almost drove him to a knee. Lionel leaned into the cut, trying to force Allystaire back.

"It has to be their choice!" Allystaire bellowed. He couldn't take his eyes off the Baron to address the Delondeur spearmen, but he yelled his words for them anyway. "How many of you want to die on a sorcerer's table? How many of you want your bodies twisted into this?"

He found a surge of strength to push the Baron back, and pressed him with a mid-level swing, swept tight. Lionel knocked it aside with obvious contempt.

"They do not choose to serve me," the Baron yelled. "They are born to it. They are born to be a sword in my hand, a shield between me and my enemies. They ought to come happily to their end if it means serving me, no matter how."

The Baron followed his words with a series of fast cuts. Faster, Allystaire was sure, than Lionel Delondeur had ever swung a sword on his youngest and strongest days. He found himself giving ground. The men behind him, Torvul and Idgen Marte among them, scattered, most making for the Temple stairs. More of the folk, including some of the Delondeur prisoners, had spilled out of the Temple to watch the duel unfolding before them.

I cannot match his pace or tire him out, Allystaire thought as he danced away from another blow. He swung, more for the sake of feeling like he fought back, trying a high line that Delondeur ducked under with the agility of a much younger man. Lionel reversed his sword and jabbed the hilt, a rough thing with a huge dark stone in the pommel, straight into Allystaire's chest.

He sprawled to the ground, but not for long. To lie there was to die, so Allystaire rolled to his left and pushed himself quickly back to his feet. He was upright in time to see Delondeur pulling his sword free from another grey and smoking wound in the earth.

He was, Allystaire noted, a bit slow pulling the blade clear.

"How many did you give to them for this strength, Lionel? How many for this unnatural youth?"

"Just one," Lionel roared, rushing towards Allystaire and swinging low. Allystaire got his blade in the way, slowed down the cut, but didn't stop it, couldn't stop it. Instead of taking him in the thigh it bit into his calf.

Allystaire stumbled away, half dragging the leg behind him. It would hurt, later. He had no time for it now. He spared a glance at Lionel's face. It was the face of a madman, all sense and understanding fled from it. The eyes were wide and bulging, the mouth set in a rictus grin.

"What was his name?" Allystaire shouted, shuffling back, putting distance between himself and the Baron.

Delondeur paused, his sword raised. "What?"

"His name. The man that was killed to grant you this strength. What was his name?"

"Darrus Cartin," Delondeur spat. "Some knightling. No one. His strength serves me better than it ever would have served him."

Allystaire heard the murmuring, the shocked sounds, both from the Delondeur line and along the steps of the Temple. He couldn't spare a glance because once again, Lionel was rushing at him, his sword a blur. He was able to catch Delondeur's edge with his flat, spreading his hand upward along his own blade, but he felt the steel shiver.

They pressed against each other, strength against strength. Sword arms were flattened against armored chests. The Gift of a Goddess strove against the blood magic of the sorcerers.

Allystaire felt his toes beginning to dig into the grass; he was losing traction from the wounded leg. He was losing, period.

"Go on, Coldbourne," Lionel whispered. "Sink to the ground, give in. Give me your head and I will grant merciful deaths to your pathetic following."

"I will give you nothing," Allystaire spat, his arms trembling from the exertion. He spun away, tried a back-hand that clanged harmlessly off of Delondeur's armor, but seemed to enrage the madman all the more.

Lionel's blade swept down in another two-handed cut. Allystaire's sword rose to meet it, caught it, turned aside, and broke off a foot from the hilt. The paladin staggered backwards with the force of the blow.

He held the broken jagged piece out in front of him, considered it a moment, then hurled it straight at Delondeur's face.

Had it been an axe, a knife, something weighted for the throw, it might have worked, taken an eye, or sunk in so deep as to end the fight.

Instead, flying awkwardly, it nicked Lionel's cheek and drew a thick line of blood beneath his eye, but no more.

Lionel smiled, raising his sword in a mock salute. "Are you ready to die, Coldbourne?"

"My name," Allystaire grated out, "is Allystaire Stillbright." He felt the Goddess's song thrum in his limbs, aching for a release.

Trip. Then move to your right. Torvul's voice sounded in his head. Allystaire didn't know where the dwarf was, but he didn't stop to ask.

Lionel charged, his sword raised above his head, preparing a two-handed cut that would split Allystaire down the middle.

He took the dwarf's advice and threw himself to the ground, then rolled to his right.

Lionel was moving too fast to adjust, and his arms were already swinging. The sword sizzled into the earth once more, sinking the first foot of its length into the ground.

And it stuck. Lionel tugged at it with both hands, but the sword didn't move.

Now. Now! Torvul's thoughts raged. Allystaire sprang to his feet and launched himself at the Baron in a flying tackle, pushing off from his good leg.

The clash of their armor was ear-splitting, like two giants made of metal thrown against one another. Allystaire felt Lionel's hands tear free from the sword, and for a moment, the shock of his attack combined with the strength of the Goddess's Gift kept his enemy's arms pinned to his side.

Allystaire was wearing a helm. Lionel was not. So when Allystaire slammed his head into the Baron's face, he felt his own nose crunch beneath his nose-guard, and half of Delondeur's face cave in.

The fight was not gone out of Lionel yet, though. Allystaire scrambled to his knees overtop of the Baron. Their hands fought for purchase and position, but Allystaire's were more purposeful. Lionel thrashed madly, wildly, with the pain of the blow he'd taken.

Allystaire smiled grimly as he realized that his left hand had brushed Lionel's throat. Still the Baron's arms crashed against him. The blows were painful. Ribs cracked. But what was pain?

Pain was merely a cost. He would pay it. When it came to killing the man Lionel Delondeur had become, the paladin would pay it and smile.

This, Allystaire knew, was part of the difference between them.

"I am willing to be hurt for them, Lionel," he roared. One of the Baron's hands wrapped around his wrist, but Allystaire focused, even as his bones grated. "I am willing to suffer for them." An errant fist brushed his jaw but he ignored it, finally seating the heel of his left hand high on Delondeur's chest, crumpling some of the grim armor beneath it and gaining the leverage he needed. Allystaire drew back his right hand and smashed his curled fist into Delondeur's face, shattering the baron's jaw. Lionel's arms fell weakly to the ground.

"You take strength from them, Lionel," the paladin bellowed. "Mine is given for them."

His right fist crashed again into the Baron's face. Lionel's armored form stilled. Again. His skull crumbled beneath the blow.

The Arm of the Mother stood up on his one good leg, staring at the ruined face of the dead Baron Delondeur beneath him. "It did not have to be this way.

You were a better man than this, once." Allystaire looked to the line of Delondeur spearmen then, who eyed him uncertainly. Perhaps one in three hefted their weapons.

From behind him, two voices cried out, each assuming an air of command. "HOLD, men of Delondeur! By order of your Baron," said one, "Baroness," the other. Allystaire turned to see Chaddin and Landen, the latter's hands bound in front of her, both rushing down the stairs.

Then the world suddenly exploded in a rush of sickly yellow light.

CHAPTER 40

The Sorcerers, the Islandman, and the Will

Iriphet and Gethmasanar had collaborated on the Rite of Blooming Blood, so they both felt it, instantly, when the Baron Delondeur was destroyed.

Iriphet let loose a loud yell of rage, as unseemly and unexpected a display of emotion as Gethmasanar had ever seen one of the Knowing make.

"GO. Go yourself and deal with this. We have seen nothing of the boy in days. Kill them all. Use as much power as you must. GO."

Gethmasanar drew power into himself, held up his hand, and vanished in a streak of yellow light.

* * *

Allystaire rolled from his back to his chest and pushed himself unsteadily to his feet. His ears rang, and his vision blurred. Around him, lancets of a hideous yellow flew from the air, striking randomly, killing fully half a dozen of the Delondeur spearmen before the rest, and Chaddin and Landen with them, could fling themselves to the ground.

One of the bolts sunk into Allystaire's left arm and burned a clean hole through his armor. It was like being stabbed with a hot poker straight through the meat of his arm.

Before he could recover his wits, or his hearing, he saw the bodies of Battle-Wights rising from the ground, twisting themselves back into vaguely man-like shapes. They hobbled and scuttled and crawled awkwardly, and they seemed weak—but there were so many.

And they all came straight for him.

He raised his fists, limping towards them. He felt three shapes go sprinting past him, heard their yelling as a distant roar.

Renard. Henri. Norbert.

The latter two were tossed aside by the Wights, thrown to the ground. Renard swung his spear clean through the first one, swept the spine out of it. He levered it through a second and was bearing that one to the ground when he screamed.

Allystaire could hear the scream only distantly, but he knew the expression on the man's face. He didn't want to look, but of their own volition his eyes slid down, from Renard's face to his chest.

A bladed Battle-Wight hand was punched straight through him, the blade gleaming wetly where it emerged from his breastbone. Then a second. Then the crowd of the beasts surrounded him and Allystaire's hearing settled and the world realigned itself.

He charged forward and knocked them aside, but he knew he had been too late, had heard the sickening sounds of blades being punched into flesh.

And then the Wights were on him, a dozen of them, more, ignoring every target but him.

Allystaire struggled against the overbearing weight of them. With three of them holding down each of his arms, his legs, and more than he could tell piling upon his shoulders, all the strength that flowed through them didn't matter. He focused on the robed form with the glowing yellow eyes that approached.

"So, Coldbourne," the figure began, and Allystaire knew gloating when he heard it. "Or is it Stillbright? So precious, the names you people bestow upon yourselves. You've been yelling for me for two nights now, boasting of how you did not fear me, calling me coward."

The sorcerer made a motion with his hand, and Allystaire roared with sudden pain as one of the Wights slid a thin finger-blade beneath his vambrace and plunged the blade casually through his forearm.

The sorcerer laughed, and with a twist of his ankle, Allystaire managed to get one foot under himself. He gathered himself, lunged forward.

Driven both by the dwindling song, his pain, his cold fury, it was almost enough. He got his knee off the ground and moved perhaps half a pace forward, dragging the mass of Wights with him. Behind him he heard gasps, cries, a startled but hopeful yell.

Then the sorcerer repeated his motion, and another blade slid straight through a seam in his armor, spearing his calf to the ground.

The Arm of the Mother sagged back to his knees, exhausted, gritting his teeth so hard against the pain that he heard them grinding, felt blood trickling inside his mouth.

"So you do know when you are beaten." The sorcerer took another half step closer, and Allystaire searched for any last reserves of strength to gather for a leap, but he found none.

Behind him he heard a shriek, crying, hysteria. He couldn't pick voices out. He knew only that he was failing them and they wept to see it.

"And more importantly, they know when you are beaten. As do your fellows—for have they not abandoned you?"

It was only then that Allystaire realized he did not know where Torvul or Idgen Marte were, and he felt a tiny spark of hope flicker to life within him.

"Never." He lifted his head in time to see Idgen Marte appear out of the darkness behind the sorcerer, knife in hand. She plunged it towards his robed breast, but with a wave of his hand and a flare of yellow in the darkness, she was flung away, describing an arc several yards upward into the air. Allystaire heard her shriek as she landed, heard the crunch of bone shattering.

"Well, that accounts for one of them. Both of you must be studied, of course, most carefully. What you managed was quite impressive, to destroy so many of our constructs. And your powers show promise. Primitive, but intriguing. Well. It is your body that must be studied." The sorcerer gestured lazily, and Allystaire felt more cold shocks of pain as the other Battle-Wights slid their blade hands into his flesh, in his side, in his arms, his shoulders, his back.

Gethmasanar opened his mouth but suddenly paused.

A low, deep rumbling sound rose in the night. A liquid sound, but not water. Something deeper.

Something like molten stone given a voice.

Torvul, Allystaire thought dimly, for thought was leaving him as blood trickled from nearly a dozen wounds. *But I've never heard him sing like this.*

The song was thunderous, bone-rattlingly deep. It rumbled through the earth beneath him. It thrummed in his ears with power.

"Ah, the dwarf. And what will be your play? Surely something more subtle than a knife in the dark. A potion, a puff of smoke? Flame? An acid?"

"No." Torvul spoke through clenched teeth, and though his singing stopped, Allystaire felt the song continuing to resonate in the air and the earth. "Only a talk with my mother."

"A prayer? If your goddess was going to deliver you a miracle, dabbler, she would've done it by now."

The dwarf stepped into the wan circle of light the few soldiers bearing torches threw, and he knelt. His potion bags and pouches were all but empty, and he had neither cudgel nor crossbow. "Her Ladyship is not my mother," Torvul said, and Allystaire knew from his tone that his face was twisted with that maddeningly knowing smile as he spoke, though the darkness hid his features.

The dwarf knelt, placed a hand upon the ground, and resumed his song. The power of it raised the hair on Allystaire's arms and neck.

The sorcerer's answering laugh was cut off when something flew through the night air and took him in the stomach. He was knocked a step backwards, but recovered quickly.

Torvul lifted his hand from the ground, still singing, pouring forth a song of deep places and old wisdom, and as his hand moved, the very earth rose from behind the sorcerer and wrapped around him, trying to pull him into its depths.

There was a bright flare of bilious yellow, and the earth melted away from Gethmasanar. He stepped forward, his hands completely alight with the yellow fire that normally trickled from his fingertips and eyes.

"STONESINGER!"

Allystaire was slipping ever closer towards the abyss of unconsciousness from loss of blood. Already he could not feel his feet, his hands. His heart was a dull throb in his chest, a faint tattoo in his ears.

But he knew the sound of fear in a man's voice when he heard it.

Torvul's song continued to coax stones out of the dirt, to hurl waves of earth at the sorcerer, who continued to cut them out of the air or deflect them with the blunt force of his power.

They were a study in contrasts. While the sorcerer cursed and raged and hurled yellow fire from his hands, his eyes, even his mouth, the dwarf knelt motionless upon the earth, which thrummed to his call.

As bolts of pure energy flew at Torvul, hunks of earth ripped themselves free of the ground and floated into the air to absorb them. Other rocks pulled free and flew at the sorcerer, and some began to strike him.

And then a second robed form materialized behind the first, and the yellow power that filled the air was joined with blue.

Suddenly it was all Torvul could do to keep himself covered. Allystaire could hear, dimly, the dwarf's voice going hoarse, could see the first bolt that slipped through his defenses.

He felt himself slide another notch towards oblivion. His vision turned grey and faded.

Allystaire heard Torvul's song grow weaker, and thought, *I am sorry, My Lady. I have failed. I am sorry, Gideon. Sorry, my son.*

And then just before his mind went blank and his heart stopped sounding in his ears, he heard an answer in his mind. A curious, distant voice, that said three words.

Son?

Allystaire?

Father?

* * *

Inside the Temple, Gideon sat up beneath the altar. He stood, his eyes widened, and then he disappeared. He had come and gone so fast that almost no one in the Temple noticed it, so intent were they on the battle that raged outside.

No one, that is, except for the Voice of the Mother, who fell against the altar, crying tears of joy.

* * *

The survivors of the Battle of Thornhurst who saw the Will of the Mother confront the sorcerers agreed that it was a terrible and frightening thing, even if the rest of the details varied.

Some said that he was a giant wreathed in terrible flame. Others, a nearly invisible outline, barely a man. A few said that he was a dragon, huge and terrible and breathing the power of a storm.

Still others said it was just a slim, bald youth in a robe, who looked calmly at the sorcerers hurling their unnatural fire, raised his hands, and said, "No."

Both of them, the blue and the yellow, ceased to attack the dwarf and turned their full attentions on Gideon, bombarding him with the power they wielded. Blue and yellow light both disappeared before his outstretched hand, as if it never even touched him.

But the two drew on more and more of their power. The skin of the one who wielded the blue energy split and cracked, the light that filled him pouring out, till he was barely in the shape of a man any longer.

And this, it seemed, began to overwhelm the Will, who stepped back, quailing against the onslaught he was trying to absorb.

It seemed, again, as though all might be lost. And it might have been, if not for the Islandman, whose name, and what he was doing there, no story and no song recorded.

* * *

His scream. That's what got him, in the end. Nyndstir had never been the quiet sort, never been one to sneak and stick a blade in the back. He wasn't some dumb inlander knight prattling about honor and facing a man straight on, but he'd never been a skulker either, not really.

So he was really freezing tired of skulking. And it seemed like the boy was having a bad time of it once Iriphet had started screaming in a language Nynd-stir didn't know and didn't want to know.

When he went for Iriphet's back, raising his axe high, intending to cleave straight through the sorcerer's unprotected neck, he wasn't sure what might happen when steel met—well, whatever the sorcerer was becoming. Because it was like the terrible light within him was consuming the flesh around it.

But he did scream, a long and bloody cry for vengeance, and he swung.

And his axe bit deep into something.

But the other sorcerer turned, saw him, and snarled. A beam shot straight from Gethmasanar's extended finger and pierced Nyndstir in the chest. It took him in the heart.

As he was falling to the ground, he had a vague sense that the battle around him had changed.

And then he felt a vast and awesome presence looking upon him.

Did I right the course?

He was met with a voice that sounded like waves in a storm on the open sea. The rage and the terror in it were so great that he could not make out any words. Then it was as if the storm parted for the sun. The roar of the ocean died, and there was only warmth.

Yes, the sunlight said, in a voice that put him in mind of his mother. *You steered true.*

Nyndstir Obertsun died a happier man than he ever expected.

* * *

When the Islandman burst from the trees, Gideon got all the opening he need-ed. Iriphet's gambit had been unexpected, trying to make himself a conduit for the very power that all the Knowing drew from, pouring it into Gideon in an attempt to burn him out.

But there was still a mortal shell there. As Gideon now understood, there had to be a mortal shell for the magic to attach itself to, for the will to work anything in the mortal world. And a mortal shell, no matter how well protect-ed, how ancient, no matter what power it housed, had little defense against an axe buried in its spine.

Gideon pulled the power straight out of Gethmasanar's body then. The sorcerer's yellow eyes winked out and he crumbled to the ground.

Iriphet was a longer time in dying. Gideon had to rework some of his newly absorbed power and use it to build a barrier around the conduit the dying sorcerer had opened. The power Iriphet's flesh had been hooked to was now a glowing ball of intense blue floating in the air.

Gideon boxed it in, shut it off, watched as it grew smaller and smaller, denser and tighter, until it finally winked out. The backlash against his barrier drove him to his knees for a moment.

Then both sorcerers and Baron Lionel Delondeur lay dead upon the battlefield. The Battle-Wights that held Allystaire's limp form collapsed, and Gideon rushed to his side.

CHAPTER 41

Two Awakenings

Allystaire awoke in a place that was bright, and yet had no source of light that he could see. He felt that he was lying on a bier of some kind, but then the stone beneath him became a bed so soft he wanted to weep at the feel of it. The weight of his armor was replaced with the thinnest, lightest linen he'd ever felt. Or was it silk?

No amount of softness could mitigate the pain of his limbs. Her Strength had fled and the days of using it were now telling. And there were the wounds. He felt as though no part of him was not bleeding. His side, both of his arms, his calf, his back, had all been punched by the bladed hands of Battle-Wights.

The pain of his broken nose was an old friend compared to the rest of him. Comforting, almost.

He could manage only a thin, airless moan. He tried to turn his head but his muscles protested and he flopped weakly against the down cushion.

"Oh, My Knight," he heard a voice breathe. Despite the overwhelming pain, the voice sent a thrill, a surge of love through him, and he managed to lift his head.

She stood at the foot of the bed he lay upon, a tear sliding down Her cheek.

"Goddess," he croaked, his voice barely audible even in his own ears. "Why do you…"

Then She was standing at the side of the bed, instead of the foot, bending over him. "I do not weep out of sorrow, my Allystaire," she said. "Though the hurts you have taken, and those of My People who were lost, are enough to drive me to it. No, My Knight, I weep for pride. Pride in my choices."

Her hand stroked his cheek, and instantly the pain of his body began to recede beneath the touch of her fingertips and the surge of longing it brought. "I am sorry I failed you," he murmured, letting his eyes close. "Is this death? Is this the next world?"

For the first and only time, Allystaire saw the face of the Goddess he served twist in uncertainty.

"You did not fail me," She replied, leaning closer to him. "The Longest Night has ended and My Will ushers in the dawn."

Suddenly in his mind's eye Allystaire could see the image of Gideon standing upon the field over his broken body. The boy had one hand upraised, the unnatural darkness rolled back from the skies, and the sun pulled itself over the horizon.

"Am I dead, then?" Allystaire wondered aloud again. "If I died in your service, saving your people, My Lady, I would ask nothing more."

She leaned closer to him. He feared to open his eyes for the dazzling radiance that loomed so close; even behind his eyelids he could feel the power of Her Light. "Your labors are not yet done. Yet as I told you at your vigil, there is but one gift I have left to give you."

The sheet that lay atop him was twitched aside, and then the Goddess's mouth was upon his and Her hands moving upon his body. Under Her kiss, Her touch, the pain, his muddled thoughts, and the question he had asked that had not been answered all fled before desire.

* * *

Allystaire woke up again in darkness. He sat straight up in a bed, gasping for air. His entire body was aflame. Not with pain, but with the insane, burning desire the Goddess's love had brought forth in him.

The bed beneath him creaked, and he saw a shadow in the room with him.

This bed, this room, was real.

His heart sank.

"How long?" he croaked.

"Nine days." Idgen Marte answered. She came forward to his bedside and sat down upon it, easing him onto his back with one finger pressed into his chest. He was too weak to resist.

"The first of the days that you lay here…" Idgen Marte's voice trailed off, low and husky in the dark. "Allystaire. I've seen a lot of dead men in my time. I would swear you were one of them. We were ready to carry you into the Temple and lay your body out. Gideon wouldn't let us."

Allystaire sat silently in the dark and let her words wash over him. "For a day?"

"I couldn't find your breath, the beat of your heart. Your wounds didn't bleed. But the boy insisted, and after what he'd done, there was no arguing. Two days later he let us into this room and you were breathing again, but, Cold take me, you weren't here. I couldn't feel you, with my mind, though I sat next to you."

"I think I—"

"Don't explain," Idgen Marte said. "The past day, as I've sat here…sounded like an eventful one. You talk in your sleep."

With Idgen Marte, Allystaire was beyond embarrassment. He swung his legs off the bed and stood.

Then Idgen Marte was at his side, helping ease him back into the bed as he fell. "We did the best we could with my sewing, and Torvul's potions once you'd breath back in your body. But you're still in a bad way."

Allystaire grunted, placed the palm of his left hand on his chest, and poured Her Gift into himself. "Am I?"

Then he stood. "How? What happened? What have I missed?"

"A moment." Idgen Marte struck flame on the end of one of Torvul's sticks, brought it to the wick of a lamp, and the room instantly brightened. She turned to face him, her left arm bound to her chest in a sling. "While I'm answering, could you?"

He nodded and laid his hand on her arm, winced as it snapped back together. She nearly fell to a knee, and he saw her bite the inside of her cheek to keep from crying out. She sank back into a chair as she started unwinding the sling that had bound her arm up.

"How? The answer, I s'spose, is Gideon. He came back. Killed the sorcerers. Says you brought him back. I expect you'll want to talk to him about that."

"I will," Allystaire agreed, thinking on his final words before slipping from consciousness. Perhaps from life. "As soon as I might."

"As to what you've missed." Idgen Marte's tone was a bit evasive. "Well, Chaddin and Landen seem set to get right back to figuring out whether Delondeur gets a Baron or a Baroness now that their father is dead."

Allystaire sighed. "How have you kept them off each other?"

"For a day or two, thinking you dead, nobody really had the stomach for a fight. And then, well, perhaps get dressed, come downstairs with me, eh?"

Allystaire nodded and reached for the lamp. He found the finery that had been made for him upon the arrival of Fortune's delegation, many weeks ago, and slipped into it, following with his boots.

He saw neither his hammer nor his sword. *Because they are both broken,* he reminded himself. He realized, finally, that he was in one of the smaller rooms in Timmar's Inn.

He descended the stairs to find the taproom was more full than he'd expected, and brightly lit with a roaring fire, lamps, and several fat candles burning upon the bar. When he saw who sat scattered around it, it was all he could do not to drop the lamp he'd carried down.

Torvul, Mol, and Gideon he had expected.

But not Ivar, Rede, or Cerisia.

And certainly not the two people, man and woman, who rose to greet him. The man was fair, with pale skin and fine blond hair that reached his shoulders. The woman was a bit shorter than Allystaire, and a good deal more slender, but there was kinship in their features. Where his were blunted or scarred, hers were refined and unblemished. Her eyes were darker even than his, and her skin lacked most of the wind and weather-burn his had sustained. Allystaire fumbled for words, and finally settled on his sister's name.

"Audreyn?"

The End of Book 2 of the *Paladin Trilogy*

Acknowledgments

Thanks to Andrew, Kyle, Gwen, Melanie, and the entire SFWP crew. Thanks again to Rion for pointing me to them. Thanks to Jacob for the map and the beta reading. Thanks to Josh, Stephanie, Yeager, Sarah, Andy, and Jason for the same. Last but always most, to Lara, who is a lamp when it is dark.

About the author

Daniel M. Ford was born and raised near Baltimore, Maryland. He holds an M.A. in Irish Literature from Boston College and an M.F.A. in Creative Writing, concentrating in Poetry, from George Mason University. As a poet, his work has appeared most recently in *Soundings Review*, as well as P*hoebe*, *Floorboard Review, The Cossack,* and *Vending Machine Press*. He teaches English at a college prep high school in the northeastern corner of Maryland.

THE ADVENTURE CONCLUDES...

CRUSADE

Book Three of the Paladin Trilogy

AVAILABLE IN 2018

Santa Fe Writers Project

sfwp.com